When he's not on a sunny Greek island spreading
terror, Steve Harris is likely to be found at his word proces-
sor in Basingstoke giving his latest set of characters a hard
time. Besides enjoying the telling of lies, he likes making
friends with dogs, fixing broken things and being asleep.
He is not a professional car thief though he does admit to
driving like a maniac.

Angels is his fourth novel and terrifying follow-up to the
bestselling *AdventureLand*, *Wulf* and *The Hoodoo Man*.

Angels

Steve Harris

First published in 1993
by HEADLINE BOOK PUBLISHING PLC

First published in paperback in 1993
by HEADLINE BOOK PUBLISHING PLC

A HEADLINE FEATURE paperback

10 9 8 7 6 5 4 3 2 1

ISBN 0 7472 4131 7

Printed and bound in Great Britain by
HarperCollins Manufacturing, Glasgow

HEADLINE BOOK PUBLISHING PLC
Headline House
79 Great Titchfield Street
London W1P 7FN

Angels
is dedicated to
Elizabeth Curthoys, Phil Holmes
and Sam 'Adolf' Carpetbiter
who gave me a mirror
which plays the Death March
when I look in it.
You rotters!

As usual, I had to pick a few brains, so Thanks, everyone. Especially, Detectives Pete Bloor and Ian Jones from Basingstoke C.I.D. who happily discussed murder, car thieving scams, Mickey Mouse driving licenses, Moody credit cards and the detection thereof; Superintendent Tim Brain for allowing them to; Stef (and his buddies who wish to remain nameless), Phil, and all the others who advised me on 'taking and driving away'. James Scully, Director of Webber's Garage Basingstoke for advice on Jaguar cars; Alfa Romeo for advice on their cars; Dave Rook for showing me Bad Pieterstal and for looking after a lonely traveller; Scott 'Arizona' Novis for bouncing ideas around with me; Jennifer Martin; everyone at Hammicks Basingstoke for services above and beyond the call of duty (and their tea and bikkies); Leanne Matthews and Tricia Canny, 'The battling Aussies'; Steve Harris the Younger and Suzanne for advice on early chapters; Gary M. Dobbs for being there; Geoff Barrs for being the Fount of Some Knowledge; and Miriam the '76 Humber Sceptre MkIII which took me 4,500 miles round Europe without complaint — look after her, Twink.

Thanks also to Flo, Cindy, Reggie, Colin Rowe of Hedge, Rowe & Bramble (for his eagle-eyed error spotting), Sarah 'Porker' Thomson, Clare Going, Caroline (no relation) Harris, Mike Sharland and Alice, Greenlight Productions and Kim Leggatt, Anne Williams, Caroline 'Twinkle' Oakley and everyone at Headline; Lynn Curtis for correcting my split infinitives (and for knowing about *Clarissa*); Steve Crisp for another fine illustration; David Grogan for helping me get what was best; Dave Girdlestone and

Clan (for the Parker books), Mr and Mrs Pipsqueak, and all my readers, wherever and whoever you are. Still thinking about you all!

Some of you will probably realise that I've taken liberties with the road layout and the geology of the Italian seaside town, Margherita de Savoia. To the best of my knowledge, seismic activity on this scale is unlikely . . . Any errors in police or criminal procedure, European routes, road numbers or locations is entirely due to my tampering with the truth.

Paul Dekker's character was partially inspired by Richard Stark's excellent Parker novels.

All editors in this publication are fictitious and any resemblance to real editors, either living or dead, is purely coincidental. The author does not share the views of Lulu Kaminsky! Okay, Twink?

And thanks to Paul Coombes who lent Dekker his Patron Saint!

'I get this kind of white-heat inside me. Something clicks inside my head and my ears start to roar and it's like there's molten metal in front of my eyes. When it clears, something bad has usually happened. Usually to someone else.'

Paul Dekker

Chapter One
Where Katie Died Next

1

The girl beside him was dead.

Paul was sitting in a stolen car in the world's worst traffic jam in a country he somehow didn't recognise at all, it was night-time, it was raining so hard that he couldn't see further than the tail-lights of the car in front of him and the girl in the passenger seat, whose name he didn't even know, was dead.

He knew it the moment he glanced over at her. She was in exactly the same position as she'd been a moment ago when he'd asked her if she was okay and she had responded in a very small and distant voice that she was fine; her hands were still clasped in her lap, she still sat erect with her head tilted back against the Alfa's headrest, but the light had gone from her eyes and her smell had changed.

Paul's heartbeat suddenly jacked up from a steady driving-a-hot-car ninety to a speed it was impossible even to take a guess at. It hurt and his mind immediately started shouting about imminent cardiac arrest.

Somewhere behind them horns began to blare and Paul's imagination presented him with a picture of the stolen Alfa 164, parked in the middle of the road with its engine still purring away, after all the traffic had gone. When the police – or whatever they were called in this strange land – turned up they would find not a car thief and his accomplice, but two corpses.

He took a deep breath. 'Sweetheart?' he said, not wanting

to believe the girl was really dead and not wanting to reach out and touch her either in case it provided him with the confirmation he badly didn't want.

The girl did not respond.

'Lady!' he hissed, realising that he had been unconsciously moving away from her – his left shoulder was now pressed tight against the driver's door. A part of him – a large part of him – wanted him to leave the car; now, this minute and without further delay because, bad as things were, they were certain to get worse if he stayed. He could *smell* this. The strange, dark country smelt bad, the interior of the brand new Alfa smelt bad and the girl smelt *wrong*.

Leaving the car, however, was not currently an option. A large and ancient coach had somehow jostled along the near-side of Paul's Alfa, leaving a gap of less than an inch. It was now stuck there belching thick, stinking fumes. The driver's door could not be opened because of the proximity of the Fiat Strada on that side. The woman in the Strada had been – and still was for all Paul knew – leaning towards the empty passenger seat of her car and gesticulating at him. Paul had been studiously ignoring her because *that* part of his mind wanted to click in and he couldn't afford to have that happen. *That* part of his mind would get him nowhere in this situation.

'Come on, sweetheart, wake up!' Paul urged, smelling the bad smells, and fighting the feeling of claustrophobia that was building in him. His heart was beating so furiously and so fast that as he spoke, the sentence was broken up into its phonetic component parts.

Slow down, heart! Paul commanded, breathing in and holding the bad air until his lungs hurt. He exhaled slowly through his mouth and felt his heartbeat lessen slightly.

A cacophony of car horns reached a crescendo behind him as Paul put out a hand – not trembling, but bouncing with arterial pressure – toward her.

She's either gonna be cooling or already cold, he thought. *This girl is very dead.*

But he could not accept that because for some reason he needed her to be alive. Something had happened that had bound them together. All he knew was that he had to get her back home and that she had to be alive and strong when she arrived.

His hand touched her cool bare arm. The girl didn't move.

He suddenly knew her name was Katie and that she'd had something to do with the boy. She'd known about the boy Paul had killed. The memory tried to slip back into his mind, but he thrust it aside. That memory would serve no purpose here.

Katie's skin was soft and silky. Paul gently shook her slender arm, feeling the bone beneath the thin muscle. The arm was limp.

'Katie!' he urged. '*Wake up!*'

The girl had no pulse. He knew all the points to check and all were still. Her heart function had ceased.

'Don't do this to me!' he shouted, and felt a mixture of anger and grief. 'Her brain stem may still be functional,' he heard a faintly rational and very dogged part of himself saying aloud. 'She may not have stopped breathing very long ago.'

Paul's own pulse was quickening again. He knew how to administer heart massage and the kiss of life but the same part of him that was freely pouring panic into him and urging him to get out of the car, railed against the notion of his doing it – in exactly the same fashion as it had when he'd killed the boy. But for different reasons this time. The boy was beyond help anyway and Paul had had to get away; this girl had to be helped.

His hands had been busy while he was thinking about it and Katie's seat belt was already undone. He took her light, cool body and dragged it towards him. If Katie was going to be restored he had to act now.

Wanting to scream with the urgency and cold fear his blood was carrying steadily around his body, he supported the girl in the crook of his right arm, his hand between her shoulder blades as he turned her torso to face him. Katie's head lolled forward when he moved her and her thick tangle of blonde hair

3

obscured her empty face. Paul cupped her left breast, placing the heel of his hand solidly against her sternum.

Not if I were you! You don't know what'll come out of there! the doubting part of his mind warned.

At that moment, the traffic surged forward around him and the drivers of the cars he was holding up all hit their horns simultaneously. Frantic and cursing, Paul thrust the corpse away from him. He was in a foreign country driving a stolen car and his passenger was dead. What would the police make of that little lot if they were to happen by to see what was holding up the traffic now? He *had* to move.

Katie fell back against him and her dead smell made him want to heave. It was a pungent odour but not of decay; it was the faint friction smell of something electrical stopped by force. Paul pushed her away, reached for the gearstick and bent his fingers back against the door panel, reminding himself for the fiftieth time or so that he wasn't in England nor in a right-hand drive car. To the best of his somewhat sketchy knowledge he had never driven a left-hooker before.

Almost boiling with panic, he found the gearstick on the wrong side, fitted it into first and let the car crawl forward slowly, gritting his teeth against the urge to stop and work on the girl and have done with it. *When the traffic stops moving!* he assured himself, and, as in all the best nightmares, this did not happen. The flow of traffic – though only travelling at five miles an hour or so – kept going.

2

Paul gulped in deep breaths and forced himself not to think about Katie being dead beside him and the chances of bringing her back slipping away with each passing second. He willed his heartbeat to slow and pushed away the *clicking out* feeling which told him that *that* part of his mind was close to taking control. If he *clicked out* here, he was likely to click back in again in a cell charged with God only knew what.

4

He tried to occupy his mind with listing the way he felt and while he was thinking of the urgent ache deep in his bowels and his trip-hammer heart which wasn't responding particularly well to the primitive bio-feedback magic he was trying to work on it, he realised peripherally that the muscle in his right shoulder was tense.

He peeled his hands away from the wheel and rolled on without steering, realising distantly that he'd been holding on so tightly that his knuckles had stiffened. If it had been light enough, he might have noticed the four deep crescents his fingernails had pressed into the fleshy base of the palm of each hand and seen how close he had been to breaking the skin; as it was, he simply massaged away the hot tingling before putting his right hand back on the wheel and his left on the muscle at the top of his right shoulder. The muscle was frozen hard. Paul walked his index and middle finger down his back across the Trapezius muscle, tracing the line of his scapula – one of the pair of bones his mother called 'the fly wings' – as far down as he could reach.

Beside him, Katie was slumped against the seat, dead.

And the traffic rolled on, a lane chock full of it on either side of him and another before him.

'STOP, YOU BASTARDS!' he shouted, and the power of his own voice surprised him. He clenched his left hand into a fist and punched the fascia of the Alfa in frustration. He hit it hard. The plastic cracked and his knuckles lost some skin and stung. This action provided exactly the amount of relief he had expected: none whatsoever. It would, Paul knew, reduce the pressure that was building inside him (and, he suspected, rapidly approaching critical mass) which would, in turn, prevent the *click-out* demon from taking control.

3

The traffic actually stopped a very short time after it had got rolling, but Paul felt as if hours had passed. He was trembling with fear and adrenalin and frustration.

He yanked up the hand brake, grabbed Katie, checked for a pulse, didn't find one, banged her sternum hard with the ledge of his hand, checked for a pulse again, did five pumps over her heart with the heel of his hand, then swung her around the other way so that she collapsed across him, face up. He pulled her jaw open and tilted her head back then probed the inside of her cold throat with a finger. There were no obstructions. He laid his mouth over her cool, parted lips and blew, then massaged her heart again.

Don't do it any more, cowboy! his mind warned. *You don't know what's going to happen. What if she's someone else when she comes back? What if they've got her? You don't know what you might be doing!*

Fighting the fear and the nausea the dead smell was giving him, Paul blew, massaged, blew, massaged and blew.

She's dead, pard. Give it up. Don't try any more.

'C'mon, you bitch! Come back!' Paul screamed. 'I can't do it without you!' Dimly, he realised he had no idea what he was talking about.

Katie did not respond.

Something had begun to chirrup in the background, below the dampened outside traffic noise; something that sounded like distant cicadas or crickets.

It smells all wrong and you're making it smell a damned sight worse, old poke! Paul's mind insisted. *You know that, don't you?*

And Paul *did* know that, but he had to get the girl back. It was a dreadful compulsion that he couldn't understand or justify. And it wasn't just to do with the fact that he was trying to make up for the boy he'd killed and it wasn't the fact that he *felt* something for the girl – which he didn't think he did – it was just an unbelievably deep-seated compulsion which had its roots in . . .

Life?

. . . something important which he couldn't remember. And that reason was strong enough for him not to *be able* to stop.

Tell you what, pard. Why don't you just let go of it? Let it drop.

6

Let her be dead and DON'T HELP HER ANY MORE! *You've helped her quite enough already. Just let her stay there until we're out of this place then we can quietly dump her somewhere. Somewhere we can be miles away from before the balloon goes up. We don't need any of this. You don't have to atone for the kid. Just leave her be and don't help her any more. You should have taken notice of what you were told old pard! But you didn't and look where you ended up. You try and help her some more, and I, for one, don't know where we'll both end up. How does Hell sound, old poke?*

Katie's chest hitched.

Paul felt for her heartbeat which wasn't present.

The girl's a zombie, Paul! Her heart hasn't beat since you helped her the first time. She's dead, and dead she's going to stay, unless . . .

Paul savagely thrust away the thoughts and continued to massage the girl's heart and blow life into her cold flesh. She *was* going to come back!

While he worked on Katie's heart, he glanced up at the traffic which was still unmoving. Out there somewhere in the rain, almost lost in the smell of *things wrong* and sound of a thousand cars champing at their bits, was the small presence of the chirruping cricket.

They're trying to come through now, his internal voice said with a distinct note of exasperation and then fell silent.

Paul glanced at the woman in the Strada who was leaning over the passenger seat of her car and watching him closely. When their eyes met, she began to shout and gesticulate while on the horn she beat out what might have been a morse code representation of the words she mouthed.

'No spikka da lingo,' Paul muttered sourly. A quick, hot anger possessed him and he badly wanted to get out of the car, go over there, yank open the driver's door of the Strada and scare the shit out of the stupid woman. He would not have to speak. His physical presence would do the trick. But this was impossible. Instead, still working on the girl, Paul rolled the electric window down and treated the woman to his best cold,

7

dangerous look. She would not catch the rage burning in his eyes, but it was the best he could do, other than setting about her car – and under normal circumstances he didn't do those kind of things. These days Paul kept his bad side under lock and key.

The look worked. Even in the dark and the driving rain, through which it surely could only have been dimly perceived, it worked. The woman's quick mouth stopped working, hung open for a second and then snapped shut. The high-pitched blipping of the Strada's horn ceased and after a moment the woman looked away. When Paul glanced over at her again she was staring resolutely out of the windscreen, minding her own business. It was well worth the instant soaking he had taken.

'Good!' Paul spat venomously and blew life into Katie.

4

The girl kicked. Both her legs jolted. Paul took her pulse again and to his dismay found it missing. *But she moved!* he complained.

Or something did, poke, his inner voice said calmly.

Katie's legs started to judder. Her hands trembled and spasmed and her neck muscles tightened, first raising her head and then tossing it back and forth. She looked to Paul as if she was very much alive and suffering an epileptic fit.

The rain was still coming in the open window. Paul glanced over at the woman in the Strada – who was still minding her own business – and pressed the button to wind up the window. The pane got halfway up and inside the door – at the same moment that Katie went limp again – the motor began to labour. The glass slowed and Paul smelled the acrid odour of melting insulation. A small part of him complained that this was a new car, while the larger part instantly connected Katie's apparent relapse to the failing motor. He took his finger off the button to see if it made any difference.

8

Katie spasmed as though she'd been hit in the stomach with a poker. Her feet began to hammer on the floor.

Paul pressed the button. The motor complained and got hot. A wisp of smoke puffed up through a tiny gap in the window's rubber seal.

Katie instantly went limp, as though she was somehow connected to the window switch.

The huge and disjointed feeling of unreality Paul had been wrestling with since waking up in this nightmare grew exponentially. None of this could be true because of two prime facts. The first was that no matter how bad he felt Paul Dekker did not allow, and had *never* allowed, any situation to run this far out of control. He had spent his life practising being on top of things. The second – and far crazier fact – was that it was simply not possible that the girl's life could be switched on and off by the use of an electric window button in a stolen, left-hand drive Alfa Romeo 164.

Coincidence, he told himself and didn't believe it.

He took his finger off the button and the girl started to kick and writhe. *You can't short out a girl's life with a dodgy electric motor!*

But her dead smell had been faintly electrical. It was now impossible for him to tell whether or not it had been replaced by another smell which would indicate that her life had returned or that it might do soon. Paul's nose was a great deal more sensitive than most people's, but he was not a bloodhound. The odour of the melting insulation in the window-winding mechanism had swamped every other smell in the car.

Katie jolted and shuddered and Paul reached for her wrist to verify his belief that her pulse had returned – because if it hadn't, the smell he'd detected earlier of being in very deep shit indeed would turn out to have been a wild under-estimate. If that, as the small but increasingly powerful *farmer-oppozite* part of him kept insisting, were true, then he was in serious danger of losing what was left of his rapidly shrinking collection of marbles.

Katie's arm was whipped away from him before he could take it. She threw herself around towards the door and shuddered and jolted against it, her limbs working frantically in spastic clawing and kicking movements.

Beside the Alfa the coach roared and shifted forwards, leaving a small gap on the passenger side of the car.

Like fucking magic! Paul thought. The girl would now be able to open the door far enough to escape.

'Katie!' Paul shouted, but the girl didn't hear or didn't *want* to hear him.

Somewhere out there in the rain and darkness, the chirruping cricket noise grew louder. Paul had the distinct impression that the irritating sound was at the root of all this.

Katie's hands were clawing at the door handle, but she seemed unable to take hold of it.

The Alfa suddenly wriggled on its suspension as if something had hit it. Distracted, Paul swivelled in his seat, certain that the car behind had nudged the Alfa.

But there was no impact noise, was there? his mind instantly complained. *Or shock. Even a gentle collision produces noise and a jolt and those two things were rather conspicuous by their absence, don't you think, old poke?*

There was still a good five feet between the rear of the Alfa and the car following; the coach certainly hadn't hit him, and the woman in the Fiat hadn't bumped him either.

The sensation, Paul dimly realised as he grasped for the back of Katie's grubby summer dress, felt more as if a force which had been pressing down on the car had suddenly been released.

The girl wrenched herself free of his grasp and Paul turned and pushed down the lock button on his own door, then smiled grimly at the following *shh-clunk* sound. The central locking system still worked.

'Henreeeey!' the girl squealed, and Paul realised that although he had not heard her voice before, she sounded terribly familiar. The locks popped up again, but Paul had been prepared for this eventuality and popped them straight back down.

The eventuality he had not been prepared for arrived at the exact moment the locks popped down.

Lightning struck the car.

5

Except that it wasn't ordinary lightning. The flash was white but not blinding and Paul had the sensation that it had happened internally rather than externally. And there was no following thunder. The effects, however, were akin to what he knew happened when lightning struck a car: the wipers juddered to a halt; the electric window motors inside all the doors (except the driver's door) wound all the windows down half an inch; the lighting circuit fuse blew putting out the headlamps, and the air was instantaneously filled with the acrid smell of ozone.

Several things that were not known effects of a lightning strike on a car also happened. The doors unlocked themselves; the engine coughed and died and the radio suddenly began to play Puccini's *Un bel di* from *Madame Butterfly* at full volume. This shocked Paul, not simply because of the deafening volume of the gentle music but also because Valerie Masterton's pure voice threw the situation even further into the realms of craziness. On top of that there was the fact that it just happened to be one of the few opera pieces with which Paul was familiar.

Things are no longer just a little out of hand, cowboy, his mind whispered, *they've irrevocably escaped your grasp. Don't say I didn't see this coming, pard, and don't blame me for it. I told you what to do!*

As he thought this, Paul felt a cold jolt which made him shudder. The skin at the nape of his neck prickled and the hairs there crept erect. The car was swamped with the odour of orange blossom and honey.

Paul hit the central locking button and nothing happened.

The girl's fingers finally grasped the door handle and in complete contrast to all her movements so far, she left the car with the agility and grace of a young gazelle.

11

The sound of Masterton singing Puccini was beginning to gel with the increasing volume of the chirruping cricket. Paul's dreadful sensation of dislocation was mingling with all the other awful feelings and smells and turning to a turgid, numbing horror which threatened to paralyse him. He knew he had to move if he was to accomplish anything other than becoming frozen in place so he began to clamber across to the passenger seat, intending to get out of the car if to do nothing else (and he was now no longer certain there would be anything else he would be *able* to do). Somehow, things had got too far out of hand far too quickly – even for Paul Dekker to fix.

The battle to keep the girl was lost. It had suddenly become too late.

As he reached the open door, the traffic began to move again. He ran out into it, ignoring the teeming rain that soaked him and sizzled on the tarmac around him, and the blaring of horns that racketed around him and the stalled Alfa.

Katie was behind the car now, striding purposefully back down the carriageway into the oncoming traffic.

The buildings that rose on either side of the wide road were ancient and dirty and seemed to be empty. The street lighting was minimal. There were pavements both sides of the roads, but they were chock-full of cars, some parked, some weaving their way past the parked ones as they tried to beat the jam.

'Katie!' Paul yelled. Somewhere very close to him, a dog barked. It's tone of voice was familiar, but he couldn't see it anywhere.

What was the significance of a single bark from an invisible dog? Or of the irritating noise of an omnipresent cricket? Paul did not know and did not care. Things had run away from him and he couldn't let them run any further. He had become brittle in exactly the same way as he had after killing the boy. A further shock might smash him into shards. Everything else was lost and it was important to stay whole.

He began to run after the girl, not because he expected to be able to get things back on track by catching up with her, but because it was the only course of action open to him.

'KATIE!' he roared, and knew that the possibility of *clicking out* was increasing with each passing second.

Behind him – although it sounded as if it was below him – the dog began to bark again; an even-paced, laconic *woof* . . . *woof* . . . *woof* the way Cindy had used to bark when she was alive.

Cindy's not dead, old pard!

But Cindy *was* dead.

Paul's legs ached and his knees were stiff from being in the car for so long and he could not run very fast.

Nothing to do with the ground getting softer under your feet, then?

Paul refused to consider this. Not even when the tarmac started to stick to his shoes and pull up with them in toffee-like strands. The girl had not yet realised she was being pursued and had not begun to run.

Woof . . . *woof* . . . *woof!* Cindy's deep voice barked unhurriedly.

Chrrp chrrp! the cricket sang.

The girl came face to face with a massive truck and stopped in front of it. She was silhouetted in the truck's four headlights, rain misting in halos around her as she stood tall, legs astride, hands on hips, like someone who has found herself eyeball to eyeball with a dangerous animal but is confident she can stare it down and make it back away. The truck driver leaned on the air-horns and the loud low bellow added credence to the animal simile Paul's mind had formed. When this failed to have any effect, the driver switched the lights on to main beam, then turned on the spot and fog lamps, creating a wall of light before her.

Her drenched blonde hair hung in a glistening tangle down her back, her thin summer dress clung to her body, becoming transparent in the inverted vee her legs described, and her bare arms shone golden in the headlights. In that moment she was the most gorgeous thing Paul had ever witnessed. There was a *perfection* about her which made him ache; which, he

13

realised later, he would be willing to die for. In that moment of incredible beauty she looked as though she had been newly struck from one of God's own personal moulds and placed there by His hand; a vision so lovely that it shouldn't have existed in this dark, bad place and yet its power was increased *because* of its surroundings.

'Katie!' Paul yelled and the word was thick and wrong in his mouth. This was not Katie at all. This was something else.

He ran through the traffic, dodging this way and that, while his mass steadily increased from a middleweight 168 pounds to a super heavyweight 260 and the tarmac tried to hold him back.

Cindy was still barking and the cricket was still chirruping and the *click-out* wanted to happen and Paul felt as lost and alone as he had done after he'd killed the kid.

'Come back to me!' he screamed, not just for the girl, but for all the things he had lost.

Katie was less than fifteen feet away from him now and his weight was increasing with each step. The dog was barking louder and the cricket was threatening to crack right through reality.

Paul reached the girl, took her cool, damp shoulders and turned her gently around. She did not resist. Her head fell and her shoulders slumped when he touched her and the feeling of beauty Paul had experienced slipped away, as if crumbling under his coarse hands. The moment in which he turned her to face him took a very long time – during which Paul felt the coolness of the girl, the heat of the truck's radiator; smelled hot anti-freeze and trouble and something very much like orange blossom and honey . . . and realised he was making a very big mistake.

But he was powerless to stop himself. His right hand cupped her chin and lifted her head in spite of his wishes.

'Katie,' he said softly.

And her eyes opened.

Except that Katie *had* no eyes.

Paul stared into two charred-black, empty sockets.

And if he had been able to find his voice he would have screamed, because the sockets weren't burnt clean or entirely empty. The shredded remains of the optic nerves lay there, terminating in fused blobs. Shreds of muscle dangled and swayed as she moved.

Katie smiled and her lips became blistered and scarred.

Paul was paralysed. His mouth opened and closed, but no words were coming out. Inside, his mind was on the run.

Katie treated him to what was supposed to be a rueful smile. It was an unwholesome, *ugly* smile and it numbed Paul's mind. Deep inside him he could feel those last few marbles beginning to roll.

'Made a mistake,' Katie said in a deep, grating voice which not only wasn't hers, but wasn't a woman's voice at all. 'Shan't make another,' she continued as Paul watched scars and blisters rise on her face. 'And you don't have to worry, *cowboy*, I can see you well enough. All I have to do is look. And believe me, little Paulie, *I'm looking!* I'm already looking further than you can imagine; and in more directions.'

Katie's tongue slipped out and licked her lips. It was a misshapen blob of grey gristle that looked like melted plastic.

'Everything's clamped down tight from now on. H Tyler is on a winning streak and there's nothing you can do about it, pipsqueak. Remember that.'

Most of Katie's teeth were gone at the front; those that weren't were dark and distorted as if they had suffered a tremendous amount of heat. Her gums and tongue blistered as she spoke and scraps of skin fell from her face with the movement of her mouth.

'There are worse things in Heaven and Hell, *old poke*, remember that,' Katie said, 'and sometimes it's difficult to tell the difference. Best if little boys don't dabble. Little boys who *do*, tend to come off worst. You're just a very small fishy in a very big pool from now on, Mr Professional Car Thief whose bottle has gone. Do you understand?'

At some point during the past few moments, Paul had released his grip on Katie and taken a reflexive step back from her. He was surprised, but not terribly, to find that the reason he could retreat no further was because Katie was now holding on to him. She wasn't holding him tightly, she was holding him with a rock-like solidity. A distant part of him wondered why the truck driver wasn't climbing down from his cab to move the obstruction.

'Do you understand, pipsqueak?'

Paul could not speak. He could no longer even comprehend the words.

Katie shook him gently and his teeth cracked together.

'What I'm trying to say is this,' she said, shaking him with each word, 'don't-fuck-with-me. Com-pren-ez vous? Let me show you why.'

She let go of him.

Cindy barked.

Katie opened her mouth very wide. Paul was no longer capable of resisting – even to the extent of closing his eyes. Far away from here, he was shattering into nothing. The smell of orange blossom and honey was cloying and overpowering.

Katie's chest hitched and her stomach spasmed as if she were going to throw up, but she made no sound. A black substance appeared at the back of Katie's throat, rising slowly from her gullet like a viscous liquid. It slid up her ruined tongue, not gleaming like wet latex as what was left of Paul's mind seemed to expect, but blanking parts of her flesh from view as though they didn't exist. The substance reflected almost no light at all. It flattened and stretched over her teeth and quickly coated the contours of her mouth. When the inside of her mouth was filmed with the substance, it became thinner and faster and ran out over her bottom lip, sheeting her chin and neck like a smooth layer of soot.

The black substance had no smell whatsoever, Paul distantly realised. This, like everything else so far, was impossible. All things had an odour.

Like a living thing, it sought its way beneath her dress. Paul watched it through the thin, rain-dampened material as it spread rapidly out across her shoulders and down her chest between her breasts where it gathered at her heart in a distinct bulge. If it hadn't been for the truck's lights outlining the girl, her chin, neck and shoulders and a vee-shaped section of her chest would have appeared to have vanished.

Katie's mouth was now stretched so far open that her jaw surely must have dislocated. The black stuff filled it completely and flowed out in a thick cable which snaked down her body and pooled on the ground to her left. The pool, only visible as a black hole in the wet tarmac, grew rapidly, not forming a circle, but an oval which stretched and elongated then began to pull itself in, drawing its edges closer together at certain points.

Cars were passing all around Paul; they mounted the pavements to get by and weaved past, angrily sounding their horns at the obstruction, but no one seemed to notice what was going on here; no one stopped to investigate and the truck's driver hadn't even got out yet.

Paul recognised the shape that was being created very early on in the process. The shape was going to become a two-dimensional representation of a man.

When he glanced back at Katie, her mouth was clean and closed. She was smiling that horrible rueful grimace again. The null substance was gone from her shoulders and only a thin strand of it remained attached to her. The taut string of empti-ness ran directly out through her dress; from the centre of her sternum to the chest of the rapidly forming man-shape on the road.

The shadow-man was now as well defined as a police chalk mark around a murdered body might have been. It had legs, a head and a trunk, but the arms were a single, confused lump. Its edges became well defined, then it changed again and quickly gelled into a sharp shape that looked like a child's paper-chain man. The shoulders and trunk narrowed and the arms and legs thinned and became pointed at the ends. The round head stretched and grew a profile that suggested a sloping forehead, a sharp, hooked nose and a small, cruel mouth.

Katie gave a small sigh and the strand of shadow that ran from her chest began to shimmer in rainbow colours.

'Creation, *old poke*,' she said in her deep male voice.

On the ground, the shadow-man was instantly enveloped in a wave of tiny flickering golden lights which ceased as abruptly as a cheap firework. The string that connected it to Katie dissolved into wisps of dark smoke.

'Do you understand now, small boy?' she asked Paul. 'Watch!'

On the wet tarmac, the patch of unreflected light that was the shadow-man began to move, flexing and testing, the way someone trying on a new pair of gloves will do. Then it became motionless. A moment later it began to slip effortlessly along the tarmac. Paul watched it vanish beneath the truck and was only dimly aware of the departure of another of his valued collection of marbles.

Out there in the void, Cindy's bark-rate had increased, and was falling in time with the chirruping cricket noise.

Should have had one with bells, Paul heard a disjointed part of his mind say and did not understand.

The shadow reappeared, but now it was on the truck. It swept up from the front bumper and flattened itself across the radiator grille. All the truck's lights died. Paul watched as it slid inside the truck through the grille. The radiator fractured as if it had been shot from a distance with a shotgun. Clouds of steam billowed out and jets of coolant sprayed out through the grille. A second later, the truck's engine became desperately unhappy and changed from a low, even throb to a sound like an angry bull in an alley full of dustbins. As the engine tore itself apart the truck's tyres began to burst with deafening explosions, each one lowering a different corner. The big wing mirrors twisted and detonated in clouds of glass. The shadow-man appeared again, slipping round from the side of the cab and sliding across the windscreen. The glass shattered and washed over Paul in a warm shower. Paul could see the truck's driver

18

now, a small man who sat hunched up in his seat with his arms protecting his face.

A section of tarmac suddenly vanished beneath the cab and the truck bounced down into it, its suspension squealing horribly. The truck and its trailer was now up to the top of its front bumper in a hole which perfectly matched its size and shape. The shadow-thing flitted across the roof of the cab which sank gracefully down to meet the cowering driver in a screaming wail of tortured metal. Both the cab doors flew off with tremendous force. One was instantly run over by a Ford, whose driver corrected the car's course and kept going, and the other sliced sideways through the windscreen of a passing Volkswagen, surely killing the occupants. The VW ran on to the kerb, hit another car, bounced back and was rammed by a Fiat which burst into flames. Within seconds the area surrounding the truck was filled with crashed and burning cars and injured people. Behind the truck, out of Paul's field of vision, the collisions were continuing.

'Mayhem,' Katie grated as the truck continued to sink into the ground. 'Think about it, *cowboy*. Think about my creations and what they could do to you, *small fish*. It would be easier if you promised not to fuck with me. Do you promise?'

Paul could not speak. Outside of him somewhere Cindy was barking and the cricket was chirruping and this seemed to have a deep significance. Someone was running out of time but he was unable to discern whether it was him or Katie or both of them. He watched in awe as the truck lurched down into the ground, corner by corner, into the hole the shadow-thing was excavating beneath it.

Katie took hold of him in her powerful hands, drew him to her so that he stared deep into her blackened eye sockets and spoke to him in the same kind of low, *menacing* tone that he had used himself on more than one occasion. 'The next demonstration will hurt you more, *cowboy!*' she seethed.

Woof woof . . . woof woof . . . woof woof! Cindy's measured tone called, merging and mingling with the chirruping noise.

19

'PROMISE ME!' Katie urged, shaking him as if he were no heavier than a bag of feathers.

And Paul suddenly recognised desperation in that tone. There was something going on here which he couldn't understand at all, but there was also something he *could* understand, even in his present crazed and traumatised state. It was something that he'd spent most of his life training himself to recognise and assess. Paul knew all about power and the way it balanced and the things that could be done to alter that balance. And whoever or whatever was now inhabiting that blistered body had made a mistake in using that particular tone because it spoke volumes. In spite of the fact that Paul had believed that things were entirely beyond his control, this wasn't the case. For some reason the thing inside Katie's body was concerned about what he might do. That thing – and perhaps it was H. Tyler who had announced that he was on a winning streak – did not want him to fuck with it. Which meant it was uncertain of the outcome if he chose to take that particular course of action.

He smiled a cold smile into Katie's eye sockets. 'I fuck with whoever I want to,' he said.

'You'll regret it if you do, *old poke.* After the next demonstration, you'll be only too pleased to promise me whatever I ask you to,' the thing said and let go of him. Katie's body tottered backwards, stumbled and fell, landing on its back on the truck-sized piece of empty tarmac behind her. The shadow-thing had buried the truck, its trailer and the driver and somehow back-filled the hole and replaced the tarmac – which was fractured into black crazy paving.

Cindy was barking.

Behind Paul the stretch of road was empty. Before him lay what looked like Armageddon. The tangle of wrecked and burning cars went on for as far as he could see and judging from the sound way off in the distance, the shadow-thing had not yet exhausted its energy. Paul could neither believe nor understand any of it. He was totally drained and numb.

Katie lay on her back on the wet tarmac, not a burned and

distorted thing any longer and not a vision of beauty; just a pretty blonde girl he had made a promise to: to look after her and get her home. A girl who for reasons he no longer remembered or understood, he had once vowed to protect with his life and to die for if necessary.

He knelt down beside her, not expecting to find a pulse and not being disappointed when he did not. It didn't mean it was over, apparently, but what it *did* mean was anyone's guess.

Paul picked her up and began to carry her through the rain; away from the mayhem back to where the Alfa 164 stood, alone in the middle lane of a one-way street in a foreign country.

WOW-WOW-WOW . . . WOOF!

Cindy had apparently just run out of patience.

6

Paul surged up through layers of darkness, fighting like a drowning man. He broke the surface, gasping for air and pushing away the hot, damp thing that was trying to suffocate him. For a long moment he had no idea where he was and his hand groped in the darkness for a pull-cord switch which wasn't there.

Woof woof! Cindy barked.

Paul found the cord in the wrong place, turned the lights on and discovered that he was not in a foreign country at all. He was simply in a foreign bed. And even this wasn't strictly true. He was in his *own* bed, the one where he had slept soundly – *And had nightmares too, poke!* – when he had been a child. It had become foreign simply because until recently he had only slept in it twice since he was nineteen. Although he had not been in it for over a month, the bed he still regarded as his own was north of the river in Hampstead in the house his darling wife had acrimoniously claimed was now to become her very own property. This bed was in Stepney in his old room in his mother's small two-storey apartment. The bed and the room had seemed much bigger in his youth.

21

Paul stood up, realising several things at once. The most important was that although he didn't own his own bed any more, he seemed to be still in safe possession of all his marbles. Secondary to this was the realisation that the dream – or nightmare – had been more powerful than any other he'd ever suffered and that although he was drenched in perspiration and shaking with emotion, he was very glad indeed to have been able to wake up from it. The other, seemingly less important things, were that the chirruping noise that had wormed its way into his nightmare was not a cricket, but the brand new downstairs telephone his mother had insisted on buying, and the somewhat astonishing fact that the Cindy dog – who wasn't dead at all – had chosen to time her barking with the phone's chirruping ring.

Paul went downstairs, frowning as his head cleared. The nightmare was still vivid in his memory, but it was rapidly being pushed aside by the fact that the phone was trilling away – and must have been for the past five minutes or more – at three-thirty in the morning.

Paul had been through a time early on in his career when he had expected to get caught – or at least hoovered up as a suspect – after every crime, but over the years of successful operation this worry had waned. It was difficult to keep believing you would get caught when the knock at the door never came.

Except, old poke, that things have changed now, haven't they?

Paul had to admit that this was true. The house in Hampstead was now worth almost half a million, which should have been enough to pay off darling Amy – and he'd been blackmailed into giving it to her while he paid off the mortgage – but there was always a chance that she had decided to spill the beans on him anyway. Amy had grown into the sort of woman to whom the term 'cutting off your nose to spite your face' wouldn't necessarily occur until after the action had been accomplished. Amy's heart had always ruled her head. And as far as the subject of Paul Dekker went, Amy's heart was very black indeed.

Out in the kitchen, Cindy barked in time with the gently trilling phone.

'Shut up, dog. I'm up and I'm answering it!' Paul said down the hall.

'Rrrruff!' the dog replied and fell silent.

Paul looked at the phone and was suddenly uncertain about actually picking it up.

But the police wouldn't call to tell you that Amy had told them all about you, would they? his mind assured him. *They'd be round here banging the door down. And anyway, Amy doesn't have the slightest idea what you've been up to in the past month, does she?*

Which meant that it could only be Jake with a problem (which was unlikely), Freddie Simmons in trouble (much more likely), or one of his mother Joan's elderly friends with some urgent bad news to impart. No one called at this time of night unless the news was bad.

Maybe Amy got herself run over, he thought flippantly, then cursed himself for even considering it. He would not wish that upon *anyone* – Amy or the poor sap driving the car.

He snatched the phone up and held it to his ear. 'Yes?' he enquired.

There was no reply.

Paul listened to the empty static hiss and wondered. Somewhere off in the distance of Telecom's network he could hear a small, burbling crossed-line voice whose words were tortured beyond recognition. Echoing pops and hisses that somehow suggested a great distance came and went. A relay clattered and fell silent. One of the reasons his mother had insisted on having the new phone was the sudden increase in background noise. She was certain – and Paul had no good reason to doubt her – that the old handset was well on its way to wherever telephones went to die. And according to her, the new one had solved the problem.

'Who is it?' Paul asked, thinking, *Not Amy, not at this time of night, surely?*

The distorted voice in the distance rose in pitch and then

fell silent. Paul listened to the reverberating nothingness and shivered. *There's a lot of room in there, old poke*, his mind whispered. *A whole* universe *of it. What do you suppose it would be like if you fell in?* Paul didn't know, didn't want to know and in the light of the nightmare which still burned in his mind, didn't even want himself having thoughts like that. He pushed it away.

'Who's there?' he asked into the distance. Considering how long the phone had been ringing, which suggested that the call was urgent, whoever it was didn't seem eager to speak. If it had been Amy on the other end, he was certain his ear would already be reeling under the onslaught – in fact, a full shouting match would probably have been in progress by now.

Paul listened carefully and could not detect any sound in the room at the other end of the line. Sometimes when callers refused to speak you could hear things happening – TVs or radios working, or electric fans, or the building's ambient noise – which would give you at least a vague idea of what type of call this was. Here, there was nothing.

'I'm getting tired of waiting for you,' Paul suddenly announced, keeping his tone free of the anger that was rising in him. Under these circumstances, he would normally have quietly invited the caller to present himself at the earliest opportunity in order to have his face torn off, but there was still a possibility that the call was for his mother and he didn't want to make himself unpopular with her. He needed to stay here for another week or so until the business in progress was concluded.

'Okay. I've had enough. I'm going now,' Paul said into the Telecom void, and put the phone down.

7

Paul went to the kitchen, ignoring the feeling of relief that was flooding through him, because the smell of *things being wrong* had not abated. He put the kettle on and made a fuss of the

Cindy dog – who lay on her back wiggling. He refused to contemplate the possibility that the telephone call had only been a part of his nightmare and that it hadn't been ringing at all when he'd picked it up.

I would have heard a dialling tone.

Unless you didn't wake up until you put the phone down, his *farmer-oppozite* voice instantly returned.

And again Paul refused to contemplate this possibility. The *farmer-oppozite* (as his mother called any thing or person that disagreed – it was from some children's story, apparently) part of him which almost always had conflicting views to his own, had been born in the dark days after he'd killed the kid and had remained with him ever since, forever trying to drag him down. He told himself that this was only natural and he wasn't turning schizophrenic. These kinds of thoughts – as the nightmare had been – were all part of his mind's way of dealing with the fact that he'd killed the kid. Although, as he well knew, it wasn't easy to do, you simply had to learn to live with things like that. He'd talked to people who knew and he'd read all the books and, by effort of will, had convinced himself that he hadn't cracked up after he'd killed the kid – even if his ex-wife and the goading part of him said he had. He hadn't cracked up then and he wasn't cracking up now. Nor had he lost his bottle as Amy and the nagging voice of his unconscious accused.

And if you needed any proof there was the small matter of the sixteen Jaguars (including two 1968 'E' types), ten Mercedes 500SLs, five Ford Granadas, two Rolls-Royce Silver Shadows and a Bentley Mulsanne Turbo that he'd successfully stolen and disposed of in the past three weeks.

All of them – except the Fords – had been taken off the street, which had reaffirmed his belief in himself. He knew no one else who could enter, start and remove a parked car, without causing any damage, in such a short time. He had apparently been born with an affinity and respect for machinery and an understanding of its internal *life*. And in return, machinery seemed to understand and welcome him. Excluding

25

the Alfa 164 of his nightmare (a make of car he'd never yet attempted to enter, simply because one had never appeared on his list) no car had ever yet broken down on him.

Paul did not normally voice this fact, even to himself, because of his superstition. He had been known to deny his superstition, but the fact remained that he always wore the same pair of jeans when he went out to work, he always took his lucky ten pfennig piece with him and he never considered the possibility of his mark breaking down on him. Paul did not like to tempt providence.

And if *that* little list wasn't enough, there were the five Fords that Freddie Simmons had ordered. Paul had a list of the parking habits of twenty-eight of this particular breed (new company cars, mainly) and could have taken all of them in a day if he'd wanted, but there was still the small and niggling matter of his nerve. A part of him – the part that had suddenly appeared after he'd killed the kid – had not yet been appeased. This part had said, *Oh, yeah, so you can still sneak up on things and drive them away when there's no real danger. Very brave of you, old cowboy. About as brave as wiping your own arse without having to call your mother to do it for you, I'd say.*

So Paul had met the ancient and wheezing Print Stokes in a pub in Fulham and had let Print breathe garlic and the fumes of Waddington's best bitter over him for the better part of an hour while he listened to the man's tedious life history – which, although offensive to Paul's sensitive olfactory nerves, was the only way business with Print could be done. For a 'very special rate of fifty-five nicker, cash up front' as Print had put it (when everyone knew this was the exact amount he charged everyone), Paul had ordered a Visa card and driving licence in the name of Michael Davis, 14 Henrietta Street WC2, which was the address of the office where Amy had worked when he first knew her.

When he collected the plastic and paper a week later, the surname on them was Spinks. When he complained to Print that he was neither heavy enough nor black enough to pass as a famous American boxer, Print shrugged it off, claiming truthfully that his memory was getting a little bit shaky these days and, a little less truthfully, that one false name was as good as another.

But Print had unknowingly increased the risk of the challenge and something inside Paul had risen to it. If he could calmly look the Avis or Godfrey Davis girl in the eye and claim not to be *the* Michael Spinks, but *a* Michael Spinks, ha ha what confusion it sometimes caused – then he would have conclusively proved that he had not lost his nerve. And privately – but he kept this away from his conscious mind in case the taunting part of him latched on to it – he doubted you could find very many car rental agency girls who knew who the boxer was anyway.

And there was no problem with the five agencies he chose and three of the five assistants who didn't recognise the name were men – which either said something about the popularity of boxing or the sporting tastes of car rental clerks.

He 'hired' each Granada for a week, renting one a day over a five-day period, and neither his Mickey Mouse driving licence nor his moody credit car was challenged – or even commented on. The cars had been delivered to Freddie Simmons' garage in Dover and were now, presumably, either sunning themselves in the Spanish Costas, where Freddie did business with a great many British expatriates, or on their way to North Africa or the Gulf States. The London version of Michael Spinks was now deceased, his identity having been reduced to a pile of ashes and a small pool of melted plastic. Let DC Dick Farris and DS Steve Jones pick the bones out of *that* little scam.

The kettle boiled and turned itself off. The dog was now asleep on her back, so Paul stopped scratching her belly, stood up, put a tea bag in a cup and poured water on it. He didn't particularly want a cup of tea at the moment, but he didn't particularly want to go back to bed either. The sheets would still be damp with his sweat for one thing, and for another he needed more time for his mind to settle. Amy had always sworn that she would wake up screaming in the middle of her nightmares, calm herself enough to go back to sleep and then fall straight back into the dream where it had left off. Paul didn't relish the thought of *that* happening to him tonight. The memory of the nightmare was not fading as dreams normally did the moment you awoke; it was hanging heavy in his mind like a real event he had taken part in – like something he had actually experienced.

Henry, he thought. *The girl – Katie – called out Henry, and the thing that got into her body said that H. Tyler was on a winning streak.*

Paul did not know a Henry, or an H. Tyler – or a Katie either, come to that. Pondering this, he took the bag from the cup and got milk from the fridge. If your brain simply made up dreams from things you'd experienced during the day, then the names, the Alfa Romeo and the nature of the shadow-thing must all have sprung from something that he'd seen or heard and forgotten about. The theme of the dream – death and destruction and hopelessness – was easy to trace. The kid he'd killed. His name had been Paul too. Paul Saunders, aged eight, known to his family and friends as Paulie.

Which was what Katie called you after she'd changed, wasn't it, poke?

'Guilt,' he said, and Cindy looked up at him questioningly through bleary eyes.

And the telephone began to chirrup again.

Woof woof . . . woof woof! Cindy said pointedly.

8

Paul ran up the hall and snatched the phone from its cradle before he had time to think about not doing it. 'What the fuck d'you want?' he bellowed and clamped his mouth shut before the words: *Why don't you leave me alone?* followed. He was surprised that this particular arrangement of words had even occurred to him and his anger rose.

'If you've got a problem,' he said in a murderous voice, 'I'd very much like to discuss it with you. I'm sure we could come to some kind of *arrangement*. I currently have one in mind that I would find very, very satisfying indeed. On your part, it would involve severe anguish.'

The big noisy nothingness answered him.

Fuming, Paul whacked the handset back into the cradle with so much force that it bounced out again, swung on its cord and hit the night-storage radiator, denting the thin tin front panel. Cussing under his breath, Paul grabbed the handset, checked the dialling tone, and thrust it back into its base. Boots and Pacific Bell could both award themselves ten points: the phone was undamaged.

It immediately rang again.

Paul grabbed it before the second of the pair of chirrups and brought it to his ear in a quick, jerking movement. This time he said nothing, merely listened to the sound of the cyberspace hissing at him while he fought to control his temper.

'I'm lost,' a distant, tinny voice said at a volume that was barely audible.

Paul's boiling anger vanished and suddenly he was experiencing something that had never happened to him before. His skin began to creep as if it were suddenly unhappy about being in contact with him. It was a warm June night and in spite of his being naked he had been sweating; now he was suddenly cold and tingling.

'Help me . . . *please* . . . I don't know where I am,' the voice implored.

'Who is this?' Paul asked, but a large part of him already knew *exactly* who this was. That part of him – which he was carefully ignoring – was trying to tell him that he recognised the female voice, tinny and distant though it was.

'What should I *do*?' the voice cried and Paul told himself that whoever it was at the other end of the phone – *And you wouldn't even have the faintest idea of* who *that is, would you, old cowboy?* – had not heard his question at all and was not necessarily

29

speaking to him either. Perhaps it was another crossed line, even if his skin *was* telling him this was not so.

Paul smelled the familiar acrid odour of burning electrical insulation and felt both the phone's leads which were cool.

'I can't *find* you,' the girl said. She sounded shocked and terribly lonely and a part of Paul recognised this and empathised with her. The crawling of his cold skin increased.

'Katie?' he asked, wishing immediately that he hadn't said this – and also wishing that he could convince himself that he was still asleep and dreaming, which he knew was not the case.

The voice was drowned under a wave of static.

'Hello?' Paul said. He could not bring himself to move, let alone put the telephone down and forget about it. He was transfixed.

The phone crackled.

Something cold touched Paul's bare leg and he gasped and jumped, realising for the first time since he'd woken that he badly needed to urinate – and now, he was so tense, he almost had. He was frightened to look down until his other half informed him that, *yes*, he did recognise that voice as being the voice of Katie, the girl of his dreams and, *no*, that was not her touching him, just the Cindy dog announcing her arrival in her usual way by bumping him with her nose. The dog now sat looking at him, her head cocked sideways in her *there's-something-fishy-going-on-here* look.

The line suddenly cleared – as much as it was going to, anyway – and the girl's distressed voice came through again.

'I can't *find* you and I think I'm dying and I don't know where I am,' she said. 'It hurts. He *did* something and I can't remember what it was. *Please tell me what to do!*'

'*Katie?*' Paul shouted. 'What's happened to you? Where are you?' A vision of the girl standing before the truck had lit in his mind, and as crazy and illogical as it seemed – and it seemed very crazy and illogical indeed – Paul distantly remembered making a pledge to protect her with his life. Not during

30

the dream, but even before that. He was overwhelmed with an urgent need to do whatever he could for her, whether or not the girl on the phone turned out to be the Katie of his nightmare. And as his mother would have testified: Paul Dekker was a sucker for a girl in distress.

I should be careful what you say here, poke, the doubting part of him chipped in. *Just don't make any promises you won't want to keep. Nothing's been done yet, and maybe we ought to leave it at that. For a while at least. Preferably for a good, long while.*

But Paul did not want to listen.

'I'm *lost*,' the girl cried plaintively. 'I'm broken and I'm lost and I think I'm *dying*. I can't find you.'

'Who is this?' Paul asked.

'Oh . . . it *hurts*!' the girl's distant voice said. 'Help me!'

'I'll help you!' Paul said. 'Just tell me where you are!'

'But I don't know. It's dark and I can't find you and it's too late!'

Paul ground his teeth as static washed the girl's tiny pained voice away from him. Another picture of Katie formed in his mind but now it was a picture of her afterwards – when she had changed. 'There are worse things in Heaven and Hell, *old poke*, remember that,' the blackened face reminded him.

'It . . . *hurts*!' the voice moaned through the static. 'I'm dying now and it *hurts so bad! Please! Promise me you'll . . .*'

'I promise!' Paul said – and found himself listening to the dialling tone.

9

'Whatever's wrong?' a rusty voice wanted to know.

Paul spun around, the phone still in his hand. His mother stood at the top of the stairs in pink slippers and a man's maroon dressing gown. Her hair, backlit by the landing light, made a white halo around her head. She clasped a walking stick across her chest.

Beside Paul, the dog began to hammer the floor with her tail.

31

Paul realised he was standing naked in front of his mother and tried to cover himself three different ways before he thought of putting the phone down. He covered his cock and balls and as much pubic hair as he could manage with his hands and stood there feeling absurdly guilty.

His mother squinted down at him. 'I could hear shouting,' she said. 'I thought someone had broken in.' She raised the walking stick. 'But it was only you,' she added and Paul thought he detected a note of disappointment in her voice. If he'd wanted any indication of from which side of the family he'd inherited his quick temper and tendency to violence, he realised, he had just received a very substantial one.

'What's happened?' the old lady wanted to know.

'Nothing,' Paul said. 'Just a phone call.'

His mother raised her eyebrows knowingly. 'Amy?'

Paul shook his head and sweat fell into his eyes. 'Wrong number.'

It was patently obvious that his mother did not believe this, but she shrugged the matter off anyway. Helen Dekker did not pry, as she was fond of saying, on the grounds that it might tend to incriminate her. 'Made enough noise about it, whatever it was,' she said, then added, 'And since you've woken me up, you make me some tea if there's any hot water left in the kettle. And put the dog back in her basket when you've finished with her too,' she commanded as she went back to her bedroom.

10

When Paul took his mother's tea in for her five minutes later, she was sound asleep. He left the cup on the stand beside her bed and went back to his own room.

He lay in his damp bed and thought about Amy and the nightmare girl called Katie who had died twice on him in one night and listened to the dawn chorus outside.

Going back to sleep was impossible.

And this suited Paul just fine.

Chapter Two
Piewacket

1

Piewacket had left home.

Robert Farmer wondered about this during the quiet moments (and he made sure there were plenty of them) when he was alone in his office and letting his underlings sail the good ship Barclay's Bank. Frazier currently had the helm and was entertaining a delegation of Pakistanis who needed to borrow two and three-quarter million in order to expand their growing hotel business in Earls Court. As far as Robert Farmer was concerned, Steve Frazier – who openly and cheerfully admitted to anyone except Robert himself that he intended to depose and replace the current manager within two years – was welcome to them. The current manager (now with only eighteen months left on Frazier's calendar) had more important things to think about.

Like Piewacket, the missing cat.

It was not unusual for the ginger tom to go walkabout, and over the years they'd housed the cat (*owned* was not the correct word in this context), he and Addy had become used to its comings and goings. There was no pattern to be discerned in them, although Robert had studied them for years – eleven of them, if his sharply honed memory still served him correctly. As far as he could tell, the cat did not respond to the seasons, the ambient temperature or the emotional atmosphere at home. His movements seemed to be completely random. Addy contended that sometimes her Piewacket (a wholly unsuitable 'baby' for a barren thirty-eight-year-old woman) simply needed to be alone, and would fly into a rage at the suggestion that perhaps the cat's hormones drove it from the house and the Sunningdale neighbourhood in search of what Robert would call 'a little pussy'.

The difference this time was that Robert didn't think that Piewacket was going to come back. Not because he had been run over or had died of old age (unfortunately there was plenty of life still left in that hateful animal) but because the time for being Addy's cat had come to an end.

And Robert recognised the powerful symbolism in Piewacket's departure. The time for being Addy's cat had come to an end, and this fact, once its implications were recognised, became a harbinger of the arrival of many new – and seemingly golden – opportunities. Time had moved on, had brought Robert closer to becoming his true self.

Robert's relationship with Addy was not a terribly good one, but neither was it a terribly *bad* one. What it was, was a terribly *boring* one. Poor Addy liked what she knew and she knew the missionary position (although she only seemed to like it vaguely and then not too often). She also knew their position on the social ladder, knew that shifting it upwards a rung or two wouldn't hurt and knew how to use her family's money and influence to do it. She knew and liked all the good and dull people who 'mattered' in Sunningdale and Ascot and she knew how to give them good and dull dinner parties.

What Addy didn't know – and *wouldn't* have liked if she had – was that for Robert the two high points of their fifteen years together had both happened on the 30th of August nearly three years before. Afterwards – a very long time afterwards – Addy had told him that she would forgive what he'd done but that she would never *forget*. And Robert had never forgotten either: for two reasons. The first was that during the half-hour aberration that randomly occurred in the evening of that hot Saturday, his true self had awoken from a deep slumber. The second reason was that afterwards Robert had been forced to become an actor because his true self had refused to go back to sleep again.

2

That August the thirtieth, three years earlier, had turned out to be a *special* day.

Robert had hated the idea of the charity fête from the moment Addy first mentioned it. He complained that the garden wasn't big enough (which it was) and that no one would attend (which they did, including the celebrities Bruce Forsythe, Michael and Mary Parkinson, and the disc jockey Steve Wright and his family). He had also complained about the cost of the catering (which Addy's bottomless current account had paid for anyway), the arrangements for the competitions and the destination of the money received: Addy had chosen a fifty-fifty split between the British Heart Foundation and the Terrence Higgins Trust, and Robert thought there should have been at least two more recipients.

But despite his attempts at derailing the whole affair – which were rooted, he knew, in his extreme hatred of the persona *Mr Addy Long*, which was how his wife's rich and well-connected friends thought of him – the fête was a success.

By half-past six, the last guests had left, the caterers had packed and gone home and only he and Addy remained in the huge garden. They sat opposite one another across a trestle table which housed a wheel of fortune betting game, the minimum stake on which had been ten pounds. The wheel itself had taken three hundred and ninety pounds between two and five. Addy was glowing with success and Robert – who had turned forty the day before yesterday, a fact of which she had been, and still was, totally unaware – was drinking whisky and simmering slowly to the boil. His secretary, Daisy May Jones, had remembered his birthday, his cousin from Australia had faxed the bank with a note of congratulation and even Frazier had sent him a card. But dear Addy had been too wrapped up in her precious fête.

35

She was tanned and bra-less in a white shirt and long, floral print skirt and she was sipping a Perrier and re-living the delightful afternoon. *Darling, you should have seen Eric in the log chopping contest! He took off his shirt and went through three in ninety seconds! He was all muscular and sheened with sweat. Lady Caroline screamed for him so much she almost wet herself and I bet I can guess what those two will be up to later on. He was so macho! No one could believe it! You really should have come out earlier.*

Mr Addy Long had spent the better part of the afternoon skulking in his study with a bottle of Glenfiddich and Piewacket for company. Addy had forced him outside towards the end to help thank everyone for coming.

'We raised almost three thousand! That's good darling, isn't it?' she said.

Robert did not reply. Three thousand was roughly what the cost of the tent hire and the outside caterers totted up to. Addy could have done better by donating this money and calling her friends on the phone.

'And everyone had such a lovely time!' she said.

Which was exactly what it was all about, Robert knew. Not money for charity, but an excuse for a party. He put out a hand towards his whisky glass and realised it was trembling. The words 'everyone had such a lovely time' were echoing inside his head as if someone had removed his brain and replaced it with a huge cavern. In the centre of this cavern, floating in the darkness, was a single, horrible and seductive thought: *You can have a good time too!*

And the good time, he knew without having to think about it, was tied in with the brand new, gleaming axe which he could see behind Addy, buried in the chopping block in front of the bar tent. A load of hewn logs were stacked up on either side of the block and the grass on which it stood was covered in wood chippings. Robert had heard the steady, wet *thwack-thwack* of the axe rising and falling and the roar of the crowd earlier in the afternoon and the sound had been strangely arousing.

He stood up, unbuttoned his shirt and took it off. There was a Nautilus in a part of the cellar which wasn't storing the family (Addy's family, that was) collection of fine wines, and Robert used it regularly. He was in excellent shape.

Addy's mouth dropped open. 'What are you doing?' she asked.

'I was forty on Thursday,' he replied. He clenched and relaxed both his fists several times, pumping up the muscles in his forearms. Veins and tendons began to stand out, ready for work. He pulled his tensed arms to his chest and felt his biceps and shoulder muscles swell. 'A landmark age. An age of change.'

Addie's face fell. 'Oh, *Robert!*' she said. 'I'm sorry . . . I didn't mean . . .'

'Everyone had such a lovely time!' he growled.

'I'll make it up to you, Bobby! I'm so sorry!'

But he hardly heard her words. The angry drunken feeling had left him and had been replaced by a cold, sober rage that had a lot to do with the axe and the emptiness inside his head. He stood on his chair, walked across the table, knocking over Irma Wilkes' antique wheel of fortune, jumped down on to the grass and strode over to the axe, whose buried head and erect shaft called to him like Excalibur had called to Arthur.

Robert Farmer could – and would – have fun too!

'Don't, Bobby!' Addy called from behind him.

He glanced back at her. Addy was on her feet, facing him, her left hand at her mouth. Her thumbnail, he knew, would be forcing its way between her two upper front teeth, which meant that Addy was worried.

The axe head glinted in the rays of the late sun but looked cold. The smooth white beech of the shaft had greasy finger marks on it but seemed welcoming. *Let's have us some fun!* it seemed to be saying to him.

Robert turned back to face Addy who was shifting her weight from foot to foot in a kind of paralysed walking motion. Her sun-tanned look of warm satisfaction had turned into a pasty kind of mottled brown. 'Robert, come back,' she called, 'You'll . . .'

'I'll what? Hurt you? I'm not going to take the chopper to

you, Addy. I'm just going to have me some of that fun you've been having all day.' He pulled off his shoes and socks and threw them aside. The grass felt sticky under his feet and the wood chippings were damp and sharp and clean.

'I'll make it up to you!' Addy called across the lawn. 'Just tell me what I can do! I promise! Bobby!'

Behind him the axe handle was reaching out for him. He could *feel* it. 'You just stay where you are, Addy!' he commanded. 'I'll want to talk to you in a few minutes. Don't try to run away because I'll catch up with you, you know that!'

'But, *darling!* Be reasonable!'

Robert unfastened his belt, looped it around his hand and slapped it into the palm of the other. The crack it made was loud enough to scare the birds from the oak tree at the far end of the garden. Addy jumped. 'Don't try to talk me down. I don't want to be a lap dog today. And I won't be reasonable. Today is my belated birthday and I'm going to celebrate it. And do you know how?'

Addy said nothing. Her hands were clasped in front of her mouth as if she were praying. Her thumbnails would now be finding the gaps between her two front teeth and her incisors. This was her maximum stress position.

'DO YOU KNOW HOW?' Robert bellowed, unfastening his trousers and unzipping his fly.

Addy shook her head.

'By putting on a show for *you*, my dear.' Robert pulled down his trousers and shorts together and stepped out of them. A distant part of him doubted if it were possible to have a larger, harder erection than the one he had just set free. The warm air and the sun felt good on it and his balls drew up into a tight pouch.

'Someone will see,' Addy said, somewhat pathetically.

'The tent people aren't coming back until tomorrow, everyone else has gone and there's a hedge all the way around the garden. Who's going to see?'

'Robert, I . . .'

He ignored her, turned and took hold of the axe handle. *Let it fly*, the axe said to him. *Use me well!*

Robert yanked the axe toward him and it came out of the block silently and easily. The block didn't even lift a corner. His ears began to sing the song of swiftly pumping blood. In a two-handed grip, he swung the axe into the air above his head and, at exactly the right moment, reversed his power and brought it scything down. The chopping block was a trunk section from an oak tree. It stood about two feet high. The glinting axe head hit the block square in the middle, swept through it as if it were plasticine and buried itself deep in the grass. Robert felt no shock. The muscles in his groin pulsed twice in a pre-orgasmic spasm and he remembered the Spode dinner service which Addy had insisted the caterers use. It used to belong to her grandmother, it was so valuable that the caterers had insisted on a letter of non-culpability for any damage which might occur to it before they would even consider touching it, and it had more pieces than a jigsaw puzzle.

And on the spot Robert decided that it ought to *become* a jigsaw puzzle.

That might be very nice, why don't you take me there! the axe said in his mind. *I only want to make you a happy man on your belated birthday!*

Robert glanced back at Addy who had pulled herself down into what might have resembled a question mark if he had been looking at her in profile. He wanted to hurt her – not simply for forgetting his birthday or for being boring or even for being a social climber – but because she'd chained him down over the past fifteen years; led him into being a shell of a man when she could have brought out his power. They could have been happy together if only Addy had seen his potential. But she either didn't possess the vision or she *had* seen his potential and had not liked what she'd seen and gone out of her way to bury it. Either way, she deserved to have something happen to her after she'd watched her best Spode china become best Spode fragments.

'I'll deal with you in a moment, my love,' he told her, and grinned fiercely when she shrank down into even more of a question mark. Addy expected to die – that much was certain.

The Spode set was currently stacked on the row of trestle tables where the buffet had been served. Paper plates and cups would not do for Addy Long. A condition of the caterers had been that they would neither take the crockery indoors afterwards nor wash it, to which Addy had replied, 'We have a perfectly good dishwasher.' By which, Robert assumed, she meant him. Robert Farmer would not be washing this particular load of expensive and delicate crockery.

Behind him, Addy had suddenly begun to understand his intentions. 'No, Bobby! Not the china!' she bleated.

Halfway up the lawn, Robert began to think of Henry Tyler, his old room mate at Cambridge. He was surprised at the sudden memory, but not totally. H. would have loved to have seen this. He had been a man who loved mayhem above all other things. The sight of a naked, sexually excited man walking towards a set of Spode china with a brand new axe in his hands would have kept him happy for weeks. H. had gone off to work in the field of artificial intelligence and Robert hadn't seen him for almost twenty years or thought of him for fifteen. H. had been unreliable at the best of times and Robert thought he was probably running drugs or armaments for a living these days.

Robert reached the table and swung the axe into the air just as Addy's arms gripped him around the waist. 'DON'T!' she pleaded. He paused, the axe still above his head, and looked down at her pink-pearl-painted nails grazing the flesh of his abdomen. His pelvic floor muscles throbbed again and the clear lubricating liquid that Addy called 'love juice' descended from his penis, dampening the linen table cloth. He wanted to have her then, but he shrugged her off him.

'*Please!*' Addy moaned and this struck him as sexual too – exactly the kind of sound she could have made and didn't.

He brought the axe crashing down into a pile of dinner

plates which exploded into shards at exactly the moment that the trestle table collapsed. The crockery slid into the centre of the vee and a great deal of the more delicate items broke with an extremely pleasing tinkling sound. But not enough.

As Robert raised the axe again, Addy placed her hands on both his shoulders, dug her nails in hard and raked them right down his back, over his buttocks and down his thighs. There was a brief sensation of stinging which was replaced by eight separate lines of extreme heat. These quickly blurred into two livid furrows of pain.

Robert brought the axe down into the china, and the axe – or perhaps only his imagination – chuckled.

'Glue that lot back together, Addy!' he shouted and hit the table again, right in the centre.

The two halves of the trestle parted company, spilling the wrecked china on to the lawn.

Robert turned round to face his wife. She was about twenty feet behind him and clutching a small milk jug to her bosom with her left hand. In her right hand she held an empty whisky bottle by the neck.

Apparently anguish at seeing her prize china reduced to rubble had overcome fear for her own safety.

'Not this one, you bastard!' she said, waving the bottle. 'You won't get this one!'

Robert's heart thudded in his chest and his muscles sang with work done and work yet to do. *Now we're going to have us some fun!* the axe whispered in his mind and he realised what had made him think of H. Those words had been H.'s octet – his eight-word motto. Robert suddenly remembered H. saying that as he lit the rag in his cider-bottle Molotov cocktail – the one he was about to fling at Stanton's cherished Morris Minor. Robert remembered the crazy look in H.'s eyes and thought that that same look was probably in his own eyes at this very moment. Back then, watching H., he had been confused and frightened, but now, at long last, he understood. Sometimes you had to let the demon in you out to play.

41

And when you did, it felt very good indeed.

Hatred and defiance shone in Addy's dark eyes as she backed down the lawn away from him.

'I believe you're supposed to *break* the bottle, Addy,' Robert told her, grinning. 'You won't stab me with the blunt end, will you?'

Addy's mouth worked, but no words came out. Robert assumed that she was trying to tell him that a blow in the face with the bottom of the bottle wasn't exactly going to do his features a power of good either.

He strode over to the table they had been sitting at and swiped the axe out sideways at Irma's fallen wheel of fortune which exploded in splinters of wood.

'Robert!' Addy called, her face aghast. 'Stop it now!'

'But I'm having so much fun, dear,' he replied mildly. The power of the axe was almost drowning him now. He lifted it and brought it down in the centre of the linen-covered table. The table fell and a distant part of him – the part that had been *all* of him before he got the good idea – started to mutter about how upset the hire people were going to be when they turned up tomorrow to collect their tents and tables. But the gleeful Robert-the-axe-man part of him didn't care about tomorrow. That shining new part of him wanted to destroy and to fuck. He advanced on Addy, who was backing towards the deep end of the pool.

Robert briefly entertained a delightful vision of Addy – who had never learned to swim, poor thing – backing right to the edge of the pool, then falling in. The water would churn in white foam as she struggled and failed to stay afloat. The vision almost brought him to orgasm and he thought that if *that* happened, his internal power would fade away and leave him wondering what all the overpowering urgency and fuss had been about – which was what usually happened to him after making love.

To prevent this from happening, he turned his attention to the beer tent and toured the perimeter, hacking the guy ropes

42

down in an easy, one-handed swing. The axe and Robert Farmer seemed to be in perfect, tireless balance, as though he'd been a lumberjack all his life. There was no stress, no nagging muscles or stiff joints, just a perfect hacking machine. When the sides of the tent were free, he went inside, intending to cut the corner and centre posts, then his eyes lit on the remains of the sale-or-return bar and he spent a minute laying waste to it.

After this he hurried back out into the evening sunshine, half expecting Addy to have used the opportunity to run past him and hide in the house – which would have been very unfortunate for her. Robert-the-axe-man had decided to confine his leisure pursuits to the outdoors – for today at least – but he was aware that he could quite easily be persuaded otherwise. There was a huge amount of wood inside that big fifteen-room Jacobean house. Enough to keep the average wild axe man busy for a week. There were acres of panelling, miles of floorboards, challenging oak beams and lots of lovely antique furniture – all of which had been supplied by Addy and her family. Robert's own contributions to *la maison* Farmer/Long (Addy had kept her own family name after the marriage and it had taken Robert five years to realise she'd done this because *his* wasn't good enough) were few. He had supplied an Axminster, all the televisions, radios, videos and other assorted electronic equipment, and three cars: a Range Rover, a Daimler Sovereign and, his pride and joy, the convertible Jaguar XJS V12 – which some total shit had stolen last week from the bank's own underground car park.

But Addy hadn't used the time to flee. She was about fifteen feet in front of the swimming pool, still hunched up into the question mark shape and she still had the milk jug and the whisky bottle. Robert's whole body started to shudder when he saw her there and he distantly thought his balls would burst. His naked skin seemed to have become a large, unbelievably sensitive erogenous zone that had been stroked and toyed with for long enough to push it over the edge into a slow, fizzling orgasm that didn't involve ejaculation. Many conflicting emotions and thoughts raced through his mind. The axe was whispering about how good it would feel if he were to apply it to Addy and another, deeper part of him knew that as much as she deserved it, this would be too quick. Another part of him wanted to have her and keep having her for as long as humanly possible, and a very distant part – now travelling on the very edges of his mind's known universe and likely to slip over at any second – wanted things back as they were before.

'Don't come any closer!' Addy said in a tremulous voice as he walked towards her, carrying the axe across his right shoulder.

'Or *what*, Addy?'

She did not reply.

We're going to have us some fun now! the dominant part of his mind told him. And Robert agreed that, yes, he certainly was going to have some fun and ceased thinking. 'Wish me a happy birthday, Addy!' he said.

She backed away, holding the bottle out in front of her like a sword.

'I SAID, WISH ME A HAPPY BIRTHDAY!' he thundered.

'Happy birthday, Bobby,' Addy replied in a terrified voice. 'I'm sorry I forgot. I really am! Oh, Bobby . . . *please don't hurt me!*'

'Put the jug down then,' he told her.

'And you won't hurt me?'

'Do as I tell you!'

Addy placed the last remaining piece of her treasured Spode service down in front of her and backed away. Waves of pleasure so intense that he thought he might faint swept through Robert's skin. His penis pulsed three times and for a moment he thought it was all over; ejaculation would surely lead to death. But ejaculation did not follow.

He steadied himself, drawing power from the axe, and approached the jug.

'I did as I was told,' Addy reminded him.

'So you did,' he agreed, not looking up at her. His eyes were fixed by the milk jug – not because of the juxtaposition of the delicate beauty of its pure whiteness and intricate floral design against the lush green of the manicured lawn, but because he was targeting it.

Robert stood tall, lifted his gaze from the jug and stared Addy right in the eyes. He placed his left arm behind his back in much the same way that Prince Charles on a visit might have done and carelessly flicked the axe from his right shoulder with his right hand. He knew without looking that the arc the axe described was smooth and graceful.

The honed edge of the axe head came into contact with the exact centre of the milk jug's lip. A moment later the axe head was buried in the ground and the jug existed only as a tiny pile of pieces.

Robert hefted the axe out of the turf and strode towards Addy who shuffled backwards on to the apron of the pool. During the afternoon, several fully dressed people had been in the pool – either thrown in or of their own volition – and the evidence remained floating there: a coloured handkerchief; an unopened but almost waterlogged packet of Rothman's King size; a lot of grass from people's shoes and half a leather watch strap. Some wag had, Robert knew, placed a tray at the bottom of the deep end and stood six crystal wine goblets upon it.

'You promised not to hurt me!' Addy complained.

'I don't recall promising any such thing,' Robert said, taking the cool head of the axe in his left hand. 'I think you ought to wish me a happy birthday and put down the bottle.'

Addy placed the whisky bottle at her feet and murmured the words required.

'Good girl,' he replied, still advancing on her.

Addy was backed right up to the edge of the deep end of the pool now and surely must be able to smell the chlorinated water behind her, even if she somehow hadn't noticed that the better part of the concrete apron was now between her and Robert.

'Take off your clothes,' he said.

Addy appeared to be in shock – which, he supposed, wasn't

terribly surprising under the circumstances. 'Why?' she asked in a lost voice.

'Because I'm going to fuck you,' he replied. '*First.*'

She didn't move.

Robert took a step closer.

Addy's heels found the edge of the pool and she gave a small cry, suddenly realising the awful position she'd backed herself into. 'Bobby, please don't hurt me!' she moaned.

The power over her was making his head sing; making him dizzy. 'Undress,' he said and for a moment her hands toyed with her shirt buttons and he thought he'd won. If she did as she was told, Addy would no longer be the dominant partner. She would no longer be a partner *at all* but something akin to a lap dog. Which would be a good step forward for his development.

But Addy's power had not been reduced to that extent – not even after witnessing the devastation he had wrought and not even in fear for her life. Her hands clasped and she began to bite her thumbnails.

'Here I come then, Addy. I'm coming to get you,' he said and swiped out at her with the axe, knowing it would miss her by a foot.

Addy leapt backwards into the pool.

Robert walked to the edge and waited for the water to clear. He began to snigger as he watched her fight her way to the surface in that clumsy fashion that only non-swimmers are able to achieve.

Addy's head and shoulders broke the surface and she gasped in air in a wet, reverse-scream, her hands floundering beside her for something solid and fixed to grab hold of. She slipped back beneath the churning surface, her body bucking like a horse with a chilli pepper in its anus.

Robert clasped the cool steel of the axe head to his chest as he watched her fight her way back up again.

The next time Addy broke the surface, he was amused to see that she was clutching one of the crystal wine glasses in her hand. She stayed at the surface for longer this time, trying to choke out water and suck in air at the same time.

'Sink or swim, Addy,' he told her. 'The only way to learn.'

When the third and final time that the drowning person of legend was supposed to bob up arrived, Robert informed her that she should have taken more notice of him when he had tried to teach her to swim. 'You understand how *handy* it can be?' he asked as she slipped back beneath the surface, her floral skirt billowing out around her. He waited to see if the old adage were true and was not disappointed to discover that it wasn't.

The water churned at Robert's feet and Addy's hands shot out of it and grasped the pool's edge. She hauled her head out of the water and choked out a great deal of fluid. When she heaved in a breath her lungs rattled. She coughed again then noticed her husband towering over her. 'Enough,' she gasped.

Robert brought the axe down from his chest, took hold of the very end of the handle, letting it hang vertically, and positioned it about four inches above Addy's left hand.

Then he let it fall.

The flattened metal and the oval of beech where the handle was mounted hit her fingers with a deadened thud. Addy yelped, tore her hand away and fell back into the water.

Robert watched as her struggles grew weaker and on the sixth time her hand left the water, he placed the handle of the axe near it, for her to hold on to.

Addy's damaged left hand found the beech shaft and clamped on to it like a limpet. Holding the axe head, Robert drew her towards him, then took her arm and pulled her out of the water. He laid her on her side and prepared to give her artificial respiration, but this was not necessary; she began to cough and gasp immediately.

Robert waited, his body and mind singing.

Eventually the wet coughing gave way to a damp laboured breathing. Addy found the strength to sit up. She looked up at her husband, her hands clamped to her chest and tears streaming from her eyes. 'Hurts,' she croaked.

'Happy birthday to me,' Robert said. He reached down, grabbed the front of her shirt and yanked it away from her, fully expecting it to tear right off her in one go. He was surprised when all that happened was that the shirt buttons all flew off and his wife sprawled forwards on to her face. She did not try to get up. Robert took the collar of the shirt and hefted it up towards him, pulling Addy off the ground as the shirt bit into her armpits.

The axe, now held in his left hand, was sending out strong messages that it would be better to get this over and done with now, this minute, and forget all the other stuff, but the spry part of his new mind was in the ascendant and it realised that weapons had a very narrow point of view. They existed for the moment of maiming and killing and nothing else mattered to them. To let the voice of the weapon speak *for* you rather than *to* you was a mistake. It would only result in a short, sharp killing spree of the type often perpetrated these days. And everyone knew what happened to the perpetrators when the weapon was sated and its voice fell silent. They were lost: more often than not to the more powerful voice of another weapon. Life was not that simple, not that black and white. Power was not built that way. The pattern was a great deal more sophisticated than this.

So Robert let the axe fall and was delighted when his new power did not diminish whatsoever. He had somehow captured the essence of the axe without it capturing him.

He hauled Addy round in a circle, hoping the force would tear the shirt, which it didn't. It simply rose in his hand so that Addy's upper body was bare apart from the harness the shirt had formed around her shoulders and armpits. The other effect was that Addy was now back on the ground, scrambling on all fours to alleviate the pressure where the shirt bit into her.

It wasn't what Robert had envisaged, but it had certain advantages. Addy's legs were scrambling up inside her loose skirt, tearing through the front of it and pulling the back down over her hips.

He hauled her across the lawn, like a man walking a recalcitrant Rottweiler, watching as her skirt slipped down over her bottom, drawing her silk Janet Reger French knickers with it. When her legs became hopelessly entangled in the material, he dropped her and yanked her free of it.

Addy sobbed and coughed as Robert spread her out face down on the lawn and the sound and her feeble resistance added to his burgeoning power.

'Wish me a happy birthday, Addy,' he said as he knelt between her legs and lifted her hips.

Addy's anus looked very small and tight and his erection looked very big. But he was also well lubricated. He dug his thumbs deep into her buttocks, stretching that most closely guarded of her secrets. Addy screamed as he forced his way deep inside her and kept screaming as his thrusting rose in speed and power.

Robert didn't reach orgasm for a very long time.

3

Afterwards, Addy didn't do any of the things Robert had expected her to.

She had fainted when he finally pulled out of her and he had carried her to her bedroom, cleaned her up (her anus had bled quite a bit more than he had expected it would), put her to bed, dressed and gone back outside, still tingling with the new power. In the refreshing calm that followed the release of the demon Robert, he understood with crystal clarity that what had happened today was merely a glimpse of what was to come. He would have to be patient and wait for the proper time to arrive; the time when this new side of him could be given its head.

He had cleaned up the broken Spode and deposited it in the dustbin – along with the remains of the wheel of fortune and his wife's ruined clothes – folded the linen table cloths and folded and stacked the tables, while a grudging respect for his wife grew in him.

Robert had known that at the very least this would be the end for them and at the very worst he could be arrested and charged with a vast catalogue of crime which would range from criminal damage to aggravated rape and buggery and possibly even attempted murder. This would mean not only the dissolution of his marriage and the end of his banking career but possibly a prison sentence – on rule 42 in a sex offenders' wing. And yet the new Robert considered that the set of new sensibilities he had gained would offset any price that had to be paid.

Addy slept for twenty-four hours and Robert took all the telephone calls of congratulation that came in and handled them gracefully, explaining that his wife had succumbed to a mild stomach upset and was sleeping it off. This amused him because it wasn't too far (as the crow flew and not as the intestinal tract wound) from the truth. During this period of grace all the incriminating evidence was removed. He settled in cash with the tent hire people and the caterers for the damage – caused by a fictitious drunk. He ran the dustbin of Spode to the dump in Windsor and buried the axe deep in a flower border close to the house.

When Addy woke up at eight o'clock on Monday evening, she didn't scream the house down or dress and get in the Rover and go home to Mummy or even calmly call the police. She came downstairs to where Robert was sitting in the lounge sipping whisky and thinking about H. Tyler who swore that his initial stood for Homicidal Maniac and would not argue when asked where the M. had got to, other than to say: 'That's just the way it is.' Addy was pale and puffy with sleep. Robert looked up at her and she simply said, 'Would you please make me a cup of coffee, Bobby? I'm very thirsty and my throat is sore. I'm going to have a bath now.' Then she turned and left the room.

Robert made her the coffee and took it to her. Addy didn't freeze when he entered the bathroom and she hadn't been sitting there crying – in spite of the friction burns that encircled both her shoulders, the scabbed knees, the swollen fingers on her left hand or the bruises around her throat (which he didn't even remember causing). Addy didn't even seem numb with shock; just tired.

Over the following three weeks the only sign that something had changed between them was that Addy was subdued and hardly spoke to him. Then she began to treat him normally again. Except that it wasn't 'normally' as in the way she had treated him before the unspoken incident, but now with a certain respect and deference that had not been present before it. For a month after that, Robert suspected she was quietly plotting to kill him.

When no attempt on his life was forthcoming, he started to think that there were going to be no repercussions at all – and, perhaps, that his attack on Addy had been so severe that she had become unable to remember it: as if her mind had excised the memory.

The problem he had faced during that autumn and down the slippery slope into winter had been internal rather than external. Now he'd levered the lid off the box inside him marked '*Demon*' its inhabitant simply refused to get back inside. Instead it performed a strange kind of osmosis and seeped through the rational workaday part of him, altering its composition. The demon was out and had become hopelessly entangled in him – had in fact *become* him. Which, he supposed later, was lucky: the unadulterated demon that had possessed him on the evening of the fête would not have allowed him much semblance of a 'normal' life. The problem was that the demon part of the New Robert was very close to the surface and eager to pop up its powerful head (teeth bared and drooling, he often imagined). During those months of learning how his new personality worked, he had had to be very careful: each time he'd seen his assistant manager Frazier, he had dearly wished to poke his fingers in those shifty eyes; in October he'd had to leave a meeting of his superiors when he became irritated with them because the heavy onyx ashtray that Simpson was using (in a non-smoking area) was calling to him, and he'd had to keep his secretary Daisy May out of his office whenever possible because each time she entered the room he instantaneously grew an erection so hard that it hurt and there seemed to be only one way to relieve it.

The New Robert had quickly become a skilled actor – he already knew all of the old Robert's lines, facial expressions, views, likes and dislikes, and while the demon lurked just below his calm surface, he strove hard to be as seamless and reassuring as he had been before.

He'd finally achieved a controllable balance by the middle of December and a part of him began to wonder if all this hoo-ha hadn't really happened and was just a product of his imagination. With the exception of the time he'd almost killed then raped his wife, his inner feelings didn't seem altogether different (judging from the books and magazines he read and films he saw) from what was considered to be normal.

On December the twenty-first that year he had arrived home at seven, found Addy standing in the lounge and they had word-lessly fallen into one another's arms – at first like two good friends that have been apart for a long time, then like parted lovers. They had gone upstairs and made love in the missionary position – Addy as silently and static as before and Robert carefully, wondering when the thing lurking beneath the surface would jump out and take over. But the thing never did jump out.

Afterwards, as Robert was dozing, Addy began to speak of the terrible thing he'd done to her in August. She had decided she would forgive him, she said, but she would *never* forget.

4

By the following April, Robert's dominance of his wife (a dominance he seldom practised since knowing it existed was satisfying enough) became the norm and slotted into place with all the other humdrum jigsaw parts of his life. By June he was as bored as he had been before he let the demon out of the box. He worked out relentlessly and polished his squash game until he became the kind of ruthless player nobody wishes to have a quick game with between work and a meal.

Robert expected the pressure to build in him until he was forced to release it with an act of extreme violence – and some days he wished for this to happen. But the only pressure was that of his acting job, and of a new personality settling into his body and the fact that Frazier was trying and failing to stab him in the back at the office. There was no climb to a point at which the demon would have to be released again.

Robert was somewhat disappointed to realise that his pretence of being normal seemed to have knocked off the demon's rough edges.

The main difference in his life was the abundance of nightmarish dreams – in which he fought and killed people to protect something undefined and unseen – and the waking sense of marking time.

Then the New Robert began to shrivel. The dreams ceased and the feeling of vitality that had been with him since the attack on Addy began to fade. At first he thought the New Robert was dying off with lack of use or purpose, then he began to understand that changes were still taking place inside him. The New Robert had sprung upon him unformed and was not dying but falling into a pupal stage, withdrawing into a hard-shelled chrysalis where he would stay until the time was right. Robert did not know what would finally emerge, or when. He began to feel empty and deserted. Now he found himself not acting to mask the presence of the New Robert, but with the unsatisfactory task of having to remain an actor to mask its departure. He toyed with the idea of trying to force his new personality into the open, then decided against it. It would all happen when the time was right.

Robert did the only thing possible. He waited patiently and watched for the signs.

5

And now a week and a half after Robert's second Jaguar XJS had been stolen from the same spot in the same car park as the first had almost three years ago, and almost three years after he'd taken the lid off the demon box and attacked his wife, Piewacket had left home.

Robert sat behind his desk linking paperclips and thinking. The first sign, of course, had been the theft of his car – although he didn't recognise it then. In the hours following the news (which had been broken to him by a very smug Frazier) he had been possessed by a kind of blind fury during which he could and would have torn off the thief's limbs had that man or woman been presented to him. But it wasn't until earlier today, when he reached the conclusion that Piewacket had left home, that he began to think that the anger which followed the theft of his car had been the first stirrings of the New Robert who had lain dormant for so long.

Now he sat in his office, linking fresh paperclips to the end of the long chain he was building, and began to track back through the weeks preceding the crime. There would surely be more clues; more random incidents that might also prove to be signs.

The roof of the greenhouse in the back garden had fallen in under the weight of the snow in February, Addy had sprained her ankle falling down the last two stairs in May and a couple of toads had moved into the garden in the spring. None of these things seemed to hold any special significance, however. Robert started to examine the minutiae of his life and found nothing special there either. Whatever was happening seemed to have started with the theft of his Jaguar.

And Piewacket had then begun to act strangely – if a cat as erratic and hateful as Piewacket could be said to have *begun* to act in that fashion. The tom's opinion of Robert had *actually* changed on Sunday the thirtieth of August, thirty-three months ago; the day after the New Robert had attacked Addy. He would no longer sit on Robert's lap, purring and pulling up threads with his claws, and would no longer even share the same room unless Addy also happened to be in it. Robert had tried briefly to heal his relationship with the cat – a diplomatic effort which had been abruptly terminated when Piewacket (who hadn't wanted to be lifted from the floor) had sunk his claws into Robert's arm, and his teeth deep into Robert's hand. On this occasion, the still-present demon had risen to the challenge. Piewacket had been flung the full width of the lounge with all the force Robert could muster. The cat hit the radiator, bounced off and lay still on the floor, leaving Robert triumphant and already plotting to bury the body where the gardener was unlikely to find it. But after a few moments, the stunned animal picked itself up, hissed meaningfully at Robert and strode from the room.

Piewacket hadn't left home after that, and had not strayed far until now. During the time that Robert was fighting for control of himself, the cat made itself known to him, often and spitefully. Piewacket apparently recognised the New Robert, didn't like what it saw and had declared war. The cat had run under his feet at the top of the stairs – apparently with the intention of making him fall, had fallen on him spitting and hissing from the high shelf in the study, and had clawed and chewed at his two most expensive suits. It had also taken to leaving dead, and sometimes quite rotten, mice (and on one occasion a rat half as large as itself) amongst his belongings.

Robert had tried to do the cat mortal damage on more than one occasion, but if Piewacket was anything, he was quick on his feet. On more than one occasion he had proven his acceleration (from a sleeping start on the drive's warm shingle) to be faster than the best standing start Robert could make flat-out in the V12 Jaguar.

They had reached an uneasy truce when the New Robert went into hiding and although they still kept a good distance between them, had stopped trying to kill one another.

But during the ten days following the theft of the car, Piewacket had become uneasy. He would wander the house, complaining vociferously and never settling. During the long weekend Robert had spent at home the cat seemed to become very suspicious of the corners of the rooms and spent a great deal of time sitting a few feet away from them and staring.

And on the Monday, he had vanished.

The time for being Addy's cat had come to an end.

And sitting there, linking paperclips, Robert realised that Piewacket's departure had coincided with a shift in the times. The world had moved – branched off, if you were a supporter of the *many worlds* theory – and entered a new phase. Now he thought about it, Robert could feel it in his bones; smell it in the air.

Piewacket had finished his relationship with Addy and that part of Robert's life suddenly seemed to be over too. The waiting had finished and things were about to move.

6

During his sleep that night, Robert dreamed of a great disruption in the earth; of new men rising and travelling to meet their shining destiny. He dreamed of the fiery angels of chaos ranked behind a blazing H. Tyler, and in the dream H. told Robert the name of the man who had stolen both his Jaguars. The man's name was Dekker and he was significant in a way that was far greater than the theft of two cars.

And during his dreams, the fully-formed New Robert Farmer hatched and absorbed the old one.

The New Robert awoke realising three important things. The first was that the laws of physics could be perverted, the second was that a thief named Dekker had stolen both the Jaguars Robert had lost, and the third was that Dekker was the only thing which stood between him and his destiny.

Chapter Three
Travellers

1

Robert Farmer would not have been very surprised to learn that in Bude, Cornwall, a distraught woman named Denise Defoe was currently giving detectives a full description of her husband Peter after having explained what he'd done.

Denise dabbed her eyes. 'Six foot two inches,' she said in response to the question the lady detective had asked. 'I can't believe *how* he could have done it. I just *cannot understand it!*' she wailed.

The lady detective – whose name she thought was Jane – laid a warm hand on top of Denise's cold one. 'Try not to think about it, love,' she said gently. 'How heavy was he?'

'Thirteen stone seven,' Denise heard her flat voice say. 'He was on a diet. He lost almost a stone.'

Yesterday night her life had been perfect. Now, here she was at eight o'clock the following morning, sitting in the dining room of her next-door neighbour's house with nothing at all left of her happy, comfortable existence. Her past life – the one that had been so wonderful until the strike of twelve o'clock when it had turned into a rotten pumpkin – lay in ruins, less than twenty feet away from her in her own house; a house to which she would never be able to return.

'Do you have any idea where he might be headed?' Jane asked quietly.

Denise shook her head. 'To the moon. To the Raj Indian

restaurant. To his brother in Phoenix, Arizona. To Hell, I hope!'

The Inspector sat on the far side of the table. So far he had not spoken to her directly and Denise hoped he wouldn't. His face in repose had a confident, self-satisfied expression that a distant part of her wished to remove with her fingernails.

A tall, fat detective peered around the door. 'We've got the album,' he said, partially inserting Denise's latest photographic record of her family in through the gap in the door. The white leatherbound album – a Christmas gift from her mother – had a smear of blood across the front of it.

The realisation that she was either looking at Clara's blood or Nicky's burned through her blanket of shock like a white-hot poker and re-lit her smouldering anguish. The room spun around her and she heard herself cry out.

Then she was being clasped against Jane's warm body and rocked gently back and forth and soothing words were being rained down upon her. She sobbed into the girl's stiff white shirt and tried not to listen to the Inspector telling the other detective that Peter was travelling in an old Austin Cambridge, registration number TYU 9G, and was probably not very far away since there didn't appear to be anywhere for him to go.

'Can you tell me . . . love?'

Denise looked into the kind face of the policewoman who was ten years her junior at least and who couldn't possibly know *anything* about the real world yet. 'What?' she asked.

'Can you tell me anywhere you think he might be heading for? Friends? Relatives? We've put out an alert on the car but it would be nice if we had some indication of where he might be going.'

Denise shook her head. She no longer knew anything about her husband.

'He got religion,' she said sadly to the young woman who would never know what it was like to sit two walls away from what used to be your whole life.

'When?' a male voice asked.

'Last week,' she said in an empty voice. 'Last week when I had a loving husband and two children and my two children had a rabbit each – one called Thumper and one called Bungee. The rabbits, not the children. The children were called Clara and Nicky. I had two children. I did have them. I love my children. Please bring them back. What kind of a God is it that allows things like this to happen?'

'Which religion?' the same male voice asked.

Denise took a shuddering breath. 'The religion of destruction, I suppose,' she heard herself say. 'The same religion everyone else gets.'

'Denise,' the girl sighed in a voice which ached with pity.

Denise started to sob.

2

The truth was that Denise hadn't paid a great deal of attention to Peter's claim that he had got religion. A working mother with two energetic primary school aged children and a husband whose butterfly mind was suckered by every doorstep evangelist and new fad that happened by (for about ten minutes on each occasion), found it difficult to keep up with her husband's passing fancies. This week he was collecting coins, the following he was building model aircraft, the next he was toying with the idea of becoming a councillor.

Peter brought in a good wage from the machinist's job he had, but it wasn't fulfilling and it didn't tap his quick mind; hence, she supposed, the flurry of varying leisure activities. Ever since she'd known him, Peter had been searching for something he couldn't define – or even take an educated guess at. Whatever it was, his job, his various hobbies and even his sex life couldn't sate the urge.

The religion, which he had mentioned in passing, simply saying 'I got religion today,' was, as far as Denise was concerned, either a joke or another nine-day wonder. Peter hadn't mentioned it again, and since the house wasn't suddenly filled with literature she assumed that it was just another of Peter's conversational gap-fillers.

Until last night, life had been about as perfect as it was possible to get for a thirty-year-old mother of two. Her family were happy, healthy, well-fed and looked after, and the little she managed to save from her job at Rumbelows provided life's occasional luxuries.

And now it had all been silently taken away from her.

She had woken at midnight, alone in the bed with a strange smell in her nostrils. The smell was not particularly strong, but it was an unusual enough change in the house's ambience to have woken her up in the same sudden and suspicious way the burning tea-towel had back in the days before they'd bought the smoke alarm. This smell, however, was nothing to do with smoke. It smelled like raw steak that was just beginning to turn sour. There was also an unpleasant undertone of excrement.

The odour, Denise thought, getting out of bed and putting on her gown, had to be coming from the bathroom where Peter was undoubtedly busy being ill. The other alternative was that one of the children was sick and he was in there with them, holding them while they threw up. Denise hovered at the door, listening. At the sound of the first retch, she knew, she would have to get back into bed and bury her head under the pillows. Her main failing as a mother was her violent aversion to vomit. She could clear loose shit until the cows came home and a bit of blood didn't faze her but the mere words *vomit, puke, sick* and *bilious attack* were enough to turn her stomach. Watching someone throw up never failed to tug on Denise's heave-string and after a five second battle to control herself, she would find herself joining them. As a consequence of this, the guy who dealt with the puke was the guy who was currently absent from his own side of the bed.

She listened for thirty seconds and heard no movement.

Denise's heartbeat began to pick up speed along with her following thoughts. There were worse things than vomit.

Her father had died of a heart attack (alone in the bathroom coincidentally – where he had been sitting on what he'd called 'the doughnut' reading *Readers Digest* and waiting to excrete whatever it was causing the pain in his 'stomach'). Peter's mother had died of angina and both his grandparents had gone in variations on the same awful theme. Peter himself sometimes suffered chest pains (although he swore they were muscle pains and only came after a bout of heavy lifting at work).

All these thoughts cascaded through Denise's mind and a vision of Peter writhing on the bathroom floor suddenly bloomed in her mind. By now he would be a blue-tinged grey; his body would be juddering faintly as its component parts were starved of oxygen. His heart would be fluttering or stopped.

Denise tore open the bedroom door and ran down the landing to the bathroom, not yet noticing the marks smeared on the walls or the stains on the magnolia paintwork of the carefully closed bathroom door.

'Please God, don't let it have happened!' she murmured as she flung the door open.

The door was not obstructed by Peter's fallen body though; she didn't have to push her way in. The door hit the wall and began to swing back but the nap of the fluffy carpet halted it. The bright bathroom light hurt her eyes.

At first, Denise's mind could not identify the thing in the bath. While it rooted through its store of recognition shapes trying to find one to fit what lay before her, relief flooded through her. Her husband had *not* succumbed to the traitor she thought lived in his chest.

A moment later her senses told her that since that red thing resting on the edge of the bath seemed to fit the shape of a hand (although it didn't fit well since there were only two digits attached to it) then it was very likely that the large lump of red stuff to which it was joined was a body, even if it did look like something that had made two journeys through Seth Brundle's teleport system in *The Fly*.

Her mind used the following moment of shock to inform her that, yes that was indeed shit smeared along the side panel of the bath and that the red stuff everywhere – in spite of her refusal to recognise it – was doubtless going to turn out to be blood.

The worst shock came when she finally admitted to herself that the thing in the bath was not her husband. The size and shape of it would not fit into any version of what might have happened to him that she cared to think of.

The truth was, she realised as she staggered towards it, now aware that her own heart might not be able to handle this pressure for very long, was that it was one of the children.

And even this wasn't the full truth.

The full truth was that the thing had four limbs and two heads. That lump of raw gristle in the bath was all that was left of Clara and Nicky.

Some time between Denise's falling asleep at eleven and midnight, someone had brought Clara and Nicky into the bathroom and had noiselessly slaughtered and butchered them.

IT'S NOT POSSIBLE! Denise's mind protested. No one could have done this in that short time and without making any noise. The kids would have screamed blue murder!

But as much as she denied it, the sight and smell of the evidence would not go away. This was not a nightmare. This was real life. It had happened.

Denise turned away and stumbled downstairs, following the trail of blood smeared on the banisters and the footprints on the carpet. She tried to empty her mind of the facts while she sought help. The fact, for example, that she had been unable to tell, not just where Nicky ended and Clara began, but *which was which*. Those things that she had tucked up in bed a few hours before as smiling children had become things that would have been incapable of any expression even if they had survived. Because along with most of the fingers of their right hands, the skin covering their heads had been removed. Not only had they been scalped but both their faces had been removed. *Torn off over their heads*, she tried not to let herself think, *like balaclava helmets*.

There was a finger on the mat at the bottom of the stairs. Denise passed by it, unaware of the mewling noises she was making, aware only that her heart might soon burst and that for no reason whatsoever her children had been butchered and her own life had been ruined along with theirs. She had not escaped at all. Having to live after this was far worse.

She expected to find the killer downstairs and hoped that she would because, before he put her out of her agony, he might be able to provide an answer to the question that wouldn't leave her alone.

The question was: *Why?*

There were traces of his movements all over the house: footprints, fingermarks, smears of blood. Denise followed the trail, hoping to die. Peter was not in the lounge, carved into shreds, and the killer wasn't there either. And they weren't in the kitchen or the dining room. She followed the trail to the front door. The Yale lock there was smeared where he'd opened it with slippery hands. Those same slippery hands had taken Peter's car keys from the hook above the phone and had neatly severed the telephone line.

Denise followed his trail to the empty space where the Cambridge had been parked, then stopped, no longer knowing what to do. She seemed to be buried deep inside herself and as much as she wished to die, she knew she wouldn't. Peter was not in the house. Peter had not been killed. Peter's car keys were gone. For a moment none of it fitted and when it *did* begin to mesh something in Denise's mind snapped.

Peter and the killer were the same person.

She turned to go back into the house, distantly intending to take a knife and run it across both her wrists, but the warm smell of blood and excrement that wafted out of the door prevented her from entering. She knew then that she could never go back inside.

Like an automaton, she walked out into the street, went next-door and rang the bell until a bleary-eyed Larry answered, quickly becoming alert and saying, 'My God, whatever's happened, Denny?' which was exactly what the shocked thing buried deep inside her had expected him to say. She felt as if she was trapped under a layer of ice, while her body acted out a scene which would have been handled identically – and a sight more convincingly – in any second-rate soap opera.

'Peter's killed the kids,' she heard her body say. 'Can I come in?'

And after that she remembered nothing until waking up feeling as if she were wrapped in cotton wool and realising she was surrounded by detectives who wanted to know things. There was a mark in the crook of her left elbow which presumably meant that someone had given her a shot of something powerful. Whatever it was, its insulating effects rapidly wore off. Now she was sitting there trying to think of places where her husband might have fled to when all she wanted to know was how could he have done such a terrible thing.

3

Peter Defoe, who was heading north-east in his Austin Cambridge, knew he was safe. He could not be detected because he was travelling with the faces and five assorted right-hand fingers of his deceased children. The voice he had been able to hear since he got religion had informed him of this sweet little piece of voodoo magic and it had been telling the truth. He had passed five police cruisers so far and although they must have been looking for him by now, not one of them had given him so much as a second glance.

The voice had also whispered to him that similar escapes to his own were being made all around the country. It had not given the details. So far, Peter knew the details of nothing except those concerning what he'd had to do. The *reasons* for his actions however, were still obscured from him. All he knew was that he would not be detected and that the other escapees numbered eleven.

4

One of the others, a muscular, thirty-nine-year-old Afro-Carribean man named Reuben Brown, was heading north from his home in Finchley in a pristine '68 Ford Mustang. The car was so gorgeous that when it was pulled (an irritating fact of life that Reuben hadn't so much grown used to as learned to live with) the police no longer invited him to empty his pockets and answer questions about his movements, but wanted to talk about the car. Since he'd taken possession of the Mustang, he'd actually met several policemen he'd liked. Reuben, however, would not have admitted this to his friends and colleagues, because Reuben was a confidence trickster.

In the boot of the Mustang were all the things he needed for a stay away; including his three passports, four driving licences, four false credit cards and a case of Wild Turkey – which was another piece of Americana in which he allowed himself to indulge. None of these items was concealed (other than being in his big brown bag) because; a) the police no longer asked to look in his boot, and b) he didn't expect to be pulled over today. Which, if things worked out as he expected, was a very good thing, because there was also a heavy strong-box in there containing the thirty-five thousand pounds he had illegally acquired in an hour and a half yesterday evening.

This particular scam had been Reuben's all-time favourite. He had stolen cars on credit cards, he had worked hard at business tricks and in his younger days he had stuck up a building society or two, but nothing before had been so beautifully simple to arrange or had given him such a tasty payoff in regard to the work done.

Yesterday evening, Reuben had washed, shaved off his moustache and had put on a security guard's uniform he'd borrowed. He had driven to Gatwick airport in the blue Transit van he'd bought for the occasion (the most expensive part of the operation had been paying for the Securicor logo to be painted on either side of it) and parked it illegally outside. He put on his peaked blue crash helmet, got out of the van and took the strong-box inside. Inside the airport's main concourse he took the strongbox to the Lloyds safety deposit box, laid it on the floor, unlocked it and took out the sign he'd carefully stencilled earlier. The sign fitted easily and neatly into the gap around the safety deposit box and it read:

THIS SAFETY DEPOSIT BOX IS OUT OF ORDER
PLEASE LEAVE DEPOSITS WITH SECURITY GUARD
WE APOLOGISE FOR ANY INCONVENIENCE
THANK YOU FOR YOUR COOPERATION

Reuben had first noticed the deposit box while he was here switching suitcases. On that particular day, he had hauled a hundred and twenty-five pounds, thirty-three thousand lire, a bottle of cheap whisky, a load of useless clothes and a dead tortoise. He was dispirited and on his way home when his eyes lit on the deposit box and his imagination started to run riot. He had returned on three separate occasions and stationed himself near it. Almost every business in the building seemed to make a deposit in it between the hours of seven and nine p.m. – which, he presumed, was when the shifts changed. Reuben didn't know exactly how much the traders fed into the box on an average day, but it looked as if it was a lot.

He had stood there in front of his sign for about five minutes when the first punter came up with a heavy bag of money. Reuben took it from him, selected a key from an impressive bunch and locked the bag in the box in front of him, sympathised with him about the inconvenience, complained a great deal about the bank's failing machinery – adding, however, that the overtime was going to help his pay packet a great deal come the end of the month – and the punter walked away satisfied.

As soon as Reuben had dabbed the nervous sweat from his face the next punter arrived.

In an hour and a half, the strongbox was full and Reuben decided that it was about time the deposit box was repaired. He spoke into his hissing fake radio, listened to the non-existent reply while holding up a hand to indicate that the woman now trying to give him money should wait, then told her that the problem had been sorted electronically. He took down his sign and stood protectively by the woman while she made her deposit, joked with her that if his information was wrong her money might well just vanish into thin air, then bent to pick up the strongbox.

At this point, he realised he'd made a stupid mistake. The strongbox was more the size of a small chest and it had been fairly heavy when he'd carried it in. Now, with the coins and notes inside it, it was impossible to lift. He cursed himself for not bringing a barrow, then quickly realised there was a very good way out of it. He called over a passing policeman and told the truth.

As far as his failure to bring a sack-barrow with him went, anyway.

The policeman helped him carry the box outside and put it in the van. Reuben thanked him, passed the time with him for a few minutes then told him he'd better get on his way because he didn't like to be alone with all that money.

The policeman told him that since no one knew he was in possession of it, he was unlikely to have it taken from him, then looked confused when Reuben said, 'Precisely.'

Now, following his nose and driving north in the Mustang for reasons which weren't entirely clear to him, Reuben grinned. It was a killer scam and he intended to use it again when this little bit of business (whatever it was) was over and done with. But that would be later; for the moment, it felt good and proper to be motoring in the Mustang and to end up wherever the ending up place happened to be.

5

The ending up place for Janice Darling happened to be the east-bound side of Membury services on the M4 motorway between Swindon and Newbury, and Janice was not terribly thrilled about it.

It was now eight o'clock on a cool morning in early June, the services were full of breakfasting sales representatives, travelling businessmen and truck drivers, and at best, Janice looked out of place. The phrase 'at best', however, no longer featured in her vocabulary.

Because unlike everyone else in the service area, Janice was not dressed for the day. Janice was dressed for the night. And not the kind of night you generally wanted to advertise publicly either. She was dressed for the kind of night that (if you were Janice Darling, anyway) you would not even tell your closest friends about.

But in situations this dire, she knew, you sometimes had to forget your principles, ask for help and damn the consequences.

Janice was currently standing in the relative safety of a plastic telephone bubble attempting to do just that. She had chosen Jane Parkin as the lucky friend who was going to drive miles down the motorway and collect her, but Jane wasn't answering.

Janice sighed, and glancing around her, replaced the handset. Passing men and women gave her lingering stares that made her want to fold up and vanish. She turned back to the phone and dialled the operator again, the vague ache in the small of her back now turning into a more defined pain.

The pain, as she well knew, was due to the fact that she had spent the last two hours staggering around this service area in a pair of patent leather shoes, the heels of which were so high she could barely walk. The lingering gazes were due to the rest of her 'special night' clothes. She was dressed in a black leather skirt so short that if she *did* walk in the shoes, it would ride up and reveal her bottom within eight steps – and even *this* wasn't the end of it. She was also wearing a transparent black chiffon shirt and a quarter-cup bra that didn't so much cover her breasts as hoist them up and hold them out for all the world to see.

Janice Darling, a twenty-four-year-old teacher of mathematics who should have been at home in Cardiff getting ready

68

for school, was in trouble. She was frightened, but she was also fuming. Her anger at the man who was the cause of this predicament was the only thing keeping her going.

'I'd like to make a reverse charges phone call,' she said when the operator answered, and told her Jane's number.

'Sorry, caller, there's still no reply,' the operator announced after ten rings.

Janice put the phone down and wondered what to do. Earlier, she had considered following a size 10 woman into the toilets and mugging her for her clothes, but she hadn't thought she could be convincing enough and the thought of actually having to *hit* someone had put her off.

Walking out of here was impossible. The nearby village of Membury was going to be of no use, and even if she got to Swindon or Newbury she wouldn't be able to get home because her cards and money were gone.

Tugging her skirt down, she thought of Gary Richman whose balls, at this moment, she would gladly have torn off.

Thinking back, Janice could scarcely believe it had happened.

Gary had phoned her at eight the previous evening while she was marking books and wondering why everything she taught 3X slid straight off their apparently Teflon-coated minds.

She had pounced on the telephone at the second ring, eager for a break.

'Let's play a game,' a voice had suggested and it was several seconds before she realised that it was Gary with an 'idea'. She had been seeing him for five months, but the 'ideas' hadn't started to surface until about eight weeks ago. It hadn't taken her long to realise that, as strange as they sounded in the cold light of day, Gary's 'ideas' turned her on. Gary was personable, intelligent, and had the kind of body and face that many women would have given their right arms to get next to. The fact that he owned a computer software business, was extremely wealthy and drove a Bentley Mulsanne Turbo had nothing to do with her attraction towards him. The attraction was purely sexual. For the first time in her life, Janice had found herself incapable of keeping her hands off a man. And Gary's body was gorgeous. From the moment he walked into the room, she found herself picturing him naked and hard for her.

'What kind of a game?' she had asked, a feeling of expectation already surging through her from her heart to her knees. She was hooked and she knew it and she didn't ever want to give it up. Some people might have called Gary perverted, but she was not some people.

'A very naughty game,' he had chuckled. 'There's a box outside your door. Put on what it contains and meet me at the end of your street at nine.'

In the carton had been the clothes she was now wearing. She had guessed that Gary wanted her to walk down the street wearing them, but there were still lines that had to be drawn. She *was* a respectable mathematics teacher in a well thought of school, after all. She had protected her modesty beneath a three-quarter length raincoat that she'd torn off herself as the car drew up.

The game had lasted deep into the night and they had 'made love' a total of four times. In between times, Gary had kept her handcuffed and blindfolded in the Bentley while he drove one-handed from one location to another. With the other hand, he had kept her on the boil, teasing orgasm after orgasm out of her. By the time he uncuffed her and allowed her to take off the blindfold (which was when she realised they were cruising down the motorway) she had been fucked (and fucked was the only way to describe it, she thought) twice in the back of the car, once whilst handcuffed to the bicycle shed in her own school and again by the side of the main road between Cowbridge and Bridgend.

It was an evening of which she had heartily approved until they had reached the deserted car park of Membury services where he demanded she get out of the car. The area might have been deserted, but it was well lit and Janice had refused.

She had expected to be punished in some way, but Gary had simply dropped his head into his hands as though he had a

70

headache and had started to mutter answers as though someone she could not hear was asking him questions.

'Yes,' he had said. 'No, not really. Of course it's something that . . . No. I think so. Yes, I'm ready. Yes, certainly. I'll still get it? It can happen like that? Okay. Fine.'

'Gary?' she asked.

'Get out of the car,' he said, looking up. His voice was so quiet and the expression on his face so intense that Janice had done exactly as she was told.

Gary got out of the car too and came round to the passenger side, moving in a stiff-limbed fashion. For a few seconds she thought he might have suffered a stroke. Gary grinned and in the orange light his face suddenly looked so monstrous that her mind told her that this time the fun had gone on just about long enough to push him over the edge. They had reached the point from which little girlies dressed up in erotic clothes scarcely ever returned unscathed.

He's going to kill me! Janice thought. She closed her eyes and waited to die. She was so surprised when he pulled her skirt up and his expert fingers began to manipulate her clitoris that she screamed and came at the same time.

'Now go to the centre of the car park,' he said in a voice that sounded like rusty metal.

'Gary . . . I . . .' she said breathlessly, then did as she was told. He would drive the car over to her, yank her in and fuck her – she was certain of this.

Instead, she had watched as the Bentley glided out of the car park and out of her life.

For the first hour, Janice had waited at the edge of the car park expecting him to return. When she was propositioned by two men in army uniforms, she fled inside the service area and hid in the toilets until she was relatively calm. By the time she thought of phoning Jane, she had given up all hope of ever seeing Gary again and had begun to curse him for driving away with her coat and her handbag which contained all her money and credit cards.

Now, standing in her plastic bubble unable to contact her friend, she didn't know what to do. Mobility was almost impossible in the heels, and when she walked, she would have to cross her arms over her breasts but she would have to drop her arms in order to pull down the tiny skirt when it rode up. Which meant that by the time she got from one end of the service area to the other, many people would have seen either her buttocks, her breasts or both. Sitting down didn't seem to be an option either, since Gary had torn off the tiny G-string she had been wearing and had cast it out of the car window early on in the evening.

'You look like an angel tonight,' that complete and utter bastard Gary Richman had told her earlier. *Some angel*, she thought and tears began to fill her eyes. She had been played for a fool.

There were only two options left now. One was to play the part she was dressed for and she couldn't really see herself doing that without throwing up, and the other was probably equally as dangerous.

But there are good people in the world, her mind told her. *You're one of them, if you want any kind of proof. There are people who will help you, even if you don't know them. Everything doesn't always have to turn out shitty, just as all men aren't bastards or rapists. There have got to be some good people out there.*

She tested this theory five minutes later in the ladies toilets on the westbound side of the services, having managed to get across the bridge over the carriageway by turning to face the windows each time she needed to tug the skirt back down. In the following ten minutes, she met three women who were, *sorry, love* but who were afraid they *couldn't help* her, five who refused to acknowledge her presence at all, one who *wished she could make money as easily as your sort*, two who apparently couldn't speak English and who looked at her blankly and one woman who offered her twenty-five pounds for sexual services.

But Janice's mind refused to believe there weren't some good people still left in the world. Her heart hammering hard, she dropped her defensive stance, stood up straight, strode purposefully out of the toilets and down the corridor, tugging the leather skirt down occasionally without breaking her stride. She met the gaze of each man who dared to look at her with a challenging steely stare of her own and walked across the car park towards the exit ramp.

Janice would hitch home.

She stood on the exit road that led back on to the westbound motorway carriageway and stuck out her thumb. The first five cars whizzed past without even slowing, then a Lada being driven by an ancient man slowed right down to look at her and Janice instantly decided that she would take a ride in this car. The man looked too old to try to take advantage of her – and if he did try, she was confident she could fight him off.

The old man driving the car might have had similar thoughts, because the car passed her at a walking pace, then speeded up again.

'Come on, *someone* stop!' Janice pleaded.

And a beige Montego pulled up beside her.

'No thank you,' Janice said as the passenger door swung open. The driver was the woman from the toilets who had offered her twenty-five pounds.

'I can take you where you want to go,' the woman promised.

'Sorry,' Janice said, as politely as she could manage, 'I think I'll wait.'

An army truck rolled down the ramp towards her and Janice brought her thumb down. The back of the truck was full of squaddies who waved and shouted and cat-called at her. A big guy in a maroon beret stood up in the middle of the mass of bodies, clenched both his fists to his chest and shouted theatrically, 'An angel! Come to me, angel! I love you!'

In spite of herself, Janice smiled when the soldier feigned collapse and fell backwards into the arms of his companions. She thought she probably would have been safer in the back of that truck than alone in a car with a single man, and when the next army lorry appeared, she thumbed it.

Its driver waved and smiled, but it did not stop.

A middle-aged woman in an Escort pulled up about twenty feet in front of her and as Janice started to totter towards it, apparently had second thoughts. She drove away when there was still ten feet between them.

'You *swine!*' Janice shouted after the car. 'I thought us women were supposed to help each other out!'

A picture of Gary suddenly popped into her mind. He was sitting in the Bentley in a lay-by concentrating on something. Her coat was across his lap and her open handbag stood on top of it. Something was clutched tightly between his hands, but in the picture it was indistinct. She got the feeling Gary was trying very hard to accomplish something.

Janice shook her head and said, 'Get away from me, you *bastard!* I don't want you inside my body *or* inside my head, ever again!'

Another car passed her without stopping. This one had a stereo so loud she could still hear it when the car was out on the motorway.

Don't want to arrive home deaf, anyway, she told herself.

The picture of Gary returned and she thrust it away. A white Citroën rolled slowly towards her and she covered her breasts with her right arm and thumbed at it with her left. A pretty woman was driving and a man with a shock of wild hair sat in the passenger seat. She met the man's gaze as the car closed on her and had the strange – somehow, *comforting* – feeling that this man knew all about her. But the car didn't slow. As it passed, the man shook his head and mouthed the words, *I'm so sorry*, then added another, which left Janice puzzled. She was so certain the last word he'd spoken was *angel* that she mouthed it herself to check that the movements matched. A feeling of sadness settled over her. *You wouldn't let anything happen to me, would you?* she thought and didn't know why she thought it – other than the fact that so far three people had called her *angel* this morning. She wasn't even sure who she had directed the thought *at*. Surely it couldn't have been the odd man in the Citroën?

Gary crept back into her head then and she knew the thought certainly hadn't been directed at him. *What's he doing?* she asked, suddenly certain that he was attempting to contact her. Telepathy, she supposed. He was sitting somewhere safe and warm and using her coat and handbag to try and send her a message, taunting her. They'd played at sending mental messages to one another before, and other than the feeling she'd occasionally had of something scraping the inside of her skull like a rasp (which she attributed to her imagination) it had not worked.

There's a whole uncharted universe around us, Gary had said on more than one occasion, *and when we understand it, we'll have the key to faster-than-light communication.*

It was all to do with Quantum mechanics, he said, and the fact that one of a pair of particles would respond instantly at a distance to something that happened to the other – as if they were still connected. Unravelling and understanding this tangled web, he maintained was going to knock science – and the computer industry in particular – into the twenty-second century. And telepathy, apparently, was a part of it.

Janice, whose mind was unable to provide her with a satisfactory picture of an atom, let alone an electron or photon, wished that Gary would fall straight into that uncharted universe of his and spend the rest of eternity communicating entirely with himself at a speed faster than light.

'Get out of my head!' she shouted, and heard a horrible wailing noise.

And realised that she was now standing in the centre of the slip road and that the wailing noise was being made by the car currently heading straight for her and accelerating, rather than slowing.

Janice screamed and leapt aside, sprawling out on the grass verge as the car passed. When she was able to draw breath again, she swore at Gary who she'd been so preoccupied with she hadn't noticed she was walking into the road. She sat up, realising that she wasn't going to have to worry about walking in the high heels any more, and managed a rueful grin when she realised that she had, as in all the best cartoons, leapt right out of them. The left shoe lay in the slip road before her, its five-inch heel a thing of the past. The car had squashed the shoe so efficiently it looked like nothing more than a crumpled plastic bag. The other shoe was nowhere to be seen.

Then she realised how close to death she had been and began to tremble. *So stand up and start hitching!* she told herself. *Do it now and do it quickly before you turn into the quivering jelly Gary would like you to become. Don't give in to the bastard!*

She hoisted herself from the ground, tugged her skirt down and began to hitch from the other side of the slip road, this time holding out her right thumb and covering her breasts with her left arm.

The breakfasters were now leaving the service area in droves but none of them seemed to want to stop for her.

The image of Gary popped back into her mind's eye and she quickly overlaid it with vivid images of her own: shopping in Sainsbury's; being in bed with Michael; arguing with the headmistress; her first period. It was difficult to swamp the picture of Gary this way but she did it, then shook her fist and snorted in triumph.

A car slowed, then speeded up again as she punched the air.

She could suddenly see her relationship with Gary with the utmost clarity. It hadn't been about pushing back the boundaries of sex at all: it had actually been an exercise in domination – his domination over her. Now she understood why he had never wanted to reverse the roles, in spite of her suggestions, cajoling and the use of her not inconsiderable charm. Michael had loved to be tied up, but Gary would not countenance it. *Because he was driven to dominate you,* she thought. *And where would it have ended up? Not two hours ago you expected him to kill you and you were simply going to stand there and let it happen.*

Janice could not argue about this; it was the truth. Now, she could not understand how this situation had arisen. She was independent, intelligent and didn't stand for any nonsense, either from her pupils, her colleagues or anyone else, male or female. *When you're not walking around almost naked, anyway*, she reminded herself. And yet the fact remained that she had stood there against the shiny door of the Bentley and waited for Gary to kill her because it seemed so logical that he should. Dying for the man who dominated you, was, she supposed, the ultimate act of submission.

'You must have been crazy,' she told herself aloud, refusing to admit to the warm, melting pleasure that had followed this act.

The unpleasant scraping sensation began to rasp on the inside of her skull. *Like rats gnawing*, she thought and said, 'Go away, Gary, you are not wanted here. This girl is looking after herself from now on,' just in case there was such a thing as telepathy and it was causing the odd sensation.

The feeling stopped immediately.

She grinned coldly, then lightened the expression for the approaching car, which just sped on by. Janice didn't care. A well-balanced, middle-aged (and possibly Christian) couple was going to come by soon: the law of averages stated this. These people were immediately going to recognise her predicament. They would not be swayed by her clothing (or lack of it), the fact that she was barefoot and had grass stains on her knees, or any of the other things that were currently working against her. These people would know their duty and they would do it. They would take her as far as they could, and if they weren't actually going into Wales, they would make sure she was able to continue her journey in safety.

Janice pictured these two Samaritans, hoping that visualising them would somehow speed up their appearance – drawing them to her like a magnet, perhaps. She would, she decided, pay them back handsomely for their help.

The names Samuel and Eileen came into her mind and fitted so well with her mental image of the couple who would rescue her in just a moment that she christened them so.

The scraping sensation began again. This time Janice waited to see what would develop. Perhaps Gary was trying to send her a message. In spite of the ill luck she had been experiencing since that bastard had cupped his head in his hands and started to talk as if he was on the telephone, her self-reliance was growing. If Gary was sending her a message, she was certain she could handle whatever it was without its having any ill effect on her. The ever-decreasing chain of events between her, Gary and death was broken and he could exert no authority over her now.

The image of him grew in her mind again. It was identical in every detail to its predecessor and more sharply defined than any of the images her mind normally pictured. And this image was moving – slightly. She could see the rise and fall of Gary's shoulders as he breathed, the occasional flicker of his eyelids as they blinked, the slight tremor in his right index finger as it traced the face of the thing he was apparently concentrating on. She still couldn't see what that thing was, but she thought it might be one of the Polaroids of her that she carried in her handbag and (since *he* had taken them during an earlier escapade) protected with her life.

Looking at that will do you no good whatsoever, she thought, actually attempting to transmit the words to him. *Your power over me has gone!*

In her mind's eye, Gary grimaced. *It works!* his voice said inside her head, but Janice suspected her own mind had supplied this piece of fancy.

Cars swished by her outstretched thumb, but Janice did not see them and heard them only vaguely. Her concentration was totally centred on the image of Gary in his Bentley.

I can hear you, Janice, his voice said inside her head.

Can you hear me telling you to get lost? she asked.

Then she listened carefully, not allowing herself to supply his answer for him.

Nothing happened.

Janice squashed the mental picture and the scraping sensation went away. Both returned almost instantly and this time the feeling was stronger. A vacuum grew in the pit of Janice's stomach and she began to feel as if she was not in control after all.

'If I ever see you again,' she said aloud, 'I shall flatten you with your own car. I intend to go back and forth over you until you resemble a large mass of strawberry jam in a suit.'

Where do you want to get to, love? a voice asked somewhere in the back of her mind. Janice ignored it. 'I shall cut off your balls and carry them in my handbag in a little velvet sack!' she announced.

In front of her, the thin man hanging out of the window of his Mercedes van looked just about as surprised as he would have been had she slapped his face with a wet fish. 'I only stopped to help,' he said indignantly. He tore his eyes away from her breasts and looked into her rather pretty (and very blank) face and told himself that what he had strongly suspected since he'd first spotted her was true: anyone standing in Membury services dressed like that and hitching a lift was not a gift from the gods at all, but someone who had gone stark staring mad. The girl's eyes were rolled up and he could only see the whites. He thought about making one more attempt at communicating with her and decided against it. This girl had trouble written all over her – rather fetching – body and face and he had the distinct feeling that if she got into his van with him neither of them would get out alive. He rolled up his window and drove away.

Janice was aware of the words *I only stopped to help* even more distantly than she had been the question about where she wanted to get to and both of them resounded in the depths of her mind in the voice of Gary Richman. She did not respond to the second sentence because she did not understand its meaning. She supposed it was some kind of a taunt which referred to her arrival at the service area.

Get out of my mind! she eventually told him, and when the image of Gary vanished this time, it did not return. This triumph was countered by the fact that the scraping ache just inside the crown of her head grew worse.

79

She opened her eyes and stared up the slip road, surprised to see that the traffic had suddenly ceased. A rather worse surprise was that something nasty had happened to her vision. Everything on the periphery of her line of sight dissolved into rainbow speckles which then gave way to darkness. The realisation that something awful had just been heaped on top of the pile of troubles she already had was not as disconcerting as the sensation that reality (which had always been so perfect and seamless) now had distinct edges. She moved her head several times in quick succession and formed the impression that the matter of everything fitted together rather like a mosaic – or a crazy-paving path. It was now composed of pieces which were held together by fizzling edges which clung to the darkness.

The disjointed sensation made Janice's mind reel. For a few seconds she felt dizzy and thought she might fall down, throw up or do both at the same time. There was the feeling of cool sticky grass giving way to hard tarmac beneath her feet, but she couldn't look down to see how one was giving way to the other because a very primitive part of her had woken up and was sending out messages saying that if she looked down and saw one of those black edges beneath her feet, she would instantly fall into it and be lost for all time.

As she moved her head, the edges of sections of reality joggled themselves into position – as if the whole shaky thing had been constructed and was now being manipulated especially for her. The ground beneath her bare feet rasped at her soles and heels, rocking back and forth like an angering sea.

Although no cars came down the slip road, Janice held her right arm out before her, the fist clenched and the thumb up in the hitching position, because it was the only thing she could think of to do that might allow her to hold on to her sanity for a little while longer.

Her arm and hand stood out against the background as if lit by spotlights. Her body was the only thing she could see that didn't have clumsy zig-zagging joins holding it together. She

80

seemed to be the only real thing left in a world that had very rapidly changed into something false.

I'm trying very hard, Gary's smooth voice said inside her head and Janice made her mind bite down hard on it. The grating inside her skull increased.

'*Damn you, Gary Richman!*' she hissed and her voice seemed far too loud. The ground continued to shift beneath her feet, but she was mastering it now, shifting her legs in a fashion that in a normal world might be considered as a kind of shuffle.

The confusion lasted a long time.

And then the universe coalesced into a single, solid entity and the ground fell still beneath her feet.

Janice gasped a sigh of relief, then realised that although she could hear car-horns blasting so close by that they hurt her ears, there appeared to be no cars whatsoever in the car park or at the petrol pumps off to her left. There was also the disconcerting swishing noise of cars passing *very* nearby, but there were no cars coming down the slip road.

Now you'll see, Gary said inside her head.

Janice began to feel a cool, strong wind blowing at her in regular, fairly powerful puffs, first from one side of her, then from the other, then both sides at once. Somewhere off in the distance behind her, Janice heard the long, heart-stopping wail of locked wheels laying rubber on tarmac as someone in a very fast-moving car tried to stop very quickly. She waited for the inevitable crunch of a collision, but it didn't come.

Now I'll see what? she asked and the grinding ache inside her head ceased. The world began to disassemble itself before her eyes, huge slabs falling away and vanishing into nothingness.

It was what lay behind the spurious world that made her scream.

In the last few seconds of her life, Janice suddenly understood exactly how far Gary's domination of her had gone.

The world devoid of traffic was a construct that Gary – apparently by telepathy – had built inside her head. It was not a real thing, but a mere mental representation which had been so convincing that it had completely fooled all her senses. While she thought she was standing on shifting ground looking up the slip road, she had in fact been moving in the real world – a world which had been overlaid inside her head.

Gary's domination over her had reached the point where he had been able to place her somewhere in the real world without her knowing about it until he chose to show it to her.

That somewhere was the white line between the middle and fast lanes of the westbound carriageway of the M4 motorway.

Janice shrieked and tottered sideways as cars and lorries swept by either side of her at high speed. Her presence had not caused the traffic to slow at all and although horrified and astonished faces stared out of windows at her and cars were deftly switching lanes to avoid her, very few of the horn blasts were directed at her. Most of them were coming from the slow lane as people pulled hard left to avoid her.

She perceived all this inside the second it took her to stumble one step into the fast lane. In the following second she looked at the silver Celica bearing down on her and already skidding and fishtailing as its driver fought against the skid which had started the moment he'd spotted her and his right foot had hit the brake pedal. The car, which had presumably been travelling in excess of the speed limit, was the vehicle which had her name on it, Janice knew. It was not going to be able to stop before it reached her and the lane to its left was full, so there was nowhere else for it to go. Janice recognised the two faces behind the windscreen and, in the last moment of her life, her lips twitched into a sardonic smile.

The occupants of the Celica were her two good Samaritans, the ones she had christened Samuel and Eileen.

The Celica hit Janice head on, snapping her knees backwards. By the time the car bounced off the centre guard rail and ran into an articulated lorry, Janice had flown up over the bonnet, smashed in through the screen with such a force that both Samuel and Eileen's necks were broken and both front seats collapsed. Janice cartwheeled over the rear seat and exited through the car's back window, taking the glass out in a complete unbroken section, which firemen would later marvel at.

As blows rained down on her from every direction and almost every bone in her body was shattered, Janice dimly perceived the vast and terrible nature of what lay behind her murder. Gary was going to profit from her death with a substantial increase in his power, but Gary was not in this alone – he was a part of something far worse; something huge and terrible and perverted. And it had to do with immortality and angels and a man whose face had been badly disfigured and a girl called Katie.

As Janice hit the tarmac and bounced up into the front of a Ford, she knew that Gary and his friends were unstoppable and was glad that she was no longer going to have to be involved.

There was a distant sound of bending metal, then darkness.

6

Gary Richman sat in his Bentley, the picture of Janice gripped tightly in his fingers, and shuddered as he absorbed great crashing waves of her energy. There wouldn't be too much of Janice going knocking on the Pearly Gates, that was for sure. He watched her dying moments closely, then winced when his connection with her was broken with a painful snap inside his head. With trembling hands, he put the photograph back inside her bag, realising that he had missed an opportunity. If he had arranged for her to be killed more slowly he might have been able to siphon off some of the power of the huge pile-up that had already started out there on the motorway. He would not make a similar mistake.

Gary took a deep breath, turned the ignition key and drove away, thinking that it was going to be a very interesting meeting indeed.

7

The other ten also felt the second surge of power in the web that connected them. It felt rather like a hot liquid pleasantly splashing up the sides of an empty stomach.

In Basingstoke, the sensation woke a pharmacist called Gordon Clement a full hour before his normal getting-up time. The moment his eyes blinked open, he was completely alert, fresh and felt like ten men. He assumed this unusual event was simply the result of a good night's sleep and a variety of pleasant dreams, none of which he could quite recall. He checked the other side of the bed to make sure there was no one there this morning, rolled out, sprang to his feet and drew back the curtains, already knowing that he wouldn't be going to work today. Nor would he be labouring in the kitchen to make up the remainder of the illegal drug for which he had already been paid.

Today, he decided, he would take the Morgan out of the garage, put the rag-top down for the first time this year and drive out into the country. Hills sounded exactly like the things he needed to see today. Maybe the Chilterns, or even the Cheviots.

By the time he'd washed, breakfasted and packed an overnight bag (because one day off sick might just as well be two or three) his mind had swung round like a compass needle and was pointing towards The Wash, where he had never been before. Maybe he'd have a look at those exotic places King's Lynn and Boston, or perhaps even Skegness.

The wind was chilly in the open-top Morgan, but Gordon thought the day would warm up, and anyway it was refreshing – invigorating even.

By the time he got to Northampton, Gordon's compass needle had changed direction again and it occurred to him that Cambridge might be a very nice place to spend a few hours.

Or perhaps, he thought as he changed down into third and overtook a slow-moving Royal Mail truck, *even a few days.*

8

One of the remaining six people who were currently heading towards Cambridge was a balding Royal Navy intelligence officer called Roger Graham. Roger, who had spent two of his three weeks' leave getting under the feet of his wife Derry, had decided to push the boundaries of his leave into AWOL territory and take an extended sabbatical.

His colleagues would doubtless consider this move to be very *unintelligent*, but as far as Roger was concerned they could all go and piss into the wind. He wasn't about to tell them that great things were afoot in Cambridge (a fact for which he had no hard evidence at all) because intelligence men, as a rule, were not renowned for their vivid imaginations. And as much as he would have liked to have shared his convictions about what was going on in Cambridge with someone, it was impossible. He could hardly explain to anyone. Even Derry (whose disbelief would be instantly suspended by even the most unlikely Mills & Boon) wouldn't believe that rather like Darth Vader he could tell things from fluctuations in *The Force*.

So Roger had kept his mouth shut, reached carefully into the void (although he wasn't certain how he did this), felt the changes taking place there and realised that the time had arrived.

9

The time had also arrived for French painter and sculptor Philippe Matisse, who was standing on a platform at Kings Cross station with a train ticket to Cambridge in his dusty right hand, and a mixed wad of francs and sterling and his passport in his grubby jeans.

Until ten minutes ago, Philippe had been working on a sculpture in marble of a naked woman. The sculpture was going to be called *Si belle comme une poubelle* – and he had been working on it all night.

During that time he had felt a blast of power hit him and this gave him the energy to continue his labour long after the point at which he would normally have been exhausted. When the second blast hit him, Philippe realised that he had been changed and had become part of something which needed investigation.

Not knowing exactly why he was doing it, only that he had to, he walked to the station and bought a ticket to Cambridge. He did not know the city, he had never been to it and he had no friends there. In fact, he hadn't ever *thought* about the place as far as he was aware.

Philippe had also brought his passport because (for some unknown reason) he thought he might soon be going back to Calais, the city of his birth, but quite how going to Cambridge – which was in the opposite direction – would bring him closer to France, he did not know.

But for the first time in his life, Philippe felt free. He had simply walked away and left his life behind him. There would be no more slavery to absent muses, no more kowtowing to gallery owners, Arts Councils and the presenters of arts programmes; no more nights lying awake thinking his whole life's work so far was nothing more than worthless crap (even if people did pay good money for it). No more explaining to people whose mother tongue was stupidity exactly what his work was about.

Philippe would not miss it.

10

Enrico Spagnol was already in Cambridge. He was standing on the cracked garden path of a large detached house in the Barnwell district. As far as he knew, he had recently pushed the doorbell. He had no idea whether or not the bell had actually rung because he was not running smoothly this morning.

The reason that his mind (and almost every joint in his body) was working like a rusty machine was lack of lubrication. What he needed at this particular moment was a very large drink – and not a drink of the variety they brewed at home, which seemed designed either to tickle your taste-buds or your nose or both. What Enrico needed was a good unhealthy slug of Jack Daniels. He wished he'd taken a drink this morning before he left home (or what he called his *place of residence* – home was actually Taranto in what the British called the Italian instep).

Enrico wished a great many things, including that he'd never gone to work in the petro-chemical industry which would have meant that he'd never had to come here and experience such unnatural delights as frost, deep snow and a winter wind that could cut you in half. In Enrico's opinion, snow was for dusting the tops of distant mountains and had no other use whatsoever. The fact that it was now June and sunny did not alter Enrico's opinion of British weather at all. The only saving graces the country had, in his opinion, were; a) petrol was cheaper, and b) so was Jack Daniels.

Enrico also wished he knew why he'd driven to this house this morning instead of going to the lab. When he'd woken up, the day had seemed full of promise and he'd rushed to get dressed, knowing that something good was in the wind. He'd even forgotten about the Jack Daniels which usually called to him first thing. Once he was in the car, some hitherto unexperienced homing-pigeon part of him had led him straight here.

Now, due to the lack of lubrication, his short-term memory was coming and going and he had no idea whether the doorbell had rung when he'd pressed it. There was a strong, acrid smell about the house of something having recently caught fire, but the windows were not blackened or cracked and there appeared to be no external damage.

Enrico glanced around the overgrown lawn and wondered what it was all about. The building didn't look as if it had been occupied recently, and if it had, its owner or tenant hadn't cared about the state of it or its grounds. The lawn was three feet high, the flower beds filled with weeds, the concrete path grew nettles in every crack and there were various broken pieces of garden furniture scattered about. The house itself wasn't much better. The paintwork had all peeled, tiles were missing from the roof in various places and the front door looked as if someone had recently forced it open with a crowbar and hadn't worried too much about fixing the damage.

He walked back up to the door and reached out for the bell, wishing for his bottle of Jack. He was no longer sure whether or not he'd pressed the bell push, let alone if the bell had rung. He had a vague mental image of having done it, but decided to do it again anyway.

He pressed the button and listened, then carefully noted the fact that he heard no bell ring.

Enrico used the lion's head knocker. The hall sounded empty. He waited, hanging on to the fact that he had knocked, and when no one answered, he knocked again.

Eventually, he got down on his aching knees, and pushing open the letter box, peered through. The acrid burnt-cable smell wafted out at him and he wrinkled his nose. Something in the house *had* caught fire recently. The fire had not been big enough to burn the house down though, or to damage the part he was now looking at. He could see a wide hallway that had no carpet or wallpaper, two doorways leading off the hall to rooms on the left (one front and one back), another doorway on the right, which served the other front downstairs room, and an uncarpeted wooden staircase. At the far end of the hall was a large kitchen. The floor and staircase were covered in muddy footprints and Enrico decided these must have been made by the firemen who had come to put out the fire. For a few seconds he wondered, *What fire?* then remembered again.

'Hello?' he shouted through the letter box, but he was certain no one was home and began to wonder at his idiocy at coming here. Earlier, it had seemed very important – now it seemed like a crazy idea.

Still peering through the letter box, Enrico decided that the best thing he could possibly do under the circumstances was drive home and lubricate himself so that he could think clearly again. When he became loose and supple he would consider the matter – and maybe consider going to the lab.

He was preparing himself for what was going to be a painful transition between kneeling and standing when he heard a movement behind him.

If it was the polizia (which was almost certain – any of the neighbours might have seen him lurking here looking a little bit too foreign) Enrico didn't know what he was going to tell them. His thoughts weren't yet slippery enough to provide him with an alibi and they surely wouldn't believe that he'd come here simply because it seemed like a good idea when he'd woken up. Getting up and running was out of the question — in fact, getting up at all was going to be a major problem. Enrico did the simplest thing possible. He crossed himself, said a quick prayer and looked over his right shoulder.

And was surprised to see a large, grinning black man standing in the gateway. He was even more surprised that the black man was holding out a bottle towards him and that the bottle looked very much like it might contain whisky.

'I have a feeling we're both in the wrong place, brother,' the black man said as Enrico made his painful way to his feet. 'Or maybe the right place at the wrong time. I have another idea, but you look as if you could use a drink before you listen to it.'

Enrico nodded, frightened to speak in case it made the black man vanish like a genie and he didn't want that to happen until after he'd felt the cool glass mouth of the bottle touch his hot, dry lips.

He walked slowly towards the genie with the bottle, not looking at the man at all; his eyes could not be torn away from the liquid inside the glass.

'I hope you like Wild Turkey, brother,' Reuben Brown said. 'It's all I brought with me.'

11

There was a story still doing the rounds in Hamburg that some years ago, when they were teenagers, brothers Erich and Josef

Spiegel had been refused admission to the Bader-Meinhof gang on the grounds that they were too violent and uncontrollable.

This kind of a reputation was useful when you were in the business of collecting unpaid debts. The word on the streets was that if Erich and Josef came to call, you would either change your ways or pay what you owed as soon as possible. People who didn't had been known to vanish.

The sum total of the people Erich and Josef had *vanished* was actually four. These had been intentional hits, but the brothers actively tried to steer their careers away from this type of work; there was too much preparation involved and a great deal of careful covering up to be done afterwards.

What drove both of them was not the actual process of causing injury (although they had become very skilled in this) but the less tangible delights of terrorism. The fact that people were terrified and in awe of them felt far better and lasted much longer than the momentary physical pleasure of a cold finger snapping in your hand or an ear tearing away from a scalp. They were paid handsomely for the work they did, but they would have done it for free. The smell and taste of someone's fear in your mouth made you swell with power.

At ten o'clock that morning, fear was the last thing on the brothers' minds. Their car, a red Mercedes saloon (the appearance of which had been known to empty a street of people), had broken down on the M11 about two miles after they had passed junction 8.

They waited for assistance, discussing the successful job they had completed yesterday. At one point during the proceedings, Erich had begun to think they'd blown it, because both the man and his wife appeared to be dead. On its own this would not have been good. Coupled with the fact that they had not yet obtained the DM500,000 payment for the pure cocaine the people had received ninety-three days ago, it might have been a disaster.

But disaster had been averted, James Sievert and his wife were now both safely tucked up in Hammersmith Hospital, alive but not well, and the brothers had received and banked the cash.

When they had finished comparing the various joys of the job (Erich was particularly proud of having so carefully nailed the Sievert dog, a stinking Yorkshire terrier called Smut, to the front door by one of its hind legs so that it was still alive when its master arrived home) they fell silent and stared at the passing traffic.

There were other things to talk about – such as why they were on the M11 heading towards Cambridge when they should have been on the M2 making for Dover and then Paris where they had business with a certain M. Foubert – but they had somehow reached an unspoken agreement that Cambridge would not be discussed.

Although they were not twins, Erich and Josef shared many very similar views. Each was aware that the *real* reason they chose to do this kind of work was for the power they absorbed, and each knew that to discuss it would somehow dissipate that power. These things were similar to the Jewish belief that the real name of God could not be spoken. Both men could recognise certain kinds of magic in the world of the mundane and both were attracted to that magic – and occasionally *made* that kind of magic, though neither spoke of it.

And for this reason, neither spoke of nor alluded to the fact that Cambridge (or something *in* Cambridge) was calling to them.

Erich and Josef had never seen Cambridge, but they both held remarkably similar imaginary pictures of it in their minds. It was a large, beautiful sprawl filled with mediaeval buildings which shone golden in the light of the setting sun. Somewhere off to the left of this sprawl was a small section that pulsed with a searing red light which possessed the power of a million suns. The light reached out for them and found its way deep inside them, tapping into the power they had already accrued and forming pictures which had the intensity of a religious awakening. The images were of a vast purification brought about by seas of fire and rivers of blood; of a new world, young and strong and fertile. A fresh world on which giants and angels would roam throughout eternity.

The vision was so intriguing that this morning, without mentioning it to one another, both of them had got into the Mercedes with the intention of going to Cambridge. Josef had driven and Erich hadn't questioned his choice of route when he realised they were going north instead of south.

The route he had chosen was the route to their destiny.

12

The two other men who were currently considering their destiny were Charles Robinson, a hospital registrar, and Dick Stevens, an ex-mountaineer who had gone up K2 with a party of twenty-three and who had returned alone, never quite the same man as he had been before.

Charles Robinson thought his destiny looked very dark indeed because one of his patients had walked and he shouldn't have let it happen, and Dick Stevens thought his destiny looked very bright because he was waiting in the front garden of a deserted house for that patient to walk by.

During the three days that he had spent alone after he'd dug himself out of the avalanche that had killed his entire party (except his darling Jenny Richt who thought she could hear someone calling later that day when the blizzard had blown up and had walked off the edge of a four-hundred-foot drop trying to find them), Dick Stevens had seen and heard things that ordinary people would never, thank God, have to experience. He had written down some of his experiences in a book he had called *When the Roof of the World Falls*, and this book, mainly due to the publicity surrounding the disastrous climbing attempt and his stormy love affair with Jenny, had become a very respectable seller indeed. It wasn't megabucks country and it wasn't enough to put towards another climb (if Dick had wanted to make another attempt, which he didn't – wild horses wouldn't have dragged him back to Nepal) but for a book of this type, he was told, the sales were remarkable. The income provided him with a comfortable lifestyle and looked set to do so for the foreseeable future.

In the book, Dick had opened his heart about his relationships with the other climbers and his affair with Jenny, how their problems and differences had been overcome, and detailed the minor incidents and mishaps that happened during the climb. He wrote in depth about the avalanche and the following blizzard during which he lost Jenny, but the book really took off when he wrote about the time after the disaster. Dick had included plenty of instances where he'd heard – and responded to – voices advising him; he'd written about the huge sheet of ice he'd found in which were frozen humanoid figures that were not men or apes; and he'd written about the strange artifacts he'd found and lost again. But there were things he did not write about.

Such as the fact that the blizzard had somehow entered him and still blew inside his head to this very day, chilling his thoughts and mental processes. Such as the fact that he had received a visitation from one of God's own angels and had discovered that Heaven was not going to turn out to be the serene and comfortable and welcoming place that everyone thought.

There were many reasons why Dick Stevens did not want to climb another mountain and the first and foremost of these was that up on K2, after talking to the angel, he did not want to die.

This was also the reason he was crouched behind a hedge cradling an ice-axe and waiting for a certain girl to go by. The blizzard inside his head was stronger today, but not strong enough to make him forget his task, which was the most important thing in his life. The angel had promised him death and eternal torment, or life, the removal of the blizzard, and eventually immortality in return for becoming a spotter and for carrying out a spotter's duty on one single occasion. When the task had been accomplished, he would have his immortality.

In his terror, Dick had agreed without asking for details. *Anyone*, he wrote (in a book chapter he later burnt), *faced with the same horrendous choice would have accepted; without thought or question of the terms of the agreement. There was no choice.*

And that had been three years ago. During those years, Dick had kept away from mountains, given up drinking, given up driving, and had planned his life around what he considered to be the safest courses of action.

He had often wondered about the nature of the promise he had made; if indeed he had made a promise at all and not hallucinated the whole episode. He often looked at his own quotation that preceded the title page of his book: *When the roof of the world falls, who knows what strangeness might fall with it?* and sometimes it made a terrible kind of sense; other times it looked supremely stupid. Had the avalanche briefly opened a way through from another dimension? Or had he just been struck crazy with the devastating loss? He didn't even know what a spotter might be, for Christ's sake.

But it paid to play safe – especially during the long days and nights when the blizzard blew hard.

And this morning he'd woken with the knowledge that it was all true and not just a flight of fancy. He was to fulfil his side of the bargain. He was to take the ice-axe and lie in wait in the garden of a certain empty house in order to rid the world of something evil that would pass by. It wouldn't be like killing a human, he knew. There would be no blood, no mess and no screaming. The thing would die at a single blow of the axe, would simply deflate like a punctured balloon, draw itself together and vanish.

Now, crouched behind the hedge and waiting for the evil thing, Dick was not certain how he would recognise it. He assumed that it would be in human form, which meant it wasn't going to be easy to tell from a real person. There was going to have to be some kind of a sign – something about it that let him know what it was.

And when the man walked by on the other side of the hedge,

Dick began to grin. The angel had spoken the truth about his becoming a spotter. He had become imbued with new talents.

Spotter's talents.

The hedge was too thick to see through, but Dick could plainly see both the man and the dog on the other side of it. The man was tinged with red and Dick thought he was suddenly seeing light of another wavelength – or maybe something that wasn't light at all. The dog was of a darker colour, almost maroon.

Dick wondered if the man was human and felt a warm trickling sensation creep across his skin as though someone had flicked a low-pressure shower head over him. He nodded and tested his theory with the following passers-by. They all gave off a similar warm-water feeling and Dick supposed that a part of him was somehow sensing the temperature of their blood. Which presumably meant that the inhuman thing that would soon pass would either be much hotter or a great deal cooler.

For some reason the blizzard inside his head suddenly abated and Dick grinned again. It was a very long time since his mind had worked with such perfect clarity. In the new silence he could hear a distant and regular *blip* which had a resonance rather like the sonar noise you always heard in old war films about submarines. Dick also found that he could track it. The noise was in the back of his head which meant that the inhuman thing was walking along a street which lay behind him. If that thing intended to come up this road, it was going to have to turn right soon, then left, then left again.

He concentrated and closed his ears to the nearby traffic noises. He could feel the *blip* getting nearer. It was still behind him, but it was closing in on him.

In a moment of doubt about his capacity for range-finding, he turned and looked at the house in case he was wildly adrift about the distance and the thing, knowing he was here, was stealing up the garden from behind him. This was not the case but his movement made him lose the tell-tale sound.

Cursing his doubt, he made himself still again and waited for the *blip* to return.

When the sound returned, it was away to his right but a little closer which meant that it was coming the way he had anticipated.

Another blood-red person walked past the hedge – a woman this time and the area around her hips was a shade darker in colour, which, Dick presumed, meant she was pregnant. He thought he could rapidly develop a great deal of skill in this role.

When the *blip* swung around so that it was off to his right-hand front side but closing, he started to form a plan of action. When the thing drew close he would stand up and wait behind the hedge very close to the gate. He would track the thing as it walked on the other side and when it reached the gateway, he would leap out, drag it backwards into the garden and kill it. This should present no problem, and according to the knowledge he'd woken with this morning there would be little resistance (if any) and no evidence to cover up afterwards.

The *blip* was closing fast now and Dick stood up and moved silently to a sheltered point behind the gate as he tracked it.

He turned his head when he estimated that the thing had reached the perimeter of the garden and was surprised to see that the monster was as blood-red and warm as all the other people that had gone by. This, presumably, was necessary if you wanted to pass yourself off as a human. The thing was masquerading as a girl, which was what he had expected. The *blip* was so loud it was almost deafening now.

Dick waited until the girl-thing reached the gateway, hooked an arm around its neck, yanked it backwards into the garden so hard he lifted it off its feet, threw it to the ground and buried the ice-axe in its midriff.

The thing did not die and vanish. It screamed long and hard and writhed on the ground, trying frantically to crawl away from him. Dick followed it and struck it again as it rolled over on to its front. This blow sank deep into its ribcage and he had to tug hard on the axe to remove it. Blood and air whistled out through the gaping hole he had made in the thing and although it had to be dying, it's *blip* was as loud and regular as ever.

'Stopp hhhhit!' the thing mewled as it tried to get away from him. 'Jhusss ssstop hhhit!'

Frowning, Dick aimed the next blow at the creature's spine, and still it didn't die, just kept crawling away from him except that its legs no longer worked.

The thing let out a long, heart-rending scream that sounded so similar to the one his beloved Jenny had made when she walked off the mountain that it set off the blizzard in Dick's head again. He hated the thing for having the audacity – even in its death throes – to remind him what could have been and in a freezing rage he brought the axe down on the back of its neck.

The thing collapsed.

Its head rolled over to face him, its dead eyes accusing.

And its *blip* sounded regularly inside Dick's head.

He stood there transfixed. This couldn't possibly have happened. It wasn't anything like what he had been led to believe. Inside his head, the blizzard increased in intensity.

'You don't suppose you killed the wrong girl, do you?' a voice asked from behind him.

Dick turned, speechless.

A tall, dark-eyed man stood in the gateway. 'It was the wrong girl,' the man told him. 'But you've done us all more good than you can imagine, so don't let it worry you. Just take off her fingers and her face and put them in your pocket. Everyone will think it was me then, but that doesn't matter because we'll both be invisible to them.'

'The *wrong* girl?' Dick repeated.

'The blip. I can hear it too. Unfortunately it occurs on our frequency. Unfortunate for her on this occasion. Take a look in her handbag.'

'Handbag?'

The tall man had it in his hands. He tossed it to Dick. The *blip* became deafeningly loud. 'Look inside,' the man advised.

Dick opened the bag and saw what it was that happened on

their frequency. The thing providing the *blip* was a call bleeper of the kind used by hospital staff. The bleeper was active and working in groups of two tones, but the first could only be heard with your ears. For some reason the second of the pair resounded inside your head.

'I expect she was hurrying to answer it, don't you?' the man said, holding out a hand. Dick put the bleeper back in the bag, dropped it and shook hands with the man. His grip was strong and his hand cool. His touch filled Dick with confidence. For the first time in two years his feeling of utter loneliness left him.

'My name's Peter Defoe,' the man said. 'And I've been looking for you. I think we're going to be spending some time together. Now, if you'll just take her face and some of her right hand fingers, I'm sure they won't be able to find you either.'

Chapter Four
Taking and Driving Away

1

Paul Dekker prided himself on being the most meticulous and careful car thief in London. He was the only person he knew of who actually *researched* his cars before he stole them. He did this for two reasons. The first and most important was that being careful lessened the chances of being caught. The second was that under normal circumstances he had no desire to take away a car that was owned by a little guy. Little guys – a social order into which Paul was born, and from which he had wrenched himself as quickly as possible – didn't often possess the kinds of cars he stole, but it could happen. There was more than one security guard, bricklayer, machinist or office-worker in London who was currently busting his balls – or her ass – to meet the payments on a very expensive Merc or Jag. These people revered and understood their cars; had an affinity with them in much the same way as he did. They owned the cars, not as casual status symbols, but for their power and beauty. These little guys who *understood* may not have been the people for whom the car manufacturers' marketing departments had intended the cars, but they were surely who the designers and engineers had in mind: people who would love them.

And Paul did not like to take their hard-won treasures from them.

His targets were the big guys; the people who drove these cars because they wanted the world to know, not that they appreciated fine engineering, but that they could *afford* it. And, as far as Paul was concerned, if the big guys could afford one, they could afford another when he took theirs away. And having to pay for a new car was the worst that could happen to them: all that generally happened was that their insurance policy No Claims Discount went down twenty percent or so. This might have been enough to slaughter a little guy, but the others would simply pay up, probably only having to add the cost to their company's running expenses.

Paul had meticulously researched the silver Mercedes 500SL convertible he was currently approaching in Harley Street. The car belonged to a rich man who was at this very moment making himself richer by administering Hormone Replacement Therapy to one of a number of wealthy post-menopausal women whom Paul had seen enter his office.

The doctor had faith in New Technology, Paul knew. If his car was anything to go by, his office was probably chock-full of computers and monitoring systems. The Merc was fitted with an extremely sophisticated alarm system which armed itself *and* operated the door locks from a remote control the doctor carried with him. Paul knew it would sense any movement inside the car through sudden changes of air pressure or heat and would alert its owner through its inbuilt radio transmitter.

What Paul knew and the doctor didn't was that the security system wasn't worth the space it had taken up, let alone the two grand or more it had cost to have fitted. The problem, as ever, was going to be the steering lock.

2

Ordinarily, Paul could have managed four, perhaps five, of these jobs in a good day, and all would have gone just as smoothly as silk. Ordinarily, Paul's concentration would have been so intense that it would have been unbreakable. Even his thoughts about the kid (*Paulie*) he'd killed – which were never very far away – would cease, and the goading part of his mind, which had called him *cowboy* or *poke* ever since, would fall silent. Ordinarily his highly tuned olfactory nerves would have been able to alert him if, in spite of his care, things were not going according to plan.

This was not an ordinary morning, however. Paul's mind was not clear and concentrated and his nose was of no use to him. The former, he assumed as he approached the Merc, was because of the latter. He had been smelling blood-red danger since the nightmare he'd had last week, and it didn't make sense. None of it made sense. Not the smell, or the dreams – of which he'd dreamed a variant for the past seven nights – or the strange behaviour of Cindy.

The dog which had suddenly developed the ability to bark in time with the bleating ring of the telephone had since begun to display even more disconcerting talents.

Like, for example, Paul reminded himself, *knowing when the phone is going to ring. What do you think of that?*

He didn't know *what* he thought of it. His mother had reported Cindy's behaviour to him the day after his first nightmare, swearing that the dog had become psychopathic. Paul had explained that she meant psychic and had laughed off the story.

But it doesn't seem quite so funny now, does it, Poke?

And it didn't. Paul didn't know how to classify it, but funny it wasn't. Because the Cindy dog *had* seemingly become psychic. And she only barked her canine approximation of the phone's chirruping sound immediately before *those* calls happened.

'I think it must be your Amy,' his mother had suggested. 'She always rings off when I answer the calls. She must want something from you.'

'She's not *my* Amy,' Paul had said for the nth time. 'And she's got everything she wanted. The house is paid off and I'm out of her life. It is over with and we have no other connection. Why would she ring me?'

But he knew *why* she would ring him. She would ring him because she had *gone bad*. Because her avarice nerve had been tickled when they moved into the house; because her opinion of him had changed dramatically after he'd killed the kid. Because he'd wanted to retire. But most of all because she had *gone bad*. The word was blackmail, but that didn't sum it up completely. If it was Amy it would be blackmail with extreme hatred.

If it was Amy.

And during the daytime Paul was able to convince himself that it *was* Amy, trying somehow to put the frighteners on him; softening him up before she threatened to blow the whistle on him . . . *unless*. But during the night-time when he awoke from one of the dreams with the chirruping inside his head turning into the bleating of the phone, and the Cindy dog barking in time with it, and staggered downstairs to listen to the huge, dark vacuum in which the girl was lost, it was another matter altogether.

It wasn't Amy.

Amy couldn't summon that pathetic *lost* tone of voice if her life depended on it. And if Amy had help – another girl to act out the part – then why was she appealing to his protective instinct, a facet of him that Amy apparently found pathetic?

At night, there were many reasons why it could not be Amy.

He only had to think about his screwed up sense of smell to know that. The blood-red danger smell which never entirely left him now was stronger when he was inside the house, and stronger still at night. On a few occasions last week he had stayed up late, waiting for the phone to ring, because things might be different if he answered the call without having to wake from a nightmare first; if his head was clear and he was alert. He'd sat in front of the television in his mother's tiny lounge watching old American movies and American Pro wrestling and American Football. And on each occasion – though at different times – the smell of danger had increased. And on each occasion, as the odour grew sharper, the placid Cindy dog had begun to act in a strange and unsettling way.

The dog, who slept soundly – curled up in its mistress's chair

102

until Paul finally put her in her basket in the kitchen – would suddenly wake up, her eyes still distant with sleep. Her hackles would rise and she would clamber to her feet and stand stiffly in the chair, gazing around the room. She would begin to growl a deep, meaningful warning and turn haltingly until she faced Paul.

On the first occasion Paul thought the dog was still asleep and probably suffering from a nightmare itself. Cindy was not the kind of dog you normally worried about being bitten by. To the best of his knowledge the dog had never displayed any sign of aggression whatsoever. She could not be goaded into biting, even in play, and when he took her out, would fall on her back into the submissive position as soon as another dog approached. She was the type of dog who would have gladly welcomed burglars into the house in the dead of night on the grounds that they might, if treated properly, pause to scratch her chest or behind her ears. But sitting there on the sofa, a single bound away from the dog, Paul watched its lip curl and started to think about defensive measures. The dog – which may have some Labrador and some greyhound in it – only weighed about two stone or so, but it was all muscle, it had a bite which regularly reduced marrow-bone to chippings and it was currently displaying a very large number of teeth.

'What's up?' Paul had asked and the dog had stiffened, its legs bowed as if it was about to leap.

'Cindy?' he'd said.

The dog didn't seem to hear him.

And then he realised that Cindy wasn't looking at him at all, but at a spot on the wall beside him about two feet above his head. He turned and glanced at the wall, expecting to see a spider or a fly moving about there – both species were nutriment as far as the dog was concerned – but the wall was clean. He looked back at the dog who was looking less and less like the *El wimpo* he knew and loved and more and more like something in a tabloid newspaper report: *She was a good and faithful dog for six years and then she attacked my son with no provo-*

cation at all, he could imagine his mother saying while he lay in hospital, his livid jigsaw-puzzle face being held in place with thousands of sutures. Cindy might have been tracking an invisible something across the wall, but there was only one person in here that she was going to sink her teeth into when the fancy took her.

Still growling, the dog jumped down from its chair, ran around the room and before Paul could move, turned and leapt at him, landing squarely on his chest. She began to snarl and snap and it took a few seconds for him to realise that she was not attacking him.

The unsettling thing was that the opposite appeared to be true. The Cindy dog, the least aggressive dog he'd ever met, thought she was *protecting* him.

Protecting him against something that clearly frightened and angered her and which she sensed Paul could not deal with. The fact that she seemed prepared to put herself between it (whatever *it* might have been) and Paul seemed to be a measure of how threatening she considered it to be. Cindy thought it was something too dangerous for a human to handle.

And whatever it was had stopped flitting along the walls and was now hanging up there in the corner behind the light fitting where two walls and the ceiling met.

The dog's body was as rigid as an ironing board when Paul tried to move it. One of her front paws was in his navel and the other was quivering on his right thigh. Paul looked up into the corner of the room and shivered as he tried to see what the dog could see. There was something about that white Y where the room's corners met that seemed very significant. Something about the three ninety-degree angles which made him think about openings. Afterwards, he would recall the strange and crazy thought he'd had that if he were to reach up there into that angle he would be able to put his hand right through it.

Cindy lunged up towards the corner, snapping her teeth together with a *clack* so loud that Paul's own teeth began to hurt, and then two strange things happened. The first was that the blood smell decreased and was replaced with something that smelt faintly like orange blossom and honey, and the second was that the dog relaxed, jumped lithely down from him, crossed the room, got back in the chair and was asleep and snoring within ten seconds.

It happened so quickly that Paul found himself wondering if any of it had happened at all. It wasn't so remarkably different from the days after he'd killed little Paulie when everything had passed in a heat-haze of unreality.

The third strange thing that had happened – which wasn't so strange since he'd been expecting it – was that the telephone had immediately begun to ring. *I can't find you*, the pitiful voice had moaned. The strange thing was that the two events seemed connected. It was as if the girl had been waiting for the other thing to stop before she could ring.

And this scenario had since recurred several times – although Cindy had chosen two of the other three corners of the room to snarl and snap at.

The longer it went on, the less Paul entertained the notion that it was his ex-wife (or an accomplice) making the calls.

All he knew was that there was a girl in trouble out there somewhere (a girl who was not Amy) and that somehow the girl had his phone number and wanted his help, even though she couldn't possibly know who he was. Somehow the girl also had access to his dream-life or his subconscious mind. There was no woman in his past or his present whose voice came close to matching the one of the girl on the phone, and no one (other than Amy) as far as he was aware who had his mother's number.

And if it sounded crazy (which it did) it was just tough. There were none of the other sensations or sounds Paul associated with temporary insanity accompanying this. In the days after the kid, Paul had seen a Jaguar smile at him, had watched the pavement in Regent Street become chequered, and heard the boy's distraught voice accusing him. Which was as close to insanity as he ever wanted to get. Now, unlike before, he didn't have the feeling that his mind was ill and he wasn't hallucinating. There were just the dreams and the phone calls. And unless his mother had gone crazy too, it wasn't a sign of madness – she had answered some of the calls. Paul wasn't sure what to make about the dog's behaviour: he didn't think it was possible to make dogs go crazy – he thought they were born that way.

He would just have to wait and see what happened.

3

As he walked towards the shiny Mercedes the doctor had just paid close to ninety-five big ones for, Paul was not concentrating on his work but considering shouting his address out at the mystery woman the next time she called. He wasn't sure whether or not she could hear him – or of what trouble she would bring if she *did* hear him and decided to come to him – and his mind was not clear and crisply focussed.

And this was about as lax as he had ever been in his approach to a theft. Last night the girl had called and announced that they were after her and pleaded for his help. And the dream part of him that had resolved to protect her with his life if necessary wanted him to act. And like his mother would have been only too glad to tell him, Paul Dekker always was a sucker for a girl in distress.

Paul reached the car and paused, glancing across the road at the windows of the building where the doctor was pumping hormones into women with thinning bones. Except for the reception area, all the windows were shaded. No one was staring out of the reception window and, as magically as ever, no one was on his side of the street.

The car was gorgeous.

How would you like to come for a ride with me? he asked it mentally and felt that the car was going to be cooperative. Paul well knew that imbuing mechanical objects with a kind of soul was disparagingly known as *animism* but like a great many other people he also knew that when assembled, a motor car became a thing which was more than the sum of its parts – a thing that had a secret inner life and which would serve you or fail you of its own volition. Depending, of course, on how you treated it. Which was one reason he didn't like to break their steering locks.

Paul placed his bag on the ground, smiling at the tell-tale alarm lights flashing inside the two-seater. If anyone had asked this particular car thief how best to protect their vehicle he would have advocated the inclusion of 'fucking great key-operated dead-locks on everything that opens' and not high-tech alarm systems like the one this baby was equipped with, because the failing with these was that the owner had to be able to get in. Which meant that the owner would have a little gadget which disarmed the alarm (and in this particular case *opened the locks*) by sending an electronically generated wave to it. Inside the car a recep-tor picked up the wave, and if it matched the pattern held in its memory, would let you in. The theory was, there were so many possible frequencies to choose from that unless you were a very lucky thief indeed you wouldn't be able to match that wave with a spurious one in a month of Sundays. This theory was fine, as far as it went. But as Paul knew very well it didn't *actually* go very far at all. Especially if you had a little grey battery-operated box in your bag which would generate a square wave.

Paul took out the box and turned it on. Dennis the Menace, who built it for him, had included a winking red l.e.d. to tell him that the gadget was actually working and that he was not standing here wasting his time because the thing had flat batter-ies. Paul thought that he might get Dennis to include a meter which would tell him how long he had to wait when he built the new one. Sometimes the device worked instantly and at others it took several minutes.

This time was going to be a several-minute job by the look of it.

Paul glanced up and down the road as his heart rate rose to a fairly quick pace – probably in the region of a hundred and twelve, he noted distantly.

They're coming after me! the girl had pleaded. *I don't know where I am and they're coming after me! Where should I go?*

Paul suddenly thought he knew where she should go. The perfect solution had just presented itself to him. When she rang tonight, he would tell her to go to Jake's. Jake Fulman was in Devon for a few days and since he hadn't told Paul why he was going, was probably upsetting the local CID down there, so his place was empty.

Paul would give the girl Jake's address, tell her where to find the key and ask her to wait there for him. He could ring her when she arrived and meet her in a safe place – probably the pub at the end of Jake's street. That way, if there was any skul-duggery going on, he would be reasonably safe. And playing it safe was a good idea, because Amy was on the loose. And Amy wished him nothing but harm and there was still a possi-bility, however slim, that she and the mystery girl had cooked up something between them. And these days, you never knew who was coming to get you.

The Mercedes' horn blipped, its lights flashed and the door locks popped open.

So much for modern technology, Paul thought, turning off Dennis the Menace's blast-box. His heart-rate jacked up to its peak, which was what he would have expected at this point, and Paul, still turning over the pros and cons of his plan in his mind, checked the street, walked round to the driver's side of the car and got in.

Which was the biggest mistake of his professional life.

Paul had an ignition lock assembly and keys for a Mercedes 500SL in his bag. They were not for this particular Merc, so the keys wouldn't fit. He would have liked to have been able to remove the whole lock mechanism from this car and fit his own before driving away and could have done it in fifteen minutes at the most. Paul didn't think he had fifteen minutes to spare though – not in this exposed position. The existing ignition switch could be overcome with the careful use of a slide-hammer. You simply put the screwdriver head into the slot, belted the weighted slide down and the force would spin the lock-barrel out. All you had to do then was insert a small screwdriver into the hole, locate the slot inside and twist in much the same way as you would do with an ignition key.

Although this would hurt the car, and although Paul did not like to damage his vehicles, it was quite often necessary due to the constraints of time. He would replace the damaged switch with the new one later, when the car was away and safe.

But before he did any damage, he tried his spare set of keys in the ignition because stranger things had happened than being able to start up an expensive car with the wrong keys.

The key slid into the barrel and for a moment he thought his patron saint, St Cunt of the Car Thieves, was smiling on him because the key went all the way in without resistance. His heartbeat increasing, he rocked the steering wheel back and forth with one hand while he tried to turn the key with the other.

St Cunt grinned and the key turned out of the steering lock position. Paul was astonished at his good fortune. He'd never known a Mercedes lock to do this before. He was also astonished to find that this was as much luck as he was going to get today. The key would turn no further.

You bastard! Paul thought, but he didn't say it aloud.

Paul wiggled the key, trying to feel it through the tumblers, but he was not a locksmith or a housebreaker and his patron saint had moved on.

It didn't matter. The steering lock was released and that was the important thing. All he would have to do now was undo the fascia, clip the ignition wires and he would be away. There wouldn't be any need for the slide hammer in the lock at all.

He had the panel off when someone rapped on the window. Paul looked up into the red, angry face of the car's owner and realised his mistake.

You forgot to walk away, old poke, his mind told him. *Perhaps Amy was right after all. You've lost it.*

And he thought his mind might be right. The radio feedback between the car alarm and the device the doctor used to arm

109

and disarm it had warned him that the system had turned itself off. Paul should have popped the locks, walked away and waited. The chances were supposed to have been that the doctor would not have the other half of the car alarm in his surgery with him and would not hear the warning bleep. His secretary might have heard the noise but would not have considered it necessary to interrupt the great man while he was busy. By the time he found out that the warning tone had happened at all, Paul was supposed to be miles away.

But just in case this common scenario didn't turn out this way, Paul was supposed to have walked away and waited to see if the man came out to reset the alarm.

And he had forgotten.

For the first time in his life he had forgotten something that important.

It's as easy as that to get caught, poke. I'm surprised you didn't do it before, the taunting part of his mind told him. *You wanted to get caught, didn't you? So you'd be able to give it all up. So you had a good reason. Well, let me tell you, the kid was reason enough!*

But Paul was no longer listening because outside the car in Harley Street a large, red-faced man in a worsted three-piece suit with a gold watch-chain across the waistcoat, was motioning him to roll down the window.

Since Paul hadn't managed to turn the ignition on, it was impossible. His heart and mind racing, he opened the door and got out of the car. Two very interested female faces were watching him from the doctor's reception area window. And a slim, middle-aged woman with ash-blonde hair who only could have been the man's receptionist was coming across the road in the bristling, tight-buttocked walk of authority.

The consultant was big and fat and red with rage, but Paul was big and muscular and cold with fear. He could have put the man down (and possibly into hospital for a long stay) with one or two blows but as close as he was to *clicking out* he couldn't let that happen. Four people would be able to supply the police with a very detailed description of him. Paul realised his fists had clenched and willed them to relax. His hands did not wish to respond and compromised by dropping into uneasy claws as if they belonged to a weightlifter about to attempt a clean and jerk.

'WHAT IS THE MEANING OF THIS?' the consultant thundered.

Paul grinned coldly. 'It means I'm taking your car away,' he said quietly.

Like a gunslinger, the consultant produced the remote control for the alarm – apparently from thin air. He pointed and shot, and behind him Paul heard the car's locks snick down. A second later the horn blipped.

'I don't think you are,' the man said, thrusting the oversized controller into a pocket that was a little too small to hold it. 'I think you are going to come inside with me while I phone the police.'

Now the man's hands were free he looked as if he was having the same amount of trouble keeping them away from Paul as Paul was having controlling his own. The doctor's face was turning pale, which was a bad sign. It was when the red flush of rage left people that they became dangerous.

'Under the circumstances,' Paul said, 'I don't think that would be advisable.'

'Advisable? You're telling me what's *advisable?* I'd advise you, young man, to close your mouth before I close it for you. I find you trying to steal my car, there are several witnesses who saw the whole thing, and you're telling me what's advisable! I can't believe the sheer gall of you people. For two pins I'd knock your teeth out!'

The tight-assed secretary looked less than thrilled at the prospect of seeing her boss in a street fight. She placed a calming hand on his arm and said, 'Mr Barrs, *please.*'

The man shook off her hand. 'He wants to . . . *advise* me!' he yelled at her.

Paul closed his eyes and took a deep breath. He wanted very badly to shut the man up, but it was impossible. He unclenched his fists again and did his very best to look calm. The rule about

111

how empty the streets would become when he wanted to take-and-drive-away had a corresponding rule which governed the process of an *al fresco* argument. This rule stated that number of onlookers corresponded directly to the volume of the raised voices. And Mr Barrs was shouting loud enough to have addressed a crowd at pre-war Nuremberg.

'I wasn't stealing your car,' Paul said as two elderly ladies ventured out of the Barrs emporium of revitalisation. *This has got their replaced hormones jumping, poke*, he thought bitterly.

'You weren't stealing my car,' the consultant shouted, 'that's rich!' He turned to the knot of people who were gathering mainly outside his surgery. 'IT'S OKAY,' he announced, 'HE WASN'T STEALING MY CAR AT ALL. APPARENTLY HE THOUGHT IT WAS LONELY AND HE WAS JUST KEEPING IT COMPANY.'

Paul glared into the back of the man's neck, trying not to target it. He told his right hand to unclench and it wouldn't. 'Do you want everyone to hear what I have to say?' he asked in his quiet, *murderous* tone.

The secretary caught the full effect of it and backed away from him, but it was wasted on the consultant.

The fat man spun nimbly around, his eyes blazing. 'You shut up and come with me,' he hissed.

'I can tell you, or I can tell everyone,' Paul said. 'Now, if you'll just hand over the remote and the keys, I'll take the car and say nothing. If you don't, I'll tell everyone.'

'Give you the keys?' the consultant repeated in amazement. 'GIVE YOU THE KEYS? WHAT DO YOU TAKE ME FOR?'

Paul judged that Mr Barrs was about two seconds away from striking out – which would be a very bad thing indeed, because if he struck out, Paul would *click out* and if that happened he would regain his consciousness some time later and there would be blood on him and his knuckles would all be skinned. And then he would have to read the papers to find out what he'd done – unless, of course, he woke up in a cell.

'Okay, folks,' Paul shouted out. 'I'm not stealing Mr Barrs' car. I'm trying to repossess it. He's eight months behind with the payments and the credit firm have hired me to take it back.'

Barrs struck out at him and Paul ducked, frantically trying not to lose control. The imaginary relay inside his head became energised and its swinging arm clicked from one set of contacts to another. Paul ducked the next blow, mentally sucking the contacts back to where they had started from. This was another first for him.

Two new things in one day! his internal voice cawed at him as the relay tried to click him out again. Paul brought it back and held it briefly as he dodged out of the charging consultant's path.

'You lying bastard!' the fat man raged as Paul danced away from him.

The clicking inside his head was speeding into a steady bee-like buzz now as both sides of him fought for control.

'It was only three! Only three!' the man said, and the fight left him. His shoulders slumped and he suddenly looked like the world's most embarrassed man. His fists fell open and his hands began to flutter aimlessly, like damaged canaries.

The peak inside Paul's head passed and he was under control again. St Cunt had smiled on him again and he could scarcely believe his good fortune. The consultant was three payments short on the car.

'You surely don't have to repossess it for three payments,' Mr Barrs complained, rather petulantly. At that moment he looked as if he could do with a little hormone replacement himself.

Paul shrugged and smiled. 'I'm sorry, those were my orders.'

The ash-blonde woman shimmied forward again now the situation had fallen back into territory she could understand and deal with. The administrator in her would smooth things over. She placed herself between Paul and her mysteriously beaten employer. 'There must have been a slight misunderstanding,' she said with a condescending buttery smoothness. 'We'll rectify it straight away. If you would be so good as to come into the surgery, I'll make the cheque out right now. Mr Barrs will sign it and you won't have to take the car.'

Paul shook his head. 'I'm afraid I can't do that. You can make the payments, but I still have to repossess the car. You'll be able to collect it from the holding area when the cheque is cleared.'

'I don't *believe* it,' Mr Barrs moaned.

'That's the way it is,' Paul said. 'The car has to go. Now, I haven't damaged it yet, and I don't want to because someone will have to pay for the damage. If I have to take the car away without your permission I'm going to have to hurt the ignition. When you settle up your arrears, you'll be responsible for making the damage good. If you *don't* settle up, the credit company will have to pay and that'll be another black mark against your name, Mr Barrs. So it would be best all round if you'd just give me the remote for the alarm and the keys. I'll take it to the holding area in Battersea where it'll be safe and sound, and you sort out your deficit and you'll be able to collect it either tomorrow or the next day. Sound fair?'

Mr Barrs looked as though he found it diabolical, but he appeared not to want to say so. His secretary turned and looked at him and he gave a slight nod of his head.

Today, apparently, was a fighting day for Paul. He'd had to fight for control of his rage, and now he was having to fight for control of his mirth. Deep inside his bag, underneath years' worth of accumulated bits and pieces that would ease his entry into cars, was a booklet of Repo notices he thought he would never need. Print Stokes had made them up for him back in the days when Print could remember the name you told him to put on a document. Paul had been meaning to throw them away for years – had in fact almost done it after he'd killed the kid and it had no longer seemed necessary to keep all the tools. Now he was glad he hadn't; his patron saint had smiled on him again. He searched the depths of his memory for the name on the notices because very soon the secretary or the consultant was going to want to know how to reclaim the car. He thought the name of the Repo agency on the notices was Jenkins, but he wasn't sure.

'Would you like to come into the office?' the woman asked and turned and shimmied back across the road without waiting for a reply, her crestfallen employer following her.

4

And ten minutes later, Paul was heading for Freddie Simmons' place in Dover with ninety odd thousand pounds worth of undamaged Mercedes equipped with its own alarm system and its own keys and (he'd found to his delight) almost all the optional extras that the manufacturers were able to provide. This was one beauty that Paul would very much have liked to keep for himself.

The sun came out just before he reached the M20 and Paul dropped the Merc's lid to let the cool breeze buffet him. The car could have outpaced almost everything else on the road, but he stayed at a steady seventy miles an hour because the question, *Is this your car, sir?* was not one that he particularly wanted to answer today. And there was plenty of time anyway.

Mr Barrs and his loyal secretary probably would not believe the finance company when they said they hadn't put out a repossession order on the car. The finance company would, however, promise to look into the matter and meanwhile would gladly receive the cheque which was probably speeding towards them by motorcycle courier. By the time they'd banked the cheque and phoned Mr Barrs back to say that they had definitely not ordered a repossession and furthermore did not use Jenkins Security in Battersea, the smell of rat would begin to taint the air in a certain Harley Street surgery.

If Paul was right in his estimation of the speed at which these things dawned on people, Barrs' secretary would not get around to ringing the Battersea call box number printed on his card until almost two o'clock, by which time he would be lunching in Dover with fourteen thousand pounds making his inside jacket pocket bulge and the car would have fresh plates all round and a new set of papers on the way.

He also estimated that someone would answer the ringing phone in the call box after the secretary's third attempt. Then the balloon would go up. By four, Barrs and his sidekick would be talking to detectives. By eight, if the CID weren't too busy, one or the other of them might be leafing through mug-shots of known confidence tricksters. By midnight, when Paul was once again sitting in front of the television waiting for the lost girl called Katie to phone him, Barrs and his secretary would have realised that the theft of a single car (even if it was a very expensive one) didn't figure very highly on the CID's list of priorities. They would not have been asked to help build a photofit picture of the criminal and the police would have been very vague about their chances of recovering the car.

Wave bye bye, Paul thought, *your baby isn't coming back to you*.

Mr Barrs' baby was in fact going to a famous (or so Freddie said), and presumably unscrupulous, writer who currently lived in Dublin for tax reasons.

Halfway along the M20 Paul realised that the thing that was wrong about the leathery smell of the car's interior was the fact that it was still being swamped by the danger smell he'd had all week and the happy feeling of good fortune he'd been holding on to suddenly vaporised like a wisp of cloud under strong sunlight.

Paul frowned. As he'd driven away from Harley Street where luck he didn't deserve had been piled on him like he was the last good man on the planet, he'd imagined that the blood-red smell was no longer in his nose. He'd had the stench of danger following him around for a week, but it was not because of the strange phone calls or the weird behaviour of Cindy, but because a part of him knew he was going to make a mistake. That mistake had come and had been casually backhanded away by St Cunt, and having gone, its smell had ceased.

Except that it hadn't ceased at all.

You wanted it gone, poke, so you imagined it gone.

It not only had *not* ceased, but it was growing stronger. And this time it didn't smell blood-red, but simply *blood*. And in spite of the fact that the Merc's rag-top was down and the moving air smelled only of exhaust fumes and warm rubber, it was getting so strong that Paul could *taste* it. Unlike the blood of pulp fiction it didn't taste coppery at all, but rather of a combination of iodine, iron and salt. It tasted so much like real blood that Paul inserted a finger into his mouth then checked it in case he really was bleeding. His saliva was clean. He inserted his right hand pinky into each nostril but there was no blood there either. He hadn't expected there to be. After the fight with Charlie MacDonald he'd had to have the leaky blood vessels cauterised. This guy's nose could now withstand something close to a nuclear attack without so much as a spot of blood.

He checked his face in the rear view mirror and glanced up and down his body, but unless it was internal (and he'd put that particular worry to bed a long time ago) he was not bleeding at all.

Paul shook his head and reached for the radio which merely screamed static at him when he turned it on. He punched all of the pre-set buttons and was treated to four different frequencies of the same screech. He changed the waveband to FM and pressed the search button. The radio found a signal and settled and Paul found himself listening to something which sounded very much like the British Telecom void. A huge, empty space formed around him, courtesy of the Merc's eight expensive speakers. Paul punched the search button again and the next time the radio settled the dial told him he was parked on the band for Radio Three where he should have been listening to classical music. Radio Three did not seem to be broadcasting today though, and neither did anything else. Wherever the tuner paused Paul heard the Telecom void.

She's trying to get through to you, poke, his mind whispered. *She isn't confined to the telephone any more, either. What do you suppose this girl is, Paul, a ghost or what?*

Paul chose not to believe in ghosts and stabbed the button again.

And deep in the void, heard Cindy barking. Not laconically as she did just before the phone rang or when it was ringing, but as if she was fighting for her life.

See what a mess you got yourself into now, poke, his mind told him. *I told you to leave it alone. You kept on answering that phone and you've been making up your mind to help the girl and now look what you've gone and went and done! That thing came out. That thing's come down from the ceiling, pard. It's slipped out of that Y and it's getting the dog! Just remember who invited it! You did Paulie, old cow-poke. You did!*

Paul fingered the button again.

I'm broken! the girl's voice hissed all around him. *You've got to help me because I'm broken and I don't know who I am or what they're doing. I'm empty! I can't pick it up!*

Paul punched the button again.

I can't pick it up without you! I've got to go . . . they're tracking me . . . they want to . . . hurt me . . . some more . . . oh God, I'm empty and it hurts so much . . .

'The aerial isn't up,' Paul announced through gritted teeth although he knew the aerial was whipping the wind about two feet behind him. 'And this cannot happen,' he added savagely.

It's happening, cowboy! his mind told him. *You got very close to the edge earlier and now you've teetered off!*

Paul reached out and turned off the radio.

Going ga-ga a-ga-ga-gain! a part of his mind told him.

'Shaddup!' Paul hissed, swinging the Merc out into the fast lane and putting his foot down. He hadn't gone over the edge before and he wasn't going over the edge now.

The Mercedes accelerated smoothly up to a hundred and twenty and the wind noise became a deep roar. The lane lines flew towards Paul in exactly the way he liked them to, approaching rapidly, stretching as they reached him then vanishing under the car. This was one feeling that had never changed for him. Speed had felt good before and unlike almost everything since he'd killed the kid, it felt just as good now. There weren't many things that still felt fresh and clean to him these days, but this was one of them. His jaw set, and his mouth pulled into a tight grin, Paul pressed a little harder on the accelerator and watched the approaching lane lines quicken. When he glanced at the speedo he wasn't entirely surprised to find that he was travelling at twice the seventy mile per hour speed limit.

The wind blustered in his ears and tousled his hair and Paul imagined it cleansing him. When his *farmer-oppozite* voice began to point out what would happen if he had a blow-out now, he crushed it with a recital of the capabilities and speed ratings of the tyres that were fitted to this car.

And as his foot touched the floor and the car hit a hundred and fifty, a picture formed in the back of Paul's clean, calm mind. The image was of the girl – Katie – sitting in another car. The car was a Renault 5 Gordini and the girl was wearing a white dress. The material was dirty and peppered with dark-tinged holes of the kind which might have been caused by a shotgun blast. The girl's eyes were blank and her movements jerky as if she was fighting for control of her limbs. She looked as though she'd forgotten everything she'd ever learned about limb coordination.

Paul judged that the Volvo up ahead of him in the fast lane was moving somewhere in the region of eighty and took his foot off the throttle and applied it gently to the brake. The brakes pulled the car smoothly down to ninety and began to fade a little. Paul lifted his foot and re-applied it hard when a big Ford swung out to tail the Volvo. A hand appeared from the passenger side of the Ford and slapped an already flashing magnetic blue beacon on to its roof. Paul had the Merc down to sixty and back into the middle lane before the unmarked police car's siren began to sound. He braked again as the Volvo and the police car pulled across into his lane, and crossed it to the left-hand lane, and watched in his mirror as the two cars rolled on to the hard shoulder.

Paul took deep breaths. His heart was pounding – somewhere in the region of one hundred and eighty, he thought – and his blood pressure had shot so high that a spot in the centre of his vision shimmered with each heart beat.

Told you you were trying to get yourself caught, cowboy! the voice accused. Paul wasn't listening; he was too busy thanking his patron saint for the fact that the cops in the unmarked car had been so busy watching the Volvo that neither had looked behind them and seen the rapidly approaching Merc. Still drawing deep breaths, he slowed the car to fifty-five and switched to the slow lane.

Where the image of the girl and the smell of blood came back to him.

Paul mentally acknowledged that his inner voice was probably right about everything. A part of him probably *did* want to get caught, a part of him probably *was* going over the edge and a part of him *couldn't* hack it any more. *So fuck it*, he thought to his doubting part. *I might as well be hung for a sheep as a lamb, mightn't I?*

'Speak to me,' Paul said and turned the radio on.

The girl did not speak. The Telecom void did not reach out for him.

The car was instantly filled with the slightly scratchy sound of Nigel Kennedy playing Vivaldi.

Paul's mind did a slow roll. He tried to generate beta waves and concentrated on slowing his heart and didn't think about the way the world wanted to dissolve around him because Paul Dekker was a man who wasn't now going, and never had been . . .

Crazy? Is that the word you're searching for old poke?

In his mental picture, the girl was trying to change gear and missing the slot. Her foot was working the clutch as though it were a pump and her hand couldn't time the movement of the stick to coincide when the clutch pedal was down. Her car was slowing and soon, he knew, horns would be sounding around her. A distant part of him was glad that he had vision but not sound because he could well remember the cacophony of that nightmare traffic jam he had dreamed and thought that hearing it again really would make him crack.

In his vivid mental picture, Paul could see the streets and houses surrounding the slowing Renault and although the details were etched finely enough for it to be reality, he did not recognise the area.

The Mercedes caught up with a rusty Datsun and Paul swung into the middle lane, realising that he had not seen it there until it was almost too late. When he'd passed it, he pulled back into the slow lane, noting that the road ahead was free and that if he kept at a constant fifty-five, he wouldn't be in danger of shunting into the car in front.

He punched one of the radio's pre-set buttons and got Jackie Brambles on Radio One, punched another and got the lunchtime news programme on Radio Four.

And in his mind, the girl had found the Renault's third gear. Her car was moving so slowly that she ought to have selected second or probably first, but she'd found *something* and apparently intended to stick to it. The car was bouncing along in a way that driving instructors the world over would attribute to 'kangaroo petrol'. But the car was moving and if she didn't stall it, would pick up speed.

You've flipped, poke. You've gone!

Paul grimaced and nodded. There was an ever strengthening smell of blood in his nostrils. He'd heard the girl – and Cindy – through the car radio and now he was entertaining the crazy notion that his imaginings were real; as though his brain had opened a window on to something that was really happening to someone he didn't know in a place he didn't recognise. He didn't *feel* crazy like he had in the days after the kid, but what difference that made, he didn't know. What he did know was that *being* crazy didn't necessarily depend on *feeling* crazy. And that, as Jake Fulman would have said, was a Catch Twenty-Three Situation, when either way and no matter what you did, you were going to be fucked.

Sometimes, Paul knew, there was nothing you could do except trust yourself and leave everything up to the pilot, that unseen driver who lived under cover in your subconscious. If Paul's pilot had been a regular kind of guy, this wouldn't have been so bad, but he knew from experience that beneath his tough exterior lay not a heart of gold, but a ruthless maniac who would strike out first and not even bother to ask questions afterwards.

'Fuck it,' he said, 'I'll find out soon enough if I've flipped,' and simply refused to consider the matter any further.

Because the girl in his imagination hadn't stalled the Renault and was now in fourth gear, cruising along at around thirty-five or forty.

I can't find you! he imagined her saying, and in his mind, her lips moved.

This already happened, poke, his inner voice suddenly announced with absolute conviction. *This is not happening now, this is a replay. I think we're watching something that happened . . . what d'you say, poke . . . a week or so ago?*

Paul had no idea what this particular facet of his mind was on about and tried very hard to ignore it. If he had been able, he would have excised this section of his mind so he never had to listen to it again. It was not constructive and most of the time it did not seem to have anything in common with him. If it was the voice of his subconscious *driver*, then he was sunk. He had toyed with the idea that he might have somehow become schizophrenic after the kid and that this was the cause of the voice, but he had dismissed it. Now, the idea began to look a little more appealing. It would mean that the voice *wasn't* part of him at all, but merely a mental aberration. Anything would have been better than having to admit that this part of him existed.

And in the street in his mind, up ahead of the girl in the Renault, a wobbly kid on a bike three sizes too large for him rode down the grass verge towards the road.

Except that it wasn't just *any* kid on a bike.

It was *the* kid.

His little Paulie, the boy who had blighted his life. The eight-year-old whose memory was never going to leave Paul alone for as long as he lived. Little Paulie Saunders who had just learned to ride a two-wheeler and who had sneaked his big brother's mountain bike out of the garden shed for a quick spin.

Paul searched his mind for the *off* button and couldn't find it, then superimposed another picture on top of the existing one, but couldn't quite blot it out. As if to prevent it happening all over again, Paul's foot lifted from the Merc's accelerator. His superimposed picture vanished and up there on the big screen in his mind, the boy was grinning wildly as the bike travelled down the bank, picking up speed. His teeth were shining white in the early morning sunshine, his mop of brown hair was blowing back as the bike got faster and steadier.

I don't want it again! Paul told himself, knowing this bald statement of the obvious would make no difference. He'd dreamed it and dreamed it, over and over, and not wanting it had not made it go away then, just as it wouldn't now.

The boy on the bike was wearing a maroon tee shirt which seemed alive in the breeze, rippling and flapping around him. He had faded jeans with the knees out and turn-ups and wore scuffed baseball boots. He was a good-looking boy with brown eyes and freckles and a scab on his right elbow. Now, as he had done a year ago, Paul had time to take in each and every excruciating detail of the boy. There was an exhilaration on little Paulie's face that was so beautiful it hurt to look at it. The bike's spokes glittered in the sunlight and dew glistened on the spinning tyres. The rear wheel had a slight buckle which made the bike tremble slightly as it picked up speed.

Paul watched the boy's stubby fingers reach for the brakes, the sunlight and shadow etching his hands into things that looked too perfect to be real. The grooves between his knuckles were shadowed and the points highlighted. There was a rind of grime under each of his fingernails.

The perfect hands took the brake levers and pulled, their

tendons rising with the effort. Paul watched the dark flicker of confusion pass over the boy's face like a shadow and gritted his teeth when realisation dawned on the boy and his expression tightened into terror.

Paul and little Paulie had both realised at the same moment that the bike's dew-dampened brakes weren't going to stop it. And by the time Paul realised that the boy was not a practised enough rider to swerve away or jump off, it was too late. The brakes were slowing the bike, but not enough to prevent it from bumping down the kerb and travelling into the road.

Paul watched the girl in the Renault closing fast on the boy; watched as the boy's muscles all tensed. The bike double thumped down the kerb, displacing Paulie's feet from the pedals. The boy was leaning back now, his legs splayed and his feet high as he tugged on the handlebars like the rider on a runaway horse might tug at the reins. His face was contorted into a desperate grimace and all the tendons in his neck stood out.

'NO!' Paul shouted.

And the vision stopped.

The smell of blood filled Paul's nostrils. He gasped in air and forced his tensed shoulder muscles to drop. 'I can't believe it!' he complained in the closest approximation to exasperation he could manage. The words sounded more like those of a whining child and did not please him.

The radio ceased to operate. Paul glanced down at it, distantly registering his heartbeat which had to be in excess of one hundred and sixty. The dial was still showing the frequency for Radio Four, but the radio was no longer making any sound at all.

Something fucking horrible is happening out there somewhere, Paul thought, automatically blaming an external force rather than admitting to his fragile – and weakening – mental condition. The feeling *that something fucking horrible* was indeed happening, was however, powerful and persuasive as was the notion that he had become something akin to a TV set able to receive all channels on one waveband.

Paul pushed his hand into his trouser pocket and searched for his lucky ten pfennig piece, suddenly certain that he'd forgotten to bring it with him today.

That would explain everything *wouldn't it, cowboy?* his goad said sarcastically. *You forgot your lucky coin. Well, well, doesn't that just about sum up what you've turned into!*

The coin was inside his pocket and touching it didn't make him feel any better at all.

Which isn't so surprising since it isn't a particularly lucky coin at all, the voice continued. *You were carrying it when you killed the kid, old poke, weren't you? Or had you forgotten?*

Paul had not forgotten, in spite of having tried very hard to do just that.

The radio burst into life again, only this time not to the sound of Radio 4 but to the Telecom void.

I think I killed someone, Katie's plaintive voice said from a great distance. *I think he's dead now . . .*

Paul looked at the radio in disbelief and switched it off.

The radio continued to hiss at him.

'This cannot be happening!' he shouted, looking back at the radio. A warm relief flooded through him when he realised he'd missed the off switch and pushed the balance button by mistake.

Watching the movement of his left hand forefinger very carefully, he stabbed at the on/off switch.

The radio fell silent.

Paul grinned viciously. 'Got you, you bastard!' he said.

And when he looked up the boy on the bike was bumping down the bank beside the motorway and rolling out across the hard shoulder into the road.

Which was not possible because the crash barrier beside the hard shoulder was unbroken.

Knowing that it was not possible did not alter the fact that Paulie Simmons, until now considered by all right-thinking people to be dead, buried and not present on the face of the earth, was currently in the carriageway in front of him, apparently set on re-enacting the accident.

Paul stood on the footbrake knowing two things. The first was that this car wouldn't skid like the Ford had because it was equipped with an anti-lock braking system and the second was that this time there would be no impact because neither hallucinations nor ghosts had substance.

The boy was leaning back now, his legs splayed and his feet high as he tugged on the handlebars and brakes. His face was contorted into a desperate grimace and all the tendons in his neck stood out. During the long moment before the car struck him, his head turned towards Paul. His mouth and eyes were round with shock and terror.

The Mercedes did not skid, just slowed rapidly and efficiently. Neither rapidly nor efficiently enough to avoid striking the boy on the bike.

Doesn't matter, Paul screamed to himself as he gazed again into the boy's eyes.

When it struck the boy, the car was still travelling at around twenty-five miles an hour.

The impact was as sickening this time as it had been before. There was a brief screech of tearing metal and a shimmy from the car as the bike went under the wheels, but what was worse was the solid, low *thunk!* the boy's body made as the car's radiator grille and bonnet stove into him.

What was worse than *that* was the fact that the boy didn't bounce off or go under the car, but flipped up on to the bonnet in something that resembled slow motion but possessed all the energy of its real speed.

Little Paulie rolled up the bonnet towards him, leaving bloody handprints on the paintwork with each rotation. The sound was awful, deep toned and damp, *thock-thock-thock-thock* and was followed by a meaty *slap!* as the boy's broken face came to rest against the screen.

The Mercedes was stationary now. Gasping in a breath that would be expelled as a scream of anger at the deadly blow of betrayal his senses had dealt him, Paul watched the light fading from the boy's eyes as the torn and bloody fingers clutched at the windscreen wiper in a reflexive need to cling on.

And just like the first time, that distant part of Paul's mind woke up and spoke to him.

There you go pard, it said. *Jake Fulman always said you were a cowboy and he was right. You'll have two notches on your six-gun tonight instead of one, you ole desperado!*

But this time, in spite of the fact that Paul was again in possession of a stolen car, he would not give in to that ultimate act of cowardice and drive away. This time he would stay and face the music because if you had any kind of a conscience at all, the memory of a hit-and-run didn't fade with time, it just hung there in the back of your mind, as permanent as a pyramid. And if you believed, as Paul had, that you didn't have a conscience, you might just find out that you were wrong. That little nagging thing might only have been sleeping and something like this might wake it up. And, as Paul knew to his cost, once woken these things could grow to *like* being awake and might decide never to fall asleep again.

Paul closed his eyes, certain that when he opened them again, the boy would be gone. This time he'd *stopped*, not simply swerved so that the boy slid off; this time he'd been willing to give himself up. It had to be the thought that counted – the intention. All that ghosts wanted was justice and the boy had now got it. This time Paul had resolved to give himself up, and his resolution should have placated the ghost. Now the boy could stop haunting him.

But when he opened his eyes again, the body was still there, the blood still smeared across the windscreen where the boy's broken head had slid across it. Those bloody hands with the little grimy nails still clung to the wiper. It really had happened again. The boy could not be the same one, of course, and there was probably no bicycle – Paul had probably imagined those things – but the fact remained that there was a dead boy on the bonnet of this Mercedes.

Trying not to look into the boy's dead eyes, or at his cracked face, Paul turned off the engine and got out of the car, realising for the first time that a queue had built up behind him. It was already two hundred yards long and was getting longer with every passing second. Way out at the back people were hurriedly switching lanes to avoid the hold up. The first five cars behind him were too tightly packed to manoeuvre their way around him and Paul realised that he was lucky there hadn't been a pile-up behind him. Many more people could have been killed.

There was an old lady sitting behind the wheel of the car directly behind him and although she was glaring at him, she wasn't sounding her horn or getting out of the car. Paul realised that she must have seen what happened and was too shocked to move.

The only person heading towards him was an irate-looking man in overalls, who, judging from the speckles of white paint over his face and hair had recently been applying emulsion to a ceiling with a roller.

'What the *fuck* d'you think you're doing?' the painter said in a voice pitched high with anger. 'You could have fucking caused a fucking *accident!*'

'I already did,' Paul said, swallowing hard and indicating the Mercedes over his shoulder. 'I think he's dead.'

'Who is?' the painter demanded, staring past him. 'There's no one else in the car.' He glanced back at Paul. 'Where is he?' he asked. 'What, did he get out of the fucking motor and then die?'

'The boy,' Paul croaked. 'The boy. He's on the bonnet.'

Way back in the queue, people began to pass the patience barrier and started that well-known exorcism routine, the laying of hands on horns.

The painter looked at Paul with a great deal of suspicion. 'That *kid* on the bonnet?' he said, frowning.

Paul nodded his head.

The painter shook his own head in disgust. 'You fucking rich bastards are all the same, ain't you?' he said. 'My mum used to say you was all as crazy as coots. Mad as fucking hatters. That fucking kid on the bonnet, my arse! Well, I dunno how *old* it is, mister, but your sort ought to recognise one of them better than anyone else. You spend enough time shooting the poor little fuckers. Get it off the bonnet and get your fucking pose machine out of the way before I dot you one. I've just about had enough of your sort for one day. First they want it coffee, then they want it white, then they don't know. You're all a bunch of inbred throwbacks with no brains at all. Now just get back in the car and fuck right off, will you?'

You been had, poke, the voice of Paul's conscience quipped happily.

Paul turned, saw the thing on the bonnet of the Mercedes and suddenly wanted to hurt someone very badly indeed. He spun around but the painter was gone, back in his van. Paul considered following him and yanking him out again, then bit down hard on the rage. It had not been the painter's fault.

It had been no one's fault but his own.

5

Freddie Simmons did not much care for the small indentation the pheasant had made in the bonnet of the Mercedes and wanted to knock five hundred off the price on the grounds that Paul was supposed to have delivered an unmarked car.

Under normal circumstances Paul would have become intensely irritated and would have obtained the full price simply by subjecting Freddie to an unspoken threat of extreme violence. The patented Paul Dekker *look* would surely have done the business, but Paul had been unable to summon it up. He had argued, but his heart hadn't been in it and he had settled for a deduction of two and a half and an additional errand simply to have the matter over and done with.

Now they were sitting in Sherrie's having lunch and Freddie, not a person renowned for his tact and diplomacy, was wondering aloud what was wrong with Paul. As if that wasn't bad enough, Freddie had chosen to do it in his worst Jewish accent.

'The guy comes in with a dented car, I deduct less than it'll cost me to have it fixed, I fix him up with a ride home, I buy him his lunch and he just sits there with a face as long as a fiddle,' Freddie intoned. '"What's wrong?" I ask him, ''cause he's not only my best wheel man, he's my *friend* and I'm concerned about him. "I'm tired, Freddie," is all he says. "I'm tired." And he expects *me*, his old pal Freddie, to believe this!'

Freddie shook his head but neglected to put the '*Oy-yoy-yoy!*' at the end of the sentence as Paul had expected him to. Paul did not complain about the over-cooked mode of speech because at times like this Freddie would be only too pleased to announce that you could '*take the boy away from the Jews but you could never take the Jew away from the boy*', and that might cause Paul to become a little anti-Semitic towards him. Which would probably have been misplaced because Freddie's origins were doubtful to say the least. The guy wasn't even circumcised.

Paul forked trout into his mouth. It tasted like minced cardboard that had been soaked in blood. This wasn't the way he'd anticipated feeling this lunchtime.

'It's the wife,' Freddie said cheerfully, stuffing pork into his mouth. 'That little bitch has been on your case again,' he said through the food. 'Tell me I'm right, Paulie!'

Paul looked up slowly. He pointed at Freddie with his fish knife. '*Don't* call me Paulie,' he said softly.

Freddie leaned away from him, holding his hands up. 'Okay, okay!' he said. 'It's just that I don't like to see you like this. You got almost fifteen grand in your pocket, you got rid of Amy – and not before time if you don't mind me saying so – you paid off your house and you got the luck of the devil, so what's wrong?'

'I've had enough,' Paul said. 'I'm going to retire.'

Freddie's face fell. '*Retire?*' he asked, spitting the word out as though he couldn't expel it fast enough. 'You can go on holiday for a few months, you can spend some of that money I've been giving you, you can buy yourself a new house and get yourself a new woman. *That'll* make you feel better. What you *can't* do is retire.'

Paul shrugged. When things started to go as badly wrong as they had today, it was time to get out. He didn't intend to end up like one of those ageing boxers who went back into the ring time and time again and got taken down every time. He didn't want to end up with steadily accruing list of 'guiltys' on his own personal charge-sheet, and he certainly didn't want to do time. But most of all he didn't want to go crazy. If quitting would prevent this, then he would do it.

'Why can't I?' he challenged.

Freddie looked horrified. Apparently it was just an expression: he was not horrified enough to stop eating. 'You just *can't*,' he said around his next mouthful. 'What would we do without you? And it isn't just me I'm thinking of. There's Jake-baby, there's Billy Pink and all the others. What about your poor old mother?'

Paul toyed with his fish. 'Jake and Billy are well able to look after themselves. They don't depend on me for a living. Nobody depends on me for a living, not even you, Freddie. If I quit, Jake and Billy will keep you well supplied. Perhaps not as quickly or efficiently, but they'll do it. Your orders will be fulfilled. And my mother doesn't need me. She won't take money from me on the grounds that it might incriminate her. I have to pay her in groceries. She has her own stash anyway. The only thing she really likes about having me around is that I take the dog out when it's raining.'

Freddie was not convinced. 'How will you live?' he asked, and Paul began to realise that Freddie's concern for him was genuine. That was another new thing to store away in his mental journal.

'I've got two hundred grand tucked away,' Paul said.

Freddie threw his hands up in dismissal. 'Two hundred!' he scorned. 'What can you do with two hundred? How long will that last you? Six months? A year? Then what?'

'That's ten years at twenty a year,' Paul said.

131

'What? *What?* Paul wants to live like a pauper? I don't believe what I'm hearing! A goldfish can't live on twenty a year. Tell me you're having me on, *please!*'

'Twenty grand a year is a lot more than most people take home,' Paul argued.

'Most people! Tell me about *most people!* You, Paul, are *not* most people. You are definitely *not* most people. Where will you live? In a rabbit hutch?'

'I'll manage,' he said.

Freddie looked at the ceiling. 'He'll manage,' he said. He thought for a moment and asked, 'What's wrong? What's happened to make you like this?'

How about telling him you killed a kid a year ago? Paul's mental voice suggested. *How about telling him you drove away from the accident because you were frightened? Frightened that you'd killed the boy and of what would happen to you. You know that's why you didn't stop. It wasn't because you were driving a hot car at all, it was because you're a coward. Because you're scared shitless of ever hearing the sound of that cell door slam shut on you. Because you might not be able to stand the claustrophobia. Tell him that you left a dying child because you don't like enclosed places. And while you're at it, why not tell him about the voices and the fact that you killed the same kid again today, except that when you looked it was a pheasant? Freddie will understand why you want to give it up then.*

'Nothing's happened,' Paul said. 'No single thing anyway. I'm just getting tired of it, and because of that things are starting to foul up. I think my moments of glory have passed. I just want to forget about it all and do nothing.'

Freddie nodded. 'I've heard people talk like this before,' he said. 'You think you lost your bottle.'

And that was almost exactly what Amy had said last year when they were still at the top of the long slippery slope that would eventually lead to hatred and separation – and, still to come, a very messy divorce. Except that Amy hadn't asked him if that was what he *thought* – she had *accused* him of losing his nerve. And done it in a fashion that suggested it automatically made him a nobody who was worse than dirt. At least Freddie had suggested it with sympathy and understanding. What made this more remarkable was that it was completely out of character for him.

And now there were three people who thought he'd lost it, Amy, Freddie and Paul himself. He hadn't been comfortable over the past few weeks while he was trying to prove himself and today had just about put the lid on it for him.

'You can't give it up, Paul,' Freddie said quietly, 'because it's in your blood. You were born to take and drive away, you're brilliant at it, you're the best driver I know. And, anyway, there's nothing else you can do. *Your bottle hasn't gone,*' he added vehemently. 'Paul Dekker's bottle *does not go.* Paul Dekker is tough – everyone knows that – he's the best and . . . and you can't give it up.'

Freddie now sounded like he was fighting to retain his own belief in Paul; as if he didn't want his illusions shattered. Paul understood, but he wasn't going to spend the rest of his life going through the motions when his heart was no longer in it. And anyway, when you were inside the living legend, looking out, you tended not to believe the hype. In spite of his reputation he was neither a superman nor a genius, just a careful car-thief who had lost his taste for the game.

And quite a few of those valuable marbles of yours, too, cowboy, his mental goad chipped in.

Paul shook his head. 'Thanks for the pep talk, Freddie, but I still intend to retire. I've had enough now. I want to quit while I'm ahead.'

Freddie shrugged and threw his hands up. 'You're crazy,' he said sadly.

Yep, hit the nail right on the head that time, didn't he, poke? Paul thought.

6

The car Freddie wanted him to deliver to Mayfair as payment

for the two hundred and fifty pounds he had not deducted from the price of the Merc, was a stolen Daimler Sovereign. It was now re-registered as another Daimler Sovereign – one that had been written off in Hastings six months ago. It was comfortable, quiet and blended in so nicely with the background that getting pulled in it was extremely unlikely. And if he *was* pulled, there would be no problem as the papers Freddie turned out were always in order.

This particular Daimler was a nice, easy, friendly car. It ran well, its paintwork had been cut and polished, the interior had been professionally valeted and it smelled of leather and good carpet.

And it also smelled of blood.

Paul had started it up, knowing that this car was going to be his nemesis. This welcoming Daimler was going to be the last hot car he ever drove. Not because after this he intended to retire and go somewhere warm for a very long time – and he had been toying with the idea of Greece during his lunch with Freddie – but because he wasn't going to *get* to retire. The car was going to kill him. This, he suspected, was the true cause of the smell of blood that had been haunting him. It had been growing stronger and stronger all day and the closer the Daimler carried him to London, the more powerful the odour became.

Up ahead somewhere there was another car waiting. A car that had an appointment with this Daimler. It might now be parked up somewhere waiting to be brought to life by its owner, or it might be alive now, droning through the city streets, or singing down the motorway. But no matter where it was, it would know, like the Daimler surely knew, of its appointment with destruction.

Paul kept the car in the slow lane because his imagination would not stop presenting him with pictures of a fast car coming towards him on the other side of the motorway. In his mind, the front offside tyre would suddenly blow as the car pulled into the fast lane to overtake. He pictured the tyre flying apart in ragged scraps of smoking rubber; watched as, still ahead of him, the car hit the centre barrier, bounced back, hit a truck, bounced off that and leapt the barrier, timing its moves at exactly the right – or wrong – times. He could feel the weight of the car as it impacted the Daimler, imagine the terrible sounds and the pain as twisted metal bit down on his legs and body.

The end, old poke, he thought.

Or perhaps the Daimler itself would be the traitor. There might be a nut working its way loose somewhere in the suspension and each uneven patch of road was helping it on its way. Maybe the steering would fail – or one of his own tyres – and the car would throw itself at the nearest solid object.

Either way, Paul was certain the end was waiting.

He drove carefully, never exceeding sixty, never breaking the old 'two-second-rule', because according to the old Ministry of Transport advertisements, only a fool broke that, and he kept his wits about him.

He told himself that he did not deserve to die and his mental voice replied that thousands of people thought that every day and still died. He told himself that there was nothing he could have done to save the kid even if he had stopped and that the accident hadn't been his fault at all, but this didn't satisfy the goad either.

Whose bonnet did he roll up, going thock-thock-thock-thock and leaving bloody handprints that someone not a mile away from here had to wash off carefully with cold water? Who might that have been, poke? You killed him, therefore you're responsible! And sometimes you have to pay the price of your actions and sometimes the price isn't just that of a few rolling marbles.

And Paul knew that if it was going to come, it would come. But he didn't intend to make it easy. Death was going to have to work very fucking hard indeed if it wanted him. When you got right down under all the shit that was currently floating about inside him, right down to the bottom line, you would find a cussed bastard who would quite simply refuse to shift. A person who would fight on no matter how badly the odds were stacked against him. A person who had proved himself – on more than one occasion – capable of chipping away at those stacked odds. Until the incident with little Paulie, that person had been the whole Paul; now there was a whole garbage tip of other stuff piled on top of him. But when the chips were down, that guy could be drawn out again, even if he was weakened and hampered by the other facets of Paul's personality.

Paul drove on, his eyes and ears more finely attuned to what was going on around him than they had been for almost a year. His heartbeat was fast, but it was rock-steady. His concentration was so intense that his mental goad fell silent and Paul began to feel very good indeed. If he had to make his exit from this world, this would be the way he wanted to feel when it happened. Not frightened, but sure and confident – the way the girl in his dreams had looked when she faced down the truck.

The thought made him think of the radio, but Paul did not turn it on.

As he drove through the London suburbs, the smell of blood grew so strong that he had to roll down both front windows. The odour of exhaust which swept in did not swamp the smell and hardly took the edge off it.

An hour later, in Mayfair, Paul parked the car on the first floor of the NCP car park Freddie had told him to take it to, locked the papers and the car park ticket inside the cubby-box, got out of the car, got his tool bag from the boot, then locked up. He checked that no one was standing nearby watching him, then bent and placed the car keys on top of the offside rear wheel. He was surprised that he'd made it here without the car turning traitor on him and even more surprised that back here in London the blood-smell was stronger.

He straightened up, glanced around the car park and saw no one who was likely to attack him to get Freddie's money back, not that he expected that kind of behaviour from Freddie, but it was sensible to play it safe when you had this kind of smell in your nostrils.

There *were* two guys – in a VW Golf about four slots away in the next row – and Paul knew as soon as he laid eyes on them that they were here to take the car, but they made no move while he stood there. Presumably they had been warned that a Paul Dekker carrying money was not a Paul Dekker who took kindly to being surprised – or even walked towards with anything that might be construed as *intent*.

Paul took the tube to West Hampstead standing well back from the edge of the platform while he waited for the train and not moving away from the wall until the train was stationary. He had already imagined how the hand would feel on his back as it gave him a good hard push.

In a back street about a quarter of a mile away from the tube station there was a shop and office on which the door sign proclaimed:

The Miles Carriage Co.
Classic Car Restoration & Repair
Better by Miles

Using the name Stephen Miles, Paul had rented the place three years ago because he didn't like having to conceal his money, his tools and parts or his lists of marks past, present and future under floorboards or behind water tanks at home. Its name was the worst joke he had been able to think of without adding the S to make it SMiles.

The Miles Carriage Co. was a 'real' business which permanently ran at a loss but somehow managed to pay its bills. The real Stephen Miles had been a forty-one-year-old single geologist who had died in a light aircraft crash in Western Samoa. Some bright spark had intercepted the notification of his death and had kept him alive on paper for profit. Paul had paid and turned him into a classic car buff who had never heard of profit, let alone made one.

But the Miles Carriage Co. occasionally turned out a restored car, due entirely to the interest of Jake Fulman and a young speed-freak called Double A – since his parents had seen fit to name him Anthony when his surname was already Anthony.

Jake, who was an excellent mechanic as well as the world's clumsiest cat-burglar when the mood took him, had been delighted by the prospect of restoring some old cars in his spare time and had recruited Double A to help. When he wasn't snorting lines of anything he could get his hands on, Anthony Anthony was a welder and bodyshop technician. Occasionally the men turned up to do a little work on their latest pet project and Paul let them get on with it. The accountant handled the income from one in four of their exploits and although the company had so far only turned out two cars through the books – a Daimler Dart and a Sunbeam Tiger – everyone seemed to be happy.

And it gave Paul somewhere to base his exploits. Of course, if anyone decided to investigate the place, the amount of money in the safe at any one time could not easily be explained away, but the same thing applied to Paul's own bank accounts (five identities, fifty grand in each except his own in which there was currently twelve hundred pounds). From the safe in the shop, the cash was regularly moved into the other four accounts.

It didn't take ten minutes to walk from the tube to the shop, and during the journey no one looked at Paul twice. He found the keys in his pocket and peered through the filthy plate glass window to see if Double A had been in. Jake was still in Devon, but the youngster had recently been hot to continue with the car that sat behind the glass. It was a 1959 Ford Popular and for reasons that were unclear to Paul, the other two had decided not to restore this one, but to street-rod it: V8 Rover engine, Holley carbs, close ratio box, limited-slip differential and the kind of paint job that Paul knew he was going to find beautiful but very offensive.

He also knew that they were going to spend more money on it than they would ever be able to recoup by selling it. He would have asked why they wanted to do such a thing to a perfectly respectable collector's car, if he hadn't known it would elicit, as a response, the old mountain climbing cliché: *Because it's there!*

Double A had been inside spraying the car sometime within the past two days. There was a lot of newspaper in there which had caught the overspray of the metallic purple paint which had been applied to the car. Paul frowned at the Ford through the window, then let himself in and went straight upstairs to the huge Chubb safe.

He felt better after he'd put the tool bag and the money in the safe, but not much better. He wasn't going to be killed for the money now, but he could still smell and taste blood which presumably meant that someone somewhere had it in for him.

He walked back to the tube and took the Metropolitan line back to Stepney Green, walked down the Mile End Road, turned into Hannibal Road and headed for his mother's apartment near the library. No one accosted him; no cars mounted the pavement and shot towards him and he didn't forget to look both ways before crossing the road.

And the smell of blood increased.

It wasn't until he had his hand in his pocket and his fingers closed around the door key that he realised he had been barking up the wrong tree altogether.

Chapter Five
Messages

1

Paul began to feel as if he was being crushed by a huge force of gravity that had somehow sheathed his body. It was centred in the pit of his stomach and wanted to draw the rest of him to it. His mind began to empty, pouring down into his stomach, and one of the thoughts that flitted past his consciousness was that he was about to become the human equivalent of a black hole.

Sometimes you didn't just pay for your sins by losing a few marbles, and sometimes you didn't pay by having one of your marks turn on you. Sometimes the price was higher. He knew that now; the overpowering smell of blood told him that.

As if from a distance he watched his leaden arm fight the incredible force of gravity as it brought his front door key up to the lock. Somewhere off in the void of his mind a warning light flashed under a sign which might have read: *DON'T DO THIS!*

But Paul could not stop himself because a part of him was intercepting his thoughts as they flooded away from his brain and a great many of these thoughts stated quite plainly that he had to be wrong. This simply could not be.

The key found the lock and slid home.

Paul turned it, his ears singing and his teeth aching. His heart no longer seemed to be beating – or even present in his chest.

The heavy arm pushed the front door open and withdrew the key, leaving Paul looking into the hall.

The Cindy dog did not bark or rush out of whatever room

she had been sleeping in to greet him. The muffled sound of the television in the lounge was not present. The apartment had a huge atmosphere of emptiness as if no one had ever inhabited it.

'She went out with the dog,' Paul heard his voice saying, and it sounded like a recording being played back at a very low speed. It possessed no conviction at all.

Paul began to walk down the – somehow *alien* territory – of the hall towards the kitchen because of the smell of blood. Deep in that null place that used to be his mind, a few remaining thoughts twinkled like distant stars and he knew that his mother would be there. She was old and unsteady on her feet. She had surely fallen whilst holding a knife and would have lain on the floor there ever since, bleeding, the dog snuggled up against her, trying in vain to heal her with its tongue. He knew when it had happened: when he'd heard Cindy barking on the Merc's radio. It was a long time ago. Long enough for her to have bled to death while her son, for whom she had probably called out, toyed with a meal of fish in a Dover restaurant and decided to retire.

But Paul could not let this be true. 'Muuum!' his sloweddown voice yelled. Defying the massive force of gravity, his right hand moved back to his jacket pocket and deposited the door key, then reached for the handle of the kitchen door.

Paul sucked in air as thick as treacle and as raw as a butcher's shop and opened the door. '*Muuum!*' his voice moaned.

But the kitchen was empty.

There was no blood on the floor, no sign of his mother or the dog, and nothing was out of place – not even a butter-knife.

Certain that his head would implode, Paul wheeled around and burst into the dining room.

The dog's basket was there, shoved under the oak diningroom table because that was where the dog liked to go for some peace and quiet during the day, the two-seater settee and the recliner were there and all the ornaments along the mantel were there. Helen Dekker and Cindy were not there.

Moving as slowly as a man walking on the moon, Paul went back up the hall towards the silent lounge. If the television and the stereo had both been on at full volume he probably would not have heard them: the ringing of his ears had become a deafening electrical buzz. His whole being seemed to be spiralling in around the black hole at the centre of him.

He felt his voice call out for his mother again, but could not hear it. The aching of his teeth turned his mouth into a red blur of heat but even this did not take away the smell and taste of blood.

Paul's hand closed around the icy aluminium of the lounge door-handle then turned and pushed. Paul staggered into the room and a crazy thought swept through his head. *IT'S NOT TOO LATE TO SAVE HER!*

Something snapped inside him and with a sound like a wooden rule being broken across someone's knee and the feeling of extreme gravity left him instantly. Thoughts began to rush back to him from every direction and his stomach seemed to have vaporised.

He had been wrong about everything – including the fact that fate had killed his mother as an act of revenge.

His mother was dead, but not by the hand of fate.

Whoever had done this had been a madman.

Paul stood in the doorway, unable to accept that what he was looking at was real. He closed his eyes and felt himself swoon, but his hands flew out and pushed against the sides of the door frame, steadying him. The thick smell of blood was rich with filthy undertones – alkalis, fluids and excreta.

It's not too late to save her!

The words rang in his mind but the picture that had engraved itself on to his retinas like a photographic negative told him otherwise. His mother, lying there on her back with the dead dog placed on top of her, was neither whole nor alive.

Cindy's guts! Paul's mind screamed. *Those aren't hers, they're Cindy's!*

He opened his eyes and was unable to believe that the

amount of blood in the room had come just from the disem-bowelled dog. And if his mother had watched someone do that to the most important thing in her life, she would surely have died of a heart attack.

Who would do this? Paul's mind raged as he went over to his mother. The carpet was slippery with blood and pieces of flesh that he tried not to look at.

It's not too late to save her!

Still not being able to believe there was any way this could be either real or actually happening, Paul knelt down in the stinking mess beside his mother and took her cold and resistant arm, intending to find out if she still had a pulse.

There were three deep cuts across the inside of her forearm that looked as though they had been made with a scalpel or a cut-throat razor. The movement of her arm made the cuts gape. The first was just below the inside of her elbow and muscle and vein had been severed. Dark blood had oozed from the injury. The second was in the middle and not as deep and the third across her wrist. In spite of the fact that the huge thought in Paul's head told him that it was not too late to save her, he did not try to take his mother's pulse. He could see the slashed artery inside her wrist, along with all the severed tendons, and there was nothing coming out of it, which meant that her heart was no longer beating and that all the blood in the room had not come from Cindy. At least a gallon of it was his mother's.

'Who?' he heard himself saying, over and over again.

He knelt there in the blood, not knowing what to do next. A part of him wanted to cry and couldn't, another part of him badly wanted revenge and yet another was still crazily insisting that it wasn't too late. But above all, he felt an overpowering urge to restore whatever dignity he could to her. He simply could not leave her splayed on the floor with her disembowelled dog on top of her.

Paul slid his hands between Cindy and his mother and gently lifted the dog. He laid the animal on the carpet beside his mother and realised the two of them had become entangled to a degree that he could barely force himself to look at, let alone attempt to rectify. The old cotton apron his mother permanently wore around the house was slashed apart and she had been disembowelled too – except that it looked as if someone had made the first incision with the scalpel and finished off the job with their bare hands.

Still on his knees, Paul shuffled back from the corpses, still unable to admit that he was not suffering from an hallucination. He had to be because Helen looked too peaceful for her to have died in this way. Her skin was waxy and flecked with blood, but her eyes and mouth were closed as if she had simply passed away in her sleep. And her complexion added to the surreal effect and made Paul's feeling of dislocation bite even harder. His mother had been seventy-one years old and her face had shown every minute of it. This morning, when he had gone out, her face had been so deeply lined that her skin had been divided up into geometric shapes that she had called 'her diamonds'. Now there wasn't a line on her face. Her complexion was smooth.

Paul closed his eyes and squeezed them tight as if the act would alter reality. The images burned on in his brain. There was blood smeared on the wall behind the sofa – he had seen it when he came in, but had not considered it. Now, behind the crashing purples and blues that swirled and burst in front of his closed eyes, he could see patterns in the smears. Shapes he recognised.

I think it's about time we phoned the police, old poke, don't you? his mind calmly suggested.

Paul opened his eyes, dragged them away from his mother and the dog and looked at the wall behind the sofa. There were words drawn up there in his mother's blood and whoever had daubed them had left fifteen or twenty shoe-prints on the sofa: where he had clambered up and down – presumably re-inking his fingers with blood – and moved along the sofa to complete his message.

The blood-words read:

DON'T HELP HER

And Paul didn't understand. Helen and Cindy were both beyond help. Both were already dead and cold.

Don't help her? he dazedly wondered as he turned towards the door. *Don't help her?*

Paul sat down on the carpet in the hall, picked up the phone, checked for the dialling tone and punched three nines.

'Emergency services. Which service do you require?' the operator asked.

'Police,' Paul gasped. 'My mother has been murdered.'

2

He sat beside the phone waiting for someone to arrive who would be able to deal with it and the thought passed through his shocked mind that things were probably not going to look terribly good for him from where the police were standing. Paul dismissed this doubt quickly. He had no motive whatsoever for killing his mother and the guy who had done it would have left traces that were going to be easy to find. His footprints were on the sofa for everyone to see. The police might view him with suspicion at first, but not when the forensic guys arrived. He was unable to consider the matter any further and slumped against the front door, wishing he'd been right about the Daimler.

When the telephone rang, Paul was so certain it would be the local police station calling to say someone was on the way, that he snatched the handset up, pushed the talk button and said, 'Hello? Police?'

It wasn't until he'd repeated the question three times that he realised he was listening to the Telecom void hissing around him.

'There are worse things in Heaven and Hell, *old poke*, just as I told you,' a deep, grating voice said to him across a huge distance.

A vivid picture bloomed in Paul's mind: the burnt and blistered nightmare thing that Katie had turned into in his dreams.

'You were warned what would happen unless you promised not to fuck with me, *cowboy*,' the voice rasped. 'And now you've had your second demonstration. Do you like it, *old poke*? Or do you regret it?'

'Who is this?' Paul croaked frantically trying to keep his mind from dissolving the way it seemed to want to. Unconsciousness would bring relief, but only temporarily. 'Who the fuck are you, *you bastard?*' he asked. '*What do you want?*'

'I only want to be left alone. You have the message, *cowboy*. You have had the demonstrations. Remember this because things can get worse for you, *old poke*. You can make the promise never to fuck with me at any time but you would be wiser to do it now. When you make the promise, and you *will* make it, I will ease your burden. Remember, Mister Professional Car Thief whose bottle has gone, you are just a very small fishy in an extremely large pool. Do you want to make a promise now?'

Paul gritted his teeth. 'I fuck with whomever I choose,' he said, 'and right now you're the number one candidate. I'm going to be coming after you now and I won't stop while I still have a heartbeat. Got it, motherfucker?'

'A very apt choice of profanity indeed,' the voice said, and the phone began to wail the unobtainable tone.

Later – much later – Paul would wonder why the killer hadn't come for him if he had worried him so much, and later still he would come to realise that the murder of his mother had been a very big mistake indeed. But for now, he dropped the phone, stared down the hall at the empty kitchen and waited for the police to arrive.

146

Chapter Six
Arlington Stephen Jones

1

If, on his way to work that morning, Arlington Stephen Jones had been pulled up by a road-rat and informed that he had been constantly driving in excess of the speed limit to the tune of fifteen miles an hour, he would have been surprised since he was thinking so deeply that he had no recollection of the journey at all. If the road-rat had not recognised him, he would simply have flashed his ID which stated that he was a sergeant in the Criminal Investigation Department and would have expected to have been allowed to continue without let or hindrance. If the road-rat had remarked upon his first Christian name, as colleagues who didn't know better sometimes did, DS Arlington Stephen Jones would more than likely have punched his lights out.

This morning, he was not a happy man. His head had developed a permanent ache, his eyes were constantly sore and Maddie was no longer talking to him. Only one of these things was a regular occurrence, but it still irritated him more than the other two put together.

Steve Jones had not slept well, or often enough, or for long enough in more than five days. This fact was the cause of the other problems. At times like this, when he *did* get to sleep he would grind his teeth, shout, swear and roll about like a man in a fever. Consequently, when he had a sticky one on at work, his relationship with Maddie was put under considerable strain.

Neither of them would leave the marital bed to sleep in the spare room because, as they would have freely admitted, they were both extremely pig-headed and each thought the other should be the one who went. Consequently Maddie slept as badly as he did.

Which was not good news because when deprived of sleep, Maddie didn't just suffer headaches and sore eyes and a feeling of exhaustion. Lack of sleep caused Maddie to undergo a radical change in personality.

He had heard of sleep deprivation being used as torture and he'd read about women whose PMT could turn them into demons but he'd never heard of a woman whose hormones could be so badly jangled by a few more hours awake.

Jangled enough for her to become violent, in fact, and if anyone should doubt it, he was currently carrying the proof under his shirt on the left side of his ribcage. At the moment the proof was a fist-shaped, red mark which would rapidly turn yellow and then black if past experience was anything to go by. It hurt each time he drew a breath.

This morning he had woken to find Maddie standing over him, glaring down at him. He had asked what was wrong and she'd pulled back the duvet and let him have it.

He had followed her down to the kitchen and warned her that he had a temper too and that it was just about reaching breaking strain, and she had simply started to throw things at him, moving noiselessly and efficiently. He had retreated, dressed and left the house because although his temper was badly frayed, the fact remained that you did not hit women, no matter how badly they behaved or how sorely they tempted you. And also because the Maddie he loved was in there somewhere and would come straight back after a couple of good nights' sleep.

And if he could just deal with the root cause of all his troubles, those couple of good nights' sleep could be duly had.

That root cause was that in his waking hours he was spending all his time in the company of two extremely awkward bastards.

The first extremely awkward bastard was Detective Constable

Dick Farris whose brain, he suspected, would provide little more room for angels to dance upon than the head of a pin, and the second was the maniac who swore black was white and – against all the evidence, such as it was – that he hadn't torn his mother and her dog to shreds.

Dick Farris truly believed that the maniac had not committed the crime which was a big problem, since Dick relied heavily on *gut feeling* and was right ninety percent of the time. Add this to the other facts that DS Jones would have so gladly incinerated and forgotten about if he hadn't been an honest detective, ha ha, and you had yourself a violent wife and a body and mind that begged for mercy.

The guy in the frame was a naughty boy, even if Dick didn't believe he was the killer. It was written all over his face and might as well have been done so in three-foot-high flashing neon letters: I AM A CROOK! But the bastard was not only not known to this particular police force, he had no form at all. And asking around didn't do too much good either. Paul Dekker was apparently some kind of an icon amongst the criminal fraternity (amongst those who would talk to the CID anyway) or maybe even a legend. No one seemed to know exactly where he was, or exactly what his scams were, but everyone had heard of his reputation. You didn't fuck about with Paul Dekker, the word was, so nobody did. Which didn't seem to be too difficult for most people since he was like the Scarlet fucking Pimpernel; he popped up and then vanished again before you knew he was there.

The last person who had seen him was Print Stokes, and poor old Print who would tell you anything for a couple of pints was getting very shaky in the memory department these days and hadn't been able to remember whether Dekker had come to him for something or if they'd just bumped into one another.

Steve suspected that Mr Dekker had bumped into Print for papers (perhaps a passport) and that Print had genuinely forgotten about it. The problem was that they hadn't found any moody papers at all at Dekker's mother's place and Dekker himself wasn't going to point them anywhere else, even to save himself from a murder charge.

'We should have cracked into him the same night we hoovered him up,' Steve had constantly told Dick Farris. 'Got to him before he recovered enough not to talk.'

But the fact was they had been as hard on him in the hours after their arrival as they possibly could have been. And the guy just stuck to the same story. Even then, he'd refused to provide an alibi by listing his movements that day.

'But I'll get the bastard today,' Jones said venomously.

Sorting it out quickly was imperative because when Maddie became Muddy there was no chance whatsoever of any kind of a love life at all, and one of the side effects of Steve's mental frustration was a huge increase in his sex drive.

2

They brought Paul into the interview room at nine-fifteen. He had known his rights from the start and hadn't wanted a solicitor. Dick read the sheet to him again, but he still refused counsel.

Dick loaded and started the tape and gave the time, dates, and said who was present. Steve Jones didn't mind how long they ran for today because it was Dick's turn to transcribe the tape. And in spite of his headache, his ribs and his sore eyes, he felt a certain careful excitement. This was provided by the odd warmth in the pit of his stomach which usually meant he was getting somewhere. This was a *real* gut feeling, not one of Dick's hunches. They sat down, facing Dekker across the table and Steve did the honours.

'Detective Sergeant Jones,' he announced. 'Sleep well last night, Paul?' he asked.

Dekker shook his head.

'Bad dreams?'

The man smiled thinly.

There was danger in that smile which could not be missed. This guy came across as very hard indeed and Steve did not much relish the thought of having to restrain him physically.

'Nice house,' Steve said, and when there was no response at all – not even a glimmer – added, 'The one in Hampstead. Where your wife lives. What was her name again?'

Dekker just stared at him.

Steve appeared to search his memory. 'Amy,' he said after due consideration. 'She's told us quite a bit about you, Paulie.'

And in less than a second found his left wrist in an extremely painful grip. It happened so fast that neither he nor Dick even saw it coming, let alone had time to react. When Steve looked up in astonishment the guy's eyes had turned wild. He glanced over at Dick, whose mouth was not a mouth, it was ajar, but Dekker was already speaking.

'Don't you *ever* call me Paulie,' he warned and his tone was not lost on Steve.

Then it was over as if it had never happened. Dekker withdrew his arm as fast as he had brought it out and resumed his relaxed, impassive slouch.

Despite still being able to feel Dekker's iron fingers around his wrists, and despite the fact that the new arrivals in his growing collection of bruises would be there to provide the proof, Steve knew that he was later going to have to listen to that part of the tape again to prove to himself that it had happened at all.

'We'll forget you did that, I think,' Steve said, floundering.

Dick's gaping mouth finally snapped shut. 'Let's go through it one more time,' he suggested to Dekker.

You're doing the typing, Steve thought. *Go ahead.*

Dick stuck a Rothman's into the corner of his mouth but did not light it. He smiled at Dekker. 'The sooner we put this to bed, the better for all of us, wouldn't you say?'

'I would say so,' Dekker agreed.

'But we can't get any further unless you'll talk.'

'And we've got enough evidence to charge you, anyway,' Steve added, ignoring the deadly look his colleague shot him.

Dekker shrugged. 'So charge me,' he said, smiling icily.

'Forget that,' Dick snapped. 'We'd rather be clear about things before we go ahead and put the wheels in motion. We don't want you to go down if you didn't do it, but you're going to have to start talking turkey. Keeping your lip zipped isn't doing you a power of good.'

'Yeah, so tell us where you were when your mother was killed,' Steve said, more to irritate Dick than because he expected Dekker to talk. If, by any slender chance, Dekker hadn't done the murder, then he'd been up to something that was going to land him in a different pile of shit if he owned up. But Steve believed the reason he refused to account for his movements that day was because they wouldn't check out. Because Arlington Stephen Jones *knew* what Dekker had done that day: he had prepared himself for the murder. One thing he had done was to go and get the weapon from somewhere – probably close by since he'd had to take it back there after the murder.

'I was out,' Paul said.

Steve nodded. 'Where?' he said, and when he realised the guy was actually going to start pulling worms from the can, wished he hadn't sounded so cynical and weary.

A shadow passed over Dekker's face. 'Dover,' he said.

Dick was straight back in there before Steve could believe the guy had given a location. 'Why did you go to Dover, Paul?' he asked.

Dekker shook his head. 'Just for a day out,' he said.

'And how did you get there?' Steve asked. *That* was where the passport old Print had made him up had to be. Stashed away in Dover, waiting.

'Train,' Dekker answered, his voice flat, his expression blank.

'How did you pay?'

Dekker smiled. 'Cash. Untraceable.'

'Why did you go to Dover for a day out? Why not up the West End or something?'

'Wanted to see the Channel Tunnel exhibition.'

Steve shook his head. 'Folkestone,' he said.

'Bus,' Dekker replied.

The Rothman's jiggled up and down in Dick's mouth. 'Can

you tell us a little about the exhibition?' he asked, sounding genuinely interested.

Dekker gave a fairly detailed description, which, in Steve's opinion only proved that he'd been there. It didn't prove when. And Dekker said he hadn't paid for anything with plastic, he'd eaten in a café whose name he didn't recall and that he doubted anyone would remember him since he was just another punter. They would have to ask around, Steve knew, and he also knew (just as Dekker knew) that it wouldn't be verifiable. The man didn't sound as if he was lying, but the alibi was so shaky Steve did not believe it.

'And you arrived home at . . . what time?' Dick asked.

'About ten minutes before I called you,' Dekker answered.

'What time would that have been?' Steve asked. His headache was fading fast now and the cogs in his brain were beginning to mesh again. Dekker could quite possibly trip himself up right here and right now. If the time of the train from Dover's arrival didn't check with what Dekker said, there would be time missing; time that would have to be accounted for. *It's always better to keep your mouth shut than to tell fibs to us*, he thought. *Unless you've got no loopholes at all in your story. Unless you've checked it out.* And he didn't think Dekker *had* checked it out. He had made the story up on the spur of the moment. Unless, of course, he had been down to stash the moody passport. He asked himself why Dekker would go all the way to Dover to hide a passport and didn't have a good answer.

Dekker shook his head. 'I don't know the exact time. When something like that happens, you don't tend to look at a clock.'

'Happens?' Steve asked.

'I mean when you walk in and discover something like that.'

Dick nodded. 'Why weren't you wearing your watch then? It's a nice watch. A . . .'

'Rolex,' Steve finished.

'Must have cost a few bob,' Dick said.

'More than a few,' Steve added.

'But you weren't wearing it.'

153

'Because . . .' Steve said and tailed off.

'. . . you were up to no good, right?' Dick finished for him. 'You were out doing a job, weren't you? Everyone knows your name, Paul. Everyone knows you're crooked. What was the scam this time then?'

Steve knew it wasn't for insurance or inheritance. Helen Dekker had the grand sum of two hundred and fifty-three pounds and thirty-seven pence in her current account and forty-eight seventy-two in the Halifax. Her death insurance – if it paid out – was worth less than the cost of her burial.

Dekker said nothing.

'Okay,' Dick continued. 'Let's just say you didn't put the watch on and leave it at that. It wasn't because you were out on a blag and didn't want anyone to see it, or didn't want it falling off and getting left behind. Let's just say you went to Dover and Folkestone and you weren't wearing your watch. Which train did you come home on?'

'Early evening,' Dekker said. 'I got home around seven. Might have been half-past.'

Steve smiled. Unless he was very lucky, Mr Dekker might just have opened his mouth and inserted his foot.

'And you opened the door . . .'

Dekker's face was pale now. 'Smelt blood,' he said as if he was talking to himself.

'Then what?' Steve asked.

'Thought something was wrong,' Dekker said. His face clouded as if some problem had just occurred to him.

'Okay,' Steve said, keeping the rhythm going. Today was the first day that Dekker had wanted to talk about the murder at all. Up until now, all he had done was to protest his innocence. 'What did you do?'

'I went to the kitchen. I thought she might have fallen. She wasn't there. I checked the dining room. Then I went to the lounge.'

'And then?' Steve asked.

Dekker shook his head. 'I couldn't believe it. I kept thinking: "It's not too late to help her", but I knew it was. I knew she was dead. And the dog too.'

'Then what?' Dick said softly.

'I moved Cindy off her and phoned you.'

'Why did you do it?' Steve asked, and nearly burst a blood vessel when Dekker responded, 'It seemed like a good idea at the time.' Then he realised that Dekker had misinterpreted his question and was referring to phoning the police.

'You killed her, didn't you?' Steve said.

Dekker shook his head.

'Why did you change your shoes, Paul?' Steve asked.

'I didn't,' Dekker said.

'You know all about the shoes, don't you?' he persisted.

Dekker shook his head again.

Dick moved his cigarette from one side of his mouth to the other. 'Did you like your mother?' he asked.

Dekker nodded.

'But you had a row, right?'

Dekker shook.

'An argument then? A disagreement.'

'I didn't kill her,' he insisted.

Steve grinned. In his estimation they were less than two hours away from a full and frank confession. 'I told you earlier that we went to see your wife. That's a nice house she lives in over there in Hampstead. Who paid?'

'She isn't my wife any more,' Dekker said.

'She said you paid the mortgage off. What was it, two hundred grand? Three? Where would a guy like you get that kind of money? D'you kill people for a living, Paul?'

Dekker leaned back in his chair and stared at Steve with eyes that were very cold and very hard. It wouldn't have taken too much more of this to convince him that Dekker was indeed a hit-man. Except that real hit-men didn't make that kind of a mess – or phone the police.

'Do you know what else she told us?' Steve asked. 'She told us that you were unpredictable and that she was frightened of you. She said you would get a kind of crazy look in your eyes from time to time and that your face would change. She said you weren't able to keep yourself under control. You call it "clicking out" she said. That mean anything to you? She said that when you got this psychopathic look – this "wild man" look as she put it – she was afraid for her life. She told us that this was the main reason you split.'

Amy Dekker had told them a number of other things too, including her opinion that her ex spent most of his life being less than two seconds away from murder and that she was not at all surprised he had succumbed to his urges.

'Amy doesn't like me very much any more,' Dekker said.

'So what about this disagreement with your mother?' Dick wanted to know. 'What happened?'

'We didn't disagree. I didn't kill her,' Dekker said tiredly.

'But you did have arguments with her. That would only be natural.'

'Not since I moved back in with her.'

'So you were holding a grudge from long ago,' Steve suggested.

Dekker shook his head.

'I'll tell you what I think happened,' Steve said. 'You were upset for some reason and you decided to top your mum. When you went out that day, you went to fetch the weapon. Not to Dover, but to somewhere nearby. Maybe you sat there brooding for a while. Maybe you had this clicking-out thing. Anyway, you came home, killed your mum and her dog, wrote the message on the wall, washed up, changed your clothes and took the weapon back to where you got it from. You were intending to leave the country then, but something made you go home again. Perhaps you'd forgotten to do something, or perhaps you thought she might still be alive. I don't know why yet – but you went back. When you got home, maybe you clicked back in again and realised what you'd done – or maybe you were just disgusted with yourself. So, not thinking straight, you phoned us and told us your mum had been murdered. Then you realised you ought to make it look like someone else had done it, so you left your other shoes in the room.'

And this, as far as Arlington Stephen Jones was concerned, was the top and bottom of it. There were quite a few loose ends, but weren't there always? The guy's wife had said he was half-crazy and you only had to look at him to know she was telling the truth. Some of the forensic and the bit about the shoes didn't quite hang together, but why should a crazy man act in a logical fashion?

Dekker was frowning now. 'Why do you keep talking about my shoes?' he wanted to know.

'One pair of heavy brown leather-soled brogues. Bit slippery with all that blood about, weren't they?'

'I don't understand,' Dekker said, shaking his head slightly.

Steve shrugged. 'Neither do we,' he said. 'Funny choice of footwear for a murder, if you ask me.'

'You found a pair of shoes?'

Steve smiled benevolently. 'Not just *any* shoes. *Your* shoes. The ones you wore to kill your mother. You remember the shoes, surely?'

'I don't have any brogues,' Dekker said.

'They were the ones you were wearing,' Steve said. 'They are the ones you stomped all over the settee with when you wrote your message on the wall. The brogues are the ones with all the blood inside them. The ones you had on when we got there are almost clean inside.'

'Are they my size?' Dekker asked.

Steve nodded his head. 'We're pretty thorough here,' he said. 'We checked.'

'Tell me,' Dick said, 'if those shoes belonged to someone else, why do you think he would have taken them off where and when he did?'

'You'd have to explain where and when he took them off before I could give an opinion,' Dekker replied. 'I have no knowledge of them at all.'

'You don't remember walking straight from the body to the

left-hand corner of the lounge and then taking them off? There was a trail of very distinct footprints.'

'The corner of the room,' Dekker repeated and nodded slightly, looking as though he was chalking something up on a mental blackboard and finally making it add up.

'Those shoes are not mine,' he finally said.

'So whose are they?' Dick Farris asked.

3

'If he opts for counsel, and he *will* opt for counsel, don't deceive yourself on *that* score,' Dick said when they'd packed Sonny Jim back off to his cell, 'they'll pull us to pieces.'

Steve was not amused. Things had gone rapidly downhill during the rest of the day. Dekker wouldn't confess, wouldn't answer questions about his trade or income, and insisted that the shoes were not his. For a time back there Steve had thought the guy would crack, but it hadn't happened.

And after the interview had been terminated, things had got worse. His headache had returned with a vengeance, his eyes felt like some bastard was throwing hot grit into them and the ache in his ribs had turned into a spike which prodded each time he inhaled. Worse still, Dick was chain smoking and being ultra-negative, and worse than that, forensic had taken those fucking shoes apart.

There had already been doubts. There was no murder weapon (bigger than a surgical scalpel, the forensic guys said, but just as sharp: thin blade between three and five inches), and the thin blade could not be found. This problem could have been solved with a confession, but there were other, more difficult ones to consider.

For example – if you wanted examples and Steve could have done without them at that moment – there had been no traces of Helen Dekker's blood in any of the flat's sinks, drains, or U bends. Which meant that Dekker had not attempted to wash it off him. There were no bloodstained clothes other than the ones Dekker had been wearing (and the stains on those were not consistent with the violence that had been visited upon the woman) and there was no blood anywhere else in the house other than the lounge where the crime had been committed and around the telephone and the front door in the hall.

Which meant that Dekker had not left the house, or changed, or done anything other than he'd said. And it got worse. The train times Dekker had given checked out and now there were the fucking shoes.

'So we'll have to let him go,' Steve said.

'Unless he coughs before our extension expires,' Dick replied, 'and I don't think he's going to do that.' Dick butted one Rothman's and lit another. He looked very tired.

'Think he did it?' Steve asked, dispiritedly. The guy had had guilt written all over him but it was rapidly becoming obvious that the guilt had a source other than the murder.

Dick sighed. 'I think he knows more than he's letting on, but I don't think he did it. I can't see how he *could* have done it. The more I think about it, the less likely it seems he *did* do it.'

Which, unfortunately, was the way Steve was being forced to feel. 'So what happened then?' he demanded. 'If *he* didn't kill her, who did and how did they do it?'

But he already knew the answer to this question: Mr Brown Brogue shoes, a man who could enter a house without being seen.

No one in the area had noted any strangers on the day in question, not even Mrs Farren or Mrs Rusk who both acted as window-monitor-cum-sentry, the former for the road and the latter for the block of flats. The two old women independently noted every movement, animal, mineral and vegetable, on their patch. Both of them had had some very interesting opinions on the odd hours at which the young Mr Dekker came and went, and both had seen him arrive home on the evening in question at the time he'd given. The two women had seen others in the area, but these (with the exception of a football pools collector) were local residents and had all been traced and dismissed from the inquiry.

It *was* possible that Mr Brown Brogues had managed to get to the Dekker residence without being spotted (this kind of thing happened all the time, as Steve knew only too well, even when there were nosy neighbours); what was *not* possible was that he had been able to leave again without trace.

There should have been bloody footprints on the path and probably all down the road too. The brogues had been soaked, and according to forensic, full up too. Which meant that somewhere there was also a pair of blood-stained socks. But not in the Dekker house there wasn't. The closest they could come to those were the two final footprints in the corner of the room. These had showed toes and the ball and heel of the foot and were smeared down their length as if the person had been wearing those missing socks.

The killer's hands, wrists and arms would have been pretty well soaked, too, so forensic said. He'd had to reach quite high to write the message on the wall, and due to the fact that quite a large section of Helen Dekker's liver had been used to daub the words, lots of blood would have been running down the guy's arms. But, of course, Dekker hadn't had enough on him. With the exception of the phone and the front door (which had borne Dekker's messy dabs) there were no hand-prints anywhere.

None of this would have mattered a great deal if Dekker had decided to confess, but he had stuck rigidly to his story.

And after the interview, forensic had struck the final blow.

They'd sawn the upper off the sole of one of the brogues and repeated the process with one of Dekker's own shoes. And the wear-prints inside the two shoes had not matched.

Dick shook his head. 'I don't know what happened,' he said. 'Some kind of a gangland reprisal, perhaps. Although what the message *Don't Help Her* meant, I have no idea.'

Steve grimaced. The question 'Don't help *who?*' had been put to Dekker many times and Steve was almost (but not quite) certain that the man didn't know who the *her* referred to. 'His wife?' he suggested.

Dick smiled. 'Would you need anyone to warn you off helping her?' he asked.

Steve shook his head. Amy Dekker did not inspire sympathy and certainly didn't come across as someone who needed any kind of help at all. Amy Dekker radiated the message that she was doing quite nicely on her own, thank you very much, and that any help offered would not only offend but would probably result in a broken arm; and the arm in question would certainly not be hers.

'Girlfriend, then,' Steve offered, already knowing what Dick would say. There had been nothing in the flat to suggest Dekker had anyone else.

'I don't think he has one. I think he's been relentlessly faithful to that bitch in Hampstead since he met her and I think he's still being faithful to her. Christ only knows why,' Dick added. He lit a new Rothman's from the butt of his old one. 'One thing's for sure,' he said, 'Dekker certainly isn't going to help us catch the killer. Maybe he doesn't even know who it is.'

'He *must* know,' Steve said shaking his head. 'The bastard must know *something*.'

Dick nodded. 'But we're going to have to let him go,' he said. 'And it's probably the best policy at the moment. You know I never truly believed he was the man, don't you?'

'Don't I just,' Steve replied, unable to keep the sneer out of his voice. To make matters worse, the bastard doing the pontificating (and thinking more clearly and logically than Steve could himself, which hurt even more) was a fucking detective constable. Not for the first time, Steve found himself wondering how their roles had mysteriously become reversed. *Who's got the stripes? Ask him that!* he thought irritably, but he kept his mouth shut because the simple fact was that Dick was the better detective.

Dick seemed oblivious of his partner's discomfort. 'What I *do* believe is that our friend Paul Dekker will be able to lead us to the killer. Just because we don't charge him doesn't mean we can't keep an eye on him, does it? He's still our number one suspect. We'll get the guy who did it, don't worry about that. We'll just let matey-boy do the leg work for us.'

Steve rubbed his tired eyes. 'D'you think he knows who did it?' he asked, not quite comprehending.

Dick shrugged and smiled.

Steve sat up, his brain chugging into action. Until now he hadn't been able to believe there was anyone else involved and he had been stuck on the same circular line of thought: Dekker was the murderer. Now he'd finally made the jump away from that belief he began to feel better – in spite of the fresh set of problems it posed.

'You *do* think he knows who did it, don't you?' Steve said. 'There *was* somebody else,' he added quietly, testing the taste of the words and nodding his head. He didn't know whether he was simply being carried away by the enthusiasm Dick obviously still felt about the case, and at that moment he didn't care. His turgid mind had begun to follow the path Dick had gone down and lots of things were falling into place.

'I know what else you think too,' Steve said. 'You think he's going to go after them.'

'Would you say the guy's dangerous?' Dick asked, his eyes twinkling. 'I would. Dangerous enough not to heed a warning written with his own mother's liver. He'll go after them as soon as we let him go and we'll be hot on his heels. Perhaps, if we're good boys, Santa will let us collar the killer *and* matey-boy for attempted murder. He looks to me like he ought to be inside – in the interests of the safety of the general public, of course. What do you think?'

Steve nodded his approval. 'Just one thing,' he said after a moment of thought. 'How do you suppose our man got out of that flat without leaving a trace?'

This, apparently, was the least of Dick's worries. As far as he was concerned, if it *had* happened, then it *could* happen.

'Looks to me,' Dick said, grinning, 'as if he just walked into the corner of the room and vanished.'

'After taking off his shoes,' Steve added, smiling because that particular problem had just been relegated to the third division. It didn't matter any more. Let forensic puzzle it out. They could – and would – catch the villain without having to know the answer to that question. 'He took off his shoes and disappeared!' he said.

Dick chuckled. 'Straight through the wall, *whoosh!* Dematerialised, or whatever it is they call it.'

'Yeah, Dick, but why didn't he take the shoes?' Steve chortled.

He shrugged and said something that Arlington Stephen Jones would remember for a long time to come. 'You ever heard of a ghost who wore brown leather brogues?'

4

Five days later, Detective Sergeant Arlington Stephen Jones was beginning to regret the earlier jokes about ghosts. In fact they were beginning to ring distinctly hollow in his ears. He was slowly developing the belief that there *were* such things as ghosts and that Paul Dekker might just number amongst their ranks.

The man was impossible to tail.

Steve wasn't alone in his failure to track Dekker; Dick and a number of other detectives had tried to keep tabs on the man and he had given all of them the slip.

It wasn't as if Dekker drove anything particularly snappy – his car was an ageing red Citroën BX16 TRS – and shouldn't have been able to out accelerate or out manoeuvre the cars following him. And even when Dekker beat them across junctions or roundabouts, they shouldn't have lost sight of him. His Citroën didn't exactly stick out like a sore thumb, but it had been resprayed in a non-standard red tone that you shouldn't have been able to miss. And as if that wasn't enough, there was a big yellow sticker in the tailgate window that read: DON'T MESS WITH THE BEST in red lettering.

But despite this, and despite the fact that even if he *had* suspected someone was following him, Dekker couldn't have known it for certain – or known *which* car it was – he had managed to slip away from all of them. One moment the Citroën would be two or three cars ahead of you, cruising along at a steady thirty-five or forty, and the next it would be making an unexpected turn into a side street or doing a dangerous U-turn into the oncoming traffic – a manoeuvre which could not be copied without breaking your cover. And by the time you got to where you'd last seen the car, it would have vanished.

Rather like one of Dick's departing ghosts, in fact.

But today, as a one-time-only last-ditch attempt, they were going to attempt a six-car tail which would not only prove that there was nothing supernatural about Mr Paul Dekker at all, but which would take them to their man.

Today was going to be the day they caught the killer.

Because in Steve's estimation, Dekker was ready to make his move.

He had been preparing for it since they had released him, Steve was certain, and now he *had* to be ready. Dick had one of his hunches – which coincided nicely with the awful gut feeling Steve was currently suffering – and judging from the way Dekker didn't seem to be in a hurry to leave on this particular morning, they were going to be proved right.

Steve sat behind the wheel of the unmarked Granada chewing his thumbnail while Dick sat beside him, chain smoking and staring at the entrance to Jake Fulman's yard.

'We've got him,' Steve said around his thumb. 'We've got the bastard this time.'

Dick grunted.

There were doubts trying to creep into Steve's mind and he fought valiantly against them, refusing to consider that an alternative to what he wanted to happen could exist.

Such as Dekker somehow giving them the slip. It couldn't happen. Not today. Not after so much preparation. Steve stared at the big green gates to Fulman's yard and tore off a strip of thumbnail with his teeth. He would not *allow* any alternative.

After they'd released him from custody, Dekker had been unable to return to his mother's flat because it was still a crime scene and forensic were still working there – somewhat sporadically now. Steve thought he'd made a big mistake in his choice of alternative residence because he'd moved into the house of a man called Jake Fulman. Which had tarnished him by association, because Big Jake was well known to the police. He had, in fact, served time twice and the arresting officer on the second occasion had been Dick.

They'd checked Jake's place over while Dekker was out, of course, but there was nothing in the house or yard which might tend to incriminate either him or Dekker.

And if the worst *did* come to the worst today, and the unthinkable happened, there would still be Jake to fall back on. Or to fall on like a ton of bricks. Sooner or later Jake would be coming home and if it was necessary Steve and Dick would be waiting for him.

Dick had warned him that Jake was almost as reticent as Dekker, but Steve thought that if push came to shove, he could make Fulman sing like the proverbial canary. 'Positive thinking,' he had explained to Dick yesterday, 'makes all the difference.'

But that was before he'd gone home to find that, like a ghost, Maddie had disappeared too. No note, no personal effects taken, car still parked in the street. She'd done a runner and she'd done it perfectly. She hadn't been in to work that day, she wasn't at either of her parents' places nor any of her friends'. Maddie, evidently, did not want him to find her.

The fact that she'd gone wasn't so bad (at least he'd been able to toss and turn without collecting any more bumps, bruises or grazes last night), but the way she had so effortlessly accomplished it kept on returning and grinning into his face. If Steve had been a superstitious man, which he most certainly was not, he might have looked upon this as an augury of things to come. As it was, it just kept chipping away at his positive frame of mind.

Three of the tail cars had been parked up near Jake's place since yesterday morning, two were on the main road, one facing either directions, and the last was placed centrally so that wherever Dekker went, it would be able to relieve one of the other cars quickly.

Dekker hadn't made any kind of move by eleven and the guys in the other cars were getting tetchy. The DI wanted to call it off if nothing had happened by one because everyone had better things to be doing, Dick had run out of Rothman's and wanted to walk to the shop at the end of the road and get a couple of packs and maybe a sandwich, and Steve had gnawed both his thumbnails down to the quick, sucked the tips until they were crinkled and was now on his second pinky.

'Shan't be two minutes,' Dick said, finally giving in to his addiction which had evidently been complaining of not being fixed for more than thirty minutes.

Steve nodded. 'Ham roll,' he said, although he thought his mouth was too dry to eat. The time had to be getting near now.

He spat out a piece of nail and watched Dick plodding towards the newsagent's at the end of the street, wondering distantly if Dick had haemorrhoids. He certainly walked like he did.

And just as Dick opened the door of the newsagent, Dekker's red Citroën shot out of the yard and handbrake-turned into the road, its rear tyres smoking and screaming and laying twin arcs of rubber.

It happened without any warning whatsoever and so fast that even as he watched the car accelerating rapidly away from him, Steve could barely bring himself to believe it.

He fought to turn the Granada's ignition keys, realising the steering lock was on, waggled the wheel frantically from side to side and screamed in frustration.

By the time he'd beaten the stubborn lock, got the car running, got moving and picked up the radio mike, the red Citroën was at the far end of the road.

'Sonny Jim's out and away!' he shouted into the mike.

'Turning right into Fulham Palace Road and probably heading for Putney Bridge!'

The end of the road was a good three hundred yards away from where the Granada was screaming that it wanted second gear as soon as possible and Steve didn't think he was going to catch it very easily. He also knew that he *would* catch it. He would catch it if it was the last thing he did.

He changed into second, floored the pedal, changed into third, floored it again and was decelerating for the junction when he saw Dick coming out the shop, a plastic bag under his arm, a Rothman's already plugged into his mouth and a match already against the matchbox. He paused when he saw the Granada, and his mouth dropped open in an expression of extreme surprise.

Steve noted, as he passed his colleague and turned into Fulham Palace Road without stopping, that Dick was able to gape without losing his cigarette.

'Got him,' Bill Thomson said over the radio. 'Christ, he's in a hurry. He's going at a real lick!'

'Keep on him!' Steve hissed to himself and flung the Granada out into the oncoming traffic, overtaking a stream of cars.

'Was that you, Jones?' the DI asked over the radio.

Steve cursed and did not reply.

'He's turned on to the 306, headed towards Barnes,' Bill Thomson said, 'and in case anyone is interested, he's driving like a fucking maniac. *Jesus*, Davey, did you see that?' he added, presumably forgetting he still had his mike button depressed. 'How the *fuck* he missed that taxi, I'll never know.'

Steve shot past the 306 and turned on to the South Circular, hoping to get up towards Barnes Station ahead of anyone else. He wound down the window and slapped the blue flasher on the roof, turned on the headlights and the siren and the heavy traffic peeled away before him.

It wasn't exactly undercover, but it was the only way to get there quickly and he could get the light back off the roof before he was likely to run into Dekker.

'He's going down Queen's Ride and he isn't stopping for *anything*!' Bill shouted, a distinct hint of admiration present in his voice. 'We're losing him. Anyone else nearby?'

'Coming up towards the junction,' Steve replied. 'How close is he?'

Then he saw how close Dekker was. The red Citroën shot across his path into Upper Richmond Road West without even slowing down.

Steve cancelled the flasher, shut the lights off, serpentined through the mess of stalled and collided cars and lorries the Citroën had left in its wake and turned into the road it had just gone down.

'Got you, you fucker,' he breathed.

The red Citroën was darting in and out of the traffic about three hundred yards ahead of him, but the conditions had forced it to slow down.

He called in to tell the others he had it and that it was still heading west.

'We're out of it,' Bill Thomson suddenly announced. 'Fucking bus hit us at the junction. We're okay but the car's broke.'

There was a brief flurry of exchanged comments from the other four cars, which Steve learned were all fairly well behind and likely to be held up in the jam at the junction where he'd first spotted Dekker.

If anyone else managed to squeeze through the mayhem Dekker had left behind him, all well and good, but if they couldn't they needn't worry. Steve Jones had the car in his sights and he didn't intend to let it get away again.

'Where are we going, sunshine?' he asked as the Citroën pulled out and had to dodge back in again. Car horns sounded and Steve grinned. 'You tell him,' he encouraged.

Taking risks and causing noisy resentment of his own, Steve gradually gained ground on Dekker. By the time they reached the A316 Chertsey Road, only a hundred yards or so separated them and Steve had become convinced that Dekker's business was outside London completely.

Unless he's going to Heathrow! he thought and announced this possibility over the radio. Although *why* Dekker would want to get out of the country if he hadn't done the dirty deed himself was anyone's guess. Theoretically he was free to come and go as he chose.

'We'll get down there,' DS Mason replied, 'but it's going to take . . .'

And his voice was submerged under the harsh hiss of radio static. Steve wound the squelch and switched channels, then reached the conclusion that he was either in a dead spot or out of range. The radios were shaky at the best of times.

But details like this were of little consequence. All that had to be done was to keep the DON'T MESS WITH THE BEST sticker in sight.

And if he's got a gun? If he's going to shoot someone with it?

Steve didn't think about it at all.

Because the Citroën was turning left.

He watched it take the corner ahead of him, caught a glimpse of Dekker inside the car, and for some unknown reason, shivered.

He's only a crook, he reminded himself. *He's an ordinary bad guy. He is no one special. What he* isn't, *is a ghost. He's an average crook and you can handle him.*

But he hadn't forgotten the speed at which Dekker had taken his arm in the interview room, or the man's cast-iron grip that had left four bruised fingerprints on the inside of his wrist and a bruised thumbprint on the outside. The bruises were still there, in fact. Nor had he forgotten the icy look in those eyes when Dekker had warned him not to call him Paulie, and these things made him slightly uneasy. If he wanted, which he did not, he could easily conjure up a picture of Dekker with a sharp, scalpel-like instrument with a blade of between three and five inches and that icy look in his eyes as he said, 'Don't mess with the best,' and didn't even bother adding what the small print on the car sticker proclaimed: ''cause the best don't mess,' because he didn't have to. The message would already have been received and understood.

169

Steve realised that he did not much relish the idea of being stuck in an empty room with Dekker, and told himself that he didn't even have to *have* the idea. There was no chance whatsoever of it happening. All he had to do was to follow the red Citroën wherever it went and shout for help as soon as Dekker got out of it.

He's an ordinary slag and when you make this turn, he'll still only be a hundred yards ahead of you, Steve thought, changing down to second.

And there was the Citroën.

Except that it wasn't a hundred yards ahead of him, it was parked at the roadside with its engine running and Dekker was sitting behind the wheel, holding it as if he was about to drive away.

He cannot know I'm following him! Steve thought, and felt cold, because he had the distinct feeling that this was exactly why Dekker had stopped here.

For a moment, Steve faltered, his right foot off the gas. Then he drove smoothly by the Citroën and forced himself not to look over as he passed it. There weren't many other options open to him. If he had pulled in behind Dekker or stopped ahead of him, he would have given himself away for sure. That was, if there was still anything to give away, and he strongly suspected there wasn't.

He imagined he could feel Dekker's icy gaze on him as he swept by the Citroën and tensed as he changed up and accelerated away because he could still feel those cold eyes boring into the back of his skull.

Rubbish! he told himself. *Even if he has spotted the Granada following him, he can't possibly know who's driving.*

That was if he was wrong about Dekker staring at him, of course.

The junction was rapidly coming towards him and Steve didn't know whether he should just pull over and wait to see what Dekker did next, or keep going. If he stopped and waited no doubt would remain in Dekker's mind at all about which car was tailing him, and Steve needed that doubt. Even if he'd spotted the Granada some time ago, Dekker wouldn't know whether there was anyone else tailing him or not. Steve didn't know if the fact that he'd been spotted would cause Dekker to abandon whatever his dark mission was, but he doubted it. Guys like Dekker had egos the size of Africa and thought they couldn't be beaten. Dekker knew he was a good driver and would probably try to shake off any remaining followers in much the same way as he was now doing to Steve.

Certain that Dekker would turn round and go back on to the main road, Steve indicated right, intending to turn right again as soon as possible and get back on the main road.

As he pulled out to the crown of the road and stopped, he glanced in his mirror. There was the Citroën, way up behind him, reversing rapidly into someone's drive. The road Steve was waiting to join was clear, but he paused, making sure that Dekker was going to come back out of the drive again. He had to pause for far too long. Worried that Dekker would know exactly *why* he was waiting, he made the turn, glancing out of the side window as he drove away.

And there was the red Citroën, straightening from another vicious handbrake-turn and rocketing back towards the junction with the main road.

'Bastard!' Steve shouted, but the game wasn't over yet. Unless Dekker went back the way he had come, of course. Steve put the pedal to the metal, threw the Granada around the next right-hand turn so violently that for a moment he expected the world outside to invert itself as the car went over on to its roof, changed up to third and grabbed the radio mike.

'He might be coming back up the A316 towards you!' Steve shouted, not realising that the radio still wasn't working until he got no reply. He flung the mike aside and stood on the brakes to slow the heavy car for the next turn.

Steve shot out of the junction into a gap in the traffic, ignoring the protests of the black VW he'd cut up, put his foot down and overtook a string of three cars.

DON'T MESS WITH THE BEST was a good two hundred yards ahead of him, weaving in and out of the traffic and moving very rapidly indeed.

Steve followed suit, knowing that Dekker would only have to look in his rear-view mirror to know exactly what was going on, and no longer caring. If Dekker wanted a race, Dekker would get a race. He was going to find out exactly how Arlington Stephen Jones had obtained the Formula Ford trophy that had stood on his mantelpiece gathering dust since his sponsors let him down twelve years ago.

The next time Steve glanced in his own mirror he was surprised to see that he and Dekker were not the only two boy racers out to play today. The black VW Golf he'd cut up was so close to the back of the Granada that he could not see its headlights or radiator grille.

The difference, Steve knew, between him and the grim-faced man behind the wheel of the VW was that Steve didn't intend to give anyone a severe facial alteration for cutting him up. He'd experienced this phenomenon before while he was on a job and on one occasion had come away with a very fat lip. These days, he knew how to get rid of the bastards.

He wound down the window, pulled the flasher to him by its cord, picked it up and slapped it on the roof. He hit the switch and started it flashing, just in case matey-boy behind him hadn't quite got the message.

Then he cursed, because matey-boy was apparently one of those psychos who didn't much care whether or not you were a policeman. These sort of guys would attack God if the notion took them.

'My fucking luck!' Steve shouted angrily.

And to make matters worse, Dekker had pulled in again. Not into a side turning this time, but just to the side of the road. He'd left the engine running again – Steve could tell from the occasional puff of dark exhaust that came from the pipe.

He pulled in directly behind the Citroën, got out of his car, and balling his fist, strode to the back of it where Mr VW Golf was currently getting out of his own car.

Mr VW Golf was about twenty-two, six one, a hundred and sixty pounds, crop-haired and heavily tattooed. He looked very angry and very stupid.

'What th' fuck you on, guy?' he said.

And then he was on his back, his eyes closed and a thin trickle of blood easing its way from the corner of his mouth.

Steve rubbed his jarred right fist, then reached into the VW and took the keys. He ignored Dekker and the Citroën, checked behind the black Volkswagen, then returned and waited for Mr VW to wake up, fighting off the urge to kick out his frustration on the still body of the idiot.

So much for covert operations, he told himself.

In a few seconds the idiot's eyelids started to flutter. Steve waited until he was recovered enough to push himself up on his elbows. Then he waved the keys in his face.

'What you doin', guy?' Mr VW whined.

'Keeping death off the road,' Steve told him. 'There's a storm drain behind your car.' He jangled the keys. 'And these are going into it. I just thought I ought to wait until you woke up before I put them in. We wouldn't want you not knowing where they were, would we?'

'Come on, guy, you're s'posed to be a cop!' the idiot complained feeling his jaw. 'You ain't s'posed to *hit* people.'

'Self-defence, I think,' Steve told him. 'You chased me while I was in pursuit, I stopped, you tried to attack me, slashing at me with your keys, and I subdued you using the minimum amount of force. All by the book, I think you'll find. And it's not my fault that when I disarmed you, your weapon fell into the drain.'

'You *can't do that!*' Mr VW shouted and for a moment Steve thought he was going to fight. But the guy just sat there as he walked by and didn't follow him to the drain. Steve fed the bunch of keys through the slats and smiled grimly at the *chink* and *splash!* that followed. *Exit one king-sized wanker*, he thought. When he went back, Mr VW's head was in his hands. 'You *cunt!*' the man said, without looking up, 'I gotta be in Harlesden at two for a job.'

'There's a bus stop back down the road,' Steve told him, and went back to his Granada. He was not terribly surprised to discover that Dekker and his red Citroën had long since departed.

He *was* surprised when, after ten minutes of listless driving towards the west, the radio crackled into life and Trevor Mason announced, 'Got him! He's on the A315 at Hounslow Heath and heading west. He's driving fairly slowly now and he doesn't seem to have spotted us.'

Don't you believe it, Steve thought, turning north-west. He tried not to admit that there was anything special about Dekker, but he was fighting a losing battle. Dekker might not be a ghost, but he was most definitely a man with a sixth sense. He seemed to have a kind of built in radar for people tracking him.

'Anyone nearby?' Mason asked.

'Coming. Keep me posted,' Steve said, not finding it necessary to announce the fact that Dekker had identified him. It had become a little bit more than a covert tracking exercise now, it had become personal.

It had actually become personal at the moment that Dekker's hand had flashed out and taken his arm, but Steve did not fool around with this dim realisation because of its implications. If you started to think about moments like that one, you also had to think about their significance. And you might discover that the reason you so badly wanted to stay on Dekker's tail although he knew you were there was nothing to do with professional pride at all. It might turn out that what you were *actually* doing was fighting a battle for power; trying to tip the balance back towards you, because at the moment your arm had been grabbed Dekker might somehow have asserted his dominance over you. And now he might just be rubbing your nose in it.

I'm coming after you, Paulie, Steve thought, ignoring the message, DON'T MESS WITH THE BEST – *'cause the best don't mess*, that was constantly flashing on and off in his mind.

'We'll see who's the best,' Steve muttered and picked up the mike. 'I'm in Harlington Road,' he said, and waited for some card to announce that 'Arlington's in Harlington', which might just have resulted in some more skin being removed from his knuckles on someone else's teeth later in the day. But no one seemed to be feeling terribly witty at the moment.

'I'd say you'll hit the 315 at about the moment he crosses it,' Trevor Mason replied. 'When we see you, we'll let you take over and shoot off another way. Okay?'

Steve confirmed it and changed down to third.

He saw Trevor and Dave's Escort cross the junction while he was waiting to make the left turn and over the next five minutes fought to catch it up. He couldn't see Dekker's Citroën at all, but Trevor kept reporting it was still there and still taking it easy and a feeling of satisfaction stole over him. Dekker was not infallible at all. He hadn't spotted old Trev with his dandruff and his psoriasis and Dave with his pipe full of smouldering Condor and they had been following him for quite some time.

There would be a chase when Steve took over from Trevor, but that was exactly what he wanted. They could forget about Dekker taking them to the killer – for today at least – what was important was that the man learned there was no escape from them. That he could not shake them off.

He finally reached the Escort. Now he could see the red Citroën way up ahead. Trevor and Dave had left a sizeable gap. Dave slowed the car and pulled over to the left. 'There you go,' Trevor said over the radio, 'take it easy.'

Dave gave him a thumbs up as he passed.

And Dekker, as if he had been waiting for it all along, hit the gas.

And Steve stood on his accelerator too.

'What the fuck's going on?' Trevor's crackly voice demanded.

'I think he spotted me,' Steve answered, and gritting his teeth, gave chase.

The two cars ran on to the M4 motorway at more than eighty

miles an hour and still accelerating. There was two hundred yards between them and Steve kept it that way. There would be plenty of time to catch up; the Granada had a bigger engine than the Citroën and quite a few more horses under the bonnet. He could pace Dekker easily now and there would be no opportunity for the man to use any more of his shaking-off tactics.

'You made a big mistake, *Paulie*,' he sneered.

The speedometer needle passed ninety and the Granada gave a tiny shimmy the way it always did at high speed then settled down. Dekker had about another ten, maybe fifteen miles an hour left in the old dog he was driving and the big Ford could cope with that easily. Steve had had the needle round to one hundred and thirty before now – although how accurate the speedo was, he didn't know.

Dekker put his car in the fast lane, passed a coach, then switched back, still accelerating.

Steve glanced at the clock which was approaching one hundred and fifteen and told himself that he *must* be gaining ground on Dekker because it was impossible that the Citroën could go any faster. He'd seen it puffing blue smoke back in town, seen it with his own eyes. *Which means the motor is tired and can't go much faster, for Christ's sake!* he thought.

And Dekker was in the fast lane again, probably flat out now.

The level of wind noise inside the Granada had increased from silence to a low rumble and according to the speedo it was travelling at one hundred and twenty-five mph. And up ahead the Citroën was pulling away.

Steve thrust his foot hard to the floor and swore because Dekker was cheating. He didn't have a standard sixteen hundred engine in that car at all. It was probably a tweaked two litre – perhaps something even bigger.

Then he grinned because the Granada was proving itself and it didn't matter a toss about what was under the bonnet of Dekker's car. He was finally catching it up. 'We'll see who messes with the best, Mister fucking Dekker,' Steve snarled. 'We'll see who comes out on top!'

The radio hissed harsh static.

'Jones?' a distant voice enquired. 'You receiving?'

It was the Detective Inspector, Steve realised. Well, he could go whistle. This particular problem wasn't about to be called off. Dekker was in his sights and Dekker was going to learn something today. He was about to learn that what his window sticker said was true, except that it didn't refer to him. There was someone better. There *was* someone better and his name was Arlington Stephen Jones.

'Jones?'

Steve ignored the radio. There was less than a hundred yards between him and Dekker now and the bastard surely must know he couldn't get away by now.

And then what? You follow him about all day and then what? Arrest him for dangerous driving? Pay him a visit and ask him who he thinks is the best now? What good will that do? Will it make Maddie reappear out of nowhere? Will it solve the case?

He had to admit that it wouldn't do either of these things, and following that, the thought occurred that all this was pointless. Unless he made Dekker pay for the trouble he'd caused. Dekker was the cause of all his problems; if it hadn't been for him, Maddie would still be at home and everything would be fine.

He hurt your arm, Steve reminded himself as he chased down the Citroën. *And in spite of what everyone says, he probably killed his mother too. He's scum. Scum of the worst type.*

The Citroën suddenly switched into the middle lane and braked hard.

Steve shot by it, and changed lanes about a hundred yards in front of it.

'You fucker!' he swore, and found that at that moment he hated Mr Paul Dekker more than he'd hated anything or anyone else in his whole life. He hated him because he was tougher, faster, stronger and a better driver than he had any right to be, but most of all he hated him for the ease with which he had tilted the balance of power between them. And he hated him for knowing it, and for displaying that he knew it in that DON'T MESS WITH THE BEST window sticker.

At the moment he thought all these things, he also had a reve-lation. He'd spent the greater part of his career trying to understand the criminal mind, but he'd never been able to get a handle on the mental state that seemed to be required before a murder could be committed. *Why don't they just walk away from it?* was the question he had always asked himself, and now he had the answer. Sometimes you just *couldn't* walk away from it. Sometimes it just wasn't possible and action had to be taken.

During that moment of revelation Steve realised how easy it was to reach the point at which murder became, not just a necessity, but the only available option.

And he also realised how good it would feel.

Dekker's presence on the planet, he realised, was for him like a terrible itch beneath a plaster cast: an irritation that had to be eliminated, no matter what the cost. Something that had to be removed.

'Don't mess with the best,' he said through gritted teeth and put the Granada into the slow lane, braking hard.

His left arm began to ache where Dekker had held it in that cast iron grip. He remembered the moment of panic and help-lessness he'd felt when the guy's fingers had tested his bones, the look of astonishment on Dick's face at how fast the guy had moved. None of this could be allowed to happen again.

Steve brought the Granada down to fifty and kept his eye on the wing mirror. The Citroën hung back, also slowing.

'Come on, you bastard, go by me!' Steve shouted, slowing to forty.

And here came Dekker, accelerating again and not even bothering to change from the middle lane to the outside.

Steve's heart was hammering so hard that his head felt ready to explode. It was a good feeling because beneath it he was as icy cool as Dekker himself. He accurately judged the speed of the approaching Citroën and when it was almost level with him accelerated until the Granada was moving about a mile an hour slower.

Dekker glanced over at him as they drew level and Steve was pleased to see that he was pale-faced and frowning. It might have been concentration, but as far as Steve was concerned, pigs might have been donkeys. Dekker was frightened and didn't look anything like *the best* with whom you shouldn't *mess*. He looked hounded. Not far off being beaten, in fact. A man who had done his best and had discovered to his dismay that his best was not good enough.

Then Dekker looked away and put his foot down.

Steve matched him, keeping the rear nearside wing of the Citroën level with the Ford's front bumper.

They were moving at around sixty now. Steve checked his wing mirror, waiting for a fair-sized gap in the centre lane. He didn't have to wait long – most of the fast traffic was changing to the outside lane quite a way back.

With a scream of rage, Steve floored the throttle and steered into the Citroën's back wing.

What happened next did not happen as he had envisaged it. He had expected Dekker to steer to the left, away from the crowded fast lane which would have caused the Citroën to roll – out into the traffic he was trying to avoid.

What happened was that Dekker accelerated and steered the Citroën towards the fast lane, straightening it out at the very last moment. The driver of the Audi he'd missed by a whisker was probably intending to travel by train from now on, and the Citroën was dented but Dekker was unharmed.

The sound of blaring car horns penetrated the Ford's sound-proofing and the traffic behind Steve slowed.

'You *fucker!*' Steve screamed, his inner core of ice suddenly becoming a fiery rage. He swung the Granada out into the centre lane, hit the gas and stove into the rear of Dekker's car which shimmied, struck a glancing blow to a Vauxhall in the slow lane, and straightened. The Citroën's rear bumper hung in tatters and the plastic tailgate had shattered but the big glass window with the DON'T MESS sticker in it stayed whole and in place, as if to taunt Steve.

Steve aimed the Ford for another blow, but Dekker threw his own car into a tiny gap in the slow lane, drove over on to the hard shoulder and put his foot down.

'I'm coming for you!' Steve shouted and steered into the slow lane, not waiting for a gap at all but knowing one would surely appear, just as he knew that when he drove down the slow lane with his lights and the flasher on, the traffic would all make way for him.

I don't know how to do it! someone said in a little-girl-lost voice over Steve's radio. He glanced at it in disbelief. It wasn't a voice he recognised or one that he cared for.

There was a smell of burning rubber in his nostrils and Steve knew he should have been paying attention to it, because there was probably a radiator hose leaking or a drive belt over-heating in the engine, but getting Dekker was more important.

Help me . . . I'm lost . . . please help me, the plaintive voice moaned on the radio.

Help her, Steve thought and knew that should have been important too. But he was catching up with Dekker again and this time was going to be the last time. Dekker had made the mistake of staying on the hard shoulder and there was nowhere he could dodge to now. When the big Ford put the squeeze on him, he was going to have to go over the edge. And at the moment that meant a fifteen or twenty foot drop into a field.

He drew level with the Citroën and Dekker turned and shook his head, then mouthed a single word at him. The word was 'Don't'.

But Steve did not intend to *don't* after all that had happened, he intended to *do*. He took the wheel in both hands and wrenched it to the left, not realising until he was committed and way beyond recovering that the Citroën had out-braked him at a rate that ought to have been impossible and had switched back to the lane he'd just left.

In the two seconds that followed, Arlington Stephen Jones realised a great many more things. The thoughts flickered through his mind like a pack of cards being riffled by a card sharp. Each and every one of them passed in a fraction of a second and each of them was crystal clear.

The first thought concerned the smell of burning rubber, which, he now knew, was coming from the front, driver's side tyre which had been fouled by bent metalwork since he'd run into the Citroën the first time. This was also the tyre that was currently supporting the better part of the car's weight.

This fact was confirmed a moment later when the tyre burst and the car began to roll, its back half flipping up like a bucking bronco.

The next important thought was to do with the voice from the radio which had pleaded for help. Steve knew now that the owner of that voice was the person whom Dekker (in his own mother's blood) had been warned against helping.

There were a great many more revelations as – in what felt like slow motion – the car cartwheeled over and massive forces started to act upon his body, but most of these were of little consequence. He learned things about his life and his behaviour that he had never understood, but there were several over-whelming nuggets of knowledge that all arrived together and cancelled the others out.

The first was that in less than a second he was going to die of a broken neck – caused by whiplash – and that it wouldn't hurt when the steering column pierced his stomach. The second was the fact that Dekker hadn't killed his mother at all.

In the last two cartwheels of his life, Arlington Stephen Jones discovered the identity, address and whereabouts of the man who had killed Helen Dekker, and worse, still, the purpose for the killing.

But the knowledge that would haunt him in the afterlife – if there was an afterlife for him – was the fact that single-handedly he had almost won a war for the wrong side.

Chapter Seven
Greece

1

Paul sat in a cramped left-hand window seat in the rear of the Dan Air 737, staring at the back of the seat in front of him, into which his knees were firmly wedged.

He had sat in this position for the better part of four hours and still had an hour or so to go. The flight was supposed to take three hours and ten minutes but like every other charter Paul had been on there had been a problem. Usually these problems were delays which meant you simply had to sit in the airport lounge kicking your heels, but today the problem had not occurred until the passengers were on the plane.

Paul was not a good flyer and although he didn't broadcast this fact, would have admitted under duress that he was a fully paid-up member of what they used to call 'The White Knuckle Club' and avoided air travel wherever possible. As Freddie Simmons – also a member of this revered institution – would undoubtedly have said, 'I'll take a boat every time. If a boat goes down, I swim. Can I *fly* if a plane falls?'

And as far as Paul was concerned Freddie was just about as right as right could be. Even if you didn't suffer the awful hemmed-in feeling of claustrophobia that had been crushing him for the last four hours, climbing aboard an aeroplane meant assigning control of your destiny to two men you knew nothing about and a piece of machinery so complex that there was a possibility of a thousand bad things happening. Those two guys in charge of your life might know how to deal with any of these problems – or they might be total lame brains who did not, and in Paul's opinion six miles up in the air wasn't the right place to find out.

He hadn't exactly been feeling relaxed when he boarded the plane and the announcement that there was a problem with one of the navigational systems had put a count of fifteen beats per minute on his already overworked heart. The sight of the guy in the white overalls, coming and going with different-sized tools and looking supremely puzzled, while the plane's passengers had sat in the smelly and cramped cabin sweating it out and watching, didn't exactly instil confidence either.

And when that had finally been sorted there was another problem. Travelling through the passengers, front to back, had come a concerned buzz of conversation. The word, Paul learned from the ugly woman beside him (whose gaze he had been trying to avoid because she was a talker), was that there was someone on the plane who was going to have to be put off.

And Paul had thought that he might know who that person was.

They had evidently not lost track of him at all. Either that or they'd put the word out about the car they were looking for and someone had spotted it parked in the railway station car park in Crawley.

2

There was no apparent logic driving the chain of events that had happened today. They had wanted to nail him, he could understand that, and he suspected they'd been trying to follow him in case he either gave himself away or knew the identity of the killer and intended a reprisal. But the other thing – the way that the detective had tried to push him off the road – defied any attempt at understanding. The best Paul could come up with was that he was certain Paul was the murderer and that

183

he wasn't going to get enough evidence for a conviction. Therefore he had decided to take matters into his own hands. It didn't sound right – it sounded crazy in fact – but it was the best Paul could do.

And the cop had paid for his craziness with his life.

Paul had pulled in after the Granada had jumped the barrier and had walked back to the scene of the accident. There were already others parked up along the hard shoulder and by the time he got close people were flooding down the bank to where the car lay on its roof. Paul had already known the detective – the infamous Steve Jones, who had nicked practically every crook south of the river on at least one occasion – was dead. The smell of his departure was borne to Paul's nostrils on the wind, mingled with the other, sharper smells of petrol, blood and burning rubber.

A young Nordic guy with flaxen hair and a waxen face, his arm around an extremely attractive black girl, had approached Paul and asked if he was the driver of the Citroën. The guy said they'd seen what happened and would be prepared to act as witnesses, and with a trembling hand the girl had given Paul a piece of paper on which she had written their names and addresses and telephone numbers. Paul doubted whether anyone was likely to call Pieter back from Stockholm if it came to a court case, but he thanked them and pocketed the piece of paper.

And then he had left the scene.

He had driven to the junction with the M25, hoping the police would assume he had turned off earlier towards Heathrow airport, and turned south towards Gatwick, wondering how much crazier things could get.

He had arrived at Crawley station with two hours to spare and had parked the damaged Citroën – which, in spite of the damage it had suffered, still ran and handled like a dream – and considered removing the number plates. He doubted this would prevent the car's identification for long – if at all – there was the non-standard colour to consider and the DON'T MESS

WITH THE BEST sticker that Amy had placed there during better times as a warning to drivers who cut her up. Paul had tried to peel the sticker away before and knew that it wouldn't come off clean. Its total removal was going to be a matter of twenty minutes scraping with a razor blade he didn't have, and the car's colour would give it away anyway. He simply locked the car, thanked it for everything it had done for him and told it goodbye.

He took a taxi from Crawley to Gatwick airport, hoping that by the time the Citroën was found he would be out of the country. If they found it early enough, he hoped they would lose some time wondering if he had taken a train to somewhere other than the airport.

Inside the airport Paul had checked in for the flight and watched the movements of the policemen and listened carefully to the tannoy announcements while he waited for his flight call on the screens. No one gave him a second glance and there were no calls for passenger Stephen Miles travelling to Greece to come to the information booth.

The recently departed Steve Jones, and his bosom buddy Dick Farris, had been right about several things concerning passports and income, but they had been wrong about the reasons that Paul did not wish to be followed and had spent so much time shaking them off.

Paul, now travelling as his alter-ego Stephen Miles, restorer of classic cars, had not known (and still did not know) how close the police had been to charging him with the murder of his mother. While he'd been fighting off the creeping claustrophobia he'd felt during his time in the cells and trying to deal with the vivid memory of the horrendous thing that had happened to his mother and Cindy, he had however had some pointers. These, based mainly around the shoes that weren't his (and the frustration that had been so evident upon Steve Jones' face), suggested that the forensic evidence didn't support the theory that he was the killer. But he had been surprised when he was released without charge. It had taken about five minutes of being out in the open air and not feeling as if you were about to be crushed by those thick walls for his head to clear and then he had realised that they were expecting him to lead them to the murderer. And when that didn't happen, they would take him in again. And again. And again.

Paul had managed to hold on to his remaining few marbles while he was banged up, but it had been a struggle. He estimated (or rather his mental *goad* estimated) that within another week of that awful claustrophobia that came hand in hand with incarceration, he would have cracked. And not just cracked in spirit, either, but *totally* cracked. Into fragments so small and complex that they would be impossible to reassemble.

Paul was well aware of the old lag's maxim, *If you can't do the time, don't do the crime!* but until now had not considered it applicable in his case. He was careful and skilled and didn't expect ever to get caught. Being banged up for the better part of a week had not only brought the wisdom of the saying home to him, it had demonstrated to him that he could not possibly live behind bars and remain sane.

And the prospect of fifteen to twenty years for a crime he hadn't committed didn't bear thinking about. Paul thought he would be consigned to a rubber room within six weeks and that the rest of his life would henceforth be lived there.

All of which meant that he couldn't go inside again.

Which meant that he had to disappear, possibly for quite some time and possibly for ever.

Running away from the police and vanishing was not the kind of retirement he had planned, but it most certainly *was* the type of retirement which stood up well against the alternative that seemed to be on offer.

So every day this week, he had gone out in the Citroën, shaken off the police and prepared for it. There was money and documentation in the safe at the Miles Carriage Co. and Stephen Miles opened an account with the National Bank of Greece, transferred a hundred and twenty-five thousand pounds into it, rushed himself a ten-year British passport at Petty France, and at Thomas Cook booked a fortnight's holiday in a self-catering apartment on the Greek island of Skiathos where he'd never been before in his life. And once he was there, he intended to stay there for a very long time, possibly spending his days lying on the beach while he metaphorically placed his mind on low ground so that all his stray marbles would be encouraged to roll back to him.

He didn't know what would happen after that and he didn't particularly care.

That would be enough.

3

And then the buzz had gone through the plane and Paul's heart had sunk. They had surely found the car, deduced that he'd gone to Gatwick, checked the boarding lists and somehow – probably by computer – discovered that Stephen Miles of the Miles Carriage Co. couldn't be on that Dan Air to Skiathos because he'd died some time ago in an aeroplane crash in Western Samoa.

And when the two uniformed policemen came waltzing up the steps at the front of the aircraft, Paul had already unclipped the seat belt that had been biting into his hips since the moment he'd sat down and was on the point of asking the woman sitting next to him to let him out into the aisle. If he had to go, he intended to do it in as dignified a manner as possible.

Then a scuffle broke out up in the non-smoking section of the aeroplane as the policemen invited a man who might have been Lebanese to come with them, and the man quite strenuously declined.

After the man had been removed from the cabin, Paul clipped his seat belt again but was unable to relax. He waited for the next announcement which would surely say that there would be a further delay while the Lebanese man's luggage was unloaded from the plane and gritted his teeth when it came because he knew the passengers would break into a fear-thrilled babble of speculation as to whether the man had been carrying explosives. He was not surprised when these two things happened almost immediately, nor particularly astonished when a self-elected spokesman from the non-smoking section demanded that the passengers be taken off the plane until the danger had passed, then refused to accept the tendered explanation (made by a very harried-looking stewardess who was sweating off her make-up and who would have to put a new face on before take off) that there was a problem with the man's passport.

If Paul had been a little nearer, he would have been sorely tempted to put the man forcibly back into his seat because when people were on aeroplanes they panicked as easily as horses and when you were sitting at the back of a cigar-tube containing more than a hundred frightened people your claustrophobia would make a break for it, feed itself off that free-flowing fear and then return to whack you right in the face. And Paul's heart was already hammering away at more than a hundred and thirty.

As it was, he ignored the questioning looks of the woman beside him, closed his eyes, breathed deeply and waited.

And eventually the plane had taken off.

4

Now there were only sixty minutes or so in which things could go wrong in the air. Paul knew there were three thousand six hundred seconds yet to pass and he also knew how long a second could take to sail by when the claustrophobia demon was constantly snapping at your heels.

To make matters worse, there was a part of him which had burning questions to ask about the nature of Steve Jones' attempt on his life. Such as: was this the first time Jones had tried to kill a suspect, and if not, what had caused such a wildly out of character act? This part of him, which Paul studiously ignored while he stared at the seat back before him because he couldn't look out of the window without that same part making him dizzy and reminding him that six miles was one fuck of a long way to fall, had some thoughts on the matter. These thoughts appertained to the mystery of the blood message on his mother's lounge wall, to the mystery of the dream girl called Katie, and to the present mental state of the guys in the cockpit.

Because this part of Paul knew *exactly* who it was he had been warned off helping and it also thought that whoever had killed his mother had somehow got to Jones and made him homicidal. And if that was the case, whoever that masked man was, he might also have got to the Dan Air crew.

But Paul wouldn't allow himself to think these things while he was still thirty-five thousand feet above the planet, just as he wouldn't allow himself the insane thought that somewhere up the road to his future he would meet a girl who had been trying to contact him through his dreams, who had his telephone number and who someone had killed his mother to stop him from helping. He had stopped all of this dead in its tracks by leaving the country, and if that was what the bastard who'd murdered his mother had intended, then he'd got his wish. Paul told himself that he did not care and ignored the black bubble of resentment which pulsed inside him.

'You okay?' the woman beside him finally asked.

'Fine,' Paul replied, still staring at the elastic-topped net in the seat back which contained a sick-bag and an in-flight magazine. There were less than three thousand seconds left for something to go wrong with the plane.

'Only you look a bit pale,' she continued, having broken the ice.

Ordinarily Paul would have turned to glare at her until she fell silent, but nothing was ordinary any more and he'd discovered, to his discomfort, that a rapid head movement in any direction would upset his finely honed (and now very sensitive, for some reason) sense of balance. His mental clock kept ticking off those seconds and with each one he became a little more tense.

'Be all right when I get off,' he muttered. The woman didn't smell bad (in fact she bore a very faint hint of Amy's old favourite *Opium* which meant she'd probably used the bath oil recently rather than the perfume or *Eau de toilette*) and she'd had the decency to keep her trap shut for more than three hours. He supposed he owed her some kind of civility.

'Perhaps I could arrange for one of the cabin crew to give you a little whiff of oxygen,' the woman said. 'I know exactly how planes can make you feel.'

Paul shook his head and wished he hadn't. He closed his eyes, took a deep breath and tried to empty his mind. 'Thanks, but no thanks,' he said and put the first three fingers of his right hand against the pulse point on his left wrist and began to count while he wished himself luck.

5

There you go, poke, we're down, you old coward! Paul's goad announced as the aeroplane's wheels shrieked on the tarmac.

The pilot immediately applied reverse thrust as he had earlier promised he would, adding comfortingly that he would be doing this as the Skiathos landing strip was a very short one.

Paul let himself breathe again when the plane had slowed to taxiing speed. His claustrophobia vanished back into its hole and he suddenly felt very light and, considering his circumstances, very positive. The last remaining hurdle was passport control. If he got through that (and he didn't expect that the airport officials would be waiting to apprehend Stephen Miles because his luck surely couldn't have turned *that* sour) then he was out of the game. Once he was inside Greece, he was his own man. They could extradite him, of course, but they would first have to hack their way through to his new identity, which wouldn't be easy since no one except Jake Fulman knew it existed (even Double A thought Paul was Mr Miles), and Jake wouldn't spill, even under torture. And even if that happened, Paul was confident that he could vanish into Europe or the Middle East before they could apprehend him.

As he walked down the steps into the warm, fragrant, flood-lit darkness of Skiathos airport, Paul felt as if a huge weight had been lifted from him.

6

The apartment he had chosen by simply nodding his head at the first selection the girl at the travel agency had offered him, turned out to be exactly as lonely and secluded as he would have wished.

The mini-bus, into which fifteen people had initially been cramped, had toured the town dropping couples off at various hotels and apartments then had taken what the tour representative had said was the island's only main road. By this time there were five people left in the bus. Both couples were booked into the Skiathos Palace Hotel and Paul had been a little bemused when he had suddenly found himself alone with the Greek driver and the rep, who had earlier introduced herself as Sandra.

'I've got you all to myself now,' she said, climbing back on the bus and sliding into the seat next to him. Sandra was a short girl of about twenty, very pretty, tanned bronze and just a little overweight. She smelled of perspiration and Sure deodorant and made it plain to Paul that as far as *he* was concerned she was *very* available, and not just for her normal range of duties either. Sandra didn't actually say this – she didn't have to. She made it plain by blithely ignoring social etiquette and invading his space. She sat so close against Paul that he could feel the warmth of her arm, her hip and her thigh through his clothing.

'How far is it?' he asked, without turning towards her.

'Not far,' she replied. 'Another few minutes. I think you'll like the place. Look, if you need to contact me at any time, the number's on a sheet in the blurb I gave you earlier. It says it's an emergency number, but you don't have to worry about that.'

Paul nodded and looked out of the window. There was no street lighting here and outside the overspill from the coach's lights, the darkness was total.

Sandra apparently wasn't getting the reaction she was used to. 'Perhaps we could meet for a drink when you've settled in?' she suggested.

Paul sensed the loneliness in her and something in him identified with it. He turned back from the window and wasn't totally surprised to find Sandra looking up at him with a face that was just begging to be kissed. Her head was inclined at the right angle, her lips were parted and her eyes had a faintly dazed look.

Sometimes it happened. Most times they were girls who reminded him of Amy who was someone he was trying hard to forget. Ordinarily he would have rejected an advance of this type (and from this *Amy* type) out of hand, but things weren't ordinary any more. Everything had changed and Paul knew that things would never return to being the way they once were.

Because you lost your battle, cowboy, his goad said. *And because they almost had you believing you killed your mum and Cindy.*

Paul ignored his inner voice and the appealing expression. 'Maybe we could meet,' he replied, looking back into the darkness. 'We'll see.'

After another five minutes of driving away from the main town the bus made a lurching left turn on to an unmade road and slowed to a crawl, picking its way through deep ruts and potholes. Sandra allowed herself to be lurched against Paul and apologised, giggling with what was meant to sound like embarrassment.

'Where are we going?' he asked.

'This place is on a kind of promontory. It's a little arm that sticks out almost a kilometre from the main road and your apartment isn't far from the end. On your right, if it was daylight and if there weren't loads of trees in the way, you'd be able to see Vromolimnos Bay. There's a good beach down there and quite a nice little taverna. It's about twenty minutes' walk. There's a better taverna closer to the road but if you go down there in the dark, you ought to take a torch or you'll get lost.'

The bus made a right turn and stopped.

'Here we are,' Sandra said.

The apartment block was neat and clean, two storeys high and looked deserted. Paul followed the rep from the bus and was once again astonished by the warmth of the night and the silence which was broken only by a few distant crickets.

The large courtyard was lit by tiny bulbs which nestled beneath red fibreglass mushrooms. There was an unmown patch of straw on the right that presumably had once been a lawn and there were a great many broken chairs strewn about in it. A flaccid hosepipe ran from the side of the block and disappeared into the patch. There was an ancient Fiat 500 parked on the untidy shingle drive and beyond this a cement mixer. Judging by the mess around it, it had recently been used.

'They've been having some alterations done, but it's all finished now,' Sandra said – a little too quickly for Paul's liking. 'I think you're going to like it here.'

More lights came on and a tall, heavily-built Greek woman appeared from one of the lower apartments. She strode across to them, snatched Paul's case from his hand, put it down, took his hand and shook it vigorously while she beamed gold teeth at him and jabbered away in Greek. She smelled of garlic and chocolate and was very strong. It was like shaking hands with a talking vice. Paul liked her instantly.

'This is Mrs Manessis,' Sandra said. 'She says you are very welcome, and that although you are booked for a one room studio apartment, she would very much like you to have the newly decorated three-room one upstairs.'

Paul smiled back at her and said, 'Thank you,' nodding his head.

'Is okay, Meester Miless!' Mrs Manessis replied. 'We look after you good!'

And later that night as he lay on his bed in the spacious white room that smelled faintly of emulsion, he had to concede that the woman had been right. She had proudly shown him each detail of his apartment, demonstrated the use of the cooker, shower and the sliding balcony doors and had left him alone, only to return ten minutes later bearing a tray on which stood half a bottle of brandy, a glass, bread, a sizeable Greek salad and two foil-wrapped chocolates.

Paul had once been to Rhodes with Amy and already knew that he liked Greece and that the natives were friendly and hospitable, but this kind of cossetting was new to him.

'Eat!' Mrs Manessis had commanded, furiously miming the action of knives and forks, and had stood over him in order to make sure he was going to do exactly that and hadn't left again until she was satisfied.

Paul lay there on the hard bed in the sparse room and thought about England. From this distance it hardly seemed possible to believe England existed, let alone admit that the things which had happened to him were true. Lying here in the warm and quiet with the windows open and the comforting velvet night waiting to steal in the moment he turned off the single light, his past life seemed less like reality and more like a half-remembered dream.

'You could get to like it here,' Paul told himself, turning out the light.

He closed his eyes, listened to the slow, steady beat of his heart pushing a good deal of brandy around his body and felt his mind preparing to throw itself over the precipice of sleep.

And for the first time since he'd heard the distant voice of Katie across the Telecom void, he did not resist.

7

Over the next four days, Mr Stephen Miles slept for more than sixty hours, forty of them in the bed in his apartment and the rest on the fine sand of Vromolimnos beach under the shade of overhanging trees.

Each time he awoke he felt a little better than he had the last time, and each time he told himself that he was completely recovered now and couldn't possibly feel any better.

The memories of England became less and less real when contrasted with the reality presented by the blinding Greek sunshine and during the afternoon of the fourth day he started to think he'd truly made it. For one thing, no one had come to get him and it didn't seem possible now that they would, and for another his marbles seemed to be all rolling back into their rightful places. But there were two things that *really* convinced him and both were to do with waking up. The first of these was that for the first time since he'd killed the boy, he'd woken up sporting an erection which tented his trunks (and to which the two naked American girls nearby were paying an inordinate amount of giggling attention), and the second was that he *hadn't* woken up thinking about the boy.

Paul smiled at the girls and rolled on to his stomach, distantly wondering if the proximity of naked female flesh had caused his erection, but feeling too good to be embarrassed. He lay there letting the sun rake his back and told himself that he was finally healed and fit and that tomorrow might be a very good day to start exploring the island. He waited and listened for his goading inner voice to start complaining, but the voice was absent.

Chapter Eight
Picking Up An Angel

1

The motorcycle he hired in Skiathos town after having spent the better part of the following morning just sitting in one of the cafés staring at the people coming and going, was a two-fifty Yamaha trials bike – except that in Europe they were apparently known as trail bikes. The owner of the business, a middle-aged man who spoke extremely good English, had started negotiations by offering him a 50cc Suzuki and looked offended when Paul simply shook his head. He explained that if he was going to go off-road he wanted something that would handle it and the Greek had agreed, looking concerned. He had thought about it for a few moments, his face clouded, then gone out through the back door, returning with the well-used Yamaha.

'She's mine,' he explained. 'All I have this big. Is too big for these . . . children, but I rent her to you because you know motor-bikes. I don't rent to anybody, but you know motorbikes. She take you everywhere. But listen. She's *mine* so you break, you pay. Okay?'

Paul nodded and used the Stephen Miles plastic and driving licence to hire it, promising the man that his beloved machine wouldn't come to any harm. The bike was filthy and well worn, but it looked like the Greek knew motorbikes too. Barring the balding tyres which all Greeks seemed to drive on, it was in excellent mechanical condition and sounded fit and healthy.

He had this proven to him five minutes later as he cruised out towards the airport where he had landed. When you opened the throttle, the bike shot away, as Jake Fulman would have said, like shit out of a tin trumpet.

The island came round in a ragged U-bend at the end of the runway, forming what would have been a long, narrow lagoon if the top of the U had been enclosed, and the road that crossed from one leg to the other seemed to be a part of the runway itself. Paul smelt burning aviation fuel and pulled up, gazing down the landing strip in case a plane happened to be taking off. If there was one, it ought to be up in the air a good distance before it got here, but he didn't want any unnecessary shocks which might make him drop the bike, because like the man had said: 'You break, you pay'.

But the strip was clear. Paul sniffed again then glanced up into the sky in the opposite direction. He immediately spotted the descending jet. It was still a long way out and Paul doubted that he was smelling its exhaust. There wasn't even any wind, and even if there had been, unless the jet had been circling in a holding pattern, it wouldn't have carried the smell here ahead of it.

He looked up at it as its approach slowly made it grow larger and the first hint of doubt appeared in his mind.

It doesn't have to be a British plane, he assured himself. *It could be from anywhere.*

But it would be a British plane, he knew, because accompanying that smell of burnt aviation fuel he couldn't possibly yet be smelling was the sharper tang of trouble.

You're just getting jittery, that's all, he thought. *Just being pessimistic. Only one person in the world knows who you are, and that man can be trusted with your life. And even he doesn't know* where *you are. He probably doesn't even know you've left the country yet.*

The plane was a Monarch 737 which most certainly had come from somewhere in Britain. Paul watched it land, ducking as it passed low over his head and concentrating on its odour. The fuel smell matched, but neither this nor the trouble smell grew any stronger in his nostrils.

Just so long as you don't start sniffing blood or rotten orange blossom and honey, it won't be anything you can't handle, he told himself, and kick-started the bike again.

And because he could smell neither of those two things, and because he had a new identity, he put the matter out of his mind and drove back towards Vromolimnos Bay, his eyes streaming in the wind and the slipstream whipping his tee shirt against his back.

Paul intended to collect his towel and trunks and find a beach that wasn't so crowded as Vromolimnos, but as he reached the bay on the south side of the promontory from where the apartment lay, he noticed a guy in a speedboat heading rapidly towards the shore-line from the small island that lay a couple of kilometres away. When he glanced back again, the boat was raising spray as its driver turned sharply away from the huddle of small boats moored out in the bay.

One of those might come in very handy, his goad said, and before he even realised it had spoken to him for the first time in days, he was heading down the track to the beach thinking that hiring a speedboat for a day or two might be very nice indeed.

By the time he'd killed the Yamaha's engine, he also knew he'd come to the right place. There was a little wooden shed on the beach with a sign propped up against it advertising the fact that here was the best place on the island to hire a boat. The huddle of small boats out in the bay were not fishing boats, as Paul had imagined, but about fifteen squarish, flat speedboats, each with a steering wheel and its outboard motor tilted up out of the water. These things were red and white and looked as if they were made from fibreglass. Paul walked down the beach towards the hut, watching the boat he'd originally spotted and deciding that the smaller craft didn't compare favourably. The boat he'd first seen was now bobbing around as its driver leaned over the side, untying the rope and float that hitched one of the little boats. This one looked like a proper speedboat. It was made of varnished yellow wood, had a pointed front, a deep draught and a raked-back windscreen, framed with chromium.

It also had an electric starter, Paul's professional mind noted after the man had hitched the smaller boat to it. He noticed too that if the boats were moored in this position overnight, and if they were kept gassed-up, they would be unbelievably easy to steal.

Paul reached the wooden hut and noticed that the door was fastened with a very large hasp through which was fitted a very large Ingersoll padlock and that there was a 'No Smoking' sign on the door. This, apparently, was why those little boats didn't get spirited away.

A blind man could have deduced that this was there their owner kept his supply of fuel, and if that blind man hadn't been able to read the sign or feel the padlock, then he surely would have been able to smell the sharp odour of the methanol that was seeping out from between the boards. The only professional question that remained was, did the boats have onboard petrol tanks, or was the shed full of the kind of metal petrol cans you could (if you didn't mind the danger, that was) carry in the boot of your car?

Paul didn't know a great deal about the workings of motorboats or about how much gas they used, but mentally opted for metal cans since they were very portable and since there was no other elegant way of filling an onboard tank. The tank of the guy's own boat might have to be filled from a drum with a pump, but Paul doubted he would want to have to do this fifteen or twenty times a day with the smaller ones.

He sauntered down towards the water line where the Greek had anchored the real boat and was wading ashore, leading the smaller one by a blue rope. The boat bobbed and tugged behind him like a slightly reluctant dog being led out into weather it didn't care for.

The man looked up. He was thin and wiry with a mop of black hair and the same kind of six o'clock shadow that all Greek men above the age of fifteen seemed to have. Paul thought he was aged about thirty, but it was difficult to tell. 'Hello!' he called, and turning away, took the rope in both hands, dug in his heels and, with a phenomenal effort, yanked the boat out of the water and on to the beach.

'How much to hire this?' Paul asked, making a quick appraisal of the craft. It was made of moulded glass-fibre, had a steering wheel and a throttle handle in the centre of the floor where the gearstick would have been in a car. There were no other controls and no ignition switch. There was also a rubber tube which ran from the outboard and lay loose in the back of the boat. It terminated in an easy-lock union which presumably connected to a petrol container.

Which means that all you have to do to steal it, is lever the lock off the shed door, take a can, hook it up and yank hard on the starter cord, Paul thought, and forcefully dismissed this from his mind. He had retired for one thing, and for another – if you wanted another and he didn't – he had no reason whatsoever to want to steal a small speedboat.

Might pay to keep your hand in though, old poke, his goad suddenly announced. *Remember what you promised*.

But Paul didn't have to remember because the only thing he had promised to do was leave the game and start afresh, somewhere else, and that was exactly what he was doing.

'Not this one,' the boat man said. 'This one has broken steering. People don't listen. Here?' He pointed out into the bay.

Paul followed the line of his finger and spotted a patch of water that was a slightly darker hue than the rest. He nodded.

'Rocks,' the man said. 'Just under the sea. I have map in the shed. When they take boat, I say: "Keep away from Skiathos, here, here, here, here!" But they don't listen and this is what happens.' He shook his head and shrugged. 'How long would you like to hire boat, my friend?' he asked, brightening.

Paul didn't know. Ever since his goad had put in its tuppence worth a fairly large part of him didn't want to have anything

200

to do with boats. 'A day?' he said. 'Two perhaps.'

'For you . . .' the Greek appeared to think about it '. . . special price. One day, ten thousand drachma. Two days, eighteen.'

Paul shook his head and turned away.

The Greek caught up with him as he walked off and took his arm, just as Paul had expected. In his old life, an act as simple as this would have pulled Paul's hair-trigger and resulted in a short, sharp shock for whoever had done it, but this was not his old life and Stephen Miles was not predisposed to violence. And in the Mediterranean the rules were different anyway – anyone could grab hold of you, whether they knew you or not.

Knowing this might have been enough to stop yourself acting, but it was not enough to prevent the internal physiological responses that had been acquired over a great many years. Paul's glands shot adrenaline into him, raised his blood pressure and heart rate and quickened his senses, and he had to stop himself from violently shrugging off the Greek's hand. The trouble with pretending to be someone else, Paul realised (and not for the first time), was that the original guy was like the Greek boatman's rocks – still there just below the surface and waiting to do damage.

Thought you were a new man, cowboy, his internal voice chipped in. *You don't suppose we're rejecting that new man, like a transplant patient might reject a new kidney, do you?*

Paul didn't answer. He would make the new man take, even if it was just as a superficial shell at first. The shell would calcify and cramp the old Paul Dekker, just as the version of him that had appeared after he'd killed the boy had cramped the original.

'Okay, just for you,' the Greek said, beaming. 'Two days, fifteen thousand.'

Paul converted the currencies. Then nodded.

'When you want to take?' the boatman asked. 'Tomorrow?'

'Tomorrow and the day after,' he said, then heard himself asking, 'Tell me, how far can you go on a tank of gas in one of these?'

The Greek frowned. 'Where you want to go?' he asked suspiciously.

Paul shrugged. He had no idea where he wanted to go or why he'd asked the question. So far he had only envisioned puttering around in this bay and maybe going over to the little island which couldn't have been more than half a mile away. A tank of gas was surely going to last that long. 'Around,' he said.

The Greek's face brightened. 'I give you tank of gas, last you all day if you don't drive top speed all the time. You can go around. You get enough gas go around Skiathos one and half time. Is plenty.' He pointed out to sea. 'Volos,' he announced shaking his head, 'is big port. Ellas mainland. Too far. You go Volos, you go Flying Dolphin hydrofoil.'

Paul nodded.

The boatman pointed north, up the length of the island. 'Alonissos island,' he said, shaking his head again. 'You want go Alonissos, you take Flying Dolphin. In boat you have big firework. You get trouble, near Skiathos, you shoot firework in air. Is bright light, someone tell me they see, I come get you. Alonissos too far. Volos too far. Is not allowed.'

'Okay,' Paul agreed, 'see you tomorrow.'

'I am here from eight in morning,' the Greek promised.

It wasn't until Paul was back on the bike and heading away from the bay that he realised that the personality of Stephen Miles wasn't being rejected by his body at all. Stephen Miles had not *taken* in the first place; the graft hadn't worked. Down there, underneath his relaxed new exterior, the sly and wary personality of the original Paul Dekker was being just as careful as ever – if not more so. Because now he was busily denying its existence, it was guiding him without consultation.

As he cruised down the road towards his turning, he suddenly realised *why* he'd spotted the speedboat and become inordinately interested in hiring one, even though he was not interested in boats. And it was not as if he was simply uninterested in boats. He had, in fact, spent the greater part of his life avoiding them

202

because as soon as he set foot on one his sensitive sense of balance would begin to complain that if he didn't get off, *now*, *this minute*, it was just going to have to make him throw up. But in spite of this, and completely out of character (for either the old Paul Dekker or the new Stephen Miles), he'd hired a speedboat for two days.

And the reason *why* was the same reason he'd paid so much attention to the hasp and the Ingersoll on the shed door and the petrol can connections inside the motorboat. The reason was that the old Paul Dekker was looking for a quick and easy way off the island in case a speedy escape became necessary.

Paul considered this for a moment, and was angry that he'd been suckered by the careful guy that lurked just below the surface. He had almost decided not to rent the boat after all when he remembered the smell of aviation fuel and trouble. Then he thought better of it. It might just become important to know how one of those little speedboats worked, and tomorrow he would find out – not just how you drove them, but how much fuel the guy kept in his shed and at what time he locked up for the night. If there was a chance you were going to have to steal something, it paid to be prepared.

Sounds like me, he told himself and smiled with something like admiration for the guy who was struggling to get out.

You can take the boy out of the criminal element, Freddie, he thought, *but you can't take the criminal element out of the boy*.

And by the time he'd reached the conclusion that it was senseless to try and subdue his own personality and had decided that Stephen Miles was never going to reach the rank of a 'real' person and might just as well stay at the level of being a convenient cover, he was a good couple of kilometres past his turning.

Paul didn't particularly care. He was feeling good about himself for once. He seemed to have come to a kind of agreement with his guilt over the boy, he felt healthier and saner than he'd done since the accident and he no longer had to train himself to react and think as a different person.

And the bonus is, he told himself, *there aren't even any telephones*

203

in your apartment block. There were other bonuses too, such as the fact that the only other residents beside him and the owners were an elderly German couple who had an equally elderly toy poodle called Fritz, all of whom were friendly, and the fact that Mrs Manessis brought him fresh eggs from her chickens each morning. It was a good place to stay and Paul intended to have a quiet word with Mrs Manessis about a longer rental before he announced to Sandra the rep that he didn't intend to go home. But the important thing was that there were no telephones in the block.

Paul considered turning round and going back to his apartment to collect his swimming kit, then decided to carry on down the main road and see if he could find the famed Banana beach, which Sandra and the others on the mini-bus had spent so much time giggling about during the trip from the airport. In spite of the fact that people regularly took all their clothes off on Vromolimnos beach, Banana beach was the island's one and only official nudist beach. Which would save Paul from having to backtrack to collect his trunks.

2

During the next twenty-five minutes Paul learned two important things about navigation on Greek islands. The first was that since the locals already knew where everything was, they didn't feel the need to erect signposts, and the second thing was that the maps supplied by motorcycle hire companies didn't necessarily bear a close resemblance to the topography of the island. Some of the roads marked on what was rapidly becoming a sweat-stained, dog-eared and crumpled piece of paper which under no circumstances should have been called a map, appeared to have been drawn by a master of the art of wishful thinking. Most of them didn't exist at all, and the ones that did were little more than meandering goat tracks.

Halfway up one of these tiny tracks, and shielded from the burning sun by overhanging trees, Paul swore at whatever town planner had drawn in the roads he would have liked to exist, tore the map into shreds and jettisoned the idea of an afternoon on Banana beach. He reasoned that he'd hired the bike in order to explore the island and decided that he would spend the afternoon doing just that. Skiathos was not a large island and by the time the sun sank into the Mediterranean Paul Dekker would never again need a map of it.

He got on the Yamaha, kicked it into life and drove slowly up the tree-covered hill, standing on the footrests and allowing the bike to ride up and down over the roots and hollows. He hoped there would be a clearing at the top of this hill (which wasn't even marked on the map) and that when he arrived there he would be able to see the lie of the land, perhaps right down to the coastline, which couldn't be very far away.

He was beginning to doubt the wisdom of this decision when the trees started to thin. Up ahead, there was a distinct line where the vegetation abruptly ceased. Beyond, the hill still rose, but up there it was just loose shale and rock. As he cruised out of the undergrowth of trees and bushes, he was mildly surprised to see that the division between bare ground and the trees was drawn as sharply as if someone had purposely arranged the sweeping circular line around the hillside with geometric precision. It looked as though a circle had been drawn around the hillside with a gigantic compass, its point set at the peak of the hill – which Paul couldn't yet see, but which he estimated to be another two hundred yards or so away.

Perhaps this isn't such a good idea, after all, Paul's internal voice suddenly suggested. *Perhaps you just ought to turn around, go back to the apartment and see what's happening there.*

But Paul didn't think anything would be happening back at the apartment because all he could smell was the sap oozing from pine trees and the pleasant, dry, dusty smell of Greek rock and shale.

The aeroplane! his goad reminded him. *Your promise! You don't need this, poke!*

And Paul slowed the Yamaha when the smell of smoke hit

his nostrils because it wasn't the sweet smell of burning wood or the stench of a bonfire, it was the smell of a house burning down.

He was suddenly convinced that the apartment was on fire.

But then it was too late to return, because in the two seconds he'd taken to identify the sudden smell (which had vanished now, anyway) his body had been busy finding a convenient place to turn the bike, and had apparently decided that the best place to do it would be over this ridge.

And now he was here, on the plateau at the top of the hill, it was too late to go back.

Because of the sudden profusion of strange odours that hit his olfactory nerves.

Because of the two men who stood on the far side of the plateau looking as though they meant business with a capital B.

And because of the girl in the thin white summer dress who stood in the centre of the flat plateau, her back towards him and her arms stretched towards the sky.

The girl was Katie.

3

Get out of here, poke, and do it now! his mental voice insisted. *You're going to regret it forever if you don't. Two more seconds and your life will be blighted forever. This'll be the end for you and me both. Believe me, old cowboy, I know. If you think killing the kid was bad, you're mistaken. In comparison to what'll happen if you don't just turn around and leave, it'll become just about as significant as treading on a snail. So get out!*

Paul reached down and turned off the Yamaha's ignition, not because he wanted to prove himself by ignoring the warning voice, and not because of a dream promise he might or might not have made to this girl, but because she looked as if she might be in some very serious trouble.

Paul put the bike on its stand and got off it, weighing up the

206

tableau in front of him which not only looked as if it had been waiting for him to arrive before it sprung into action, but looked and smelled completely wrong.

Don't do this, cowboy!

The light was different. This was not the normal Greek brilliance that etched everything on to your retinas in fine detail, but the softer, surreal light you only ever saw just before thunderstorms. Everything looked as if it was lit internally rather than from outside. Half expecting to see clouds over the hillside, Paul glanced up into the clear blue sky. Except that there was something present in the sky which hadn't been there before. Something that was so barely discernible that it looked as if it had been constructed of the finest, clearest glass that had ever been manufactured. He could not make out its shape, its beginning or end, but only that it existed. And that might have merely been one of the little tricks the light was so fond of playing on your eyes.

'Katie!' Paul called, and his voice sounded flat, as if it had been spoken in a roomful of cotton wool.

The girl stood in the centre of a rough ring of ancient boulders which protruded from the shale and stood knee-high in smooth parabolic shapes. They looked like huge rock bullets that had been buried to their necks. And like bullets from the Wild West films of Paul's youth, there were six of them – except that these were placed in what would probably have been all six corners of a hexagon if they'd been viewed from above.

Corners sounds about right, poke! his goad said. *The guy who killed your mother and Cindy knew all about corners, didn't he? So now you know too, why don't you get the fuck away from here?*

But it was far too late to leave now. There were those two men on the far side of the clearing and although they presently seemed to be transfixed by the girl in the centre of the rocks, they meant to do her some serious damage judging by the weapons they were carrying. The smaller of the two, a wiry, bearded man, was carrying a long black knife and the other held a length of what appeared to be metal pipe to his chest.

The men smelled dangerous, but Paul didn't think they would pose too much of a threat because they were also radiating the sour, sweaty smell of fear. These were the people who had arrived on the plane he'd seen land earlier, Paul realised. They were too pale-skinned to have been here any longer.

He stood there, waiting for someone to move and smelling the peculiar *dead* smell that came from the girl. The girl looked as though she'd already been through the mill. There were scratches and abrasions on her arms and legs, the back of her dress was dirty and the mane of yellow hair that tumbled down her back didn't look as if it had seen a brush for a month.

There are worse things in Heaven and Hell, old poke, the voice of the nightmare Katie repeated in his mind. *Best if little boys don't dabble.*

'Katie?' he called again, not liking the dreadful flat timbre of his voice. The girl didn't seem to hear him.

'Don't touch her!' one of the men warned. 'She's dangerous!'

'I came to get her,' Paul said in his curiously compressed voice. 'You won't be getting to touch her either.'

'You don't understand!' the guy with the beard said. 'You should . . .'

The man's voice ceased in mid-sentence as the air pressure around Paul increased to what surely had to be two or three thousand millibars. He felt as if he was being crushed and sucked in air which was thicker than treacle and tasted of ozone. His ears were screaming and he could barely move.

Something glittered gold at the base of one of the bullet-shaped stones, then faded.

Worse things, old poke, a voice reminded him. *Worse things . . .*

Paul's head tilted back as he gasped for air. The huge, almost invisible thing in the sky was stretching down, rearranging reality into a shape which might have been a funnel.

A shower of red sparks jetted out from the stone Paul had seen glitter and the one diagonally across from it glittered gold and faded, then expelled its own shower of red sparks.

In the centre of the circle, the girl's hair began to fly as though a strong breeze had formed around her. Her hands clutched at the air as if she were trying to scramble upward and her dress whipped at her legs.

Another of the stones shot red sparks, then another.

A very calm and disassociated part of Paul's mind calmly informed him that this wasn't happening at all and that he had surely been wrong about regrouping his collection of marbles because this was a very vivid hallucination indeed. Another part of his mind – the part that had viewed Stonehenge as something more than a simple collection of big square stones when he'd visited it at eight years of age – was informing him that now he knew what they were for.

And the glass-like thing which Paul could both see, and see *through* – as if it wasn't there at all – drew steadily downwards, centring itself over Katie.

Paul heaved in another breath and watched a series of dark colours sweep over the six rocks, starting at the points and washing down to the bare earth where they vanished.

Then the rocks suddenly became six points of darkness that was so total it hurt to look at them. They seemed to suck the light away from Paul's retinas and in doing so, left their own anti-images burned there.

The acrid smell suddenly increased to a level which threatened to make Paul throw up, and a perfect hexagon of blinding golden light lit like a fence around the points of the six rocks. Red sparks sizzled from the golden beam at each corner and vanished into the darkness of the rocks.

And the spout of the invisible funnel reached down. Except that now the spout was hexagonal and Paul knew it would be exactly the same size as the shape described by the golden light. He could see up into the tube now, but one look was enough to inform him that he would never want to take another. When you looked at the hexagonal tube from outside, you could see right through it, but when you gazed up at the *inside* you found yourself looking at a vast and perfect nothingness that threatened to unhinge your mind. There was *nothing* in there and it went on for ever. There would be something coming through that emptiness soon, Paul was certain of that, but what it was going to be and where it would be coming from he did not want to know.

The tube slid down over Katie and met the golden hexagon with a shriek that could be heard even through the constant screaming in Paul's pressurised ears. Sheets of lightning flew horizontally out from the join, bending and earthing themselves. Paul's body started to tingle as though he was being vibrated apart and he caught fire.

He tried to shout and expelled thick air in a cough which hurt his lungs. He beat his left arm with his right and the blue fire went out in the shape of his hand then relit itself like a joke birthday cake candle. He hit himself three more times before he realised that the blue fire was cool and harmless and was apparently of the variety that belonged to Saint Elmo.

He let it burn and, fighting against the tremendous resistance of the leaden air, forced his way around the perimeter of the hexagon, because over there on the other side he could see the two men – who were also burning – walking towards it and whatever they intended to do was going to be something he had to stop.

Paul tried to force himself into a run, but the best he could manage was a fast shuffle and he arrived at the black stone the men had been heading towards too late to stop the guy with the metal pipe dropping it against the rock.

There may have been a flash and bang – afterwards Paul wasn't certain. All he knew was that in the space of half a second he had seen enough raw power run down the length of that pipe to reduce it to vapour. And once the power had found a way to earth, the removal of its conductor had not halted the flow. All three men had scrambled away as the earth beneath their feet liquefied. There had been a brief sensation of extreme heat and the hairs inside Paul's nostrils had been singed. After this he had experienced a huge tearing sensation and an almighty thump in the guts that had put him here on the ground fighting for breath and knowing he had to get to his feet before the other two men. The only other thing he was currently certain of was that whatever had been happening had been violently terminated.

Paul didn't realise that he wasn't only stunned, he was also blinded, until someone took hold of his right hand and began to saw at his index finger with a knife.

4

Out there behind the patchwork quilt of flashing pastel colours that had been dropped between Paul's eyes and the world someone announced, 'We did it! It worked!' in a shaky and surprised voice. The fuzzy words beat against his ears like a stream of rice falling on a taut snare-drum skin. They were possessed with an echoing resonance and the vague rattle of snare-wires.

Paul thought all this during the moment it took to ball his left fist. During this moment he also concluded that his hearing had been permanently damaged and that since he was going to be fighting blind, St Cunt was going to have to divert a great deal of luck in his direction in a very short space of time if he was going to have any chance of getting out of this alive.

He snapped out his left fist in a hooking punch, towards where he estimated the man was, twisting his body to the right. St Cunt might just have started paying attention, but he wasn't smiling yet. It was a start and better than nothing. Paul's fist missed the face of his assailant completely, but it glanced off the top of his shoulder. The man shouted and the cold blade fell away from Paul's index finger.

'Careful, Dick!' one of the men shouted, and even through the hissing echoing rain the voice brought to his ears, Paul identified the strong West Country accent and knew he wouldn't forget it. The owner of the voice sounded as if he were out of range, but the man named Dick was still nearby, either scrambling away from him or scrambling towards him once more.

A part of Paul's mind was shouting that good old Dick out there behind all those swimming colours had tried to cut off one of his fingers and this information was banging like a fist against the button in Paul's mind marked *Rage*. He threw another punch towards Dick – with his aching right hand this time – but this one missed completely. He scrambled towards the source of the noise and struck out again, realising a moment too late to take evasive action, that the other man was approaching from his left.

The man was wearing soft shoes. Paul realised this a moment later when one of those soft shoes hit him hard in the lower abdomen, and his bladder and penis lit with extreme heat and a painful tingling sensation which may or may not have meant that he was pissing himself. Paul didn't know, and at the moment he didn't care. The part of him which kept a tally of the damage he gave and received during a fight chalked this one down and noted that it was a good thing that the blow hadn't been struck by a good old hiking boot which would have caused more damage.

Paul ignored the threat to his left and crawled towards the sound of Dick, who had evidently dropped the knife and was trying to snatch it up. He snapped out another right-handed punch and this one connected with something solid enough to be a thigh. Dick yelped.

'I've got him!' West Country shouted.

And gave away his position.

Paul fell on to his right side and kicked up his left leg. His shin bone connected with West Country's and it hurt, but the other man was yelling and the part of Paul keeping tally marked it down as a success.

'Look out!' Dick yelled.

Paul struck out again. Missed. Swore and leapt towards the sound of Dick's voice, but Dick was gone.

Then West Country kicked him again.

This kick was well aimed and forcefully and precisely delivered. It not only lifted Paul from the ground as the soft shoe stove into his stomach, but it knocked the breath out of him.

Paul hit the ground and his arms gave way beneath him. His chin hit the shale and in his mind the tally-man marked down one against. His arms were trapped, folded beneath him, and would not move. He tried to gasp in a breath and couldn't. It took all the remaining oxygen his bloodstream possessed to try and propel himself along using his legs. Paul had perhaps moved six inches before these too gave out.

Told you, old cowboy, his mental goad announced. *Why didn't you just turn the bike around when you had a chance?*

The pastel shades before his eyes were darkening now and their neat seams were disappearing as they turned into a single black sheet.

What are they gonna do now, poke? Cut off your fingers, I expect.

Paul fought to stay conscious and tried to breathe while he waited for them to kick him to death or plunge a knife in him.

'I think *I'll* do this one,' West Country said, out there in the darkness.

Paul felt himself being rolled over on to his back and could not resist. *What size shoes, old poke?* his mind asked him.

One of the men took his right hand.

'Doesn't he have to be dead first?' Dick asked nervously. 'He's still blipping.'

West Country chuckled. 'Might be more interesting this way,' he said.

Find out what size they are! Paul heaved in a breath and realised he didn't have the faintest idea of what he was thinking about.

'What about the girl?' Dick said. 'Shouldn't we . . .?'

'She'll wait. She won't be going anywhere now. I think we've already done her enough damage, but we'll take her face and fingers too, just to be sure. In fact . . .'

Paul's hand was released. It fell to the ground, which seemed to be a very long drop.

'. . . I think it might be interesting to do it in reverse order here. I think I might take his face first.'

Paul gasped in another shuddering breath.

'It's okay, boy,' West Country assured him. 'It won't hurt.'

And as the knife was applied to his forehead, just below his hair line, a number of things happened. Paul's vision cleared and he found himself staring up into the perspiring face of West Country whose eyes had the radiance of a Born Again Christian, and whose teeth had fastened on to his bottom lip in concentration. Paul felt strength trickling back into his limbs and the part of his mind that had been banging on the *Rage* button began to bang even harder because the owner of that chilling expression of utter concentration clearly intended to cut around the edges of his face and peel it away like an orange skin.

Paul's blood pressure surged, his heart squeezed hard, three times in succession, and he felt as though someone had suddenly turned him through fifteen degrees inside his body. He knew what was coming next. In his mind he heard himself explaining – perhaps to Amy, years ago, or maybe to some poor unfortunate soul who was about to witness him in action: *Sometimes I get mad. I get this kind of white-heat inside me. Something clicks inside my head and my ears start to roar and it's like there's molten metal in front of my eyes. When it clears something bad has usually happened. Usually to someone else.*

Paul listened to the roaring in his ears and let his mind empty. If he had wanted to stop it happening, it would have already been too late. But Paul didn't want to stop it at all. On this occasion, the maniac that lived beneath the real Paul Dekker was welcome to come out to play.

Paul took a deep breath and gazed up into the glassy eyes of his attacker.

Two seconds later he clicked out.

5

Dick Stevens, who had gone up K2 with a party of twenty-seven and come down alone with a blizzard blowing through his mind, watched as Peter Defoe rolled the man over on to his back. Dick had been watching the man carefully ever since he had driven on to the hill top and although he looked beaten now, and although Dick had heard his *blip* cease earlier and had mistakenly thought he was dead, he still wasn't sure about him. The man looked out for the count, but he was still *blipping* and his psychic colour was deepening which was something Dick hadn't experienced before. He would very much have liked Peter Defoe to have killed the man before taking his face and fingers, but Peter seemed confident, and so far Peter had been exactly right about everything, down to the moment at which the man would appear.

As Peter crouched over the man, Dick glanced at the girl who lay still in what had once been the last usable magic circle in Europe and which was now no more than a scattering of ashes. Even the bullet-shaped rocks which had defined the hexagon were ruined. They hadn't so much become pillars of salt, as Dick had at first told himself, but piles of black ash which were steadily dwindling with each puff of moving air. Dick had been promised magic and he'd seen magic. Had *fought* magic and won. Soon, he knew, the blizzard would be taken from his mind. It had been promised and that promise would be fulfilled, just as the promise of his immortality would.

Dick did not know whether or not the girl was finished. She had no psychic colour, but she'd had none when he'd first seen her. He thought she had been dead already and was being driven by God knew what awful force. He'd known that there was something wrong with her the moment he'd first picked up her monstrous *blip*. But that *blip* was gone now and he was glad to get it out of his mind. And although it didn't matter a jot about whether the girl was dead or not because she was no longer a threat, Dick promised himself that he would take her face and fingers anyway. It was not necessary because neither he nor Peter had touched her before her death, but he would take them anyway. As mementoes, perhaps.

215

'What about the girl?' he asked. 'Shouldn't we . . .?'

Peter grinned at him. 'She'll wait. She won't be going anywhere now. I think we've already done her enough damage, but we'll take her face and fingers too, just to be sure. In fact . . .'

Dick watched the idea crawl into Peter's head. Whenever this happened, his face rearranged itself as if a large invisible beetle was picking its way across his features. Dick didn't care for these moments much because they made Peter look inordinately ugly and shifty. Rather like the kind of man who might suddenly turn on you when you least expected it, in fact. The kind of man who might take it into his head to see that you didn't live to see the wondrous things promised to you by the angel which had fallen through the roof of the world during the avalanche.

In fact, the expression Peter wore when he was getting an idea personified the way the angel had made him feel, both times they had met. Up on K2, the angel hadn't had any facial expressions, and on the second occasion, in Cambridge, it hadn't had a face to speak of (or any wings, robes or even a halo come to that), but on both occasions (and he was certain it was the same angel both times) he had felt he was in the presence of a being that might well welch on any deal you made with it.

In a more elegant way, he had confided this to Erich, one of the two German brothers he and Peter had travelled out with, while they stood at the back of the plane by the galley queuing for the toilets. Erich had been very amused. He had laughed and shook his head, then slapped Dick's back and told him he should have been called Thomas. 'You know what holds these things up in the air?' Erich had asked, then without waiting for a reply, had answered, 'Faith. With a little faith you can move mountains, Thomas!'

But Erich wasn't the one who had agreed to act as a Spotter, once and once only, in return for removal of the mind-blizzard and eternal life. Erich wasn't the one who had tried to fulfil his part in a bargain, only to have the blizzard still raging inside him because of a mistake anyone could have and probably *would* have made. The fact that he had not killed a monster but a human made little difference as far as he was concerned. He had done the deed. But this had not been acceptable as his part of the bargain, in spite of what the contract had implied. The rules (changed as far as he could see) were that it had to be a monster. So Dick had not been able to retire and enjoy his rewards, but had instead been sent out again after the same monster.

When he got back, he decided that after this cold wind inside him had been removed, he would demand extra recompense for the extra work he had done, and if that didn't work he would try to make another deal to get that extra thing.

He already knew what it would be. It would be the only thing he'd truly wanted since he climbed his last mountain.

He would ask for Jenny Richt to be brought back.

In his mind he saw her staggering through the blizzard, just ahead of him as she answered the calls that only she could hear and told her lost companions that she was coming for them. He watched Jenny, visible only because of the bulky red anorak she was wearing, trudge two paces through the snow and knew these were the last two she would ever take. Then there was a blur of descending red material and Jenny was gone.

I want her back! Dick thought slowly through the blizzard in his mind.

In front of him, the invisible beetle had crawled across Peter's face and into his mind and he was dropping the unconscious man's hand.

Dick watched the man's hand fall and hit the ground, open-palmed and relaxed. A long time seemed to have passed since Peter had said, 'In fact . . .'

'. . . I think it might be interesting to do it in reverse order here. I think I might take his face first,' Peter said.

Dick was unsure of what part the man – whose name, he remembered, was Paul Dekker – had been playing in this.

Someone had explained it, but all that seemed a very long time ago and a great deal of snow had piled up in his mind since then. He couldn't even recall if it was Peter or the angel who had informed him. All he knew was that he and Peter had to locate the 'girl', follow her *blip* when she made her move, and destroy the junction while she was in it. He thought Dekker had been sent to help her take the power, but he didn't know who had sent him or why they had arrived here separately. The important thing was that the monster masquerading as the girl was destroyed and that had been accomplished.

Dekker gasped in another shuddering breath and his psychic colour darkened.

'It's okay, boy,' Peter assured him, positioning the point of the knife on Dekker's hairline, 'it won't hurt.'

Peter might have had the Spotter talent of being able to hear the *blip* of a monster and to distinguish it from that of an ordinary human, but Dick knew he didn't see the colours. 'Watch it, Peter, he's darkening!' he shouted, and the moment his mouth snapped shut, Dekker's colour reached black, rippled and flashed like a fluorescent lamp being turned on and suddenly clicked to a brilliant white.

Dick's bag was over on the edge of the clearing where he had left it. Inside was a coiled nylon rope, crampons, cleats, hooks, pitons and the ice-axe with which he'd carried out his first – abortive – monster killing. He'd brought all the other stuff to cover the ice-axe and prove that he was a serious climber – and even though there were no mountains on Skiathos, no one in authority had questioned it. This was just as well, because the bag also contained the face and right-hand fingers of the girl he'd killed. They might have been wrapped in clingfilm and covered in tinfoil, but that hadn't stopped them working their own particular brand of magic. They might not have made you physically invisible, but this didn't matter. Being able to come and go without anyone noticing you were there amounted to the same thing anyway. It had worked just as Peter had assured him it would. Now, he was glad he had gone to the trouble of bringing the ice-axe with him. He was certainly going to need it.

Because now that Dekker's psychic colour had lit up white, the monster in him was coming to the fore and although Dekker might have been beaten, the monster wasn't dazed or groggy at all. Judging from the growling sound it was making, it was wide awake and very angry.

In the moment it took for Dick to turn away from Peter and Dekker, he saw Dekker's left arm flash out at a tremendous speed. It was an open-palmed push, rather than a punch and the cup of Dekker's hand caught the point of Peter's chin and snapped his head back so hard that it surely must have broken his neck.

Dick sprinted over to his bag, snatched the ice-axe from it, and ran back towards Dekker, surprised to see that Peter was not only still alive, but scrambling across the scree on all fours and trying to get to his feet while Dekker chased him and tore at his shirt.

'Get him, Dick!' Peter shouted. 'Quick!'

Dekker leapt nimbly forward, rabbit-punched Peter who fell limply to the ground, then froze, standing over him as though not knowing what to do next.

Dick charged up to the inert monster, swung out with the axe and killed Dekker with a single blow. The ice-axe hit him in the side, between his ribs and his pelvis, swept through muscle and intestines and exited somewhere near his navel. There was a satisfying moment of jarring resistance as Dekker's flesh was parted.

When he started his swing, Dick was so certain that this was going to happen, that he believed it *had* happened. What he did *not* believe was the evidence of his eyes which told him that Dekker was not in the act of falling down dead at all and hadn't even taken a hit. Dekker was, in fact, getting up off the ground after diving away from the axe's sweeping arc at the last moment.

'We don't have to do this,' Dekker said in an icy voice as he walked slowly towards Dick. 'We really don't.'

Dick nodded. 'We do,' he replied, and when Dekker was close enough, swept the axe down towards where his shoulder joined his neck.

And was surprised to find that not only did Dekker have hold of his right wrist in a grip that was so powerful it had stopped the axe about three inches away from its target, but that he hadn't even seen Dekker's arm move.

Dick was not a muscular man but he was extremely strong. He had spent a great deal of his life hauling himself up mountains, and since his retirement had kept himself fit. And yet his arm was locked as solidly in position as it would have been if concrete had set around it. In the heart of the blizzard in his mind a tiny part of him complained that Dekker could not possibly be so quick *and* so strong. Dick recognised this part of his mind well; it was the part of him that had kept him going up impossible climbs when any sensible person would have retreated. It was the part of him that insisted it would not be beaten, no matter what the odds. And because of this, Dick kept hold of the ice-axe in spite of the crushing pain which wanted him to drop it; in spite of the knowledge that Dekker's grip was somehow more powerful than the bone and muscle of the wrist that had dragged him to the top of most of the world's highest mountains.

He concentrated all his strength into his wrist and fingers and pushed down against Dekker's grip. Dekker's elbow bent a little and the axe moved half an inch closer to his neck. When Dekker finally tired and his muscles quit on him, the force with which the axe would hit him would surely take it right down into his chest. And in spite of the fact that Dekker's face showed no expression at all, while his own lips were curled, his teeth were gritted and his brow furrowed, Dekker's muscles would be the ones to give first because Dick wouldn't allow it to happen any other way. Now the bastard had begun to speak. But what was more demoralising was that his voice didn't bear the first signs of strain.

'I want you to leave me alone,' Dekker said quietly. 'I don't ever want to have to look into your face again. I don't want to hurt you and if you don't want to *get* hurt, you'll do as I say. If you choose not to leave me alone, you'll regret it. Believe me.'

'I-uh-don't-uh-think . . . *so!*' Dick grunted and bent Dekker's elbow another half an inch. His own muscles were screaming now, but Dick was used to that. He estimated that he could hold on for another three minutes before the strain began to turn the chemicals into crystalline waste products which would quickly weaken his arm. But that had to be happening inside Dekker's body too, whether he was possessed by a monster or not.

But in a few seconds it wouldn't matter because behind Dekker, Peter was picking himself up. Dick balled the fist of his free arm and let Dekker have it. And found his left wrist snatched from the air. He moved closer to Dekker and brought his knee up, but Dekker was already turning away and the blow caught his thigh.

'I warned you,' Dekker said, and releasing his grip, pushed Dick away. Dick brought the ice-axe down at him in a short, chopping movement, and Dekker parried it away, stepped in through his open defence and jabbed at his face with his left hand, three times in quick succession.

Dick's head snapped back a little further each time he was hit. His vision blurred at the first blow, his nose exploded at the second and the third took out at least two of his front teeth and perhaps more – the gap of soft and bleeding gums felt as though it was a mile wide. Dick staggered backwards, spitting blood and teeth and hacking out again with the ice-axe, and missing, and slashing back the other way, and each time Dekker was out of range, and each time he came back in and let loose another flurry of blinding blows.

But Dick would not be beaten. He dropped the axe, turned like a boxer so he would be leading with his left hand and began to box the way they had taught him at Eton all those years ago. It didn't save him from the astonishing amount of punishment he was taking, but he did get a few good hard jabs of his own in and it was keeping Dekker occupied while Peter recovered.

It seemed to go on for a long time, Dekker landing shattering blow after shattering blow. It was like fighting a machine. The monster in Dekker apparently didn't feel pain. You may just as well have punched brickwork. And just as Dick's internal blizzard grew to the point of enveloping him completely and he teetered on the edge of unconsciousness, there was Peter, coming quickly towards them from behind Dekker.

And although Dekker couldn't have heard him approach – and even if he *had* heard him approach, couldn't have known his exact position – Dekker turned gracefully, caught Peter's outstretched hand, yanked him towards Dick, then, moving just as smoothly, kicked his legs out from beneath him and whipped his arm back, spinning him head over heels. Dick's last conscious thought was that Peter's feet were scything down towards his already badly damaged face.

6

Paul clicked back in, experiencing the usual panic and dread at having to face what he might have done. It took several seconds for his reeling sense of balance and his spinning vision to settle, during which time his heart had jacked up to a speed at which he didn't want to take a guess and he had registered pain, the smell of sweat, ash and blood and a horrible silence.

You've done it this time, old poke, he thought as his vision cleared.

He was squatting beside the Yamaha on the edge of the plateau – which was no longer composed of grey rock and shale, but of black ash. There were three motionless bodies sprawled there – the girl in the centre of what had been the hexagon, and the two men off to the side, one lying on top of the other. He was certain that they were all dead.

Paul stayed where he was, breathing deeply and trying to piece together what had happened. The best explanation he could manage wasn't very good at all. He seemed to have been drawn here in order to help the girl – which presumably had meant stopping the two men from killing her by doing what they had done (and this matter would have to be thought about later – if he tried to address it now, someone would find him still here much later, probably babbling crazily). And if this was the case, if this was what someone had murdered his mother and her dog to warn him off doing, it hardly seemed necessary. He had not prevented it from happening; had not understood *what* he should be doing until it was too late. Whatever it was, it was all over now and apart from his *clicking out* which had apparently saved his life and put paid to the two men, he had lost the battle spectacularly.

You should have turned round when I said, poke, his goad said. *Isn't it funny how wherever you go these days, dead people keep on turning up? What are you going to do with these three?*

Paul inspected the gash in his right forefinger where one of the men had tried to cut it off. It had bled a great deal and looked as if it would start again the moment he flexed his finger but the blood was trying to congeal there and Paul thought he might get away without having to have it stitched. He took a tissue from his jeans pocket, moistened a section and laid it over the cut and wrapped the rest of the tissue around it. Then he stood up and played back his internal register of damage. Other than the cut finger, the usual grazed and stinging knuckles and the deep ache in his stomach where he had been kicked, there was surprisingly little. He'd come round in a worse condition many times after *clicking out* and . . .

. . . you hadn't even killed anyone, isn't that what you were going to think? You're not just a car-thief any more cowboy, you're a murderer too. Tot them up, poke, why don't you? There's little Paulie, your mum, Cindy, Katie and these two guys. Not bad for a retired car-thief who's lost his bottle!

This wasn't what Paul had been going to think. He had been about to tell himself that he'd often woken up in a lot less trouble, but what his goad thought was true enough.

Fighting the urge to kick the motorcycle into life and drive away as quickly as possible, Paul went carefully over to where the men lay and became more cautious when he got close enough to realise they didn't smell right at all, not for injured and unconscious live people or for very dead ones. What they smelt like made Paul very uncomfortable indeed because it was the smell he'd detected in his nightmare just before Katie had undergone her awful metamorphosis. It was the smell of rotten orange blossom and honey.

Paul stood still for a long time, smelling the air for any hint of a change while he studied the two bodies and listened to the complete silence. When he was satisfied that nothing was suddenly going to change he squatted beside them and rolled the taller one (whom he now knew was called Peter) from his old ice-axe-wielding friend Dick and examined them. They both had a fair amount of damage to their faces and perhaps a broken arm or two but neither looked as if they had been hit over the head with anything hard and there were no gashes or puncture wounds which might have suggested that the maniac inside Paul had finished them off with the ice-axe.

Neither of the two men had any respiration at all, or even the faintest heartbeat, but they didn't have the electrical friction smell of the recently deceased or the fruity decomposition odour that Paul knew set in a very short time afterwards. Their limbs were loose and their foreheads were cool and damp. Their lips were tinged with blue – which might have suggested they'd both died of heart-attacks or suffocation but this didn't seem likely, especially in the light of the speckled substance both men had in the corners of their mouths.

This was something else Paul remembered from his nightmares and something he liked even less than the smell. He felt a sudden urge to touch the matt black shadowy substance to prove to himself that it really did exist and fought it off because his *farmer-oppozite* voice was shouting that something like that was going to be harder to wash off than crude oil and once you got it on you, you might have to watch as it spread its way across your skin, vanishing you into a black nothingness, piece by piece.

Paul did not want to think about that totally odourless substance, which couldn't have existed because *everything* that did had a distinctive smell. He tried not to remember the way that substance had flooded out of Katie's mouth in his nightmare and become some kind of a *being*. A thing that might reduce a Mack truck to a wheezing wreck in less than thirty seconds and bury it beneath the tarmac in another thirty. He did not want to think about how something like that could exist outside a nightmare, or what it might be able to do to a person, in much the same way as he did not wish to think about the glassy tube that had swept down from the sky with an eternity of emptiness inside it.

He didn't want to touch the 'dead' men again either, but it was necessary because in spite of the craziness that had happened, the men were real *(real enough to try to saw off your finger, poke, anyway)* and had to have been involved in some way with the death of his mother, even if they hadn't committed the murder, and they might be carrying documents which would provide clues which might lead him to the source of all this shit. Paul knew that there were a lot of mights involved and that he should really be doing something for Katie – who could, as much as he doubted it, still be alive – but he couldn't tear himself away yet. He lifted Dick's leg (after inspecting it for any of the shadowy substance) and studied his shoe. And knew that Dick hadn't murdered his mother because Dick's foot was so large that he would certainly have to have his shoes and boots hand-made. These weren't the feet that had left size nine toe and heel prints beside the brogues in the corner of his mother's lounge. The man called Peter was wearing size tens. Paul had to measure his own shoes against them to prove that they were the wrong size and when a part of him reminded him of Cinderella and the glass slipper, he began to feel the departure of at least one of his prized marbles. If either man had worn size nine shoes, even if they had been brown leather brogues, it would have proven nothing. Nine was the most popular shoe size on the planet.

Paul threw down Peter's leg, and began to search his cool wrong-smelling body. There was a passport in the back pocket of his jeans which gave his name as Peter Defoe from Bude, Cornwall. Its date of issue was yesterday. It was either an excellent forgery or the real thing. Paul looked for all the tiny signs which would give it away if it was moody, and couldn't see them. What finally convinced him, was the smell. This passport even smelled like the real thing. If it was a fake, then it was the only forgery he'd ever seen which didn't smell well-handled. Which meant that it had been rush-issued at Petty France in much the same way as his own passport had. Which although properly issued (like the Stephen Miles passport Paul was using), didn't necessarily guarantee that Peter Defoe was the guy's real name. It didn't matter either way, Paul would never forget the name or the face.

Peter Defoe had a wallet which contained several thousand drachma, fifty-five pounds sterling, a driving licence in the same name and a family group picture in which Peter Defoe stood in bright sunshine with his arm around the waist of a pretty women while two grinning children stood in front of them eating candyfloss. On the back of the photo, in neat handwriting were the words, *Me, Denny, Nicky and Clara, EuroDisney August 1992.*

The Peter Defoe in the photograph was slightly overweight, bearded, grinning and relaxed. He didn't look like the kind of man who would kick you unconscious and then remove your face, but then he didn't look that way any more. The picture wasn't yet a year old, but Peter Defoe had changed a great deal since it was taken. He'd lost weight, and his beard, and his friendly expression. His face was now gaunt, his body more muscular, and his hairline had receded by almost two inches.

Wondering what could change a man from a jolly parent to a pared-down psychopath inside a year, Paul put the picture back in the wallet and the wallet back into Defoe's trouser pocket. The man looked as if he had been training since that trip to

EuroDisney, perhaps training to play a part in the plot against Paul Dekker.

Paul wondered whether this thought was paranoid and decided that it wasn't. If he'd wanted proof, he would only have had to look at the list inside his head which was about forty items long and getting longer and more complex every day. At the head of this list of facts, although being jostled by up-and-coming snippets of proof, was the number one truth that read: *Helen Dekker murdered – son suspected.* Currently holding the number two position was the one that read: *Detective tries to kill chief murder suspect.* And there was more, if he'd cared to look. At the moment Paul did not have the time nor the inclination, because he had thrust his hand into one of Defoe's jacket pockets and was in the process, not of learning how a man could change from a jolly parent to a pared-down psychopath inside a year, but of the kind of results you could apparently expect when this happened.

Paul withdrew the lumpy but neatly folded plastic bag and had almost unfolded it into the twelve-inch polythene square it would eventually become before he realised what was inside, and was then unable to quit. In spite of the cold hand inside him that closed around his heart and squeezed very hard, his hands finished flattening out the bag.

Inside was what was left of the face of one of Defoe's children. Clara. Paul tried hard not to recognise the mess he was staring at, but in the photograph Clara had a birthmark over her left eyebrow and so did the misshapen piece of flattened flesh he was looking at.

He would have done this to your *face, poke,* Paul's goad calmly told him through the raging flood of confusion in his mind. Out there before him, his hands were turning the bag over and showing him that the other side showed another face and that this face had belonged to the man's other child.

Paul fought to retain his self-control as his hands folded the bag along the creases and stuffed it back into the man's pocket. He no longer wanted to know any more about Peter Defoe, but his hands wouldn't stop searching until he'd found the collection of rotting fingers which lay loose amongst the small change in the man's trouser pocket.

It was magic, cowboy, Paul's goad told him, but Paul did not want to know about magic of any variety. He'd seen enough things today to unhinge the most unimaginative of minds and he did not want to see, hear or think about any more.

But he could not stop himself searching the other man.

The other man carried fingers too, along with his passport. The old style passport that Richard Stevens carried still had eighteen months left to run and had been well used. Richard Stevens, who had been born in Manchester on the twenty ninth of September 1949, had listed his occupation as 'Climber'. And judging from the stamps in the passport he'd been to most of the great mountain ranges of the world. This passport also seemed to be the genuine article. Paul mechanically stuffed it back into the climber's pocket, not understanding how these two men had become involved in his life, or he in ending theirs. None of it made any sense at all.

Except that the girl had somehow been the link.

'You'll never know now,' he told himself, standing and turning to face the cause of all this. Paul's heart sank when he looked at her. Poor little Katie, sprawled face down in the ash, her tangle of yellow hair now blackened and her dress singed and stained. A part of him had been hoping that she would have survived the catastrophe, but that tiny flame of hope had only been able to exist for as long as he avoided looking at her. Now it guttered and was snuffed out and Paul's cold heart ached as he approached her.

He believed the voice of the lost girl he'd heard on the telephone had been this girl's voice. He had no proof and would *never* have any now – it was too late for that – but he chose to believe it anyway. The dead girl was certainly the one he'd had with him in the Alfa Romeo of his nightmares. Her dress was the same and Paul knew that when he bent down to turn her over he would smell that faint friction smell like an electrical motor that had been stopped by force. The smell that would tell him she was dead and that he had failed her and that a trip in a stolen Alfa Romeo wasn't going to be enough to bring her back to life.

Paul went towards her, aching with something that might have been pity but surely couldn't have been grief. Perhaps it was merely the emptiness of chances passed but not apprehended, or possibly for the way he had failed her. He seemed to recall something about a promise he had made to protect her with his life, but he did not recall actually *making* the promise. Either way, none of it really mattered now. It was all over.

He knelt down beside her and took her slender arm, feeling the tender muscle and fragile bone which lay just beneath the coolness of her smooth skin. Her fingers were long and thin and as he turned her wrist to search for the pulse he already knew would not be present, they reflexively formed a shape that suggested they might be pointing at the sky, perhaps in accusation.

Paul didn't want to think about what he'd seen appear in the clear blue sky a hundred feet or so above him or about what was supposed to have happened inside that red hexagon of light. Perhaps it was for the best that it hadn't worked out.

Paul glanced over at the dead assailants who had not been metamorphosing into shadow-men as his mind had been suggesting they might, but who were simply lying still, like dead men ought to, even if they were carrying magical icons.

He rolled Katie on to her back and gently brushed ash from her face. She was – *she used to be*, he corrected himself – quite pretty. He felt another surge of inner agony that he didn't allow himself to recognise and thought, *Her red shoes* . . . then caught the thought because it didn't make any sense at all. Paul Dekker did not have a car any longer, so the dead girl's red shoes could not still be in back of it.

Paul felt the girl's throat, then her heart, then wondered if he ought to try to resuscitate her. He thought about the amount of time that had passed and concluded that not only was it too long but that the girl's neurological circuits had probably been burned out when the hexagram – or whatever it was – had been shorted. The air still hung heavily around them, smelling angry and out of balance, as if it had been shredded by something massive. Paul got the feeling that another insult to reality in the immediate area – *Such as trying to bring back the girl, poke* – however tiny might cause a disproportionate reaction.

But it seemed important to do *something*.

It's about time you quit thinking about this dead girl and started thinking about yourself. Just get on the bike and get out of here and leave everything be. If you do that, you'll be out of whatever game this is. Just don't try to bring her back, because you might just manage it.

Paul looked at Katie's streaked face and again felt an overpowering – if somewhat misplaced – urge to protect her. Could she be brought back to life? His *farmer-oppozite* voice seemed to think so. He placed his hand beneath her neck and lifted. Katie's head seemed lighter than was possible. It tipped backwards as he lifted and her lips parted. They were blue-tinged with cyanosis as the two men's mouths had been, but Katie didn't have the soot-black substance at the corners of her mouth. Paul felt a terrible urge to kiss the girl. He could already taste the cool resistance of her lips, the electrical tang of her mouth's moisture.

So who are we now, cowboy? Prince Charming? I don't think so, poke! Prince Jonah the kid killer, more likely. And she doesn't look much like Snow White, either. Is she as white as snow, as red as blood and with hair like ebony? Or does she look just a little more like a ghost, old poke. Perhaps you ought to leave her alone.

The girl's eyes were closed. Paul badly needed to know what colour they were . . .

Used to be!

. . . and didn't know why. He lifted one of Katie's eyelids, half expecting to be gazing into an almost empty socket the way he had in his nightmare. But Katie – if that was her name – used to live behind eyes that were pale green.

'Sweetheart?' Paul said, still cradling her head.

She won't answer you, poke, she's very dead. Just put her down and let her be. It wouldn't do to . . .

'Do what?' Paul asked aloud, but his goad had shut up shop and – as Jake would have added – shit in the shutters, and he was in no state to order his own conscious thoughts, let alone chase around after the ones that his subconscious blasted through to him in bits and pieces. He could no longer think clearly about anything, except that it was rapidly becoming evident that the only thing staying here any longer was likely to get him was caught. Katie was dead.

He pulled her to him and her cold face nuzzled against his neck, making him ache with sorrow. He put his left arm under her legs, his right around her shoulders and scooped her off the ground, not really knowing why he was doing it except that he felt he couldn't leave her out in the sunshine and would lay her in the shade.

She was light. He stood easily and strode out of what had once been a magic circle, passed the bike – which was still ticking as it cooled, proving that he hadn't been here for ever, which was how he was beginning to feel – and walked towards the tree line.

And as he started down the hill, the girl moaned.

It's just her breath shifting, he told himself, but he paused and felt for a pulse which didn't exist and which surely wasn't going to start again after all this time. The girl was dead and had been for perhaps twenty or thirty minutes. If she suddenly came back to life now, she wouldn't be the girl she once was. Too much degeneration had already taken place inside her brain. She would probably be horribly disabled, not only physically but mentally too.

'Katie?' he said, and pictured himself standing naked in the hallway, that first time she had tried to reach him. A kind of bond had been formed between them then – perhaps even before then, somehow – and it was this that was preventing him from simply laying her down and leaving her. There had been a bargain struck, a deal made, and Paul had not yet carried out his part. He was only dimly aware that this was so, and then wasn't certain if he only felt like this because of the pointlessness of everything that had happened.

Katie's eyelids fluttered.

Paul hurriedly carried her to the shade of the nearest tree and gently laid her down, no longer knowing whether he was going crazy or had already gone, and no longer caring.

Because the girl was alive.

In spite of the impossibility of it, there was still a tiny pinprick of life left in her. A minute glimmer which might be fanned into flame if only he knew what to do.

Leave it alone! his goad warned. *You don't know what's going to be in there if she wakes up again, and worse than that, you don't know what might come creeping out. So just leave it. Remember what happened to your mother and Cindy . . .*

'Katie?' Paul whispered. His heart was hammering like a machine press and his blood pressure was through the roof. The *click-out* demon was rising, but Paul wouldn't let it queer his pitch this time. This was too important. He had sworn to help her and he would.

Why don't you just let go of it, pard? his goad complained. *Why don't you just let her be dead? Let it drop. We don't need this. You've helped her enough already. Don't help her anymore!*

The girl lay there, not bursting back into life, or even flickering. Paul tested her for a pulse and considered massaging her heart.

DON'T DO IT!

And because his internal voice was screaming at him, and also because of his promise and because he remembered the way the thing in his nightmare had warned him against it (and how that thing – or something it had sent – had subsequently murdered his mother and his dog), and because he would not be beaten, Paul did just that.

Ignoring the screaming in his mind, he hit the girl's chest, pumped her heart, then tilted her head back, opened her mouth and probed the back of her throat with an index finger that was steadily dropping blood again, then put his mouth over her cool lips. She tasted of burnt electrical insulation, his own blood and something which might have been jasmine. Paul breathed into her, watching her chest expand, then took his mouth away and watched it fall.

The girl expelled the breath in a long sigh.

Paul felt for a heartbeat, didn't find one, pumped three times, then breathed into her again.

The girl's eyelids fluttered again.

'Come on, sweetheart!' Paul urged, massaging her chest. 'Come back to me!'

And as he brought his open mouth down towards hers, she gasped in a shuddering breath of her own.

'Yes!' he said. 'Come on, do it again! Breathe for me! Come *on and breathe!*'

And now he knew what his task was. In spite of what his *farmer-oppozite* voice told him and in spite of what every other damned thing seemed to be warning him off doing, his purpose was solely to bring back the girl, to blow air into her, to give her life. This was the compulsion that had been driving him since his first dream of her. He didn't know *why* and he didn't care about that. For the moment, simply knowing his purpose was enough. For the first time since killing the kid, Paul felt a sense of shape and purpose to his life. And it felt good.

Air rattled into Katie's lungs and wheezed out.

'Good girl!' he encouraged, glancing back up hill in case those two dead men had made a similar recovery and were heading down towards them, but all there was to see up there was the dusty Yamaha, gleaming dully in the sunlight.

Her wrist was in his hand again and his index fingers were walking it, searching for the pulse point. Paul didn't even realise he was doing this until his fingers registered the cold hard fact that there was no pulse in the girl's wrist.

Paul did not think too deeply about this because Katie was

233

breathing, heaving in big irregular ragged gasps and letting them go in long sighing shudders, and people who were breathing had pulses. You might not be able to put your finger right on the spot, but they certainly did have pulses. Paul watched his right hand slide up Katie's cool skinny arm and grasp her bicep so that his thumb was placed on the Brachial artery – the one that a doctor would compress with a blood pressure cuff. He absently watched his hand squeeze gently, watched the gash in his index finger beginning to yawn and the way fresh blood oozed out and fell in blooms upon the girl's pale skin. In spite of what his thumb told him, he refused to admit that there was nothing passing down that artery and when he found his fingers applying themselves to Katie's breastbone, quickly moved them away.

Because, cowboy, the girl's heart isn't beating, right?

'She's breathing,' he answered. People whose hearts weren't beating didn't breathe and this girl was breathing.

Katie's eyelids flickered.

'Good girl! Come on, angel! Come back to me!' he urged.

Her legs began to twitch as if she were being electrocuted. The smell of burning insulation increased and Katie's hands reached up, her clawed fingers trembling and Paul's blood glistening on her wrists. Her hands found one another and clasped.

Paul felt as if the world had suddenly tilted through ninety degrees. The feeling of falling and vertigo only lasted for a moment and later, when he could think again, Paul would wonder if the feeling had been caused externally, rather than as his own reaction to the pressure. The sensation, he would think, might have been caused by something arriving, tearing its way through from outside reality.

Katie's eyes opened. They were a deeper green now than they'd been earlier. They were beautiful eyes. This was something else that Paul would think very deeply about much later. Now, there wasn't time to think at all.

'Yes!' Paul shouted as the girl's features tried on many expressions in quick succession. Her hands reached up towards him and fastened on to his biceps and Paul did not allow himself to register how cold they were because anyone with half a brain would have been able to see that the girl was alive. It would just take a little while for her circulation to attain its maximum effect.

The girl gasped as though she'd been holding her breath for a very long time and when her eyes finally met Paul's there was a confusion in them which was so huge it was painful to look at.

Sucker! he heard his goad tell him. *A girl in trouble and you're putty in her hands. Forget it! We don't need this. You don't have to be anyone's knight, you don't have to prove yourself any more. I forgive you for the kid. It wasn't your fault you killed him, it was his. You could have done nothing for him, even if you'd stopped, you know that, don't you? I forgive you for the kid, so just leave this girl here – and she can't* really *be a girl because she's just been dead and she still doesn't have a pulse – and go away as quickly as possible because like the nightmare Katie said, you're just a very small fishy in a very large pool now, Paul. You can't handle this one, it's too big!*

But Paul was looking into the pain and fear in Katie's green eyes and Katie's green eyes seemed to be talking to an even deeper part of him than the place his mental goad lived.

Somewhere deep inside him, beneath the seething *click-out* maelstrom and beneath many years' worth of firmly built protective layers, was a part of him that was as small and shy as a naked child, and which had once been as pure as newly fallen snow. This stained thing, which might have been the keeper of his heart, or perhaps his soul – and during the hours of daylight Paul believed in neither of these things – was the part of him that linked with the girl and which ached to serve her. There were no good reasons, other than redemption perhaps, and Paul didn't believe in this either. That deep part of him was simply a sucker for a girl in distress and it was the central core around which were hung all the other things that made up Paul Dekker, it could not be denied.

The girl whimpered.

'S'okay,' Paul said, 'I'm here. You're safe.'

When she spoke, her voice was distant and shocked. It was also the voice Paul had heard across the Telecom void. 'I don't know what to do,' she whispered. 'Everything has gone wrong.'

Paul touched her cool face. 'It's gonna be okay, sweetheart,' he promised.

Katie clutched at her heart. 'It *hurts*,' she moaned. 'It hurts and I can't *stop* it. I'm not supposed to be here now. The angel . . . was supposed to . . . come and . . .'

Paul glanced back up the hill. He did not want to hear anything about angels that were supposed to come. 'We ought to get you out of here,' he said. 'D'you think you can stand up?'

'It's ruined,' Katie moaned. 'It's *dead*! How can that *be*?'

Paul didn't answer the question because he assumed that she meant the angel that was supposed to come. He knew exactly how it could be dead – or whatever the angel equivalent of dead was – someone had shorted out its way into this dimension while it was coming through.

Things were beginning to slot together for him now and the more things that fitted, the less he liked it. The girl had come to this hill in order to drag an angel from wherever angels lived and the empty eternity he'd seen inside that tube was its way through. He didn't know why anyone would want to do such a thing – always assuming that it was possible – and he didn't *want* to know. It was starting to look as if his goad (and the monstrous Katie of his nightmares) had been right all along. He was out of his league.

Instead of answering, Paul bent down and scooped the girl up in his arms. Her arms linked around his neck and her cool face nestled into his sweaty chest. 'I'm dead too,' she murmured as Paul carried her back towards the Yamaha. 'I think I am. I don't think I'm attached to my body any more. It's broken. It's broken inside and I don't know what to do. The angel is dead and I don't know what to do.'

'Quiet,' Paul said gently. 'Relax. I'll look after you.'

They reached the top of the hill and Paul paused, but the two men who'd apparently killed the inbound angel between them were still there, still dead. They had become detached from *their* bodies in a more permanent way.

'Where do you live?' Paul asked.

There was a long silence after which the girl haltingly replied, 'I have to get to Fleet.'

'Here,' Paul said, trying to keep the terrible urgency he was feeling from his voice. The place looked and smelled dead and finished, but there were still alarm bells ringing inside him and the faint smell of *something on fire* still lingered in his nostrils. 'Where are you staying here?'

Katie sobbed. 'I don't remember,' she said. 'I don't remember *anything*. I live in Fleet. Except that I don't live *anywhere* any more. I don't know where I am and I can't come back and I can't *go*. I think I'm dead and it *hurts. Help me, please!*'

'I'm trying to, sweetheart,' Paul said, suddenly wondering if she would be able to travel on the Yamaha's pillion. There were no rear footrests which would be a problem. Her legs would either get burnt on the bike's exhaust or her feet would fall into the chain or the rear wheel. But it had to be the bike, because carrying her all the way down the hill and back to his apartment was going to be a bigger problem. In the back of his mind a picture was trying to form and it was related to the odour of burning wood. He was beginning to suspect that the two men he had killed had not flown in alone on that aeroplane. There might have been others, and those others, as the visual part of his mind was now picturing, might just have set fire to the wood that surrounded the hill.

'I can't hold on,' she said. 'It's too *slippery*. Oh, *Paul*.'

And her body went limp.

Like fucking magic, Paul thought.

He didn't know what to do. The part of him that strongly objected to everything that had happened to him this afternoon – which was a very large part of him – was warning him that there were only a certain amount of impossible things it was prepared to stomach in any one day and it was already feeling very full and extremely queasy. It warned him that it had hold of his marble bag and that for his own sake, it might just have to invert it and release its pull string because in spite of his claustrophobia, a few years in a rubber room would be a cake-walk in comparison to what was happening now.

Paul doggedly set the girl down on the back of the Yamaha's seat, and holding her steady, sat on the front and tried to arrange her limp arms around his waist so that she would hold on. He tried not to notice that her breathing had stopped again as he linked her fingers together around his waist. Paul started the Yamaha and the girl began to topple backwards as soon as he pulled away. Cursing, he stopped, pulled her arms away from his waist and draped them over his shoulders, yanking them downwards so that her body was levered forwards against his back. He linked her limp fingers again, checked that her feet were clear of the ground and the motorcycle, then selected first gear and pulled away, holding her wrists in position with one hand while he steered with the other.

It wasn't perfect and it wasn't quick, but it worked. Paul rode slowly into the tree line, already looking for the smoke which would confirm that the wood was on fire.

Five minutes later he bumped down the goat track and back on to the main road, vaguely surprised that the trees hadn't been set alight. He told himself that he was simply smelling a forest fire that had broken out somewhere else on the island – probably spontaneously – and wondered why he was unable to believe it.

He assured himself that he had things under control and that St Cunt was up there smiling on him as usual, and was unable to believe this either.

Five minutes after this he discovered why.

Chapter Nine
Sandra Rook

1

Being a tour operator's representative had not turned out to be quite the bundle of non-stop laughs Sandra Rook had anticipated when she flew out back in March. For starters, the weather hadn't been terribly good. One of the first things her employers had neglected to tell her (and there were many of these things) was that there was a good reason why Skiathos was renowned as one of the greenest islands in Greece, and that it had nothing to do with where they dumped their waste. What it did have to do with was the amount of rain that fell between November and May. Sandra, who had flown out without even bringing a sweater, let alone a raincoat, had learned the hard way that lush vegetation and pine forests meant lots of the wet stuff falling from the sky.

They had also neglected to tell her that her 'office' would consist of a single rickety desk and a cranky telephone in a minute office which she would have to share with three representatives from other companies. That would have been bad enough on its own, but the office had a roof which leaked when it was raining, a supply of water that tasted like shit and which you would only consider drinking if you wanted to fly home on a Medicare stretcher, a toilet that was permanently blocked (and Sandra would have dearly liked to have known which of the others was able to produce turds of such gigantic proportions that they regularly had to be poked away with sticks by the unfortunate caretaker, Nikos), a photocopier that might have worked back in 1970 but had long since become a home for the local insect life, and a fax which only ever seemed to send messages to a sweet factory in Turkey, no matter what number you dialled.

To make matters worse, there were the other reps. Matt, the other English rep, had a body that women (and certainly this woman) would have killed for – only to find they'd wasted their time. Matt, who had also recently begun to display a capacity for whining that would surely have brought Job to the point of violent retribution, was homosexual. Like almost all the people who signed on the dotted line as tour reps, Matt had come to Greece in search of a killer tan, a very busy sex life and a lot of *falling-down water*. He was rightfully disappointed, Sandra (who had also come for those things) supposed, because he had been employed to go to Mykonos which he said was *very camp indeed* and had ended up here when his firm had suddenly pulled out of that island. Unfortunately for Matt, almost every other gay man in Europe also knew about Mykonos, and booked holidays there rather than coming here. Which, Sandra thought, was the reason he was getting a little more tetchy with each passing day.

The others who shared the office were a German girl called Monique who had awful breath, a moustache and a morose temperament and, worst of all, Riley, a statuesque Norwegian girl who, to Sandra's chagrin, was like a magnet for any passing unattached male – and some who *were* attached.

Riley's easy success with the best-looking of the men irked Sandra and she spread the word that those huge turds that mysteriously appeared in the toilet, often appeared mysteriously after Riley had been in there. This wasn't true (they seemed to appear of their own volition) but it was the only retaliation Sandra had and it made her feel a great deal better about her predicament.

And her predicament was detailed in a long list of complaints that was currently sitting on her rickety desk awaiting the height of the season before she fought to make the fax machine send them back to head office. The document complained of the many administrative faults Sandra had discovered since her arrival, it complained about the poor quality of the accommodation that many clients were having forced upon them, and it listed the amount of backhanders she'd had to hand out and deals she'd had to make in order for things to run properly. Sandra had constructed a card-house out of the company's inadequacies, and she intended to make them pay for it and pay handsomely. She had discovered that not only was she the lowest paid representative in her office, she was the lowest paid amongst any of the others she met. It wouldn't last for long though. Because when the height of the season arrived next month she was going to threaten to pull the base out of the card-house unless the company agreed to a sizeable hike in her pay cheque.

But it hadn't all been an uphill slog. Over the months since she'd arrived, Sandra had got her fair share of the things she had come for: sun, booze and the men with rattlesnake hips, but so far she'd never had one who made her go weak at the knees in the same way Stephen Miles had done. And he had generated this effect in her just by being close to her.

Which was one of the reasons she found herself puttering up the main road towards Vromolimnos on the ancient, rusty and barely roadworthy Honda PC50 moped the company had so generously supplied as her transport. There were other calls she could make on the way, but it was Stephen Miles she wanted to see. On the day of his arrival he had *almost* promised to take her out for a drink. Sandra would have been the first to admit that it had been under duress, but sometimes a girl had to revert to using her feminine wiles – especially with the strong, silent types. *Still waters run deep*, she told herself as she approached the apartment where the aged Gallagher couple were staying, and grinned. It was true what they said about the quiet ones – they really were always the worst. And Sandra thought she could bring out the worst in Mr Stephen Miles.

She had grown moist for him that evening in the mini-bus and if she'd had her way, would have fucked him into oblivion that same evening. And when she'd seen him roar past her office on Yiannis' big trials bike about ten minutes ago, her libido had woken up again and wanted to come out to play. So she thought she would pay him a call. She went to see Yiannis who confirmed that he had rented out his own bike to Meester Miles less than twenty minutes ago, and who said he thought Meester Miles knew motorcycles, but who didn't have the faintest idea where Meester Miles might have gone on it, and she decided that he had gone back to his apartment, which was the first thing people *always* did after hiring a bike. Most of the motorbike accidents she'd dealt with since May when the tourists had started trickling in happened in the minutes after the act of hiring the bikes. Almost without exception the hirers were on their way back to their hotel or apartment when the accident happened. There seemed to be some kind of a law that governed this. People always went home to get beach gear or cold drinks to take with them on their travels.

But first she would have to visit the Gallagher couple who were both in their eighties and not so much infirm as falling apart. The old boy had arthritis in both his knees, an unspecified heart condition for which he daily took countless pills and a huge appetite for alcohol which, according to his wife, he wasn't allowed to mix with the pills. Mrs Gallagher was called Glenda. She was one of the heaviest people Sandra had ever seen and when she sat, which was most of the time (and Sandra wasn't a bit surprised about this), she formed a large, lumpy triangle which hid whatever unfortunate piece of furniture she chose to rest herself on. Sandra, who wondered how the woman had fitted into the aircraft seat on the way here, had mentally christened her Jabba, after Jabba the Hut in the Star Wars film, and on more than one occasion had found herself on the brink of addressing her as such.

Things wouldn't have been so bad if the couple had been booked into one of the large hotels where every facility they might have needed was less than a hundred yards away, but for some unknown reason they'd booked a self-catering apartment which was two miles away from the town and a steep climb up a track away from the main road. The company brochure had noted that the situation would have suited those 'fond of walking' and had warned that a torch would be needed if you envisaged finding yourself outside at night, so it was the Gallaghers' own fault they had found themselves there. Neither of them had complained and both seemed to be very happy with the accommodation, but Sandra was certain that at least one of them would be returning home *inside* a case, rather than carrying one. Sandra did not relish the prospect of her first death. Matt had had one last month – a drowning – and had been badly shaken.

Sandra turned off the main road, got as far up the track towards where the Gallaghers were staying as the moped would take her before its engine was overcome by the strain and gave up (Sandra never pedalled because it was inelegant), swung the machine round – because the first time she'd visited this place she'd suddenly found herself out of control and going backwards down the hill again – and parked it neatly on its side stand.

She walked the rest of the way, wondering, as always, what Matt's problem was. The block contained seven apartments and the owner, Mr Papodoupolis, had named it The Seven Muses. Matt had complained vehemently that two apartments and two muses were missing, but Sandra couldn't see it. Matt had groaned with exasperation, rolled his eyes and told her to 'look it up', but she had never found it necessary. Seven apartments, seven muses. It was all quite logical.

She was hammering on the front door of the Gallaghers' apartment when Marie the maid came bustling by, her arms bundled full of sheets and pillow cases. 'Yassou, Marie,' Sandra said.

'They've gone out,' Marie said in Greek.

Sandra paused in mid-knock, her fist clenched in the air like a Black Panther salute. 'Out?' she said, and a mental image of her own sweating body riding the lean, mean Stephen Miles machine broke into fragments. It simply wasn't possible that the Gallaghers had gone out. The sun was shining full-blast midday-heat out here and it wasn't for the faint-hearted, let alone the *weak*-hearted. Even the Greeks, who didn't take off their top-coats until half past May, stayed indoors when it was this hot.

'Out?' Sandra repeated.

Marie smiled. 'Yes,' she nodded, dumping the sheets in her linen truck, 'they said they were going to walk to the beach.'

'You saw them leave?' The nearest beach was Vromolimnos and the walk would surely kill them.

'Of course,' Marie said.

'How long ago?' *They'll both be dead by now*, she thought.

Marie shrugged. 'Twenty minutes. Half an hour.'

'Thanks, Marie, I'd better go and look for them,' Sandra said, hurrying back towards the moped. 'They'll kill themselves in this heat,' she called over her shoulder.

2

Mr Jim Gallagher and his lady wife Jabba were not on the road on the way to Vromolimnos beach, they were not *on* Vromolimnos beach, and they were not present on the main road for half a mile or so in either direction.

Sandra spent the better part of half an hour searching for them, concluded that they'd made it down the track to the main road and had jumped into a passing taxi (if jumped was the correct word in their context) and gone to town. She wondered about going into town and looking for a taxi with badly damaged suspension on one side and then asked herself what she was worrying about. It was their holiday, their lives and health, and she was not responsible for them. She wasn't their nurse and if they decided to walk about in the midday heat – or even fling themselves off cliffs – it wasn't *this* rep's lookout. Let them kill themselves if they wanted. Sandra Rook was not employed to stop them.

Reaching this conclusion, she realised, as she headed back towards Stephen Miles' apartment, did not remove the worry about her clients from her mind, nor ease the daunting idea that she might have two dead bodies to deal with before the end of the day.

By the time she turned off the main road and on to the track which led to the apartment block in which Stephen Miles was staying, she was a good deal more sweaty than she had anticipated, she had surely left it too late to catch him before he went out and her sexual fantasy was in ruins.

The only thing that drove her onwards was her libido, that low-down genetic message which shot fire into her loins on at least fifteen days of every month and made her want to fuck like a bunny-rabbit. It was now patently obvious that she wasn't going to spend the rest of the afternoon locked into a sweaty scene with Stephen Miles, but she would do the next best thing and leave a message on his door. Perhaps he would meet her tonight when she'd had time to freshen up and forget about the Gallaghers. Stephen Miles was one fish she did not intend to let get away.

Sandra drove carefully up the rutted track, trying to put the Gallagher couple out of her mind. The closer she got to the Xinaris apartments where there was a very slim chance that Mr Miles might still be, the easier it became. As she rounded the last twist in the track, her heart suddenly thumping and butterflies taking flight in her stomach, she managed to forget all about them.

This lasted for the fifteen seconds it took her to enter the drive of the Xinaris apartments, pass the overgrown front garden and turn into the forecourt immediately in front of the building.

There was a great deal going on in the forecourt and none of it had anything at all to do with her fantasy about Stephen Miles. Sandra's brain refused to take in what was happening there, or verify what her eyes were seeing and simply repeated, *Oh, there they are!* over and over because the mystery about

245

what had become of the Gallagher couple had been solved. The Gallaghers were there in the forecourt of the Xinaris. Impossible as it seemed, they had found their way from their own apartment to another rented by the same company and almost three miles away. And they had walked it in the midday heat.

Sandra's limbs then emptied themselves of strength and turned to rubber. She fell off the little Honda and sprawled in the gravel on her face, tasting it and feeling it scrape flesh away from her cheek.

Sandra experienced the sharp shock of disbelief all adults feel at unexpectedly finding themselves flat on the ground and her brain started to work again. In the following moments as she spat gravel and tried to get her arms to push her up off the ground, she realised that she'd made several bad mistakes which she could have avoided and a part of her complained bitterly that, *No one on earth could have been prepared for this and avoided it.*

What she *should* have done was to have turned the PC50 round in as tight a circle as possible and wound the throttle open, left the scene and gone for help.

Because the Gallaghers weren't alone in the forecourt. Mrs Manessis was there and so were two tall blond men. And the two tall blond men were in the act of killing Mrs Manessis while the Gallaghers clung to one another, apparently frozen in place by what was happening before them.

Sandra tried to gather her strength, but the sound of the two men killing Mrs Manessis steadily sapped it. Sandra hadn't thought a great deal about crimes of violence or murder, but those she'd seen played out on the television or the movies were always noisy. There should have been screaming and raised voices accompanying the scene, but none of this was present. Which made what could be heard far worse.

The men – who, Sandra realised, must either be brothers or twins – were beating Mrs Manessis with sticks, one of which might have been a rake handle and the other of which surely belonged to a pick-axe. They were conversing quietly in German as they worked on the woman in a considered, almost thought-ful, way. It wasn't a frenzied or hurried attack at all.

Sandra pushed her hands under her, realising she could hear birdsong and the distant roar of powerboats towing skiers down in Vromolimnos Bay. Crickets chirruped in the under-growth and there was a large green lizard skittering across the flagstones in front of the building. She could hear all this plainly and it was punctuated with steady thuds which, if she had closed her eyes, might have sounded like Mrs Manessis beating a carpet.

The two Germans had paused for a moment when Sandra turned into the forecourt and fell off the moped, then calmly exchanged a few words and gone back to work. Her presence – and the presence of the Gallaghers – had obviously not thrown them which meant that they intended to kill her and the elderly couple too.

Sandra got to her haunches, and against her better judge-ment glanced over at Mrs Manessis who should have been screaming or unconscious. What she was doing was kneeling before the men trying to defend herself. She had not curled herself up in a small ball, but was trying to take hold of either of the weapons as they crashed down on her with clockwork monotony. Each time she managed to grab one of the sticks, the other would crash down on her fingers or swing into her face. There was blood running from the woman's nose, her lips and cheeks were split and two of the fingers on her right hand were frozen at impossible backward angles, but still she fought on.

Get out of here, Sandra! she told herself.

One of the Germans – the one with the pick-axe handle – took a pace away from the woman, spoke in a calm voice, then nodded in her direction. The other German glanced over and smiled.

'Do something!' Mrs Gallagher finally wailed. 'For God's sake, someone, *do something!*'

Someone did do something. Her husband slid to the ground like a deflating balloon. Sandra doubted very much that this was the kind of thing Jabba had had in mind. The old boy's heart had evidently had enough and pulled the plug. There was someone else going to do something the moment those Germans turned away from her. Sandra Rook was going to attempt to break the fifteen hundred metres world record.

The German with the pick handle raised it over his shoulder like a man about to take a swipe at a large tree with a very sharp axe and brought it down on to Mrs Manessis's upturned face.

Sandra didn't want to see the result, but didn't turn away quickly enough. She had once watched a butcher at work on a side of beef with a meat cleaver and the sound of the pick handle hitting the woman was almost identical. Mrs Manessis ceased to have a face. Sandra saw it fold into itself. Before she looked away the image of the woman's forehead wrapped snugly around the hickory shaft burned itself into her mind.

Sandra was on her feet by the time Mrs Manessis hit the ground and her legs were sprung to sprint her away. It seemed to take a very long time to make that first push forwards, and she glanced over at the two men as her muscles bunched with incredible force. They were walking unhurriedly towards her now, even as Mrs Manessis settled into the grass. They were smiling, looking not a bit like two men who had just beaten a woman to death but as if they had just watched a good film with a happy ending.

But they weren't going to get her.

Sandra shot forwards, her feet biting the gravel and propelling her towards the entrance.

And as her head turned back from the Germans she realised that Mrs Jabba-the-Hut Gallagher was going to ruin it all for her. Mrs Jabba wanted to be taken along too, and was coming straight for her, her massive flabby arms outstretched and sweat sheening her horrified face.

'DO SOMETHING!' she bellowed.

Sandra did something. She turned to her right as sharply as possible. It wasn't sharp enough. One of Mrs Gallagher's meaty hands slapped into her arm and clung on like a limpet.

It was like being suddenly manacled to a brick building. The resistance was total. Sandra skidded round in a circle, already trying hard to shake herself free, while her feet fought to propel herself away. The woman's grip hurt.

'Let go!' Sandra screamed.

'Do something!' Mrs Gallagher screamed back. 'My husband has collapsed and they've killed that lady *and now they're going to kill me! Do something, for God's sake!*'

Sandra glanced over her shoulder. The smiling Germans were less than twenty feet away now and still coming. 'LET GO OF ME!' she shouted into Jabba's face, and to her surprise the woman released her.

I'm going to get away, Sandra thought, starting to run and glancing back. *She let me go and they aren't running after me. I've done it, I'm free! I've got away!*

And could not believe it when she found Mr Gallagher's body in her path. Sandra was certain, even as she sprawled to the ground again, that she had been running to the right of the dead man to the tune of ten feet, but here he was right in her way.

I don't think you're going to be getting laid tonight, my girl, a calm part of her observed. *Not unless you disentangle yourself from this dead man and are up on your feet again within the next two seconds or so.*

Close behind her there was a noise like a baseball being struck, a small sigh, and the sound of something large and soft collapsing. Fluid spattered down on her. Sandra did not know if it was blood or sweat or something worse and didn't want to know because she was up and if she didn't hesitate for even a moment, if she didn't turn around, she was going to make it.

One of the men said something in German, but Sandra didn't care because she was away. The entrance to the drive loomed in her vision and once she was through it there was going to be no stopping at all.

Sandra pushed off her right leg, dug her left in and was very surprised when her right didn't power forward but moved just six inches then hit something very hard. She was spitting out gravel again before she realised that one of the men had inserted his piece of wood between her legs and tripped her up.

She scrambled onward on all fours, screaming so loud that her ears popped. *That'll stop them!* a part of her mind crowed. *That'll bring someone running to see what all the fuss is about!*

Then her ankles were being grasped.

Sandra kicked out and shook off the hands, screaming again.

Something hard hit her in the centre of her back and her arms dropped her to the ground.

Tears stung her eyes. 'Bastards!' she hissed. She tried to scream again, but couldn't draw enough breath. Then one of the men sat down on her back, crushing her. The hands took her legs again and pulled them down flat. Sandra fought to breathe while she waited for someone to hit her head. In a second or two it would be all over.

But the blow didn't come.

Behind her, the two men held a brief, calm discussion and Sandra distantly decided they were weighing up the pros and cons of raping her before they killed her. She half hoped they would. It was going to take them a while to rape her and someone would surely come by during that time. In the back of her mind she entertained a brief fantasy of Stephen Miles turning up on his big bike. Stephen Miles was exactly the kind of man you hoped for as a rescuer. She had no doubt whatsoever that he could and would handle these two. He had that kind of look about him. She doubted there were many people who upset him and thought that those who did probably lived to regret it.

So where are you? she pleaded.

But the legendary Mr Miles wasn't going to come and save her. It didn't take a great deal of knowledge of the way things happened to work that one out. Heroes were only available to writers of film scripts and paperback books, and even if he did turn up, one of the Germans would simply draw a gun and shoot him.

The Germans didn't begin to tear off her clothes though and after several seconds of silence during which she fought for breath, Sandra allowed herself to begin to hope that she was going to live through this. She couldn't find any good reasons, but the knowledge that they hadn't killed her yet was enough to keep her going.

One of the men lifted her left leg, bending it at the knee, and the one sitting astride her (not facing her head as she had thought, but facing the other direction) shuffled down her back to her waist, allowing her to breathe in. Sandra had no idea what they were going to do to her except that apparently they didn't intend to beat her to death as they had done with the others.

Something cold touched her calf muscle and the two men traded a few laconic words. Whatever they were going to do they weren't getting excited about it. Sandra knew it didn't follow that it wouldn't hurt.

The cold thing moved and it felt as if one of the men was writing on the back of her leg with a ballpoint pen. The man who was pinning her to the ground leaned down towards her legs and Sandra gauged that if she brought up the heel of her free leg fast enough, she could break his nose. After *that*, there was no plan, no follow through. Sandra couldn't think about it. She was too terrified to act and too terrified to stay still.

But deep inside her, she was raging at the injustice of all this. She had done nothing to deserve it, and neither had Mrs Manessis or the Gallaghers. There were three people lying dead within twenty feet of her and this part of her inquired if she was going to allow herself to become the fourth. The answer, of course, was no. Putting this refusal into practice, however, was a kettle of fish of another kind.

Sandra forced aside the information that the cool thing – which was now resting at the back of her knee – had begun to sting agonisingly, and brought her free leg up as far as she could, as fast as she could.

The desired effect was attained.

Sandra didn't know where in the face she'd hit the German with a heel made solid by plenty of barefoot walking over the past months, but she knew how good it felt and heard how much it hurt the man. He yelped and fell off her.

Sandra scrambled up to her knees, sensed the other man behind her and brought her right elbow back, hitting him in the groin. Then she was on her feet and her mind was yelling in triumph about how easy it had all been. The German with the bleeding nose reached out for her and she brought back her right leg to kick at him . . .

And found herself on the shingle again, her left leg stinging and somehow totally beyond her control. She reached down to the site of the pain as both Germans got up, realising that pricking she'd felt there had probably been an injection of something to paralyse her.

'Are you okay, Erich?' one of the German asked.

'Ja, Josef. You?'

Sandra heard them speaking but paid no attention because her fingers had found the site of the injury they had inflicted on her and her mind was reeling. *Must have been sharp*, she thought dizzily. *That must have been sharp!* Because there was a deep gash at the back of her knee which ran from one side to the other and it was gaping open. And inside that gash, her fingers had found four severed stick-like things that a distant part of her mind informed her were tendons. These things should have been joined, but the upper part just slid about inside her when she tried to move her leg. Somehow, they had cut through her tendons.

Sandra felt her strength running out of her with the awful knowledge.

When they turned her over and began to work at the back of her other knee with what surely had to be a scalpel, Sandra did not resist. A few seconds later she fainted.

When her senses returned to her, Sandra could smell paraffin and the acrid stench of burning.

Her legs felt wet and ached right up into her groin. When she remembered what had happened, she almost fainted again.

But you're still alive! she told herself and forced herself up on to her elbows. When she saw what was happening, she wished she hadn't woken up at all.

Behind her, the Xinaris apartment building was ablaze, as were the bodies of the Gallaghers. Beside her, the overgrown front lawn was ablaze too and that dark shape deep within the flames, she knew, was Mrs Manessis. Sandra looked around for the two men, but they had done their work and gone.

And they didn't kill you, she reminded herself. *They've crippled you – perhaps for life and perhaps not – but you're still alive*.

Sandra knew what she had to do. The gate was about twenty feet away and if she was going to get out of here without being burned to death, she was going to have to crawl on her elbows. And it would be a close-run thing because the lawn was burning all the way down to where the entrance was and soon – very soon – the hedge that marked the boundary of the garden would catch.

Sandra tried to move her legs and failed, then dug her elbows into the gravel and began to drag herself along.

Before she had covered ten feet, the hedge ahead of her was ablaze and the flames were licking out towards her from the garden at her left. She crawled across the drive to her right, away from the flames and towards the border hedge which ran the length of the drive.

It wasn't until a channel of fire lit across the opening at the end of the gravel drive that Sandra realised the source of the paraffin smell. The Germans had left a trail across the driveway so the fire would spread to the hedge on her right. This hedge had been soaked too.

What was worse than the prospect of having to crawl on her

elbows down a ten foot wide corridor through the fire which would shortly be raging on both sides of her was the last sadistic trick the bastards had played on her.

She wasn't going to be able to get out. She knew that now. At best it would involve crawling through the slender channel of fire that crossed the driveway and although it might have been possible to do it without getting burnt to death under normal circumstances (and she didn't have a clue about what *they* might be in such a situation), she wasn't going to be able to do it.

Because the slimy wetness that clung to her wasn't just her own blood, sweat and urine, as she had first thought, it was something much worse.

Those two bastards had soaked her in paraffin too.

As she crawled towards her death, because it was the only option open to her, Sandra wondered if she ought to be praying.

She was already halfway through the Lord's Prayer when she wondered what kind of a God would do this to her and stopped.

During the rest of the crawl she simply wished for the man called Stephen Miles, except that the smoke and the hot air in her lungs was confusing her and she kept thinking he was called Paul Dekker.

Come and save me, she thought as her hands reached across the channel of fire in the gateway and dragged her body forward. *Come and save me, Paul Dekker!*

But Paul Dekker did not come.

Chapter Ten
Running Away

1

Paul knew that his patron saint had deserted him as soon as he could see the tree-covered promontory on which his apartment block stood. Now he knew where the burning smell had been coming from. There was a pall of smoke drifting slowly skyward through the greenery and he estimated that the fire that was making it was situated, not somewhere quite close to the Xinaris apartments but right on the spot.

So now what? he asked himself. Whoever it was who wanted the girl dead (and he was no longer sure that *dead* was the right word – perhaps they wanted the *whole* girl) was being very thorough. This wasn't being perpetrated by one or two crazies, this had the feel of an organised operation involving a number of people.

Paul dismissed the question that occurred to him next, which was, *Who are they?* in favour of the better one, *How many am I dealing with?* Because that was the important thing. He already knew what they wanted; at the moment there wasn't time to wonder about *why* they wanted it.

He estimated that there were probably four or six of them. He'd already despatched two, which meant *(If the two on the hilltop don't get up like Lazarus and walk, that is)* there were at least another two remaining. They weren't good odds, but Paul thought he had a chance because evidently these people were not professional killers. If they had been and they had wanted him and the girl dead, they would have concealed someone with a high-power rifle in the woods at the edge of the clearing. Paul knew he would not have spotted someone with a gun. Two shots and it would have been all over.

So why didn't they do that?

Paul didn't know for certain but thought that they might want the girl back in one piece, even if she was no longer truly alive.

So just give her to them cowboy, his goad suggested.

Paul thought it was too late for that now. He had a strong suspicion that they would kill him anyway. They'd already killed his mother and he'd already killed two of them, so it was too late. Paul thought it had become too late at the moment the girl had appeared in his nightmare. It was something to do with killing the kid. Perhaps he was still trying to atone for it, to redress the balance by doing something good for once in his life. *Or perhaps you're still trying to prove you haven't lost your bottle,* his mental voice chipped in. Paul didn't know and at the moment he didn't care. All he knew was that he didn't intend to be shoved about by anyone or anything, no matter who or what it was and that if someone or something wanted to take him on they were going to have a damned good fight on their hands.

He turned off the main road and drove slowly up the track towards the apartment, holding the girl's arms in place with one hand and steering and using the throttle with the other. He kept to the centre of the road and kept his eyes peeled because whoever had set light to the apartment building might still be around and he didn't want to be taken by surprise.

Paul wasn't remotely surprised to find that it was his apartment block on fire and that the garden, hedges and surrounding trees were also burning. He stopped the motorcycle when the heat grew fierce on his face and looked from the burning building to where its entrance had been. There were a couple of Greeks there, talking animatedly while, Paul presumed, they waited for the fire brigade, or whatever passed for it on this island. At first, he thought the thing they stood beside was a lump of smouldering tree trunk that had somehow been thrown out of the garden and on to the track, perhaps by an explosion. Then he realised what it was and looked away. That blackened thing had once been human and what he'd thought was a branch reaching out towards him was a charred arm. It was the bracelet that gave it away. Paul recognised it the moment he saw it. It was a chunky gold identity bracelet and he'd last seen it on the plump wrist of Sandra, his tour rep.

Mayhem, that's what you were promised in your dream! his goad said. *Still looking forward to putting up a good fight, cowboy? You want to take on people who do this?*

Paul glanced over at the building which had contained practically everything that Stephen Miles had owned in the way of papers and money. His cheque book had been in the building. His passport and two of his three credit cards were there. Even his wallet and all his money had been inside. All that was left of Stephen Miles was the driving licence – which the motorcycle hire guy had wanted to keep and which Paul had eventually talked him out of – and his Visa card.

Paul was beginning to feel badly stunned and dog-tired with shock, the way he had after discovering his mother's body. He couldn't afford to have that happen again. He took his hand off the bike's throttle and in the automatic checking motion of a man with something valuable to look after, reached round to pat the back pocket of his jeans where his Visa and licence were.

The first pat did not work. *Missed*, Paul thought distantly, and equally as distantly noted that this was strange. Stranger things had happened and if he'd needed proof, well, it was there in front of him to see.

After the second pat – which also missed – Paul felt terribly cold. Not only was there no comforting bulge of plastic bent to fit a buttock there, there was no bulge at all. His jeans no longer even *had* a back pocket on the right-hand side of his trousers.

And now the Greeks had noticed him and were hurrying towards him, shouting and waving.

Paul swapped hands, using the bike's clutch with his left while he held on to the girl's arm with his right, and when he was moving, swapped back and opened the throttle, swinging the Yamaha round through one hundred and eighty degrees.

What now, cowboy? his mind enquired as he rolled away from the two Greeks, and Paul didn't know.

2

There were two one-thousand drachma notes stuffed into one of his pockets, along with a wad of tissue paper and his lucky ten pfennig piece. Paul discovered them shortly after he parked the bike in Skiathos town.

Getting the girl off the bike was a problem and caused a great deal of interest among the occupants of the nearby cafés. He was certain that when people came asking, as they were certain to, there would be many witnesses to his having been here with the girl. This was something which could not have been avoided.

Katie was as limp as a rag doll and he had to hold her in place while he put the bike up on the centre stand, then drag her off the pillion backwards. He had considered lifting her leg over the seat and taking her off this way, then decided his first idea would be best. But Katie's dress had become entangled in the broken off stalk which had once been the bike's left indicator and he'd torn the material trying to extricate it.

When he finally stood her on her feet, being careful to hold her straight so that she looked a little less like someone who was dead and a little more like someone who had perhaps fainted with the heat, he glared over at the occupants of the nearest taverna, fully expecting a spontaneous round of applause. A dozen or so faces stared at him through sunglasses and he began to wonder if his pursuers were already here, waiting for him, then dismissed the thought. Even if they were here, they could do nothing in front of all these people.

Except, perhaps, release one of those shadow-men, like they did in your nightmare, or several, like they did in Margherita de Savoia!

Paul didn't think that would happen and was puzzled by his mind's reference to the place with the strange name. Paul didn't know where it was, what it was or what had happened there. The reason he'd come into town was because it was the best option on offer. Everything had gone badly wrong, he needed some thinking time and he didn't expect anyone to make a move on him with all these people about. The down-side was that for anyone looking for them, he and Katie were not only easy to see, they stuck out like the sorest of thumbs. Paul's face, hands, bare arms and clothing looked exactly as if he had been in the fight to end all fights, there was a cut along his hairline (he'd noticed in the bike's only wing-mirror) which was drying now, but which had left his face streaked with blood, and his right-hand forefinger was still steadily weeping. And if that wasn't bad enough on its own (and Paul thought it was) the girl accompanying him was wearing a filthy and torn dress, both her knees were cut and she appeared, to all intents and purposes, to be quite dead.

They were not the kind of couple, Paul realised dryly, who could pass unnoticed.

He just hoped that the police didn't turn up while they were still here. He wasn't sure if the arsonists had left evidence behind that would incriminate him, but it was a distinct possibility. Getting him arrested would probably be a good move because then, while the Stephen Miles identity was crumbling to dust under the scrutiny of the authorities, someone would turn up to collect the girl.

It wasn't good being here, but the alternative – hiding out on a deserted beach where no one would see them – was worse. Paul didn't know if the people who were out to get him and Katie were able to track them somehow, but in the light of everything that had so far happened it seemed possible and on a deserted stretch of sand they might have turned up and finished off what they had started.

Katie was still breathing. Paul resisted the urge to feel for a pulse, assuring himself, as he had done before, that people who were dead didn't breathe and people who *did* breathe had pulses. Katie was simply unconscious. There was enough heavyweight impossibility for him to wrestle mentally with at the moment without adding to it.

'Come on, sweetheart,' he said to her. 'We have to go and sit in this café. Can you walk?'

Katie did not respond. People were watching.

'Come on, darling, you're going to have to help me, I can't get you over there alone.'

Katie sighed. 'It . . . *hurts,*' she said in a small voice. Her eyes didn't open.

Paul's mind was reeling but there was a small, hard shell of practicality inside him which didn't need his imagination. 'Good girl,' he heard himself encourage. 'We'll stop it hurting. All we have to do is get you over there in the shade. You'll feel better out of the sunshine. Just help me and try to walk. I'll hold you.'

One of Katie's legs took a step forward and Paul held on to her, steadying her as she moved and the other leg followed. She walked like a baby taking its first steps and seemed to have no sense of balance at all. Paul formed the impression that whatever had happened to her up on that hill had wiped away her memories of walking.

'I'm dead, Paul,' Katie said quite distinctly, and he pretended he hadn't heard it because the better part of him believed her.

'Just over here,' he said, guiding her under the awning of the café. When he glanced up, everyone in the place was paying very close attention to them.

'We fell off the bike, *okay?*' Paul announced in a voice that made it very clear that if it wasn't okay someone else might soon be hurting just as much as he did, and probably more.

Those who weren't watching from behind the safe barrier of mirrored lenses looked away; those who were, adjusted the position of their heads and looked on from an angle. The result was better than Paul had expected.

He shuffled Katie up to an empty table, thankful that she

didn't sigh and expire again until he'd got her into a seat as far back from the road as possible.

The Greek waiter appeared beside them almost instantly. 'What can I get you?' he asked in a perfect Australian accent.

'A large shot of brandy and two Sprites,' Paul said.

The waiter turned to Katie. 'And for you?' he asked, increasing the volume, presumably for the benefit of the café's other patrons. He might just as well, Paul thought, shout that this woman had been very badly beaten and that no one who had done something like that to a pretty girl was welcome to come into his café and threaten his customers.

The waiter looked very surprised indeed when he found his wrist suddenly locked in an iron grip and even more surprised when he looked down and noticed that the index finger of the hand that was currently threatening to break his ulna, his radius or both was bleeding profusely and that the blood was running down his arm. He turned to look at Paul moving his head very slowly and carefully. His expression suggested he didn't much care for the look on the face of his most recent customer.

'You speak English, don't you?' Paul asked him icily.

The waiter nodded.

'Then listen to this very carefully and watch my lips in case of any difficulty. My wife has sunstroke. We've fallen off the motorcycle. She doesn't feel very well and she just wants to sit here quietly and sip a cool drink. Both of us want to be left alone. Neither of us wants trouble. Neither of us wants anyone else to get hurt. Get it?'

The waiter got it. He nodded.

'I've already ordered for both of us. Now bring us what we asked for and leave us alone. Understood?'

The waiter, who had been surprised at the speed with which his arm had been taken, was surprised again at how quickly it was released. If it hadn't been for the blood still running down his arm and the ache deep in his wrist bones he would have doubted it had happened at all. While he was living in Australia he'd seen all the old Bruce Lee kung-fu films and heard the stories about how Bruce had reckoned he could reach out and close someone's eyelids with his fingers before they could move to stop him, and he had classified them as bullshit of the first order. It wasn't possible for a man to move as quickly as that. Except that it *was* possible and he'd just undergone a demonstration of exactly how possible it was. He hadn't wanted the man and the weird woman in his taverna to begin with – he knew they were trouble the moment they rode up on Yiannis' bike – and now he wanted them here even less, but it looked as if they intended to stay and, glancing down at the blood on his wrist, he supposed they had every right to.

'Would you like to use the washroom, sir?' he asked politely. 'Or I could bring you a damp cloth, or perhaps a plaster for your finger.'

'Just get us the drinks and leave us alone,' Paul said.

3

During the following three hours, Paul sipped brandy which burned his stomach and didn't calm his mind, kept a close eye on Katie and the street, and wondered what he'd got himself into. The word 'supernatural' wasn't one that he cared for a great deal – was one that he'd tried to avoid since the odd events in the days that followed his killing the kid – but it was the only one that came close to describing what had been happening to him since that first weird dream of Katie. There was something fucking horrible at work here and as much as he would have liked to put it out of his mind and simply keep himself to himself, he was going to have to do the opposite thing and find out what it was and what it intended to do about it.

There were worse things in Heaven and Hell, Katie's nightmare voice had announced, but there was something else that Paul remembered as he went over the events time and again looking for a pattern. That something else was the reason he'd psychically (or subconsciously or unconsciously or whatever

262

you wanted to call it) signed up to become the guardian of a girl who – to put it mildly – was suffering from something very serious indeed. That something was a chink in the armour of the terribly burned thing that Katie had metamorphosed into. It had said, 'Made a mistake. Shan't make another.' Which meant there was at least a glimmer of hope because it wasn't the kind of thing you would normally expect a supernatural being to say. The thing behind all this, whatever it eventually turned out to be, wasn't all powerful or infallible at all. Paul remembered refusing to promise not to fuck with it, remembered its tone of desperation. *If it was that good and it didn't want you fucking around with it, it would have put paid to you in the first place. It would not have had to resort to demonstrations of its power in order to discourage you.*

The problem was, he didn't know how good it *was* or what it *could* do. Or, come to that, what its problem was. The thing evidently had an axe to grind as far as Katie was concerned, but what it all meant was anyone's guess. According to Katie, she'd come to Greece to pick up an angel. Paul wasn't even sure what an angel was supposed to be, unless it was in the biblical sense, and he didn't recall anything from his long distant Sunday School classes that said anything about angels inhabiting people's bodies. He thought they were huge things with halos and wings and that they had flitted around in ancient times bringing glad tidings and calming people who were *sore afraid*.

All he could deduce from the available evidence was that Katie believed there *were* such things as angels, she'd come to get one (and it wasn't difficult to imagine one coming down through that emptiness that had appeared in the sky) and had somehow vacated her body so that it could happen. Apparently the bad guys hadn't wanted it to happen because, like some interdimensional bounty hunter, the angel was coming to round them up. So they'd tried to shut the door on it, and they had succeeded. Why they hadn't all gone home happy afterwards was anyone's guess, as was what they intended to do next.

Paul caught the waiter's eye, snapped his fingers and found

himself with a fresh brandy in less than thirty seconds. Katie's original Sprite still stood on the table in front of her, warm and flat. She was still breathing but she had not moved since Paul had arranged her position an hour ago. At first she had sat bolt upright, her eyes closed and her hands in her lap, then her muscles had gone limp and she had fallen back in her chair, her head tipping back and showing her throat while her hair fell on to the table of the people who were sitting behind her. Paul had retrieved her quickly, muttering apologies to the Scandinavian guy who now had plenty of dusty blonde hair in his pizza, and had arranged her so that her elbow rested on her seat's armrest and her head rested in the palm of her hand. She still looked unconscious *(dead isn't a word we use around here any more, is it, poke?)*, but it was the best he could do. People were still coming and going and the pair of them were still attracting plenty of attention, but so far, it was so good. Neither the police nor the supernatural squad had turned up and wanted to do business. Paul watched the people go by and wished that Stephen Miles had lived a lot longer. Stephen Miles had been a man with no problems at all. Stephen Miles had been one of those happy holiday makers who were walking about out there, bronzed and tanned and enjoying themselves. Paul wondered what Stephen Miles would have been doing if his life hadn't been so rudely interrupted.

Paul knew exactly what *he* intended to do next and he wasn't particularly enamoured about it because a part of him (and he wasn't sure if it was the professional thief who he'd tried to pension off or the maniac Paul Dekker who took control when he *clicked out*) had known it all along and had planned for it. Paul thought back to the moment when he'd spotted the speedboats in Kolios bay and was unable to recall the transition from Stephen Miles back to the skittish Paul Dekker who had apparently been looking for an escape route even then. The change had been seamless and it raised more questions which were difficult to answer, such as, *how had he known he might want to leave the island by the back door?* There was no way he *could* have known, but he had. The more he thought about it, the more it hurt because there seemed to be a subconscious part of him which knew a lot more about all this than it was letting on and it was impossible for him to access that part.

Paul toyed with the idea that he was collecting information from his dreams and then dismissed it because it didn't matter. All that mattered was that he'd identified an escape route and now he was going to have to take it. The only way to deal with all the other shit which floated around inside his head threatening to bring him to the boil (and he had been struggling hard to keep calm and stay in control ever since picking up Katie) was to ignore it.

4

The taverna became crowded at around five and was still crowded when it began to get dark. Paul drank another three brandies which did nothing to dissipate the bowstring tension in him and merely made his stomach sour. He had forgotten what time the boat-hire man said he shut up shop but thought it was unlikely to be before eight and would probably be well after nine by the time all the boats had been secured and the guy had finished locking up. That meant another hour of inactivity while adrenaline was steadily being released into Paul's body and he slowly slid up his internal scale towards the point marked *click-out*.

By a quarter to nine Paul was very close to screaming with frustration. He had to move and move now, and if the time was wrong, it would just have to be.

He called the waiter over, paid the bill and gently shook Katie. 'Sweetheart? You awake?' he asked, aware that there was more than one person in the taverna waiting to see how the girl would leave. The words *'in a coffin would probably be appropriate'* occurred to him and Paul thrust them out of his mind because they made his senses reel and because Katie *was not dead and never had been*. The fact that he hadn't been able to find her heartbeat didn't prove a thing.

What about her smell, cowboy? Doesn't she still smell dead?

Paul sniffed and smelled brandy and Greek cigarettes and pizza. Beneath those strong odours was the smell of hot electrical insulation and a faint odour that Paul found difficult to place. He frowned, asking himself if he thought it was vanilla? It was a pleasant, *fresh* smell. But the girl still smelled as if she was dead.

Katie sighed. 'I have to get back . . .' she murmured, her head still cupped in her hand where he had placed it. Her eyelids didn't even flutter. 'You have . . . to get me back . . . they said.'

'Get you back where, and who said?' Paul hissed, teetering on the edge of panic. He had expected *(or hoped, poke)* that the girl would wake up but there was a horrible distance in her voice that chilled him. She sounded as lost and far away as she had across the Telecom void, and an image had grown in Paul's mind of the essence of the girl floating in a dimension of total darkness, able to see her body across a vast distance, but unable to get to it.

Katie suddenly straightened up, jolting erect in her seat as if she'd suddenly become attached to a live wire.

Now look what you've done, cowboy, Paul's goad complained. *You've brought her back. Or you've brought* something *back, and even if it's only her, you don't know where she's been or what's happened to her. What if her face suddenly becomes terribly burnt like in your dream? And you know that wasn't a dream, poke, don't you? That, let me tell you, was a* premonition. *What if she starts to cough up those shadow-things?*

Katie juddered and writhed in her seat as the muscles of her face spasmed her features into an ugly parody of themselves. Her right hand flew out and knocked her glass of flat Sprite clean off the table. Paul heard it smash on the ground, and was distantly aware that the waiter was hurrying towards them and that the taverna had become almost silent as its customers turned to see what the commotion was, but he was transfixed by the girl. The friction smell increased to an unbelievable level.

266

Paul's heart squeezed three times and he felt himself twist inside his body. *You're going, cowboy!* his goad warned, and he sucked in his cheeks and bit them hard. The pain stopped the *click-out* happening but he was still skewed inside himself and knew that he was only hanging on to himself by a thread.

Katie's sharp movements ceased abruptly. Her hands fell on the table and her face turned towards Paul. He drew in a deep breath and held it, willing his heartbeat and blood pressure down.

'What happened?' someone behind Paul wanted to know.

'Thrown a fit,' another voice replied. 'Epileptic probably.'

Katie's eyes opened. They were clear and green and very distant. For a moment Paul was certain she was looking at him, then was certain she was looking through him and at something he could not see. The electrical odour was fading now and Paul was thankful for that small mercy.

Katie's mouth drew up into what Paul supposed was meant to be a smile but which was actually a frightening grimace. 'I got back,' she said in a voice so slurred the words were barely distinguishable.

Paul's favourite taverna owner was knelt beside them now, sweeping the broken glass into a dustpan and muttering to himself in Greek.

'You have to get me out of here,' Katie said slowly and carefully, 'because they know what happened and they're coming for us.' She slumped forward, and Paul thought she'd gone again, but she put her forearms down on the table with a slap and caught herself. Her tangle of blonde hair fell across her face and Paul found himself reaching out to push it back for her, then stopped himself. He knew her skin would be cool and he was still only one notch away from *clicking out*.

'Is she okay now?' the voice asked from behind Paul. He wanted to turn round and tell the guy to shut the fuck up, but was unable to do it. Katie was currently conscious and he was certain that the moment he took his eyes off her she would slip back to that other state.

'What's happened to you?' Paul heard himself ask. 'Will you

be okay?' He realised he didn't want to know the answers to either of these questions and was pleased when he didn't get one.

'Get me out of here,' Katie said, grimacing, 'because I haven't got long.' She threw herself upright again and was shaken by a series of furious spasms.

'Heeeere she goes again!' the voice behind Paul announced, in a passable imitation of the guy who introduced Johnny Carson on the Tonight show – and found his next words, which would have been, 'What the fuck d'you think you're doing?' choked off as he was hauled to his feet by his throat.

'Let go of him!' a voice shouted and Paul clicked back in again, feeling dizzy and disorientated and finding himself holding a young man up by his throat with his left hand while his right was clenched into a fist and probably less than a second away from doing that regular all-American face some serious damage. The table he'd dragged the guy across was dripping spilled beer and the sound of breaking glass still resounded in his ears. Paul pushed the American back down into his seat and glanced at his three companions but none of them looked as if they wanted trouble. In fact the three pale faces had all found somewhere else to look rather than face him.

'Stay there!' Paul warned, realising that this was exactly what all four of them intended to do.

'That's enough!' the taverna owner said. 'I don't want you here any longer. Please leave!'

Paul turned in the direction of the voice and noted that the Greek with the Australian accent was being brave from a distance. He turned back to Katie who had stopped shudder-ing and was now bent over, her hands clenched and her elbows in her stomach as if she was in great pain.

'Are you okay?' Paul asked.

'I can't hold on for long,' Katie said in her slurred voice. 'I'm not fixed and I haven't found out how to do it. We have to leave. Quickly.'

'Can you walk?'

Katie looked up at him, tears streaking her face. She smiled and this time it *was* a smile. It was a smile that was so pathetic and helpless that Paul thought his heart would break.

'You'll have to help me,' she said in a tiny voice, 'I've forgotten how.'

5

Katie died again just before they turned off the main road to Kolios beach. Paul knew it was going to happen the moment the faint vanilla smell of Katie's living body vanished. The girl was clinging tightly to him, her cool arms locked around his waist and her face pressed against his back. She didn't shudder when she died or make a sound or show any sign that she might be going. It was just that her smell changed and the tension left her body. Paul slowed the bike, thinking she might well let go of him and fall off, but her arms remained tightly locked around him.

Paul passed the beach turning, not allowing himself the thought that there was a dead girl clinging to him; not allowing himself any thoughts except for the ones which were necessary to deal with the immediate problem of getting off the island. He drove on until he reached the road which had led to his apartment, turned up it, drove off the road into the trees and pulled up. He lifted Katie off the pillion, laid her on the ground and hid the bike deep in a tangle of bushes where it was unlikely to be seen from the road. Then he returned to where he'd left the girl and picked her up.

It was a good twenty minutes back to the beach and during the long walk, Paul kept his mind carefully blank. Katie was light and felt very fragile in his arms. Her breathing was shallow and she had no heartbeat. This was something else Paul did not allow himself to consider. He plodded on through the darkness, listening for noises and constantly and carefully monitoring the ambient odours for any sudden changes. But if they were being sought, they were still a while away from being found, he thought. Nothing seemed amiss.

Paul's heart sank when he reached the beach. It was dark except where the lights of the houses around its far edges shone, their reflections shimmering on the water.

And except for the blazing strip, where the two tavernas stood next to one another about two hundred yards away from the speedboat hire shed.

Paul paused for a moment, doubting the veracity of his vision. He was certain he would have noticed the two tavernas the last time he was here – if they existed – and had almost managed to convince himself his mind was playing tricks when it became evident that the two brightly lit buildings were not going to go away.

Cursing his patron saint for allowing this stroke of terrible luck, he joggled Katie up in his arms and trudged down the beach, knowing that he was going to have to go through with it. There wasn't going to be any other way to get off the island tonight and they *had* to go. The police would undoubtedly be looking for him by now and what was left of the supernatural squad had probably been trying to find them since their pals hadn't returned from the top of the magic hill. The girl had told him that 'they' knew what had happened (although he didn't want even to imagine where she might have come by this snippet of information) and he tended to agree. If they hadn't found out by supernatural means, it was certain that by now they'd found out by normal ones. He was going to have to take a boat and break into the hut for fuel, even though there were people nearby.

Paul carried Katie to the shed and laid her down on the sand beside it, quickly sitting down next to her when he realised they had been followed by a young couple – presumably on their way to one of the tavernas. He tensed as the couple drew close but there was no danger smell, only the pungency of aftershave and perfume clashing. The couple strolled past, arm in arm, and greeted him with an accented 'Good evening' as they went by. Paul nodded to them because he didn't want them to know what nationality he was if anyone asked them about the incident

270

with the speedboat later on. Not that it was going to make a great deal of difference, he supposed. He'd already left a trail a blind man could have seen. His Stephen Miles credit card and licence had been left up on the hill with two men who were almost certainly dead, at least one person (and possibly more) had burnt to death in the apartment where Stephen Miles had been staying, the guy from the bike shop would soon start complaining about his missing motorcycle which was last seen in the possession of Stephen Miles, and there were a good fifty people in town who'd had their evening upset by a man, in the company of a very strange girl, answering Mr Miles' description. Paul decided he might just as well have stood up and announced that he was going to steal a boat while he was in the taverna.

The owner of the speedboat business had evidently had his shed broken into before, Paul thought. There wasn't anything lying about nearby with which you could lever out some of the shed's wooden slats. Paul wished for his tool bag. A small nail-bar would come in handy here. He fingered the boards on the side of the shed that faced away from the tavernas, then felt all the back ones, but none of them were loose. But by the time he'd completed the task, his mind had entered thieving mode and become fertile: it had already come up with a solution and was awaiting the next problem.

He was going to have to swim out into the bay in order to bring one of the boats back, and if his memory served him correctly the boat he'd seen coming in for repair had had an anchor in the back. With one of those, levering off a few boards would be easy.

As Paul took off his shirt and jeans and espadrilles which – apart from the 'Bonking Pig' print boxer shorts he was wearing – were the only clothes he now owned, he hoped that the boats were moored with the anchors still in them. The anchors weren't needed because the boats were tied to floats, but he hoped the owner hadn't been bothered about taking them all away and storing them inside the shed. Paul wondered about it and didn't know what he would have done. It would have depended on the local crime rate – and in Greece local crime was supposed to be very low indeed. On the bus, when she was delivering the standard lecture, Sandra had said that the only people who committed crimes on Skiathos were the tourists.

Paul remembered the gold identity bracelet on that charred arm and again experienced the cold feeling of disbelief and denial that any of this was happening.

One more for your list, cowboy, his mental goad said. *How many people is that who have died around you lately? And what about Mrs Manessis and her husband and the two elderly Germans who lived in the block? I expect we can add them to the list, too, can't we?*

Paul ignored the voice and dived into the tepid water.

When he reached out and took hold of the nearest of the speedboats, he half expected floodlights to come on and hundreds of people to start shouting at him. This didn't happen, of course, but Paul considered it a good sign because he always felt that way before he stole something. That fear had kept him sharp over the years – had made him one of London's best car thieves in fact – and it would keep him sharp now.

He glanced back at the shore, then at the tavernas, then all around the bay. There was no movement. This was a good thing for more than one reason: if the supernatural squad turned up while he was out here, they could simply whisk Katie away. He was painfully aware of this, and was depending on good old St Cunt of the Car Thieves to prevent it happening. In the light of how his patron saint had been looking the other way when the kid on the bike had shot into the road, it was not a safe bet, but there was no other way. The boat had to be brought back to shore and he couldn't have dragged Katie out there with him.

There was no anchor in the back of the boat, and no engine mounted there either.

Paul ducked under it and came out between it and the one next to it. 'Just about par for the fucking course,' he muttered and went under again.

The third boat had an outboard motor fitted, but no anchor. And neither did the fourth. Paul was now in the centre of the cluster and knew that if he found one that had everything he wanted, getting it out between all the others in the dark was going to be a task that was nigh-on impossible. It would mean untying perhaps six or seven different boats, one at a time, moving his through them, then tying them back up again.

He took a deep breath, went under and swam to the far side, asking whoever it was you had to ask for a favour. And whoever it was, was listening and gave him what he wanted. The boat on the far perimeter of the cluster had an outboard and anchor and someone had carelessly left a paddle there too. Paul considered climbing aboard and paddling back, then decided not to press his luck. Whoever had granted the favour (*your guardian angel, perhaps, cowboy!*) might have also left the paddle as the bait for a trap. Paul swam to the nearest float, pulled the ring – to which four ropes were tied – out of the water and picked at the knot, realising now why it had taken the boatman so long to unfasten the one he'd brought in for repair. The knot was tight and his fingers were wet and slippery and sore. He trod water and fought with the knot, glancing back at the shoreline (where he could see the dark shape of the hut but no sign of Katie at all) then looking out to sea at the lights twinkling distantly on the horizon. According to the map that came with the motorbike, those lights were coming from Skopelos. Paul wasn't sure how far away it was, but that was the direction he intended to go. Somewhere beyond that lay a peninsula of the mainland where there was a village called Platania. It might have been five miles away or it might have been fifteen, but he was certain they would be there while it was still dark, and away across the mainland before anyone discovered the missing boat.

'Got you, you bastard!' he growled as the knot finally gave way. There was a part of him that didn't care two frozen dog turds about the trouble he might or might not be in, and the things that had happened and those that might happen, and this part was interested solely in the task in hand. This part of him was currently very happy because it was doing what it excelled at and doing it right. The feeling was good. Paul was grinning when he wrapped the boat's mooring rope around his waist and tied it.

Towing the boat was extremely difficult and to make things worse he found himself fighting a current which had aided the outward journey. Paul was a strong swimmer but it had been a long and arduous day and before he'd even covered half the distance, his muscles were pointing this fact out to him. By the time he was halfway back to the beach he was uncertain if he was going to make it and a few moments later he knew he wasn't. He swam back to the boat and wasn't particularly surprised to find that he no longer had the strength to haul himself out of the water. He hung on to the side, cursing and gasping for breath, and waited for some strength to return to his limbs while the current gently guided the boat back in the direction it had come from.

What should have been a ten-minute exercise took over half an hour to accomplish, and by the time the boat's bow crunched up on to the sandy beach Paul was exhausted.

He yanked the boat as far out of the water as he could manage, took the small anchor out of the back and went towards the shed, paying out the anchor's rope as he walked. The far end of the rope was attached to the boat and he hadn't untied it in case those gently lapping waves bore the boat back out to sea. He didn't think he was fit enough to swim out and get it back.

Katie was lying in exactly the same position but her smell had changed again. Paul noticed this while he was still twenty feet away from her and hurried over to her. The odour of hot electrical insulation had increased and the smell of orange blossom had returned.

You know what happens now, cowpoke? Her face changes. That's where the burning smell comes from. It isn't the smell of her death, it's the smell of the way she died originally. Think about that, poke.

But Katie's face didn't turn into the eyeless thing of his nightmares and the rotten orange smell didn't augur any other terrible thing. No shadow-men streamed forth from her mouth. She was simply a slender girl in her mid-twenties . . .

Who is no longer breathing.

Paul placed his hand in front of the girl's nose and mouth and felt nothing – no disturbance of the air at all. His heart sank. No heartbeat – or as he preferred to think, a heartbeat he couldn't quite find – he could live with. If you were breathing you were alive, it was as simple as that. Even if you didn't seem to be home, you were alive because breathing was a totally pointless exercise for a corpse. Dead things did not breathe.

Paul felt his blood pressure increase in direct proportion to the panic that was blooming inside him.

Got this far! he thought. *This can't happen. This isn't* supposed *to happen!*

He knew what he was going to have to do next and he didn't want to do it because his mind was screaming that he'd been wrong all along, and that the girl had been dead since he carried her out of the ashes of the magic ring, and that when he placed his mouth over hers, her lips were going to be icy cold and they were going to taste of rotten orange blossom, and even if something did come back it wasn't going to be Katie.

He turned his cheek to her mouth and still didn't feel any air coming from her. The girl was still.

'Katie!' he urged.

She's dead, poke! There's nothing you can do for her. She's gone now. Slipped away. Even if she was clinging on before, she's lost it and she's gone now. Gone away. So why don't you just leave her be, break into that shed, get some fuel and get the fuck out of here? They'll blame this one on you too, you know that, don't you? And they'll be right. All these deaths are yours, *Paul. They belong to you. See what happens when you start off by running down a kid on a bike? It escalates. You might not have been caught for it, but someone, somewhere, knows you did it and has chalked it up. And this is the result, so make the best of a bad job and just get yourself out of here.*

But Paul could not do that because it wouldn't make sense. There had to be a pattern here and Katie ceasing to be and starting to rot did not fit into it. The girl could not be dead or everything that had happened since the first nightmare had been pointless. He put his hand under the girl's neck and pulled it upwards, tilting her head back so that her airway would be open. He told himself that he'd done this before, earlier in the day, and tried to empty his mind, but his *farmer-oppozite* voice fought back.

Did you? it asked. *Are you, old cowboy, old number one car thief, one hundred percent certain that you did do this earlier? Ask yourself that. And while you are asking yourself that, think about the days after you killed the kid. You needed treatment, didn't you? But did you get any? I don't seem to recall that happening. I seem to recall you walking about in a shadow world where impossible things happened. Where you weren't sure what was real and what was not. Wasn't that when your marriage finally got put to bed? When you cracked? What if you didn't get better? What if it's still going on? What then?*

Paul thought about it and admitted that he might well have cracked back then, and argued that it hadn't been like this. Everything had been grey and dirty and badly drawn. The hallucinations had not been convincing, even to his distressed mind. What he'd seen today was very convincing indeed.

His fingers walked the girl's throat, searching for a pulse he knew he wasn't going to find, then he leaned over and enclosed her cold mouth and nostrils with his own mouth and breathed life into her because when you came down to it, there was no option. It wasn't a matter of whether it was the right or wrong thing to do, or whether it was really happening or not. For all Paul cared, he could be locked up in a rubber room in an asylum right now and dreaming all this. When you got down to it, none of it made one iota of difference.

Because he was *compelled* to bring back the girl. There were many reasons for this. But, he knew, the compulsion would have been just as great if there had been no reasons at all.

Like his mother had said, her boy was a sucker for a girl in distress.

Hasn't this got past the distress stage, poke? his mental goad asked.

But Paul wasn't listening, because he was busy breathing life into the girl and massaging her heart.

After fifteen minutes he was beginning to believe he'd left it too long this time.

After thirty he was certain that Katie was dead and not coming back again.

Ten minutes after that Paul began to realise there was no point in flogging dead horses and that as his goad had so rightly pointed out, things had gone somewhat beyond the distress stage. Irrevocably, in fact.

Ten minutes after *that* Paul began to tell himself that he was truly insane if he thought the girl was going to come back now. Her brain was surely dead from oxygen starvation even if other parts of her body had survived – and he sincerely doubted that there was any viable tissue left at all, now.

After another ten minutes Paul felt his marbles begin to roll away, one by one. His arms ached from the heart massage, from the swimming and the fighting, his stomach hurt where he had been kicked and burned where the cheap brandy lay in it, his back ached and his shoulder muscles were all locked up tight and enough was enough. He badly wanted to stop.

And could not.

Chapter Eleven
Lulu Kaminsky takes a Trip

1

It was Lulu Kaminsky's forty-second birthday and when she met Gary Richman on the escalator going up towards the entrance of Holborn tube station she was not only extremely angry, she was a woman with a mission. The mission, though only vaguely planned in her mind, included punching out the lights of a woman named Caroline McGuiness and then stuffing the six hundred and fifty sheets of paper which were currently weighing down her shoulder bag (and her shoulder) into every orifice that Ms Squeaky Fucking Clean McGuiness had.

Being this angry was not a new thing for Lulu; she had been bubbling under the danger mark since her twenty-fifth birthday when that rat who had promised to love, honour and obey her (and if that wasn't quite what he'd promised then it damn' well should have been!) had vanished off the face of the earth. And he *had* vanished. Johnny Kaminsky, ex-holder of the European middleweight title for boxing, had walked out and disappeared taking half his wife's money, and all the detectives (and all the king's horses and all the king's fucking men, come to that) she'd hired had managed to come up with exactly no trace of him at all.

During those long lonely nights when her bed was warmed only by men of less than twenty years old (poor sex technique but *extremely* fast recovery time) she had comforted herself with the thought that the small semi-circular scars on the first and second knuckles of her right hand had been caused by her knocking the sucker's two front teeth clean out of his head the day before he vanished. *Some boxer!* she would tell herself, and then she would glow, promising herself (and meaning it) that if she ever saw the motherfucker again she would tear his testes right out of his scrotum and crush them to pulp while they were still attached to his body.

What irritated her most about the bastard – and what had fuelled her anger for the past seventeen years – was the fact that she would never be free of him. Lulu Kaminsky, who had become the world's third most successful author of Shopping & Fucking novels at the tender age of twenty-two (and who had stayed in the top five ever since by sheer brute force), had become successful while she was married to the boxer and had been railroaded by a succession of publishers into keeping the surname she hated when she wanted to use her maiden name of Jones.

Lulu blamed it on the publishers, but it wasn't simply that she'd been pushed around. NO ONE (and in her mind those words were spelled out in capitals) pushed Lulu Kaminsky around – and as angry as she was at being stuck with the name, she was not stupid: there was a good reason why Ronald McDonald didn't suddenly become Ronald Fisher or Ronald anything else, and that reason was product identification. You change the name, you lose sales. And Lulu liked sales.

The anger that was marring her forty-second birthday (other than the background irritation of somehow having got that old without noticing it coming) was caused by Caroline McGuiness, her present British editor – but not present for very much longer if Lulu had her way, not as her editor and perhaps not as *anyone's* editor.

The six hundred and fifty pages in Lulu's shoulder bag was her new blockbuster novel, *Masquerades*, the third of a series of four for which she had been paid an advance of nine and a half million pounds sterling. There was two point three seven five million pounds' worth of book in that shoulder bag and Lulu had been working on it for fourteen months. The book was finished, polished, complete in every way, and a fortnight ago it had been delivered (ahead of schedule by two months) to the publisher.

Dick Francis, so they said, had a clause in his contracts which forbade any editing. Lulu wished she'd thought of this one before signing her last contract, but when you were acting as your own agent (Lulu thought agents were, to a man and woman, scum of the worst sort) there were bound to be minor things you missed and back then, when little Jane had still been her editor, it hadn't seemed necessary. A simple note enclosed with the manuscript reading, *Touch this and suffer hereafter!* had been enough to preclude anything except the most delicate of corrections (split infinitives and people's eyes changing colour were the ones that crept by her most frequently). But Jane had left the fold (and rumour, although Lulu didn't believe it, had it that she'd only signed on with Penguin on condition that they promised never to publish a Kaminsky book) and Lulu had found herself saddled with Caroline McGuiness.

The girl – who had seemed a little mousy and in awe of her – had taken over from Jane as senior editor shortly after Lulu's previous book, *The Sins of the Daughters*, had started selling in lorry-loads of paperbacks and had only spoken to her twice since. The first time was to say that Simon & Schuster, Doubleday and HarperCollins had agreed to an auction for the American rights to *The Sins* with a million-dollar floor and would she be at home on the fifteenth to take the calls? The second time was to ask for permission for a quotation – which Lulu had denied without hesitation, suggesting that the writer ought to be able to come up with a good sentence of his own if he had half a brain.

Things had remained cordial until this morning when the *Masquerades* typescript had come back looking as if it had been present at an explosion in a ballpoint factory. Caroline Squeaky Fucking Clean McGuiness had gone through the typescript, not with the customary pencil (which could be erased) but with a pen, and had struck out every occurrence (and there were many) of the words, fuck, cunt, cock and motherfucker, and where she had thought it was really necessary had inserted alternatives between the lines. Boner had been replaced with the word erection, as had hard-on. The quoted speech that had urgently pleaded, 'Fuck me, *now!*' had been replaced with the non-sexist (and infinitely crappier), 'Make love with me, *now!*'. Whole paragraphs had been struck out. Every other sentence had been re-worded.

Lulu had opened the express delivery package at midday, looked at the way her work had been ruined and told herself that she'd always wondered why she was supposed to type double line-spaced and now, after all this time, she had the answer. That was her last clear thought before her rage reached the point of Armageddon.

Three hours later she had found herself bound for London courtesy of an Intercity 125 and was only dimly aware of what had happened during the time that had passed.

The journey down from Inverness was a long one but not long enough for Lulu's anger to abate. She simmered gently throughout the journey and had vented a little of her rage on anyone who had had the misfortune to impinge on what she considered 'her space' from the moment she stepped out of the carriage.

It was getting late when Lulu went down into the tube – almost eight – and she didn't expect to find her target still in her office, but that didn't matter because Ms Squeaky Fucking Clean had been unfortunate enough to provide Lulu with her home address and phone number 'In case you need me out of hours', and it was to this address that Lulu intended to go. Whether murder would be committed or not when she arrived, was something that she was still uncertain about. What she most definitely *was not* uncertain about was that Caroline McGuiness would live to regret applying her ballpoint to the work of Lulu Kaminsky.

Over the years, many people had told Lulu Kaminsky that she wrote in a very visual style and that the movies and television adaptations of her work had never quite come up to how they'd imagined the characters and settings would look. Lulu was pleased by these comments because those moving pictures never looked as good to her as did the ones that lit up on the screen in her mind. Visualising (sex scenes mainly) was Lulu's forte and when, halfway up the escalator, Gary Richman turned and spoke to her, she didn't respond because she was engaged in a very pleasurable visualisation. It involved Ms Squeaky Clean McGuiness having a rolled up tube of manuscript pages rammed right down her stupid throat.

'I expect you'd like to meet the man who stole your Jaguar,' the voice said again.

Lulu's reverie shattered into sharp shards. She realised that the man's crotch was at the level of her waist and balled her fist to strike out at it because it was an easy and open target and the owner of that crotch (although it wasn't going to be in working order for quite some time to come, she thought) had just announced that he was the man who had stolen her green 'E' type roadster convertible three weeks before.

But Lulu didn't just let him have it because she made the mistake of looking up to experience the range of expressions that would pass across his face when she hit him.

And it was a face she recognised.

Her fist stayed clenched but her mouth dropped open.

'Gary?' she asked.

Gary Richman smiled down at her. Here was the man who had provided a great deal of the sexual source material for her first three novels. She'd had a violent and filthy three-month affair with him more years ago than she cared to remember and hadn't seen or heard from him since. The eponymous heroine of her first book *Clarissa* had been an innocent who was corrupted and turned into a masochist by a man called Gary.

And now here she was staring into the handsome face of the man who had taught her every deviation she knew; the man who had shown her the pleasure that lay behind the ugly term 'hogtied and fucked'. As soon as she laid eyes on him that phrase bounded back into her mind and hung there in a most disturbing fashion.

Lulu's fist unclenched itself.

'It's me, Lulu,' Gary said, grinning.

'What did you say about my car?' she asked. 'You didn't steal it, did you?' Things were happening deep inside her. She was five seconds away from being nineteen again. She remembered sitting on that handsome face, realised she wanted to do it again, *now, this minute* . . . and felt herself blush.

Gary shook his head. 'I didn't, but I bet you'd like to meet the man who did. I bet you have something in store for that poor chap.'

Lulu nodded. There were many things, all of them bad, but she couldn't bring any of them to mind at the moment. She was moistening rapidly and her head was starting to swim. Words, those little objects she had built a vastly successful career out of, had deserted her. Gary Richman had improved with age. He looked wealthier and more confident than she'd ever imagined he could.

'Chemistry,' Gary grinned, reading her mind. 'Still there, isn't it?'

'What a coincidence,' Lulu said breathlessly. Distantly she thought she might soon start to drool.

'You want to meet him?'

Lulu didn't know where she was. The escalator had gone. She had the distinct feeling that if she was to look around she was going to see the long white beach of a tropical island. There were fresh smells assailing her nostrils – coconut palms, the salt smell of the water, suntan oil. She could hear the water lapping at the beach, just as she would like to lap at Gary, whose eyes held her firmly in their grasp.

I am on holiday, she thought and didn't look around to

confirm it because she knew it was true and because everything she needed for that holiday in paradise was held in the dark eyes of her lover.

'I can arrange for you to meet him but you have to tell me now,' Gary said, his voice rather irritable.

Something in Lulu that hadn't been there when she was nineteen, and rapidly being turned into a masochist to Gary Richman's sadist, objected wholeheartedly to this particular tone. In fact, it *resented* this tone. Lulu Kaminsky might have once played at being a masochist and she might still like to be hogtied on the odd occasion, but *nobody* fucked her around.

'Don't push me!' Lulu warned and would have grinned to herself at stealing Sly's famous line if she hadn't suddenly realised two things.

The first was that she was almost at the top of a very tall escalator and not on a tropical beach at all, and the second was that the man who had stolen her Jaguar was most certainly dead because in spite of her choice of words a moment ago, Gary Richman clearly intended to push her backwards down the escalator so that she would be able to meet him.

Gary's hands didn't flash out like her ex-husband's had done until she'd started to hit back, but simply came slowly towards her face, palms out like a priest about to bless her.

Lulu clenched her fist, remembering that Gary's crotch was within easy striking distance, and was surprised when she felt a sharp pain in the left side of her head. Lulu's mental image of her fingers curling into a fist and that fist flashing out and hitting his crotch didn't turn into reality as she had expected. Her right arm just lay limp, her fingers flapping against her thigh.

Stroke! she thought in disbelief. *He's made me have a stroke! How did he do that?*

Gary's hands were warm when they covered her eyes and cupped her face.

'I won't hurt you,' he promised, and pushed gently.

Lulu felt her head tilt back and was unable to resist. She badly wanted to tear the bastard's arms off but wanting, as she'd so often pointed out, wasn't getting. She curved back slowly until she was staring, inverted, at the huge distance down to the bottom of the escalator.

By the time she realised Gary's hands were not pushing her and that he had not touched her at all – at least *physically* – she had passed the limit of her balance and there was only one way to go.

There were people following her up the escalator – not many, and the nearest was over twenty feet behind her – but Lulu was certain she was not going to go all the way down. Someone would stop her. She would live.

Lulu toppled over backwards and the top of her skull hit the edge of the metal stair about six steps behind her. The edge of the stair was cold and sharp and her head broke when it made contact. Lulu felt something shear off her and thought it might have been a chunk of skull.

As her legs flew over her head, flipping her into a clumsy backward somersault, Lulu realised she was soon going to come to a halt. Soon she would hit the people coming up the escalator behind her and she was going to stop. She was seething with rage now and a part of her was busily calculating how quickly she was going to be able to get up and deal with the mother-fucker who'd made her fall. She was hurt, but she couldn't be badly hurt because she was still conscious and she was feeling no pain.

Her knees – which had seemed to take five minutes to pass across her field of vision – came down on the edge of a stair too. As Lulu's body whipped her over backwards again, she tried to scream at the hot wires in her knees and found she had no breath.

And then she was upright – tilting back at an impossible angle, but upright and staring up the escalator to where Gary stood, smiling down at her as he walked on the spot and stayed where he was.

'Lady! Your *head!*'

Lulu assumed the voice belonged to the person who had

caught her and who was trying, even now, to make her stand up on her own two feet. That man sounded very shaken and seemed to want to get rid of her as soon as possible. Lulu wasn't surprised. It had been a shock for her too. She caught her balance, tested her knees – which seemed still to be usable even though they hurt badly – and grabbed hold of the hand rail. She was two steps nearer Gary and her rage was rapidly approaching critical mass when she realised that the man who had snatched her out of her death-dive and stood her back on her feet so smoothly that he must have been a gym instructor was still bleating away behind her.

What do you want? A fucking medal? Lulu wondered and swung round to face the man.

And wished she hadn't because something horrible happened at the back of her head where she'd cracked it on the stairs. Something felt as if it was coming out.

The guy three stairs down didn't look well at all, Lulu thought as her right hand came slowly up to check the damage at the back of her head. In fact, he looked positively *green*. There was a little blood on his shirt and Lulu thought he was one of those squeamish types. She would have been sorry she'd bled on him if it hadn't been for his extremely stupid expression. He had the kind of face, Lulu thought, that would only be improved if you were to hit it with a housebrick.

She quit thinking about the stupid guy when her hand reached her head. She quit thinking about Gary too, and about Ms Caroline Squeaky Fucking Clean McGuiness and all the other battles there were to be fought and wars there were to be won. There wasn't room for any of this because Lulu had a very big problem indeed and she was having trouble dealing with it.

The problem had to do with the back of her head and Lulu couldn't quite fathom it out. She had expected her fingers to report blood back there, perhaps a little torn skin and maybe a lump. At worst she'd expected a gash that might require the insertion of one or two stitches (it had felt a little hot and wet around there and she'd thought there was probably blood running down her neck).

But the messages her fingertips were sending back didn't say any of these things. What they said was unbelievable and impossible. What they said was, *Your head is okay up to* here, *then it stops being okay all the way across to* here *and it doesn't just stop being okay, it stops being present.*

When she was a child, Lulu had been very fond of Easter eggs. But they had to be filled with chocolates or some other confection or she had felt cheated. She could plainly remember receiving hollow ones. You could tell there was nothing in them because they didn't rattle and when you took the foil off, the two halves were joined along the seam. The first time she had collected one of these – from some aunt or other – she had broken a section out of its shell on the fireplace and had inserted little fingers which searched for the goodies inside and reported that nothing was there. Lulu had felt sublimely cheated.

Which was the way she felt now as her fingers probed deeper and deeper into the gaping hole in the back of her head.

My brain has all come out, Lulu thought, but this was not true. Some of it was still present. She touched something that felt like very lightly scrambled eggs and lights flashed in front of her eyes. She moved her fingers across the mangled surface of that thing and heard orchestral music and saw a dinosaur.

Lulu's fingers were inside her head up as far as the knuckles which surely wasn't possible. None of it was possible because if her brain had been *that* damaged she wouldn't be conscious and standing here on the escalator with her fingers in the hole where it had been.

Lulu's right hand came out of the hole and moved round where she could see it. Her fingers were bloody and there were quite sizeable clumps of yellowish-white tissue there.

Blew your nose and blown your brains out, Lulu thought, and wondered what this part of her brain did.

She looked down at the green man who had caught her. Her

right hand was on its way back to the hole now, pausing at her shoulder and informing her that she no longer had to worry about where the missing tissue had gone because she was wearing it.

'I don't think I'm going to get away with this one, do you?' she asked the man in a conversational tone.

The man's mouth opened and shut. When Lulu fell towards him, he didn't catch her this time, just stepped aside.

It was a very long way to the bottom of the escalator.

Every jolt and bump was agony.

Chapter Twelve
Lulu Kaminsky Fights Back

1

Paul smiled when Katie began to breathe again and quietly congratulated himself, ignoring the swooning feeling of unreality that had been stalking him since he'd rescued her.

Since the day he'd killed little Paulie Saunders he'd read a great many medical books – at first to try to assure himself that the kid had died instantly (as the newspaper reports had claimed) and had not suffered, and later in order to convince himself that he was not going insane. The books had been no comfort to him whatsoever and had merely fed his latent hypochondria. Over the months following the death of the child, Paul had learned a great deal about physiology and psychology and psychiatry. Now, kneeling over the body of a girl who was able to breathe – and somehow to survive – without the benefit of a circulation, he tried to forget everything he knew because the fact that the girl was alive didn't just insult the neat order in which his brain tried to keep all this information, it dealt it a deadly blow.

Beneath his exultation at not having lost the game after all, Paul felt the departure of a few more of his valued collection of marbles and simply let them roll, telling himself that John Lennon hadn't been too far off the mark when he'd sung, *nothing is real* in Strawberry Fields all those years ago. None of this could possibly have been real, but it could not be denied because no matter how your mind railed against it, it remained unassailed and quite firmly in place. All he could do was to accept it and keep on keeping on as if it *was* real.

He watched Katie for a few moments, then picked up the boat's anchor and got to work on the thin timber of the shed.

The boards protested terribly as he levered them away from the shed's framework and Paul stopped twice to check that no one had been alerted. There was loud Greek music drifting down the beach from one of the tavernas and the shouts and screams accompanying it suggested that everyone there was too involved in dancing and having a good time to notice the sounds he was making. He doubted they could even be heard over the music.

He removed three of the boards, bent down and peered through the gap, wishing he had a torch. The inside of the shed was in total darkness. Paul had a couple of books of matches in his trouser pocket which he'd swiped from the tables of the taverna, but there was no chance of using these for illumination. Judging by the powerful smell of oily fuel wafting out of the shed, he and Katie would find themselves fifty feet in the air in very small pieces the moment he drew a match along the strike.

He took his face out of the gap and put his arm in. And his hand fell straight on to a fuel can. A full fuel can. St Cunt was smiling again.

In another twenty seconds Paul had loaded two full cans and the anchor into the speedboat. He hooked the tube that came out of one of the cans to the easy-lock connector which led to the outboard and squeezed the little rubber bulb several times to prime the motor, while he wondered if two cans would be enough. He thought they should be. The owner of the business had told him that a full can would be enough to take him around the island one and a half times and it surely couldn't have been that far to those lights that were winking at him from Skopelos. Two cans would be ample to make it to the mainland.

He jumped out, waded into the warm sea and tugged the boat back into the water, wondering if he ought to secure it before going back to get Katie. There was no wind which meant it wasn't likely to drift out very far and as always happened when a theft took longer than he anticipated, there was an urgent ache in his guts which made him want to leave the area as quickly as possible.

Paul waded ashore and hurried up the beach, fighting off the feeling that he'd forgotten something very important and ignoring his inner voice when it calmly suggested that it might have been to do with the change of smell. It couldn't have been anything to do with the change of smell because there hadn't been one since he'd levered the first board off the hut and the powerful fuel odour had hit him.

'Katie!' he called. 'Time we got the fuck out of here!'

There was something wrong with the shadowy space where he'd left her. It took another two paces before Paul allowed himself to believe what his eyes had been trying to tell him.

Katie had gone.

2

Paul's mind did a slow roll.

There goes another one of those marbles, cowboy!

He took a deep breath because his heart was squeezing painfully and his mind was trying to fold in on itself. A large part of him was gaily informing him that none of this had happened at all, probably all the way back to before he'd taken the first phone call from the girl, and Paul badly wanted to believe it but he couldn't because . . .

It'd mean you're just about as crazy as it's possible to get, right?

. . . whatever he was, he wasn't insane and never had been. Not even in the weeks after the kid.

Okay, can you see any evidence of her?

There was an indentation in the sand where she'd lain but Paul didn't point this out because he knew his mind would argue back at him that he might just have made that hollow himself.

'Katie!' he called. 'Katie!'

She doesn't exist, so why don't we just take ourselves out of here?
Just get in the boat and go.

Paul grinned because that Jiminy Cricket voice that had popped up in his mind after the accident, and that had been trying to grind him down ever since, had made a mistake. He wasn't crazy and there was a girl and everything that had happened really had happened otherwise there would be no need to *just get in the boat and go*.

'Katie!'

She's gone. Leave it.

But Paul would not and could not leave it. Katie had forgotten how to walk properly and could not have gone far, even if she'd regained consciousness. Suddenly, he knew exactly where she had gone. He turned and ran around the corner of the shed, certain that somehow she'd found her way behind it.

'Got you, you *motherfucker!*' said a voice that wasn't Katie's.

Paul saw the board heading for his face the moment before it hit him.

3

'You'd better talk fast and you'd better make it convincing, pipsqueak,' Katie hissed into his face.

Paul was only dimly aware of what had happened. His vision was blurred and his nose, though clear, felt as if it ought to be bleeding, which meant someone had caught him a good one in the face. This was not unheard of for him, but it was an occurrence so rare it commanded respect for whoever had managed it.

The person who had managed it was sitting on his chest. It appeared to be Katie, except that it couldn't be because her olfactory signature no longer smelled of any of the delicate fragrances he'd smelt before, like jasmine or vanilla – or even the cloying rotten orange blossom she'd reeked of in his nightmares. Even her dead smell had gone. Katie now smelt of sour sweat, high-tar cigarettes and garlic. And her face seemed to have changed, the features becoming coarser in a way he couldn't quite put his finger on. There was no further time to wonder what had happened because Katie's right fist flashed out and hit him on the side of his jaw.

It was a blow she couldn't possibly have struck. Paul had been hit by some very experienced street-fighters in his time and he couldn't remember one who had a more powerful punch. For a few seconds after the blow had been struck, he couldn't remember anything at all; his mind billowed and cracked like a sheet in the wind. When his vision lit again he could taste blood in his mouth and one of his lower molars was loose. He moved his jaw and was surprised to discover that it wasn't broken.

Katie grabbed hold of his hair and hoisted his head from the sand.

'What did you fucking well do?' she demanded. 'Where am I and how did I get here? Start talking or you'll get some more.'

'Greece,' Paul said groggily. His wits were out there some-where, but until he could collect them there was nothing he could do. He felt as if all the strength he'd had left had been used up by absorbing that tremendous right hook.

'Greece? *GREECE?*' Katie screeched, yanking his head back and forth. 'How did I get here? *I'm supposed to be in London!*'

'Something happened,' Paul said. His head was clearing now and the nature of the problem had presented itself. As crazy as it sounded, and it *did* sound crazy, that wasn't Katie sitting on top of him and weighing a good two stone more than she had when he carried her here, it was someone else. Someone else was inside her body and whoever it was had arrived carry-ing everything they owned, right down to weight and strength.

'I'll say something happened, pipsqueak! I'll say!' Katie looked at the sky and bellowed, 'I don't know how you did this, Gary, but if you value your internal organs, you'll make it stop right now.'

She glared down at Paul. 'Are you him?' she demanded.

293

Paul tried to shake his head but she had too firm a grip on his hair.

'ARE YOU?'

'Who?' Paul croaked. The situation was about as out of hand as he wanted it to get but he didn't seem to have the strength to get her off him. It felt as if someone had parked a truck on top of him.

'GARY FUCKING RICHMAN!' she screamed and punched him in the side of the throat with the extended knuckles of her left hand.

The pain was terrible. Paul gasped for breath, knowing that he was likely to die here if he didn't do something quickly.

'Stop it, Katie,' he groaned.

'Katie? What's with the fucking Katie business?' the girl screeched. 'My name isn't Katie, my name is LULU. GOT THAT, GARY? NOW TAKE ME BACK!'

Paul winced and tensed for another blow which didn't come. Lulu had made a discovery.

'This isn't my body,' she said in a shocked voice. 'I'm not in my body!'

'You're in someone else's,' Paul croaked. 'Where were you before?'

'London,' Lulu said. 'I was going to see my editor. Look, this can't happen. You can't go into someone else's body. You *can't!*'

A puzzled look crossed the face of the girl who was no longer truly Katie. She raised her right hand and Paul thought she was going to swipe at him again, but her hand paused in the air, hovered there for a second, then gingerly touched the back of her head. 'Right,' she said, and nodded to herself as though she suddenly understood a great many things.

In that second Paul knew that wherever this woman had come from, she didn't intend to go back again.

She leaned close to him and breathed garlic into his face. 'If you're not Gary, then you must be the asshole who stole my Jaguar,' she said, and her tone wasn't just threatening, it was homicidal.

She sat up, placed both her hands around his throat, straightened her arms and leaned forward. Paul's air supply was instantly and efficiently closed off.

The face hovering above him was sweating and bulging with veins and it wore an expression so ugly that Paul could barely believe it could have been made out of those delicate features. 'You shouldn't have done that,' she said. 'You shouldn't have stolen my Jaguar. I loved that car, you *motherfucker!*'

She squeezed hard and her fingers dug into his neck while a pair of extremely strong thumbs pressed on his adam's apple. Paul's head felt as if it would explode at any moment. His ears sang.

He brought up his forearms, clenching his biceps against the weight of the girl. It hurt, but not as badly as what was happening to his throat did. Paul willed himself to reach the point at which *click-out* would occur, but for some reason the maniac inside him didn't seem to be present and the pressure wasn't building up in him in the usual way.

The girl's knees rose as Paul's muscles strained and he made claws of his hands and grabbed her bare thighs, digging his fingers in as hard as he could and pulling them one away from the other while he distantly registered that her flesh was warm.

The girl cursed and increased the pressure at his throat. Black spots bloomed in front of his eyes and his arm muscles were screaming but Paul kept pulling and digging in his fingers.

'You shithouse!' she hissed, and shuffled her left leg off his right arm.

Suddenly his throat was released. Paul gasped in a breath and lost it again as one of the girl's fists stove into his stomach. Paul turned himself violently to the left and the girl went over.

And Paul *clicked out*. Except that for the first time in his life he didn't lose consciousness when it happened.

It was an eerie feeling – as though a large part of him had suddenly become someone else – but he couldn't think about it, not simply because the girl was scrambling towards him, foaming and hissing like a rabid animal, but because the hyperdrive level of consciousness he'd been flung into precluded all unnecessary thought. His sense of smell had gone, his pain had vanished and his mind had miraculously cleared itself of all the heavy luggage it had been dragging around for so long.

The feeling was good.

He caught the next blow that came toward him, catching Katie's small fist in his hand. There was a terrible strength in those slender fingers but Paul was stronger. He squeezed, not hard enough to break, but hard enough to hurt.

The girl squealed and slashed out at him with her left hand. She was fast but she was furious now and it wasn't well aimed. Paul blocked the blow with his forearm and then brought it down quickly, wrenching the girl's shoulder and turning her away from him. He yanked her right arm across his body and Katie rolled on to her back, hissing and spitting like a wildcat as he rolled on top of her and pinned her down. The girl couldn't have weighed more than eight and a half stone to his twelve but she almost managed to buck him off. Paul was cold and efficient. He hit the side of her jaw, hard. The girl's head snapped to one side and the fight went out of her. When her face turned back towards him there was a thin trickle of blood running from the side of her mouth. The girl's eyelids flickered and finally opened.

Katie's eyes, which had been green, had changed colour to a brown that was so deep it was almost black. Her delicate features had coarsened somehow. When she spoke there was blood on her teeth. 'I going to kill you, you *motherfucker!*' she spat.

And Paul watched his hands go to work, knowing what they were going to do and knowing that he would be unable to stop them even if he wanted to, which he did not.

His left hand pinned Katie's head to the sand by her throat and his right pressed down hard over her mouth, its palm blocking her nostrils. Katie made mewling sounds deep in her throat and started to buck and writhe but Paul's hands had her nailed down and kept her nailed down.

Her hands found his arms and her nails tore at his flesh. It didn't hurt at all, but Paul felt the score-keeper deep inside him chalk up the damage and knew that he would be feeling the pain later.

Then he clicked back in again. The sensation felt as though someone had taken both his shoulders and given them a good, hard wrench to the left but there was none of the disorientation he usually felt. This time he knew exactly what he'd been doing.

And this time he didn't stop doing it.

He suddenly became aware that the girl's flesh was warm, that he could feel a quick, powerful pulse where he was squeezing her throat. A small voice in the back of his mind announced, *This girl is alive now. You've been trying to get her back all day and now you have, you're killing her.*

But Paul could not release his grip. Did not *want* to release his grip.

Katie suddenly twisted her head to one side, dislodged his hand and gasped in breath in a short backwards scream. Paul let her exhale then blocked her mouth again, pushing harder this time, and feeling Katie's lips part under his palm. He pushed until he could feel her teeth pressing against his hand and locked himself into position while she struggled.

A small hiss of air escaped from Katie's right nostril and a part of Paul was pleased to note that the seal was still good – when she tried to breathe in again, both her nostrils collapsed against the vacuum.

Her nails scratched away at his arms and Paul knew some of the cuts were getting deep and he also knew they weren't going to be getting much deeper because the more time that passed without Katie breathing, the less accurate and more frantic her movements were getting. The strong pulse at her throat was quickening now and the pressure had got so high that he could feel the arteries moving his fingers slightly.

Katie's knees came up and hit him in the back. Paul didn't move.

297

Her frantic movements became more powerful and Paul knew that she was making a last ditch attempt to shake him off her and that it would seen be over.

Then she went limp. Her brown eyes opened and looked up at him with an expression of total hatred.

She's going to die if you don't let go of her soon, a small part of Paul thought, and he mentally nodded to it: *Exactly.*

The girl's pulse was getting quicker and weaker. Her chest was hitching beneath him, still trying to draw in air, but Paul wasn't going to let that happen.

What if you're wrong? he asked himself, then thrust the doubt aside. He was not wrong. The girl was going to have to be killed.

After another minute the girl went limp. Her chest stopped heaving, her arms and legs stopped kicking and hitting and she stopped trying to move her head. Her eyes still stared up at him in pure, distilled hatred and Paul didn't release his grip because he thought he knew what was coming.

And it did. Her final assault wasn't just frantic, it was ferocious.

Paul rode it, counting the seconds and feeling as if someone was twisting his own life away. He had called himself a murderer before, but then there had always been ifs and buts to stave off the accusation with. This time there weren't going to be any. There was no accident here, no *click-out* to blame it on. He was fully conscious and completely aware of what he was doing and why he was doing it. If he hadn't been a murderer before he most certainly would be in a few seconds. The ex-car thief whose bottle had gone, was finally going to make the grade.

And in those final moments as he crushed the life out of the girl, it didn't feel quite so good any more.

The next time the girl stopped moving, Paul knew she wasn't going to start again. Her pulse faded, beat a couple of times arhythmically, then shut up shop and quit. He watched the light in her eyes flicker and vanish and smelt the familiar smell of a life brought violently to an end.

It wasn't her, he told himself as he let her go. As sure as he was of this fact, it didn't make him feel any better. It had been *someone* and they might have been someone awful and murderous but they'd had life. A real, warm, pulsating life, like the one little Paulie Saunders had had until he'd rolled up the bonnet of the stolen car Paul had been driving. And Paul had taken this life in favour of something cold and distant, something that was not supposed to be. Kneeling there astride the dead girl, and feeling very lonely indeed, he wondered if the thing he'd promised to serve and protect – with his own life if necessary – might have been not a girl in distress or something angelic, but a demon.

4

Katie's features changed as Paul watched, no longer certain he'd done the right thing. They didn't rearrange themselves as he'd been certain they would have to, but simply relaxed as though the distortion had been caused by something oddly shaped inside her skull, which like ice was now melting away.

Her flesh was still damp with sweat, but it was cool again now. When he had found the courage, Paul lifted one of her eyelids. Her eyes were rolled up but he could see a section of iris. It was difficult to tell the exact colour in this light, but it had certainly changed from the dark brown to a lighter shade.

There were four distinct finger marks dotting the right side of her throat and a large abrasion on its left side where his thumb had been pressing and his nail had dug into her skin. Her lips were swollen and split and there was a rime of blood around both her nostrils.

You finished off the job those two guys started up on the hill this afternoon, I'd say, poke, his goad told him and Paul thought it might be speaking the truth this time. He'd caused her a great deal of damage.

And that's only what it looks like from the outside, killer. What do you suppose her lungs and throat look like from inside?

Paul didn't want to think about it. *There was no other way,* he thought back at his doubting half. *Someone took over her body and intended to stay there. I had to get rid of her to get Katie back.*

But now he'd removed that someone – murdered that someone, if you liked, and he did not like – he was no longer sure that Katie would be able to come back.

He got off her body, tilted her head back into the position for mouth to mouth – something he seemed to be doing every five minutes just lately – and inserted his finger to check the airway was clear.

Katie's tongue was swollen to roughly twice its normal size. Paul began to feel very cold. *You fucked it up this time*, he told himself as he checked for a pulse. *You fucked it up good and proper.*

Then he filled his lungs, pressed his lips to hers which felt cold and swollen and tasted salty with her blood, and began to breathe into her.

And Katie sucked. Her arms came up and wound themselves around his head like the tentacles of an octopus, locking his mouth against hers, and Katie breathed in, long and hard and deep. Paul's lungs emptied themselves and Katie still sucked at him, drawing the air out of every last branch and byway of his chest. Paul tied to draw away long before it started to hurt and Katie's head followed him up, her mouth locked against his, her teeth meshed into his teeth, stopping him from closing his mouth.

And when Paul's lungs began to scream, she began to probe his mouth with a tongue which was hard and misshapen and which tasted and felt like melted plastic.

They were both on their knees when she finally let him go. Paul drew in air, choked it out again and gasped in some more, his ears ringing and lights bursting before his eyes as he fought to stay conscious.

When he looked up at her, Katie's face had gone.

She had become the charred nightmare thing that had haunted his dreams. Her lips were blistered and scarred, her eyes had been burned out of their sockets and her skin hung in crisp tatters on damaged flesh which wept pus.

'You didn't listen, *cowboy*,' she said in that deep, grating voice he remembered so well. 'You ignored the warnings and there's no going back now. It's too late for you, *old poke*. I know where you are now. I've found you, *little fishy*, and I won't lose you again.'

The Katie-thing licked its lips with its awful grey tongue and Paul's stomach tightened. He could still taste it, there inside his mouth.

'The girl is mine,' the thing said. 'Remember that, small boy who had to dabble. The girl is *my* angel and I *will* have her.'

Paul's head was shaking slowly from side to side in denial. 'You won't have her,' he heard himself say in a flat and dangerous voice.

The Katie-thing grinned a terrible sneering smile. 'Because you made a promise. Ask yourself when you made this *promise* and who you made it to. You have no idea, little boy. You know nothing. Understand this, *Paulie*, you are powerless to stop me. I'm on a roll now. I'm on a winning streak and you don't even know the rules. What can you do against me?'

Blackened eye-sockets studied him. Paul stared into them, his mind reeling. He felt as if he had become marbled with ice and there was a sharp pain between his eyes that was spiking deep into his brain.

'It doesn't have to be this hard,' the Katie-thing said and Paul knew it didn't. It really didn't have to be such a battle. There were easier ways to skin a cat. He felt himself relax slightly, then tensed again when the spike in his brain drove itself deeper.

'It doesn't have to be a war,' the thing said.

Something which felt like a coarse file was rasping against the inside of Paul's skull. It hurt like a bastard. The smell of jasmine and vanilla filled his nostrils. *It doesn't have to be a war*, he thought.

'The girl is dead and there's nothing anyone on the planet can do about it, you know that, don't you?'

Paul felt himself nodding. The voice didn't grate so much now; it was starting to sound velvety.

'She can't be brought back to life. You know that, don't you?'

And listening to the persuasive voice, Paul *did* know that. If only that bastard with the file would stop shaving bone from the inside of his skull he would probably be able to confirm it verbally, too.

'And what good is a dead girl to you?'

Paul thought about it and couldn't quite put his finger on what good a dead girl could do him. He was dog-tired and it would feel good to be able to throw in the towel at this point.

The spike between his eyes dug deeper and the rasping on the inside of his skull increased.

'Give her up, Paul. She's no use to you and you have nothing to prove. You already have my respect. Give her up and make it easy on yourself.'

The sensation of his skull being scraped away ceased and something happened in the spot where the pain had been. It felt – rather than sounded – like short-wave radio static and Paul found that he had a question. After he'd asked it, he wasn't sure if he had posed it, or the *farmer-oppozite* part of him that liked to disagree for the sake of disagreeing, or whether it had come from elsewhere.

'Why don't you just take her?' he asked.

'Are you offering her to me?' the Katie-thing asked.

Paul shook his head. He wasn't offering anyone anything. He was asking a very pertinent question. What he'd meant to ask was why wasn't this thing just taking her because there wasn't a damned thing he could do to stop it happening. 'She's not mine to give,' he said.

'Give her to me. Give her up!' the thing commanded.

Something was coming towards Paul very rapidly and from a very great distance and it was coming to fill the vacuum that had formed inside his head where the scraping and the burst of static had been.

'She's yours to give! NOW GIVE HER TO ME!' the Katie-thing shouted.

And the thing that had been heading towards him arrived

inside his head with great force. Paul staggered backwards and sat down hard on the sand under the onslaught. It didn't finish arriving for what seemed like a very long time. It was hot and smelled of jasmine and vanilla and it burst in his brain and showered down through his whole body in what seemed to be a rain of hot golden fragments which eased their way through nerve and tissue until they touched something deep inside him. When it had finished, Paul felt achingly lonely, but the spike had gone from between his eyes and he suddenly understood. Katie was *not* his to give away, and he was not hers. But they *were* linked. To give her away he would have to break the promise he'd made to her – or perhaps a promise they'd *both* made. And if he broke that promise he wouldn't just be giving away the body of a dead girl, he would be giving away a great deal more – he would be surrendering a war he'd sworn to fight.

'You can't have her,' he said.

'I won't let you keep her,' the Katie-thing raged. 'She's mine and I'll have her. Now that I've found you, I'll always know where you are. I'll be watching you and I'll make sure you suffer hell for this, *old poke*. And you'll know you can't win because you've lost it. I'll be watching you, and I'll thwart you at every turn and when I have you, I'll have the girl too. You'll live through a million miseries, *old poke*, I'll see to that.'

'Take her now,' Paul said, 'if you think you can.' He smiled into the Katie-thing's face, 'and I won't lose any sleep over the million miseries. My ex-wife already made me live through those.'

And Katie fell backwards into the sand.

Moving like a man who has been run down by a truck and who is surprised to have survived the experience, Paul picked himself up and checked the damage register. There was nothing new apart from the ache just beneath the lid of his skull where the essence of Katie (or whatever it was) had entered and passed through. Paul did not check the marble counter that lived next door to the damage counter. He might have gone gaga again and he might not have done but he didn't intend to lose any sleep on that score. Things had gone so far beyond rational explanation now that there wasn't any point. He would just have to make do with trusting his guts and believing what he saw and heard from now on. Any other approach would be a waste of energy and it looked as if he was going to need as much of that particular commodity as he could lay his hands on.

He dropped to his knees beside Katie and didn't take her pulse. This was something else he didn't intend to do any more either. Katie was not breathing, but she was back in the same shape as she'd been before he started to give her artificial respiration. He considered doing it again and told himself that the resistance he was feeling to putting his lips to hers was only natural under the circumstances. Instead of trying to kick-start her by breathing into her, he simply took her small hand, held on to it and spoke to her in much the same way as folk beside hospital beds spoke to their comatose relatives.

'Katie, I know you can hear me and I want you to come back,' he said gently.

Katie did not move.

'I know it's probably not going to be very comfortable inside that body now and I'm sorry, but I had to get rid of that other woman and she didn't want to leave,' he continued, being very careful not to let the full weight of his words sink into his brain. When his *farmer-oppozite* voice started to chant *rubber-room, rubber-room*, Paul squashed it instantly. There were marbles rolling and he simply let them go. If he had to go crazy to get through this, he was quite prepared for it now. He was going to come out of the other end of this in one piece and if the smile on his face when it was all over turned out to be the smile of a man who was going to spend the rest of his life weaving baskets or turning chair legs on a wood lathe, then so be it. That didn't matter.

This did.

'Katie,' he said, suddenly certain that this was going to work, 'come back to me now.'

And Katie heaved in a breath.

It rattled horribly, but it was a breath.

Another followed, then another.

When he scooped her up off the ground, her green eyes opened and she drew her bruised lips up into what he imagined was supposed to be a smile.

Paul felt a warmth in the pit of his stomach which had been absent for a very long time, and somewhere in the distance of his cluttered mind heard an alarm bell begin to ring.

Don't you go . . . his goad started, and once again Paul crushed it. He smiled back at the girl and ignored the fact that her skin was as cold as marble.

'You okay, folks?' a voice asked.

Paul wheeled round and found himself fifteen feet away from an elderly couple who were coming towards him, arm in arm. He hoped they couldn't see the state he and Katie were in.

'Fine,' he replied in a voice that sounded as ragged as sandpaper. 'We're just going for a little boat trip,' he said, already on his way down to the beach.

'Have fun!' the man called after him, and Paul heard the woman say, 'Oh, and he's *carrying* her. Isn't it *romantic!*

And there was a part of Paul that wished it was.

Chapter Thirteen
Bedtime at Freddie's

1

Freddie Simmons was fond of telling his associates that he hadn't made it to where he was today without being extremely careful, and he was right. Where he was today was a twelve-room ranch-style house (which he referred to as a mansion) with a floodlit pool and tennis courts (and an indoor pool in the basement). The mansion was set in five acres of prime Kent countryside eight miles outside Dover where he carried on a legitimate car dealership and also ran an artfully concealed trade in exporting stolen quality cars.

Everything Freddie did, he did carefully. 'Careful,' he had often told Paul Dekker, 'is my middle name.'

And this fastidiousness – as tiresome as some of his colleagues found it – was the main reason why, at fifty-three years of age and after twenty-seven years of very dodgy deals indeed, Freddie had a clean criminal record. There was a certain amount of luck involved, he would admit, but care and attention to detail tended to create its own luck. Freddie's oft quoted motto was that, *Being careful pays dividends*.

And the statement had been proven true because not only had he never been caught selling stolen vehicles, but Freddie's house was the only one within a two-mile radius that hadn't been burgled within the last eighteen months. While other people fitted burglar alarms to their houses, hoping that the sight of a small metal box on an outside wall would be enough to discourage thieves, Freddie had carefully made his own home something close to impregnable. While he was at home, nothing could move between the high perimeter wall surrounding his property and the house without him (and inside thirty seconds the police) knowing about it. As soon as they stepped on to his property they would be bathed in bright light and recorded by security cameras from various angles. That was if they managed to gain entrance, of course. Anyone who attempted to get through the electrically operated front gates or over the walls was going to be in for a shock. Literally. There was an electric cow-fence set just below the top of the wall on the inside – where it wouldn't be detected until you put your hand on it – and several strands of this were also interlaced with (and partially insulated from) the mesh of the front gate.

Ian King, the area postman, would have borne testimony to this: he had once made the mistake of leaning back on the gate while waiting for Freddie to come out and sign for a parcel. He had intended to turn to face the sun, to relax and smoke a cigarette while he waited. He turned round, leaned back, and found himself sitting on the gravel amongst his scattered Silk Cuts feeling as if someone had bullwhipped the skin from the back of his neck. He had still been sitting there like that when Freddie had come out, and if he had felt just a little better than he did, would have boxed Freddie's ears. As it was, he expressed his shock and dismay, and by (quite eloquently under the circumstances, he thought) threatening to 'sue the shirt right off your back, you cocksucker!' Ian King had left ten minutes later, wiser for his experience and a great deal happier. The happiness had a lot to do with the burn on his neck, which throbbed and stung, but which had somehow sent him away with five hundred pounds in his pocket. The next time he had gone to the house signs had been erected which read: ELEC-TRIFIED GATES – DO NOT TOUCH.

But Freddie's security system didn't depend on his being there in order to operate – any break-in attempt would be automatically filmed and the police alerted. And just in case they didn't turn up quickly enough, Freddie had installed one or two other horrible surprises. There was a second, lower wall around the perimeter, two feet inside the wired one. Freddie had intended to keep guard dogs in this corridor but he wasn't a dog man and didn't relish the thought of being mistaken for a stranger by several Dobermanns, so the dogs had never been bought. But if you wanted your ankles broken or your toes badly bitten, scaling the outer wall of his property and jumping down into the bare dirt corridor would still be a good way of going about it because Freddie had installed quite a number of very nasty gin-traps there.

This evening (and it was still evening until two-thirty in the morning as far as Freddie was concerned), he was locked up tight in his mansion and he was not thinking about his security system at all. It had never yet been breached, it was never likely to be breached, and all the green lights on the board in his bedroom were pulsing in their regular, hypnotic fashion. Freddie lay on his bed, a glass of brandy in one hand and a cigar in the other and stared at the twinkling tell-tales, not even seeing them.

Freddie was busy feeling lonely.

His last relationship had begun and ended in the same spirit with which he conducted his business deals: carefully.

He had carefully dumped Lori, his third wife, when he had grown tired of her six months ago. 'Compatible' wasn't a word Freddie had considered when he married her a year ago; when you got to your fifties and were marrying a twenty-three-year-old blonde who listened to Hammer and Lukey Luke and the 2 Live Crew and all that other rap crap they called music, and who chewed gum and swore like a navvy, 'compatible' was a word you tended to avoid. But *'careful'* wasn't. Lori had been a mistake who was gone, if not yet forgotten. But because he'd remembered to be careful she would be easier to forget than wife number two who was still connected – like a leech – to his bank account. Lori had been young enough and green enough to sign the pre-marital contract his lawyers had drawn

308

up and now she was up in London with nothing but the clothes he'd bought her, the Lotus Eclat he'd generously let her take away and the twenty-year-old black guy she'd cuckolded him with. Unlike wife two, she would not be asking for half of everything and maintenance forever after.

Since then, Freddie's personal life had been bleak, if not empty. Since Rachel it had always been bleak, and having other women always seemed a little like fixing a sticking plaster over a gash that needed stitches, but sometimes – for a little while at least – those plasters provided relief from his misery.

And in the six months since Lori had gone down the road, that relief had been provided by a string of blondes who had been eager to make his acquaintance and even more eager to prove to him that they could match his sexual tastes. Girls like this were easy to come by when you had money, and they weren't, as most people seemed to think, horrible old whores either. All of them had been beautiful (and Freddie had shot videos to prove it), all of them had left him worn out in bed, and all of them had been extremely sweet to him.

But none of them had had a personality that interested him in the slightest. When he had become immune to the sexual analgesic each of them had provided, he went out looking for another.

Because there were things that weren't easy to come by, even when you had so much money you didn't know what to do with it next (and Freddie'd had a good few ideas in his time). The most important of those things was finding people you wanted to spend time with. Almost without exception, Freddie had found, these were people who didn't give a toss about how much you were worth.

The last woman in his life whose company he had really enjoyed had been his first wife, Rachel, whose sex drive had been somewhere in the twice a month region rather than the 'at every available opportunity' excesses of Carla, the last blonde, and Rachel hadn't been what you might have called skilled – or, at times, particularly enthusiastic. But Freddie hadn't had to forgive her these things because it simply didn't occur to him that they were things that *needed* forgiving. Rachel was bright and had a razor sharp wit and was the most fun person to be with that he had ever met.

On its own that would have been bad enough now that she was gone. What was worse was that for once in his long and careful life he had forgotten his prime rule and had allowed himself to fall hopelessly in love with her. Freddie had loved Rachel with all his heart and now, two new wives and six blondes who could all fuck like rattlesnakes later, he was still in love with her and thought he always would be. But life was a bitch and a sadistic bitch at that and he couldn't have Rachel back because of the things that money couldn't buy.

It wasn't true that money couldn't buy you love: Freddie knew it could buy you something so close as to make no difference (but that it seemed to preclude your return of that love), but it *was* true that money couldn't buy you happiness (and would merely ease your suffering). More importantly it couldn't buy you that most precious gift of all, *life*.

In the dark downhill months after Rachel had been diagnosed as having leukaemia and became more pale and tired the harder they fought to save her, money *had* made her suffering a little more comfortable. It had also transported her across the Atlantic for quick marrow transplants by the world's finest surgeons, therapy in the world's finest clinics – and from there to Mexico for less orthodox treatment. But it hadn't been able to prevent her dwindling life-force from fading to a glowing ember, then finally extinguishing itself.

Afterwards, Freddie had tried to drink her out of his system, then to gamble her out, then to fuck her out; and none of it had worked.

Now, lying alone on his big circular bed with the satellite dish pointing towards Eutelsat, and the television trying to show him pictures of yet more girls who liked to suck cocks doing their thing, Freddie stared at the green lights on the security panel and thought of her.

310

And when he'd finished dabbing the tears from his eyes he began to think of someone else whose company he had enjoyed and whom he wasn't likely to be seeing again. This was someone else who didn't seem to give a toss about money: that living legend who sometimes seemed to burn with the fires of hell, Paul Dekker.

Freddie relit his cigar and frowned, wondering where Paul was now. He certainly wasn't on the other end of the phone in London at his mother's place where he'd been since that bitch he'd been married to had thrown him out. Freddie had had three unpleasant experiences on the telephone while trying to contact him and had been forced to quit. It looked very much as if someone up there didn't want him to get in contact with Paul and Freddie was acutely attuned to this kind of message.

He'd phoned Paul's mother's number two days after Paul had delivered what he'd claimed was his last ever car. There was a buyer in Amsterdam who badly wanted an early Pontiac Trans-Am and Jake Fulman wasn't at home and neither was Billy Pink. Freddie had been a little relieved. In spite of what Paul had said about the other two men being reliable, the fact was that Jake was clumsy and Billy Pink was downright care-less. Either one was likely to turn up with the wrong model or with a damaged example of the right one. Trans-Ams weren't easy to come by and they weren't exactly low-profile when you were spiriting them away either. It was the kind of job at which Paul would have excelled and Freddie was glad of an excuse to phone him. He'd wanted to call him and try to talk him out of retiring but hadn't thought Paul would respond kindly to it. Freddie, who hadn't got where he was today without an ability to manipulate people, was a skilled enough amateur psychologist to know that when you told Paul Dekker he *had* to do something, he would simply refuse. If you let him know you *wanted* him to do something he would probably refuse. It was something to do with his insecurity, Freddie thought. Paul didn't like anyone to fuck around with him and was driven to stamp his authority on everything.

But there was more than one way the proverbial cat could be skinned.

If you were to call him and sympathise with him and tell him it was a shame he was out of the game because you had an extremely difficult job that you couldn't get anyone to do, you would be appealing to two parts of Paul that he had little control over; two parts of him that he would probably be glad to see the back of. The first was his seemingly inbuilt urge to help people out (and Freddie had often jokingly suggested to him that he had missed his vocation and that he really ought to be an Automobile Association mechanic), and the second was his strong sense of professional pride. Although he wouldn't admit to it, Paul Dekker thought that he wasn't simply the best car-thief in Britain, but the best in the world.

And because Freddie knew that a retired Paul Dekker was going to be an unhappy Paul Dekker (and that his own export business was going to suffer, of course) he had made the call.

And found himself talking to a man who wasn't Paul at all, but who apparently knew all about him and who wanted to know all about Freddie too. Within the first five seconds of the call, Freddie's internal trouble radar had spotted and identified a detective. He had kept the call short and sweet because the word 'indisposed' when applied to Paul's inability to come to the phone sounded very much like a metaphor for 'under arrest', and the gravity (and grindingly slow speed) with which the detective spoke suggested that someone nearby might just be trying to trace the call.

So Freddie had rung off and begun to call around. Word had it that Paul had been murdered. Word had it that Paul had murdered his mother. Word had it that they had both been murdered – it had been in the papers. No one knew anything for sure and Freddie wasn't about to phone Paul's local nick for any confirmation in case no one had been killed at all and Paul had been arrested in connection with the theft of a number of automobiles.

And a few days later he'd rung Jake's place and, surprise,

surprise, found himself talking to a man who wasn't Jake at all but knew all about him and wanted to know all about Freddie too . . . and so on and so forth.

And tonight he'd tried to ring the offices of the Miles Carriage Co. and had failed. The line was apparently out of action and all he'd heard down the telephone was a huge distant hiss that might or might not have carried the burbling voices of other telephone lines. For a few seconds Freddie had thought that one of those distant voices might be addressing him and the hairs at the back of his neck had stood erect. The words echoed indistinctly and they might have been a snippet of conversation when someone had asked, '. . . are you coming too?' or they might have said, '. . . coming for you too', and they could have been a threat, but Freddie didn't consider them in great detail because his back felt as if someone had just tipped icy water down it and when that happened it was time to hang up.

He'd thought about it for a while and constructed a scenario in which Paul had been hoovered up by the CID for many and various car crimes and had split a seam and spilled. Detectives were already at the Miles Carriage Co. and they already knew all about Freddie Simmons and were warning him that they were coming for him too.

It had taken all his courage (and several glasses of brandy too) for him to lift that receiver and phone the Miles Carriage Co. again, but now he was glad he'd done it because on the second occasion he'd got straight through and found himself listening to the hoarse, snapping and horrendously enthusiastic tones of Double A, Jake's speed-freak side kick. Long before Freddie had been able to steer the conversation around to what terrible things might have happened, he already knew that it was nothing serious, because Double A (who he'd never met) was wittering on about the 1959 Ford Popular he was working on and explaining just how difficult it was making Anderson racing's four-into-two-into-one exhaust manifolds fit under the Pop's bonnet. According to Double A, no one had been at the Miles Carriage Co. today except him (and he could have done with a little help, he could have told you) and God was in his heaven and things were all right with the world – and probably the universe too, for that matter. Jake was still in Cornwall fishing and wasn't due back until tomorrow or the next day and he hadn't heard from or seen Stephen Miles in weeks. Double A said he hadn't been visited by the police and that he'd heard of Paul Dekker but didn't know anything about him and hadn't heard anything about any murder, but then he didn't read papers unless they had *New Musical Express* or *Viz* written across the front, so the Pope might have eloped for all *he* knew.

Now feeling very relieved, Freddie rang directory enquiries and asked for the number of the police station in Stepney which was where Paul would be if he had been arrested and was awaiting trial.

The desk sergeant – or whoever had answered the phone – must have been tired, Freddie realised. They were not holding anyone going by the name Paul Dekker, the guy had said, and had informed him that no one using that name had been charged and sent for trial within the last three weeks. While Freddie was busy feeling even more relieved as he told himself, *That means that even if they did pick him up, they released him without charge*, the desk sergeant asked him why he wanted to know. 'I'm looking for him,' Freddie said, without thinking.

And to his amazement the sergeant replied, 'And you're not the only one.'

Which meant that Paul was out and about.

Now, lying here on his bed and staring at the glimmering security lights and trying to suck his cigar back into life, Freddie wondered where Paul was and wished the gate intercom would bleep and a hoarse voice would announce that, 'It's me, Paul,' because when you were with him, some of that relentless energy and supreme self-confidence would rub off. When you were with him you suddenly didn't feel sorry for yourself any more; you felt full of vitality and exhilarated and your mind would start to teem with plans. When you were with Paul

314

Dekker you felt as if you were sharing the glare of the spotlight that seemed to shine on him.

And there weren't many people who made you feel like that.

2

When Freddie woke up a while later, it was from a dream in which Paul Dekker had been dancing cheek to cheek with Rachel, who, Freddie seemed to remember, he had resurrected. Rachel didn't look good in the dream; she was alive but her body was little more than a decomposing bag of bones and the white satin dress she'd been buried in was in tatters. She kept on smiling at Freddie as the two of them turned and her teeth were rotten. And in spite of this he still wanted her very badly.

Freddie shook the dream out of his head but was unable to quell the stomach-twisting longing. He glanced at his cigar – which had gone out instead of killing him in a blaze as it might have done – thanked God, then wondered why he'd bothered.

His mouth was sour. He sat up and sipped at the brandy, then swiped the fallen cigar ash off the bed. The satellite station he'd tuned into had quit showing pornography now because the gasping and groaning had stopped. He glanced at the security board on the wall, then switched his bleary gaze to the television to see what delights were in store for him now.

In spite of the fact that his subscription card to the twenty-four-hour film channel was valid (if illegal in this country) and was still housed in the slot, the TV picture had become encrypted. There was no sound, so sign of a picture, and, surprisingly no written German entreaty which might have been informing him that his card was out of date or that it needed to be inserted.

There was just interference there of the type that Freddie had only ever seen in cartoons and on satellite: big black and white Zs.

Freddie glared at the screen then found that he didn't care

if all the gremlins in the universe were inside his television and satellite receiver chewing up bits of electronic stuff. They were welcome to it.

He lay back on the bed, shut off the television with the remote and closed his eyes, already knowing that sleep, that rarest of commodities these days, was shooting down the road away from him, rather than stealing up to him with its warm and drowsy blankets.

'Fuck it!' he said and sat up, his left hand already reaching for the half-smoked Havana in the ashtray. The cigar made him cough but the brandy soothed his throat. The question was, what could he do now? He knew from bitter experience that if he put himself down and tried to sleep he would almost make it before he began to itch, and that once the itch started – perhaps on his nose or ear – and he gave in and scratched it, sleep would become very unlikely indeed. Because every time you scratched that itch it would pop up somewhere else; somewhere difficult to get at so that you would spend the next hour writhing about chasing it around your body.

And yet his eyes felt as if the Sandman had been by several times already and was down to the sharp sand now, with gravel to come – which meant that reading was out of the question – and he felt too tired to get up and do those things everyone advised insomniacs to do.

And as he sat there trying not to remember that rotting Rachel, something began to scratch.

3

There were many things that Freddie Simmons did not like. One of them was not being able to sleep, another was not having Rachel, and there was an almost endless list of lesser irritations. There were not many things that he feared. On occasion he had feared Paul Dekker (which was why he didn't short change him) and he was frightened of being bitten by dogs, which was why he didn't ever get any, and scared of drowning, which was why he seldom used either of the pools, but the thing that Freddie hated most was *RATS*. Rats were important enough in his mind always to think about in capital letters. When he was a kid, too stupid to know danger when he saw it, he had cornered a rat in the porch of his house. It was a big brown rat of the species *rattus norvegicus* – the kind that might make you pray for a piper, and it had had yellow teeth. It backed up into the corner of the porch and it showed him those teeth like an angry dog might have done. Then it had attacked. It wasn't true (at least as far as Freddie knew) that rats went for your throat – it would have been an impossible jump for a creature that size – but it was most certainly true that they resented being cornered.

The rat leapt forward, not up at his throat, but simply forward towards the nearest part of him. And that part happened to be the leg of his trousers. The rat caught the sharply pressed crease of his first pair of long trousers between its jaws and bit hard. Freddie had screamed and leapt backwards, but the rat's jaws were locked and it hung on, its heavy body swinging round and swiping his other leg. Freddie could remember that feeling, even now; its body hitting his other leg then swinging back and flicking off his other calf as he tried to run away backwards, then stopped and frantically tried to shake it off. The rat's tail swished and its tiny claws scrabbled at his trouser-leg seeking purchase and all the while its beady eyes stared up at him.

And when he finally got the rat off him it wasn't because the animal had let go but because the material of his trousers had torn clean away leaving a hole the size of a sixpence. The rat dashed away and Freddie was glad of that. He cried a little because he was shocked and also because for the first time in his life he had met something that had possessed a fury with which he could not compete. And since that day he'd made sure that rats and Freddie Simmons weren't ever anywhere near one another – and learned all sorts of other nasty things about them, like the fact that they'd carried the plague; like the fact that you could catch fatal diseases from their urine. Rats were no go.

Which was why every muscle in his body tensed when he heard that scratching up in the corner of the room.

4

For a few seconds Freddie stared up at the ceiling in terror, knowing that there was a Rat the size of a cat in his attic and that there was only a layer of expanded polystyrene insulation chips, a thickness of plasterboard and a little artex between that monster and his room. It could have been worse – the scraping could be happening directly over his head instead of fifteen feet or so away in the furthest corner of the room, but in his panic Freddie didn't consider this much of a blessing. There wasn't likely to be much to choose between a huge Rat falling down right on top of you and one that came down over there in the corner then rushed across the room at you. In fact, if you happened to be some kind of a demon whose job it was to set up something like this, you would go for the distance every time. The horror would be much worse when your subject found himself looking at that monster coming towards him and *knew* he would be unable to run away.

The scratching ceased but Freddie did not relax. Rats were intelligent – everyone knew that. The Rat somehow knew that he'd heard it and now it was keeping still or perhaps moving stealthily to a different position up there. It would remain quiet until he began to believe he'd imagined the whole thing, then it would start all over again.

Freddie didn't move until the cigar burned short enough to begin to heat his fingers . . . *coming for you too!* the garbled telephone voice said in his mind. He tore his eyes away from the ceiling and looked in a bemused kind of astonishment at the cigar and thought, *There must be a draught in here*.

In one of these warm, tipsy moments when you were no longer quite sober but not yet drunk, Freddie had invented a subject called Cigar Physics. It had a number of prime rules which dealt with the smoking of various kinds of Havanas, King Edward's and cheaper brands, and all of them were quite true. One of these rules (number seven, in fact) was that: *The resistance of cigar ash to leaving the cigar and falling into the ashtray is directly proportional to the amount of force used to flick it.* Rule 7b stated that once you'd taken the cigar away from the ashtray, that resistance suddenly ceased and the ash would immediately fall – usually on to you. Rule 1 was: *Cigars do not burn down of their own accord.* You had to work at keeping a cigar burning. If you didn't suck regularly, it would simply go out.

Freddie gazed at the hot end of the cigar which should have been dead ash but which was glowing brightly and again thought, *There must be a draught*, although this was impossible. Freddie didn't like to be cold and the house was fitted with the best triple glazing money could buy. Not double glazing, but *triple*. The house was so thoroughly sealed up that your ears would pop if you closed the doors too quickly.

He leaned over to the ashtray and stubbed the cigar out, now able to *feel* that draught on his face. There was a smell on that cool breeze, but his nose and palate were full of smoke and brandy and he couldn't yet place it . . . but it was there all right.

The Rat did not move. Freddie waited five long minutes and then began to doubt that he'd heard it at all. Perhaps he'd been half asleep and imagined it. The moment he had this thought, Freddie tensed, expecting the Rat to take the cue and commence operations again, but this didn't happen.

Nothing happened.

And that was worse.

Freddie told himself that if he was really concerned, he could leave the room – go downstairs or something – then he remembered that film *Alien* and reminded himself that the Rat might be anywhere, waiting for him. It might already be in the drinks cabinet, waiting for him to try to soothe his nerves with more brandy. The moment he dropped the lid, out it would shoot, yellow teeth bared as it ploughed into his throat.

You're being extremely silly, he told himself, and sat up on the edge of the bed. Knowing he was being extremely silly, however, didn't prevent him from feeling extremely scared. He was alone in the house with a Rat.

But was there a Rat? Have you heard it since?

Freddie admitted that he hadn't, but he'd already worked out the reason for this – the Rat had found a better way through. Perhaps it had forced itself down the cavity wall and had found a way in downstairs. Freddie thought of going downstairs to check and immediately decided against it. He thought that halfway down the stairs he might put down a bare foot onto something warm and furry and alive and he knew that if that happened, he would simply die of the shock.

The draught, Freddie realised as he sat on the edge of the round bed, was blowing across him from the corner of the room where the scratching noise had come from. This was impossible because there was no window on that side of the room and there was nowhere else for a breeze (and it *was* a breeze now) to come from. Freddie sniffed and noted that the smell was something like rotting citrus fruit.

Goosebumps pricked up all over his body as he gazed up into the Y of that square corner and Freddie decided that, irrational or not, now would be as good a time to leave the room – and possibly the house – as any. He had a strong feeling that the Rat was still up there, perhaps gnawing at the point of that corner from the inside. That was where it was going to come through, he was sure.

He stood up on legs that felt as if they belonged to someone else (someone half crippled) and put on his dressing gown, wishing again that Paul were here. He was certain that Paul didn't have irrational thoughts in the middle of the night and wasn't frightened of Rats. Paul would know how to deal with something like this. His car keys were downstairs on the radiator shelf by the front door. The door into the big garage was situated nearby. If he could just get down there, pick up the keys and get into the garage, he could be out of here. Perhaps he would come back again when it was daylight – after the Rentokil man had been, that was.

He glanced at the door, wondering if the Rat was behind it waiting for him, then glanced back up into the corner of the room, suddenly certain that the proximity of a Rat had driven him insane.

5

As Freddie stared up into the corner where the three planes met (at ninety degrees) and drew a Y (with all angles at ninety degrees) not unlike the inside of a Mercedes Benz emblem, the corner reversed its perspective. It was no longer the inside of a point, but the *outside*, as though a huge pressure from behind had pushed against it, like a finger into a rubber glove. And yet the shape of the walls had not changed to accommodate this new shape. It was a geometric impossibility, and it hurt to look at it.

Three nineties, Freddie thought, trying to tear his eyes away. His hand was on the cool brass door handle in front of him, but he couldn't lever it down, just as he couldn't take his eyes off the impossible thing in the corner of the room. There should only have been three ninety-degree angles up there, and all Freddie knew was that what was up there now added up to a great deal more than two hundred and seventy degrees. Freddie didn't know how many it took to support that impossibility, but it had to be a lot. Possibly in the order of thousands.

Enough to drive you insane anyway, he thought distantly.

There were many insane thoughts raging through Freddie's head at the moment and they included the certain knowledge that whatever was going to come through that point in a few seconds, was going to be no ordinary Rat. It was either going to be something *masquerading* as a Rat, or the very God of Rats itself. And if it wasn't that, there was another strong possibility. Freddie knew the power of positive thinking – regularly extolled its virtues, in fact, telling his colleagues and friends that if you *wanted* something badly enough, you would get it, by and by. There was a kind of psychic (or physic, as Jake would have said) law that governed it. Positive thinking had quite often worked for Freddie and now he thought he might have been *wanting* something he hadn't fully considered the consequences of getting.

That something was the return of Rachel.

He remembered his dream of Paul Dekker dancing with his dead wife, who was no longer dead but still rotting, and he knew with the utmost certainty that if she came back to him through that point it wouldn't be to love him, but to curse him and tear him apart for bringing her back in that condition.

And as he watched, the point (that was somehow still a proper corner too, just as it had always been) opened, like a three-petalled flower sensing sunlight and suddenly blooming.

Freddie didn't see what lay on the other side of that blossoming hole because he'd wrenched his gaze away from it and was looking dumbly down at his right hand that wouldn't do as it was told and open the door. But he did smell the odour that was carried out of the chasm or hole or whatever it was on a warm breeze. The smell was not the damp wood and paper smell of Rats nesting, but the smell of charred human flesh, rotten fruit and the acrid odour of burned-out electrical equipment.

Freddie tried not to picture what this might mean and concentrated all his attention on his liver-spotted right hand and the cool brass door handle beneath it while the thought, *RUN AWAY!* flashed on and off in the visual part of his mind.

For an instant, Freddie was certain that someone had removed his entire arm, from shoulder to finger, and replaced it with an identical plastic facsimile which contained no working parts at all . . . then he felt a tingle in his fingers, realised distantly that for some reason the brass handle was rapidly warming up, and his arm came back to life.

He almost had the door open when the voice from behind

him said, 'I wouldn't go out there if I were you, you never know what might be waiting for you.'

Freddie let go of the handle because the huge, flashing *RUN AWAY!* thought now had a very large Rat superimposed upon it, and as if mounted on a rusty gimbal, he swung creakily around to face the source of the voice.

It's all a nightmare. A nightmare is all it is! Freddie assured himself. The corner of the room, where the ceiling met the far walls, was back in its original position and looked just as if nothing untoward had ever happened to it.

And yet there was a man standing there.

Freddie glanced over at the security panel, which told him that the system was all up and running and that it had not been breached.

And yet there was a man standing there.

That's why it has to be a dream, Freddie told himself. *If someone is here, they must have come through the security net because people don't arrive through cracks in the fabric of your house. And if someone got through the net and missed all the traps, then that someone has to be the product of a brandy-laden nightmare and not real at all.*

But he was forced to admit that the man didn't look anything like the product of a nightmare. He was dressed in a suit and looked confident, handsome and charming. He looked, in fact, like a man who ought to be your friendly neighbourhood bank manager, from the top of his neatly coiffed head, right down to the tips of his brown brogue shoes.

6

'My name is Robert Farmer,' said the man, who until Piewacket the cat had left home, had sailed the good ship Barclay's Bank and who had been known to his wife's rich friends as Mr Addy Long, 'and something very strange and wonderful has happened to me.'

Freddie blinked at him. He was vaguely conscious of his blood running downhill, away from his brain, even though his heart was hammering fast enough to pump Niagara Falls back the way it came.

'I can walk through walls,' Robert Farmer smiled. 'Remember that old series *Kung Fu*, with David Carradine? They used to say at the beginning that a Shao-Lin priest was said to be able to walk through walls, but you never saw Grasshopper do it, did you? You saw him walk on the rice-paper without making a mark, but I can tell you that it's child's play in comparison. David Carradine never did walk through walls, to the best of my memory . . .' he appeared to think about it, then grinned '. . . but then again, he wasn't as well connected as I am,' he finished.

'Who . . . who?' Freddie heard himself say. The edges of his vision were pulsing now and there was a pain all the way down his left arm. He tried to think positively and was totally unable.

'I think I already explained who I am,' the man said, his smile fading. 'Robert Farmer. Ought I to spell it for you? R-O-B-E-R-T F-A-R-M-E-R.'

'How . . .' Freddie's mouth wouldn't work properly and the outrage he badly wanted to feel over the invasion of his privacy just didn't happen. All that happened was that the blood drained from his brain, the pain in his arm increased, the fear he felt grew exponentially and a deep and burning urge to urinate grew in him.

'What you want to know, I think,' the man said, 'is how I got past your security system? As I already said, something strange and wonderful has happened to me. After a lifetime of dull orderliness I have found my vocation. I have become a disciple, you see. I am one of twelve who walk with the Angel. There are certain benefits attached to my vocation, and one of them is the ability to move, rather like God, I suppose, in mysterious ways. It's only local, I'm afraid, but you must admit that walking through walls is impressive. I'm having *such* a lovely time.'

'Don't hurt me,' Freddie heard his voice plead. He was

ashamed to hear the cringing tone and wished that the pain –
which was surely the onset of the decent-sized heart attack he'd
been warned about – would hurry up and kill him.

Robert Farmer spent a moment looking bemused. 'Hurt you?'
he said, frowning, then his face changed and he smiled again.
This smile was a not a pleasant smile at all, but the smile of a
sadist who has just imagined a new *twist*.

Freddie backed up against the door as Robert Farmer reached
into his pocket. Freddie expected a knife to appear and wasn't
disappointed. The part of him that wasn't gibbering in fear or
assuring him there were a thousand worse ways to die than of
a cardiac arrest, was surprised at the size and shape of the knife,
however. The knife wasn't the huge glittering Bowie favoured
by the maniacs in the horror films he often watched on satellite TV, or even one of the phallic in-and-out flick knives that
seemed to be so popular with the Italians. The knife wasn't even
shiny. The weapon was the kind of thing Freddie had always
fondly imagined you would stick a pig with to make it bleed
as per the saying. It was a matt black four-inch stiletto, the blade
of which was no more than half an inch wide at the handle. It
tapered down to the most acute point Freddie had ever seen
on a knife. A knife like that, he knew, would slide into you as
easily and effortlessly as a shark would slip through water. He
distantly wondered what it would feel like.

'I won't hurt you,' Robert Farmer said. 'All you have to do
is talk to me. Can you do that?'

Freddie nodded. 'I can,' he whispered breathlessly. The
door handle was under his hands again and this time he thought
he could open it and go through it before the man reached him.
He didn't know what would happen after that and at this
point, he didn't care. All he knew was that he had to get away.
No one showed you a knife like that in a situation like this unless
they intended to make you bleed like that proverbial stuck pig,
even if they claimed the opposite.

'I want to know all about Paul Dekker,' Robert Farmer said.

'I don't know him,' Freddie said, and when the man arched

his eyebrows and quizzically tipped his head to one side, added, 'Anything about him, I mean.'

'Then tell me what you do know. I need to know his weaknesses. What are they? I need to know how he can be . . . uhh . . . compromised.'

Freddie's mind reeled. Paul Dekker *had* no weaknesses, but if he were to tell the man this, that stiletto would be applied to him, sure as eggs were oeufs.

Unless you can get away.

And before he knew what he intended to do, the door was open and he was through it and hammering across the landing towards the stairs.

It was a twenty-foot run to the top stair, and during each pace Freddie expected to be brought crashing down, and during each pace the pain in his chest and arm grew fourfold. Then he was at the top of the long staircase and down at the bottom was the door to the garage and the radiator shelf with the big bunch of car-keys on top of it. Freddie knew that once he got down there and into the garage he was going to have to fumble all through those keys to get the right one to start the car, and that while he did it, Robert Farmer would be coming steadily towards him, that sadistic smile distorting his handsome face, then the automatic garage doors would refuse to open and that he was going to have to rev up the car and drive straight through them . . .

But suddenly he thought he could do all that and still come out ahead.

There were twenty-eight stairs there which meant fourteen steps if he took them two at a time.

In his mind, he saw himself in the car already, churning gravel out on the drive and heading towards the opening of the front gates. It was going to be a simple matter. And if his chest still hurt when he got away, he would drive straight to the hospital. He was going to get out of this alive and intact and Paul Dekker was going to have to answer some very serious questions the next time Freddie Simmons got hold of him.

Back in his carefree days, he and Rachel had made a game of racing one another up and down the stairs of whatever place they happened to be staying and had once been caught doing this in one of London's better class hotels while making as much noise as a couple of school kids might have done. They had been told off and had been as shamefaced and guilty as those school kids would have been. After the manager had gone Rachel had said, 'But I beat you anyway!' Had Rachel been here today, there was no way she would have been able to beat him. This was going to be the stair race to end them all.

But in his panic, Freddie had discarded his first and foremost rule. If the circumstances had been a little less pressing he would have told himself that since his carefree days he had become older, heavier and somewhat less fit, even if you didn't count the pain that was surely a heart attack. He probably would have concluded that going down the stairs one at a time in the normal way would be sufficient if he did it quickly enough.

And if this had been the case, Freddie would have got away alive and intact, just as he had imagined he would.

Two paces and four stairs down from the top, Freddie's feet quit being fleet and started being stupid. The left (on the side of him that hurt, and wasn't *that* just a barrel of laughs) kicked into the right and the right came down awkwardly. Freddie instantly reverted to going down in one steps, but he was moving too fast. His left kicked forward again, wrapped itself around his right ankle, and then he knew he was going to be disqualified from this particular stair-race because he was cheating by taking to the air.

The flight was shorter than he expected. He crashed down on to his chest still eight steps from the bottom and ground to a halt. There was blood in his mouth, one of his teeth was gone from the front at the top and there seemed to be about an eighth of an inch shaved off the left hand side of his tongue where his jaws had snapped shut on it. This wasn't the real problem – the real problem was that his heart attack (although it felt like someone had fed his ribcage through a hydraulic press) didn't appear to want to put him out of his agony. His bastard heart was going to keep him alive for long enough for Robert Farmer to do whatever he wanted to him.

'Another strange thing,' Farmer said from above and behind him, 'when you become enlightened, you realise that everything is possessed of a kind of life. I believe they call it animism. Imbuing inanimate objects with human characteristics. It's not quite right, but I can assure you that everything has a life of its own – including your feet, I shouldn't wonder. And do you know what? No, I didn't think you would. This knife, the very same one with which I took the life out of Paul Dekker's mother Helen, and his little doggy Cindy, can speak. It spoke to me when I visited the Dekker residence, just as the axe spoke to me when I first discovered there was more to life than Addy and her Spode chinaware. And it's speaking to me now. The trouble with weapons, as I'm sure you know, Mr Simmons, is that they are manufactured to cause injury and death. They have a life of their own and voices of their own. Naturally their outlook is a little narrow, but their voices can be most persuasive. This stiletto, for instance, is strongly suggesting that you might feel a little more cooperative towards me if I were to use it to wheedle your left eye from its socket. And besides that, it's telling me how good I would feel while I was doing it.'

'Ungghh,' Freddie said. The hydraulic press was busily stamping out shapes which might eventually become tin lids from the sheet metal his ribs seemed to have turned into.

He felt himself being turned over and was unable to resist. He half expected to be picked up and carried somewhere a little more convenient for the torture to be done, but Farmer left him where he was and squatted down beside him.

'There's a man in Cambridge,' he said, inspecting the point of the stiletto, 'who used to be my friend when I was in university. His name used to be Henry Tyler. We used to call him H. H has opened doors and those doors can never again be closed. Opening those doors lost him his life, but he is not dead. H has undergone a metamorphosis. He has been transmogrified. He has become . . . something more than human. Do you understand?'

Freddie didn't have the slightest idea about what the man might have meant because he was having shapes painfully punched out of his chest by a huge imaginary press. He said nothing until Robert Farmer reached down and slapped him hard across the face, then, wishing he could just die and be done with it, right here and right now, he said, 'Yuhhhng.'

The man slapped him again. 'No, I don't think you *do* understand. We have *all* become something more than human, but H made himself deiparous. Do you know what that means? That means "to bring forth a god". H gave his life opening the doors and bringing forth the god, and therein lies our problem. Your good friend Paul Dekker has possession of something we need – something which belongs to us. And I want you to tell me how we can make him return it. Dekker is not an ordinary man. He is driven by demons of his own construction. What I want you to do is to tell me exactly what those demons are. Do you understand?'

Freddie nodded. He didn't understand at all but the point of the stiletto was wavering an inch away from his left eye and even though the left side of his body was cramped with pain he could imagine exactly how the point of that knife would feel as it was applied to the lens of his eye. There would be pain that would make his cardiac arrest seem like a mere pulled muscle.

Robert Farmer smiled down at him. 'So tell me everything you know about him.'

Through the red haze of pain, Freddie began to speak, knowing that he wasn't going to be able to come up with the goods. There wasn't too much to tell about Paul and what he did know was difficult to impart because each time he stalled to fight for a breath he didn't think he was going to be able to draw, his friendly bank manager slapped him hard enough across the face to make his ears ring.

''S'all I know,' Freddie eventually wheezed.

'You didn't tell me anything,' Robert Farmer complained, his even features swimming in the air above Freddie. He was frowning and that looked like a very bad sign.

''S'all I know,' Freddie repeated. 'Truth.'

Robert Farmer bent down until his nose was almost touching Freddie's. He smiled. 'Then you didn't know very much, did you?'

Freddie shook his head. The pain in his chest seemed to have subsided a little. He tested his arms and legs and found that they all moved and seemed to be in a reasonable condition. He wasn't going to be able to put up a fight against this man, but now he'd told everything he knew, there was a chance (however slim) that he might be left alone. And if that happened there was still a chance of survival.

'Since we're so freely swapping information, Freddie, and since I like you, I'll tell you something else about becoming more than human. I can absorb blood. Give me your hand and I'll show you.'

Freddie didn't move because Robert Farmer's eyes were changing and his expression was becoming enraptured. Freddie had seen enough pornographic movies (including the ones he'd made himself with a string of blondes) to be able to recognise the *wanting* expression that would steal on to a person's face in the moments directly before orgasm, and Robert Farmer's features had arranged themselves in his way. But his eyes had become cold and steely and his head was cocked to one side as if he was listening. The man believed that his knife spoke to him and Freddie thought it might now be suggesting some very nasty things. The panic and terror which had been swamped by the pain in his chest, now rose like a geyser and flooded through him. He *was* going to die. He'd fulfilled his part of the bargain but the man was still going to use the knife on him.

'You promised!' Freddie moaned. 'You said you wouldn't hurt me!'

'I don't recall promising any such thing,' Robert Farmer said.

'Don't hurt me!' Freddie pleaded.

'A little pain is good for the soul,' the man replied, grinning. 'Watch closely and marvel,' he added.

The man lifted his left hand and brought it into his line of vision. He placed the sharp tip of the stiletto on one of the lines on Freddie's hand between the knuckle of his forefinger and the web of his thumb. 'This is the heart line,' he announced. 'It says you died of a broken heart. You died years ago, Freddie, you know that. Now watch carefully.'

The point of the stiletto dented his flesh and then pierced it. It was a small point of sharp pain at first, but when it was forced against tendon and bone the pain became a searing fire. Freddie tried to move his hand and didn't have the strength. He tried to hit the man with his right hand and couldn't get the angle right. Then he just lay there and screamed, the tears blurring his eyes as he watched his hand become unzipped all the way across the heart line. Tendons were severed, one by one, pinging like breaking piano wires as bolts of white lightning shot up his arm and found his heart and his brain.

Then the knife was gone and the man had hold of the four fingers of his hand and was bending them backwards so that the massive gash opened up. Freddie could see the ruined tendons and nerves and bone in there amongst the free-flowing blood which spattered onto his face.

Then Robert Farmer's face swam into his field of view and the man wiped the ruined hand down it, from forehead to chin. Then he turned and gazed deep into Freddie's eyes. 'Watch,' he said.

And for a moment Freddie forget his pain because the blood – his blood – that was smearing the man's face, broke up into tiny globules like oil on water and were absorbed into the man's flesh.

'I've got some of you now,' Robert Farmer said. 'Some of your power or energy or essence or whatever you want to call it. I've got it and do you know what? *Now we're gonna have us some fun!*'

'Don't,' Freddie murmured. He could see the knife in the man's eyes now, as clearly as if Robert Farmer *was* the knife, but he could see something else in there too, something colder and harder and sharper than any knife could ever be. Right down at the back of Robert Farmer he glimpsed something that might have been a spark of the god that someone he knew had brought forth.

And then all he could see was the stiletto coming down towards his right eye.

But Freddie didn't die. He didn't die even after he was blinded and the stiletto drove down through his navel like a cold spike while Robert Farmer carefully explained that there was a price to be paid for everything and that this was the price that had to be paid for knowing Paul Dekker and being likely to help him if he'd asked for help. He didn't die when the man announced again that, *'Now we're gonna have us some fun!'* and then locked his mouth over Freddie's own and sucked out Freddie's air.

Freddie died when the cold, hard, sharp thing that might have been a spark of a god touched his soul.

Chapter Fourteen
Katie Comes Back

1

By the time the first fuel can ran out and the motorboat's outboard coughed and died Paul was beginning to suspect that he'd finally worked out something logical about all this. It wasn't a big something, and it wasn't yet proven, but any glimpse at all of the pattern behind all of these seemingly arbitrary happenings was something of a windfall. Even if you did have to ignore the departure of more of those marbles in order to believe it.

Paul had expected to be sunk, out here in the sea, and that (so far) hadn't happened. Katie had not been possessed by any more people, living or recently dead, and had not metamorphosed into the charred thing that seemed to be the source of all this madness. His greatest worry had been the memory of his dream in which the shadow-man had poured out of Katie and wrecked and buried the truck. Most of the other things he'd dreamed about had happened (which made the dream a premonition, he supposed, somewhat less than enthusiastically) and he'd expected this particular one to be next. There were good reasons for this, the main one being that he'd seen that black substance on the lips of the two men he'd killed up on the hill. If one of those things could destroy and bury a large truck in a matter of a minute, a small speed boat (and its occupants) would become history in very short order.

But this hadn't happened and Paul thought he knew why.

It was because Katie was still breathing.

Which meant that the thing that *was* Katie (and you could call it a soul, a spirit, a life-force, an essence or whatever you damn well wanted to – it all amounted to the mind-boggling fact that after *this* there really *was* more to come) was still resident inside her body however deeply she was buried there. When Katie's body was breathing, Paul thought, Katie was *in* or at home and they were safe. Which meant that inside the average body there was only enough room to accommodate one immortal spirit (or whatever expression you chose). Katie had been gone when she'd been up on the hill trying to pick up the angel (and Paul was still not ready, able, or willing to think about this aspect of the problem), she'd been gone prior to becoming possessed by the woman calling herself Lulu Kaminsky, and she'd still been gone when she had turned into the burnt thing that wanted her so badly.

So as long as she kept on breathing, nothing bad could happen.

Paul wasn't happy about the logic of this, or about the questions it raised, and it wasn't proven, but it was the best he had to go on. He just hoped the theory would hold until they got back on dry land.

2

He switched the petrol cans, knocked the outboard into neutral and pulled the string, hard. The engine coughed and spluttered – and just when he thought it was going to die, caught and began to rev smoothly. He put it back into gear and went forward to the driver's seat.

Katie was still slumped in the passenger seat, her head tilted back. He examined her carefully, relaxing slightly when he noticed the rise and fall of her chest. He pulled the throttle handle and the boat dipped its stern and raised its bows and set to work.

Paul steered, occasionally glancing over at Katie's serene face which looked beautiful in the light from the pale moon and stars. The warmth he'd felt earlier – the strange butterfly warmth in the pit of his stomach – began again and his *farmer-oppozite* voice warned, *Not this time, old poke! Not with this one! And anyway, she's not even beautiful, not really. She wasn't this afternoon, so she can't be now. And this is one you really don't want to let get under your skin. The girl is, to all intents and purposes, dead, cowboy. There's even less future in this one than there was with Amy. So don't even think about it!*

But Paul *did* think about it. He couldn't help himself.

3

There were lights off to his right, and a lighthouse flashing on the same side a little further up. Paul didn't know what village that was over there because the map he'd got when he'd hired the motorcycle didn't have a great deal of the mainland marked on it. All he knew was that there was a peninsula that hung down near Skiathos and that the nearest mainland town to the island was called Platania. They had passed Platania about half an hour ago. It would have been the quickest way to the mainland, and travelling up the peninsula from there, in a car, was the logical route, but Paul wasn't sure how much the bad guys knew about his and Katie's whereabouts. He suspected that if any of those men who had been chasing him back on Skiathos had suspected he'd made a dash for the mainland, they would have concluded he'd go straight for Platania. In fact, they may have arrived there already and been waiting for him.

So they were going the long way. All Paul knew from the map he'd seen was that the land down here was shaped the same way as your hand would look if you laid it down on a table with your fingers pointing towards you. The thumb was the strip of land on his right and at the top, where the web of the thumb curved round to meet the fingers, there was a big port called Volos. That was where all the supplies that came to Skiathos started from. And there was likely to be a little more safety and a lot more cars in a place like Volos than there would be in a one horse village like Platania. It was possible that if the bad

335

guys had been waiting in Platania and he hadn't shown up that they would go on to Volos, but Paul intended to be pretty hard to find from now on.

Unless, of course, what the burned Katie-thing said was true, old poke.

Paul had to admit that this was a possibility. He could remember the words the charred thing had said back on the beach: *Now that I've found you, I'll always know where you are.* It was a possibility, but Paul thought the thing had been telling lies. The only way he would find out for certain was if he was intercepted before he made land.

4

When Katie woke up, the lights of Volos were getting very close and Paul was heading towards land to the left of the port because there was quite a lot of shipping coming and going and all of it seemed to be intent on running him down. He supposed he ought to be showing lights like all the other vessels were and hoped that no one (like the angry guy on the ferry who had shouted at him in Greek through a megaphone, or the fishermen whose trawl nets he had fouled for a frantic five minutes during which he struggled to disentangle the outboard's prop before the boat caught up with him) had reported his presence to the coastguard.

Paul smelt her waking up, which was a first for him. The rotten orange blossom smell vanished and the honey smell increased. There was a tiny hint of vanilla beneath it, like a hint of a subtle and expensive perfume. These odours found favour with Paul's olfactory nerves. They were smells that somehow suggested life and vitality.

The girl yawned and stretched like a contented cat.

Paul slowed the boat and turned towards her.

'You awake?' he asked and the question seemed unbelievably stupid. This was a dead girl he'd just put the question to. He refused to think about it.

'Where are we?' she asked, her voice dry and scratchy. Paul thought that might have something to do with the way he'd recently strangled her to death and refused to think about this either.

'Greece,' Paul said and pointed towards the lights. 'That's Volos over there . . . I hope. We're making for land just to the side of it. We need a car. There are people chasing us.'

The girl turned towards him and studied him intently while her right hand examined her neck. 'Are you Paul?' she asked finally.

He nodded.

'Did you save me?'

Paul looked at her. Then he shrugged and looked away. 'I think so,' he said. 'At least I tried.'

'Did you . . . I mean, was I . . . *dead?*'

'I don't know what happened,' Paul said, steering the boat and staring into the lights. 'You were up on a hill. People were trying to hurt you. I took you away.'

'I was dead and you brought me back to life,' Katie said. She reached out and placed her right hand on his left forearm. The hand was cool and strangely thrilling. Paul glanced at it and looked away. *You can't!* his goad insisted, and for once in his life Paul agreed.

'Oh God, I dreamed about you coming for me,' she said. 'I knew you were there. I've known you were there for a long time. Thank you. Thank you for everything you've done.'

When Paul glanced at her again he expected to see that she was looking at him in the way a teenage girl will look at a centre-page spread of the newest teenybopper idol – the way the dead holiday rep had looked at him. But she wasn't looking at him like this at all, she was looking at him as if they shared a gorgeous and happy secret. Her green eyes seemed to be alive with light and her face was not blankly enraptured but majestic. For a moment Paul withered under the power of that expression, then found he was returning it. And for a moment after that he wondered if it were possible that he and the girl had been bound together not just since her first telephone call, but for many years. Perhaps many centuries or perhaps forever.

Then the moment was gone and the girl's face clouded. For a second Paul felt as if something like a warm knife had been withdrawn from his heart and that he'd simultaneously been tossed from the top of a skyscraper.

Don't let this happen! his goad said sharply, but Paul thought it had spoken too late. The bond between them – whatever its nature – had already drawn them closer together.

'Something happened,' Katie said. 'Something else. Do you know what?'

Paul shook his head.

'It's like I'm fractured. I'm not right inside. Something broke me and now I have to do this.'

Paul's heart began to speed. 'Do what?' he asked.

Katie shook her head. 'How can I do it if I can't remember?' she spat in a petulant voice. 'What do you think I am?'

For a moment Paul thought Lulu Kaminsky had come back and he throttled the boat right down and prepared to get rid of her again, but it wasn't necessary. The sudden spurt of fire was over in a second. Katie slumped back in the seat and sobbed. 'I don't know wuh-what's happening at all,' she complained. 'What do they want from muh-me?'

'Who?' Paul asked. 'Who are *they?*' But a large part of him didn't want to know.

'If I can't bring anything back with me, what's the point?' she said, looking at him with hopelessness in her eyes. 'When I'm *there* I know *everything* and when I'm huh-here, it's all gone. How can I duh-do it? What's the point of buh-being an huh-huh-huh . . . oh *God!*'

'Calm down,' Paul said gently – as much to himself as to Katie. The information that the girl was in Greece in order to pick up an angel was resounding inside his head and he was trying not to think that if it hadn't been ruined by the two men up on the hill, he just might be sitting here next to one of God's own. If that kind of thought didn't push you over the edge, you had to be over it already.

'I need some water,' Katie said. 'I'm so duh-dry I can't even cry properly. My body's dried out and my throat hurts and I can't even think straight.'

'We'll get you some water soon,' Paul promised. 'Just breathe deeply and try to keep calm.' Katie drew a dry, rattling breath that hurt to listen to and Paul followed suit, willing his hammering heart to slow down.

There was another fishing vessel in their path – Paul thought Sandra the dead rep had called this type of small boat a caique and had pronounced it the way Freddie Simmons referred to himself: *kike*. Paul couldn't see floats, but there had to be a trawl net – or whatever they called those nets that dangled beneath the water like walls – around somewhere, so he turned away from the boat and back towards the lights of Volos.

When his heart had slowed sufficiently to allow him to talk without the words quavering as they came out of his mouth he asked Katie what she *could* remember. It was important to find out anything she knew.

She swivelled towards him and gazed at him with a hurt look in her eyes. 'From when?' she asked.

'From any when, sweetheart,' Paul said. 'Anything at all. Your name and address. Your age. Anything will do.'

She shook her head. 'My name is Kate Straker. I'm twenty-four years old and I used to live in Church Crookham near Fleet in Hampshire until . . .' she tailed off.

Paul glanced over at her and Katie looked away. 'Until when?'

'Oh God! Henry says I'm a *bad* girl. Chris has gone. I think he's killed Chris. Henry wants me to love him and I *want* to and there's this kid in the road. Oh God, the *kid! How did he get there? I can't stop!*'

Paul broke out in goosebumps that must have been the size of eggs. He didn't know who Henry was (although he could make a good guess) but he knew all about the kid in the road.

He'd lived through this twice himself, and he'd had the dream *(better make that* premonition, *old poke)* about Katie running down a child. It could not be the same one. It wasn't possible, even if his mental voice insisted it was.

Katie fell silent.

'You okay?' Paul asked.

'I know what happened to me now,' she said in a flat voice. 'I remember.'

'What?' Paul asked, already knowing he had to listen to her say it. If only to prove that he wasn't insane. *Or not alone in your insanity, poke!*

'I died,' she said. 'Not when I ran the kid over and crashed the car – I was already dead when I did that. I died earlier. There was fire. Something came through and it killed me. *Oh, Christ, it hurts!*'

She folded up as if something had hit her hard in the stomach. 'He used this body!' she moaned. 'He used this body and he broke it. It's cracked and tainted and I *can't stay here! I'm going away again!*'

'DON'T!' Paul shouted. DON'T SLIP AWAY! HANG ON!'

'Oh, Paul, don't make me stay alive!' she moaned.

Paul let go of the boat's wheel and took the girl in his arms. He drew her to him and rocked her and whispered in her ear that he would look after her and that everything was going to be all right because he was here and he would see that it was so.

And eventually the girl relaxed.

'What else can you remember?' he whispered as her breathing became even again. They were almost at the harbour now. Paul steered the boat to the left, towards a dark patch of land at the edge of the port. The sky was beginning to lighten now. It was gone four-thirty and Paul expected dawn in the not too distant future. There was a chance they would be able to slip away unseen. What was going to happen next rather depended on St Cunt of the Car Thieves.

'We have to go back,' she murmured into his chest.

'To Skiathos?'

'To Cambridge.'

'You live in Church Crookham,' he said.

'It happened in Cambridge,' she said.

Just before the boat nosed up on to the dark beach (which was busy with fishermen, and crowded with nets and boats that floated in the shallows) Katie spoke again.

'They're doing something to me, you know,' she said. 'Something I don't like.'

'Who are?' he asked.

'*Them,*' she said simply. 'Where I've been.'

'Where have you been?' Paul asked, throttling down and guiding the boat between the anchor lines of the fishing caiques.

Katie thought about it, then looked up at him. She grinned sadly. 'Heaven, I s'pose,' she said. 'I died and I crossed the great void and I went to Heaven. I was a bad girl, but I still went to Heaven and when I got there they made me promise something. They said I was special and that I had to come back. Some of me anyway. I'm a special case. I'm half here and half on the other side of the void. It's like being carved in two because there's a part of me on the other side of the void and it knows everything, but I can't access it. There's stuff trickling through in little tiny snippets and not much of it makes any sense. All I'm certain of is that I'm stuck between the two sides and I have to set everything to rights before I can get *unstuck.*'

Paul glanced at her and found that his belief in this came easily. The girl was dead and alive at the same time; caught between two states of existence. It didn't sound crazy at all (no crazier than some of the thoughts that had gone through his mind, anyway); it explained a great deal, in fact. What any sane rational person might have thought about it was neither here nor there because any sane and rational person would, by now, feel much the same way as Paul did. Ready to grasp at anything that fitted the situation.

'But they're also doing something to me. They're changing me, bit by bit. I have to go away soon so they can finish. Finish changing me into something I don't want to be. You know what I think that is, don't you?'

Paul nodded. He knew exactly what it was.

Katie sighed. 'They're changing me into an angel,' she said.

5

With these words ringing in his head like the tolling of great bells, Paul pointed the boat at a free patch of beach, gunned the engine, cut it and swivelled the outboard up out of the water so it wouldn't collect sand or get damaged. The boat hire guy would eventually get his property back and Paul's respect for the inner life of vehicles demanded that the boat was not returned damaged. And besides, the boat had served him well.

It crunched up on to the beach, and ignoring the open curiosity of the majority of the Greeks who were present, Paul leapt out and dragged it as far out of the water as possible, then found a decent-sized rock and tied the mooring rope around it.

'*Kalimera, kapitan!*' one of the fishermen called. He was sitting on the beach amongst a pile of netting, smoking. 'Circumnavigation?' he asked. A number of his colleagues apparently found this highly amusing. Paul glanced over at them, waved and smiled, hoping that no one arrived here in five minutes with questions to ask. *So much for keeping a low profile, poke*, his mental voice said.

The beach smelled of fish and tar and diesel fuel. As he helped Katie from the boat, he breathed deeply, but there was no smell of blood and no smell of trouble on its way.

'Will you be able to walk?' he asked her.

Katie looked up at him and treated him to the hurt smile she seemed to be so good at. He was certain she was unaware that it spoke directly to his heart. 'I knew how to walk for twenty-odd years,' she said in a voice as dry as dust, 'and forgot how to do it in less than a month. You'll have to help me. I could crawl like a baby but I don't have the balance or limb control. I'm going to have to re-learn. I don't seem to fit inside my body any more. I've gone the wrong shape or something.'

Paul helped her to her feet, lifted her out of the boat and set her down gently on the beach. He stood beside her and put his right arm around her slender waist and pulled her left arm around his, clamping her hand tightly to his hip with his own hand. 'Here we go,' he said. 'Right foot forward.'

'Bravo!' a heavily accented voice cheerily called from nearby. 'Romantico!' There was a half-hearted chorus of wolf-whistles and a couple of the fishermen clapped good-naturedly.

'It's like being inside a jump-suit that someone's sewn-up at the wrists and ankles,' Katie said, and an image of the black, pointed-limbed shadow-man jumped into Paul's mind.

They trudged unsteadily up the beach as the dawn broke, looking, Paul thought, rather like the only two survivors of some terrible maritime disaster – he with his torn and dirty tee shirt, skinned knuckles and cut forefinger that was still seeping blood and countless bruises and scratches, and Katie in her torn white dress, grazed knees and bruised throat.

There were plenty of cars parked along the road behind the beach, but they were still in full view of the fishermen so taking one of these would be imprudent – and besides, something inside Paul had identified with the group of fishermen; for some strange reason he'd felt safe on that beach, as if he was amongst friends. Most of the Greeks he'd come in contact with seemed eminently able to create this particular ambience and a part of Paul (a terribly lonely part which most of the time went unrecognised) suggested to him that when this was all over it might well be a good idea to come back here to stay; to carry on as he'd meant to when he'd been Stephen Miles. The possibility of this (as unlikely as it was to ever happen) was strangely comforting. Paul hadn't *belonged* anywhere or to anyone for longer than he cared to remember.

Unless you count our Katie here, his inner voice reminded him. *You've been trying to belong to her ever since you first heard her voice, if I recall correctly. And you know, of course, what belonging to her – or her belonging to you – will mean?*

343

Paul thought it might mean never getting the opportunity to settle in Greece – or anywhere. He had the distinct impression, in fact, that since yesterday he was seeing everything for the last time.

He put this thought out of his head. There was only one way to approach this, and that was to take it as he arrived at it.

Katie's head was lolling and her legs were moving as if she was very drunk and it was difficult to walk. He asked her if she was okay and got no response. When he tilted her head up, her eyes were closed (and her lips were dry and cracked which reminded him that she was dehydrating and really did need that water), but she was breathing, and when he moved on, she tried to match his step which presumably meant she was still in there somewhere.

There was a jumble of square whitewashed houses up ahead, and a parade of shops. Several roads turned off the main one that presumably led to the centre of Volos and Paul thought that one of these was going to bear fruit. The Greeks got up early and it was almost light, so he would have to be quick if he was going to take a car without being seen, but he thought he could do it. Having to take care of the girl while he was hunting was going to be a problem though and if anything went wrong, running away was going to be out of the question. He briefly considered sitting her down and leaving her somewhere safe until he came back with a car, then remembered what had happened when he went to steal the speedboat and jettisoned the idea. He didn't want to return to find Lulu Kaminsky waiting for him – or perhaps something worse.

He manoeuvred Katie down the first side street and smiled grimly. St Cunt was still up there somewhere, and he was awake and looking out for his own. Garages were apparently an unheard of thing throughout most of Greece; the street was lined with cars.

Not for the first time since he'd taken the boat, Paul thought of his tool bag which had contained all the goodies you needed to get into almost any car in the known universe. Stealing a car unequipped was a little like a carpenter trying to build a bookcase from a standing oak with his bare hands. Or it would have been if people were conscientious about security. The only crimes committed on Skiathos, Sandra Rook, the rep who had been unfortunate enough to have a certain Mr Miles in her last group, had said, were those committed by the tourists. She had also opined (accurately, Paul hoped) that the general level of theft in Greece was a great deal lower than that in most of Europe. He was depending on it, because if you didn't expect to get your car stolen, you were going to be a lot less likely to bother with the rigmarole of locking it each time you got out.

The first car he tried was a Subaru pick-up with something that looked like the tasselled hem of a curtain framing the top edge of the windscreen. The owner of this vehicle had apparently not heard what Sandra Rook had had to say about the crime rate in this country because both doors were very firmly locked and both side windows were wound right up tight.

Paul walked Katie down the line of cars, trying doors as he passed and cursing silently to himself. His heart leapt when he saw the dusty red Citroën BX16 and for a moment he was certain that it was *his* Citroën and that, like Trigger would have done for Roy Rodgers, it had somehow *known* and sped here to save him.

But although this Citroën was easily as old as his, it was not his. For one thing, it had had a far rougher life than any car of his had ever had. The paintwork was dull and both the front wings were dented. The wiper blade was missing and there was a thin rind of street dust across the screen which looked as if it hadn't been touched for months. It was left-hand drive, too. Paul took Katie to the front door and tried it, knowing already that it would be locked, but fascinated by the coincidence. The car possessed the same smell as his had done – he could detect this from the outside – and the upholstery was the same grey shade. *It wasn't left here for you*, Paul's *farmer-oppozite* voice cut in before he could entertain any flights of fancy about how this might have happened. *It's just an ordinary common or garden*

Citroën BX16 that belongs to some Greek who abandoned it here when it broke down because he's having to get parts shipped from France. The owner probably lives in this house right here and if you hang about admiring his car for very much longer he'll be out here wanting to know what you're doing.

But Paul wasn't listening. He was dragging Katie to the back of the car to see if it had the suffix TRS and an idea was lighting in his mind.

And there it was. It was a BX16 *TRS*. His heart started to race and Paul knew that if he held out his hand and studied it, it would be bouncing with arterial pressure. He half expected to see a sticker in the back window which would be the Greek equivalent of DON'T MESS WITH THE BEST, but was undaunted to find there was nothing in the back window but a hairline crack.

The battery will be flat anyway, his goad informed him. *Flat as a pancake. And even if it isn't, the car won't start.*

But the idea he'd had was stronger than all these doubts and now he'd had it there was no going back. He knew, without having to check, that every car on the street was going to be locked. In spite of Sandra's glowing report, this was an area in which people were security conscious. The areas around ports in every country of the world had greater crime rates than the average.

It's a waste of time!

'We'll see,' Paul muttered. The idea sounded good. Very good indeed.

If Katie had woken up and told him that there was a distant look in his suddenly very dark eyes, a deep furrow between his eyebrows that hadn't been there a moment ago and a strange, twisted smile on his face, Paul wouldn't have been the least bit surprised.

He was a man who loved his work.

6

Andreas Thrivilas, the seventy-two-year-old fisherman who

had enquired of the Englishman if he had made a circumnavigation, had grown up in Crete. He did not hate the Germans *en masse* for what he had watched the Nazi soldiers do to his father and mother (and a great deal of the other villagers) during the war, just as he did not hate his fellow Greeks for what one or two of them had done to him during the Generals' Regime. He hated the German soldiers who had slaughtered forty-six of his village's people and he hated the two men who had subjected him to unbelievably brutal torture while he was jailed in Athens during the Regime, but when, as a child, you'd watched people shot for nothing, and when you later found yourself with four of your toes and four of your fingers lopped off (by someone you *knew*, for the Lord's sake!) for no good reason either, a little hatred was only normal.

The latter crime against him had been avenged though (by another, he was glad to say), and in a way, the earlier crime had been avenged too, so his hatred was a small, hard shell in the back of his mind and it wasn't directed at any one person. What it *was* directed towards were the people who would shuck off their humanity like an old coat in return for a little power. These people who would turn into torturers and murderers in return for a little 'authority'. For Andreas, this was the true essence of evil.

During his later years as a political activist, before he gave it all up for a calm life at the mercy of the ocean, Andreas had become able to identify this potential for evil in his fellow humans where it was present. It was not present in everyone, but there had been enough of it in enough of his colleagues to discourage his own quest for power.

But life wasn't all dark. Andreas was also able to identify the *good* men. Almost all his circle of sea-going colleagues seemed to have this quality. The two strange English who had beached their boat here and wandered off like drunken lovers had been in possession of it too.

Andreas glanced over at the boat and nodded. This wasn't the first time people had made it here from Skiathos in one of

Antony's little motorboats, and he doubted it would be the last. It was, however, the first time they had arrived so early in the morning, and had tipped the outboard up out of the water and properly secured the boat. The Englishman had had respect for the vessel and that was good. Andreas told himself that when he was certain the two people weren't coming back (usually they returned half an hour later and then ran out of fuel at sea trying to get back, but these had looked as if they'd intended a one-way trip only) he would ring Antony and tell him the boat was safe. No one would bother with the police because by the time the paperwork was all done, you would have lost two working days. He glanced over at the boat again, then turned back to the two men who were striding down the beach towards him and his colleagues.

They were Germans – he could tell, even from this distance – and they weren't German tourists who, for the most part, felt embarrassed about the war and carried on as if it had never happened, although from time to time they seemed to treat Greeks with a little extra respect. These particular Germans looked as if they would be very comfortable in jackboots.

'*Kalimera!*' Andreas greeted them. Although appearances could sometimes be deceptive, he didn't expect them to be in this particular case.

'Where did this boat come from?' one of the Germans demanded as soon as they were close enough for speech.

During his time of being a sea-dog Andreas had noted a kind of hive mind amongst sailors. At times there seemed to be an unspoken means of communication between them. It was probably simply because they were a tightly knit brotherhood, but Andreas preferred to think there was more to it than this. Whatever it was, it was working its magic now. None of the others had paid the slightest attention to the approach of the two men and none of them looked up now. The message had gone around: *Leave it to Andreas*, and that was what everyone intended to do. But there was a tension among the men too, a tension that hadn't been there earlier.

'*Kalimera!*' Andreas called again, pretending not to understand. He could speak German fluently, but there was no need for these two to know that unless he wanted them to.

The two men looked so similar they might have been twins. They also looked exactly like the kind of person Andreas hated. Two people who had sold their souls for power.

'*Kalimera*,' one of them said, '*Sprechen Sie Deutsch?*'

'Little piece of,' Andreas replied in German. 'Perhaps I'm better English to speak?'

'It's okay, Josef,' one of the men said quickly in German, 'the dumb fuck doesn't know enough German to understand us.'

Andreas smiled vacantly and sunnily. There were a variety of sharp implements on his boat and a part of him wished they were all currently protruding from these arrogant bastards. All he would have to do was call and inside three minutes the minced carcasses would be on their way to sea to feed the fishes.

'How long here has this boat been?' the one that wasn't called Josef asked carefully.

The trouble with English, Andreas noted, still smiling, was that foreigners tended to transpose it until it was barely recognisable. English was a mountainous language to learn and these two bastards were still in its foothills.

'Why do you ask?' he enquired.

'What do they want, Andreas?' Yiannis called from the boat where he was unloading fish.

'Apart from a severe beating, it remains to be seen,' he replied in Greek. Yiannis chuckled. 'Just say the word!' he called happily.

'What did he say?' the one called Josef asked suspiciously.

'I asked him what time the boat came in. He says about two hours ago. I was here but I don't have a watch.' He showed them his wrist. 'When the sun goes down, I wake up and go to work,' he said. 'When it's daylight and I'm tired, I sleep. Why do I need the time?'

'It is impossible,' Josef said. He turned to his brother and

349

spoke in German. 'They say two hours ago, Erich. They could not have arrived two hours ago. It's too quick. Half an hour maybe.'

'Why should they tell us lies?' the one called Erich replied in German.

'I don't know,' Josef replied, 'but they are certainly lying.'

'Do you suppose they know about Dekker and the girl?' Erich asked.

'Know what? What *can* they know? Do you suppose these people have been visited by a host of heavenly angels in fiery chariots who brought them glad tidings? These are *fishermen*, Erich.'

'They might know something!'

'They can't!'

'Dekker might have told them something, or the girl. They might be trying to protect them.'

Andreas followed this exchange like a man at Wimbledon following a particularly exciting rally between the number one and number two cedes. Although he had trouble with the word 'chariots' and the word 'host' he was able to get the drift of the conversation and the phrase, *And Gods walked in the lands* slipped, unbidden, into his mind. He felt a certain resentment about the denigration of his chosen profession, though – Joseph and Jesus had both been carpenters, hadn't they? And some of the disciples had been fishermen.

'The girl is in no state to tell anyone anything, and what do you suppose Dekker might have said?, "I need you to help me because this girl has become a channel between this world and the next, through which terrible or holy things may be drawn"? And do you suppose they would have thought him anything more than a lunatic?'

Erich shrugged.

'These are just stupid fishermen who are telling us lies because we are foreigners,' Josef said.

'Old man,' he said in English, 'about this you must very carefully think. How long ago did the boat arrive?'

The two Germans seemed to have the knack of rubbing him up the wrong way, Andreas realised. First they had knocked fishermen (some of whom had been amongst the twelve, in case they'd forgotten), then they had intimated that fishermen were stupid, and now they'd called him *old*, which he most certainly was not. But the big, beaming grin did not leave his face because throughout his life Andreas had wanted to witness divine intervention. He had prayed for it during his childhood days when people not unlike these two had lined up and shot forty-six people he knew, and he had prayed for it again when he was imprisoned and under torture. It hadn't happened on those occasions, and since Andreas had reached the conclusion that it wasn't going to and thought that being on the sea in a thunderstorm was the closest he would ever get in this life to seeing the hand of the creator at work. But now he'd heard a second magical phrase and in his mind it joined the first and jangled there like Christmas bells: . . . *this girl has become a channel between this world and the next through which terrible or holy things may be drawn* . . . *And Gods walked in the lands.*

Andreas felt very crazy and ten times as jubilant. The man – Dekker (and that was a name he would never forget) – was the guardian of a girl who could bring forth Gods. And these men evidently wanted to stop that from happening. But the girl was the important one. Andreas had spoken to two very special people this morning on this very beach and he only knew the name of the man. He *had* to know the name of the woman. *I have truly seen the divine hand at work*, Andreas thought. He felt a strong urge to follow where they had gone and smiled at himself; it was evidently in the genes of fishermen. He knew how to pay for this glimpse of something very special, and that was by protecting the two people.

'How long ago?' Josef wanted to know. 'Two hours it can't have been. Less it must be.'

'Perhaps . . . an hour,' Andreas said.

Josef nodded at Erich. *Now we're getting somewhere*, the expression said.

'But I feel it was longer,' Andreas replied, willing Dekker and the woman to be away from here. 'Two men came,' he said. 'Young men. Boys really.'

Erich looked at Josef in astonishment.

'In this boat?' Josef demanded.

Andreas nodded. Each passing second they were a second further away.

'Andre?'

Andreas glanced over towards the boat. There were perhaps fifteen faces turned towards him now.

Andreas shrugged and waved that all was okay.

And when he looked back, found himself staring down the barrel of a Walther PPK. These guns had once been all the rage. It was the fault of the writer and film-makers of James Bond. Andreas' heart lifted a beat, but he was not frightened. He had stared down the barrels of bigger guns than this in his time and refused to speak. He had, in fact, had the barrels of bigger hand-guns than this one thrust so far down his throat he had gagged and so far into his anus he had screamed. And he had not spoken. And he was not dead.

'Who in the boat was?' Josef asked. 'A girl and a man?'

Andreas smiled. And nodded. 'I spoke to them,' he said. 'And if you tell me the name of the girl, I will tell you what they said to me.'

Andreas didn't care whether they shot him or not. If he could only discover the name of the woman, he would die a happy man.

'The girl is named Kate,' Josef said.

Andreas nodded. Kate was a good enough name for a woman who could bring forth demons or Gods. Dekker and Kate. They were on the side of the just Gods, he knew. He hoped Dekker would be able to fight like ten men as his name seemed to suggest, because it looked like he was going to have to.

The gun moved closer to his nose. Andreas didn't look over Erich's shoulder because he didn't want to make a move that might alert the two men – or blow his head off – but on the periphery of his vision a number of Greek fishermen, moving in unison due to that hive mind they seemed to possess, had silently noted the weapon and were just as silently closing in on the two Germans.

'What did they say to you?' Josef asked.

Andreas thought about it. He didn't know which way Dekker and the girl intended to go – or how they intended to get there – but they obviously knew they were being pursued and it would surely be a good thing if he sent the Germans in the wrong direction. But which way could he send them? They had come from Skiathos through the night, so they had travelled north. Andreas expected they were heading for the airport at Thessaloniki in order to get out of the country, but he wasn't sure. He didn't want to send the Germans south in case that was where they had actually gone. His friends were closing in and if he could just stall the Germans for a few more seconds he wasn't going to have to tell them anything at all, except, with any luck, goodbye.

'*Schnell!*' Josef said. '*Hurry!*' He pushed the Walther against Andreas' cheek.

'JOSEF!' Erich suddenly cried.

Andreas didn't know what had alerted Erich because the fishermen had made no sound, but then it was only academic because Erich knew and he was reacting. Andreas had never seen anyone move so fast. One moment the man Andreas had come to think of as the less intelligent one of the pair was standing passively beside Josef, a frown furrowed deep in his face as if he didn't quite understand what was going on, and the next, there was a gun in his hand and he was turning and dropping to his knees.

Erich fired and Yiannis fell.

Afterwards there was no sound except the echoing *crack!* of the gun shot.

Josef had not moved a muscle, but a smile had spread across his face.

'Lie down everyone,' Erich said with hardly a trace of a

German accent at all. 'Or I will shoot you all.'

Andreas had expected pandemonium. In his mind he had seen the fishermen scatter and run – some of them towards him and his German friends – and he had seen them being taken down one by one. But this didn't happen and as his friends all dropped to their faces on the beach, he thought he knew why.

It was because of the hive mind. When Erich had fired, Andreas had suddenly known what to say to satisfy the Germans. It had arrived inside his head as if the sound of the shot had driven it there and Andreas knew it was *right* and that it was going to save a great deal of killing. And the strange link between him and his friends had somehow told them this too.

'They said they needed to get to Delfi,' Andreas said. 'They wanted to get there quickly. To the Oracle. I don't know why.'

Josef nodded. 'What else?' he demanded.

'I gave them my car. I have a cousin in Delfi who will collect it from the car park they are going to leave it in and return it. They are already on their way and they have a half-hour start.'

'Why to Delfi?' Josef demanded.

Erich glanced over his shoulder. 'Because of the place,' he said in German. 'Because it's a weak place like the one on Skiathos. They are going to try to bring another angel through.'

'Delfi is dead,' Josef complained.

'Perhaps they can make it work once.' Erich said. 'We can't let it happen.'

'I think he's lying,' Josef said.

Erich looked back again. 'We can't take the chance!' he hissed.

Josef stared into Andreas' face. 'I would kill you, old man, for what you have done!'

Andreas saw his finger tighten on the trigger and for a crazy moment wanted to correct him and tell him that what he meant was, *I am going to kill you for what you have done.*

But he didn't speak. Andreas was content now and prepared to die. He'd waited all his life to see the hand of God at work, and he had done better than that. He had not only witnessed it, but he had actually *helped* in fulfilling God's wish. This was a good enough reason to have lived a long life and he was satisfied. If he was going to meet his maker he would be able to stand there and say, 'I did what I could,' and be proud of it. There was a part of him that wished he really had been able to give Dekker and Kate his car. Then his part would indeed have been rounded, seamless and complete. As one of his English friends might have said, *That would have just about put the tin lid on it.*

For one last time, Andreas looked at his beach and his friends – including Yiannis who, he hoped, would be waiting to meet him on the other side, and then he closed his eyes.

'Leave it!' Erich said in German. 'You!' Andreas heard him shout. 'Give me your car keys!'

Andreas' hand automatically went to his jacket pocket, and he paused when he remembered he'd just told the Germans he'd given his car to Dekker and the girl. Even if he gave the Germans the car it probably wouldn't get them very far. It probably wouldn't even start. It had been running badly the last time he'd driven it, and that had been five months ago so the battery was bound to be flat. He didn't much need a car these days and if he hadn't kept getting the feeling that he might need it one day he would have sold it long ago.

'Which car?' Erich suddenly said, and Andreas was surprised to hear a voice answer, 'The Strada. Up there!'

Andreas opened his eyes and was surprised again. He was no longer staring down the barrel of the Walther and the two Germans were hurrying up towards the road where George's Fiat Strada was parked. He hadn't heard either of them move away from him. George was up on his knees pointing the way. He looked incredibly angry. All the other fishermen were quietly picking themselves up – in unison.

The third – and most stupendous – surprise was that Yiannis was getting up too. He was shot through the left shoulder and his jacket was soaked in his blood but he was alive.

Andreas quietly thanked God.

Someone threw a rock in the direction of the Strada as it departed and George complained.

'Stop bickering and get the police and an ambulance for Yiannis!' Andreas shouted, suddenly feeling very good to be taking charge.

7

With that strange grin fixed to his face, Paul walked Katie back to the driver's door of the dusty red Citroën, knowing it was going to work. It wasn't a method he had practised, or even done more than once, but Paul knew deep in his heart that it would work.

Back in the bad old days, when he had still lived in a big house in London with a bad woman and things had looked settled, if not quite rosy, Amy had accomplished the impossible by locking herself out of her car. The car in question was the red Citroën BX16 TRS to which Arlington Stephen Jones had taken such exception.

The car had electric central locking, which meant that you couldn't lock yourself out since you needed to put the key in the lock and turn it to lock all the doors. You could lock yourself *in* simply by pressing down one of the lock buttons alongside the windows, but unless something went horribly wrong, you could get out again just as easily by pulling the button back up. There were only two good ways to lock yourself out of this particular car, and both of them involved locking it and then losing a key. If you had two keys (which Amy did), then locked the car and lost a key, all you had to do was take the other key from where you kept it (on a hook in the kitchen in this case). But when Paul arrived home on this particular day, for some reason which was never clearly explained (when Amy got mad, the tough retreated – if they knew what was good for them), she had locked the first key inside the car with the second then lost the second. For the sake of any passing policeman, there was, of course, no tool in the house that could be remotely construed as being fit for the purpose of illegally entering vehicles. After a heated discussion with Amy who didn't want even the merest mark on the car and who wanted to call out a mechanic from the main dealer, presumably because she didn't trust her husband's skills, Paul had said, 'Okay, you do whatever pleases you,' and had slapped the door of the car. He didn't slap it hard and he wasn't even facing it at the time.

And with their characteristic *sher-clonk* noise the locks had popped up.

Paul had been delighted. After the key had been retrieved (and Amy had retreated), he had spent the better part of an hour trying to reproduce the phenomenon. He found the palm print he had made, and targeted it, and slapped the door again in the same place and with the same amount of force. It had not worked again.

But now, standing there beside the other Citroën BX16 TRS, Paul was certain he could do it again. All he was going to have to do was slap in the right place with the right amount of force.

He turned his back to the door, closed his eyes and hit the door just below the lock.

When nothing happened, he turned and inspected his hand print in the dust and told himself that perhaps he ought to hit it a little lower. There was a car coming down the street and Paul waited for it to go past before he tried again.

Nothing happened.

The battery's flat, just like I thought, his goad said.

Paul ignored this negative part of him because just lately it had managed to be almost one hundred percent wrong, and if you wanted proof, he was not dead, he was not mad and the speedboat had not drowned him.

He slapped the car again, and in spite of the clear need he felt to hit it harder (because you didn't *decrease* the force you were using when the desired result wasn't forthcoming, but *increased* it), pulled the blow at the last moment. A child, patted this gently, would have thought you were pleased with it. The Cindy dog wouldn't even have awoken from her after-noon nap.

And, apparently, the car didn't notice it either.

Paul turned round to see if he'd struck the door in the right place, not listening to his goad telling him that it wasn't going to work, because it *was* going to work and he was going to be driving away in this car inside five minutes even if it meant taking a rock to the side window in order to get in.

'Come on, darlin',' he muttered and thought he saw a tiny vibration shimmer through the car. It was probably still settling after the slaps he'd given it.

Now the locks are going to pop, he thought.

And was surprised when they didn't.

'What do you want, a magic spell!' he asked the car. 'I'm not going to hurt you. Much. Now come on and open!'

So much for animism, poke.

He placed the palm of his hand on the door panel where he thought the spot was, then jiggled it to one side until it felt comfortable. Then he gave a little push.

And the locks popped up.

Paul didn't congratulate himself. He was either very lucky or very skilled or a combination of both but there wasn't time to think about it because he'd just heard a noise – from the direc-tion of the beach, he thought – which had sounded very much like a gunshot. There could have been a thousand reasons for that noise but Paul knew that nine hundred and ninety-nine of them were going to be the wrong ones. Someone – proba-bly the person or persons who had seen fit to burn down the Xinaris apartments and set fire to Sandra the rep for no good reason – had found the speedboat and was attempting to shoot information out of the fishermen down there.

He hustled Katie round to the passenger door, and ignor-ing the smell of sand, dust and something that might have been gone-off fish that was billowing out of the car, sat her down in the seat. He tried to put a belt on her, gave up when he realised it was severed down at the business end, and scooted back round to the driver's side and opened the door as far as it would go. He didn't want to have to do this and it hurt his professional pride, but there wasn't going to be time for a clean job now. He was going to have to put his foot against the bar of the steering wheel and push until the lock broke, then he was going to have to kick the plastic nacelle that housed the ignition switch until it broke and he could get at the wires. It was the kind of 'joyrider' trick that he hated and the car would probably remember it, but it was the only way.

He leaned in, took the wheel and wound it away from him, expecting the steering lock to click into place. It wasn't until the wheel had gone through almost a hundred and eighty degrees and the tyres were scrubbing against the kerb that Paul realised – with a serendipitous shock which was both surprising and pleasurable – that the lock was either broken already or else it had been removed.

He leaned back to kick at the plastic housing around the ignition – had, in fact, jockeyed his foot into the right position for the kick – when he noticed the wires dangling out of the hole beside the ignition switch. For a moment he saw bared copper ends, just waiting to be touched together, decided that someone had known he was coming and wondered why they hadn't just left the doors open for him, then the truth dawned.

The wires were not hanging loose just waiting to be twisted together and touched with another which would turn the starter – they ran down beneath the nacelle and were held in place with a loop of insulating tape that was peeling away. This car had either been broken into previously, or its owner had been suffering from problems with the ignition and combined lock. The lock had been broken and the ignition . . .

Paul got in the car, still not believing the sunny mood in which St Cunt must have woken up today, and groped under the plastic housing.

. . . was worked by the small, uninsulated toggle switch which was dangling beside the handle that opened the bonnet.

Paul drew the switch out, held it in one hand and clicked it to the first position with the other. On the dashboard the warning lights lit. The radio began to play – Puccini's *Un bel di*, again, Paul noted with a chill. He only hoped it really was going to turn out to be One Fine Day, and not one fine nightmare as it had in his dream.

He held his breath and moved the switch to the next position – which was sprung, just as he had hoped – and the position which worked the starter. He held it there as the engine was spun, now not quite so certain that things were going to turn out okay after all. The guy – or guys – with the gun couldn't be too far behind him now, and the Citroën didn't sound exactly like it was dying to go to work. The battery was pretty tired and the engine only spun slowly.

These Citroëns had auto-chokes and according to the manual which came with them you weren't supposed to put your foot on the accelerator while trying to start them under any circumstances. The manual didn't exactly say, *You touch the gas: you walk!* but that was close enough to what it meant. But Amy's old car – the one he had been allowed to take when she got her new Merc – had always responded kindly to a touch of throttle when it was being reluctant and he could think of no reason why this one shouldn't react in a similar way.

He let the switch back to rest the battery for a few seconds, pressed the throttle pedal down about an inch and tried again.

And in a cloud of blue smoke the car started. It didn't run evenly, but it had been standing a long time and Paul thought it might settle down once the cobwebs had been blown out of it. Under the bonnet the hydraulic pump was clicking like a bastard and for a second Paul thought the car's suspension was gone. Then the back of the car creaked up off the ground like an ancient camel might have done, and after a great deal of extremely loud clicking from the pump, the front eventually followed suit.

'Here we go then,' Paul said, glancing over at Katie whose eyes were still closed. He hit the clutch, selected first and the car slid gently out of its parking space.

As the car nosed out of the junction on to the road that ran past the beach, Paul saw a blue Fiat rapidly pulling out of a space back down where they'd left the boat. Its driver wound the wheel round hard and the Fiat did a tyre-smoking one hundred and eighty degrees, bumping up, then down the kerb on the far side of the road, and sped away into the distance.

Paul stopped the car and stayed where he was, watching. It was dangerous to wait here in a stolen car, but going out on to the road might be even more dangerous. He was pretty sure who was driving that Fiat and he wanted it out of sight before he drove away. Because one of the two people who were inside it might just be looking back when the Citroën pulled out of the side-turning and one of them might think that the only other car moving on the road at the moment was worth investigating.

But there was another reason Paul glanced in the rear-view mirror to make sure the road was clear behind him, and that was because something told him that the Fiat would be heading back this way in a moment anyway and he trusted this feeling.

In his time, Paul had read a great many articles on the psychology of driving and knew the theory that the moment a person got behind the wheel of a car, that person would undergo an instant, and sometimes radical, change of personality. Mild housewives could become power-drunk maniacs, respectable businessmen would suddenly revert to something akin to the law of the jungle. Seventeen-year-old kids would try to drive you off the road. Paul had seen the process in action many times – although never as vividly drawn as the picture of utter lunacy Arlington Stephen Jones had described. One of Paul's most closely guarded secrets (and, he thought, one of the reasons he was still alive today) was that once behind the wheel of an automobile, he too underwent a change of personality. He didn't become a maniac who wanted to carve people up (although he could and would do it if absolutely necessary), but he did change. Once he was behind the wheel, he became a cold and steely driving machine which seemed to be attached to the soul of the car in some strange way that enabled him to push it to the edge of its performance envelope (and sometimes beyond) without mishap.

But there was more to it than that. When he drove, his perceptions seemed to be heightened so that he could think ahead – not just in the normal way, but as if he could see into the very near future. He would know where gaps in the traffic were going to appear and what other drivers were going to do next – even before those other drivers made those things happen. When the cops had been tailing him he'd known everything that was going to happen, occasionally as much as twenty seconds in advance – including what result the actions he'd taken *now* would have. Some of this might have been the result of many years of driving, of course, but there was more to it than that. When Paul got behind the wheel, he became *aware*.

And that awareness was telling him that in a moment that blue Fiat Strada was going to do another one-eighty turn and come right back towards him.

He waited until he saw the car's brake light flash red, then took his foot off the clutch and allowed the Citroën to glide back into the side street. He parked it tight against the kerb, but left the engine running, and leaned across to Katie. She didn't respond when he called her name, so he wound her seat into the lowered position so that she wouldn't be visible if the people in the Fiat happened to look this way. Then he stabbed at the button for the electric window on his side. The motor protested and then the window freed itself and rolled down.

Paul lay down with his head in Katie's cool lap and listened.

The Fiat zipped by a few seconds later.

Paul waited until the noise of the car had faded to a distant hum, then sat up and drove back out into the road. He had no idea where the people in the Fiat might have been heading and he just hoped that it wasn't going to turn out to be the same place where he and Katie were headed.

The Citroën's petrol tank was half empty – or, if you wanted to take the optimistic view, half full. It would get them quite a way, but Paul was short of money and Katie possessed nothing except the tattered remains of the clothing she was wearing, which meant he was going to have to rob someone. He thought of his back pocket again, where his bank and credit card ought to be, and shook his head. Taking money from someone wasn't something he was looking forward to, but it was going to have to be done. And if it had to be done, he would do it.

Paul turned right on to the main road, following in the Fiat's tyre tracks and only now realising that he had no map and only a vague idea of the Greek mainland's geography. It came down in a rough vee shape – he knew that – and it was joined on to Yugoslavia in the north. He was pretty certain that Albania and another one of those previously communist countries, perhaps Hungary or Bulgaria, had taken a hand in drawing up the borders, but he wasn't sure where they were or how easy they would be to cross into. The easiest border had to be Yugoslavia, and from there it would be a straight drive all the way across to France and England, but that would be what they expected him to do. The alternative was to try to get across to Italy on a boat and take it from there. But whatever way you looked at it, there were going to be problems. Like having no passports and no money, if you wanted examples. Paul didn't know how easy it was to cross borders in these fine days of a United Europe, but he did know that the last time he'd taken a car into France for Freddie they'd scrutinised his passport very thoroughly indeed.

Italy was probably a good bet for gaining some time.

Paul changed up to fourth, smiled as the car finally saw fit to run smoothly, and took the road that was signposted Larissa and Trikala because another one of the talents that manifested itself the moment he climbed into a car was an almost infallible sense of direction. He would have to head west if he was going to find the coast and then get a ferry over to Italy, and the road to Larissa and Trikala would almost certainly take them west.

Until Katie began to stir, Paul had forgotten about the water he had promised to get her, just as he'd forgotten his own thirst (and you could add hunger, pain and fatigue to that list too).

Things like that tended to happen when he began to drive.

9

Paul used the last of his money buying two bottles of water in a supermarket on the outskirts of Larissa. He was now the proud owner of a ten drachma piece, his lucky ten pfennig piece (which, all things considered, hadn't been working too well just lately) and two bottles of very cold water that sloshed invitingly as he walked. The water had been in the shop's chill cabinet and once he was out in the sunshine, condensation misted the bottle. Paul had intended to give both bottles to Katie because he thought that her need was likely to be greater than his, but his dehydrated cells did not agree. Paul bit down on his need – there was no chance of getting any more water (or any more *anything*, come to that) for a while – and Katie's metabolism was running in the realms of mystery. Depriving her of one of the bottles of water might be a very bad thing. There was no way of telling.

It was only a hundred yards back to the car and if Paul hadn't found himself raising the bottle to his parched lips to moisten them with the condensation, he might actually have made it. Now his cracked lips were damp there was no going back.

He pulled the top off the bottle and swallowed a mouthful of water, vowing that this would be the only one. The water vanished into his body like a single squall of rain would disappear into the sands of the Kalahari desert. *More!* his body screamed.

Paul fought a brief mental battle and lost. If Katie needed

more water than he had left, he would get it for her. If he was going to protect her he was going to have to keep himself able to do the job, and if that meant drinking the water, that was going to have to happen.

And if Katie needed more water he would get it for her. He was going to have to rob someone soon anyway; bringing the moment forward wasn't going to make much difference.

The first litre bottle was empty by the time he got back to the car.

Katie couldn't hold her bottle. She reached out for it as Paul climbed back into the car (now starting to feel very tired and hungry) and dropped it as he handed it to her. Paul picked it up and gave it to her again and again it slipped from the grasp.

Katie gave him a wan smile. 'I can't work my fingers properly,' she rasped. 'I can't get myself into them yet. I sometimes think I never will.'

'You'll be okay, sweetheart,' Paul assured her as he retrieved the bottle again. 'Just give it time.'

Katie was flagging badly. She didn't seem able to move properly at all and Paul thought that she might be on her way out again. Her head was lolling as if her neck muscles were too weak to hold it up. 'Is it time?' he asked and tried hard to ignore the cold knot of fear in his intestines. Just before they'd stopped to get the water she had told him she would know when it was time for her to leave again and had suggested that he tie her up, 'In case anything happens after I've gone back.' She hadn't been able to hazard a guess at what might happen when she left her body, but Paul had – and he didn't relish the thought of another visitation by Lulu Kaminsky while he was driving at seventy miles an hour.

Katie shook her head. It rolled around like it belonged to a paralytic drunk. 'Not yet,' she said. 'Things to do first. Water. *Please.*'

He tore the seal from the bottle, put his left hand at the back of Katie's neck and supported her head while he held the bottle to her lips.

She coughed out the first mouthful and moaned that she couldn't swallow. Paul looked at the dark imprints of his fingers on her throat and thought he knew why. 'Try again,' he said. 'Don't *try* to swallow, just let it happen. It's supposed to be a reflex action. Just relax and let it happen.'

This time Katie's mouth filled up with water and overflowed. She looked at him with an expression of such exquisite despair that Paul felt as though something inside him was tearing. His heart ached for her. Somewhere in the back of his mind his goad was complaining that this wasn't supposed to happen, but he ignored it. He put the bottle between his thighs, pushed Katie's chin up and stroked her throat the way he'd done with the Cindy dog to make her swallow her worm tablets. The action was supposed to stimulate the swallowing reflex. He didn't know if it would work on humans (and it hadn't worked particularly well with the dog who would dutifully swallow and then gob out the tablet) but it was worth a try.

Katie swallowed.

Then she coughed.

Then the corners of her mouth flickered into a brief smile. 'More,' she said.

It took the better part of twenty minutes to get the whole litre into her but her swallowing reflex returned early on. Paul made her sip slowly because he wanted the water to stay down. After the first five minutes Katie's dry, rasping cough turned into a moist, loose cough (which he supposed was pretty good for a person he'd choked to death last night) and after the second five minutes he felt her neck muscles come back to life and take back the weight of her head. Paul did not remove his hand from the cool nape of her neck and did not ask himself why.

He wasn't sure whether or not he was imagining it, but as Katie drained the water her skin seemed to take on a new lustre and her features seemed to change from being slightly pinched and taut to being . . . healthy – although healthy wasn't a good word to use in these circumstances, he supposed. But the overall effect was that she seemed to bloom, like a cut and fading

366

rose suddenly having had the dying process reversed.

By the time the water had gone, something indefinable had changed about her. If she had been pretty when he picked her up, that quality had increased somewhat. She still wasn't the thing of aching beauty he'd seen in his dream but she looked a great deal better for the water. A part of Paul began to feel terribly guilty about drinking the other litre.

'Do you need more?' he asked when the bottle was empty.

Katie thought about it. 'Soon,' she said. 'Not yet.'

Her voice sounded a lot less harsh and scratchy now and Paul was thankful for that. Her throat ought to have been badly damaged after what he'd done to her, but it looked as though that hadn't happened. Paul didn't ask himself why, just accepted it. It was easier that way.

'I forgot,' she said, favouring him with that wan smile again.

'Forgot what?' Paul said, starting the car.

'Forgot to drink,' she said. 'I don't think I've drunk anything since it happened. That's a very long time. Too long to last without water. I'm lucky I didn't . . .'

Her face fell. 'Oh,' she said.

Paul looked away, put the Citroën into first and let out the clutch.

10

Paul thought it was Dickens' Mr Micawber who had always claimed that 'something will turn up' although he wasn't sure. Whichever character it was didn't matter; what mattered was that the sentiment was correct.

The thing that Paul had been waiting for turned up in the hills on the far side of a tiny village called Trigona. That thing was a tiny white Opel Corsa hire car which was parked on the side of the road. The people who had been in it were a little way ahead of it busily snapping off shots of the view.

The couple were in their mid-twenties, Paul thought, and probably American since they were both wearing baseball caps.

The guy was about five ten and looked quite athletic – as if he'd played a lot of football in college and had tried to keep himself in shape afterwards. The girl was a little shorter and wearing shiny stretch leggings but looked just as fit.

Paul stopped the Citroën behind the Corsa and got out. The girl glanced over at him then went back to taking her pictures.

Paul went to the driver's door of the Corsa, opened it and withdrew the keys which they had carelessly left in the ignition. People believed their holiday representatives and didn't expect to be robbed while they were in Greece.

'Hey, Scott!' the girl called in a shrill American accent, but Scott had noticed what was going on at the same moment as his girl and was hurrying back. Paul hoped their minds would now be draining of logical thought as they perceived the threat because both of them had cameras and it would be easy to take a shot of him to show the police. He could take their films, of course, but he didn't really want it to get that nasty. He didn't like face to face robbery at all, and he had no desire to hurt either of these two.

But if it came to it, he knew he could and would.

Scott didn't look like a man who saw a lot of violence or one who was likely to cause any if there was a way around it. He had an open, honest face that was now showing two parts fear and one part outrage.

'What're you doing, man?' he demanded as he hurried up to where Paul stood beside his car.

'He has the keys,' the girl said. 'Give them back!'

Scott didn't try to take the keys, but stopped about five feet away from Paul.

'I'm sorry about this,' Paul said, 'but I'm in a great deal of trouble and I need help.'

'Just gimme the keys and we'll talk about it,' Scott said reasonably, holding out his hand. He didn't look as if he truly expected to get the keys back and he wasn't going to be surprised.

'I haven't got the time,' Paul said. 'Except to say that I need money. I don't want to hurt either of you. I just want some money.'

'We don't have any,' Scott said, 'only plastic.'

Paul shook his head. 'Just give me the cash you have and the dollar traveller's cheques. You'll get reimbursed for the cheques. The alternative is that I drive away with your keys. It's quite a hike back to the last town and it's a very hot day.' Paul knew the threat wasn't particularly convincing – these two looked as if they could walk that far before breakfast – but he was hoping they didn't want the hassle. If they thought they could cope with it, he would have to get a little heavier.

Scott's face became thoughtful and Paul knew that he was weighing up his chances. He also knew that if the charge came, it was likely to be the kind of charge an ex-American footballer would make. A kind of forward-facing rugby tackle. This guy might have been well muscled but he wasn't a street-fighter.

'You don't understand,' Scott said, sounding as if his patience was wearing very thin and that he did indeed fancy his chances. 'I just told you, we have no cash. Our cheques are back at the hotel, too.'

Paul didn't need the furtive sideways glance that Scott made to inform him that the woman was approaching him from behind – a part of him had been aware of her progress as she snuck out of his field of vision. He'd thought that she was going to attempt to make a run for it, but a glance at her determined expression had changed his mind. This was one of those women who didn't want to be typecast; who had long ago decided that the role of victim wasn't one she was going to adopt. This was a woman who had probably started off going to self-defence classes so that any passing rapist who mistook her for an easy mark would rue the day of his birth, and who had excelled and then followed with karate classes. This was a woman who believed she was about to perform a perfectly executed round-house kick to his kidneys while her boyfriend or husband or whatever he was charged in from the front. Paul felt the pressure rise inside him and knew what was going to come next.

'Don't make me ask you again,' Paul said quietly. 'Just give me the money.' He caught Scott's gaze then and watched it falter. Paul knew that his own features had now become hard and cold – rearranged themselves into that murderous gaze that Amy had been so eager to tell the police about.

'Don't, Stacey!' Scott suddenly warned.

Paul *clicked out* and was again surprised that the transition didn't black out his normal level of consciousness. It was simply as though his body and all his senses had been thrust roughly into overdrive. Paul Dekker speeded up and the world about him slowed correspondingly. He spun, caught Stacey's leg as she kicked out at him and hoisted it into the air. Stacey fell over backwards and landed heavily on her shoulders. Paul turned again, leaned to one side as Scott approached, charging head-down-arms-out, and with perfect timing, stepped aside and kicked Scott's legs out from under him. Scott fell on top of Stacey who was on her way up again and both of them rolled in the dust. Neither of them was going to be seriously hurt, but Paul doubted they'd want to fight any more.

'Just give me the money,' Paul said.

Stacey's nose was bleeding when she got up and there was a gravel rash down one of Scott's arms and across his right cheek.

'You *bastard!*' Stacey said venomously. She struck out at Paul with a fast, clawed hand and shrieked when she realised that the reason why she didn't have four fingernails full of his skin was because her hand had been brought to a point-blank stand-still in mid-air by the strong hand which had appeared out of nowhere and clamped itself around her wrist. She tried again with her left and her radius bone smashed into a forearm that hadn't so much been brought up in defence but seemed as if it had simply appeared there out of thin air. It was like taking a swing at a concrete bollard.

'Leave it, Stace!' Scott said.

Paul let go of her arm. She tried again. This time he squeezed the bones of her right wrist until she squealed. She didn't try to hit him again when he let go of her, but drew back until she

370

was behind Scott. He looked as if he would dearly like to give it a shot too, but apparently his judgement was better. 'I'll get the money,' he said.

Paul took two hundred dollars in cheques and twenty thousand drachmae – which amounted to about two hundred sterling, give or take a few. It wasn't enough, but it would buy food and the shelter he was looking forward to. He felt as if he could sleep for a week.

'Okay, now could I please have the keys back?' Scott said shakily. He looked as if he badly needed to cry but was frightened to do so. Paul wasn't sure if it was him Scott was scared of crying in front of or the woman. Either way he felt dreadful about the whole thing. Perhaps next time he would take an unattended handbag.

'I'm sorry,' he said, 'but I'm going to have to drive away with them. I'm going to take them four miles down this road and leave them there. I'll pile some stones up in a pyramid and leave them on top so you can find them there. If I give them back to you now, you'll have set the police on to me within fifteen minutes. If you choose to walk to where I leave the keys I'll have an hour start at best, half an hour if you run. If you decide to go back to Trigona, I've got about three-quarters of an hour or so to get on my way. I'm sorry.'

Scott made a half-hearted lunge for the keys, missed by three feet, and gave up.

Paul walked back to the Citroën remembering the gun-shots he'd heard on the beach and thinking, *they ought to think themselves lucky because it might have been those people following us who stopped them. Instead of being scared and two hundred quid lighter, they could very well be dead.*

11

By the time Andreas Volissou arrived home from the police station in Volos, Paul and Katie were hacking down the winding E90 between Ioanina and Vrossina in the creaking Citroën and

Scott and Stacey Anderson were in the police station in Trikala – miles away in the wrong direction from where they had been mugged – trying to get the message across to the local police chief through a café owner who had been drafted in as interpreter. The police chief was having trouble understanding what had happened in regard to the car-theft that hadn't quite taken place and the interpreter was getting tetchy. Neither Scott nor Stacey now expected the thief to be apprehended, and the following day both would be kicking themselves for somehow neglecting to take the number of the red car the thief had been driving. But they would tell themselves it could have been worse; all they had lost was their pride, two hundred dollars and twenty thousand drachmae. In Los Angeles people were killed for less every day.

People, however, were seldom killed in Volos – or even shot at and wounded – which was the reason why Andreas and his friends had spent so long with the police when all they wanted was to be at the hospital with Yiannis. Yiannis, who had lost a little blood, broken a collar bone, and who was now busy swearing vengeance against the Germans the moment he got out of hospital, had been duly visited and the fishermen had gone home.

When Andreas turned into his street, he was immediately aware that something was different and he tensed, thinking that perhaps the Germans had found him out for a liar and had returned to exact their revenge. But the street was quiet and nothing seemed out of place . . . except that something was different. Missing, perhaps. Andreas stood on the corner wondering what it was, then walked up the street deciding how he was going to tell his wife what had happened. She surely wouldn't believe him; he could barely believe himself. It all seemed a very long time ago now, as though it had been a dream. Andreas shook his head, wishing there had been more he could have done. He had witnessed the God of good at work this morning and he had managed to pervert the course of the God of bad that had followed in its path, but he still had the nagging feeling that there was something else he should have done; something more.

It wasn't until he was almost at his gate that he realised what was missing from the street and when he did, he was filled with a glow of warmth that he expected would remain with him until his dying day.

There *was* more he could have done, and he had done it. He had accomplished this by neglecting to get rid of the red Citroën BX16 TRS that had stood inert beside his back gate for the past six months. He'd had no further use for it and had been meaning to sell it, except that he thought (as he'd constantly told his wife when she nagged him) that it might come in handy some day.

The car was gone.

And Andreas thought he now understood why he'd been so loath to get rid of it. It *had* come in handy.

Dekker and Kate had taken it.

Andreas grinned, knowing immediately that the car would take them as far as they wanted to go in it. It hadn't wanted to work for him (had locked its steering wheel against him so often that he'd had the lock removed, in fact) but it would certainly work for them. Many things now fitted into place for him: now, he also knew the reason the car had played him up for so long. It hadn't wanted him to drive it. It had been trying to save what it had left inside it for this very day.

For Dekker and Kate.

12

Paul had expected either to get Jake or Jake's answering machine, but neither of these things happened. He'd stood sweating in the tiny telephone cubicle in the OTE office in Ioanina and dialled in the 0044 international code for England, dropped the zero from the London prefix and wound Jake's home number into the ancient dial . . . and found himself listening to the Telecom void. At first, he'd tensed, expecting a message to come sweeping across it into his ear – a message that would prove he'd gone ga-ga because it would be from Katie who was awake and sitting on a bench where he could see her. When this didn't happen he thought he might get a message from the thing that wanted them both dead, but this didn't happen either. There was a flurry of distant foreign voices and then that vast, somehow *live* silence.

It's tracking you, Paul's mind told him. *It'll speak when it finds you reaching out into the void.*

And because he was almost certain that this was true, Paul rang off. He looked over at Katie, who smiled at him, gave her an *everything's okay* wave and tried again, hoping that the thing would need a certain amount of time over an open line before it could target him. This time he got straight through to Jake's number. It rang distantly, three times, and just when Paul thought the answering machine would cut in, it was picked up.

'Hello?' a voice said. It sounded bouncy, as though the journey up to the satellite and back had distorted it. It was not Jake's voice.

'Jake there?' Paul asked. He heard his own voice twice – as he spoke it and as it echoed in his ear. The effect was extremely disconcerting.

'Who's calling?' the voice responded.

Paul frowned. 'Is Jake there?'

'You tell me who you are, I'll get him for you.'

'How about you telling me who you are and why you're answering the phone?' Paul asked, knowing it was the police. He only hoped Jake hadn't gone and done something stupid.

'My name's Mason,' the voice said. 'Harold Mason, and I'm answering Jake's phone because Jake is indisposed.'

Paul rang off, cursing.

When he got the line back again, he called Freddie Simmons whose answering machine announced that Freddie was dead drunk and wasn't able to come to the phone but would be delighted to call back when he'd sobered up if you cared to leave your name, number and a message of your choice. 'It's Paul,' he said. 'I'm in trouble, I'm going to need help. I'll call again.'

Then he rang Freddie's dealership and spoke to Mae, Freddie's long-time secretary. Mae sobbed a lot. 'We huh-only just fuh-hound out,' she managed before becoming unintelligible.

'Found out what?' Paul demanded, thinking that he knew already.

'Fuh-Freddie's duh-head. Muh-hurdered. They fuh-hound him this muh-morning!'

'I'm sorry,' Paul said, knowing exactly why Freddie had been murdered. Because he could have been relied on to help out. Freddie knew people all over Europe and beyond. People who would have aided one of Freddie's own, regardless of the law.

That's another one to add to your list! his goad told him. *It didn't turn out to be un bel di after all, did it? It's only eleven-thirty here and only nine-thirty at home and the day already turned out shitty, didn't it, poke?*

'How many more?' Paul thought, and was surprised to hear his *spoken* words bouncing down the phone to Mae.

'Pardon?' she said.

'Nothing,' Paul said, and rang off before she wanted to know who he was and where he was and what he knew about all this. He tried the Stephen Miles number and couldn't get through, then he tried Jake again and got the same policeman. Paul asked if Jake was still alive, but the policeman refused to comment on anything until such time as Paul had identified himself and Paul didn't intend to do *that*.

In desperation, he rang the number of Jake's sidekick, Double A. Double A was sure to know all about it if anything had happened to Jake.

The number rang but no one answered it.

Paul left the booth, paid his bill with the drachmae he'd stolen and sat down beside Katie who looked a great deal healthier than she had earlier.

Not bad for a dead girl, Paul thought, and since there was no *poke* suffix to the thought, wasn't sure if it had come from him or from his separate, doubting side. It was getting difficult to tell which was which just lately. The fracture in his mind that had occurred when he'd killed the kid seemed to be knitting together as were the other separations: Paul Dekker the cool, calculating car-thief, and Paul Dekker the *click-out* demon. He wasn't sure if this was entirely a good thing to happen at this moment because there seemed to be a lot of evidence that the splits in him had linked him to Katie and he didn't want those links broken.

'How are you feeling?' he asked. He was hot and sweating like a pig, but Katie wasn't showing so much as a bead of perspiration. Her leg felt very cold against his. It was a little like sitting in front of an open refrigerator and Paul found himself distantly noting the fact that she was still dead. He wasn't sure what else he had expected.

'I'm okay,' she said. 'I need some more water, but otherwise I'm okay.'

'Do you have to eat anything?' he asked. His own stomach was growling busily.

'I don't think I'm meant to,' she said. 'I'm . . . y'know . . . and I think my energy is coming from . . . the other place. I don't feel hungry. I just need water to stop me drying out. I don't know why.'

'We'll get some,' Paul said. 'Don't you worry about a thing.'

Katie put her cold hand on his thigh. 'Paul?' she said, gazing up at him with eyes as green as emeralds.

He fought an urge to take hold of that hand, lost and curled his fingers around it not listening to the part of him that was screaming about it being as cold as marble. 'What?' he asked.

'I've got to go away soon, and I'm frightened of what will happen to me . . .'

'You'll be okay,' he cut in, because he was frightened too.

'. . . but most of all I'm frightened that you won't be here when I get back.'

Paul smiled. 'I'm not going anywhere without you,' he said.

'Will you promise to wait for me to come back? No matter how long it takes?'

Paul promised and was surprised when she squeezed his hand.

For a moment Katie's face lit up in a gorgeous grin. 'I got back inside my hand,' she said. 'This one, anyway. The other's still a bit funny.'

Then the smile was gone and Katie shuddered and cringed and her face seemed to rearrange itself somehow. Her cold fingers bit into Paul's knee and she began to breathe harshly. *'I think they might know where we are now!'* she said suddenly. *'The phones. Something to do with the telephones!'*

Then she relaxed and gave him that pathetic smile of hers. 'It hurts when I find out stuff like that,' she said. 'I don't know where it comes from. It's like my mind reaches out and breaks through a stretchy membrane. I think it taps into something on this side. It's not from . . . over there. I think we'd better leave soon enough. They found us.'

Paul wanted to try the phone again before he went because if they (whoever *they* were) could target him and Katie through the phone links, he didn't want to have to use the phone again somewhere else. He tried the phone again, still couldn't get through, and sat down beside her again, wishing he knew what they were up against.

'There's a way of finding out,' Katie said, and Paul was so surprised by the answer that for a few minutes he didn't realise he hadn't asked her the question.

'How?' he asked.

'We have to find a mortuary or a chapel of rest,' she said quietly. 'I can't remember what happened to me, but we can force back the memories. But you may not want to do it.'

Paul already knew he didn't want to do it, already knew that he *would* do it, no matter what it involved – and there was only one thing it could involve. You didn't find much variety in chapels of rest. 'Tell me,' he said.

Katie sighed. 'It's probably dangerous,' she said, shaking her head.

'Tell me.'

'We have to use a body. A corpse. Wake it up and make it talk.'

Paul's mind was spinning. It felt like a downward spiral. 'A *Greek* corpse?' he said.

'It doesn't matter about the corpse. It just has to be fresh. It doesn't matter what nationality it is because it won't speak in its mother tongue. It'll speak in another way. It'll talk through us.'

'I don't understand,' Paul said.

'We have to link with it. The three of us have to join up. The corpse will be a channel between us and the information we need. We'll understand it when it speaks.'

Paul shook his head. 'Can't we just link without a third . . . person? Just me and you?'

Katie smiled at him. 'I'd like that. I think we can, and I think that we soon will, but then you'll find out about me. You'll find out what *I* know. What we need to find out now is what *they* know. Or some of it. Our side can wait until later. This is urgent.'

His mind still spinning, Paul went back to the call box for one last try before they left. This time, his patron saint smiled on him.

13

An hour later, at the same time that Scott and Stacey were talking to the police in Trikala and Andreas was discovering that his car had been stolen, Paul and Katie had left Ioanina and were hammering down the empty E90 towards Vrossina in the creaking Citroën.

Back in town, Paul had changed one of Scott's traveller's cheques – a process which hadn't been aided by his lack of a passport to back it up. Some Greek exchanges didn't bother with identification when you changed cheques and some did. Paul happened to pick one of the ones that did. They were going to remember him in there if anyone came looking but after he'd complained loudly that he'd never needed his passport to change money anywhere else and that he would just have to take his business elsewhere, the bank teller had given in and changed the two hundred dollars worth of cheques for him. The teller, a young Greek in jeans and a tee shirt who carried out his business while munching his way through a giant tuna salad roll (which had made Paul drool), hadn't even checked that the signatures on the top and bottom of the cheques were identical. This was a good thing because Paul didn't have the capabilities of Print Stokes and they weren't similar at all. Paul lightened up when the cash was in his hand and asked the teller where he'd got the roll, then went to the shop and bought three.

He also bought four litres of chilled bottled water, a road map of the Greek mainland and a breadknife. He sat in the car poring over the map while he ate the roll and Katie sipped at a litre of water. He wasn't particularly surprised to find that they were headed directly towards the west coast – the Ionian coast – and a town called called Igoumenitsa from which (according to the map) ferries sailed to Corfu and to Brindisi in Italy. Paul wasn't altogether sure how far up the ankle of Italy Brindisi was situated but he thought it was probably down at the bottom somewhere, perhaps even on the heel of the boot. What he *was* sure about was that his infallible sense of direction would navigate him through Italy just as easily as it had taken him across Greece. What he was also sure about was that when he got to Naples, the meeting place he'd arranged during his final phone call, help would be there waiting.

Then he thought about the prospect of using a dead person as an oracle – of *linking* with a dead person (and two dead people if you counted Katie) – and the part of him that called him *poke*, spoke up.

Perhaps you'd better say if *you get to Naples, cowboy!* it suggested.

Chapter Fifteen
Double A In a Fix

1

The huge black man wasn't the kind of person that Double A, *never* Anthony Anthony as his warped-minded parents would have preferred, would willingly have opened a door to. Not the big sliding front door of the Miles Carriage Co. – through which the black man had come unnoticed – and not the side door, and certainly not the door of his flat. The black man was going to be trouble. You could tell by the deep insincerity of his wide, friendly grin and by his body language which was frantically signalling, *I'm an okay guy*.

There were circumstances under which Double A would have admitted that he suffered from paranoia – he took a great deal of amphetamine sulphate, methadrine, cocaine (when he could raise the cash), any other chemical upper that ended in the letters 'ine' and quite a lot of Ecstasy too, and paranoia was one of the bastards that walked hand in hand with the regular use of these stimulants. Then there was the paranoia associated with *possession* of these illegal substances; everyone started to look as if they might be plain-clothes CID or police narks and each approach by a stranger could leave you pumped up with adren-aline and trembling, even if they only wanted to know the way somewhere.

But knowing that the black man was someone who should be avoided like the plague had nothing to do with Double A's paranoia, which had begun to clash and crash like cymbals. You didn't need that hair-trigger mental condition to know that this guy was big trouble. A blind man could have seen it from five hundred yards.

At the moment Double A was straight (but carrying a packet of sulphate crystals with which he intended to make his evening go like a rocket). He felt his right hand go to his overall pocket and close around the packet of crystals in a kind of automatic reaction and he fought the urge to crush it into his fist and withdraw that fist, ready to dump the packet when the man took his eyes off him for a second because this man did not look like he might be a policeman. Policemen (and Double A had had plenty of experience of that particular brand of kill-joy in his twenty-one years) *never* used the body language this man was using. They came in full of confidence and superiority and tried to make you cringe. This man looked more like a drug dealer who had a proposition to make, an offer – possibly of the variety which could not be refused – and the fact that he was black had nothing to do with it whatsoever. It wouldn't have mattered if he'd been green or purple: Double A had seen that body language on all sorts of folk and all of them had been in possession of axes to grind.

Double A stood and looked at the black man looking at him and wondered if running away would be the prudent thing to do at this point. If it hadn't been for the fact that he was standing next to his pride and joy – the '59 Ford Pop with the V8 Rover engine – he would have abandoned ship there and then and fuck what might have happened to the Miles Carriage Co. in his absence.

'Nice car,' the man said.

Double A nodded slowly, wishing he hadn't chosen to slide the big glass door back in order to test the engine, then remembering Phil who had tried to tune a running Renault in a closed garage and whose girlfriend Liz had dragged him out of the engine compartment ten minutes later with the shapes of various engine details burnt into his forehead. At least opening the door had left him with a wide escape route if it became necessary.

'Heard it running from down the street,' the black man continued, sounding impressed. 'Sounds like a mean mutha.'

Double A nodded again, sizing up the gap to the left of the man. If he was right-handed this would be the one to go for.

'What's under the lid?' the man asked.

And now the man had pushed Double A's professional pride button. He was aware that it was happening and totally unable to prevent himself responding. 'V8 Rover,' he said. 'Oversize valves. Ported and skimmed head. Balanced and Tuftrided crank. Lightened flywheel. Holleys. Fast road cam. Anderson racing manifold and exhaust. You name it.' Double A found himself smiling. 'This car is going to be very quick,' he finished, suddenly wishing he'd simply told the man to mind his own business. The smile left his face. *Watch this guy, he's slippery*, he told himself.

'Drive an old Mustang, myself,' the black man said, nodding. He looked to Double A as if he was thinking hard – perhaps listening since his head was cocked to one side.

Double A tried to order his muddy thoughts. He was not at his best when he was straight and he knew it. The black guy was trying very hard to win his confidence – seemed to have a natural knack for it, in fact – and if he wasn't careful he was going to find himself in very big trouble.

'How far away is this car from being on the road?' the man suddenly asked.

About twelve feet or so, I'd say, Double A wanted to reply, but there were no quick-witted mean-mouthed chemicals in his bloodstream giving him courage and the guy was a little too muscular for his liking. 'How do you mean?' he asked, wondering when the guy was going to get around to the reason he was here. He already felt outclassed and that horrible feeling in the pit of his stomach, he realised, was fear.

'Could it be driven on the road?'

Double A nodded quickly, suddenly believing that he was going to get an offer for the car and clinging to that idea. 'It'll go okay but there's no ticket on it or any tax.'

'Where's the owner?' the black man asked.

Double A didn't like the tone of this question a great deal. It had been asked innocently enough, but it somehow sounded threatening. As if the guy knew exactly where the owner was and that it was far enough away for him not to arrive and queer his pitch. 'I'm the owner,' Double A replied.

'Of the garage. You're not Miles, are you?'

'He's not here. I use these premises and pay him a cut of the profits.'

'Where is he?'

Double A shook his head. 'I don't know,' he said.

The black man cocked his head again. 'He don't know,' he said and grinned up into the corner of the workshop. Then he came towards Double A, cutting off his chance of an easy escape.

'My name's Reuben Brown,' the man said, extending a huge hand, 'and I'd like to buy that there machine of yours.'

Double A looked at that great hand for a long time, wondering what to do. He felt sluggish and wished he'd taken a line of that sulphate a bit earlier. His paranoia was throwing up images of what was likely to happen – all bad things – and the guy was not good news, but there was a large part of Double A that dearly wanted to believe that good old Reuben Brown only wanted to buy the car.

He took the hand and instead of being pulled quickly towards the man (whose head would dip and turn his nose to strawberry jam), found it being vigorously pumped up and down. It was a good firm handshake and if Double A's paranoia hadn't been running rife he would have been able to tell from it that Reuben Brown really was the good guy he was pretending to be.

'It's going to cost you eighteen grand when it's done,' Double A said in a tone he hoped conveyed disdain. If there was one thing he didn't intend to do it was sell this car.

'I'll take it off you now for fifteen,' Reuben Brown smiled.

Double A shook his head, knowing now what the trouble was

going to be. 'It ain't for sale,' he said, wondering how he intended to stop the man simply taking the car away from him. Reuben Brown was easily six feet tall, probably weighed fifteen stone and looked very much like a going-to-seed boxer. Double A was five six and weighed a little under nine stone. Jake Fulman's often quoted opinion was that he had seen more fat on a french fry. Double A knew he had a good power to weight ratio and he was quick and strong for a little guy, but being a quick and strong little guy in this situation would be akin to putting a motorcycle up against a battle tank. The only good course of action would be to head rapidly in the other direction.

Reuben Brown leaned against the Ford's purple bodywork that was still eight coats of paint away from the mirror shine it would eventually have and said, 'I know you ain't quite finished it, but I would very much like to pay you the money, now and in cash, and take this baby off your hands. This vehicle is just what I've been looking for.'

'Don't lean on the paintwork, man, it's still soft,' Double A said. There was a distinct tremor in his voice. A part of his brain was busily totting up how much cocaine his cut of the money would buy him and arguing that he wouldn't have to tell Jake or Stephen Miles how much he'd sold the car for which would considerably increase the length of time he would be able to spend out of his tree, while the paranoid part of him told him that selling the car would be the worst thing he could ever do.

Reuben Brown glanced inside the car and smiled. Double A knew he wasn't smiling at what he saw in there because the inside of the car hadn't been done yet. There were two moth-eaten bucket seats in there and the original bench in the back. The plush upholstery, the quilted headlining and the little maple steering wheel were things yet to come. Reuben Brown was smiling because he'd seen the keys in there.

'I'll tell you what, Anthony,' he said, 'I'll give you the whole eighteen and promise not to set the cops on you. How about that?'

Double A felt as if he had suddenly been drenched with water straight from the Antarctic ocean. *Cop*! his paranoia shouted because the man shouldn't have known his name or anything else about him. But the man had to be a bent cop because he was trying to make a deal *not* to set the cops on him. Which was a whisker away from being crazy because bent cops wanted paying – they certainly didn't want to give you eighteen thousand pounds for a car which wouldn't be worth more than twelve even when it was finished. In fact, Double A had had his heart set on keeping the car because privately he didn't think he and Jake would recoup their expenditure when it came to selling time. He thought they would be lucky to be offered ten or eleven.

'I didn't tell you my name,' he complained.

Reuben shook his head. 'You didn't have to,' he said.

'I don't get it,' Double A thought and was surprised to find he had spoken the words. A large and garish picture of a crowbar had lit up in his mind (or a nail-bar, as Jake would have insisted, but certainly not a jemmy) and he was wondering where he'd last seen it. He thought it might be on the bench behind him which would mean travelling a good ten or twelve feet in a backward direction and he thought that the black man would probably notice what was happening long before his hand closed around it.

'A little bird,' Reuben explained, 'twittered in my ear and told me a few things about you and Jake and Mister Stephen Miles. It told me enough about Mister Miles to frighten me, in fact. Here's a 'did you know' for you: did you know that Stephen Miles is an alias and that the man's real name is Paul Dekker? No, I thought not. What about this: did you know that Paul Dekker is wanted for the murder of his mother and is thought to be armed and dangerous? No? There are a great many things you don't know, aren't there? Okay. The police would be very happy to talk to you about Mister Dekker and they would probably also be interested in a few other things too. How about this: Anthony Anthony's flat contains a gram of cocaine, almost half a pound of amphetamine sulphate, two hundred and forty-seven tablets of extremely good quality Ecstasy, three hundred blotters of acid and a sizeable amount of your old favourite, methadrine. You're not just using, you're *dealing*.

Double A's head was shaking hard. 'I don't deal and I don't do acid,' he said. 'And my flat is clean.' Dealing drugs was impossible if you suffered the level of paranoia he did and the packet of sulphate in his overalls pocket was the last he had. He had been intending to make a few calls later this evening to replenish his supply.

Reuben smiled that nice guy smile again. '*Was* clean,' he said. 'Your flat *was* clean. I have a friend called Gordon Clement. He's from Basingstoke and he used to be a chemist at a drug firm. I met him in Cambridge along with a dozen other very interesting people and we've all been putting our heads together to decide what to do about you, Anthony. You don't understand, do you? I can tell by your confused expression. Let me make it simple. Gordon Clement has been busy making things for us. We bought the cocaine, of course, but Gordon made the other stuff. And he is now in your flat stashing away all those lovely chemicals in places where you probably won't find them until after the police arrive. Those drugs *are* in your flat and it *will* look to the police as if you are dealing.'

Double A's mind was spinning. 'Don't believe you,' was all he could think of to say.

'I'm trying to make it easy for you,' Reuben said. He patted his pocket. 'In here is a list of all the places the drugs are hidden in your flat. All you have to do is sell me the car for eighteen grand and I'll give you the list and you can do whatever you like with the drugs. How about that? Sounds good? It ought to! Especially when you consider the alternative. The alternative is that I just take the car away from you without paying and then phone the police and tell them about you and Dekker . . . and more importantly about the drugs.'

Double A's head was still gently shaking. He didn't have anything to say. For some reason he had been expertly stitched up and he couldn't think why. And worse than that, it didn't add up. If they'd wanted the car that badly, why hadn't they just stolen it when he wasn't here? Why had they gone to all this trouble? There was only one explanation. Double A knew this explanation existed but he was more frightened than he'd ever been in his life and his mind was turgid and wouldn't let him know what it was.

The black man straightened up, told Double A to wait there and walked to the back of the car, bent down behind it and came back with an attaché case which he laid down on the floor in front of him. 'Here's the money,' he said, smiling confidently. 'All eighteen thousand.' He knelt down, snapped the catches, opened the lid and turned it so that Double A could see the cash. There were twenty neatly banded blocks of twenty pound notes inside the case. Reuben picked up two of them and put them in his jacket pockets. 'There's the money,' he said, getting up. 'And if you want something else to help you make up your mind . . .'

Reuben Brown's right hand slid beneath his jacket and Double A watched, certain he was going to find himself staring down the barrel of a gun in less than two seconds. His muscles were all frozen in terror and he thought he might piss his pants when the gun was pointed at him. In that moment the thing in the world he least wanted to happen was for him to wet himself in front of that great grinning bastard. Double A started to get angry.

This didn't stop his bladder trying to evacuate itself when the guy's hand flashed out in front of him. Double A locked the muscles of his pelvic floor and prevented it happening, but not before a good squirt dampened the front of his boxers. He had jeans on over the shorts and overalls over the jeans so it wasn't likely to soak through so the black guy could see, but that wasn't the point. The point was the shame and the awful feeling of having been betrayed by your body. His anger grew when he realised that he wasn't looking at a gun at all, but at a small transparent bag containing a fair amount of white powder.

'A sample of what's waiting for you at home,' Reuben said. 'All the way from Bogotá.'

He threw the packet and Double A was surprised to see his own hand snatch it from the air. He pulled the self-sealing strip open, wet his finger and tasted it.

'Snort yourself a couple of lines,' Reuben suggested.

Double A turned his back on the man and walked to the bench, expecting to be clubbed around the head or shot in the back at every step.

Neither of these things happened.

Double A took a Haynes manual from the shelf above the bench, laid it down and poured a little of the powder on to it. He made two lines of it with a steel rule, rolled a piece of notepaper then turned back to Reuben, intending to invite him to take a line first. He certainly didn't mean to snort any of this stuff because he doubted there was any cocaine in it at all. Which was one good reason for tasting things before you put them up your nose. His friend Parker had died at a party because of some bad coke and since then Double A had been rigorous in the tasting routine. He had come across bad gear on more than one occasion and had become able to identify some of the substances it was cut with, such a talcum powder and, on more than one occasion, Vim. Double A had once tasted cocaine to which, for some obscure reason, strychnine had been added and he had never forgotten the tell-tale bitter taste. This cocaine tasted very much like it might be entirely composed of strychnine and Double A thought that one good snort might result in his death a few pained minutes later. The fact that the man had held such a low opinion of him that he expected him to fall for this shot anger into him and his head finally began to clear.

When he turned back to invite Reuben Brown to take the first line, his mind had not just allowed him to access the logical explanation that almost certainly lay behind all this conflicting evidence, it had whacked him right between the eyes.

It was all a confidence trick.

The man wanted the car, but he didn't intend to pay for it at all. The money in the attaché case was probably as fake as the bag of cocaine and it was extremely doubtful whether there was anyone in his flat planting drugs for the police to see. If any of this had been true it would not have been necessary for the man to try and kill him with this powder that was supposed to be cocaine.

Double A spun round keeping his face carefully blank.

And this time found himself staring down the barrel of a revolver.

'Try it,' Reuben Brown suggested. 'I'm sure you'll grow to like it. Especially in view of the alternative.'

Double A turned back to the Haynes manual with the two lines laid out on it. The crowbar he'd been thinking of earlier was on the bench at his right, within reach, but now he didn't know what good it was likely to do him.

'Snort that cocaine, Anthony,' the man encouraged. 'It'll make you feel *reaaal goood*!'

Double A's fevered and angry mind briefly considered two ways of dying. One was to snort the substance in front of him and the other was to die trying to get out of this mess. He was very frightened but he was even more angry and the feeling of dampness at his crotch filled him with hot shame. The mixture of emotions was a potent cocktail and if Double A had been a fighting man, which he most certainly wasn't, he would have turned round, knocked the gun from the man's hand and punched him hard in the crotch and fuck the consequences.

Double A dipped his head towards the lines of probable death and tried to feel the force like Yoda or Obi Wan would have suggested if he had been Luke Skywalker. He wasn't entirely surprised to find that since he was not Luke Skywalker there was no force to feel. He made a tube out of the notepaper again and *was* surprised to discover that he had taken the tube in his left hand when he was right-handed.

'You'll love this,' Reuben promised. 'Best buzz you ever had.'

Double A suddenly understood that there was a third option

open to him and that his body had evidently chosen to take it. He fought with it for a second, then accepted it, crazy as it seemed, because this option was to refuse to die.

He put the tube into his left nostril and positioned it over one of the lines of powder, then he turned off his mind.

He right hand snaked out and grabbed the crowbar and Double A stood, bringing the bar out in a swift semi-circle behind him, turning into the arc.

The crowbar missed the gun by a good eighteen inches, but the blow was good enough anyway. The forked nail-puller on the end of the crowbar's crook smacked into the point of Reuben Brown's elbow. The man screamed and jumped back, dropping the gun.

The gun's butt hit the workshop floor leaving the barrel pointing up towards the region of Double A's guts, and in that long, slow movement he envisaged it going off and imagined how it would cartwheel backwards with the recoil as the slug tore through him.

But the gun didn't go off.

It shattered.

'Plastic!' Double A screamed, suddenly angrier than he had ever been in his life. 'Even the gun was a fake!'

One of Reuben's big fists was hooking towards him. Double A smacked the crowbar down into it, pulled it back, and as Reuben Brown hunched up, yelling and cradling a hand that was surely broken, brought it down again on the man's temple.

The black man gave a tiny yelp and hit the ground, hard.

Double A stood there in a daze, expecting him to wake up in a few seconds and wondering what to do when he did. He didn't really want to hit him again. If you made a habit of hitting someone that hard with a piece of steel this weighty you were going to find yourself with a very large corpse on your hands.

The man didn't get up though and panic started to flood through Double A who wanted to become a murderer about as badly as he'd wanted to piss his pants. He tried to make himself do something – like perhaps see if the man was still breathing – but the best his body could do was to present him with a packet of sulphate which his hand had taken out of his overalls. Double A dropped the crowbar, tipped a little pile of crystals on the back of his shaking hand and snorted. When his left nostril stopped stinging and started feeling good, he repeated the process with the other. He put the packet away, took a couple of deep breaths and stood still until he started to feel like Superman. His head cleared miraculously and his hands stopped shaking and started thrumming with power.

'Okay,' he sighed, feeling a smile tickle the corners of his mouth. 'Now what?'

Double A thought he could see the man's back move with his breathing but wasn't certain if he was seeing this because he *wanted* to see it. Sometimes those things happened after a good hit. He moved carefully to the side of the man in case he just happened to be playing possum and gently poked him in the ribs with the toe of his Doc Marten's. The big guy didn't move. Double A poked harder and when there was no response, ventured a gentle kick. The man groaned and Double A nodded and left him alone.

He didn't know what to do next. He briefly considered tying up the man then questioning him and found that he didn't really want to know the answers to any of the questions he had and wasn't confident that the man wouldn't wriggle out of his bonds. He looked around the workshop for inspiration and spent a motionless twenty seconds devising tortures for the man which could be applied using the various tools which hung there. Then his paranoia snapped him out of it. Old Reuben would wake up soon and when he did he was going to be very pissed off.

Double A decided that leaving the premises while he still had a chance would be a very good idea. Standing here and waiting for developments (however good it felt simply to stand and feel triumphant) was an act of extreme stupidity. The man was dangerous. He might have been carrying a suitcase of funny money and a toy shop gun, but the chemical he'd tried to make Double A snort was most certainly real.

Double A asked himself the question: *Can I get this guy outside the building and then keep him out?* and immediately answered, *No*, which was a shame since the man was likely to do damage to the premises when he woke and found his quarry had fled. The building might have belonged to Stephen Miles (or the legendary Paul Dekker if the man was to be believed) but Double A felt responsible for it and its contents. Jake Fulman (and Stephen Miles by association, he supposed) were the only people who had ever thought enough of him to bestow this much responsibility on him and he didn't want to let them down, even under these circumstances.

You can't just fuck off and leave him here, he told himself, then had one of the bright ideas that were apt to come after a good snort. He *could* just fuck off and leave him here. He went to the bench, held his breath and dusted the lines of powder off the Haynes manual into the sink, replaced the book on the shelf, then checked on Reuben who was still inert.

He quickly picked up the case containing the money (in case it turned out to be real money after all) and put it in the boot of the Ford Popular. He got the crowbar from where he had dropped it and got into the car. The car seemed to be at least one of the reasons Reuben had come and Double A didn't intend to let him have it. He put the crowbar on the seat next to him and turned the ignition key.

The starter wound and before Double A could even picture what he was going to look like when the engine refused to fire and Reuben got up and started towards him, the V8 burst into howling life.

Double A pumped the throttle a couple of times and the sound and feel of the power as the engine came on cam and the ragged tickover changed to a deep-throated roar, brought him out in shivers. He hit the clutch and whacked the gearstick towards where reverse ought to be. The straight-cut cogs caught with a metallic *chonk*! and Double A let out the stiff clutch pedal. The car shot backwards out into the street, Double A winding the wheel hard to left, then letting it straighten. There was a squealing of locked tyres from behind him and he tensed, realising he'd pulled out in front of someone and expecting a collision. But his hands and feet were busy and a second after the impact should have come he was in second gear and barrelling up towards sixty along the narrow street. He did not look in the rear-view mirror to see what had become of the car that had nearly hit him.

At the end of the street he tried the brakes for the first time, knowing that they were not going to work and that he was going out across the busy main road, but the car dug in its anchors and slowed rapidly, leaving him stopped at the junction. He turned left, accelerated down the road, then pulled up beside the phone box he'd been heading toward.

He got out of the car shaking with adrenaline and speed and in surprise at the car's power. He'd known it was going to be a mover, but he'd never driven anything quite so rock-solid and quick – the '59 Popular ran like a rocket on rails.

He hurried to the phone box, pulled a handful of change out through his overalls from his jeans pocket and dropped it all over the pavement. Coins tinkled and spun and rolled off in every direction. Double A jettisoned the idea of ringing the police direct, yanked the handset off the hook, punched in three nines and asked for the police. He told them that an armed man was breaking into the premises of the Miles Carriage Co. '*Right now so you'd better be quick*!' then hung up when they asked him who he was.

He went back to the car, toying with the idea of going back to see what happened, then rejecting it. The car was not road-legal and it wasn't exactly low-profile, either. It stuck out like shit on a Savile Row suit, in fact. And besides that, he was carrying sulphate and a suitcase full of what was probably funny money.

Double A decided to go back to his flat in Wandsworth, and as soon as he was back behind the wheel of the Pop suffered an attack of the screaming meemies. He couldn't go home in case that guy really had been telling the truth about the stuff being planted in his flat. What if there had been another guy and he'd been sitting on Double A's sagging sofa awaiting a phone call from good old Reuben? What if the time had passed and now the guy (Gordon Clement, his name was, it was lit up like neon in Double A's head) had planted the drugs? What if the guy was waiting there with a gun – not a plastic one from a toy shop, but a real, honest to goodness Colt .45 or Luger or whatever these guys used?

He reached the end of the street and turned left, moving slowly in the heavy traffic and fighting his paranoia. Why had they wanted the car? Why had they wanted to kill him? The only rational explanation was that Stephen Miles was mixed up in something very nasty indeed (and this became more likely in the light of his true identity being Paul Dekker who, legend had it, no one fucked around with because Dekker was mean) and that whoever Reuben was working for thought that little Double A was a part of Dekker's gang.

He made the left turn, dimly realising that he had gone round in a circle and that in thirty seconds or so he was going to go past the end of the street where the Miles Carriage Co. was situated. At the very moment of this realisation, he heard the wailing of a police car approaching from behind. This time he did look in the mirror. The cop car was coming down the centre of the road and the traffic was parting to allow it through. Double A pulled over and encouraged the cops in the car to get the fucker, then told himself it couldn't have been the cops he'd summoned because there was a fire truck hot on its tail and he hadn't asked for one of those.

But the pair turned down the right street anyway.

As Double A drove slowly past the turning he wasn't entirely surprised to see fire gouting out of the open doorway of his work-shop. The fucker had obviously come round quicker than he'd anticipated and torched the place. This knowledge drove a cold spike of fear through the sulphate warmth inside Double A's shrunken stomach. *You can't go home now*, he thought as he passed the turning, *it won't be safe.*

And there was a part of him that thought it might never be safe again.

2

Since Double A had discovered the delights of chemical stimulants five years ago when he was still a sweet little sixteen, he had suffered the consequences. There was an immutable law which demanded balance. This metaphysical law stated that under normal circumstances you sometimes felt good and you sometimes felt bad, but mostly you simply felt okay. On average this worked out evens, providing the necessary balance. The law also said that if you made yourself feel good artificially then you would have to feel artificially bad afterwards to redress the balance. These were the rules of the come-down and anyone who'd ever woken up with a hangover after a good night out could have told you about them. With speed it was worse because speed made you feel like Superman and the better you felt, the greater the pain that followed. There were other downs to take into consideration too when you were a speed-freak.

Your teeth tended to fall apart for one. In his lighter moments, Double A would tell you he had enough metal in his mouth to make a fiftieth scale model of the Eiffel tower. There were other things too, like constant mouth ulcers, nose bleeds, the erosion of the septum (which until it had started to happen to him Double A had thought was something you coughed up in the mornings rather than the piece of gristle between your nostrils), a non-existent appetite and a liver which would turn you yellow when it wanted to be left alone for a while.

But if you wanted to feel like Superman, these were things you had to get used to. What Double A had never managed to come to terms with were the things the doctors called psychoses. The nagging paranoia was difficult to live with (although if you believed everything and everyone was out to get you, you weren't likely to be far wrong) but the visual sensory distortions were another thing altogether. Double A did not like, and never had liked, hallucinations. Seeing things that didn't exist and were not happening made life very difficult indeed, which was one of the reasons he'd only tried acid once. Double A didn't suffer from many hallucinations, but when he had one he remembered it for a long, uncomfortable time. It felt as if someone else had control of your brain.

And he was having one now.

It had to be an hallucination because there was no way that Reuben Brown could have got this far away from the Miles Carriage Co. by now and be looking so sprightly and fit. He was striding down the road towards West Hampstead tube station when he should have been in hospital having the wound in his head stitched and X-rayed. For a moment Double A wondered if he really had hit the man around the head, but as he passed he saw the white pad of gauze plastered to the man's temple.

Double A stopped the car a little further down the road, locked the doors and left the engine running while he watched Reuben Brown heading towards him. He began to shake with fear and anger as the man approached and ignored his mind when it kept telling him this couldn't be happening, because it was. He became certain that the man was not an hallucination when he recognised the car and veered across the pavement towards it.

Double A rammed the stick into reverse, backed up until he'd passed the man and kept going until there was fifty feet between them. Reuben stood on the edge of the pavement watching him and grinning.

Just you stay there! Double A thought. *Go to hospital, go directly to hospital, do not pass go, do not collect two hundred pounds!*

He put the Pop into first, rolled forward, changed up into second, floored the accelerator and let the clutch go. The Pop screamed forward at a sickening speed, shimmying and laying rubber and leaving thick black smoke behind it. Double A wrestled the wheel to keep it from flipping out sideways and when he estimated he was close enough, yanked the wheel to the left and mounted the kerb. He had intended just to put the left-hand side up on the pavement, but Reuben Brown, who evidently hadn't got where he was today by being slow-witted, was already hammering back across the pavement so Double A followed him.

Pedestrians scattered as the Pop slewed sideways across the pavement and straightened. Reuben was heading for the nearest building, but Double A was going to make damned sure he didn't make it.

The front nearside wing caught Reuben Brown's arse, lifted him from the ground and threw him across what remained of the pavement.

Double A didn't see what happened next because he was busy missing pedestrians and fighting the car back down on to the road where it belonged.

3

The four staff in the open-plan office of Miller, Eskine & Bader, solicitors and commissioners for oaths, saw exactly what happened next. The plate glass window at the front of their office imploded with a noise like that of a bomb going off.

At the back of the office Jeremy Miller, the sixty-seven-year-old senior partner, stood up behind his desk, winced and sat down again, clawed up two handfuls of paperwork and quietly began to die. The shock caused a sudden increase in his already high blood pressure and finally burst the aneurysm which had formed in an artery inside his brain a month earlier and given him splitting headaches ever since. The other two partners and the two secretaries would not notice the departure of their esteemed leader until five minutes later because when the window imploded a huge black man flew through.

The man came into the office in a curved trajectory, looking for all the world as if a moment before he had been on his hands and knees searching for something on the ground. His lips were pressed tightly together and his face bore a frown. The image would be forever burnt into the memory of Emma Eskine and sometimes, over the next three years, she would wake up from nightmares involving the man.

He hit the tough grey carpet amongst a great deal of broken glass, fell onto his face, twitched three times and lay still.

'What the f. . .?' David Miller said, almost swearing, remembering where he was, and finally, not caring '. . .ucking hell is going on?' he shouted.

Emma Eskine, who was going to find herself senior partner in five minutes (and who would be so busy washing her hands that she wouldn't understand), stared out at the anxious crowd on the street who had gathered outside the missing window and were staring right back in at her.

'A car hit him,' someone announced needlessly. Emma didn't think he'd chosen to jump through a plate glass window as an act of suicide.

'Hit and run,' someone else said.

Emma seemed to be the only moving person in a sea of stillness. The other members of staff were all frozen in the positions they'd been in when the window burst and no one outside seemed particularly anxious to enter. She crunched her way across the broken glass and knelt down beside the man – who surely had to be dead – distantly noting that another pair of tights had gone west as soon as they'd come into contact with the glass. 'Did anyone get the car number?' she asked, taking one of the man's hands. No one had, which was a pity because this man was dead and the driver ought to be facing a murder or manslaughter charge.

'It was a black car,' a voice said from the depths of the crowd. 'I saw it all happen.'

'It was *purple*!' someone else argued and a heated discussion broke out.

Emma felt the man's throat. Her hand came away bloody. There was no pulse. She was glad he hadn't landed face up. Emma had managed to get to the ripe old age of forty-three without ever seeing a real life dead person and somehow it didn't seem to count if he was face down. She told herself this as she stood up. There were two large round holes in her tights through which her pale knees showed like twin moons. Emma glanced down at them, noted that there were several splinters of glass impressed in her flesh but that there was only a single tiny pinprick of blood on her left knee, and looked out at the crowd.

It was then that Daisy Souza, the twenty-two-year-old secretary whom David Miller had been shafting for the past six months, started to scream. 'I'M CUT!' she wailed. 'HELP ME, SOMEONE, I'M BLEEDING!'

Emma glanced over at her. There was a superficial wound on Daisy's left cheek which had presumably been caused by flying glass. At some time during the past few seconds Daisy had felt the wetness on her face and touched it to see what it was. Now she was holding the hand up in front of her face and screaming in a fashion that suggested she truly believed she was going to die.

'Shut up!' Emma shouted at her. 'You're okay. It's just a little cut!'

David was up on his feet now, hurrying towards the girl he was about to dump his wife and two children in favour of. He took her in his arms and held her, but Daisy didn't stop screaming. Someone crashed in through the door, saw the chaos and quickly left.

'Phone the police and an ambulance,' Emma commanded over her shoulder, and James 'Douglas' Bader, who reassured his clients with a cool confidence that had now totally deserted him, grabbed the telephone, fumbled with it and dropped it over the front of his desk. While he was hauling it back by the wire, Emma looked around for something to wipe the blood from her hands with.

'It was a *green* car. It had fat wheels,' someone shouted from outside. 'Is he dead?' someone else wanted to know.

There was a balled tissue up the left sleeve of Emma's shirt. She was going to get the shirt sleeve bloody retrieving it, but there was nothing else around to wipe her hands on – unless you counted the dead man at her feet or the carpet that was already ruined and Emma didn't want to touch the man again or risk collecting glass splinters in her fingers. She had the dead man's blood on her and for all she knew, that blood might be carrying the HIV virus. So far, there was no place on her – other than the unlikely pinprick on her knee – where that virus could gain admittance to her body so it was important not to be cut. Not biting her fingernails, rubbing her eyes or picking her nose until she'd given her hands a good wash might also be good practice, she thought distantly, though she made a habit of none of these things.

By the time she'd undone the button of her shirt sleeve and got out the wad of tissue, James had dialled emergency, got through and was babbling incoherently into the phone, David had managed to reduce Daisy's screaming to a ragged sob, Jessica, the senior secretary, had stood up and sat down again three times, her mouth working like that of a goldfish, and the crowd had stopped jostling and arguing about the colour of the perpetrator of this crime's car and fallen into an expectant silence.

Are they expecting him to get up, or something? Emma thought. 'He's dead!' she shouted. 'The police and an ambulance are coming and there's nothing to see! *Now go away!*'

She took the tissue in her left hand and started to dab furiously at the blood on her right . . . and then stopped.

Part of her right hand seemed to have disappeared.

Emma looked at the ragged black hole in the centre of her palm and her mind reeled. When Emma had been a child out in Kent in the days when the appearance of blacks of African or West Indian extraction was still a strange and rare enough experience to warrant writing up in your diary, her mother had told her that if you touched a black man, his colour would come off on your hands. A very tiny and distant part of Emma that would forever be a wide-eyed child now woke up and started to crow that mother had been right.

But this wasn't the shiny brown colour of the dead man on the floor, this was a blackness so total it seemed to reflect no light at all. It was blacker than soot. It looked like a hole into the deepest, darkest night you could imagine. Emma was certain she would be able to insert her fingers into that hole. *Stuff came off him*, she thought. *He had stuff on him*!

She dabbed the black spot with the white handkerchief and the linen caught the disappearing disease too. Then she began to rub frantically at the substance, only dimly aware that she was spreading it and flatly refusing to believe that each time the black stuff touched the blood something happened which looked like a tiny prism of light twinkling and bursting.

It cannot be moving, she told herself, trying frantically to hang on to her rationality. *This stuff, whatever it is, cannot be alive or spreading out across your hand. It cannot be fusing with this man's blood and making your hand vanish as it does it*!

There was a noise at her feet. Emma thought that her feet might have somehow got to be several miles away because that was surely the distance the sound of glass crunching and tinkling had travelled.

Somewhere in the distance behind her, Daisy began to scream again.

The noise of the crowd quickly grew from a disturbed muttering to a frightened roar and Emma decided that the police and the ambulance must have finally arrived.

'Emma!' James called from miles behind her.

Emma tore her eyes away from her hand and looked towards the sound of crunching glass.

And at her feet the dead man was picking himself up. He was on all fours, looking up at her with vacant eyes. The black substance she had on her hands was flowing from his mouth and running down beneath his clothes like strange, thin black blood. The man pulled himself to a crouch and his mouth began to work. 'I . . . I'm, . . . okhaay,' he announced in a harsh and sibilant voice. But he could neither be okay nor alive because the collision with the window had torn his cheeks to tatters, the right side of his throat hung open and there was a long sliver of three-eighths of an inch thick plate glass protruding from his right temple. The wound there was two inches wide and the glass had surely pierced his brain and killed him instantly which was the reason his heart hadn't pumped out eight pints of blood into the carpet.

The man stood up and Emma saw rainbow prisms shimmer about his body. It was like watching flashbulbs go off in a crowded football stadium.

He took hold of the shard of glass protruding from his skull and winced as he eased it out of his head. There were scraps of flesh and blood and the black substance on the glass as he pulled it out.

Emma watched in total disbelief as the sliver of glass fell to the floor and broke.

'Not dead, just hurting a little,' the man said, and treated her to a smile that would haunt her dreams for years. Then he turned and walked towards the opening where the window had been. The crowd parted magically as he stepped over the low wall and out into the street. And then he was gone.

When the police arrived, they found Emma in the toilets frantically trying to wash 'the black stuff' from her clean and red-raw hands.

4

Double A could barely believe what he'd done. Even after he'd parked up the Pop on a trading estate well away from the scene of the crime he'd committed and piled most of the remaining sulphate up his nose, he was unable to understand what had possessed him.

He'd felt a kind of righteous anger at seeing Reuben Brown sauntering down the street and running the motherfucker down had seemed to be exactly the thing to do. Double A wasn't quite sure how it had all happened, and the terror and panic he had expected to feel afterwards had set in, but he couldn't remove the thought from his head that running down the man had been the right course of action to take.

He sat in the car, shaking and watching the traffic passing through the estate in case one of them turned out to be a police car looking for a chopped, purple '59 Ford Popular. There was a part of him that badly wanted to dump the car and run away – where to he didn't exactly know – and another part that vehemently complained that dumping the car was exactly the thing that Reuben and his buddies would have wanted him to do. He had to keep the car – it was too late to think of dumping it now because if anyone had taken its number (and he hoped that in the confusion no one had) the police would already know his name and address and every patrol car in London would be looking out for it. Which meant that it wasn't safe to drive it and that it wasn't safe to go home.

But he had to keep the car. He searched his fevered mind for a *because* that would give him a single good reason to keep the car and there wasn't one. It would be crazy to drive around in it.

Double A considered this for a moment and told himself that it might be crazy to keep the car but it was nothing like as crazy as what he'd done with it an hour ago. He would keep the car. If the police tried to pull him, they would have to catch him first and if there was one thing to which those size nines down at the bottom of his ankles were supremely suited, it was running away. If a cop attempted to pull him, there wouldn't be any doubt as to whether his number had been taken. If that happened he would dump the car and run away and deal with the fresh set of problems then.

Double A started the car again, being very careful that he didn't think too deeply about this sulphate-aided logic which probably had more holes than Emmenthal cheese because deep down inside of him there was a bright fire raging that had nothing to do with chemically altered consciousness and everything to do with the intuition that he had just won the first round in what was going to be a long battle.

Double A drove off the estate and headed towards Jake Fulman's place down in Hammersmith because Jake was supposed to be coming back from the West Country either today or tomorrow and he might be able to suggest a way out of this fix. Jake obviously knew a great deal more about the comings and goings of the mysterious Stephen Miles than he had let on and Double A thought he was likely to be able to explain exactly what was going on.

But Double A didn't turn into Jake's yard, just cruised past, because there was a car parked up about fifty feet away from Jake's place and there were two men inside it, one of whom was smoking a pipe. It had gone lunch-time now so they weren't there eating their sandwiches, that was for sure. There was a chance they were insurance salesmen, but it was only a slim one. All the insurance men Double A had ever met drove flash cars and this one was a bog-standard Ford Escort of exactly the type in which you would expect to see CID carrying out deep cover surveillance. On several occasions Double A had noted the presence of a car very much like this one lurking within photographing distance of the flat of Declan the Dealer and Declan was now serving a seven-year stretch.

He parked the Pop round the corner and walked back, ready to run for it if the Escort's doors showed so much as a sign of being opened. The guys inside it could be baddies or they might be police. Double A was plumping for police.

And when he was within ten feet of the car he was *certain* they were the police. He was also certain that they were here after Jake and not him because although both men looked at him long and hard as he passed, their stares were ones of bored suspicion rather than of recognition.

Double A got a long look in through the open gates of Jake's yard as he walked by and wasn't surprised to see another Escort parked on the cinders behind the house. Two men were leaning on it soaking up the sun and smoking. Both of them looked over at him, failed to recognise him and looked away.

The police evidently wanted to talk to Jake Fulman quite badly. Double A thought that when he pulled up in his Range Rover, the guys in his drive would go for him while the other car blocked the entrance so Jake couldn't reverse out again when he realised what was going on. This didn't necessarily mean that Jake (who had a reputation for his clumsy burglaries) had left his mark behind him somewhere in the not too distant past, though. If you lived within fifty miles of London and you came home and found your valuables missing and the house looking not just burgled but as if a cyclone had passed through, the first person the police would want to interview would be Jake. Jake, who would never make the grade as a cat-burglar and who preferred a nail-bar to a skeleton key every time, had improved and refined his technique considerably since the days when he had gained his reputation, but still spent much of his time being accused of crimes he had not committed.

But the fact remained that Jake wasn't going to be available for at least twenty-four and possibly forty-eight hours because the police evidently intended to question him.

Double A wondered if he ought to wait at the end of the road for Jake to turn up so he could warn him, and decided that it wouldn't work. There were two ways Jake could enter the street and he was bound to choose the wrong one to guard. And even if he did get lucky and stopped Jake, he was certain that the police would catch on if he hung around.

Double A walked to the end of the road, went into the shop and bought himself three packets of sugar-free gum because he badly needed to chew (and when there was no gum in his mouth his teeth simply ground together) then walked around the block and went back to the car with another bright idea glowing over his head like a hundred watt bulb.

There was a certain confidence growing in him now. Obviously the CID hadn't received an APB – or whatever they called them – to look out for a short skinny speed-freak driving a purple '59 Ford Popular, or someone would have been chasing him by now. The cops in the car outside had seen it cruise by and hadn't given chase – or, apparently, called in to say they'd seen it. Which was good news in the extreme. The bright idea which occurred to him on his way back to the car was that he could go home and hang around outside for a while, casing the place in a similar manner to how he had done it here. If there was no sign of danger, he would be able to go indoors and at least collect a few of his belongings before he had to go on the run or whatever was going to happen next.

He drove back to Wandsworth, parked the car two streets away from the block of flats he lived in and toured the area, chewing hard, fighting off the fear and looking for pairs of men in Ford Escorts or people who might be in league with Reuben Brown who was now likely to be in hospital with severe injuries or, quite possibly, dead.

An hour later Double A had run out of speed and gum and had seen nothing untoward. His heart rattling along like an electric sewing machine, he ventured into the foyer of the building and looked up the stairs. It took a great deal of courage to make himself start up them.

His flat was on the third floor. There were twenty-six steps between each floor (which was double thirteen for those possessing the paranoia bug) and Double A was careful not to linger on any combination of thirteen, passing quickly across the landings and pausing halfway up the flights when the pressure became too much for him.

At the top of the third flight, he took a deep breath and walked round the corner into the corridor that led to his flat. It was as empty as it always was. Double A started to feel relieved. If there was one thing he wanted more than anything in the world it was to sit down on his own toilet in his own bathroom and take a good, long, slow dump.

He checked the stairwell behind him to make sure no one had followed him up, punched the air in silent triumph, took his keys from his pocket . . . then paused at his front door.

The door was closed and locked and didn't look as if it had been tampered with in any way, but he'd been being cautious all afternoon and it might pay to keep it that way. Being careless could easily lead to grief, as good old Reuben Brown could have told you.

Double A dropped to his knees, carefully pushed back the letter-box flap and peered down his hall and into the lounge. No problem!

He stood up, unlocked the door, went inside and closed and double locked it, then strode down the hall to the lounge where he would be able to find something to read while he took his dump.

Double A didn't see the thing that stove into his guts the moment he entered the lounge but he certainly felt its impact. He bent over, dropping to his knees and realising vaguely that his bladder was evacuating itself again and that this time there was going to be no stopping it while he fought the crushing pain that had robbed him of his breath.

Then something snapped down hard on the back of his neck.

And as Double A's vision flashed blue and went out, he thought, *They got me!*

Chapter Sixteen
Raising the Dead

1

By eight that evening, Paul had organised almost everything. The last thing he had done was dump the red Citroën in a back street. It seemed a little like abandoning a good friend and he had felt almost as sad when he left it behind as he had when he'd abandoned his own at Crawley railway station – what seemed like months ago now. It had been a good car and Paul hoped its owner would get it back before people started taking pieces of it away for spares.

They had spent the better part of the afternoon sitting in the only open taverna on the sea front waiting for the shops and banks to re-open for the evening. The sun felt good on Paul's face and the beers he drank eventually found their way beneath his guard and soothed him to sleep. His dreams were pleasant and in spite of the fact that he was only out for about two and a half hours, he felt refreshed and alert when he woke with Katie's cool hand on his arm and her voice telling him that the bank across the road looked as if it was about to open.

He had changed the rest of the dollar cheques into cash (this particular bank was one of the ones that *didn't* ask for your passport) then booked himself and Katie (as Mr and Mrs Stephen Smith) into a hotel on the sea front, paying cash in advance for one night only. When the hotel owner who was doubling as the receptionist politely (but suspiciously, Paul thought) inquired as to what had happened to the pair of them, Paul had tiredly repeated the story about the motorcycle accident. It wasn't until they got upstairs into their room and he looked at himself in the bathroom mirror that he realised why the proprietor hadn't looked as if he believed them. The dark-eyed person that stared back at him from the mirror looked like someone who had been through a very dirty war. By comparison, Katie, whose dress now looked like something Pam Hogg might have designed in one of her wilder moments and then attached with a sharp instrument and a hoover bag full of dirt, looked clean and tidy. Both of them were grimy and the idea of a good long shower was almost irresistible, but that would have to wait. If they wanted to keep a low profile they both needed new clothes. The arse of Paul's jeans had torn where the pocket had been ripped off and his boxers were showing through, his espadrilles were ruined, and his shirt was torn and filthy.

Katie lay down on the double bed and sighed like the world's most tired woman.

'I've got to go out,' Paul told her, and asked if she thought she would be okay. She hadn't said a great deal since she'd asked him if he wanted to try to use a dead person to get some information, but she was looking in fairly good condition – taking everything into consideration. She seemed to have managed to find her way back into all the limbs of her body now, except her left hand which sometimes flapped about like a dying fish and sometimes hung limply like a dead one.

'I'll be okay if you promise to come back to me,' she said.

Paul knew why she wanted him to promise to return and why she hadn't been saying much. It was because he had not yet agreed to rush out with her and find a dead person to wake up. She thought she had found the line over which he was not willing to step; thought she might have spooked him badly enough for him to want to fade away and leave her. The idea of stealing into a morgue in the dead of night and trying to wake up a freshly deceased person didn't exactly fill Paul with pleasure, but it didn't repel him either, and this was one of the reasons he hadn't agreed.

Things were moving just a little too swiftly for him to assimilate them and trying to use a dead person to 'scry', as she had called it, seemed to be lifting the lid off a very dark and deep chasm. And once you shifted the lids of these kind of things they very often didn't want to go back again. A part of Paul *wanted* to see that dead person walk and talk and this frightened him. It was something to do with the *power* you would be exerting over life and death and Paul couldn't get it straight in his mind at all. He didn't know if it would be a good thing or a bad thing, but he suspected it would be bad. Unless it was imperative that it was done, he didn't trust himself to take part because he thought he might be different afterwards.

The fact that he had already brought Katie back to life a number of times ought to have convinced him otherwise, he supposed, but this seemed different somehow. For one thing, whatever dead person they chose would be someone who wasn't involved in their battle.

'I promise I'll come back to you,' Paul said and went out.

When he returned at eight he was wearing new espadrilles, a cheap pair of new denim jeans, a tee shirt with a picture of Corfu printed on the front and a place called Kavos exploding out of the southern point of the island in bright colours, and he was carrying a plastic bag.

He sat down next to Katie and said, 'I bought two tickets to Brindisi. The boat leaves at five in the morning from the dock across the road.' He took the tickets out and showed them to her. 'We're going to have trouble getting through passport control, but we'll worry about that when we arrive.' He folded the tickets and put them in his back pocket. 'And I got you a new dress. Hope it fits.'

He pulled the dress from the bag and held it up. It was a plain, short, white summer dress almost identical to the one she was wearing. Almost, but not quite. This white dress was the one she had been wearing in his first dream of her.

Katie smiled. 'Thank you,' she said. 'It'll fit, I'm sure. What else did you get?'

Paul shook his head. 'Nothing,' he said.

'In the bag. Something heavy.'

'Oh, that.' He put his hand in the bag, withdrew the thing and held it up for her to see.

It was a brand new crowbar.

'There's a funeral parlour just down the road,' he said. 'I don't know whether there's anyone in the chapel of rest, but there are flowers being delivered. We're going to need this to get us in tonight.'

And then Katie was in his arms, her own arms around his neck and pulling his mouth towards hers. She kissed him, long and deeply, and her cool mouth didn't taste of death and decay, but of vanilla and orange blossom and life. Paul didn't pull away from her until he was so hard he thought he would burst.

2

It took less than ten seconds to jemmy the door of the chapel of rest. Paul inserted the flat end of the crowbar by the lock and pushed and after the merest pressure, the lock popped undone. The wood of the door and frame didn't even split.

Paul checked that there was no one passing and no lights burning in the funeral parlour itself, then opened the door. Katie went in first and Paul followed, closing the door after him and setting the deadlock so even if Mr Funeral Director himself turned up with his Yale key, he wouldn't be able to get in. He groped in the darkness, found the light switch and flicked it. Katie stood about six feet in front of him with her hand already on the brass knob of a door – *the* door. She had showered and put on the dress he had bought her and there was a lustre in her tangled mane of yellow hair and a languid grace in her movements. Her bare arms and legs shone golden in the dim light and Paul felt an almost overpowering urge to have her – an urge which was heightened by the incongruity of the crazy situation they were in.

Not now, not ever, he told himself. *Katie is not yours to have and to hold and she never will be. You are here to protect and serve her and that's where it begins and ends. Anything else is folly, and probably dangerous...*

But his erection did not subside until he followed her into the room where the coffin stood open.

The room smelled of flowers and formalin. Paul knew about the 'hygienic treatment' that undertakers liked to give to bodies. Pumping out the blood and replacing it with a preservative stopped the rotting process – or at least slowed it down until the body was disposed of. The undertaker who had taken care of Paul's mother had wanted to do this to her and when Paul had refused, the man had unconsciously wrinkled his nose and suggested that in that case it might be wise to visit her sooner rather than later. Paul had not visited her at all. There didn't seem any point.

This coffin was dark, burnished wood – probably mahogany veneer, Paul thought – and was lined with quilted white satin. He went over to where Katie stood, staring down at the body, and took her cold left hand.

The dead person was a handsome Greek boy in his late teens. He was dressed in his best suit and his hands were clasped at his waist. His hair had been washed and blow-dried and someone had shaved him – probably since his death – and applied a little make-up: mascara to his lashes and powder to his face. His fingernails were clean and trimmed. His shoes were shiny.

'What happens now?' Paul asked.

Katie turned to him with a distant expression that made his heart race, and shrugged. 'I know, but I don't know,' she said. 'It's like everything else. It's inside me but I can't remember it. I just have to do what feels right. I think we have to join hands.'

'I've already got your hand,' Paul said. His voice shook with his heartbeat. If his libido had wanted proof that Katie was no normal sexy girl in her mid-twenties, all it had to do was peer out of his eyes right now. And yet there was still something in

412

her face that was attractive. Paul thought it might be raw power that was fizzling away behind those clear green eyes; the kind of power that would draw you in and then zap you into nothingness if you let it. For a moment Paul felt like a fly grazing at one of those ultra-violet bug killers they hung up in the restaurants around here.

'All of us,' Katie said. 'Go round the other side and take his hand. I'll take this one and you and I hold hands across him.'

Paul put down the crowbar and the bread knife he'd brought with him and did as he was told. Katie was changing somehow, tapping her inner resources and bringing them forth. It was scary but it was also magical. Paul began to believe she could make this boy sit up and recite the Rime of the Ancient Mariner if she wanted to.

He took Katie's hand then reached down for the boy's, telling himself that it wasn't going to be much different from the way that Katie felt. Except that it was. The boy's hands were stiff and very cold and the texture of them was wrong and they didn't want to let go of one another. Paul shook the teenager's right hand away from his left and pulled it towards him. It was like bending a tree branch.

When Katie took hold of the Greek boy's other hand Paul received a shock that felt like a jolt of static but which went on for a good five seconds. There was a part of him that badly wanted to let go of those two cold hands and get the hell out of here.

Now what are you getting yourself into, cowboy? his goad asked as Paul's pulse rate shot up through the one forties and into the one fifties. Paul didn't know.

Katie closed her eyes and Paul waited for her to start to chant or say some incantation, but she merely pursed her lips as if she was concentrating hard. Paul's mind tried to tell him that he could see the emerald green of her eyes shining through the closed lids, but he bit down on the thought and looked away.

And that was worse because the place he chose to look at was the boy's face and his eyelids had begun to flutter.

Good time to leave, the goad thought and the larger part of Paul agreed. You had to draw the line somewhere. He was a second away from bolting for it and knew just how relieved he was going to feel when he got out of this cloying atmosphere into the warm and fragrant Greek night with its cloud of bright stars. He relaxed his grip on both the hands he had hold of and felt a bright spark of panic as they both instantly increased theirs.

It isn't possible! his mind screamed.

But it was possible and it was happening, right before his eyes.

The Greek boy's lids fluttered and he gasped in a breath that sounded something like the last of the bath water gurgling down the plughole. The breath was expelled in a kind of raspberry through the boy's lips and Paul remembered something else he'd once learned about the way bodies were laid out. Undertakers didn't like you to gape, so they sewed your mouth shut by inserting a needle and thread up between your front teeth and lip and driving it through your septum where your nose joined your face. Then they made a loop down inside the front of your bottom jaw and pulled it up tight so your mouth shut. Paul presumed they tied a knot where your front teeth were then closed your lips over the thread. If this boy was going to talk, that thread that was making him expel his breath in a dry fart was going to have to be severed.

But there was no further time to consider whether he ought to try to tell Katie because the boy's eyes opened and they were looking directly at Paul. They were dark and dry and milky and they looked at him like they knew him and hated him.

The boy's lips parted, revealing the black loop of thread. He drew a breath and spoke a single word in an arid voice. The word wasn't in any language that Paul had ever heard before – it certainly wasn't Greek or English or even Latin – and yet it was a language that Paul understood as easily as if it had been his mother tongue. He doubted he could speak it, but he could understand it.

There was only one translation of the word and if anyone

had asked Paul what the corpse had said, the only truthful reply he could have given was, 'What?' But although that was the literal truth of the single word there was much more information contained within it. It was a question, an accusation, a threat, and an invitation all rolled into one. It evidently meant that the corpse was going to talk.

As Paul waited for Katie to ask a question – and gradually realised that the only person likely to be asking questions around here was him – the corpse began what looked as if it was going to be a long, slow (and probably painful, if the dead boy could feel anything) transition from lying to sitting. Paul could hear the movement of muscles soaked in preserving fluid trying to work as they used to – probably as recently as yesterday. The boy sat up surrounded by many faint sounds that reminded Paul of paper bags rustling and old cloth tearing.

The boy slowly turned his head toward Katie and Paul heard bone popping and tendon creaking. And as the boy's head turned away from him, Paul saw the reason he was here. This youth hadn't died of a heart attack or disease, he'd been in a very bad accident. The undertaker, knowing that the relatives weren't likely to inspect the corpse too closely, hadn't done a very good job on the back of his skull. Whatever had hit this boy had hit him very hard indeed. His hair was missing and his skull was ruined. It looked as though someone had worked on it with a chainsaw. There were pieces of it missing. Paul's stomach squeezed and he knew, without a shadow of a doubt, that the boy had been hit by a car.

This is what little Paulie looked like, his mind whispered.

The corpse spoke the word again, to Katie this time, and Paul tore his gaze away from its damaged head to see what she would do. And then he looked away again because there was a faint emerald tinge showing through her eyelids and she was vibrating slightly.

Paul glanced at that damaged head again and then closed his own eyes. He wasn't entirely surprised to find that instead of seeing purple and blue after-images against a black background, he found himself looking at a flat, faultless green sheet. A sensation accompanied this which felt like several more of his marbles rolling away from each other. Paul purposely didn't think about it, just as he refused to consider the implications or the actuality of what he was doing. The only thing that seemed certain was that you couldn't do things like he'd been doing since yesterday and expect to live to tell the tale. Paul refused to consider how he felt about this either.

Katie didn't speak. Paul knew he was going to have to do it and he searched for his voice. The smell of death and formalin was making him want to throw up and he thought he might do so the moment he opened his mouth. There was a smell of engine oil beneath all the other odours and that almost pushed Paul over the edge because somewhere on this dead youth there was a spot of lubrication from the vehicle which killed him and a part of Paul's mind was repeating, *He's still got its oil on him!*

Paul cleared his throat. 'We brought you back because we need to know things,' he said.

The corpse turned back to him. It's flat, opaque eyes held his gaze. It spoke again in the strange language. 'Then know this and remember me,' it said.

And Paul was no longer in the chapel of rest holding hands with two dead people but outside in bright sunlight, striding past the taverna where he and Katie had spent the afternoon. He was nineteen and feeling good because he had two loves in his life: a girlfriend named Katerina whom he loved and intended to marry, and a 250cc trials bike – upon which he intended to take the other love of his life to the beach this afternoon. He had a job on the ferries which was okay but which kept him away from home for days at a time, but today he wasn't thinking of work because his shift was over and now he had three days in which he could please himself. And he intended to do a great deal of pleasing.

He called out to John who was on the other side of the street and suddenly decided that he would kill the half an hour until Katerina was free by catching up on the gossip John would have.

He turned abruptly, stepped off the kerb – and suddenly John was shouting at him. Screaming at him.

Like a man in a dream, he turned to his left, knowing there was a puzzled frown on his face. The car that was coming at him, now laying rubber as its driver braked, was a white pick-up. He felt a moment of confusion because the road had been clear when he looked, then there were many thoughts cascading inside his head like a great fountain. The chief of these was the information that for the first time since he was able to walk he had stepped off the kerb *without* looking. Below this there was an angry feeling that his body and mind had betrayed him and that it was too late to make amends. Then there was the feeling that the driver of the car had betrayed him too, because that car was surely going to hit him and delay his date with Katerina, and jostling with this was the certain knowledge that he wasn't going to be hurt. He was going to collect a bump and he was going to remember that white pick-up until the day he died, but he was going to walk away.

Then this was all swept away by a great all-encompassing fear and an urge to jump, and jump at the right time.

And he did jump. As the front of the car reached him, he leapt higher than he had ever leapt before and brought his legs up like a long-jumper. And the bonnet of the car passed under him. For one glorious moment he thought he'd made it. Then his knees went through the windscreen and he felt his legs tear as he was tossed over the roof of the cab, the world outside him rolling into a huge colourful blur. He felt blood spatter his face and saw a leg – his left – above him, now absent from the knee down and gouting blood. Then he bounced on something which might have been the back of the pick-up. Then, as the world blurred again, he caught a glimpse of another car. A car which had smashed into the back of the pick-up and lost its bonnet. He whip-lashed backwards down into that open engine and felt hair tear from his head and heard the screaming scrape of something metallic moving fast against the back of his skull. Then there was a jumbled blur of thoughts and memories which turned into a huge electric shock. Then there was silence.

Then Paul was back in the chapel of rest, still feeling the sensation of his hair being torn out by the fan belt of the crashed car and the agonising scrape of the old fashioned steel-bladed fan against the back of his already cracked skull.

'Remember me,' the corpse said, and turned away.

Paul thought it was finished but for a few moments was unable to speak. 'Wait,' he said eventually, and it turned back.

'What?' it asked, again showing him the thread that held its jaws closed.

'You have to answer my questions.'

'Ic alufool kalamoon,' he said. *I won't.*

'We won't let you go until we're finished,' Paul told it. He gave up trying to keep his heartbeat in the one fifties and let it go. If they found him dead here in the morning, so be it. He was beyond caring.

'Let me rest,' the corpse said. 'I have far to travel.'

'Not until you answer my questions.'

'Then ask.'

Paul's mind blanked. The only question he could come up with was, *What's happening?* and he doubted very strongly that this was going to be specific enough. 'How many are there following me?' he asked.

'Two live, two neither live nor dead. More wait ahead.'

'How many more?'

The corpse curled its lips. 'There are thirteen in total, of course. One leads, twelve follow.'

Thirteen, Paul thought, *four behind, nine in front. And when you kill them, they don't die, they still keep coming.* 'What do they want?' he asked.

'What is theirs.'

'Katie?'

'The Kate body is empty. It is a channel.'

'What do they want her for?'

'The Kate body is altered. It is a doorway across the void.

418

It is deiparous. It can be used to birth gods and angels and sprites.'

That sounds about right, Paul thought. *Crazy, but right.*

'Who is the one who leads?' he asked.

The corpse spoke a word that fled from Paul's mind as soon as he heard it. It was a sound that was both beautiful and unpleasant. A sound that made you feel colder than ice. It was a sound that summed up his feelings about the burnt Katie-thing quite precisely.

'What is he?' he asked, already knowing the answer.

'A black angel.'

'And he's in Cambridge, leading his flock,' Paul said to himself.

The corpse did not reply.

'Where is he?' he demanded.

'He is in a man body. He is half-born. The man body is crip-pled.'

'It's name is H?' Paul asked.

'The body was Henry Tyler. The body was opened unto the angel. Henry Tyler is gone. The black angel has the body. It is half-born.'

'How do we deal with it?'

'It will not deal.'

Paul rephrased the question. 'How do we overcome it?'

The corpse held him with those hateful eyes and spoke in its foreign language. 'The black angel cannot be overcome.'

'What are its weaknesses?'

'None.'

Paul thought about it. He didn't think that the corpse would be able to lie, but the existing evidence suggested that good old Henry Tyler, the man who had apparently told Katie she was a bad girl, and the man who had now been replaced with a black angel, *did* have weaknesses. He (or his agents or disci-ples or whatever you wanted to call them) had tried to scare Paul off and the angel itself had tried to make a deal with him. It was possible that the corpse didn't have access to all the information, of course. Paul didn't know where this stuff was coming from and had assumed that the corpse was either plucking it out of the ether or had somehow become connected to the world beyond. There was another possibility, however.

'How much do you know?' Paul said.

'I know nothing,' the corpse replied. 'I say what I see.'

'Where are you looking?'

'Through the doorway.'

Which meant that the corpse was dredging the parts of Katie's mind to which she had no access. Paul didn't know if those parts were over there inside her skull or situated 'on the other side of the chasm', but that didn't matter. Katie wasn't yet complete, so there was no reason why her knowledge should be.

'Can you tell me the location of the four who follow me?' Paul asked.

'No,' the corpse said. 'Coming. Not close.'

'Those who wait?'

'The black angel is in Cambridge. The others are scattered in the land. They . . . wait.'

The corpse closed its eyes. 'Set me free,' it grated.

'What is the black angel's aim?' he asked.

'Mayhem,' the dead boy said. 'Set me free now. Enough!'

'Go!' Paul said.

The dead boy leaned back into his coffin with a series of creakings and poppings and let out his last breath in another dry, rasping fart.

Paul placed the boy's hand on his stomach, then took the other out of Katie's hand and laid this the way he had found it. He had expected to feel triumphant but he felt dirty and queasy. *Remember me*, the boy had said. Paul didn't think he would ever be able to forget, even if he wanted to.

Katie still stood like a statue, her head tilted back, her eyes closed and her hand holding on to thin air where the boy's hand had been. Paul could see no green light showing through her eyelids and began to believe he'd imagined it. It felt more comfortable that way.

'Sweetheart?' he said.

Katie relaxed. Her eyes opened and she looked confused. 'Something cold,' she said. 'There was something cold in me, feeling my brain. What happened?'

'We did it,' Paul said. 'Now let's get out of here.'

3

Katie slept as soon as her head touched the pillow of the double bed in the hotel. Paul didn't. He felt as if he was being pulled apart. For one thing, there was a naked girl beside him whom he badly wanted to wake up and make love to (even if she had flesh as cold as winter and no pulse at all) and he knew he should not. For another thing he had brought a corpse back to life and had it read parts of Katie's mind she couldn't get to herself. Anyone who could sleep under those conditions was going to have to have been previously sedated.

The dark angel, he thought. *A thing from the far side of death. A thing from Hell?* He didn't know what he thought about Heaven and Hell – except that the concept was far too simple for his liking. If there was a world beyond death to which everyone went (and he had been forced to believe this was true, whether he'd wanted to or not) he doubted it was going to be a simple split between the good guys on one side and the baddies on the other. He felt more comfortable believing that on the other side of the chasm was another world, perhaps a little like this one, where the good guys and the bad guys would live side by side, if a little uneasily. A world where life differed, perhaps, and where people were aware of things they could not perceive while they were here, but just another world in an endless chain of other worlds through which immortal souls would pass.

Paul imagined being a goldfish whose whole world was a deep, dark pond. A human being could walk up to that pond and push a hollow tube down into it and the fish would be scared and amazed in the same way as he had been when he'd seen the tube descend out of nowhere up on that hill. For the human it wouldn't be anything out of the ordinary. For the fish it would be a miracle. But if the goldfish suddenly became human, it would be a fresh world where this kind of miracle would be as nothing. *And if it then got turned back into a fish, its brain wouldn't be able to recall or explain what had happened when it was human,* he thought. *And if the fish returned to the pond and was half fish, half human, the other fish would call it a being from across the void. They'd call it angel.*

It was soapbox philosophy – or theosophy, rather – and Paul knew it. He also knew that thinking of himself as one little fishy in a very large pool (as Henry Tyler had once informed him in a dream) made him feel a great deal more comfortable about the whole thing.

When he finally fell asleep, it was safe in the knowledge that he had lived in worlds before this one, and he would live in worlds after it and that in each of them he would be bonded to a girl he now knew as Katie.

And when he woke at four-thirty to the sound of the ferry's low bellow announcing its arrival, he woke with tears in his eyes and the clear memory of having recently been dreaming that he was pleading with some far-off greater being. His words still rang in his ears: *Please God, I want her back when you've finished with her. Please send her back to me!*

Chapter Seventeen
Double A Takes a Trip

1

Consciousness took quite a time to return to Double A, and when it did it came back to him bit by bit, and cautiously, like a deer that has recently been scared away from its favourite forest clearing.

His hearing came back first and by the time his still-closed eyes began to register light outside, he knew he'd been listening to a deep, measured breathing that held a faint whistle for quite a while. If Double A had been capable of thought at that moment, he would have known there was an opportunity to escape and the words, *He's asleep* would have crept across his mind.

And he would have been wrong.

If, as Double A's senses had crept back to him, his sense of smell had also returned, he would have been able to save himself a great deal of mental anguish, but his sense of smell was one of the things he had traded off against his need to feel like Superman; several years' worth of constant chemical insult to his nasal passages precluded him from detecting all but the most pungent of odours.

By the time he *was* capable of thought, Double A's terror had reached such a degree that his neural networks might as well have been absent.

When he became aware that he was not alone on the sagging sofa where he'd been placed; not because the weight beside him was causing him to tilt to the left instead to the right which would have normally been the case (his mind was not clear enough to register this), but because his left hand was touching something that was warm and firm and probably the source of the breathing, Double A began to feel warm at his crotch.

A second later he realised that he was pissing his pants and a second later everything that had happened to him came crashing back. In the space of one day he had survived one attempt on his life, he had turned into a merciless killer, he had shoved more junk up his nose than he ought to have done, and he had been caught by the would-be assassin's accomplice who had already hit him hard enough to knock him cold for what seemed like two days (and hard enough for him to wake with drying blood in his mouth) and who evidently intended to extend the torture for God only knew how long.

The final straw was when Double A finally opened his eyes.

And saw the dead man sitting in the chair opposite him.

Double A screamed long and hard . . . and fainted away.

2

There were two of them. Double A found this out shortly afterwards because the one who was alive (and who had been sitting beside him) slapped his face, hard.

Lights flashed behind Double A's eyes and part of him informed him that if he would please just give it a great bit hit of sulphate or something similar it would make sure it looked after him and things would look just fine and dandy for him.

Double A wasn't sure he hadn't voiced this opinion. His mouth and throat felt as if he'd just said something.

'You must be joking me!' a voice said from somewhere above and before him. 'Wakey wakey, rise and shine!'

This time Double A heard the hand swooping down towards him. He thought of good old Reuben Brown and knew that it had to be him out there taking a swipe at him because the other guy was most certainly deceased. A hit of sulphate wasn't going to make *him* get up and walk. Double A screamed to himself that it couldn't be Reuben out there because he'd put the guy 'hrough a plate glass window at twenty miles an hour or more and had the dent in the '59 Pop's wing to prove it. It was crazy, but in that moment Double A believed it. Who else could it be out there? Double A tried to play dead for a little longer and the hard hand hit him around the face.

'Wake up, you little bastard!'

There was something familiar about that voice.

Of course, it's Reuben's!

Double A tasted fresh blood in his mouth.

Cheek's cut probably. Nose is probably bleeding a bit too. Stings!

The hand hit him again, but not so hard this time. Reuben was tiring of his game.

If I just had a snort I'd be fine! Make a break for it then, he thought, dazedly.

'Okay,' the voice said. 'I didn't want to have to do this, but if it's what you want, if it's your little heart's desire, then who am I to stop you?'

There was a pause which was followed by a rustling noise.

And when the man grabbed Double A's hair and tilted his head back, Anthony Anthony suddenly realised he'd spoken the thought and given Reuben a good idea. The stuff back at the Miles Carriage Co. had been hot and there was no reason why Reuben shouldn't have more of it.

'No!' Double A moaned.

'You said you wanted it!'

A finger pressed powder into Double A's right nostril. His head was released.

'Suck that up! Go on!'

Double A held his breath.

The finger found his left nostril and plugged it with powder.

'Wake up, you little bastard, and suck up that dope.'

Double A opened his mouth and took a breath. His nose was stinging and he suspected the poison was beginning to work.

You just let good old Reuben kill you, he thought to himself in astonishment, *and you didn't fight back. You didn't even open your eyes.*

But he hadn't breathed the stuff in yet. Not far enough anyway. There were only a few specks of the powder eating into his mucus membranes way up there in the back of his nostrils; the rest was chewing at his damaged septum.

I'm playing dead, he told himself and then thought, *Yes, and in a few seconds you won't have to act either, it'll be real! If you don't do something!*

Double A did something. It wasn't much but it was better than nothing and it was quite an achievement for a man who was paralysed with terror because he was being killed by someone he'd killed earlier.

He closed his mouth and blew hard through his nose.

The deadly powder shot out of his nose and blew down across his lips and chin. It was going to be dangerous to inhale again now, either through his nose *or* mouth. This knowledge lit in his mind in words of fire. One single little inhalation was going to mean poison pouring into him. He had hardly realised the irony of this when the man shouted. 'You little *swine*!' and grabbed him again.

This time Reuben wasn't so gentle. More powder was thrust into his nostrils, a strong hand held the back of his head and another clamped itself over his mouth.

'Suck it up!' the voice commanded.

Double A held his breath until his lungs screamed and garish puce and purple starbursts began to swim before his eyes, then he learned why few people attempted to commit suicide by simply refusing to breathe: it couldn't be done. When your body decided it was going to have to breathe in, it would do it regardless of whether you wanted it to or not.

Two good nostrils full of powder blasted their way up into Double A's mucus membranes and down his throat.

Double A waited for the agony as whatever corrosive agent the powder contained started to work on him, peeling away his flesh . . . but this didn't happen. It was rather like inhaling a nostril full of minute, fresh snowflakes.

If this is the way it feels, I don't mind, he thought and began to grin.

3

Double A realised he hadn't been poisoned at all but rather had been done a very big favour at the same moment he opened his eyes. The powder was the best cocaine he'd snorted in a very long while.

'What?' he said in delight and confusion and disbelief.

The face he was staring up at was not the dark face of dead Reuben Brown, the man with the plastic gun, the suitcase full of funny money and a plastic bag full of death, but the plug-ugly mug of Big Jake Fulman, a man Double A had not expected to see again. For two pins Double A could have kissed it.

''Bout time too,' Jake said.

Double A sat up, looking from Jake to the man in the chair and back again while he unconsciously fingered the rest of the cocaine from the rims of his nostrils and vacuumed it up them. He ached, his stomach hurt and his neck was going to complain each time he tried to turn his head (from now until doomsday by the feel of it) and his clothes were soaked in urine, but he felt good. Not for the first time Double A noted that it was amazing what a fillip a little snort of powder could give you when you were feeling down and out.

'Jake,' he said, still not quite believing his good fortune. A part of him (old Mr Paranoia) was telling him that this was just another *halucy* and that Jake's features would soon ripple and become Reuben's, but Double A did not believe it.

'In person,' Jake said.

'What happened?' Double A asked.

Jake grimaced. 'Funny that. I was about to ask you the very same question, ducky.'

Double A shook his head, an action against which his neck complained vehemently. 'I dunno,' he said, 'there was this big black guy. I killed him.'

'Snap,' Jake said. 'Except mine was more medium-sized and white.' He pointed his finger over his shoulder at the dead man in the seat. 'Who is he, why did he try to kill me, why are there cops crawling all over my house and yard, what's happened to the workshop, and did I stick the right white powder up your snout or are you going to flake out and die on me in two shakes?'

'Where is it?' Double A asked. 'The powder, I mean.'

Jake took a paper bag from his jacket pocket which looked as if it contained at least two ounces. 'This is what I gave you. Any good?'

Double A held out his hand and took the bag, his disbelief growing. He nodded, peering into the bag and wondering if his eyeballs were going to fall right out of his head and roll around in there gathering up cocaine. 'Excellent,' he said distantly. *There's enough here to erode your septum right out of your nose*, he thought. *Enough to make you a one-nostril human being. Enough to kill you with ecstasy.*

In the distance Jake was speaking '. . . and this . . . and this . . .'

Double A looked up and saw two more bags, both plastic zip-lock ones. One was full of amphetamine sulphate crystals and the other contained sheets of printed blotting paper.

'. . . and there was some other stuff but I already flushed that down the porcelain megaphone. I was gonna do away with this lot too, but you came home and I got distracted.'

'Hitting *me*,' Double A complained, dipping a finger into the bag and tasting the powder. It really was true. The stuff was good cocaine.

Jake shrugged. 'Thought you was one of them,' he said. 'Time I realised you was you, it was a bit too late. Damage was done.' He shrugged again. Jake Fulman was not a man to whom the word 'sorry' came easily. 'Are you okay?' he eventually asked.

'I'd be feeling a lot better if you hadn't hit me,' Double A said, snorting a pinch of the coke.

'Better safe than sorry,' Jake said. 'Matey-boy was armed.'

When Double A looked up he found himself looking at a gun which was identical to the one Reuben had threatened him with – except this one was equipped with a silencer.

'That's not a real gun,' he said disdainfully. 'It's plastic.'

'Oh,' Jake said sagely, and squeezed the trigger.

The noise which followed sounded rather like the sound Double A expected a real muffled gun would make. Something smacked the sofa beside him and deep inside it a spring twanged. Double A's tired nose detected a smell that was either gunpowder or cordite.

Beside him, a small, black-edged hole had appeared in the sofa.

Double A suddenly remembered that crap he hadn't taken earlier. Now seemed like a very good time to go and take it.

'Wake up, my little chicken,' Jake said irritably. 'Someone's dropped a cartload of pig shit on us and you and me are going to have to deal with it. Go get washed and changed because we're in a hurry.'

4

Double A was not a man who liked the idea of communal toilets, communal changing rooms, or anything else communal, and especially showers. One of the reasons for this was that he was uncomfortable with his body. In Double A's opinion some bodies were made to be seen naked and some were made to remain unseen. What little there was of his fell into the latter category. A long time ago Jake had started to call him his little chicken, not because of cowardice but because he thought Double A looked like one. A starved one. Jake had a point, he supposed. What Double A didn't like most about his body was having other people stare at it.

Which was exactly what Jake was doing now. Double A

stood in the shower thinking himself lucky that Jake hadn't thought it necessary to shower too, otherwise Jake would be a lot closer to him than he was.

He was currently sitting on the closed lid of the toilet, talking.

'I was going to spend another three days down in Looe,' he said. 'The shark fishing's good, the sea was calm and there was this big house I was casing. I'd already done two others and I thought I'd make it a hat-trick before I came back. But I went to bed last night about midnight and I started to get these fucking horrible nightmares about that house. It was called Black Rock and I kept on dreaming that every time I set foot inside it something horrible was coming after me. I kept on waking up and then going back to sleep and dreaming the same thing again. And each time I was further inside the house and by about the fifth time I could hear this yelling, like someone wanted me to help 'em. Like they were in trouble. It was a girl. I dunno which girl because there were loads of 'em there. It was like a haunted house where loads of girls were trapped or entombed or something, but there were only a few I could hear. But there was one voice calling louder. Except that sometimes it was a *different* voice, but I knew it was the same one. Dreams are fucking weird, ain't they?'

'Yeah,' Double A agreed. If it wasn't for the craziness he'd experienced today (and even then, only if there was no chance of Jake seeing him) he might have placed his forefinger against his forehead and wound it round and round. But there had been craziness today and it looked set to continue and there was a part of him that sympathised with Jake. The man sounded embarrassed but as if he had a real need to get this thing off his chest. Double A owed it to him to listen, but he would have done it anyway. Because old Reuben hadn't just been a conman, he'd been an expert who knew that the best tricksters were the ones who wove a thread of truth through their lies. And Reuben had been telling the truth about Gordon Clement the pharmacist from Basingstoke who was supposed to have been in his flat hiding drugs. If Jake hadn't turned up unexpectedly,

Clement, who was still sitting in the lounge just about as dead as a doornail could get, would have planted the drugs and called the police. And where would poor Anthony be now? Hiding his head under his wing, poor thing, while the detectives constructed a case against him that would put him away for fifteen at least.

'Then, when that stopped, I could hear another voice. Paul's.'

'Dekker?' Double A asked, inspecting the dark bruise that was coming in his midriff where his saviour had planted his knee firmly into his guts.

'You've heard of him,' Jake said.

'Mr Stephen Miles,' Double A said. 'Dunno why you had to keep it a secret from me. Reuben the conman knew who he was.'

'Less known, less said,' Jake muttered darkly. 'They don't call you rocket-gob for nothing.'

'They don't call me rocket-gob at all,' Double A complained.

Jake chose to ignore this. 'Anyway, lemme 'splain this to you. I hear Paul shouting out that he needs to get a hold of me. And he's in the back of this dark house and I'm running and he's saying, "Look behind you, Jake!" And I'm turning and seeing shadows behind me, like what you get in football stadiums when they got all the lights on. Lots of different shadows chasing me. And I'm running but it's like I'm running on the spot. I can't get to him to help him because my shadows are holding me back. Whaddya make of that little lot?'

Double A shook his head. He wanted to tell Jake that he was as crazy as Joan of Arc, but for one thing he didn't think Jake would know who she was and for another there was something about the dream that spoke to a deep, dark place inside him and brought him out in shivers in spite of the steaming water that was coursing down his body.

'So I wake up and it's three o'clock in the morning and I says to myself, Jake, you just had a . . . whaddya call it . . . premolution? A premolution. So I call Paul's mum's. He's been staying with her since that Amy threw him out. No reply. I call

431

my place and there are cops there. I don't tell 'em who I am, because you can tell cops a mile off. I call Amy. And you know what?'

'The cops think he killed his mother,' Double A replied. 'Reuben knew that too. He's missing, isn't he? D'you think he did it?'

Jake paused for a moment. 'And Amy's mother answered the phone. Amy's dead. Murdered in her bed.'

'Christ,' Double A said. He was beginning to understand what he was into now and he didn't like it in any way whatsoever. Someone (and it might be Paul Dekker and it might not, but judging from what Reuben had said, it wasn't) was going around killing everyone Paul Dekker knew.

'And then I called Freddie.'

Double A knew what came next. 'And he's dead too. They tried to kill me and presumably they would have tried to kill you too if they'd known where you were.'

'Looks that way,' Jake said. 'Anyway, I still had this leftover feeling from the nightmare that I had to help Paul, so I got dressed, checked out of the hotel, came back to town, dumped the booty with Dan Coley and went over to the workshop. The fire was out by then, but I didn't stop because the cops were like bluebottles around a nice fresh turd. I didn't know where to go next, then I *did* know where to go.'

'Here,' Double A said, turning off the faucet. 'Pass me a towel.'

Jake got up and gave him the towel. 'And I ring on the doorbell, and lo and behold . . . I'm staring down the barrel of this gun.'

Double A got out of the shower and dripped on the floor. It was getting a little too scary now to worry about being coy and Jake didn't look as if he was the least bit interested in the width of his body. His eyes were distant. 'What happened?' Double A asked.

Jake shook his head. 'I was psyched right up. I'd have punched out Tyson, Evander Holyfield, Frank Bruno and several others without it even crossing my mind that I might get hurt. I let him have it, boy.'

'While he was pointing a gun?'

'I was looking at the wrong end of guns while you were still filling your Pampers with green goo,' he said, 'and this guy wasn't someone whose piece fitted in his hand. You can tell when they're likely to shoot you. It's in their eyes, but it's also in their hands. The gun'll fit there like it belongs. The guy was crazy enough to do it, but he wasn't clear-headed enough to know his moment. His moment passed about two seconds after he opened the door. He who hesitates is well fucked, ducks. He should have shot me on sight but he paused. I hit him. Hard. Very hard indeed.'

'A lot?' Double A asked, awestruck at what was a genuine revelation. The only time he'd encountered violence at Jake's hand was when he made a huge and costly blunder and then it amounted to nothing more than a gentle cuff around the head. Jake was one of the most placid men he knew. He looked like a man you wouldn't think lightly of upsetting (and consequently people *didn't* upset him) but to Double A he was just a regular guy who knew his cars and did the odd cat-burglary (although the word 'cat' ought to have been replaced with the word 'rhino'). Jake took people's possessions, but he made a point of not hurting those people physically.

'Just the one,' Jake said. 'Once was enough. I used to box. You didn't know that, didya?' He smiled briefly. 'Heavyweight. Not very accurate, but I packed a bit of a punch. Still do. Gave up after it happened the first time. Lost the killer instinct, see. Gotta have the killer instinct if you wanna win fights. Need a strong chin, too. Strong chin, I had, but the instinct had gone.'

The revelations were coming thick and fast now. Double A already knew what the 'it' was that had happened, but he still had to ask. 'You killed someone?'

Jake nodded. 'Yeah. One punch. Just like matey-boy in there. Twenty-two he was. Name of Anton. Charlie Anton.

Promising boxer. See, the ole skull's thinnest where the jawbone latches on. You pop someone a stiff one on the jaw, it rattles through that thin bit of skull and k.o.s 'em. You see 'em fall down stiff on the telly. 'S'what happened to Charlie Anton, 'cept I popped him a better one. A much better one. Bust his jaw, jawbone drove up into that thin bit of bone and bust that, and when Charlie fell down stiff, it was because he *was* stiff. A stiff. Know what I said about knowing when folk with guns mean it because there is a look in their eyes and their gun fits their hands?'

Double A nodded.

'I seen that look on Charlie's wife's face . . . and the fit of the gun in her hand. She came after me later. Two years later, just about when I'd put it to the back of my mind. I'd long since given up being a punchbag for other boxers and I'd already signed on as a 'prentice grease monkey. I opened my door one day to a knock and there she was. I didn't even know her. "This is for Charlie," she says and lets me have it. Yvonne, her name was. I found that out later.'

'You were *shot*?' Double A asked in total astonishment, but now Jake had come clean there was no stopping him. He was already pulling his shirt up and unbuttoning his trousers. The four bullet wound scars were long since healed over, but Jake's flesh was indented where the slugs had struck him. There was one just above his navel, one near his right hip, one low on his abdomen and the last was in the top of his right thigh.

'She started low and worked her way up,' Jake said. 'It was a six-shot army issue revolver. I forget which one but I ain't forgot how it hurt or how I bled. They dug the first two bullets out of the door frame, the third hit me in the leg, and like I say, she worked her way up as I fell down. If she'd aimed true to start, the fifth or the sixth bullet would have killed me. As it was they managed to put old Jake back together again. This scar here is from the surgery.' He pointed to a faint line that ran down his belly. 'That's the kind of trouble hitting people

434

on the chin can get you into, ducky,' he finished. 'And today, history repeated itself.'

Double A found fresh underwear in the airing cupboard and a clean pair of jeans which needed ironing. They would have to do. 'Meaning that you expect to get shot at now?' he asked. He thought of the bag of coke and decided that a top up would be a very nice thing.

'Meaning that this time it went in reverse. I just meant to knock him down and he ended up dead and I regret that, but I'd have been shot if I hadn't hit him first and I don't intend to get shot. But that story is just an aside. It just proves that things revolve. They go in cycles. History repeats. And it makes me feel better about my . . . premo . . .'

'. . . nition,' Double A finished for him.

'What it doesn't make me feel better about is the black stuff that came out of him.'

'Black stuff? Blood?' Double A asked.

Jake shook his head. 'Nope, just black stuff. Like soot. Came out his mouth, trickled down his chin and then stopped.'

Double A shook his head. 'I didn't see any black stuff,' he said.

Jake shrugged and went on. ''Magination prob'ly. Anyway, he's dead. So I drag him into the lounge, take his gun and his bags of dope and start flushing them down the toilet . . . and then I hear someone coming. I nip back in the lounge, hide by the wall, a body comes through and I hit this one too. Knee in the guts, whack on the back of the head. And it's you. I drag you over to the sofa, thinking, Well, Jake, you've just gone and done it a third time, and you gasp or moan or something and I'm just composing myself again when the phone rings. I dash over there and pick it up thinking it's more of these lunatics and don't speak. And a bouncy voice comes across saying, "Tony? Tony, is that you?" And I don't speak for a bit because that guy I just killed might be Tony for all I know. "Tony?" the voice goes, and I'm thinking I recognise it but I still don't trust myself. And then it goes, "Double A? I know it's you. No need to panic. It's Stephen."' Jake tailed off, looking flushed and elated.

'Paul Dekker,' Double A said grimly. He didn't like the turn this conversation was taking, or the look that was trying to get itself settled on Jake's face. This was the face of a guy who would lay his life on the line for his friend. Double A thought he knew what the trouble was and he already had an answer for it. When you got right down to it and forgot all the shit like people's guns not fitting their hands and black stuff running out of their mouths after they'd died, it was quite simple. Good old Paul Dekker, the underworld's Scarlet Pimpernel, had bitten off more than he could chew with an organisation that couldn't be handled. Paul Dekker had upset the Mafia (who were, after all, the only people able, at the drop of a hat, to produce the kinds of quantities of drugs he'd seen today) and there was only one thing you could do when something like that happened: go far away, lie low and stay there. You couldn't fight the Mafia. Except the look on Jake's face was telling him that Jake thought you *could* fight the Mafia – and live to tell the tale.

Jake said, 'I say "It's Jake, Paul," and he tells me he's in trouble and needs help. He's in Greece and on his way to Italy and he wants us to go down to Naples and fetch him.'

Double A shook his head. 'Not the Cosa Nostra,' he said. 'You can break all my arms and legs, but I still won't go. Those guys kill you. Look at what's happening to all Dekker's friends and relatives if you don't believe me. Look at what's happened to me today.'

Jake shook his head. 'That ain't the problem, pal. The Mafia don't kill your ex-wife, for one thing. And for another, when you've killed one of them, they don't stop looking for you afterwards. You might be lucky for a time, or maybe for years, but sooner or later someone somewhere will spot you and they come. This ain't Mafia . . .'

And Double A got the distinct feeling that Jake was omitting the words, *This is something worse*.

The problem of what to do with the body was resolved in a way that neither of them expected. Jake had suggested just leaving it where it sat and dealing with it later, but Double A wanted it out of the flat. They were still arguing about it when Double A strode from the bathroom intending to do three things: a) treat himself to a good, deep snort; b) look for signs of the mysterious black stuff on the body; and c) to see (after the hefty snort) whether the body looked as if it would fold up enough to fit in the old steamer trunk in his lounge where he kept his clothes.

When Double A reached the lounge with Jake hot on his heels, he stopped so quickly that Jake ran into his back and shunted him forward another two paces.

'Oh,' he said, remembering his fantasy about Reuben Brown picking himself up out of the shattered remains of the plate glass window.

The dead man was gone.

'He *was* dead,' Jake said quietly. 'He had no heartbeat and he was definitely not breathing. He was dead. He *was*.'

Double A collected the bag of coke (which the dead man had left without collecting, and that was a funny joke because corpses probably went better with coke), took a pinch and fed it up his nose. Then he took another, then another. When he began to thrum like a taut string, he turned back to Jake, who looked as if he could do with a snort too, took a deep, shuddering breath and asked, 'What exactly *did* Dekker say about the nature of the trouble he was in?'

Jake shrugged. 'He said there were four guys tailing him and some coming towards him. There's a total of thirteen which means we're likely to be up against less than eleven.'

Double A shook his head. '*No*,' he said, 'the *nature* of the trouble, not how many are going to be trying to kill us.'

Jake shook his head. He looked as if he'd started to have problems with what they might be up against, too. Dead men didn't get up and walk. 'He just said that there was this girl. They're trying to kill her and Paul doesn't want to let them.'

'Oh,' Double A said, knowing his face said more. Thirteen people wanted to kill one girl – a girl who must have done something pretty fucking terrible, if you asked him – and Paul Dekker had decided to stop them doing it, probably simply because he wanted to jump her bones (or already had and wanted to do it some more). And these thirteen people had already killed Freddie Simmons, Dekker's wife, probably Dekker's mother too, judging from what Freddie had said the last time he'd called, and they'd also tried to kill little Anthony Anthony who had spent his life steering clear of trouble. All for a girl. *They must want her dead pretty badly*, he told himself, and couldn't think of a reason.

'He didn't say *why* they wanted her dead? Or *who* they were?' Double A asked.

'He didn't have to,' Jake said somewhat defensively. 'Lemme 'splain. If Paul does something, he does it for a good reason. I don't have to know the details – I can find those out later – all I have to know is that Paul's in trouble and that's good enough for yours truly. Paul's my friend and when your friend is in the shit you get on and help them out of it. I'd do the same for you. I'd expect you to do the same for me.'

'He didn't say anything about the *rules*?' Double A asked.

Jake's eyes gleamed dangerously. They were the eyes of a man who intended to fight a war on behalf of a friend, to the death if necessary. 'Rules? What the fuck are you talking about?' he said impatiently.

Double A didn't reply because his paranoid mind was drawing up the rules independently of him. The rules of engagement in this particular war were loaded against them. Thirteen against three. Four if you counted the girl. And when you killed off one of the opposition, you weren't lowering the odds because that corpse just got up and walked away. These kind of rules might have been drawn up by the guy who made the *Night of the Living Dead* movie and its sequel. A part of Double

A protested vehemently against the possibility of this happening in real life, but his paranoid part knew it was the truth. *They'll come after you*, he told himself, *slowly, but as relentlessly as machines. When you stop, they'll still be travelling. And they'll follow you wherever you go.* He thought about it and made a decision. 'I ain't coming, man,' he said.

Jake looked as if he had been slapped. His mouth dropped open. 'What?' he said.

'You want to go to Naples and get yourself killed, you go. I ain't coming. I don't even know where Naples is, other than it's in Italy somewhere, and I don't want to end up being dead there.'

'You're in it, my little chicken, whether you like it or not. I know it ain't your choice and I know we don't really know what we're up against, but sure as eggs make turkeys, you're in it. You been tagged and you're in.'

'And now I'm calling it quits,' Double A said.

'You don't quite catch me; they'll get you anyway, *ducky*,' Jake snarled.

Now Double A was seeing another side of dear old Jake – the side that had once frightened people. The dangerous side. Jake hadn't lost his killer instinct at all; it had been hiding just below the surface. Jake suddenly looked angry enough to knock down walls with his bare hands. Double A thought of him killing a man with a single punch, and in spite of himself, he broke out in a thrill of goosebumps.

'They might, they might not. If I go to Naples, they will for sure.'

Jake inspected his knuckles with darkly glittering eyes. For the first time, Double A noticed they were skinned where he'd hit Gordon Clement the gun-toting chemist. He felt the thrill again and shook it off because when he felt it, he actually *wanted* to go along with Jake and fight for Dekker and the girl. *It's this kind of thinking that makes guys like you rush to the recruiting offices each time a war breaks out*, he told himself. *And we all know what happens to those in a rush to fight.*

They come back in body bags, or horribly burnt or crippled.

'I ought to break *your* jaw, ducks,' Jake said, still inspecting his grazed knuckles. 'But I won't. You wanna run away, you do it. But I'm going and I want the car because I'm going overland. So just give me the keys to the Pop and I'll go.'

I'll give you the whole fifteen thousand, Reuben said in Double A's head, and he remembered how badly the man had wanted to take that car off him (badly enough to kill him, in fact) and how fiercely he had refused to let it go. The car was important. So important that Reuben had come to take it away. Double A's coked-up-to-the-max mind then made several quantum leaps of intuition that he would later remember as having seemed like solid logic at the time. Reuben had wanted the car, ergo he'd wanted to take it *away* from them. Which meant that the other side (who Double A had already christened *the baddies* in his mind) had known the car would soon be heading for Naples. In spite of the fact that this presupposed the baddies could see into the future (to some degree at least) it meant that they found it necessary to disable him and Jake. Which meant that the baddies must be entertaining a certain doubt in their minds as to the eventual outcome. Thirteen against three and they weren't certain they were going to win if Jake took the Pop down to Naples. Double A felt his internal balance swinging back. It stopped when each side was level. What swung it heavily down on the opposite side and made up Mrs Anthony's son's mind for him was what Jake said next.

'We won't need you anyway, chicken. We can handle it alone. I'm pretty handy when I need to be, and Paul . . . Paul can fight like ten men.'

And there it was. Paul can fight like ten men, Double A thought, suddenly wondering where his passport was. Not three against thirteen, at all! Paul can fight like ten men. And Jake makes eleven and I make twelve . . . and the girl makes the whole fucking sum up to thirteen. Even fucking Stevens.

'I'm coming,' he said, and didn't realise until a moment later that he was beaming like a lighthouse.

'YOU DON'T QUITE CATCH ME!' Jake roared, thumping the counter of the Hovercraft check-in desk with a fist that now seemed to be almost permanently clenched. The girl behind the counter looked worried – as did several members of the queue which Jake had jumped. A middle-aged guy had protested that Jake ought to get to the back of the line and Jake had challenged him with a smile, then told him, in a quiet, simmering tone, that those were very nice teeth and that if he still wanted to be in possession of them when he got to France, perhaps he ought to shut his trap and keep it shut. This wasn't exactly the low-profile Double A (who was intending to take the bags of coke and sulphate with him across the water) had wanted to keep, but he had to admit that it was impressive. Big Jake looked (and moved) like a steam locomotive whose boiler was pressurised almost to the point of explosion, and so far everyone he'd come in contact with had recognised this and treated him accordingly; no one wanted to be present when the boiler eventually blew. Double A had just been towed along in Jake's wake, alternately cringing and grinning.

'LISTEN TO ME CAREFULLY,' Jake told the girl. 'I HAVE TO GET ACROSS TO FRANCE THIS EVENING. IF I'D WANTED TO GO THE SLOW WAY I'D HAVE GONE DOWN TO THE SEALINK OFFICE AND GOT ON A BOAT WITH NO TROUBLE AT ALL, BUT I'M IN A HURRY WHICH IS WHY I'M HERE. DO YOU UNDERSTAND?'

'Yes,' the girl said, 'but . . .'

'AND I DON'T CARE IF YOU ARE BOOKED UP SOLID BECAUSE THERE ARE THREE FLIGHTS BETWEEN NOW AND SHUT DOWN TIME AND NOT EVERYONE IS GOING TO TURN UP FOR ALL THREE. THERE WILL BE AT LEAST ONE CANCELLATION OR "NO SHOW" AS YOU CALL THEM, BETWEEN NOW AND THEN, AND I WANT THE SPACE. THE MONEY'S IN FRONT OF YOU, IN CASH. NOW TAKE IT AND GIVE ME TICKETS!'

The girl looked as if she wanted to cry and was just about managing not to. 'I can't issue tickets for a flight when there isn't one for you to get on,' she insisted.

'I'VE CROSSED THIS FUCKING CHANNEL ON THE WRONG FUCKING HOVERCRAFT ABOUT A THOUSAND TIMES BEFORE!' Jake shouted.

'No need for that kind of language!' a disgruntled voice said from somewhere in the queue.

Jake spun round. 'WHO SAID THAT?' he thundered. No one had, apparently.

He turned back to the desk. 'IF I TURN UP EARLY FOR A CROSSING AND THERE'S A HOVERCRAFT ABOUT TO GO WITH A SPACE ON IT, DO YOU OR DO YOU NOT LET ME GO ON THAT ONE? YES YOU DO. SO WHAT IS THE PROBLEM WITH THE TICKETS? IT DOESN'T MATTER WHICH *FLIGHT* IT SAYS ON THEM SO LONG AS YOU'VE GOT THEM.'

The girl shook her head. 'Sorry, no space, no tickets.'

Jake nodded. 'Okay, what time's the next flight?' he said evenly.

'Forty-five minutes,' the girl replied.

'And if I come back in half an hour and there's a space, you'll sell me tickets?'

'Yes, but I wouldn't bother,' the girl said, letting her true feelings show now that the end of this particular tunnel was showing light, 'because this time of year the show rate is almost one hundred percent. You'd probably be better off going down to the Sealink offices like you said.'

'I'll be back,' Jake said, 'and there will be a space.' He turned to Double A, said, 'C'mon, chicken,' and strode out of the office.

'Where are we going?' Double A said when it became clear they were heading away from the car and toward the gates they'd come in.

'We're going to make a space,' Jake said.

The cars were already turning up for the next crossing (what the hovercraft people liked to call a 'flight') but Jake, who had stationed himself on the corner of the turning into the hover-port, waited until twenty-five minutes had passed before he stepped off the kerb and flagged down a car that was indicating to turn into the port. 'Wait here,' he told Double A, and hurried over to the car as the driver wound down his window.

Double A couldn't hear what Jake was saying, but he guessed from the body language what was happening. Jake was shrugging and doing a great deal of hand waving and head shaking. This then stopped and he started making signs with his hands as though he was issuing instructions.

A few seconds later he stood up, walked out into the busy main road and held up a hand, stopping the traffic. Then he signalled the driver of the car he'd stopped, who did a U turn back onto the main road and drove away.

Jake had a contented smile on his face when he returned. 'There's our space,' he said.

'What happened?' Double A asked.

'I told 'em there was a problem with the apron that goes into the water. They now think there's a craft grounded on it, blocking it, and that all further flights will be going from the Seacat port back down the coast. They think that there's plenty of time to get there because I said everything'll be forty minutes late.'

'They won't get back here before we go?' Double A asked. Jake smiled again. 'I doubt it, I've sent them in the wrong direction. They're going *away* from the Seacat port.'

7

An hour later, having survived a crossing the captain (or pilot) had described as moderate (apparently doublespeak for rough) and having gone through the Calais passport control without raising more than the suspicion you'd expect when you were driving a purple '59 Ford Popular with an engine that sounded exceedingly pissed off when it was off cam and that screamed with rage when you blipped the throttle, Double A found himself in a zen-like state of calm.

The officious customs guys hadn't searched the car, but Double A's mind had leapt and gibbered and somersaulted because he was certain they would and that as a consequence he would spend a good few years being buggered in a French prison. They'd given the car a quick once over, and he suspected they would have taken it to one side and pulled it apart if it hadn't been for the fact that it was getting late, they looked as if they'd already worked a long shift and had probably had as little as half an hour to go.

The drive down to Dover had been quite taxing; Jake drove like he did everything else – with a great deal of force – and the crossing hadn't exactly made Double A feel wonderful (although another snort would soon put *that* right), but when they'd got out on to the European mainland he'd suddenly begun to understand something. That something was that he was sitting on the wrong side of a car on the wrong side of the road in a foreign country and that Jake hadn't been driving like a maniac at all back in England. Compared to what he was now doing, he'd been driving very carefully. Double A had shouted, 'Look out, man!' a couple of times, realised he was being ignored and relaxed in the certain knowledge that the bad guys wouldn't be getting him at all because Jake was going to kill him first.

When, after more than ten minutes of Jake's playing high-speed dodgems, Double A found that he was still alive, he unzipped the fastener of his bag of sulphate and tasted it. It tasted fine. He snorted some. It was a more ragged buzz than the coke and it hurt more afterwards but it filled you with enthusiasm and energy. 'So where are we going?' he asked Jake, whose sweaty face was furrowed in concentration.

Jake threw the Pop around a corner so fast that Double A's head was forced all the way across to his left and came to rest against the side window. Once again he marvelled at the job they'd done on the car. Jake was in second now, with his foot hard down, and the motor was shouting. *Banzai*! Double A thought.

'Naples,' Jake muttered.

Double A winced as Jake missed third and cogs grated. *Grinding 'em down to fit*, he thought. 'Is this the way to Naples, then?' he asked as they bumped over the same section of railway line for what must have been the third time. He had a sneaking suspicion that Jake had very quickly become lost, which wasn't what he'd expected; the man had run cars to Belgium, Spain and Germany for Freddie so he ought to be able to find his way out of Calais by now.

'Not exactly,' Jake said, hitting the brakes hard and thrusting Double A forward against his seatbelt.

Double A glanced over at him questioningly, but Jake didn't look back, just took a peek at the mirror, swung the Pop round the corner and accelerated away again. Here was a man who had refused point-blank to take a plane to Naples (which would have meant a two-and-a-half-hour journey rather than the twenty-odd hours of driving they were going to have to do) because he was frightened of flying. A man who apparently thought there was more chance of being killed in an aeroplane crash than there was driving round Calais like a demented version of Nigel Mansell.

'So which way do we have to go?' Double A asked.

'Getting on the motorway out of here would be a good idea,' Jake said. 'The A26. It goes all the way down to Strasbourg on the German border.'

'Then what?'

'Then we go south to . . . Switzerland, I suppose, then . . . Italy?'

'Don't you know?'

'Do you know how to get to Italy?' Jake changed gear and the car screamed, accelerating away. 'I don't. How should I know where it is, I've never been there before. We'll have to get a map sooner or later.' He flung the car out into the oncoming traffic, squeezed through a gap that ought to have been too small . . . and wasn't, and overtook the car in front.

'D'you know where this motorway is?' Double A asked.

'Yep.'

'Is it far?'

'Nope.'

Lights turned red in front of them. Jake ran them.

'Are we going towards it?'

Jake shook his head.

'Didn't we ought to be?' Double A said. There was a single paranoiac warning bell going off inside his head now.

'We will be,' Jake said. 'Just as soon as I shake off this Renault that's tailing us.'

Double A's heart sank. He turned in his seat and saw the reason why Jake had been criss-crossing the town and port of Calais. It was a Renault 5 Gordini judging by its flared air-scoop arches and its size was diminishing rapidly as Jake put the Pop's pedal down hard.

'The guy's good,' Jake said, hanging a right without warning. 'His car's slower than ours but he's managing to hang on. He must know all the short-cuts. Thought we'd lost him twice, but he keeps popping up again as if he was there all along.'

Jake hung another right – into a side-street this time – and powered away. 'If I'm right,' he growled, 'we should meet him coming towards us. I *know* there's a way through this way. He'll have turned left when he saw us turn. He's gonna get the shock of his life when he sees us.'

Double A suddenly understood what Jake meant when he spotted the Renault, a way down the road but heading towards them very quickly. There was no traffic between them and it, which in Double A's opinion was a very bad thing.

Because Jake put the Pop in the centre of the road and hit the gas.

'Do or die time,' Jake said.

And Double A suddenly thought it was likely to be the latter option for them because the guy driving the Renault put his car in the middle of the road and hit the gas too.

8

Dying wasn't as bad as it was cracked up to be, Double A thought after the collision. There was life after death after all, and even the crash hadn't really hurt. He had stared into the bright headlights of the oncoming Renault for as long as he could stand it, then, when he realised that neither Jake nor the guy in the other car intended to give way after that, he had squeezed them shut, watched the after-images and waited for it.

And it wasn't too terrifying at all. There was a sensation of swerving, which had pressed him hard against the Pop's door handle, then a shrieking of tyres, then the big bang. All those physicists were wrong, as far as Mrs Anthony's boy was concerned, because the big bang wasn't the start of life at all, it was the end. Unless you counted the start of the new one, he thought stupidly. There were some unexpected parts to the experience though; he had fondly imagined that angels would come and bear him away to heaven, or to a place of judgement, anyway. What he had not expected was still to be able to hear the sick throb of the Pop idling. Neither had he expected to feel as though a good deep snort of cocaine would straighten him out. Things like that surely weren't supposed to happen when you were dead.

'OPEN YOUR FUCKING EYES AND GET IN THIS FUCKING DRIVING SEAT!' an angry voice shouted. It was not an angelic voice at all. Double A opened his eyes and although he wasn't now exactly surprised to find he was still alive and still sitting in the passenger seat of the '59 Ford Popular, he was a little surprised at the pang of regret he felt at not having made it to the other side.

'What happened?' he said, already fishing in his pocket for the bag of sulphate or the bag of coke; whatever his hand touched first would be good enough.

'Get in the driver's seat,' Jake said, opening his door. 'If anyone comes, take off. Meet me at the motorway entrance.'

Then Jake was out of the car.

Double A pulled a plastic bag from his pocket and slipped across the car to the driver's seat, considering the words *dazed and confused* which summed up the way he felt with phenomenal accuracy. He tipped a white powder on to the back of his

447

hand, not knowing what it was and not caring, then he put a nostril to the line and hoovered it up. It was coke. A few seconds later, Double A's mind cleared and he understood what had happened. Somewhat belatedly, he began to tremble. A second after that, he wanted to throw up. He sealed the plastic bag, replaced it in his pocket, leaned out of the door that Jake had left open and shouted 'HOWWW!' at the tarmac. Nothing came up, which was another speed problem Double A was very familiar with. You tended to get the dry-heaves when you forgot to eat and consequently you sometimes spent a long time trying to relieve your stomach of something that wasn't even present in it. Double A shouted at the pavement again, spat out something that might have been bile, spat again as his mouth suddenly filled with saliva, then swallowed. His stomach, apparently satisfied that the ritual had been properly observed, settled down again to its usual state of discomfort.

Double A lifted his head and peered back down the road in the direction Jake had gone. It took a few seconds to sink into his mind that the crazy heap of garbage Jake was fighting with almost a hundred yards away, was actually something that a minute ago had been a perfectly serviceable Renault 5 Gordini. This was what happened when you played chicken for real and lost. The car's driver wasn't just going to be dead inside that tangle of steel, he was going to be pulped.

Jake was on top of the wreckage, bent double and tugging at something that might have once been a door. Double A looked at the skid marks the Renault had made. They led across the road and up the pavement and met a factory wall at an angle of thirty degrees or so, where they ended. But Double A's eyes could still trace the way the car had gone afterwards. The wall sported a large section of paint-smeared cracked brickwork where the Renault had hit it, and the facing had been knocked off the bricks all the way down to where the wreck now lay. The car and its driver had literally been wiped out.

Could have been us, Double A thought, and then pushed the thought aside because his stomach squeezed up into his throat.

Back down the road, Jake was pulling pieces of metal away from the car and casting them aside. The voice of Double A's paranoia spoke up and suggested that not only was Jake intending either to finish the guy off if he was still alive, or to tear pieces off him if he was dead, but also that it was pretty likely that people had been working a night shift on the other side of that big, cracked wall and that they were very likely on their way round the block to see what had happened. And even if that didn't happen, there must be someone else in this road somewhere, even if it was an industrial site and it was midnight. What if someone had seen the whole thing and taken down the Pop's number?

The panic bug started to gnaw at Double A's guts and he gunned the Pop's engine, realising that the only thing preventing him from driving away and meeting up with Jake at some unspecified later time, was that he didn't have the faintest idea as to where the motorway was.

'Come on, Jake!' he hissed to himself. 'The guy's dead, leave him alone!'

Then he thought about another dead guy. Another two dead guys in fact: Reuben Brown and his accomplice Gordon Clement. Both had got up and walked, which meant that this guy would probably be able to, too. Which made it even more dangerous for Jake to be down there fiddling with him.

'Hurry up!' he called down the street, remembering not to use Jake's name because walls had ears and one of them might actually be listening.

'Back up here, chick!' Jake shouted.

Double A's hand trembled when he closed the door and both of them started to shake like jellies when he reached out for the Pop's wheel. For a second or two he didn't think he was going to be able to drive at all. Then his feet found the pedals and the Pop's engine note became clear and Double A's own mind cleared with it.

The Pop rocketed backwards up the street and Double A brought it to a halt about a foot away from where Jake was climbing down off the wreckage. Jake came towards the Pop, then paused and fished in his pocket, withdrew something Double A couldn't see and turned away.

Then he was running back towards the car. Double A leaned over and opened the passenger door and Jake leapt in. 'AWAY! NOW!' he shouted.

And Double A dropped the clutch and let the Pop fly.

It wasn't until they were at the far end of the street and the remains of the Renault burst into flame that Double A realised what Jake had been doing. Jake had been turning his back against the wind. The thing he'd withdrawn from his pocket had been a matchbox. He had torched the car.

'One down,' Jake said calmly, 'fuck knows how many to go. Or why,' he added.

'Christ, Jake,' Double A said.

'Turn right here, chicken,' Jake said. 'Left at the end. What's the problem?'

Double A was going to say the problem was that they'd just killed a man and set fire to him, but it was rather late in the day to be complaining about it. For one thing the guy had wanted them dead, and for another both of them had already killed people inside the last twenty-four hours. 'Nothing,' Double A said. He offered a silent prayer to the god of cocaine. If it hadn't been for the drug in his brain he might have gone stark staring mental by now.

'Turn right,' Jake said. When Double A glanced over at him, he was peering at a printed piece of paper.

'His passport, ducks,' Jake said, sounding pleased with himself. 'Just curious to know who he was. Rather have known why the mother wanted to run us into the wall, but this'll have to do.' He squinted at the passport. 'It's all in French. Matey's name was Philippe Matisse. Twenty-eight years old. Says here he was an artist. Arse-*hole*, I would have said.'

'Was he dead?' Double A asked, 'When you got back there?'

'As a do-diddly-oh-do,' Jake replied. 'You don't wanna know about it, surely, chicken? Not with your constitution?'

Double A shrugged. He didn't *want* to know, but for some reason he *had* to.

'His head was off,' Jake said. 'That's about the size of it.'

And when Double A glanced at him, Jake was grinning and holding out his hands to demonstrate the physical aspect too. His hands were a head's width apart. Jake's face looked pale and shocked behind that fixed grin and there was a strange light gleaming in his eyes. Double A looked back at the road, all sorts of strange thoughts running through his brain as he pictured the decapitated man. In the space of twenty-four hours or so, both he and Jake had turned into murderers. Letting things get out of control was as simple as snapping your fingers. A part of him wanted to curl up in a tight ball and wait for someone else to take control of his destiny from now on, but there was another part of him which felt strangely exhilarated – and Double A doubted it had anything to do with the drugs. The look in Jake's eyes was scary because Double A knew that if he cared to crane his neck up and peer into the rear-view mirror so that he could see his own face, an exact replica of that look would be shining in his own eyes. And he thought he knew what that look meant. The thing that Jake had lost after putting an early end to the life of a boxer called Charlie Anton, had returned. And how. Jake had got his killer instinct back. He looked like a man who intended to go the full distance, no matter what the odds.

'I gotta theory, chicken,' Jake said. 'Turn right! Wanna hear it?'

Double A made the turn. He had theories of his own. None of them was particularly pleasant. 'What?' he said, pushing the car rapidly up to maximum revs, then changing up a slot and reversing the process as they approached a roundabout.

'Take this turning here. Here! Christ, boy, are you stupid? Go round the roundabout again! It's marked the A26, for God's sake!'

Double A took the turning for the A26 and sped up the ramp. The two-lane motorway was deserted. Double A hit the gas and the Pop growled and leapt forwards, pressing him back against his seat. The car's zero to sixty time was around six seconds, which was pretty good, but the noise level inside it must have been about a billion decibels, which wasn't very good at all – especially if you had to sit in it for more than a thousand miles. Double A brought the car up to about one ten, then glanced over at Jake.

'What?' Jake asked. His voice was lost in the wind noise and the racket the Pop's V8 and straight-cut gearbox was making.

'Your theory,' Double A shouted.

'SLOW THE FUCKIN' CAR DOWN THEN! I AIN'T GONNA SHOUT!'

Double A took his foot off the throttle and let the Pop's speed fall to sixty. It still wasn't quiet, but it didn't get much quieter from here down to twenty.

'Right, well, lemme 'splain,' Jake said. 'You know you hit that black bloke over the head with the crowbar and killed him?'

Double A only wished he'd been able to forget dear old Reuben. 'Yeah,' he said. 'But I dunno whether he was dead or not.'

Jake nodded. 'He was dead all right. Just like the guy I took out in your flat. He was dead too. I felt his pulse and there wasn't one. He wasn't even breathing or anything. He was dead, and so was your black guy.'

'Possibly,' Double A admitted. He thought he knew what Jake was likely to say next and wasn't sure he wanted to hear it. He had entertained such thoughts himself. It was proving difficult to clear his mind of the image of the Pop hitting Reuben and Reuben sailing through the plate glass window – and his own imaginary notion of what had happened afterwards.

'And so was our dear Philippe in the Renault.'

'So what's the point?' Double A asked eventually.

Jake reached over and took hold of Double A's forearm and squeezed it to emphasise his words as he spoke. 'The point is, those guys were *dead*. Mine definitely was, and I don't doubt that yours was too.'

Double A nodded, feeling again like his life had turned into a low-budget movie. He thought briefly of those scientists who liked to call themselves quantum mechanics. There were a few, he knew, who believed in a concept they called the Many Worlds theory. The gist of the theory was that each action you made caused the world to branch off into another version of reality. Double A wondered what he might have done – or what Dekker might have done – to split them all into a reality where dead people got up and wandered off. Then he wondered if all this was simply the work of his own, overtaxed mind. With any luck, he'd be lying at home on his bed, dreaming all this. In a few hours he might just wake up. And that would feel good because he didn't want to have to think about what was going on here.

Jake squeezed his arm, hard. 'And they *came back to life*!' he said enthusiastically.

Double A shook his head. Something inside it was being stretched to breaking point as he tried to wrap his mind around this statement. And yet it seemed to be true. 'They couldn't have been dead,' he protested.

'They *were* dead, chicken, make no mistake. Remember I said I saw that black stuff trickling out of that guy's mouth?'

'Yeah,' Double A replied. *Thirteen against thirteen*, he thought, *and they can kill us, but we can't kill them because they just get up again. That's fair, isn't it? Isn't that just about the fairest thing you ever heard?*

'Twelve now,' Jake said.

Double A turned and looked at him. Jake was wearing an expression not dissimilar from the one Jack Nicholson had sported throughout most of the film, *The Shining*. 'I didn't say anything,' Double A said.

'I saw you think it, chicken. There's only twelve now. Your Reuben might have walked, and Gordon Clement might have skipped out of your flat while we were busy, but dear old Philippe is about as dead a duck as a dead duck can be. I told you his head was off. It ain't gonna fix itself back on his shoulders, is it?'

Double A's stomach was protesting again. He swallowed hard, wishing he had some gum left. His mouth was as dry as the Kalahari.

'Nope,' Jake continued, 'he ain't coming back to life 'cause he's too badly damaged and because Jake made sure that he stayed that way. If old Phil gets up and staggers around now, he'll look something like a walking rasher of burnt bacon. But I don't think that'll happen, know why?'

'Why?' Double A croaked.

'Because of my theory that these folks ain't coming back to life at all. They might get up and walk about and make out they're alive, but it ain't them in their bodies, it's something else. It's something to do with that black stuff I seen coming out the mouth of the guy in your flat. That stuff appears – where from is anyone's guess – and after that they get up and go. Henceforth and from then onwards, they ain't human no more. They're what you might call zombies, if you like that word. The people are gone, and something else is moving them about like puppets of itself. And the next part of my theory is that this thing, whatever it is, that's driving these bodies, can only get in 'em when they die and only if they're not too fucked up at that point. Old Phil ain't coming back to life, 'cause his head's gone and he's been crisped. And you know what else I think? I think that it's this thing that wants Paul out of the way. There ain't a good reason I can think of at the present moment, but barring the gaps around the edges, it all seems to hang together. I also think that Mister Chief Bad Guy is stretching himself to his limit doing all this and that's why he's been so busy running round taking out everyone who knows Paul. He's up against it and he knows it. He's scared of losing. Which means, my little chicken, that we're in with a pretty good chance. Sounds mental, don't it? Do you think your old pal has finally teetered over the edge?'

It did sound mental, Double A knew, there was no other way it *could* sound. Unfortunately, it also sounded pretty close to the truth. *Zombies*, he told himself. *Never thought you'd find yourself in a world where you killed people and they turned into zombies, did you?* Again, he hoped he was asleep and that all of this was a bad dream brought on by a little too much of the brain powder.

'How about this for mental,' he said. 'Dekker fights like ten men, that's what you told me earlier. That's why I decided to come after all. There are – or were – thirteen of the baddies. There's you and me and the girl Dekker's got with him and Dekker himself. Even Stevens, I thought. And if there were only thirteen of them, we're already ahead to the tune of one.'

Jake squeezed Double A's wrist. His hand felt warm and very hard. Double A could feel the power in that hand and it comforted him.

'So if we wake up in the morning and find ourselves in straitjackets in a loony bin, will we be surprised?' Jake asked.

'Nope,' Double A said.

And Jake nodded. 'Better put the pedal down then, chicken, Naples is a long way off!'

Double A put everything else out of his mind and lost himself in the driving.

Chapter Eighteen
Where Katie Died

1

No one wanted to check Katie and Paul's passports when they climbed the gangplank on to the ferry at six the following morning, and there was no good reason why anyone should have. The ferry's first stop was Corfu and you didn't need a passport to make that internal journey. Presumably the Italians would do all the checking, which was going to make getting off the boat an experience Paul could have done without.

They found seats in the bar and Paul bought two litres of water for Katie and a can of Coke and two packets of crisps for himself. The cafeteria didn't open until eight and Paul was hungry. He intended to be first in the queue for breakfast when the time arrived because just lately his stomach seemed to have spent most of its time being ignored and Paul was never certain when he was going to get a chance to fill it again.

The bar began to fill with people. There were a lot of young, mainly American back-packers who looked bronzed and fit in shorts and tee shirts, a smattering of Greeks wearing their Sunday best and a few families of Italians who all seemed to have at least five children. By the time the boat set sail, there wasn't a spare seat in the bar.

A bearded American in his mid-thirties had settled into one of the seats on the far side of Paul's table. He smelled of Aramis aftershave and sweaty socks and Paul hoped he didn't take it into his head to let his hot feet feel the air. The guy was a talker and quickly engaged a pair of young back-packing Californian blondes in conversation. His name was Charlie, Paul learned, and he was in real estate in Seattle. Every so often, Charlie told the girls, he got the urge to travel and left his business in the care of his underlings and headed east. No, his business contacts didn't mind, he said, because every so often he would call one and tell him or her where he was and what he was doing and he'd found that they were always thrilled to hear of his exploits.

Paul wasn't particularly thrilled to have to hear them too, but there wasn't a lot he could do about it.

He listened to the story of how good old Charlie had been mugged in Seville and left penniless, how he had broken his ankle skiing in Klosters, how he had been thumbing a lift in Milan and had gotten picked up by a raging queen driving a stolen car but despite the Beretta the Italian had been carrying had managed to escape with his anal sphincter still intact, and Paul began to dislike good old Charlie immensely.

The girls, however, seemed charmed, and by the look of him, Charlie expected to bed either or both of them before the sun rose again. He was wittering on about how much he was looking forward to being back in Naples again now. Evidently nothing untoward had happened to him in that city since he didn't immediately relate a tale of disaster. Paul listened closely in case he was able to pick up any information about the place. At the moment he wasn't even sure which coast of Italy Naples was on, and he was soon going to need to know. Paul wondered whether he ought to forget the animosity he felt towards the man and try to pick his brains when Charlie said a sentence which contained the magic phrase 'Napoli night music'.

And suddenly Paul didn't want to talk to him at all. He already knew what *Napoli night music* was: the ceaseless sound of car horns. He'd dreamed it in that first dream of Katie. Paul felt a mind-wrenching déjà-vu at having an old memory of something this guy was going to say weeks into the future. Paul had known that good old Charlie was going to say this before the man himself had even decided to drop everything and go to Europe.

Fighting off the unpleasant sensation, Paul turned back to Katie, who had been quiet and thoughtful since he'd told her what the dead youth had said, and asked her if she was okay.

'I know H Tyler,' she said quietly. 'I know I know him, but I can't remember him at all.'

'I don't think it's him we have to worry about,' Paul replied, equally as quietly. 'I think it's what's *in* him.'

'I know it all,' she said, 'but it's as if someone has divided my brain in two and all that stuff is on the side I can't get to. I won't know what to do until I can remember exactly what happened. There's a way of fighting back, but I don't know what it is. I don't even know why I have to go back to Cambridge.'

'Because that's where it is. That's the root of the trouble,' Paul said.

'It has no weaknesses,' she said. 'It won't make deals. I think I might be wrong. We're going back to it when we should be going away from it. It wants me so it can birth itself properly into this world, and we're going back towards it.'

'They were going to kill you, up on the hill,' Paul said. 'Which would suggest it doesn't need you for that.'

'If it doesn't use me, it'll have to make another,' Katie replied thoughtfully.

'Can it do that?'

'It did it once, didn't it?'

'Did *it* do that, or was it H Tyler?' Paul said.

Katie shook her head. 'I don't know.'

'I'll tell you what I think,' Paul said. 'I think it wants us both gone and intends to kill us. It may be half-born and stuck inside H Tyler's body, but I don't think it needs you to get it out. If one person's been made who is deiparous, another can be made. H can use that other person. I think he wants us dead because he's frightened of competition. He thinks we can beat him – send him back to wherever he came from – and I think that he's missed his chance of using you and he knows it. If he was going to use you, he'd have to do it before you finished . . . being changed. Once you're changed you'll be his equal and he wants to stop that happening. If we can just keep you out of harm's way until whatever is happening to you is completed, we'll be laughing.'

Katie gave him her wan smile again. 'I don't think it's quite that simple,' she said. 'You see, I won't actually be his equal.'

Paul shook his head. 'I'm sorry?'

'I think I was off the track when I said they're making me into an angel. I don't think it's going to be quite like that. I dreamt about it last night and so far everything I've dreamt about has turned out to be true.'

'I don't understand.'

'The angel is *dead*, Paul, they already killed it. H's equal has already been vanquished.'

'But . . .'

'Angels are different. They're not human. They never were and they never will be. I *am* human and I can never be an angel. It's going to be like a secretary filling in for the boss while he's away. They're going to give me the powers but I'll still be Kate Straker underneath. I'll be just like a little car with a big engine. Neither fish nor fowl. Neither human nor angel. I'll be a kind of half-breed. And I don't know whether that'll be enough.'

Across the table from Paul, Charlie was in the middle of another interesting tale of his heroic exploits and the girls beside Paul were giggling. The real world seemed impossible to fall back into. Paul felt as someone had inserted a sheet of glass between him and it. 'It'll be enough,' he said.

'You're getting fainter,' Katie replied.

'It'll be enough,' Paul said, loud enough to halt the conversation in front of him. Charlie looked over at him. 'Nothing,' Paul said and the American carried on his conversation as if there had been no distraction at all.

'I can't hear you,' Katie said, and when Paul looked back, her eyes were clouding and quickly becoming distant.

'Katie?'

'She okay, man?' Charlie asked.

'She looks a little ill,' one of the girls said.

'It's time,' Katie said in a small voice. 'I have to go now.'

'Not yet!' Paul said. 'Not *here*!'

Katie's eyes closed and she slumped back in her seat. She exhaled a small breath and didn't take another.

'She's quit breathing!' the other blonde girl said.

'It's okay,' Paul said. 'Leave it!'

But it was too late because Charlie had reached across the table and taken hold of Katie's limp wrist and was searching for a pulse. 'It's not okay, she's *dead*, man!' Charlie said. 'It's not okay at all.'

'She'll be all right,' Paul warned. 'Leave her alone.'

The three Americans began to babble. One of the girls wanted to know if she'd had a heart attack and the other wanted Charlie to give her mouth to mouth. 'He knew she was going and he just let her,' Charlie was saying to no one in particular in an extremely surprised voice. 'He just let her die.'

Paul stood up when Charlie stood up. He knew that Charlie was going to try to save her the same way as he had: heart massage and artificial respiration. 'Don't!' Paul warned.

'Someone has to do *something*!' Charlie said. 'Get out the way!'

And then Charlie was moving the table aside.

There were perhaps a hundred people crowded into the bar. Only two of them saw Paul's fist flash out and hit Charlie on the point of his jaw, and neither of them was Charlie himself. One was the American girl called Sara who thought she'd got lucky because Charlie had been addressing her about sixty percent of the time and her friend Deborah about forty percent, and the other was an Italian businessman on his way back to Taranto. Afterwards, Sara was unable to believe that the Englishman had actually *hit* Charlie because the punch had taken so little time to accomplish it actually looked as if nothing whatsoever had happened at all – except perhaps a flicker in the ship's

460

lighting – and the Italian (who spent most of his home life glued to the sports channels) wondered if the Englishman was a boxer he ought to recognise and spent an idle half-hour trying to place the face.

Charlie jolted back as though he'd just been stung by a wasp, then toppled backwards like a felled tree.

Suck on that! Paul thought.

'Fainted,' Deborah said disdainfully, then looked back at Paul. 'Is she really dead?' she asked as her friend turned her attention to Charlie who was being picked up off the floor but who wouldn't regain consciousness for another minute or so.

Paul nodded. 'I've been expecting it. If you'll excuse me I'll have to get her out of here.'

And while everyone was wondering what had happened to Charlie, Paul gathered up Katie in his arms and left the bar.

2

Several things that Paul expected to happen after he'd knocked down the American, didn't happen, and he was grateful for this. Charlie apparently hadn't woken up with his blood boiling and come looking for revenge; no one seemed to have seen fit to alert the boat's staff of the incident, or of the death of one of its passengers.

Paul carried Katie forward towards the bows of the boat because the bar they'd been in was at the back, the sun decks were crowded with people and most of all because he didn't want Charlie or either of the American girls to discover that he hadn't taken the corpse to the infirmary at all, but had laid it down in the shade. That was behaviour that really would have sent out an alert.

It was windy on the flat piece of deck aft of the boat's forward capstans and consequently there were only a few die-hards sitting there; the rest had presumably left with the intention of finding somewhere to sit that was a little less blowy.

Paul laid Katie down in the shade (although not out of the

461

wind) against the low metal partition that prevented the passengers from wandering in amongst the machinery and sat beside her feeling very tired – and very frightened because when she had gone this time, she had gone completely. Katie was no longer breathing, and when *that* happened there was likely to be trouble ahead.

He sat there for a time, waiting for something else to find and inhabit Katie's body. For all he knew Lulu Kaminsky might still be out there awaiting her chance to climb back into the vacant body. Or perhaps this time the black angel would come home to roost. Paul doubted that particular nasty would show up, because if it was able to it would have done so already, but there was something else it could send on its behalf and Paul didn't relish that thought at all.

The corpse of the young Greek guy had told him that Katie was a channel, and Paul had no reason to doubt it. She had slipped away from herself and Lulu had slipped back from the dead to occupy her. So there seemed to be no reason why the other thing (or things) shouldn't show up now that her body was vacant again.

Those other things were the shadow-men he'd seen an example of pouring out of Katie's mouth in his first dream of her. One of them had wrecked and buried a truck in very short order and he didn't doubt that one could perform something similar on a boat of this size. Two would definitely sink it – and put paid to the lifeboats too.

This didn't happen while he waited, and Paul doubted that there would be much he could do if she did suddenly start to cough up shadow-men by the dozen, but he had promised to look after her body while she was away, so it was important to shake off the warm, sleepy feeling that seemed to be paralysing him.

He sat beside her, holding her cool hand, guarding her from God only knew what, and trying very hard not to notice how beautiful she looked, even when her spirit (or whatever it was) was absent.

You can't fall in love with this girl! he told himself, and a part of him argued that it was already too late to stop, he'd gone, hook line and sinker, and that just like his mother had always said, he was a sucker for a girl in distress. The sucker to end all suckers, in fact.

3

And when he woke, ninety minutes later, from what he thought was a deep, dreamless sleep, the news was still good. There was no black sooty stuff oozing from Katie's mouth, she hadn't been possessed and the ferry's big diesel engines were still throbbing away and powering them through the sea towards Corfu and Italy.

And although the sleep had been deep and dreamless, Paul found himself teeming with half-formed ideas and snippets of knowledge.

The first and foremost of these was that Katie was not going to birth a shadow-man or be possessed by any entity while she was here on this boat. She was going to stay just as she was. Paul smiled grimly as he remembered the reason he'd dreamed up. It was because that old saw about ghosts not being able to follow you over water, in some peculiar way that he didn't understand, held at least a grain of truth. He was certain of this and that certainty was backed with proof. Katie had been gone for a good two hours and nothing had taken her vacant body. Which seemed to indicate either that she could not be possessed while she was on water, or that a body of water somehow prevented Henry Tyler (or the Dark Angel he'd become) from tracking them.

They could, of course, be waiting for the right moment, but Paul doubted it. If they'd been able to act, they would have done so already – there was nothing to be gained from waiting. This fact also put another of Paul's worries to rest: since he hadn't woken up in the sea with bullets in him, none of H Tyler's band of merry men was present on the boat.

There was more information too; items that swam just outside the reach of his memory like small fish dodging a child's net.

The source of this stuff was something he would have preferred not to think about, but he was unable to stop himself. Katie was a channel, the dead Greek boy had said, and this suggested that she was somehow connected to another place. You could call it Heaven, or you could call it another dimension if you liked, but the upshot of it was that she was linked to a *somewhere else*. Like the man who currently owned Black Rock (the house in Cornwall Jake Fulman had had nightmares about) had thought before him, Paul envisioned a metaphysical hollow tube that extended from each human being – a tunnel, the presence of which people were not aware during their everyday lives. It sounded crazy, but Paul doubted there was a person alive today who hadn't read reports of people who'd had near-death experiences and found themselves inside a tunnel, moving towards a light. Paul's mind whispered that, *Yes, it was crazy, it was very crazy indeed . . . and probably dangerous*, but he couldn't stop himself building on it, even if it was wrong. He imagined that during a person's life, the tunnel was unattached to another reality and simply snaked about like a loose hosepipe with the water turned up high – perhaps through many realities which were layered in bands like stacked books – and that a connection wasn't made with any of these realities until that person's body ceased to function.

Paul gazed at Katie and shivered. *What if she doesn't come back?* he thought.

You're a car thief, old poke, so maybe you'd do better leaving the philosophy or the metaphysics or whatever they call it well alone. Maybe you just ought to stop building yourself a house of cards that'll fall down in the breeze and think about what you ought to be thinking about, his goad said tartly.

But the realisation about what went on down on the car-deck in the bottom of the ship had also come to him while he was asleep – and there was plenty of time yet to find out if it was right. There was something more to think about; something he couldn't quite get a handle on, and making up stories about things he couldn't prove and didn't quite understand was bringing him nearer to that thing. It was something so simple that it was teetering on the edge of his memory's tongue.

Paul stood up and stared out across the dead-flat sea. They were passing a seemingly endless range of huge, barren brown hills, way over to the right, and he watched them for a while wondering what kind of people might live in them, if any. He ached all over, his finger was still throbbing where a mad mountain climber called Dick Stevens had tried to sever it, his mouth was dry and his mind was tired and expelling his marbles in a steady stream. Katie lay dead at his feet, her tangle of blonde hair whipping in the breeze and the faint smell of diesel exhaust filled his nostrils.

And his mind wouldn't stop building on the tube theory.

Perhaps, if those mystical tubes existed, it would be possible, under certain circumstances to connect that snaking hosepipe to other realities. Or perhaps some folks' tunnels leaked, allowing knowledge or thoughts or beings through from other realities. Like Heaven and Hell, to name two. Perhaps you could use your tube to tap into the surface of Ganymede or entwine it with another person's in order to read their thoughts telepathically.

There is a notice on the car deck. Several notices in fact, old poke. Perhaps you ought to go and read one of them. You may well find that St Cunt smiles on the wicked.

Paul didn't intend to do that just yet – there was something else that had to be done first. It was simply a matter of remembering it. It was something to do with heads. He shook his own head. 'Can't remember,' he said, and thought it might be something to do with two other things he was going to have to do fairly soon. The first was to find out where the toilets were – he couldn't remember when he'd last used one – and the second was that he was terribly thirsty, which meant that Katie probably ought to be watered too. He didn't really know if pouring water into a corpse (which was what she had become, whether he liked it or not) was something he should do, but he was certain that letting her dehydrate would be worse.

Which meant, of course, that he was going to have to leave her, which was something else he was doubtful about.

She's dead, poke, she isn't going anywhere!

But someone might just discover that she was dead (Charlie or one of his girlfriends for instance, or one of the die-hards still sitting here in the wind).

But Paul suddenly realised he knew a way round that one too.

He walked over to the nearest people, a young German couple who were sitting huddled under a blanket staring at each other with the kind of expression that strongly suggested their hands were inside one another's underwear. They didn't notice he was there until he spoke, then they both jumped as if they'd been stung.

'Excuse me, but do you speak English?' Paul asked.

'Sure,' the boy said, grinning and looking embarrassed. His girl giggled. Beneath the blanket quick adjustments were taking place.

Paul smiled at them. 'I wonder if you could do me a favour?'

'Of course,' the boy replied politely. 'What would you like for me to do?'

Paul pointed at Katie. 'That's my wife over there. She doesn't like travelling on boats – she gets ill.'

The boy nodded. 'Seasick,' he said.

'She should eat ginger,' the girl suggested.

Paul shrugged. 'She's taken several Dramamine – seasick pills – and they've made her sleep. I have to go away for a while and I was wondering if you would keep your eye on her for me.'

The boy frowned as he translated. 'Keep my eye on,' he said slowly. 'Ah! Watch her for you. Let her come to no harm.' He nodded. 'Of course! No problem, as they say in Greece.'

Paul thanked them and walked away, wondering if he was

doing the right thing. When he reached the corner of the super-structure he turned and was pleased to see that the German couple were taking their task seriously. They had moved quite a bit closer to Katie and were both sitting up as alert as guard dogs. No one was going to rob or interfere with her without getting past them first, apparently. When Paul turned, the boy waved at him and finished the gesture with a sloppy salute. Paul waved back and went along the side of the ship to where the door was.

The inside of the boat was like a maze and the signs which directed you to the aging vessel's various facilities had apparently been placed by a person with no knowledge of the English language whatsoever. Paul quickly discovered that he wasn't going to find the toilets by following the signs which directed you there, so he spent ten minutes following his nose while he cased the boat. This too seemed important and it had to do with those mysterious signs which – according to Paul's *farmer-oppozite* voice – hung on the car deck. By the time he arrived at the toilets which served the cabins 198—243 (those without en suite, he presumed) Paul had seen and memorised all the gangways, staircases, offices and levels of the good ship *Poseidonis*.

Afterwards he went to the forward bar and bought a sand-wich and two litres of water. On his way back to the forward deck he lingered by one of the staircases which led down to the car-deck, wondering. A chain hung across the stairwell and a sign attached to it warned: NO ENTRY TO PASSENGERS WHILE SHIP IS AT SEA. The signs were down there waiting for him, but it didn't seem to be the right time yet. There was something else to do first and at the moment it seemed more important.

He hurried back to the bows of the ship and was relieved to see Katie still in the same position and the young Germans still sitting there on guard. They saw him coming, waved and moved back to their original place.

'Thanks,' Paul called to them as he sat down beside Katie.

'No problem!' the boy called back, grinning. He threw the

467

blanket over the girl, and crawled under it himself. The girl squealed.

Paul gazed at the play-fight going on under the blanket for a while, feeling very lonely. A part of him wished for a life as simple and enjoyable as that while his goad whispered to him that those days had finished for him the moment little Paulie Saunders had come slapping his way up the bonnet of a stolen car.

'Sweetheart,' he whispered, leaning close to Katie's corpse which smelt acrid again now, 'I don't know if you can hear me from where you are, but I'm going to give you a little water. I hope I'm doing the right thing.

He put his finger to her cold, blue-tinged lips and parted them. He expected to feel a stiff resistance when he tried to prise her jaw open – rather like the arm of the dead Greek boy had felt – and was surprised when her mouth opened smoothly and without resistance.

He broke the seal from one of the litre bottles, pulled Katie to him, cradling her head against his chest, and fed a little water into her mouth. The water ran down her throat, but there was no swallowing reflex. He gave her a little more, suddenly certain that it was running into her lungs and that she would be drowned on her return.

If she comes back at all, that is! his goad said. Paul ignored it because it didn't seem like a separate part of him at all any more, just the normal doubting part that everybody had. It hardly seemed credible that the more marbles he let roll away from him, the saner he was getting, but it certainly felt that way. *Perhaps*, he thought, *you're just getting more comfortable with your insanity. You are protecting a dead girl and you did question a corpse last night.*

And this thought reminded him of that other important idea he'd dreamed up – the one about the heads. The phrase, *Put your heads together* occurred to him, as did the phrase, *Two heads are better than one*, and in the light of what he was now think-ing, those phrases were very scary indeed.

Go for broke, he told himself. *Try it*!

But it was another hour before he was able to force himself to do it.

4

Feeling very tired and very afraid because he didn't really expect to survive what he was going to have to do, Paul tore his eyes away from the young German couple who were evidently showing him the way and looked at the girl in his lap. For the past ten minutes the Germans had been locked together in a long, slow, open-mouthed kiss. Paul had known from the start that putting his head together with Katie's wasn't going to be as simple as just resting his own forehead against hers and holding her hands and asking her questions, but he wasn't sure he could do what was necessary while she smelled like a burned out electric motor. That smell on its own would have been enough to contend with, but it was a little worse than that. Since she'd departed this time she'd been changing; this time she also had the smell of the truly dead. There were changes taking place inside her and Paul thought that if she didn't come back soon, she wouldn't be able to come back at all. Her body was beginning to decompose.

He looked at her blue-tinged lips and the flat tone of her skin and shook his head.

Then, fighting to keep his screaming mind quiet, he brought Katie nearer to him so her head was in the crook of his arm, parted her cold, dry mouth again, took a deep breath and held it, opened his own mouth as wide as it would go . . . and closed his eyes.

Then he dipped his head to meet hers.

Her coldness slipped into his body through his mouth. It was like drinking from a tainted mountain stream except that the freezing feeling didn't gather at his stomach but radiated out from it, gripping his guts and making his spine feel as if a gentle tap would shatter it into fragments. Paul felt himself sliding into a violent, endless shiver that he knew would kill him if it continued for long enough.

Stop it! his goad complained, but out there, on the windy deck in the sunshine, his chilled arms were gripping Katie to him more tightly and he was unable to make them quit. His mouth pressed harder against hers and the coldness hit Paul's legs, turning them from warm flesh and blood to immovable chunks of carved ice. He felt his balls crawling up closer to his body the way they would if he waded into freezing water, then begin to ache; a deep agonising pain that extended up into his abdomen.

Paul let his breath out, forcing it into Katie's lungs and when he drew it back again, his own lungs burned with the cold and his whole being filled with the acrid smell of burning insulation.

Talk to me! he commanded mentally. *You have to talk*!

But Katie did not respond.

The freezing feeling touched his heart then, and he felt it contract in a long, slow squeeze. It didn't hurt, but it felt as if it wasn't ever going to relax again.

Paul breathed into Katie's lungs again, distantly aware that some of the air was escaping through her nose – he could feel it freezing his cheek out there on the sunny deck. With any luck he would draw in a little oxygen when he inhaled and perhaps he wouldn't die of asphyxiation.

The next breath he drew was colder and there was still no sign of any part of Katie showing up – and no good reason why any of her should. She was gone away completely.

Talk to me! he thought again and decided to quit before it was too late. His heart was relaxing, but it was doing it as slowly as a cramped muscle and it wasn't going to be enough to keep his brain supplied with oxygen, even if he did draw some through Katie's nose.

Paul opened his eyes.

And was horrified to discover that there was no difference to his vision. Blue and purple blotches swum there against darkness.

He closed his eyes again and tried to move his mouth away from Katie's, but his neck muscles were frozen into position and he found it impossible to move at all.

That's it then, poke. When this boat docks they're going to find you two locked together. Two lovers who had a suicide pact, his goad muttered.

Paul's heart squeezed again and something cold and sluggish that might once have been his life's blood, crawled up his carotid artery and stretched out icy fingers to his brain.

And Paul became Katie, back before it all happened.

5

Kate Straker had joined the tiny band of people who called themselves the Escape Artists when she was twenty-three and was working for a company in Cambridge called Artifact whose main aim was not, as the name suggested, the acquisition and sale of antiques, but to nurture and develop computer systems which would change the grandiose claims for artificial intelligence from science fiction into science fact. Kate was a computer science graduate who had turned down a research fellowship to work for Chris Maine's Artifact for what turned out to be entirely the wrong reason.

She had done it for love.

When she drove up the road towards H Tyler's house on the day before her twenty-fourth birthday, she wasn't entirely sure of what nature that love had been. Chris was a good-looking guy who had money and a great many mind-boggling ideas about crossing the frontiers of computing, but when you took him away from his lab on the science park and held him up to the light, his character was so thin you could see through it. He had no interests other than computing, not even the ones that young and healthy lovers were supposed to have. Chris loved her, of course, but she had long ago discovered that he didn't love the whole set of disparate elements that made up Kate Straker at all. What Chris loved was a very small part of her indeed. The part that was able to leap large hardware problems at a single, intuitive bound. In some ways it seemed a lot worse being loved for her mind than it would have been if he'd treated her as a simple sex-object.

But when she stopped to think about it, the problem was six of one, and half a dozen of the other, and she was as guilty as him, because she'd fallen for Chris's brilliance in exactly the same way. The discovery that you could fall in love with a single aspect of someone hadn't come until it was too late. And neither had the equally surprising discovery that those whose talent burned brightly in one area often paid for it – and paid heavily – in other aspects of their lives. When it came to life outside computing, Chris was as dull as ditch-water.

And over the months that followed Kate had begun to crave excitement – not necessarily of the sexual kind, although some of that wouldn't have gone amiss from time to time – but any kind of excitement.

If the times really did produce the man, as the saying went (usually when talking about Winston Churchill), they chose an excellent time to fling H Tyler at her.

The virtual reality consultant had been drafted in to work on one of Chris's pet projects. Chris had been excited about obtaining the man's services. H Tyler, he said, had worked for NASA on their virtual reality schemes, he had worked for General Electric on theirs, he had done research at MIT and Bell Laboratories, had since become the world's foremost VR and AR freelance.

The only experience Kate had had of virtual reality had been a couple of years ago on a trip to London when she had found herself in the Trocadero centre watching teenagers killing off one another in the Virtuality game. Four of them had been sitting in the cockpits of machines which looked a little like the rockets you used to see in fairgrounds, wearing a peculiar kind of space helmet which covered their heads down to their grim mouths and which extended out before their eyes. Kate was familiar with the artificial reality concept: you put the helmet on and a 3D screen built into it would show you computer-generated pictures. How artificial reality differed from ordinary computer-generated images was that the ones you saw inside the helmet were dynamic. If you turned your head to the left, the image you saw changed correspondingly, supposedly scrolling seamlessly, and when you looked back, what you'd been looking at before would still be there. The idea was to create a computer reality that had all the hallmarks of a real world. Like genuine artificial intelligence, the theory was nice, but the practice left something to be desired.

Kate and three of her friends had queued up to play. Her friends enjoyed it, but Kate had gone away less impressed than she'd expected to be. The 3D had hurt her eyes, the weight of the helmet had given her a neck ache, and the computer scrolling made you feel dizzy and ill if you turned your head at anything more than a snail's pace. It was early days, and this was supposed to be the first machine of its kind open to the public in this country, but it looked as if there was a very long way to go before the people working in the field were able to present you with a reality you wouldn't be able to tell from the real thing.

Kate had composed a list of searching questions to ask the world's foremost VR freelance when he arrived.

She had expected H Tyler to be a clean-cut, handsome, bespectacled American guy dressed in a Georgio Armani suit and Gucci shoes. He would be arrogant and confident and would not be kindly disposed to criticism. She was right about the arrogance and confidence, but wrong about the rest. H Tyler turned out to be a wild-eyed, wild-haired Englishman who wore a ripped leather jacket, jeans with the knees out and battered baseball boots. H Tyler might have been in his late-thirties or early-forties, but he looked as if he belonged in a rock band rather than the plush offices of Artifact.

Katie's first opinion of him was that he was ugly. Her second was that he was uglier than she had first thought and an upstart too. Her third opinion of him – which was that something stirred inside her each time she looked at him – came later. Much later. She would be able to pinpoint that time to the exact hour: it was three a.m. on the night she'd seen him launch a Molotov cocktail at a 911 Porsche (which apparently belonged to one of his oldest enemies) and had stood watching it burn.

H Tyler – his name was Henry but he called himself H after a cartoon strip character in a tabloid newspaper whose H stood for Homicidal Maniac – did not try to seduce Katie. Not at first anyway. He simply engaged her in energetic arguments which were to do with the work they were both involved in, and defended his beloved artificial reality. H Tyler might have been ugly and pushing forty, but Katie had been able to see how he'd gained his reputation. He was brilliant, he was unconventional, and he spoke with a passion that was entrancing. Watching him in full flow must have been like watching Adolf or Churchill give a speech; his dark eyes lit with the glow of some deep and terrifying flame that roared inside him.

And it was H who introduced something else into her life that Chris couldn't provide. Excitement.

The Escape Artists, he told her, the first time he invited her along to a meeting in his house, where a bunch of 'amoral people' who were 'into getting out of it'. They were all low-life party-animals of the worst kind, H had said with an obvious affection, and the only thing they had in common was a burning desire to set themselves free from the constraints of an existence which was deadly dull, hence the name. H said that he'd spent his whole life trying to escape from one thing or another and that if Kate was interested he could 'show her a few things'.

Kate had not accepted his first invitation because she thought the 'few things' H wanted to show her were likely to be those that lived beneath his worn-out jeans. But later, after a particularly dull week in which she began to despair of ever sorting out her relationship with Chris, she accepted another, safer, invitation – to meet the gang in a pub – because she was building up a head of steam which needed to be blown off.

The Escape Artists turned out to be a varied collection of

very clever people, both male and female, with ages that ranged from nineteen to fifty. Many of them had worked with H at one time or another. There were drop-out students from the university, students who were still there, computer people, biologists, people who happily introduced themselves as thieves or drug runners, a sprinkling of people who were allegedly working on novels and several girls whose manner of dress suggested they might make a living using their bodies. The Escape Artists weren't the emotionally stunted group of losers Kate had expected; most seemed to have an enthusiasm and zest for life which seemed to negate H's claim that they wanted to escape from it, and many of them seemed to burn with the bright creative fire that H himself possessed. Kate spent the evening getting drunk, talking herself silly and having the best time she could remember since she was at university.

And when H invited her to a party at his house the following weekend, she accepted without a second thought.

This time she saw another side of the Escape Artists. The getting out of it, that H had mentioned earlier, included the prolific use of a great many illegal substances. It wasn't so different from some of the parties she'd attended at university and she had smoked dope before, so she told herself that when in Rome it was better to act like a native, and got herself high.

And by the time she discovered some of the other things the Escape Artists were partial to, she was being swept along on a warm, cosy tide and didn't want to leave it.

She did decline to take part in the display of uninhibited sex that spontaneously erupted on the lounge floor before her and at first she'd watched the five participants with a mixture of embarrassment and dismay. By the time the feeling had changed to warm excitement, H had been sitting next to her on the sofa asking her if she'd seen the door with the padlock on it. Kate had. The locked door was just inside the hallway of the house and opened on to the other front room – the one you couldn't see into from the outside because the windows had been white-washed. H asked if she'd like to see what lay behind that locked door and Kate had said she would. He told her that if he allowed it, she would be the first member of the Escape Artists – other than him – who had set foot in the room. Kate had replied that she wasn't sure she was a member of his club anyway, and H had replied that she would be soon. Behind that door lay the real escape, he said.

'So show me,' Kate replied, tearing her eyes away from a sexual act that should have been impossible but apparently was not. The image of the padlocked door which now hung in her mind was pulsing as if its wood was living flesh.

'Soon,' H smiled. 'First we're gonna have us some fun.'

Kate expected him to touch her then, but H stood up and said, 'I know a good game that you can play.' He pointed at the writhing bodies and grinned. 'It's nothing to do with sex, I'm afraid, but it has something in common: it's fun. I can show you how to have real good fun, if you'd care to learn. You strike me as being a girl who could use a little . . . excitement!'

And five minutes later, Kate had gone out with H and a boy called Martin and done something she had started the evening thinking she would never do. She had purposely committed a crime.

Kate Straker, a clean-living, twenty-three-year-old girl who wouldn't say boo to a goose in case it took fright, had stood in front of the plate glass window of a tobacconist's shop with a housebrick in her hand and her heart thudding in her ears and known she was going to enjoy this more than anything she'd ever done before.

A musician called Nick Lowe had once penned and sung a hit record in which he claimed to love the sound of breaking glass and when Kate, using all the power she had in her arm, let that window have it with the housebrick, she discovered she knew exactly what dear old Nick had been talking about. She had followed H and Martin through the broken window, and as the alarm bell rang, had crunched through that broken glass and filled her pockets – and a plastic carrier bag – with cigarettes she would never smoke. And the feeling was wonderful.

She had hated herself in the morning, of course. She had thought of the owner of that shop, dragged from his bed and forced to reckon up what he had lost while the glass crunched under his feet, and she had vowed that she would never do such a thing again.

And that night she had lain in bed beside Chris and thought of the mysterious padlocked door through which no other member of the Escape Artists had ever set foot, the five people banging their brains out on H's lounge floor while she smoked dope – and of the sound that plate glass window had made when it felt the brick. And most of all she recalled the shivering shit-scared excitement that had put the soggy cannabis-high to bed and had replaced it with a feeling she knew no drug would ever provide.

And two days later she had gone back.

It had been downhill from then on.

And now, here she was three months later, on the day before her twenty-fourth birthday, hurrying over to H's house early on a Saturday morning.

Kate was a changed woman. She still lived with Chris and still felt something for him, but her heart and body, and probably her soul too by now, belonged to H. In those three months, she had done a thousand things with H Tyler – and *to* him and *for* him – most of them bad and all of them exciting. She had vandalised cars and property, burgled shops, committed arson, lied, cheated and stolen, and all of these things had thrilled her with an orgasmic intensity and made her feel as if she had woken up into the real world – the one in which she had somehow managed to stay asleep until H came along.

And she had found out what lay behind the padlocked door.

She had been disappointed to find that the delights H had hinted at – the *total* escape – had been more of her stock-in-trade: computer hardware.

H's secret project turned out to be just another virtual reality machine and the reason he had targeted her and drawn her into his world of quick and easy thrills was the same reason Chris had become her lover. H wanted her, and he wanted *all* of her, but Kate had no doubt that he would have happily done without her body if he'd been able to carve out and keep the part of her mind he wanted. Because the machine didn't work properly.

He told her about the problem with the machine on the day he first let her into the room and had waited for her to stop shouting at him before he smiled and said that before she made up her mind she ought to try it out because although it needed refinement, she wouldn't be disappointed. Kate had listened to his spiel, told him she doubted it, and agreed to try it anyway, simply because of the impressive hardware he'd had installed in the room along with a massive power supply the electricity board must have asked some very serious questions about when he'd requested it. She asked him where the hundreds of thousands of pounds' worth of equipment had come from and received H's standard reply that, 'There are ways of getting hold of things.'

You didn't just get hold of machinery like this – which was better than anything Chris had at Artifact – and neither did you just get hold of a bunch of DEC Alpha chips which drew 43 amps a piece and which got so hot they needed cooling with liquid nitrogen – but the gang was all here and looked as if it was going to run, so she thrust the thought from her mind.

'Where's the helmet?' she asked.

H smiled and showed her a pair of goggles that might once have been intended for gas welding. They were connected to the computer by a cable that was perhaps a quarter of an inch in diameter. 'Don't need a helmet for this one,' he said. 'Don't need a body suit or a brain-mapped electrode head net. All we need are these. This isn't kid's virtual reality we got here, this is the grown-up stuff. Why go to all the bother of making an artificial world with computers when your own brain will do it about a million times more efficiently?'

'You're talking about hallucination,' Kate said.

'Reality is reality by common consent,' H said. 'An

hallucination we all share, except that it's an hallucination of all the senses in harmony. If your brain can think you up an alternate world, that's the machine to use. This machinery stimulates your brain through your optic nerves and provides a framework for the new reality.'

'Like hypnosis? If you were to hypnotise me and tell me I'm on an aeroplane, I'd think I was, right?'

'Something like that,' H said, grinning. 'Put the goggles on and find out.'

Kate watched H power-up the computer then put the goggles on. There was a sensation of something flashing rapidly in her eyes and then it ceased.

And the goggles were gone and she was sitting on the chair in H's secret room, just as she had been before, except she was no longer wearing the goggles. She felt an odd disjointed sensation. 'What happened?' she asked. 'Did I pass out?'

'No, you didn't,' H replied, 'you're still conscious, but you're in an alternate reality. And it's just like the real thing, isn't it?'

A moment later Katie realised that although she could see H standing in front of her, his mouth had not moved and his voice seemed to be coming from beside her. The unpleasant, disjointed feeling jarred her.

'You still have the goggles on, and your brain will resolve the problems in a moment,' H said. This time his mouth moved with the words although the voice still came from elsewhere. Katie looked towards the source of the voice and saw the stool H had been perched upon. It was empty.

'Yeah, I'm here,' he said. 'I'm sitting on this empty stool. You just can't see me the real me on the stool in your reality because the machine has suggested to you that I'm somewhere else. This is just a test. In a moment you'll see the representation of me in front of you vanish because the computer will suggest to you that I'm going to do it.'

And as Kate watched, H Tyler winked out of existence.

'Good, no?' his disembodied voice said from a position to her left. Kate turned her head and was surprised to find that

H wasn't there. He no longer appeared to be in the room at all. Kate's disorientation began to turn to a feeling of dizziness and nausea, but a part of her mind was marvelling at H's accomplishment. The computer-generated room was perfect in every detail; indistinguishable from the real item.

'Good,' Kate said and her voice sounded hollow and flat as if she was hearing it through the walls of another room – which, she supposed, she was. 'It's not exactly an escape though, is it?' she said.

'We can generate alternate realities,' H replied, his voice suggesting that he was walking away from her. 'This is just a test rendering.'

Kate's mind was whispering to her that a computer-generated version of reality could not be as perfect as this, not even using the impressive hardware that H had in this room, and that it had to be a trick. She moved her hands out in front of her and studied them. They were her own hands, there was no doubt about it at all. H could not have programmed images of her hands so she was actually looking at them. They looked, felt and moved exactly as her own hands did and Kate suddenly understood that it *was* all done with trickery. H had somehow hypnotised her, then unhooked her from the computer and left the room while she'd been unconscious. She was simply hearing his voice over a series of remote speakers. He had also presumably hypnotised her to see an image of him that winked out of existence a few moments after she had spotted it. It was all simple hypnotism and had nothing to do with the computer at all. Kate began to feel horribly cheated.

Then she put her hands to her face and discovered with a cold, jolting shock that H's goggles were still covering her eyes.

'*What's going on*?' she demanded.

'Relax,' H said. 'Don't panic and don't take those goggles off yet because we haven't finished having fun. What's going on is exactly what I said is going on.' H's voice now came from behind her. 'There are only two people who've escaped reality to this degree, Katie, and you're one of them. Impressed, aren't you? Wait until you take off the goggles. *Then* you'll be impressed. But before you do *that*, have a look at our problem.'

Kate fought off the shivering chill and her mind did a slow downward spiral as she stared at her hands through the opaque goggles. It was impossible, but she could see every tiny detail.

'I thought you might be able to give an opinion about the corner of the room,' H said. His hand snaked out from nowhere and took her right wrist. Kate turned to her right and found him standing next to her, grinning. A pair of goggles covered his eyes and wires trailed away from them to the computer. 'Hi,' he said. 'I thought I'd join you.' This time his voice came from his mouth.

Kate didn't know if this was the real H or another spurious image of him and her brain felt like it would burst if it had to cope with any more sudden changes of reality. She felt as if someone was revolving a sharp instrument, right down deep in her brain. 'I don't know what's real and what isn't,' she said shakily. 'I want it to stop.'

H nodded and grinned. 'Yeah, it gets you like that the first time. We'll stop soon. Just have a look at this and we'll stop. For now.'

He took her hand and pointed her forefinger up into the left corner of the room. 'What do you see up there?' he asked.

'The corner,' Kate replied.

'What else?' Take a line of sight down your finger.'

'There's a crack in the plaster on the ceiling.'

'Okay, now how long would you say that crack is?'

'About three inches.' She turned back to H who was nodding. 'So?' she asked.

'That's my problem,' H said. 'What *is* it?'

Kate shook her head, felt the weight of the goggles and the wire and experienced another cold jolt that reminded her she wasn't in the real world at all. 'It's a crack,' she croaked, fighting to find her fleeing balance.

'No, my little pipsqueak, a crack is *not* what it is.'

481

'I see a crack,' Kate insisted.

'Where there is no crack,' H replied. 'I did not programme a crack.'

'You said you didn't programme the room at all, but simply suggested directly to your brain what it should see,' Kate complained.

'The programme is the list of instructions to your brain,' H said, squeezing her arm. 'I didn't include a crack up there!'

He sounded excited and awed and there was something else in his voice, too, something which Kate wouldn't be able to identify until afterwards, but which frightened her.

'Isn't it just a crack in the plaster of the real ceiling?' she asked.

'The real ceiling isn't cracked,' H said. 'And I *wasn't* imagining it. I've seen it before and thought I was hallucinating it, but I wasn't. It exists. Our artificial reality is cracked. And each time we use the machine to give us this version of reality, the crack is larger!'

'I'm stopping this,' Kate said, 'right here and right now!' She tore off the goggles.

She felt a horrible snapping sensation as she broke her connection with the virtual reality circuit – as if her body had been stretched taut like an elastic band and had suddenly been released. Her balance fled and something hard hit her from above. It took a few seconds for her to realise that the hard thing was, in fact, the floor, and that it had hit her from below.

She looked up at H, who had removed his own goggles and was swaying like a drunk trying to stand on the deck of a ship in very rough seas. Then she looked up at the corner of the room. 'There *is* a crack,' she said, as she tried to collect the shattered pieces of her mind. 'There it is!' She felt as though she'd been dismantled, taken into another universe and reassembled, then dismantled again and brought back. Somewhere during the round trip, some of her parts seemed to have been put back in the wrong places. She'd taken LSD with H a few weeks previously, but in comparison with this, the 'hole in her reality' she'd felt afterwards had seemed like a pinprick.

'The other problem,' H said, 'is that taking off the goggles doesn't end it straight away. You have to wait for your brain to re-adjust. The crack you're seeing is the virtual reality one. It doesn't exist in our reality. Just sit still and watch it.'

Kate sat on the floor and fixed her gaze on the crack. Over the following five minutes, the crack faded until it looked as if it had been drawn in 3H pencil. Then it vanished. After it had gone, Kate wasn't sure of the moment when she could no longer see it, because that crack seemed to have burned its way into her brain and a part of it seemed to have remained with her.

'That's it,' H said from beside her. He was grinning and he looked exhilarated. '*That's it*,' he repeated. 'Thanks, Kate, I know what it is. Look, you've got to work with me on this!'

And although Kate was also thrilled, a part of her wanted to tell him to shove it, because whatever kind of virtual reality he'd managed to produce (and it was more *alternative* than *virtual*) it was going to be dangerous. But Kate didn't speak because another dangerous and thrilling thing was happening. H's hot hand had somehow – without her noticing it – found its way to the inside of her cool, bare thigh and it felt good and she didn't want it to stop.

And after they had made love on the floor amongst the wires and goggles and with the Cray humming and the cooling liquid nitrogen hissing through the bank of Alpha chips beside them, Kate realised that she *would* work with H on the problem with the computer. From now on, she would willingly do whatever H suggested to her.

And now, slowing the car and indicating to turn into his driveway, on the Saturday before her twenty-fourth birthday, she realised that the list had been a long and varied one. And that there was not one item on it, one suggested task, that she had not delighted in undertaking.

During the previous three months, H had told her that his main aim in life might have been escaping reality (and he'd had many ideas on this since the day she first tried out the system that lay behind the locked door) but that his secondary aim was

483

to corrupt Kate. And Kate had been willingly corrupted and had loved every moment.

She changed down to second and turned into H's drive, surprised to see Chris's Lotus already in the driveway. *He wasn't supposed to be here*, she thought, and her heart sank, because this was going to be a showdown, and one that she could have done without, because this morning she and H were going *all the way*.

Chris knew. He must have known that she and H had been lovers for a good long time now, but he hadn't mentioned it or even alluded to it. Perhaps he'd thought it would all blow over and that eventually she would tire of H, dump him and change back into the person she used to be. Evidently Chris had become tired of waiting for it to happen and had taken matters into his own hands.

Which meant, Kate realised, as she turned off the engine of her car and gazed at the back of Chris's Lotus, that H's final stage in escaping reality was going to be delayed.

Kate, who not so long ago had suffered nightmares about the hallucinatory crack in H's ceiling, could hardly bear to entertain the thought of a setback which would prevent her seeing that crack again. Today was supposed to be *the* day. The day that she and H peeled back that crack and saw what lay behind it. After that first time, H had developed a theory about the crack and instead of working on a programme to get rid of it entirely, they had set about making it larger. Because H said (and deep in her bones Kate knew he was right) that what was on the other side of the crack wasn't just a virtual reality, or even an artificial one. What was behind it was an *alternate* reality.

A real, honest to God, *Somewhere Else*.

And Kate didn't have any idea what it was, or even if she and H would get back from it again or alive, or either of the two, but she didn't care. She meant to see that *Somewhere Else*, even if it was the last thing she did.

And if things went according to plan, she meant to walk in that fresh universe too.

But Chris was here and that was BAD spelt in capitals.

The questions, *What if he's hurt H?* and *What if he's run amok and damaged the equipment?* ran through her head as she approached the front door and she tried to lay them to rest. There was no smoke billowing out of the house, for one thing, and for another, Chris wasn't likely to have attacked and hurt H. H was tough and Chris was not a fighting man. If Chris had gone in guns blazing, he would already have left with a bleeding nose and some loose teeth.

Which meant they would be talking, heart to heart, Chris putting his case logically (but with that pleading undertone she knew so well) and H arguing his side with his faint sardonic smile attached to the corners of his mouth.

Now, Kate thought, *would probably be the best time to tell Chris that he's history as far as this particular girl is concerned. Just tell him that it's over and that you won't be coming home again.* She owed Chris more than that, she knew, and she also knew that she wasn't going to be able to pay it. He would argue and perhaps cry, but she'd have to handle that. Eventually he would realise he was beaten and leave. And then she could get on with what she and H had planned for today.

Kate had her own key to H's house (and her own key for the padlocked door, too, although she didn't know why H bothered to keep it locked any more because after she had agreed to work with him on the project, he had disbanded the Escape Artists). She quietly let herself into the hall and stood in the doorway listening.

There were no raised voices – no human voices at all, in fact. Just the low voices of the power supply to the room where the computer lived and the whirring voice of the machine itself. Hard disks, fans and, from outside, the pumps which fed the liquid nitrogen around the bank of Alphas.

He's in there already, Kate thought, and felt chagrin at the prospect that H might have started without her. Perhaps he'd abandoned her now he had what he wanted from her in the same way as he'd jettisoned his pals in the Escape Artists when she'd happened by. 'They're not right for this,' was the only explanation he'd given when she'd questioned him. Perhaps she had suddenly become *persona non grata* too.

Or maybe he was giving a demonstration to Chris.

'H?' she called, suddenly not wanting to go any further into the house until she had more information. 'Chris?'

The two of them might have killed one another. Or Chris might have killed H. It was unlikely, but it was possible. She had the distinct impression that something was wrong.

And then H came out of the computer room, grinning. 'Hi,' he said, 'we're gonna have us some fun today!'

Kate looked at him and saw sweat beaded on his forehead and dark stains in the armpits of his shirt. His face was pale and his movements erratic somehow. There were marks on his bare forearms that looked rather like the ones you would go home with if you visited her Auntie May and tried to pick up Marmalade, who wasn't so much a cat as a feline offensive weapon. Her heart sank.

'What happened?' she asked.

H shrugged. 'Just setting up,' he said. 'I'm terrified, but I'm ready to walk.'

H had claimed he was going to walk through that crack when it was open when, in fact, if either of them was going to get through it, they were going to have to haul themselves up into it. They'd tried to bring the crack down the wall, but after a fruitless week of manipulating, the computer had come to the conclusion that the computer and the crack didn't have a great deal to do with one another. The computer's virtual reality (or their own, with the machine's help) might have caused the crack, and it might be getting larger each time they used the machine, and staying longer afterwards, but they had not been able to manipulate it at all. The very bottom line (that neither of them admitted to) was that all they had really done was to use the machine enough to allow the crack to grow.

'What happened?' Kate asked again. Her mind was suddenly filled with images and thoughts that she didn't like.

'Nothing happened, pipsqueak,' H said, smiling.

'Then where's Chris?' she asked.

H touched his left forearm with his right hand. There were more scratches on that one, she realised.

'Chris had to go,' he said.

'Where to?' she demanded. She now had a pretty good idea how you might get those kind of scratches on your arms without visiting Auntie May and Marmalade. You might get them, for instance, if you were pinning someone to the floor, strangling them with both hands. The person underneath would try very hard to encourage you to let go, and in desperation that person would undoubtedly resort to using his fingernails. She could picture the scene quite easily. Since she had been taking hallucinogenic drugs and using H's machine to encourage her brain to conjure up alternate realities, images like this one came to her a little more easily than she was comfortable with. She imagined Chris on the lounge floor, pinned there by H and turning blue as he batted and scratched at the arms that were robbing him of his life. He would be in there now, his mouth open and his lips and tongue dark. H had killed him, Kate was certain of it. It would have been a sacrifice.

'You killed him,' she said flatly.

H shook his head. 'No, he had to go. I told him about you and me and he said he had to go for a walk. To think it over.'

'So we have to wait for him to come back,' Kate said, still seeing an image of the man she had once loved lying dead on H's lounge floor. The worst thing about it was, she no longer cared. It wasn't really important if Chris were dead or alive: what *was* important was to see through that crack. But there was another problem.

'No. He won't be back until three-thirty. We can go ahead,' H said. 'The machine's ready. All we have to do is step inside and hook ourselves up.'

'You killed him,' she repeated. It wasn't Chris's death that was important, it was the *reason* for his death. H had almost certainly killed him, and H would have done it for a reason.

And she didn't think that reason had anything to do with the triangle the three of them made.

'What aren't you telling me?' she asked.

H shrugged. 'Okay, we had a bit of a to-do. I hit him.'

'You know what I mean,' she said.

'No, I don't think I do.'

'He's in the lounge, isn't he? Strangled.' And before H could reply, she opened the door and let herself in.

And there was Chris, on the floor, just as she had imagined he would be.

Kate tried very hard to feel shocked and terrified and outraged and robbed as she stood there and looked at her dead lover, but she didn't feel anything other than a momentary fluttering inside her and a slight suspicion that H knew something that she didn't. If H's secondary task in life had been to corrupt her, she realised, he'd done a wonderful job. The fluttering sensation had doubtless been the last of her innocence departing. *You're fooling yourself*, she thought. *The last of* that *departed a long time ago*.

'It'll be okay,' H said from behind her.

'You mean we'll get away with it? Murder?'

'That's what I mean.'

Kate thought she knew why H thought they'd get away with it. H thought that once they went through that crack in reality, they weren't coming back again.

'I can't do it,' she heard herself saying, and knew that it was a lie. 'Not like this. Not now.' But it was just words. Just guilty talk to cover the fact that she felt no guilt. The more she thought about hooking up to the computer, the less significant Chris's death seemed and the more exciting the prospect of walking in fresh lands became.

H nodded at her, grinning all over his pale face. He looked like a schoolmaster who had just watched his favourite pupil fight through a tough final exam and had been mightily relieved at the outcome.

I passed, she thought. *I don't know right from wrong any more.*

Or, rather, I do *know, but I've chosen to do wrong because it has a great deal more to offer.* 'Okay,' she said. 'I'm ready. Take me away!'

Kate found herself looking at the crack even before she'd put on the goggles. It was there up in the corner of the room and it *wasn't* there at the same time. It ran about a foot in three directions, with its centre in the point the two walls made where they met the ceiling. The crack had been there for a fortnight now, regardless of whether you were hooked up to the computer or not.

The only trouble was, the only sense it could be perceived with was that of sight. Both she and H had tried to touch it, but there was nothing there to touch – it simply felt like a smooth corner. They had both tried to listen to the crack and both sniffed the air around it, as if the odour of the universe that lay behind it might waft through. But nothing could be heard and all that could be smelt was the odour of hot computer, plaster and whitewash.

But when you hooked up, it was a different matter. On the last three occasions they had used the machine, the crack in the three ninety-degree angles had swollen slightly, as if there was something behind it, pressing hard. The last time – Thursday night – the crack had looked like one in a dam might have done as it got ready to burst. The prospect of both of them drowning in whatever flooded through that crack had occurred to Kate, but H was adamant that this wouldn't happen. Kate had noted this and added it to her list of things that H apparently knew that she didn't. She didn't know what he was keeping from her, or why, but she knew there was something. But deep down inside her, she trusted him to look after her. All would be revealed if she was patient, and if, when the time came, it turned out to be something terrible, then it would just have to be. The risk, as H well knew, was the thing that thrilled her most of all. Maybe she would die and maybe she wouldn't. In the thrall of the adrenaline she had become addicted to, Kate didn't much care.

'Ready?' H asked, sitting down beside her facing the crack. He toyed with his goggles and looked very sick and very happy.

'What's going to happen?' Kate asked. Her heart was hammering and she felt very hot. Her hands were trembling and she *wanted* it. Whatever it was she wanted it to happen to her.

'Let's see,' he said, and put his goggles on.

Kate followed suit and held on to his arm as the disjointed feeling thumped her between her shoulder blades. In another universe she gasped in a breath of warm air. When she looked up into the corner of the room she shrieked.

The corner of the room hung in towards them like the point of a three-sided pyramid, its sides split with ragged black cracks.

'It's coming,' H said from beside her and his voice sounded exulted and scared. 'Here it comes!'

What did you do? Kate thought. *What did you do to make it do this?* But she already knew what he'd done and she was suddenly forming a very good idea of what was going to happen.

The corner stretched noiselessly out of the wall and down towards them. The three planes bulged and the cracks widened. Kate could see in through them now. Behind them lay perfect darkness. And in that perfect darkness something existed, something of which she could only see a very tiny part. It sparkled and glinted pure gold, seethed like showers of a firework's burning powder in a wind.

'It's mine!' H shouted. 'IT'S MINE! I'VE DONE IT!'

The point of the room came down towards them at a forty-five degree angle and stopped about ten feet away from them. The thing inside it pushed and the material of the walls and ceiling bulged as if they were made of rubber.

'TAKE HER!' H commanded and Kate, terrified and exhilarated beyond belief, didn't understand the text of this message until a fine, razor-like split of sparkling gold had formed at the tip of the corner's point. Then she realised that H had planned – probably all along – to sacrifice her to the thing behind that stretched section of wall.

490

A thing? a small part of her asked. Kate had expected to see another reality, not a *thing*. She had expected a door to open to a Somewhere Else, a door which they could go through, not a door to admit a *thing*.

'H?' she heard herself ask.

'COME ON!' H shouted.

And the tip began to open, like the petals of a flower bud blooming.

Behind it, the *thing* moved, swirling in dazzling sparks of pure gold, pressing itself against the opening like a baby fighting to be born.

'You knew about this,' she heard herself say. 'You *knew*!' For a moment she watched the angles of the wall and ceiling peeling themselves back while the understanding that this was what H had been after all along sank in. He had wanted to become something greater than human. He had wanted to escape, not necessarily from reality, but certainly from his body. And she also understood that H did not care for her whatsoever. She was just another useful piece of equipment to be employed and dumped as necessary. And it looked as if she was here, not to gaze on another universe, but as a birthing aid to this glittering thing.

Will I still be me? she asked herself and replied that if that thing came into contact with her, she wouldn't be anything at all afterwards. It would be a good way to go, she decided. One glorious burning moment as that thing touched her, then nothingness.

'TAKE HER!' H commanded.

And the walls peeled away and Kate caught a glimpse of the glittering thing's face passing the hole. It was a male face and it was so beautiful it could have made you cry. It was alien but it seemed human too. It was surely an angel, one of God's golden beings. She and H had tapped into Heaven itself and if she had to die to bring that angel into this world, or to get herself into the place where it lived, she wouldn't have a second thought.

Its gaze swept the room as its head turned and for one

mind-numbing second Kate found herself locked in its dark and empty eyes.

And behind them raged the fires of Hell.

Then it had turned away and Kate knew how it felt to be damned and lost.

'NOW WE'RE GONNA HAVE US SOME FUN!' H screamed. 'COME TO ME!'

But the dark angel didn't intend to go to H; Kate had known this from the moment it had looked at her. With its smouldering gaze had come knowledge and realisation. H hadn't wanted to take her into a strange and wonderful land at all but had intended all along to make her the final corrupt sacrifice to this *thing*. The dark angel that was fighting its way through that blossoming gap was going to have to kill one of them in order to take the body of the other and H had set her up to be the one who was killed.

But that thing, which was made infinitely more awful by its golden glittering beauty, had other ideas. It had looked for an earthly body to inhabit and it had chosen hers. In a few moments, it was going to jump across the gap from its dimension to this one like a high-voltage electrical charge, but instead of hitting and killing her to get to H, it was going to be the other way around. And if the thought of being shoved out of her body and into the eternal Hell this thing surely came from was bad, the prospect of having to share her body with it was even worse.

It's too late to stop! she thought.

But her hands had decided otherwise.

Kate didn't know there was any fight left in her until she realised her hands were in the air before her, not shielding her face from the dark angel's dreadful gaze as it rolled in the constriction of its way across to this universe, but coming towards her eyes, her fingers clawed as though they intended to pluck them out.

Then she felt the warm plastic of the goggles beneath her fingers, and her hands tore them from her face.

'NO, KATE! DON'T!' H roared, and his voice was merged with another voice and amplified beyond belief. H's voice was now swamped with deep grating tones that sounded like the tortured metal of a massive suspension bridge about to collapse in a hurricane. Kate's ears rang with the words, long after they'd been spoken, long after she realised . . . that removing the goggles hadn't snapped her back out of the alternate reality that the computer had encouraged her brain to imagine.

Now, as Kate stood on legs as unsteady as those of a newborn colt, she realised the full extent of H's mind-fuck trick. The virtual reality that his machinery encouraged your brain to conjure up was so convincing because it was in no way virtual. It *was* reality. Somehow, H had managed to make your mind tap in to other places which were not pretend, but actually *real* and in existence.

And up there in the centre of the room, about ten feet away from her, was a bulging, inside-out corner which was silently peeling apart under the pressure from the huge golden thing on the other side of it.

'DON'T, KATE!' H screamed in that horrendous voice.

Kate tore her gaze away from the geometric obscenity in the centre of the room and glanced at H, not knowing what to do except that she ought to run, further and faster than she had ever done before.

'YOU CANNOT STOP ME!' H roared, doubling up in his seat as if he had been punched. His hands flew into the air and fluttered at his temples as if the pain in his head was worse than the one in his guts.

'Bastard!' Kate shouted. 'You knew!' She threw her goggles at him, hard.

'NOOOO!' H screamed, and his hands reached out to catch them.

Kate watched them sail across towards him, knowing that he was going to miss them and miss them by miles. She wanted to turn away and run now, and she *was* moving, but slowly as though she suddenly weighed a million tons. Too slowly.

The goggles hit H in the chest and Kate saw a tiny puff of blue smoke rise from the inside of the eyepiece. Behind her, the computer's gently whirring voice rose a note.

Crashed your toy! Kate thought triumphantly. Her body was turning and her feet were beginning to bear her away towards the door, but her head was still facing H, so that she was looking at him over her shoulder. Her nostrils were suddenly filled with the odour of burning electrical insulation. The huge computer began to complain. A blue crackle of electricity pulsed around the rim of H's goggles.

And Kate turned her head and found herself looking into the dark, blazing eyes of the angel.

IT IS TOO LATE. YOU ARE MINE. This time Kate heard the voice *inside* her head.

H began to scream, in his own voice now.

Something inside the computer ground to a halt with a metallic fan-like clattering.

MINE! the angel said.

Kate suddenly felt as if a weight had been lifted from her. It wasn't going to be necessary to run now, because the computer was going down and the *thing* wasn't going to be able to jump the gap after all. It would just have to go back to whatever hell hole H had tapped into. It wasn't going to be able to get through. Not to her now she'd taken off the goggles, and not to H now that his own had short-circuited.

She tore her eyes away from the angel and looked back at H who was still in his seat, as taut as a bowstring and clutching her smoking goggles to his chest with clenched fists. To H's right, the display on the computer monitor rolled, settled, then winked out. Some modules of the computer were still running, but Kate didn't expect that to remain the case for very much longer. Circuit breakers were going to blow in very short order and if they didn't, all she was going to have to do to cut the power completely, was run across to the huge switch-fuse on the far wall and pull the handle.

MINE! the angel said inside her head.

A second might have passed since one of the machine's fans had clattered to a standstill. During that second, Kate also considered many courses of action and realised that her body had made up her mind for her – once again she felt an irresistible urge to run.

As she began to turn away from H again, the computer fell silent.

And the monitor imploded, then threw out shards of glass and pieces of burning circuit board. H took the full force of the explosion, but pieces of glass nipped and burnt Kate's arms and legs and long before she was able to register that she was bleeding from superficial wounds the room's electricity supply went wild.

None of it should have happened. At the first sign of trouble the breakers should have turned off the power, and at the very worst there should have been one large jolt of electricity finding earth, one flash and bang it should have been all over.

Instead of this the room lit with blue slashes of power which leapt from the computer's casing to the monitor, from the switch-fuse to the liquid nitrogen pipes, from the cases of Alpha chips to wires halfway across the room. Blue fire danced along the length of the computer and fed itself up and down the outsides of the wires, lighting the carpet and scorching the walls.For a few moments the room was full of blue lightning travelling randomly back and forth as if possessed of a life of its own. The acrid smell of burning wiring and ozone filled the air.

And as Kate watched, a thick, ragged strand of power found H's right foot and seared up across his body, tearing his clothes apart and furrowing through the flesh beneath them. It opened a charred and sizzling rent all the way up the right side of his body to his neck and across his face. Sparks and boiling saliva and pieces of tooth shot from his mouth.

And H's goggles exploded from his face.

What was left beneath was a mess of blackened, burned flesh. His eyes had gone and his flesh was peeling like melting plastic.

From the corner of her eye as she crossed the room, Kate saw the inside-out part of the room bulge. *You can't!* she thought. *Too late!*

And, like a trip-wire, a tendril of free power found her ankle. Kate's leg muscles stopped working and she fell to the ground.

To her right, H was screaming and jolting in his seat; above her, the three planes of what had once been the ceiling were still peeling back.

And the angel came through.

It wriggled in the opening H had made and then it was free. It was huge and golden and it was through and that was all Kate had time to make out because it moved at an impossibly fast speed and it was coming at her. One moment it was head and shoulders through the hole and the next it was a golden streak that ran all the way between the hole and her and then it hit her like an express train.

There wasn't time to wonder how it had got inside her. There wasn't time to wonder *anything* because suddenly it *was* inside her and she was in the most severe pain that she had ever experienced. It was like being burned alive from the inside out and being stretched in every direction, while she was crushed in every direction simultaneously. Kate felt herself reach her elastic limit and begin to tear, the way a child's sweater would if a body-builder forced his way into it. And her life force was being compressed into a space that was far too small for it.

The stench of burning electrical equipment filled her senses and her brain flashed with searing gold heat. She felt a rip travel up what must have been her soul itself. It moved like a live thing and molten fingers followed its course, opening the slit.

Then there was another sensation of being slammed against something and the angel left her. Kate saw it arc over to H, not with her eyes – because she no longer seemed to have eyes – but with another part of her, a part that didn't seem to depend on her physical body to relay images to her.

The impact knocked H from his chair and he writhed and

bucked on the floor as electricity danced around him and golden sparks showered from his body.

I'm dead, Kate thought.

And darkness settled around her.

When her senses returned, she was still on the floor of the room where it had happened, but H was gone. The fires were out and the stinking devastation around her was lit only by the murky light that found its way through the whitewashed window. Kate was naked. The white dress she'd been wearing and her underclothes lay strewn around her. She could not think clearly, about what had happened before she blacked out or about what might have happened since. She had no idea as to how long she might have lain here. She was filled with an overpowering urge to get away and a strong sense that it would have been much better if she had died some time within the past hours or days. She sat up slowly and every part of her body screamed at her that it had been terribly violated, but the thing which filled her with frantic fear was the sensation that deep inside her very being something was twisted and torn and horribly *open*. Whatever had happened here seemed to have ruptured her soul – a part of which seemed to be inside her and the remainder of which seemed to exist somewhere in a void. All she knew was that she had to get out and get out fast.

She was surprised to find that she could stand, not surprised to discover that her balance wouldn't settle and that the torn sensation increased as she moved. Her arms and legs were scratched and cut and sticky pieces of burned skin clung to her stomach, thighs and breasts. There was a taste of burned meat in her mouth that she thought would remain with her forever. Brushing off the scraps of flesh made her dry-heave. A part of her whispered that the taste of vomit in her mouth would be preferable to the taste of charred meat, but she could not throw up and her mouth was too dry to spit.

Moving slowly and clumsily and with the feeling of panic growing in her until she thought she would scream, Kate pulled on her knickers and tried to fasten her bra. Her fingers felt like gloves without hands inside them; her hands themselves seemed to be situated somewhere up inside her forearms. It was impossible to fasten the bra so she left it hanging around her and pulled on the dress. It was peppered with tiny burn-holes and stained with blood and ash. She shoved her feet into her red sandals then fell to her knees. She thought she heard something stir in the room above as she clawed her way up the door frame to a standing position and Kate stood still because it was important that whoever it was up there didn't hear her leaving. She no longer knew who might be up there or what they might do to her, except that it would be terrible.

She fought off the panic until she was certain she hadn't heard a sound for five minutes at least and then she went out into the hall. Her car keys were still where she had left them on the ledge of the little window on the right side of the front door and she tottered towards them, sliding her right shoulder down the wall to hold herself upright. When the cool keys were in her hand, she reached for the knob of the front door lock and found she could not close her fingers around it tightly enough to turn it.

Hurry it up or H will come! her brain thought – apparently on her behalf – it didn't seem as if it belonged to her at all. She didn't know who H was. She presumed he was the thing upstairs that she had to escape from.

He's an angel! her mind thought.

She doubted this very strongly because that thing upstairs had damaged her internally and that the damage was of the kind that could not be repaired surgically. The damage was deeper than physical. The damage was to that torn, flapping thing that wasn't even inside her body any more, but somewhere out in a deep void. Except for the fact that if she didn't get away the sleeping thing up there would do more damage to that part of her, everything else was very hazy indeed.

Quick, he'll come! she thought, but her fingers could not work the oval knob.

In desperation, Kate took the knob between her teeth and

twisted her head. She fixed her fingers through the loop of the handle and pulled back, with her teeth and hands. And the door opened.

Too late, a voice said inside her head. Kate recognised the grating tone but couldn't place it. *You've been a bad girl, Katie*, it said, *very bad and it's too late to run. You're mine and I will have you. I gave you the gift of birth, Katie. I made you special. I made you deiparous, Katie, and now we are bound together because I enabled you to birth gods and you gave birth to me. I am your son. And your lover. You will give the gift of birth to many more gods, Katie. Not the gift of life, but the gift of birth. And it will please you. You are mine, little girl, and I am yours. The deed is done and it is too late to undo it.*

'Dekker,' Katie said aloud, not knowing what it meant. It was a comforting word that she remembered from distant dreams of peace and safety. An almost magical word. A word of hope to cling on to as she clung on to the open front door and looked at the sunlit world outside. It looked thin and faint as if it might soon cease to exist.

The grating voice in her head laughed. *Dekker!* it finally spat with derision. DO YOU THINK I DON'T KNOW ABOUT DEKKER? DO YOU THINK I HAVE NOT PLANNED FOR DEKKER? GODS WILL WALK AGAIN ON THE FACE OF THE PLANET, KATIE, AND DEKKER WILL NOT STOP THEM. DEKKER IS BUT A MINOR HINDRANCE, A MAN WHO IS SPLIT IN TWO, A MAN WHOSE COURAGE AND SANITY DESERTED HIM A LONG TIME AGO.

'A man?' Kate whispered, and stepped out into the sunlight.

It took several minutes to open the door of the Renault 5, get in and get the ignition key to fit in the lock, but the voice didn't speak to Kate again and the man (or angel) called H didn't rush down the stairs to stop her running away.

Because it's already too late, she realised as the car finally started. *Because Dekker is a man whose courage and sanity deserted him a long time ago.*

Kate put a foot on the clutch and pressed it down, her leg shaking like a jelly. She reached for the gearstick and felt the extremely unpleasant sensation of her hands moving from where they seemed to be trapped inside her forearms. They slid greasily down the insides of her wrists and fitted themselves into her real hands. *I'm getting back inside myself*, she thought. The fit felt loose, but her fingers were working again.

She put the car into reverse and shot out of the drive into the road, winding the steering wheel around. She had no idea where she might be going – except that it was *away* – or what she was going to do when she got there, but she didn't have to think. It was the right thing to do and she did it.

The words *Dekker* and *south* came into her mind. Kate slowed down for a junction, tried to change gear and the cogs crashed and ground before they finally accepted that second would do instead of third. She turned left and found herself on a housing estate she didn't recognise.

Dekker! she thought, changing gear. Her right leg was too weak to hold the clutch down and she worked it like a pump, trying and failing to coordinate her gear shift movement with the moments when her foot was down. She eventually found third and dropped the clutch again, unaware that she was now travelling slowly enough to warrant having the Gordini in second or first, and only vaguely aware that the car was bouncing and juddering along. Eventually the motion became smooth and she changed gear again. This time she managed to select fourth without mishap.

Dekker! she thought again. *South*! It was hopeless. 'I can't find you!' she moaned.

And up ahead of her a wobbly kid on a bike three sizes too large for him rode down the grass verge towards the road. The boy was grinning wildly as the bike travelled down the bank, picking up speed. His teeth were shining white in the early morning sunshine, his mop of brown hair was blowing back as the bike got faster and steadier. The kid was wearing a maroon tee shirt which seemed alive in the breeze, rippling and flapping about him. He wore faded jeans with the knees out and turn-ups and had scuffed baseball boots on his feet. He was a good-looking boy with brown eyes and freckles and a scab on his right elbow. The bike's spokes glittered in the early morning sunlight and dew glistened on the spinning tyres.

Kate took all this in during the second before she realised that the boy was going to come straight out in front of her and that she was going to run him down.

She hit the brakes and the clutch and the car's nose dipped.

Up on the verge, the boy realised that the wet brakes weren't going to stop the bike and his expression changed from joy to terror.

'NO!' Katie screamed as the bike bumped down the kerb and into the road.

Her trembling legs both ceased to function at the same moment. The car jolted as the idling engine tried to slow it but she was still travelling in excess of thirty miles an hour and the engine's resistance was lessening.

The boy was leaning back now, his legs splayed and his feet high as he tugged back on the handlebars.

Katie screamed and wound the steering wheel hard to the left because it was the only way to miss the boy who was now in the road and less than half a second away from death.

The Renault's tyres squealed and Kate's hands were jolted off the steering wheel as the car double-thumped up the kerb. The world outside became a green and grey blur. Something hit the car hard and Kate thought it might have been the boy. The steering wheel spun before her as the front tyres caught in something and altered their direction. Kate screamed and tried to take the wheel and tried to find the pedals with her feet. Nothing worked.

The car bumped down the kerb again, careered across the road at a diagonal and Katie saw the thing that was going to end her life.

The lamp post was an old-fashioned concrete one. The Renault 5 Gordini hit it at thirty-two miles an hour and wrapped itself around it. Kate was not wearing a seat belt. The window had gone by the time she flew through it. Kate felt a tearing

501

sensation as she arced through the air and tore through a privet hedge. She landed on grass on the other side of the hedge and skidded almost fifteen feet on her back before she came to rest at the feet of an elderly woman who was sitting in her garden reading the newspaper.

Katie opened her eyes, registered the shocked expression of the woman, who was now half sitting and half standing, her paper still in her hand, and then her vision and hearing faded.

For a time there was perfect darkness and perfect silence, then there were sirens and movement and urgent voices and pain which shot through her chest. Then there was the smell of disinfectant and bright lights and more urgent voices.

And then there was more pain and Kate wanted to tell them to let her die because her soul was ruptured and it would be the best thing for her, but she couldn't speak because she was too far away and she had to find someone called Paul.

And some time after that, her heartbeat stopped for the final time.

Kate relaxed and let herself die.

Then there was nothing.

Chapter Nineteen
A Deal For Double A

1

Double A sat back against the dented wing of the Pop, looked out across the busy parking lot of the service area and swigged down a mouthful of extremely cold Coke. His bottom fitted nicely into the dent Reuben's arse had put in the wing and the steelwork had warmed in the midday sunlight – which was a good thing because Double A was freezing.

This was Switzerland, apparently. Double A hadn't seen much of the scenery so far because the pedal had been jammed to the metal and when you were travelling in excess of a hundred and thirty, you had to keep your eyes glued to the road. Jake hadn't seen any of the scenery either, because Jake had fallen asleep directly after the Swiss border police had finished going through the car and had finally seen fit to hand back their passports and allow them into the country.

2

Getting into Germany had been easier – once you'd navigated your way round the winding one-way system that seemed intent on taking you everywhere and anywhere except across the border. When Double A had seen the border post, he had slowed the car and stuffed his stash-bags into his underpants, knowing that a finely wrought look of guilt was stealing on to his face. Jake was no help because he was out cold and didn't respond to the digs Double A gave him in the ribs other than to turn away and grunt. When Double A rolled up to the building in the first light of dawn, the passports clutched in his sweaty hand, his had been the only car there. He stopped where he thought he was supposed to stop and waited for a while, peering into the building's dark windows, then his nerve had cracked and he'd hit the accelerator and gone for broke, every nerve in his body screaming that he'd fucked it now and they were shortly going to be caught and thrown in jail.

Jake had woken five minutes later, sleepily informed him that he'd heard the crossing at Strasbourg was no longer manned, suggested that it might be a good idea to head south from here and had promptly gone back into a deep sleep from which it was impossible to rouse him.

3

Getting into Germany might have been easy, but getting out again presented Double A with certain difficulties. He had done Geography at school – had passed GCSE in it, in fact – but knowing the mean annual rainfall in Addis Abbaba and what the staple diet was in Thailand and which countries specialised in which crops, wasn't a great deal of help when all you wanted to know was which way was south. He had been pretty sure that Switzerland had actually been south of Germany, but there weren't any signposts that said: *Switzerland 250km* – they all directed you towards towns whose names didn't ring any bells at all for him. For a time Double A had followed his nose. He blasted through a tiny town called Oberkirch and another called Oppenau whose chalet-type buildings were the kind of things you'd expect to see in Switzerland, but he was pretty sure he wasn't there yet. When he found himself heading towards Baden-Baden, he knew he was still in Germany because there was a satellite TV station that broadcast from there. At which point he abruptly decided that he must be going in the wrong direction and turned round. There was no logic to support this snap decision and no evidence to prove that he was right, Double A simply did it because it seemed like a good idea.

The roads were very hilly and had sharp hairpins in them, but the Pop clung on tight, its fat tyres occasionally squealing. The thing that pleased Double A most of all about the car – which had, after all, covered more than six hundred miles without ever having previously been tested on the road – was the fact that he'd got the radiator and oil cooler fixed right first time. He'd done similar cars before and all of them had a tendency to over-heat, but this one's gauge needle resolutely stayed just to the left of the normal mark, no matter what you did to the engine. The Pop had growled and screamed its way through more petrol than Double A cared to think about (and the same applied to him and his own brand of fuel) but it was still working without so much as a minute drop in the oil pressure.

Eventually Double A had found a town called Biberach and a signpost pointing towards a town called Freiburg. And on the far side of Freiburg there was an entrance on to a motor-way called the A5. Making up his mind which side of the motorway to get on was the easiest decision he'd made since he'd woken up yesterday morning (although it seemed like a month ago now) and decided to go to the Miles Carriage Co. to work on the car. One ramp on to the A5 was signposted Strasbourg, and the other Basel. Double A's mind might have been beginning to show signs of fatigue by now, and he didn't know where Basel was, but he did know he didn't want to see Strasbourg again, so he took the other ramp.

And half an hour later he and Jake had been explaining to the Swiss border police that they were on their way to Naples for a custom car meeting and that although they couldn't lay hands on the car's certificate of roadworthiness or the green card insurance right now, both were in the Pop somewhere. And while they did this, they both tried to look tired and inno-cent (and Double A also tried to look as if there weren't two bags of illegal drugs stuffed into his underpants and that his jeans were bulging just there because he was one of those lucky people who happened to be extremely well endowed). Both of them noticed the way the guards' holster straps had become magically unclipped giving them instant access to their guns, and neither of them had truly expected to get away with it without having to fight their way through. The Swiss guards had taken their passports and car-keys away, put them in a bare walled room and told them to wait.

Throughout the ordeal so far Jake had acted in exactly the opposite way to what Double A had expected. Instead of raging and shouting the odds and flinging his arms about, he had let the men walk all over him. Jake had sat down on a seat in the little room, closed his eyes, leaned back, and said, 'If it comes to it, leave it to your Uncle Jake. He'll put both of them out of our agony.'

And Double A had replied, 'Okay, they're all yours,' realising with a cold shock that not only did Jake intend to kill the men if things got sticky, but that without any hesitation at all, Mrs Anthony's little boy would be quite prepared to do (or at least try to do) the same thing. Mrs Anthony's little boy didn't even know Dekker – and had only met his alias Mr Stephen Miles on a few occasions. He asked himself what all this was about, then, when some huge and burgeoning reply had begun to form in the middle distance of his mind, quickly withdrew the question. It wasn't just to do with Dekker at all. There was much more to it than that. Too much for little Double A to learn in his presently fragile and paranoid state anyway.

A little later, after Jake had fallen asleep again (and it seemed as if nothing short of a nuclear attack would keep him awake if he was tired and wanted his kip), Double A had heard the rattle of a dog's chain and scratch of claws on concrete, and he'd known they were going to have to fight to get away because the Swiss guards had brought out a sniffer dog and that dog was shortly going to become very excited about the traces of cocaine and amphetamine sulphate that it was surely going to find in the car. Double A knew he was bound to have lost some in the grooves of the driver's seat and on the floor.

But it hadn't come to a fight. Either the dog was a dummy, or it had been trained to sniff for cannabis or heroin or something else – perhaps explosives. There had been no kerfuffle outside, no dog howling at its find or excited voices. Eventually, Double A heard the dog being put back in its pound and shortly afterwards the goons had returned, all smiles and passports. Neither Double A nor Jake asked why they were being allowed to go without the correct paperwork, and neither of them mentioned it afterwards; Double A because his paranoia informed him that it might be extremely bad luck to do so, and Jake for reasons of his own. Probably similar ones.

And after that, Double A had put the matter out of his mind and driven, hard and fast.

4

Stopping at this service area had been necessary. For one thing, the thirsty Pop had needed fuel, and for another, Double A was starting to fall apart and it was getting dangerous for him to drive.

The hallucinations had started inside one of the massive tunnels the Swiss bored through their mountains. They weren't the crawling horrors Double A sometimes had, but they looked set to turn into them if they were left unattended for any length of time.

Lengthy wasn't a good enough word to describe some of those tunnels; they went on long enough to make you despair of ever seeing daylight again.

Double A had managed the first ones – although they were bad enough – but each successive tunnel seemed to go on longer and by the third or fourth they were making him want to scream. The tunnels were brightly lit, which gave them a surreal effect to start with, and every so often you came across huge fans which hung from the arch of the concrete tunnel liners and made a roaring noise as if they were attempting to vent the pits of Hell. The tunnel liners were sections of curved concrete and the effect of the joins passing you every few seconds was hypnotic and made you dizzy.

Double A's sense of spatial awareness took a turn for the worse in the first few and he found himself drawn toward the barriers to his right as if they were huge electromagnets. He had slowed down to fifty, then to forty, then to twenty-five, but he'd still felt as if he was being sucked to the right. In the third tunnel he'd found himself trying so hard not to steer into the barrier that he'd over-compensated and the Pop had drifted across the line and entered the outside lane while a car was trying to pass. The resulting blast of air-horn, magnified by the tunnel, made Double A scream and his automatic twist of the car's wheel almost put the Pop into the barrier he'd been trying so hard to miss.

And from then on, it had got worse. Inside the next tunnel Double A had seen mist appear on the outside of the windscreen. He'd put the wipers on, but they simply juddered across what had to be dry glass. Then the mist had tried to form itself in geometric shapes, then it had begun to glow blue, then it had broken up into globules of water that had streamed up the outside of the windscreen and vanished, only to reappear *inside* the top of the screen. Double A couldn't wipe it off (he knew it didn't exist, but he tried anyway) and he couldn't imagine it away.

In between tunnels, when his eyes weren't playing him up, his paranoia seized the opportunity to give him a hard time. Double A began to imagine that someone was trying to track him using their mind as a kind of psychic radar to find his own. He felt its scan pass over him twice before he entered the next hole in the mountain. *Didn't get me!* he told himself, and started to see bugs crawling up the Pop's sidescreens. They were the size of cockroaches, but pink and glutinous as if they'd shucked off their shells. They left sticky trails behind them.

And Double A had decided it was time for Jake to wake up and take over. A few minutes later he had parked the car in this service area and had shaken Jake violently until he'd woken up.

Jake filled the tank at the self-service pumps, sweet-talked the cashier until she'd let him pay for the petrol in French francs and then sweet-talked her into changing more of the francs he'd taken from the corpse of Philippe Matisse into Swiss money. He'd driven the car to this parking space, thrust the money into Double A's hand, told him to get food and drink with it and then gone back to sleep.

Now, sitting here in the warm dent and feeling very cold as the drugs wore off, Double A's mind began to talk seriously to him about just who might be in this service area waiting for him. Everyone looked suspicious, but that wasn't anything out of the ordinary as far as Double A was concerned. Before he could spot one of the bad guys coming at him, that bad guy was going to have to be aiming a gun at him or hammering towards him in a car. Double A felt the mental radar sweep pass across him again and stuck up a mental middle finger at it. *Go whistle*! he thought, not knowing if he was communicating with that huge and horrible thing he'd purposely avoided thinking about earlier, or if he was simply talking to himself. Either way, there was no reply.

He took another swig of his Coke, wet Coke, this time, not powder, and belched. There was no food in his gut and hadn't been for around thirty-six hours. And as Double A well knew, man could not live on speed alone. The speed would use your body for fuel for a little while, but you couldn't carry on doing it indefinitely. Sooner or later you had to replace what was being burned up by feeling good or you would be enjoying a spectacular collapse of your body. You could sit and marvel as your internal organs shrank away to provide you with the energy the speed told your body you could have. And if you pushed it too hard for too long, one of those wonderful devices, your liver or your heart, would decide it had put up with enough, thank you very much, and now it was putting its foot down and refusing to play any more. And if you let that happen you might live to regret it but you surely wouldn't have time to regret it for long.

Which was the reason for two things Double A intended to

do. First he was not going to poke any more speed into his body for as long as he could manage, next he was going to fill his stomach with food, no matter how uncomfortable it felt (and it was going to feel very uncomfortable indeed, he knew that from experience), and then he was going to sleep for eight or more hours.

He looked at the carrier bag of rolls and fruit he'd bought in the service area's shop without enthusiasm. With a positive sinking feeling, in fact. The reason why doctors had once prescribed uppers as diet pills was that once you had them coursing through your bloodstream, your stomach seemed to shrink itself to about the size of a grape and your appetite went west. Even thinking about eating made you uncomfortable.

A few minutes earlier, Double A had found himself in the restaurant intending to storm up to the counter, grab a plate of hot food and whack it down into his belly before his belly had time to notice what was going on. He stopped just inside the door and found himself staring, his mouth open. It was impossible to discern how the restaurant worked or what they had to eat. It didn't have a single long counter like English ones, where you walked along and took what you wanted from the glass cabinets or stopped by the hot food section and told them you wanted pie and chips or sausage and egg. The counter was arranged in a lying down, outlined E shape and there were high stools arranged all around the extending legs of the E. The inside of the outlined E was where the staff served you.

There were a sprinkling of customers around the counter, eating things that Double A could not put a name to. On the far side of the second leg sat two large muscular men who might have been truckers or who might have been something else. Both of them stopped eating and started staring at Double A as though picking him up and snapping him in half across their knees would give them a few moments of pleasure. Double A looked at them, then looked away. There were no menus on the counter but there were pictures of various dishes on the E's back wall. Below them was a description of what they were. For the first time, it sank in that Mrs Anthony's little boy was no longer safe in England but in a place that had a different language and different food. So far, everyone he'd spoken to (Jake and two sets of border guards) had spoken English. Double A realised with a numb dread born of his paranoia and extreme fatigue, that out here, he was going to be unable to communicate. None of the pictures of food rang any bells for him, and suddenly the thought of eating any of it with those two men watching his every move made him want to scream.

Double A had left the restaurant and found the shop. It was well stocked with rolls, crisps, biscuits, cans of soft drink and fruit, which were all things he recognised and understood. Feeling a huge relief, he had gathered up enough to feed both himself and Jake for another twenty-four hours or so, and had spent all of Jake's Swiss francs paying for it.

Now, sitting on the car with the carrier bag in one hand and a roll in the other, the thought of putting bread into his dry mouth made Double A's stomach squeeze in a defensive demonstration of what it intended to do to him if he actually unwrapped that cheese and ham roll and tried to eat it.

But he was going to try anyway. Just as soon as he'd finished watching the car that his paranoia had just drawn to his attention.

The car was a white BMW. One of the faster looking ones. Series 7 three-point-five litre, Double A thought. It had dark tinted windows and was cruising slowly around the lot as if whoever was in it was looking for a particular spot to stop. It had already passed several empty slots which were nearer the entrance to the restaurant and shops and was serpentining its way through the ranks of cars towards where Double A and the Pop were parked.

Double A put the roll back in the bag, put the bag on the ground, picked up his Coke from the car's bonnet, swigged it, belched and hammered on the Pop's window.

Jake did not wake. He had crawled into the back seat and was curled up into the nearest approximation of the foetal position he had been able to manage. He looked serene. Which would have been fine if it wasn't for the fact that he'd refused to let Double A drive any more and had taken the car keys out of the ignition and put them in his pocket to prevent Double A getting behind the wheel again while he finished his kip.

Double A glanced at the approaching BMW and pulled the Pop's door open. 'Jake!' he called, realising his voice was rising with hysteria. He felt as if he was stuck in one of those nightmares where one simple action had to be accomplished to avert disaster and when you tried to do that simple action it turned out to be impossible. Double A's simple action was to wake Jake.

Here they come! his mind screamed. *Forget Jake, he can take care of himself. Just run for it!*

Double A glanced over his shoulder. Sunlight was winking at him from the bonnet of the BMW which was one lane away and closing.

'JAKE!' he shouted, leaning into the car and shoving him.

'Seven o'clock?' Jake asked blearily.

'Wake up. Someone's coming!' Double A almost screamed. He looked back towards the BMW and saw the two truckers coming out of the service area. How they'd been found this easily, he couldn't imagine. Except that he *could* imagine. He could imagine it very well. That sensation of having been scanned by a mental radar hadn't been a warning that he was reaching exhaustion point at all, it had been real. Someone had homed in on his mind. How it worked didn't matter because it *had* worked and here was the evidence coming towards him.

'The keys!' Double A said. 'Quick, gimme the keys! They're coming!'

'Don't catch you,' Jake said, frowning as he fought to get himself to a sitting position in the cramped back of the Pop.

'They're *here*!' Double A screamed. 'They're *fucking well here*!'

Jake finally caught on and began to scramble towards the door. Anyone else, Double A realised, with a feeling of doom at how late it had suddenly got, would have simply tilted the front seat

512

forward to get out; true to his nature, Jake was climbing over it. It was going to take too long. He and Jake would both be shot dead before Jake even got out of the car.

Double A stood back to give him room to get out and looked over his shoulder at the BMW which was in their row now, and heading towards them. A cramp hit his stomach and Double A bent and shouted his Indian greeting: 'HOWWW!' He spat a few dribbles of cold Coke which tasted much the same as it had when it had gone down, then straightened against the tight pull of his guts.

The BMW pulled into the space on the far side of Pop.

'This one, chick?' Jake said, finally clambering out of the car. He looked like a man who had woken up in the midst of something he didn't quite understand and didn't know how to deal with. Double A's feeling of doom became all-encompassing. This was going to be the end. He tried to speak and couldn't, so he pointed across the lot at where the two heavily built men were.

Jake nodded, frowning. 'And them. Got you. Leave it to your Uncle Jake.'

'Keys!' Double A moaned, clutching his stomach. 'Drive away!'

But Jake was apparently intending to stand and fight.

It wasn't until the BMW's passenger door opened that Double A realised that Jake had a crowbar in his hand – or what Jake would have insisted was a nail-bar. For a second Double A could not understand where he'd got it from, but then a distant memory surfaced and he saw himself getting into the Pop with the crowbar after hitting Reuben with it. He had brought it with him in case it had turned out to be a murder weapon. He had forgotten all about it until now.

And that crowbar might have cracked old Reuben a good one over the head, but it wasn't a magical piece of steel and as far as Double A knew wasn't going to be a great deal of use when the shooting started. *Good try, Jake*, he thought, *but it ain't gonna work.*

Jake stood where he was and slapped the curve of the crowbar into his left hand. He did not run forward to hit whoever was going to get out of the BMW before they had time to set foot on the lot, which in Double A's opinion would be the best course of action, and he did not race over towards the two men who looked as if they might be truck drivers.

'Drive away!' Double A gasped.

Jake shook his head. 'Nope,' he said, and grinned.

The expression of total confidence on Jake's face made Double A want to faint. He *tried* to faint and didn't. He was going to be forced to stand here rooted to the spot with fear while the bad guys took the pair of them apart.

The BMW's door opened a little wider and Double A found his eyes drawn towards it. What appeared in the doorway was surprising because of what it wasn't. What it *wasn't* was Reuben Brown. Or the huge burgeoning thing Double A had almost let himself imagine last night. Neither was it the crushed leg of Philippe Matisse, or the besuited ones of the chemist whom Jake had killed.

What it *was* was an incredibly long, incredibly shapely pair of girls' bare legs. They were set off by feet pointed into shoes with heels so high they surely couldn't be walked in. Dumbstruck, Double A watched the legs come out of the half open door, watched the knees press together as their owner pushed herself up out of her seat. The owner of the legs turned out to look like someone who had only recently reached the age where she was a couple of summers too old to grace the cover of *Vogue*. She was wearing a tiny metallic dress which showed off almost as much of those legs as there was to show. She got out of the car, tugged at the hem of her dress and closed the door.

The guy that got out of the other side of the car was a big, good-looking man dressed in a loose summer suit that must have cost more money than Double A had ever seen.

Jake tossed the crowbar back into the Pop and turned to Double A. 'Won't be needing this,' he said.

Double A's eyes flicked from Jake to the couple and back again. His head felt as if someone had hit it with a bag of lead and his stomach had become a vacuum. 'Wha . . .?' he murmured. Halfway across the car park, the two truck-driver types were climbing into a Japanese four-wheel drive of the type Jake either called Hitachi or Sony.

'False alarm, chicken,' Jake said.

Double A didn't believe him until he'd watched the Hitachi jeep leave the car park and followed the girl's swivelling hips all the way to the service station's doors.

He turned to Jake, who was smiling. 'What happened?' he asked, feeling like the world's most stupid person.

'Who was that black guy?' Jake asked.

'Black guy? What black guy? Reuben?'

'Naaw! Y'know, chick, the one that kept on about his dreams. Prince. Martin something or other Prince.'

'Luther King,' Double A said.

Jake nodded. 'Yeah, Martin Luther King Prince. He had a dream, didn't he?'

Is any of this really happening? Double A asked himself. Unfortunately, it seemed as if it really was. 'Yes,' Double A heard himself answer.

'Well, I had one too,' Jake said. 'I was busy dreaming about that Black Rock place. Remember that house? The one I told you I was going to knock over, down in Cornwall?'

Double A nodded. The imaginary mental radar beam swept by him again, and he mentally ducked it, hunkering his mind down into a tight ball.

'I was dreaming about it again when you woke me up.'

'So?'

'So that's why I was confused. I didn't think we were in trouble. They're not in on it, see?'

Double A shook his head. He didn't see at all. He wished for a few capsules of Valium which might put him out of this misery for several hours.

'You don't catch me, do you?' Jake said, as if it was the

simplest thing in the world to understand. 'They don't *know* me. I know them, because I was casing the place, but they don't know *me* from Edam.'

'Who don't?' Double A almost screamed.

'Jack and Sophie Verglas,' Jake said. 'And if that isn't the fucking weirdest coincidence I've ever been witness to, then I'm an unkey's monkel.'

Double A took a deep breath and tried to calm himself. 'Jake,' he said, 'put it in short words and just tell it to me as simply as you can. Please.'

Jake frowned. 'Well, there I am dreaming about that Black Rock place, and stap me if the people who live in it don't drive up and park alongside the car I'm having the dream in. I must be side-kick or something. Those two rich bastards you just saw get out of this here BMW are the people who live in that house back in Cornwall. There was a bloke once who knew how that worked, that kind of coincidence. I can't remember his name. Anyway, I knew it was them. For a minute I thought they was in on it too, but then I knew they weren't. And I knew the two guys who came out of the building weren't ours as soon as I spotted them. The dream, see? I had a dream.'

'Fine,' Double A said, not understanding any of it. His body was shaking with fatigue and the last squirts of adrenaline it had been able to produce. He sat down on the warm tarmac and leaned back against the Pop's front wheel, because standing and thinking were out of the question at the moment. 'Good,' he said, closing his eyes. 'Fine.'

'You okay now?' Jake asked.

Double A wasn't okay and couldn't talk or think any more. He nodded his head anyway.

'Right,' Jake said, climbing back into the Pop. 'I'm going back to kip. Wake me up when you're ready to roll and we'll get going again. There's no real hurry at present, so you just sit there until you're ready.'

'What d'you mean, there's no real hurry?' Double A asked.

Springs twanged in the back of the Pop as Jake settled down.

'Paul ain't gonna be in Naples to meet us today,' he said.

Double A sighed, and asked the question that formed on his lips even though he knew exactly what the response was going to be. 'How d'you know?' he asked.

'I had a dream,' Jake said.

5

Double A sat against the Pop's wheel and thought about it all for a time. Eventually he cracked open a fresh Coke and took the cellophane off one of the rolls. Eating under these conditions felt rather like the way Double A imagined he would feel at being woken up in the middle of the night and being forced to eat wood and sand. *It'll get easier after the first few mouthfuls*, he assured himself. After the first few mouthfuls – washed down with Coke because he had no saliva to call his own – it didn't get any easier at all. It got quite a bit harder in fact, because now his stomach was trying to send the food right back where it came from.

But Double A managed to keep it all down. It sloshed around uncomfortably in his stomach and it was cold, but he managed to keep it where he'd put it. And he even managed to keep it down when his mind remembered and began to sing, unaided and against his wishes, a two ball song that one of his old girl-friends had often recited to him.

> *Rhubarb and custard,*
> *snot and bogey pie,*
> *All mixed together with a dead dog's eye,*
> *Stir it, stir it, stir it quick,*
> *Wash it all down with a cup of cold sick.*

Double A was okay until it got the line about cups of cold sick, and then he had to stand up and walk about a bit, because that was exactly what seemed to be lurking in his stomach – except that there was a good litre there rather than a cupful.

He didn't give his mind a chance to repeat the rhyme and after a time he began to feel a little better. Well enough to sit down on the tarmac with his back against the car again, anyway. That was a distinct improvement. He turned his face to the sun, listened to the soothing hiss of cars passing on the motorway – or autobahn or whatever they called them in this neck of the mountains – and the gentle comings and goings in the car park, and closed his eyes while he thought about Jake's dream and kept his mind out of the way of that imaginary radar sweep.

And after a little while, Double A crossed the border between conscious thought and unconscious thought and had a dream of his own.

The dream started off in the cellar of Jake's famous house in Cornwall, Black Rock, where he was standing in the corner, paralysed and screaming, while the man from the BMW chased after his wife, striking at her with the buckle end of a leather belt. Mrs Verglas was quick, in spite of the fact that she was still wearing those impossibly high heels, but she wasn't quick enough. Her long, gorgeous legs were running with blood where the belt had hit her. She was screaming, Double A was screaming and there were many other voices screaming too. There was an ancient table set up against the wall opposite Double A and on it was a large reel-to-reel tape recorder which played gentle music to accompany the screaming. Double A knew that besides playing the soundtrack, the machine was also recording the screaming. Upstairs, Paul Dekker's distant voice was shouting for Jake.

Then he was in a bar on a boat and Paul Dekker was lashing out at someone. The punch was so quick he barely had time to register it before it had come and gone. Double A was impressed.

Then he was in an office he did not recognise. He glanced up at the plate glass window and it imploded and Reuben Brown flew through, an expression of supreme surprise on his face. And seconds later one of the women in the office was getting up from where she had been kneeling beside Reuben and her face became a picture of horror as she spotted black stuff on her hands. Double A knew exactly what that black stuff was that the woman was trying so hard to wipe off her hands. It was the stuff Jake had seen coming from the corpse in Double A's flat, just before the corpse had walked.

And then he was in a room that was horribly twisted, as though one of its upper corners had somehow become turned inside out and split apart. There were two other people in the room – a man wearing a pair of gas welder's goggles and a girl who was so lovely that Double A ached for her and feared for what might happen to her. But there was no time to consider who or what the other people were because Double A's eyes were drawn to the tortured corner of the room.

The corner bulged and Double A finally saw the thing he had been preventing himself from seeing since last night. The thing was an angel – the one that had brought Reuben back to life with the black stuff, the one that had brought the chemist back to life too. It was a huge terrifying golden thing that rippled with a billion megawatts of power. It was immortal and indomitable, inescapable and cruel. Hell burned in its dark eyes.

And those eyes turned towards Double A and held him in their fiery gaze. *You have taken one of mine*, the angel boomed inside his head. *And for this you will pay, my little chicken. And you will pay handsomely and for a very long time.*

Double A stood rooted to the spot, quivering.

And now the angel was looking at him from a man's body – *the* man, the one who had been wearing the welder's goggles. Except that now the goggles were gone and so were the man's eyes and most of his face. He was in the same room, but the geometric absurdity in its top corner had gone and the walls were cracked and scorched and the carpet was burnt. It smelled as if some huge electrical device had shorted out. When the angel-thing spoke, its voice was no longer mellow and huge, but rasping and evil.

There is another way. An easier way. All you have to do is come to me. Be mine. I can promise you pleasure beyond belief.

The angel's misshapen mouth twisted into a cruel grin. *Or pain beyond endurance.*

And Double A felt some of that pain and screamed for mercy. It felt as if a million living fish hooks had been planted inside his digestive tract and were tearing their way out of him. Tissue tore, muscle and nerve were severed, but the hooks never worked their way to the surface.

'Stop it!' Double A squealed, and the words rose from his throat, thick with his own blood which sprayed the room and the angel. For a moment the blood danced on the angel's skin in shimmering rainbows and then was absorbed.

'Stop!' Double A pleaded again. His insides were shredded to tatters, and he surely ought to be dead, but he didn't die and pain didn't lessen. Sinew by sinew he was being torn apart. His lips swelled, as lumpy, bulging living masses invaded them like worms and forced their way out in blossoms of blood and skin. His right eye tore through its centre and blinding white light seared down his optic nerve and tore at his brain.

Come to me! the angel said.

And the pain was gone and the angel was gone and Double A was whole and undamaged again. The girl stood before him, looking at him in the coquettish way he'd seen Princess Di looking in some of her photographs. Something about her, something Double A couldn't quite put his finger on, struck him as achingly beautiful. She was prettier than Princess Di and she had deep green eyes which shone with the promise of the best sex Double A had ever experienced, but there was more to it than this. Much more. The girl promised Heaven.

Then her cool hands were around his neck, pulling his mouth against hers. Double A accepted her cool, flicking tongue into his mouth. She tasted of oranges and honey. Then she stood back, smiling, and he was quivering with lust as her hands traced lines down his chest, down across his belly in a vee shape that was going to end at the part of him that was hottest and hardest. The girl's hands paused at the waistband of his jeans and he felt the pressure against his abdomen released as she deftly unbuttoned him and opened his fly.

And then he was on his back on the charred floor, naked and shivering, and the girl was straddling him, holding his cock in her cool hands as she lowered herself on to it. She moaned when he entered her and Double A gasped. She was wet and cool and firm against his hot, hard cock. The sensation was so intense it was almost unbearable. 'Don't move yet,' Double A whispered, but the girl just smiled that promising smile. She leaned down and kissed him long and slow, then took her mouth from his, took his hands, pressed them to the floor and began to fuck him.

Double A managed to hang on for five deep, slow thrusts and then he came, wailing as he burst apart with pleasure. But the girl didn't stop fucking him and Double A didn't stop coming. She drew him deeper inside her than he thought would have been possible and he was still coming and she was reaching orgasm too, thrusting against him and panting and squealing and moaning.

'Come to me!' she said and there was no longer any girl or any Double A, just a single mass of fizzling, screaming ecstasy which seemed as if it would go on forever.

6

'Come to me!' a voice encouraged.

Distantly, Double A realised it was neither the voice of the girl nor the voice of the angel. It was, however, a voice he recognised and it seemed to be coming from another world.

'Come to me!' it whispered.

And Double A woke up.

He became conscious of two things at exactly the same moment and both of them slapped his face with the same amount of force. The first was that the voice he'd been listening to belonged to Reuben Brown and the second was that he'd come in his pants.

'Hard old world, ain't it?' Reuben asked as Double A focused on his face. Reuben was squatting down beside him, his elbows on his knees, his face cupped in his hands. The first question that Double A's mind raised was whether one of those big brown hands of Reuben's had had anything to do with the sticky mess that was currently soaking out through his underpants and staining his jeans. Double A decided he would rather die than find out that Reuben had wanked him to orgasm.

And it looked as if dying might be one of the things that was very shortly going to be expected of him. Reuben might once have been a confidence trickster who had threatened people with plastic pistols, but Reuben had recently undergone some changes. The eight-inch matt black blade of the commando's combat knife that lay on the tarmac between Reuben's feet was going to turn out to be very real.

Double A took all of this in within the two seconds it took for him to make the transition from deep, relaxing sleep – to abject terror. Reuben had changed in other ways too, he realised, as his eyes flicked from the huge knife to Reuben's face and back again. There was a sizeable dent in his forehead that looked as if it might have been made by a strike with something like a crowbar and there was a ragged slot in his temple. Through his terror, Double A knew exactly what had brought this fatal wound into being. He could picture Reuben getting to his feet after flying into that office through its plate glass window. There was a shard of that plate glass filling the spot in his head, a shard long enough to have given him a clumsy lobotomy. A shard that had ended his life.

Double A was as sure of this as he would have been if he'd witnessed the scene from inside the office rather than having imagined it. And if he had doubted his fevered imagination, one look into Reuben's eyes would have provided all the confirmation he needed; they were flat and dull and misty, almost to the point of being opaque. Double A had last seen eyes like this on a dog that had lain dead for a week beside the road near his flat.

Reuben was dead.

And Reuben was squatting beside him philosophising upon the nature of the world.

Double A glanced at Reuben's dead-dog eyes again, then back to the knife, certain that this time he wasn't going to be able to move a muscle. The knife was there for the taking and he wasn't even going to be able to snatch it up.

Scream! he told himself. *Jake will wake up if you scream and Jake's got the crowbar in there . . . and the gun he took from Gordon Clement.*

Double A opened his mouth, intending to give the loudest scream the world had ever heard and knowing that it wasn't going to work. His breath would get trapped in his throat and all that would escape into the world would be a tiny squeak. He tried it anyway and was not surprised at the resulting sound.

'So what's it to be, pipsqueak?' Reuben asked, smiling. The smile did not reach his eyes. 'Are you going to come home with me, or am I going to have to fix it so you hurt? The girl's real and she's yours to use, you know that, don't you? And you know she's real because you know who she is.'

Double A nodded. He knew exactly who the girl was in the same way as he'd known about the piece of glass that had killed Reuben. The girl was the girl Dekker was trying to protect.

Reuben sniggered. 'She can show you Heaven, pipsqueak. Or I can take you to Hell.'

'What do I have to do?' Double A heard himself ask. He was shocked because he had not intended to speak at all – hadn't even thought it was possible to speak. On the other side of the car, the door opened. Double A felt the car moving against his back. The other guy was round there, getting into the car, and Jake was still asleep.

'Absolutely nothing,' Reuben replied. 'That's what you have to do. Exactly nothing at all. Easy, ain't it?'

But the guy was opening the car door and Jake was asleep. *So shout. You know you can.*

But just like the man said, Double A did nothing. The

proposition was interesting. And it had to be that stopping him doing anything because he could think of no other sound reason not to act. It was because the girl was gorgeous and he wanted her. He *ached* for her. And it wasn't a lie. He *could* have her. But only if she could be taken away from Dekker. Only if Jake could be stopped from taking the car down to Naples. Two things. And the beauty of it was that he could make these two things happen by doing nothing at all. Two easy things to do nothing about in exchange for an existence which would make you scream with ecstasy was a pretty good deal as far as Mrs Anthony's boy was concerned.

'And it'll be a good, long existence,' Reuben promised, as if he'd just listened to Double A's train of thought. 'It'll last for ever. Imagine that.'

Double A imagined it. Forever with a girl like that. He started to get hard again.

'There's my man,' Reuben said. 'A guy who's finally begun to think straight!'

Behind Double A, Jake grunted with surprise. There was a noise that reminded Double A of the sound a coconut would make when hit with a wooden ball and the springs of the Pop's rear seat complained.

'Just sit still, Anthony,' Reuben said. 'You know you're doing the right thing. You have made your mind up, haven't you? You are coming home with us. No doubts or regrets?'

Double A shook his head. He had no doubts or regrets at all. Just a single question. 'Will there be cocaine?' he asked in a small voice.

Behind him, Jake cried out. The Pop rocked. Gordon Clement was evidently a little pissed off that Jake had shot him and was now getting his own back for the inconvenience.

Reuben grinned. 'More cocaine than you could shake a stick at,' he promised, 'and as pure as you can imagine. If you need it, that is. Anything you need will be yours. But I doubt you will need it because you're going to feel pretty damn' fine without it. I feel pretty damn' fine, Anthony. And I'm getting better.'

Double A heard the coconut being struck again inside the car. He didn't think about it because there was sound accompanying it. Sound that suggested Jake was hurting. Jake would feel better soon, Double A was certain. These days no one had to feel bad for long. You only had to look at Reuben to know that.

'I'm sorry,' Double A said.

Reuben's smile left his lips. 'Sorry? What d'you mean *sorry* boy?' Reuben demanded as if he'd just heard a word that wasn't in his script. Double A caught a glimpse of something black and dull on his tongue when he spoke.

'Sorry for what I did to you,' Double A said, glancing down at the knife. He knew why it was there now. It had been a test. Earlier, he'd thought about trying to snatch it up and stick it in Reuben, but he had resisted the temptation. If he'd gone for it, Reuben would have got there first and he would now be suffering. But he'd passed the test because he hadn't gone for it.

What you did *do was cave in*, a part of his mind whispered and Double A quickly shuttled the thought away. It was very important that he didn't allow himself to think things like this. He had no idea why.

'That's okay,' Reuben said. 'Sometimes I hurt a little, but I ain't dead.' He said this ponderously as if he wasn't really quite sure what state he was in at all.

Oh, you're dead all right, Double A thought, and squashed this stray note of dissent too. He did not allow himself to address the question that followed the thought which was: *If Reuben is really dead and his body is a puppet of something else, why does he think he's alive?* Because it surely wouldn't be a question which Reuben would take kindly to if he picked it up in that telepathic way he seemed to have.

The Pop rocked against Double A's back as if its occupants were a pair of sex-crazed teenagers parked up in a lover's lane. The seat springs were protesting and Jake was growling and squeaking like a fighting dog that has met its match. It was not a pretty noise.

'It don't have to be a hard old world at all, do it?' Reuben said. 'It's what we make it. If we want it to, it can be easy.'

'As pie,' Double A agreed. He knew this without a doubt. His comedown had gone and he was feeling warm and tired and very content. He could sit here in the sun all day, if that was how long it took.

For the signal to come?

'What signal?' Reuben asked.

Double A shrugged. 'Sometimes, when you're coming down after a good session, you get weird thoughts. Can't help 'em. Sorry. It doesn't mean anything that I know about.' Except for the fact that he no longer felt as if he was coming down, this was the truth.

'Right,' Reuben said. His dull eyes settled on the knife and his face relaxed.

'GET THE FUCK OFF ME!' Jake's muffled voice shouted. The words were spoken with extreme anger, but also with an odd pleading tone that Double A had never heard Jake use before. He didn't think about it. The sweeping band of the odd mental radar passed over him again and Double A reflexively withdrew his mind from its path. It wasn't looking for him now, and if it had been, it wouldn't have mattered because he had already been found. He wondered why he'd tried to keep himself away from it, then put it out of his mind.

'I can't remember what happened to my car,' Reuben said.

Double A peered at him. Reuben's eyes were fixed upon the knife. 'Staring' was the word Double A would normally have used to describe it, but it was inapplicable here; the eyes were unseeing. Double A didn't think about it until afterwards, when he would realise that Reuben was neither quite alive nor quite dead and that the thing controlling him was struggling to do it. Reuben's driver had momentarily diverted its attention elsewhere (probably to Gordon who was killing Jake) and what was left of Reuben himself was voicing its thoughts.

What Double A *did* think – and couldn't keep himself from thinking – was that the signal was about to come.

Reuben didn't pick this one up at all, just stared at the knife. 'It was a Mustang,' he said. 'I loved that car.'

And Double A heard the signal and moved, without any prior plan of action whatsoever. He was astonished that he moved at all and if the glaring discrepancy that seemed to have occurred in his mind hadn't thrown it off balance, he might have resisted because he really *did* intend to swap sides.

One moment the big knife was on the floor between Reuben's feet and the next, Reuben was toppling backwards and Double A was standing over him, his hands thrown into the air like an old lady who has just taken the fright of her life while he thought, *My God, what have I done?*

What he had done was to snatch up the knife and plant it in Reuben's left eye so hard and so fast that all he had been aware of was a single blur of speed and force that made his tired muscles scream. And he had struck true. The evidence lay before him, not bleeding and not moving. Reuben was unlikely to move ever again. The knife had sunk into his eye right up to the hilt, and its pointed black tip had come out through the back of his skull. No black substance trickled from Reuben's mouth and Double A didn't expect it to. He'd finally finished the job he'd started when he'd dotted the man over the head with the crowbar. Reuben was beyond repair.

Double A ran around to the other side of the car, realising distantly that he had successfully fooled himself over the last five minutes. Fooled himself so completely that he'd believed he was changing his alliances, while beneath that a part of him that was unconscious had known exactly what to do. Exactly what was right.

Jake was in trouble. Gordon Clement, a man he had once killed with a single blow, had wrestled the crowbar away from him and was pinning him to the seat with the straight end of it, and pushing down rhythmically, as if he expected the sharp end of the bar to pierce Jake's chest at any second. Both Jake's hands were locked around the bar as he snarled and spat and tried to keep this very thing from happening.

Why didn't you use the gun? Double A thought. But Jake had been sleeping and the man had surprised him.

Clement was standing half in and half out of the car, leaning around the tilted front seat and into the back while his feet sought a firm purchase on the ground outside. His stance was that of a man trying to pull a truck along on a rope.

Double A didn't quite know what to do. He wasn't going to be able to pull the man off Jake from this position, and kicking his legs out from beneath him might simply supply the added force he needed to push the bar through Jake.

He balled his fist and punched Clement in the kidneys as hard as he could. Two things happened that Double A did not expect. The first was that Clement did not shout or move or even seem to have noticed when he'd been hit hard enough to make him piss blood, and the second was that something in Double A's own right forefinger cracked and shot a bolt of pain up his arm.

'Fucker!' Double A screamed, shaking his hurt hand. Something clicked inside his head and Mrs Anthony's son felt the first genuine white hot rage of his life. He bent down, took Clement's ankles in his hands, put a foot against the side of the car to brace himself and heaved.

Jake shouted.

And Clement came out of the car like an eel. Double A rolled with him as he snaked and struggled on the ground. The crowbar was no longer in his hands, but judging by the strength he seemed to possess, he wasn't going to need it. Double A brought his knee up hard into Clement's crotch and wasn't terribly surprised to find it had no effect. Neither was he surprised to find that he could move and punch and kick at a speed which equalled Clement's own. Clement was stronger, but then he was bigger.

They rolled across the tarmac and Double A suddenly found himself face to face with the man. Just before Double A dipped his forehead into the man's face, he caught a strong whiff of him. The man smelled like the burning electrical equipment he'd smelled in his dream. Double A's head snapped down and he felt some of Clement's teeth crack – knew that he was going to have the marks of those teeth in his forehead for some time to come. Clement's head flew back, bounced off the tarmac and he went limp.

Double A didn't stop to think about it. He was up and away before the man had a chance to move again.

Jake was in the driver's seat of the Pop when Double A stood up. His face looked as if he'd gone ten rounds with a better fighter. His eyes were puffed up, his lips were swollen and there was blood running from his nose and the corner of his mouth. The skin was torn from all of his knuckles and blood was running down his wrists.

Double A leapt over the bonnet of the Pop, fell, rolled and got up again as the Pop burst into life. He flung himself in through the passenger's door and fought to stay put as Jake dropped the clutch and the car made a screaming semi-circle. He clung on to the seat, reached out to the door and slammed it as Jake straightened the Pop.

'Motherfucker,' Jake said.

Clement was on his feet again now and running, but Jake didn't intend to let him get away again by the look of it. The Pop screamed forward. Double A closed his eyes and then opened them again.

'Live and learn,' Jake hissed, and the Pop caught Clement's back. The thud made Double A's stomach squeeze. Jake hit the brakes. Clement shot forward, flying like a spastic Superman, hit the tarmac face down and skidded to a halt about ten feet in front of where the Pop had stopped. He started to get up.

'Not this time, Sonny Jim!' Jake said and dropped the clutch again. Clement whacked into the front of the car again and bounced off, rolling down the tarmac. He started to get up again and Jake rolled the Pop forward and hit him again, gently enough just to knock him back to the ground. 'Now fuck off!' he said, and put his foot on the throttle and let go of the clutch. The car did a sickening double bump over Clement and Jake brought it to a halt and peered into the rear view mirror.

Double A turned to look out of the Pop's back window. Clement was bust and no mistake. But he wasn't dead. His arms and legs were flapping like tentacles as he tried to get up again. He wasn't going to make it, Double A was certain of that. His limbs now had more breaks than a three-part mini-series.

'He ain't dead, chicken,' Jake said, but Double A wasn't really listening. He was now scanning the car park for witnesses. He had expected a crowd by now with all the racket that had been going on, but squealing tyres and thumps were apparently something that people in Swiss motorway service areas were well used to. The man and woman that Jake had called Jack and Sophie were standing outside the entrance to the restaurant area watching intently and so were a couple of teenagers who had just climbed out of a tiny Fiat 500. Nobody was coming running towards the 'accident' and anyone else who might be in the car park would be way too far away to get the Pop's number. Someone might be able to give a description of the car to the police, of course, but that was a risk they would just have to take. The police in England hadn't been efficient enough to warn the ports or catch them, so there was no reason why the Swiss should be any different – especially as they would, with any luck, soon be out of the country. Double A crossed his fingers.

'He ain't dead *yet*,' Jake corrected himself. 'Missed his head.'

A second later, Jake put that right.

Six seconds afterwards the Pop was back on the motorway and doing sixty. The engine roared like an enraged tiger as Jake changed up and hit the throttle.

For some time, Double A kept one of his eyes peeled for police cars, while the other kept tabs on the speedo. Jake took the Pop up to a wind-buffeting 125 and kept it there.

If they didn't get pulled for a murder, they might for speeding, he told Jake. Jake asked him who was driving the car and told him to shut up.

'Why didn't you shoot him?' Double A asked, closing his eyes.

They were entering a tunnel and he still couldn't face the walls closing in on him while they rushed by. He hoped he would be able to handle it after he'd slept.

'Why aren't we locked up at the Swiss border?' Jake replied.

Double A thought about it. 'Dunno,' he eventually conceded.

'Because we weren't carrying a gun,' Jake said. 'I dumped it in the toilets in the Hoverport in Dover. It's in the cistern in the third cubicle from the left – unless anyone's found it yet. I left it behind because for one thing, I thought we might be pulled, and for another, I wasn't sure about you.'

'How do you mean?' Double A asked. The tunnel lighting was still streaking past him, lighting bright stripes on the insides of his eyes.

'You don't really wanna know,' Jake said.

Double A thought about this. 'Yes I do,' he said.

'I thought if we brought the gun, you might start popping shots off at people, willy nilly. Guns talk.' Jake sounded embarrassed.

Double A felt daylight against his eyes and opened them again. It hurt but not as much as the lie Jake had just told him. The real reason Jake hadn't brought the gun was that he hadn't trusted his little dope-fiend friend, that was a dead certainty. Jake had stashed the gun because something had told him – quite correctly as it had turned out – that Double A might throw a weird attack and that the gun could quite possibly be used against him. 'I wouldn't have shot you,' he told Jake.

Jake just grunted.

Double A wondered how he could explain the trick his mind had worked on him. That trick had stopped him going to Jake's aid, but it had surely saved both of them. He hadn't really been going to change sides at all. Not really.

And with the words *not really* rattling around inside his empty head, Double A drifted off to sleep.

This time there were no dreams.

Chapter Twenty
Italy

1

Paul's connection with Katie broke with a snap, as if someone had aimed a taut elastic band at a point deep inside his brain and then let it go. He fell away from Katie, not yet sure whether he was him or her, and lay down on the deck of the boat, her limp head on his chest, while he gasped in deep breaths of warm air. He could still feel each and every pain that she had experienced and every emotion she'd had. It was as if he'd just lived through those things as Katie herself had done, and in real time. His heart was hammering away well in excess of a hundred and forty and he felt exhausted and ill.

It's getting late! Better go down to the car deck and have a look at those signs, his goad reminded him, but Paul wasn't ready yet. He looked at his watch and was surprised to find that only ninety minutes had passed. What had seemed like months had fitted into the timespan of the average feature film. But this film hadn't exactly been light entertainment.

'Now you know,' he said, staring up into the cloudless blue sky. The only part missing was the time between Katie's death and her leaving the hospital and getting to Skiathos. He imagined that this had happened in much the same way that her flight and crash had happened – on something that was more or less auto-pilot. She had evidently woken up in hospital (perhaps even in the morgue) and walked out, got money and a passport from somewhere – where she lived perhaps, Chris wasn't exactly going to stop her, was he? – and got on a plane.

He now had the history and that was all fine and dandy and fitted together like a jigsaw with his own experiences, but what he didn't have was the answer to the problem or, come to that, a good reason for his presence in this. The link seemed to be the boy, little Paulie Saunders, whom he had definitely killed and whom Katie too thought she'd killed. As real as it had looked, it was impossible for him to have died twice in exactly the same manner. It looked as if Paulie – or his ghost – had actually been placed in front of Katie's car in order to make her crash and die. And perhaps as a symbol that Paul would recognise and understand – another example that the forces who were manipulating Katie needed him. What did Paulie represent? Innocence coming to grief? The guilt both he and Katie felt? The chance of a return to that innocence for both of them by righting the wrongs they had both done? He thought that this was probably the case.

Except that there's more to it than that, isn't there, cowboy? Much, much more!

Paul didn't know what the rest was. He wondered if his actions were being manipulated by forces he couldn't perceive or understand – forces on the other side of Katie's *void* – and doubted it. Persuaded, perhaps, but that was all. The only force directly trying to manipulate him was that of H, the guy who had sucked a huge golden thing from another dimension into his body. Paul decided he was taking part in this of his own free will and that it was only his promise to the girl which bound them together. He could stop now if he wanted to. He would lose the girl (a matter he refused to contemplate on the grounds that when you added emotional involvement into the equation it didn't work out even at all), his mother and Cindy would have been murdered for nothing and H would get his way. Paul Dekker, a car thief whose bottle hadn't quite gone after all, would lose what somehow seemed like a golden chance to atone for the hit-and-run on the kid by putting back some good into the world, but even this didn't seem to be important. What was keeping him going, he decided, was sheer bloody-mindedness. H, or the thing that H had become, wanted him to stop and had killed in order to make him stop – and in so doing had hit Paul's stubborn button. As Freddie Simmons would gladly have told anyone prepared to listen, Paul Dekker wasn't a man who took kindly to being pushed around. Paul Dekker did what Paul Dekker wanted to do and advising him against it would only make him dig his heels in and fuck the consequences. What was keeping him going was the fact that H, or the black angel in H's body, wanted him to quit.

More than that, too, poke. But Paul refused to consider the emotional aspect or the other, more ancient links he had imagined. All that mattered was the cold, *get-even* rage that burned inside him. *Justice will be done*, he thought, *and if you can hear me, H, I'm coming after you.*

He lay on the deck with Katie's cool, tousled head on his lap, and breathed deeply, concentrating on slowing his heart and clearing his mind while he told himself that he hadn't fallen for the girl.

When he was as calm as he expected to get he remembered the car-deck and immediately began to feel an urgent need to get down there and see what it said on those signs. He laid Kate down on the deck, caught the eye of the German boy and nodded at her still form. The German understood and gave him the thumbs up.

Before he went inside the boat, Paul finished the water from the bottom of the bottle.

It didn't take away the taste of burning electrical insulation.

2

Paul stepped over the chain and the No Entry sign that prevented passengers getting down on the car deck and walked carefully down the stairs, feeling in his pocket for his lucky ten pfennig piece. He felt better when he had it in his hand and before he'd reached the first landing on the way down, the tearing feeling he'd shared as the black angel hit Katie (and which he expected to last forever) had gone.

By the time he went through the door and on to the car deck, his mind had flipped into the mode he enjoyed best and was beautifully concentrated.

There was no one at all on the car deck. He hadn't expected to see passengers there, but had thought there might be one or two seamen, smoking cigarettes or passing the time until the ferry got close to the port. Seamen would have been a problem, but he was lucky.

Paul threaded his way through the tightly packed cars, heading towards the ferry's bow door. Halfway there he glanced at the wall to see his left and felt his face light up. It was as if a weight had suddenly been lifted from his shoulders. The old magic had begun to work again and St Cunt had seen fit to smile that benevolent smile once more.

Dreamed it up! he told himself. And now he remembered that priceless piece of information he hadn't quite been able to access.

The signs, one of which he was looking at now, grinning while his fingers busily turned over the ten pfennig piece, were evenly spaced down both sides of the deck. They read:

PLEASE LEAVE YOUR CAR KEYS IN THE IGNITION
IT MAY BE NECESSARY FOR STAFF TO MOVE YOUR
VEHICLE

The piece of information was the simple fact that people travelling in ferries don't expect to have their cars stolen. Paul frowned, suddenly wondering if people travelling in ferries would take any notice of these instructions, even if they didn't expect anyone to steal their cars. Leaving your door unlocked might not result in your car being gone when you came back to collect it, but there had to be a pretty good chance of your stereo or other valuables going missing. This was presumably why passengers weren't allowed on the car deck during the voyage – if anyone stole anything it had to be the crew. Which was probably a good reason why none of them were here either. Paul wondered why they hadn't just locked all the doors to the deck – that would have kept everyone out.

He pushed between two left-hand drive Fiats, clambered over the bumper of an Audi and tried the door of a red Citroën BX16TRS, because he thought someone might have left this particular car here for him. But the driver of the Citroën had been a bit more security conscious than the signs on the wall bade him. The car was locked and the keys were not in the ignition. Worse than that, the car was a good five ranks from the bow doors. Paul didn't bother trying the old slap-on-the-door trick because he didn't think it would work and he had the distinct feeling that St Cunt had made other arrangements for him here. Somewhere closer to the front, in fact. As he wove his way forward he remembered spotting the purser's office and this too seemed significant. He wasn't quite sure how it all fitted together yet, but he was getting used to that particular affliction now. Sometimes, as he well knew, you simply had to be patient. All would be revealed in the fatness of time, as Jake would have said.

Wondering if Jake had bought his plane tickets yet, and how long it would take him to get to Naples, Paul fought his way through a tiny gap between a Daimler Sovereign and an Opel Manta. Every door he'd tried so far had been firmly locked. No one, apparently, believed that it might become necessary for staff to move their cars. Everyone suspected – as Paul had – that leaving the keys in and the doors open might just be an invitation to a thief. He passed another two locked cars – a Greek-registered Subaru pick-up and a French-registered Granada with an empty boat trailer attached to the hitch – then he stopped. His bottom jaw might have dropped in surprise – afterwards he wouldn't be sure, and now his mind was too busy understanding everything to consider how he looked. Before him lay the front rank of cars. And in the centre of that front rank, in the prime position for leaving the ferry, was the result of St Cunt's smile.

The car was a one-year-old British Racing Green V12 XJS Jaguar convertible and the top was down and the keys were in the ignition. It was right-hand drive and had a GB plate on the back.

Paul stood looking at the car for a moment, then hurried over to it and climbed in. Being back in a Jag felt very good indeed. The car seemed to fit him like a glove. Paul opened the cubby box and found the car blurb, maintenance booklet and assorted ticket stubs. The green card insurance document was not present as Paul had hoped it would be, but there was something which was just as good – the car's registration paper. The car was owned by a Mr Philip Lock who lived in Stratford-upon-Avon. He'd registered as the car's owner last year. Paul put the document back in the cubby box, took the keys from the ignition and climbed out of the car. He threaded his way back through the tightly packed deck and left the same way as he'd come.

There were quite a few people milling about in the area where the purser's office was. Some of them were already positioning cases at the large metal door on the left side of the corridor and Paul assumed that there must be an hour or less before the ferry docked. Which wasn't really long enough. He hoped there was time.

He joined a line of people queuing up at the purser's office and ground his teeth as the minutes sailed by and the queue didn't seem to get any shorter.

He turned round and saw that there were another five people waiting in line behind him. The guy directly behind looked as if he might be English.

'How long till we dock?' Paul asked.

'Comment ça va?' the man replied.

'About forty-five minutes,' an American voice said from behind him. Paul froze, but this was a young blond guy and not good old Charlie.

'Thanks,' he said, taking a deep breath and mentally forcing his heartbeat to slow. The old *click-out* demon was scurrying around under his skull and he didn't trust himself to let it out.

He had controlled it before but wasn't certain that this new ability had become permanent. Waking up in the brig wasn't going to help him or Katie.

It took another ten minutes for him to get to the front of the queue. Which meant that he had thirty-five minutes, minus however long it took Philip Lock to answer the call.

'Yes?' the guy at the window said. 'How much?'

Paul suddenly realised that he ought to change some money into Italian currency and dragged a wad of notes from his pocket. There was less than twenty-five pounds' worth left which meant he would have to rob again soon, but if this went the way he intended, two birds could easily be killed with the single stone.

The guy gave him his lire – what looked like an astonishing amount – and Paul folded it and pocketed it then said, 'I have to get in contact with one of the passengers. His name is Phil Lock. It's urgent I speak to him. Could you put out a call for him to come here?'

'Do you have something of his?' the guy asked.

Paul shook his head. 'I have to tell him something important.'

The purser slid a sheet of paper and a pencil towards him. 'Write message,' he said, 'I will pass on.'

'I have to speak to him personally,' Paul insisted. 'And quickly,' he added.

The purser shrugged theatrically and looked pointedly around Paul at the queue.

'It's *urgent*!' Paul growled. He felt that cold, hard feeling creeping across the inside of his skull. It would be reflected in his eyes, he knew. His murderous look.

It worked.

'Okay,' the purser said, giving up. 'I call him here.'

'Now,' Paul added.

The purser nodded. 'Now,' he repeated.

And while Paul watched he made the announcement, first in Greek, then in Italian, and when Paul was almost mad enough to fly through the window and tear his head off his shoulders, in English.

'In English again,' Paul said.

The message was repeated. 'Okay?' the man asked, his face dark with anger of his own.

'Fine,' Paul said, hoping the man had heard the call to the purser's office. He also hoped he was wearing a belt and a long-sleeved shirt and that he brought his wife or girlfriend with him when he came.

Five minutes later an agitated-looking sandy-haired Englishman in his early-thirties appeared. He was carrying a large bag and a dark-haired girl followed him carrying another. They paused in the corridor, looking at the queue.

'What now?' the girl asked.

'I don't know, do I?' the man answered impatiently. 'I suppose we have to queue.'

This would be them, Paul knew. A warm glow was building inside him. These two were going to be no problem at all. The girl wouldn't take it into her head to fight like Stacey had and the guy looked like someone who resolved to get fit in the coming year each New Year's Eve and who never actually got around to doing it. He might fight, but he wouldn't win.

Paul walked over to them. 'Hi!' he said.

The girl looked up at him from the depths of her bag where she was searching for something and started. Phil was still staring daggers at the queue in front of him.

'Phil!' the girl said, nudging him.

'Stop poking me in the ribs, Barbara,' he said angrily.

They looked to Paul as if they'd recently had quite a heated disagreement – possibly about whether they should answer their call to the office. Phil hadn't wanted to come by the look of things.

'What?' Phil finally asked.

'Me,' Paul said, smiling what he hoped was his broadest grin. It felt wrong on his face and probably looked as fake as plastic fruit.

'And who are you?' Phil asked.

'I'm the guy who put the call out for you,' Paul said. 'I've got the keys to your car.'

Phil was not terribly amused. 'You *what*?' he said.

'Found them up on the deck. I thought you'd like them back.'

Phil held out his hand.

'They're in my cabin,' he said.

Phil looked supremely confused. Paul could see his mind trying to fit things together and failing.

'Someone got them out of the car,' he said, shaking his head as though he'd just seen the hand of God reach down from the skies and squash his best friend for no reason whatsoever.

'You probably brought them with you and they fell out of your pocket,' Barbara suggested.

'I left them in the car,' Phil complained. 'I remember doing it. There's a sign down there saying you have to leave them in the ignition.'

'Reflex, probably,' Paul said. 'Anyhow, they were lying on the deck and I picked them up.'

Phil shook his head. 'Well, go and get them,' he said acidly.

'They're your keys not mine,' Paul replied mildly, 'and you lost them so I suggest you come and get them.'

'For Christ's sake!' Phil said.

'We'll be arriving soon,' Barbara said. 'Why don't we just go and pick them up?'

Phil shook his head, still trying to work something out. Paul knew exactly what it was and purposely didn't think it in case Phil picked it up telepathically. It was a glaring hole in his plan and it was important that Phil didn't make the connection. He looked tired and angry and he also looked like a man who didn't get conned very often, if at all. Paul hoped that even if he did have the thought, he would explain it away to himself. Right now all Phil knew was that he had lost his keys (in spite of remembering not taking them out of the ignition) and that this man had them in his cabin.

'Okay,' Phil finally said, as if he was giving in to an unreasonable child. 'Lead me to them. You wait here, Barbara.'

She glowered.

'You come too,' Paul offered. 'I'll carry your bag,' he added, putting out his hand. And once Barbara had handed it to him, it was too late for him to protest.

He led them down to where he had seen the cabins and took them down a long, empty corridor.

'Where *is* this damn cabin?' Phil asked.

'Just here,' Paul said. He halted in front of the shower cubicle he'd spotted earlier.

As Paul turned to face him, realisation dawned on Phil's face.

Paul knew exactly what he'd remembered. He'd remembered that his bunch of keys didn't have a name tag or the car number on them and therefore he couldn't have been identified from them.

'What . . .?' he said.

And Paul hit him hard on the point of his open jaw.

Phil topped backwards into Barbara.

'Phil!' she squeaked, as he slid down her legs.

Paul shook his head. 'Sorry,' he said, and snapped out a fist at her too.

Paul's patron saint was working his balls off today. Almost fifty seconds must have passed between the moment he hit Phil to the moment he dragged Barbara off the corridor floor and into the shower where her other half was slumped – and no one came down the corridor at all.

Working as quickly as he was able in the confined space, Paul took off Phil's belt (another stroke of blindingly good luck) and his shirt and trousers. He laid him on his stomach and looped the belt around his neck. He tore off one of the shirt's sleeves and tied one end of this to the loose end of the belt. They he knelt and pulled Phil's legs up behind him and looped the other end of the sleeve around his ankles. It wouldn't strangle Phil while he was unconscious, but if he tried to move when he woke up he was going to be extremely uncomfortable. He tied Phil's wrists behind his back with the other shirt sleeve, and gagged him with a strip torn from what was left of the shirt.

Barbara woke up while he was peeling her dress off her and began to whimper. Paul didn't have the heart to hit her again; like his mother would have said, he was a sucker for a girl in distress. But this was one girl whose distress he couldn't possibly end.

'Be quiet,' he said, 'I'm not going to rape you and I'm sorry I had to hit you. It's just one of those things. I'm going to have to tie you up and gag you though. If you just do as I say and keep quiet, it won't hurt.'

Barbara did as she was told. He didn't tie her in the same way as he'd bound Phil, but he didn't expect her to struggle as violently. He gagged her, tied her hands behind her back and then sat her on the floor and tied her ankles.

'Comfortable?' he asked.

Barbara shook her head.

'Never mind. They'll let you out soon. Passports in the bag?'

Barbara shook her head again, but Paul looked anyway. The passports were in the bag. He took them both, hoping the Italian immigration officials would allow them entry without studying the documents – people's passport photos rarely looked like the people themselves, but even if you made allowances there was no way that he and Katie were going to pass for Phil and Barbara. Paul crossed his fingers and looked upwards towards where he hoped St Cunt was beaming down on him.

There was money in the bag and Paul took this too, ignoring the pleading glances Barbara was shooting at him and feeling like the world's biggest bastard. There was a notepad and a pen in Barbara's handbag and box of Elastoplast. Paul took them all.

He tore off a sheet of paper, wrote OUT OF ORDER on it in capitals, and took the backing strips off four of the plasters. Then he thought about it and tore another open. This one he wound round the wound on the forefinger of his right hand. Hitting good old Charlie had made the wound weep a little and hitting Phil and Barbara (and the fevered tying-up) had made it bleed.

He stuck the other four diagonally across the corners of the sheet of paper, went out into the corridor, closed the shower room door and attached the paper sign to it. Perhaps, if he was lucky, no one would decide to take a late shower in this particular cubicle.

3

The boat tied up in Brindisi fifteen minutes later. Paul had taken a good long look at the dock as the ferry wound its way in against the apron and he thought that his luck might well hold. There were lane lines marked along the tarmac which led the departing traffic alongside a large building. There were a few straggler cars down there from the last boat and the officials seemed keen on getting rid of them before this one started off-loading. Paul saw more than one car go through with the authorities only giving the occupants' passports a cursory glance – and a couple where the passports weren't opened at all.

Now, sitting in the Jaguar with Katie beside him and Phil and Barbara's passports in his lap, Paul began to believe that getting into Italy was going to be simple. He breathed deep and even, kept Phil and Barbara out of his mind and his heart-rate down in the nineties.

Then the doors were opening and the sunlight was blinding him after the gloom of the car-deck and Paul's mind whispered that he should be very careful because it might not be that simple after all.

Beneath the fumes of the boat's diesel engines and the exhaust from the cars already starting behind him, Paul noted, somewhat distantly, that Italy had a different odour to Greece. The heat smelled the same, but there was a crisper undertone to the odour. Italy already smelt slicker and faster than Greece.

Paul watched the ramp slide out of the boat and when the cars on either side of him started their engines, he started his. He didn't intend to be first off the ferry – somewhere about tenth or twelfth would probably be the optimum – but he wanted to get used to the feel of the car. The Jag started on the first turn of the key. The tickover was smooth and the car sounded good as he revved it. This car would take them a very long way in a short amount of time, he thought. It was a good car.

Then the odour changed and Paul smelled trouble.

He glanced at Katie whose seat he'd tilted back to make her look more natural (as if she was sleeping, he hoped) but she hadn't moved and there was no black substance trickling from her lips.

But the respite is over now, you know that, don't you, poke? he asked himself. *In a few minutes you'll be back on dry land and then it'll start. Katie's not in her body, and if that thing finds out where she is, it'll start sticking it to her – and you – in very short order!*

Paul knew. And he was ready. He touched the button on the Jag's door and adjusted the tilt of the seat, then shifted it forwards slightly. Phil was one of those people who like to drive with their arms and legs straight out in front of them. Much as it made you feel you were a racing driver, it wasn't the optimum position, either for balance or long drives. He wriggled himself down in his seat, sniffed the air and found it still had that taint of trouble.

Get through it when it comes, he told himself.

Then they were pointing at him. The ramp was down, the Jag was parked dead centre and the sailors who were here to direct the traffic off the ferry wanted Paul to go first.

He paused, not knowing what to do.

Then they started shouting, waving at him to move. Behind him someone gave him a lengthy blast on their horn.

Paul pushed the shift into drive and went carefully down the ramp.

The passport control guy was waiting for him. After a single glance at him, Paul knew what the trouble was going to be. This official was one of that breed of men who dedicated their lives to giving the rich a hard time because he wasn't one of them.

And he had just spotted two people in a rich man's car.

Paul thought about making a run for it – and would have done just that if it hadn't been for the vehicles blocking the exit. The camper was nose to nose with an articulated truck which, for some reason, was trying to enter the port through the exit. Behind the camper was a large Dodge and alongside it was an English-registered MG Midget, whose owner had apparently grown impatient quite early on in the proceedings and had tried to overtake the camper on the wrong side. There was another official striding towards the jam. Which meant that his buddy, Mr I Hate the Rich, was going to have plenty of time to give Paul's car a going over.

'Hi!' Paul said, pulling up beside the man.

'Anything to declare?' the man asked. 'Armaments? Proscribed drugs?'

Paul grinned and shook his head. Over at the exit gate the official was shouting in Italian at the truck driver. The truck driver was giving as good as he got.

Why don't you just shut up and back out of there? Paul thought.

'Open the boot, please,' the customs man said.

Paul hit the button.

The man walked around behind the car.

'Where is your luggage?' he asked from behind the car.

Paul didn't reply.

The customs man – or immigration or whatever he was – came back to Paul's side of the car. Up ahead, the truck driver was still arguing with the official. Now he was gunning the truck's engine as though he meant to drive through and plough all the other vehicles out of his way.

'Luggage?' the man asked.

'Stolen,' Paul said.

The man smiled briefly. The fact that their luggage might have been stolen had given him a moment's pleasure but if it was at all possible, he was going to compound their misery. 'Passports?' he asked.

Paul handed him the passports. His blood pressure was

rising along with his heartbeat and if things didn't soon resolve themselves he was going to *click out*.

'Sometimes I get mad,' he said to the official, who hadn't yet opened the passports and discovered that the people who were currently bottom of his list of favourites weren't even the *right* people because he was now staring at Katie.

'Yes?' he said, distractedly, glancing back at Paul, then back again at Katie.

'And you know what happens?' Paul said, drawing deep and even breaths.

'No,' the official said. 'Your wife . . .?' He said it in a tone of puzzlement: *Something's bothering me about your wife. Funny, but she doesn't appear to be breathing . . .*

'I get this kind of white-heat inside me,' Paul said. 'And my ears start to roar and it's like there's molten metal in front of my eyes. It's happening to me now.'

'Is she . . . *well?*' the official asked.

Paul heard this through the roaring in his ears. He felt a huge, unseen hand reach out and twist him through fifteen degrees inside his body. His damage register lit up and reported zero and counting. His mind was emptying.

'No, she's dead at the moment,' he heard himself say. He wasn't going to stay conscious through this, he knew it. He'd thought he had it under control, but the Dekker underneath still had some tricks up his sleeve.

'Dead?' the man asked.

Up ahead the truck began to back out of the exit.

'Get out of the car,' the man said from beside Paul. Paul was staring at the confusion of vehicles ahead of him, not seeing them clearly any more. There was a waterfall of molten metal coursing down across his field of vision. He fought not to let it happen. His blood pressure reached its peak and his heart pulsed hard, once . . . twice . . . and Paul fought it down. 'People get hurt,' he gasped.

'Get out of the car!' the man demanded.

Paul saw a blur of grey to his right and knew the official had drawn his gun. 'Don't make me show you,' Paul heard himself say.

And now there was shouting, from way away. Paul knew what he would see if he turned to his right. He could see it well enough in his mind without having to look and probably with a greater clarity. Phil and Barbara were up on the top deck of the boat, surrounded by uniformed officers, and they were screaming that the Jaguar down there with those two imposters sitting in it, was their rightful property.

'OUT!' the man shouted.

Paul turned towards him and took the brakes off the *click out* demon.

And once again didn't lose consciousness, just handed over the controls to a part of him that only seemed to be able to exist in extreme circumstances. He was still twisted inside himself and he was still looking through a sheet of molten bronze and his mind was empty, but the other Dekker had clarity and power. Only two things mattered to that cold, calculating maniac, and the first of those was the gun that was being waved far too close to his face. Not far too close for comfort, but far too close for the Italian's own good.

Paul watched his right hand flash out and snatch the guy's wrist away from him. The gun came into the car, pointing high; the Italian followed, crashing into the Jag's door and toppling forward against his arm. Paul heard the crack of bone breaking, just before the guy's muscular spasm of pain caused him to squeeze the trigger of the gun. The shot took out a section of the overhanging asbestos roof. Fragments rained down in front of the office the guy had come from. Someone else's gun barked and the piece of Paul that was attached to the soul of the Jaguar winced on its behalf. If the Jaguar had been an animal it would have roared in pain at the shot which hit its flank. The rear wing was punctured. As he took the customs man's hair in his left hand and dragged his face across to the centre console Paul distantly realised this – and he also knew that whoever was shooting was doing it from somewhere over by the ferry.

He levered the man's broken arm back and the official screamed and let go of the gun. It fell into Katie's lap. The official who had been sorting out the traffic snarl-up was sprinting back this way now, fighting with his holster as he ran, and there were more people coming out of the office looking very surprised indeed. The maniac inside Paul glanced up ahead at the camper which was now edging forwards in a manner that suggested the driver had developed a thing against the guy in the MG and wasn't going to let him past under any circumstances. Paul's left hand thrust down hard and the customs man's face smacked into the gear shift housing. When Paul dragged him up again, the cigar lighter had bent over and there was a semi-circular flap of flesh hanging from the man's right eyebrow. His eyes were as distant as any Paul had ever seen. He let go of the man's broken arm and pushed him away from the car. The man tottered backwards and sat down hard.

Another shot hit the Jag, low in the door sill this time. People were coming at him from every which way but the exit was clear and there was only one problem remaining. That problem was the official who had been running back towards them. He had quit running now, his gun was out and he was blocking the way, his legs spread and the gun held up in both hands just like they did it in true-to-life cop films. The expression on his face stated, *Someone here is going to die and it isn't going to be me.*

Paul pushed the lever into drive, hit the throttle and the Jag rocketed forward. Another shot zinged off the tarmac behind him as he pulled away and Paul heard a girlish scream. He glanced in the rear-view and saw one of the office guys on the floor, writhing like a damaged snake.

The guy in front drew a bead on Paul as he approached. Paul saw him squeeze and ducked. The shot made a hole in the windscreen at the exact level of Paul's eyes. Chips of hot glass fell on his face. Another two shots hit the screen, these high on Kate's side. The fourth shot ricocheted off something inside the engine, and then the Jag was moving too fast and was getting too close for the guy's liking. He leapt to his left and rolled, loosing another shot at the car as it passed.

Two seconds later, as Paul turned right and tore rubber along the one-way system, the sharp reek of petrol hit his nostrils and he realised he'd clicked back in again. Each time it happened the two separate parts of him seemed to merge with one another a little more. Eventually, he supposed, the various facets of Paul Dekker would turn into a single entity.

If you live that long, old cowboy! his goad said.

Paul glanced in the mirror. He was pretty certain no one at the port had been quick-witted enough to get in a car and give chase, but it paid to check.

All that lay behind him – through a mist which had, for some unknown reason, formed on the rear-view mirror – was the string of cars he'd barged by.

Paul saw a sign which said Taranto, and swung the Jag round a left so sharply that its tyres complained. Taranto would be the right way, wherever it was. If there was one thing he could depend on, it was his infallible sense of direction. In that moment Paul knew he would get to Naples, even without the aid of a map, even without knowing where in Italy it was. Thinking Naples and driving in what felt like the right direction would be enough. It was a crazy thought, he knew that, but he accepted it. If the dead could come back to play, he could navigate his way to places without knowing where they were.

He doubted the Jag was going to take him all the way though. The petrol tank was pierced and gas was leaking from it. He just hoped that the hole was high and not at the tank's bottom. And besides that, every cop in southern Italy would be out and about looking for him in about ten minutes, so he was going to have to dump the car soon, whether he liked it or not. He hit the brakes for the next roundabout, took it fast and carved up an Alfasud on the way out. He floored the throttle and the Jag's engine coughed and misfired.

Don't do this to me, darlin', I need you! he told the car. And the engine began to run smooth again.

When he glanced in the misty mirror again, he saw that the guy in the Alfasud had a case of the Arlington Stephen Jones'. He was barrelling along about a hundred yards behind, clearly intending to give the Jag or the guy in it – or both – a hiding they would remember for a long time.

The road straightened and Paul put the pedal to the floor. The Jag kicked down a cog and put a large distance between it and the Alfasud in a very short time.

Paul hit the brakes hard, took another corner, accelerated, squealed round another roundabout and powered away down the next straight. In another five minutes he was on the Via Appia, according to the signposts.

And the Alfasud was still following him. It was a long way back now, but it was still there, still moving very quickly. Paul glanced at the speedo which was registering ninety and gently brought the Jag up to a ton, then to one ten.

The next time he looked in the mirror, the Alfa had gone.

And so had the road and the Italian countryside.

Paul tore his eyes away from the rear-view, not believing what he'd seen. The road in front of him was long and straight and steady, but according to the reflection in the mirror what lay behind him was a large town, built in the midst of rolling green hills, and behind it, a golden sea sparkling in low sun.

Can't happen! Hallucination! he told himself. He looked in the Jag's side mirror and saw a snippet of the same scene. The buildings were of a design he didn't recognise, but they *did* seem to be very familiar. It was no town he'd ever seen, he was sure of that.

He slowed the car slightly and twisted round to look over his left shoulder. And there was the road behind him, and down there in the distance was the Alfasud, still following him at what must have been its maximum speed.

Going crazy again! his goad shouted, as he turned back to the road, but Paul knew that he wasn't. He couldn't be *going* crazy any more because he'd already gone about as crazy as it was possible to get. He hadn't felt a marble rolling for quite a while and that had to be because the alley-bag was empty. Crazy didn't count any more.

He glanced into the misty mirror again and saw the same alien scene in the same perspective which meant that he wasn't getting any further away from it. The edges of the scene were sparkling where the image met the mist that ringed the mirror. Paul looked away because it was impossible to look at that vista for more than a few moments. It hurt something deep inside him, filled him with a dreadful yearning to walk amongst those alien buildings. A part of him felt as if he was a homesick child looking at a picture postcard of his place of birth. A place that he hadn't been back to for a very long time. It would feel very good to go there, he knew, and he also knew exactly how you could accomplish it.

All you would have to do was close your eyes and yank the steering wheel hard in either direction.

Katie would be there, waiting for him.

Paul reached up for the mirror and wrenched it to the side so that he couldn't see in any more. Then he put his hand out into the thick slipstream and twisted the door mirror, putting thoughts of seeing Katie, his mother, Freddie, and maybe even the Cindy dog again, out of his mind. People had jumped under trains because of thoughts like those.

He turned and saw that the Alfasud was slipping back into the distance now, its driver apparently having decided he wasn't going to be able to catch the Jag after all. Paul smiled and turned back.

Katie was still dead. Her wild blonde hair writhed around in the wind like Medusa's snakes and her white dress was rippling against her limp body. Her eyes were closed and her lips were parted slightly. She looked beautiful and serene. Paul felt a warm surge in his stomach when he looked at her and this time didn't instantly fill his mind with other minutiae in order to swamp the sensation and the thoughts that followed. For the first time he allowed himself to re-work the equation about why he was doing this. It was no longer simply that H wanted him to stop and had killed (and was still killing) to achieve that aim, and it wasn't just Paul's own bloody-mindedness. And it had gone somewhat beyond being a sucker for a girl in distress. It had turned into a single-minded, aching kind of love that, if he was truthful with himself, was more powerful than anything he'd ever felt before.

Paul wasn't altogether sure what kind of love you could feel for someone who was dead and who was going to return (if he wasn't deluding himself on this count) changed.

How about unnatural love? his goad chipped in.

Whatever it was, and however it was going to turn out, he could no longer deny that he was feeling it. He wondered where the living part of Katie was and what was happening to it. Could she be in one of those buildings in that strange and beautiful seaside town he'd glimpsed in the mirrors? And if she was, what was happening to her?

Paul suddenly felt an overpowering urge to touch her. He took his left hand from the steering wheel and laid it on her bare left thigh. Her flesh was as cool and still as marble and the sensation made him want to cry. It was hopeless; an affair that was already over before it had started. Katie was dead.

I'll get you back home, sweetheart, Paul thought. *And I'm sorry. Sorry for what's happened to you and sorry about what's happening to me. I just can't do anything about it. I'll try not to make it too complicated for you if you come back. I'll try not to make things too difficult.*

The moment Paul removed his hand from Katie's leg, something happened. It wasn't just that her coolness had invaded his arm, which it had, and it wasn't just that the Jag's engine note changed, which it did. There was a momentary sensation of downward pressure, as if he had just driven across a line where the ordinary atmosphere butted up against a pocket of extremely high pressure air. Paul's ears popped and he felt movement in his sinuses which began to crackle and hurt. His sense of smell deserted him and he felt giddy. In that moment Paul knew they'd found him.

Not here! he thought, and put his foot down, half expecting to be able to speed through that odd patch of air and escape on its far side.

The Jag started to labour, as if someone had placed a very steep hill in front of it, and the pain in Paul's sinuses grew. He glanced over at Katie, but she hadn't moved and there was no black substance coming from her mouth. His heart started to hammer. Out in front of him, the smooth, flat tarmac began to blur.

And an image began to form in his mind. The image wavered, as if being seen reflected on the surface of a lake, and for a moment Paul didn't understand what it represented. Then it cleared.

The man was sitting in a Bentley Mulsanne Turbo, his eyes closed and his fingers pressed lightly to his temples. The man was not H. He was good-looking and well dressed. He looked like a very successful businessman.

Paul tried to shake this image out of his head and only succeeded in very nearly losing his balance completely. The Jag was suddenly heading across the road towards the far verge. Paul steadied his head – if not his seething sense of balance – and caught the car, correcting its path smoothly. Kate's head rolled away from him so he could no longer see her face.

Paul took his foot off the accelerator and gently applied the brakes because although he could almost drive sleeping, the accent was on the word 'almost'. If the image inside his head grew much clearer it was going to swamp his vision.

The man was called Gary Richman. As the picture of him sharpened and the Jag slowed to forty, then thirty, then twenty-five, its engine labouring, Paul collected details about the man. Gary Richman was in England and not parked a couple of miles down the road, as Paul had suspected. Richman had not located the Jag, but had been informed of its whereabouts by H. Paul didn't know how this had been accomplished and it didn't matter. What mattered was that Richman knew where he and Kate were and was somehow pinning them down with the force of his mind.

So what *can happen?* But he knew this too. Richman was one of H's good men and true and was exerting some kind of force on them so that H could concentrate on bringing something through from the other side of his void. And Paul knew where the only entrance was – through Katie.

Paul felt a scraping ache inside his head, as if someone was inside his skull with a rasp. It hurt like a bastard. Screwing up his eyes, he pulled the Jag to the side of the road and stopped it. Keeping going wasn't going to do any good. He didn't know *what* was going to do any good now that they'd found him and Katie.

It was getting hard to breathe in the heavy air. Paul wanted to get out of the car, but the agonising scraping sensation in his head precluded all movement. All he could do was sit where he was and learn about Gary Richman. If Richman was using a kind of psychic radio waveband to pin him down while H had his way with Katie, then he wasn't in full control of it: it had subcarriers and from these Paul picked up snippets of information. Richman had mentally dominated and murdered a girl called Janice Darling. Janice had walked out of Membury Services and on to the M4 motorway believing that she was still in the service area. The worst shock for Paul was that Richman had also been responsible for the death of Lulu Kaminsky and that she hadn't arrived in Katie's body by chance.

Get out of my head! Paul thought, and a moment later understood the irony of having thought these words. Janice Darling had thought them before him.

There was no response from Richman. He just sat there in his car, concentrating, Paul glanced over at Katie and saw her move. He started to become desperate and willed himself to *click out.* But Richman had somehow put the dampers on this, too.

Getting out of the car seemed to be very important. A small part of Paul thought that Richman was somehow using the car to accomplish his connection. Paul tried to lift his arm to take the door handle, but his arm was heavier than lead and immovable.

Paul closed his eyes and concentrated his mind on Gary Richman. Trying to get Richman out of his head was impossible and Paul ceased his resistance. He let the image grow large and crystal clear, let the outside world fade away until there was just him and Richman.

Beside him, Katie gasped. Her arm flew out and struck Paul's thigh, but he didn't open his eyes. He could do nothing to aid her. All he could do was fight to break the link the only way he knew how. Using Richman's route to him, he reached out across more than two thousand miles with his mind, and planted what he hoped would be immense pain in Richman's eyes.

It worked. Inside his head, the image of Richman wavered as the man clapped his hands to his eyes. A moment later the pain was returned and Paul hissed in agony. On the seat beside him, Kate jolted.

And then Paul heard Richman's voice for the first time. *Too late*! it crowed.

Suck this! Paul returned and aimed a dagger of thought at Richman's throat. This time Richman squealed. It sounded rather like a cat being strangled and Paul was pleased. Until the sensation returned. It was agonising. Paul directed another jolt of pain at Richman, distantly realising the outcome was going to be dependent on one of them being able to stand a measured amount of pain for longer than the other. Because Richman wasn't sending that pain back to Paul – it was his own transmitted thoughts that were affecting him. He might have been laying into the other man, but he was laying into himself to do it.

Paul struck out venomously with his mind. He would be stronger. He had to be.

4

When the break in the link came, it did not come in the way

Paul expected. There were noises outside the Jag. Paul was aware of them only peripherally; in the same way that he was aware of the blood in his mouth where he'd bitten the insides of his cheeks and in the same way as he was registering the fact that something nasty was happening to Katie. His mind was almost entirely concentrated on giving Gary Richman the beating of his life, even though it meant taking the beating of his own life. Paul concentrated hard on striking out at Richman while he tried to raise his anger to the level at which he would *click out*. If he could only make it happen, his own pain would cease and he would be able to crush Richman completely without bothering about what happened to himself until later. For the past twenty seconds or so, he had been teetering on the brink, fighting against Richman's block which was preventing it happening.

Someone spoke. If Paul had been able to pay more attention to the voice, which seemed to be coming from completely outside his universe, he would have known that the owner of that voice was male and that he was not a happy man.

Paul shot another dagger at Richman, caught the pain and howled, unaware that the Jag's door was now open, or that hands were reaching for him – a little less certainly than they had been a moment ago.

5

When he left Italy for good, two months after marrying Giulietta, James Jackson, a black American serviceman, had left more behind him than the half-caste bun that was growing in his wife's oven. He had also left his rage, the quick anger that had caused him to dump the woman over a minor argument. The child, christened Giuseppe, had grown up with his father's rage in his genes and his mother's disdainful treatment of him to compound what he liked to call his Latin temperament.

Giuseppe, now twenty-four, had grown up angry – there had been no alternative open to him. He had been the worst student in all his school classes and had been expelled twice. Giuseppe had left his home in Verona at sixteen and had drifted round the country for four years leaving a wake of broken relationships and busted noses behind him, before settling in Brindisi where for a while he'd made a living from thieving.

Nowadays he made a better living by pimping for eight black girls whom he ruled with an iron fist. Giuseppe was strict with his relationships and rather fond of punishing his girls for the slightest misdemeanour. He was aware that some of them talked about him behind his back and knew that those of them who liked to think they had brains had developed a theory that he hurt them to vent his anger at his black father and his bad mother, and Giuseppe thought they might be right. And because he thought they might be right, he chose those particular girls to punish more often than the others. It gave him a great deal of pleasure.

One of the things that didn't please him at all was being cut up by other drivers. There were limits which he would allow, but the foreigner in the Jaguar had overstepped the mark. Ordinarily, Giuseppe wouldn't have acted unless the car had been travelling slowly and locally – then he might have cut in front of it, pulled it up, handed out a beating and forgotten it. But on this occasion, his anger had been magnified by the sight of the blonde girl riding in the rich man's car. He'd only caught a glimpse of her, but that single passing glance had enraged him. The girl was better looking than any of those he'd ever had, and if he was truthful with himself, any he was ever likely to have. And Giuseppe was enraged because the only thing that got you a good-looking white girl like that was serious money, and the driver of the Jaguar evidently thought that this kind of money stopped you having to show any consideration for other road users.

Giuseppe had started following the Jaguar with the simple intention of making its driver a little less attractive to the opposite sex by removing some of his teeth, but as he tailed the car, driving the Alfasud very hard in order to keep up, he had become more and more angry, and as his anger grew, so did his ambition.

By the time he saw the Jaguar ahead of him, parked by the side of the road, he had decided to beat the guy to a pulp and then fuck the brains out of his girlfriend in front of him.

He had slowed down as he approached the Jag, frowning. There was something strange about the look of it, he told himself. The spot of air surrounding the car seemed to be shimmering in a kind of heat wave. For a second, he thought he saw the wave solidify into a transparent dome, then he shook his head and the dome was gone. Sometimes when he got really upset he saw things happening that looked a little like this. Once, when he was giving Linda a good whipping, he had actually seen red. Not metaphorically, but *actually*.

He drew up behind the Jag and got out of the Alfa, scowling. The people in the Jag were on some kind of drug, they had to be. They pulled over to fix and there had been something wrong with the stuff. Giuseppe had lost two girls to hot-shots in the past two years and both had looked a little like this before they'd died. The people in the fancy open-topped car were writhing around as if they were in agony.

But before they finally went, Giuseppe Jackson would make their agony something they would recall throughout eternity.

He strode up to the car and was surprised when he got the distinct sensation that something heavy was pressing down on him. It felt as if he'd walked into a field of extra heavy-duty gravity where the air had become twice as thick. In the car the man, whose eyes were squeezed shut, yelped and the sound seemed deadened, as if Giuseppe had cotton wool in his ears.

He shrugged off the odd sensation because on the far side of the car the blonde girl had slipped right down in her seat and her dress was bunched up around her crotch. Her legs were spread wide and they were long and smooth and white. Her body was writhing as if she were either in the throes of an all-encompassing sexual ecstasy or tremendous pain. Giuseppe didn't care which it was because as far as he was concerned both were equally erotic. He felt himself begin to get hard. He was going to enjoy this.

He reached out to open the Jag's door and caught a jab of static which made him swear and withdraw his hand.

Something's going on here, he thought. *Something fucking peculiar*.

But whatever it was, it would have to wait because he was first in line to teach these two a lesson.

He took the door again – no static this time – and opened it.

And the man let out an ear-splitting howl. It made Giuseppe's own eardrums tingle even though the sound was deadened. He paused for a moment, uncertainty scything through his anger. Then the split healed and he took hold of the man's hands and yanked him out of the car.

The man fell to the ground and curled up in a tight ball, moaning.

Giuseppe glanced up and down the road, making sure the traffic was far enough away not to see what he was doing, and kicked the man in the kidneys, as hard as he could.

The rich guy gasped and began to unfold, just as Giuseppe knew he would. He walked over the man's body, told him, in Italian, that he was just going to have to fold right back up again, and planted the toe of his shoe into the man's belly. The rich guy folded.

There was a car coming. Giuseppe waited for it to pass, then kicked the man again. His foot connected with the guy's sternum this time and the blow hurt his toe. He swore and kicked again with the other foot. The heaviness in the air seemed to have gone now and Giuseppe felt correspondingly lighter and fitter and, now that he noticed it, sexier. He looked down at the guy, then over at the girl in the car who had stopped moving, and decided that if she wasn't as dead as she looked, he would drag her into the cornfield by the side of the road and fuck her so hard she wouldn't walk for a week.

He left the man on the ground, went round to the other side

of the car, opened the door and hefted the girl out. She wasn't heavy, but she was as floppy as a rag doll and felt a little cool to the touch. She may even have been dead. But it was too late for him to stop now, he knew that. The idea that she might be dead spoke to a deep part of him and thrilled him beyond measure. It would be a strange and perhaps enlightening experience. Except that he knew she wasn't really dead. Maybe she would be, afterwards. Maybe he could lean on her neck the way he did with Linda, except that this time he wouldn't stop leaning.

The girl smelled of burning. He realised this as he dragged her across the verge towards the field. It didn't matter. Nothing mattered except getting her into the field and forcing his bulging cock into her cool body and fucking her until she either woke up screaming or actually died.

Giuseppe didn't quite see what happened next. There was a blurred flash of black to his left and then he was falling through space. It was a black universe in which purple stars swirled and burst while he sailed downwards through it.

He didn't wake up for a very long time.

6

Paul spat blood. He thought he might piss some too, the next time he took a leak. His chest hurt and one of his kidneys was bruised, almost everything he had ached and he felt as if the inside of his head had been raped. But the important thing was that he was still alive, still able to act.

He glanced at the gun in his hand, the one the customs man had dropped into the car. He'd come very close to shooting the Italian with it. As Jake had always maintained, when you got a weapon in your hand it would begin to talk to you. Paul had tried not to listen to the gun's voice, but it had been close. He had been at the point of pulling the trigger when he realised he should be thanking the Alfasud driver for that kick in the kidneys; it had broken his link with Richman. Instead of shooting the man, he'd simply pistol-whipped him with the gun. Even that had been almost hard enough to kill, he suspected. He clicked the safety and tossed the gun back into the car then picked up Katie, who was still cold and still not breathing. He put her gently back into the Jag, thought for a moment, then collected the gun and shot the Alfasud through the radiator. He didn't expect the man to wake very soon, but it was better safe than sorry.

Wearily, he climbed back into the Jag, noticing the pool of petrol that had formed beneath it. It wasn't going to take them very far.

And the police will be looking for it, too, remember! his goad said.

Paul started the car and drove, quickly and automatically, ignoring the lingering scraping feeling inside his skull. Richman might be able to make the link with him again, but he didn't think it would happen yet. Judging by the way *he* felt, Richman was going to be in no state for a return bout for a little while yet. And H had failed to birth anything through Kate, too. Paul didn't know whether this had anything to do with his resistance to Richman – and he doubted it somehow – but the attempt had failed. With any luck they'd have a little free time before anything else happened.

It wasn't until the sensation inside his skull finally ceased that Paul questioned the route he had been taking since the last attack. Until the uncomfortable feeling left him, he'd been certain that he was heading for Naples; now he was certain he was going in the wrong direction. It was getting dark and he was tired and hungry and thirsty. He kept driving in spite of the feeling that Naples was getting further away and was surely a long way over to the left.

And it wasn't until he rolled into the town whose signpost announced it as Margherita de Savoia that he understood what had happened.

Gary Richman had won the mental battle after all.

The intention had been to squash Paul's sense of direction and to keep him away from his friends. And it had worked. There was sea to Paul's right, which meant he was now headed north or north-west up the Adriatic coast when he should have been crossing the ankle of Italy – probably on the Via Appia, off which he had turned hours ago – to the other coast where he was now certain that Naples lay.

What happened? he heard himself asking in his dream.

Margherita de Savoia blew up, that's what! the voice of his memory whispered back to him.

Paul looked at the narrow main street which ran between tall brick buildings. He had never seen it before and yet it all seemed very familiar. The light was fading rapidly now and the buildings and the people on the streets all looked threatening, as if they knew what Paul was bringing to them and they didn't want it. Each pedestrian they passed turned to stare and their expressions didn't look particularly welcoming.

And Paul wanted to be here even less than the town and its inhabitants wanted him here. There was an answer, he knew, and that answer was simple. He would just turn around and take the car out of Margherita de Savoia and head for the opposite coast of the country. If it meant driving all night, he would drive all night.

Paul put his foot on the brake, already feeling better at the prospect of leaving this town. Being here felt bad and wrong. It was a place where anything might happen. It was a place . . .

Which might explode?

. . . he would be happy to leave.

Paul pulled in to the side of the road, waited for the traffic to clear, then swung the Jag around in an arc. The car's turning circle wasn't tight enough to get round in one go, so he backed up and tried again. When he'd completed the manoeuvre, he felt as if a weight had been lifted from him. He put his foot on the accelerator, thought, *Goodbye, Margherita . . .*

And the Jaguar ran out of petrol.

Chapter Twenty-One
Enrico

Enrico Spagnol sat in the bar in Margherita de Savoia, a cold and untouched pizza ai funghi before him and a big glass of Jack Daniels in his hand. He was back in the land he'd dreamed about so often when his aching joints had been gripped by the icy claws of a British winter but he was not at home, nor had he visited his wife and children since he'd been back. He didn't expect to visit his wife and children ever again now, but if it was at all possible, he was going to fit in a quick trip to Taranto before he flew back to England. Taranto was a place he missed quite badly, but, like his family, it was now a thing of the past.

A great deal had changed for him since he'd woken up sober one spring morning in Cambridge and gone to a house that looked deserted and as if there had been a fire. He no longer worked for the oil company who had sent him to Cambridge, he no longer harboured a desire to make enough money to pack it all in and retire to Sicily, and he no longer had any ties with Italy at all. He had become a part of something else now, something that transcended ordinary ambitions and hopes. Part of a new family whose ties were greater than those of his own. He had joined the immortal family of the New Human. The coming race. The breed that would rule the planet through eternity.

But although a great deal had changed since he'd come face to face with the angel that wore the body of H Tyler, some things had stayed the same.

Like his need to be lubricated with Jack Daniels to get him going in the mornings and to put him to sleep at night. The drink was the only thing that alleviated the pains in his rusty joints, and calmed the trembling in his hands. Once accepted into the brotherhood, he had expected to be miraculously cured of the pains that haunted him whenever there was not a bottle close at hand, but this had not yet happened. It would, soon, but there was important work to be done first. The new era would commence when the man called Dekker was removed and the girl Kate was returned to her rightful owner. Then, miracles would abound.

Enrico thought about eternal paradise on earth as he sipped his drink. There was a lot of stuff he was hazy about, but this would not always be so. His mind was clouded when he was sober and he had only been in the presence of the angel when he was not drunk, so things were bound to escape his grasp. And besides that, he doubted that Jesus' own disciples had understood half of what he had said.

But once the new age began and he was cured of his ills and had immortality bestowed upon him he would become enlightened and take his place at the right hand of the new God. He was a disciple and, like the master, disciples had to undergo hardships. The price the angel had had to pay had been purification by fire; his own price was a great deal less. It was to serve the master and to live with his pain until Dekker was dead. Enrico could accept this. The Jack Daniels made that acceptance a little easier, just as it took the edge off his pain. He put the cool lip of the glass to his mouth and sipped at the fiery liquid. Soon, the way would be cleared and the new age could begin.

Dekker and the girl were here. Enrico had picked that up across the strange mental network to which the disciples were linked. He didn't know who had located the two of them or how the broadcast had arrived, but you didn't need to know how a car worked in order to drive it – or how a rifle worked in order to fire it, for that matter. He knew it in the same way as he'd known each time a disciple had been vanquished. It was just one of H's minor abilities and not really a miracle at all.

Enrico sipped at his drink and savoured the liquid. As in any war, casualties had been expected, and this war was for higher stakes than any that had so far been fought upon the planet. Dekker and his followers had fought well, so far. The disciples were down to nine now (if you didn't count the fact that some of them seemed to have died and been restored, and Enrico didn't because H was an entity with power over life and death and it was quite possible he could bring his disciples back to life again). But even if something went wrong and the three dead could not be resurrected, nine would be enough. Nine against three could not fail. It was not possible that three could overcome nine, whether you looked at it drunk or sober.

And that was good, because Enrico didn't want to become dead. What he wanted was the same thing any right-thinking adult wanted: a seamless eternal existence in which the word 'death' had been struck from the vocabulary. And he was going to be one of the first humans ever to accomplish this.

And all he was going to have to do to earn his place in H's new scheme of things was to pick up the girl Kate after Dekker had been killed.

Enrico had a hired Ford parked out in the street with which he was to take the girl back to the border (where she would be collected by another) and in it there was a rifle which he had obtained from an address on the other side of town. He wasn't quite clear about how the rifle might fit into his task, since Dekker was going to be stopped right here in Margherita by H himself, but he had a feeling it might be important. What part the weapon had to play in this would doubtlessly be revealed in the fullness of time. Knowing it was in the back of the Ford made Enrico uneasy though. He *could* shoot – better with Jack Daniels inside him than without – and once, more years ago than he cared to recall, he had belonged to a gun club where he had been a crack-shot target man of near Olympic standard, but those rifles had been balanced and specialised .22s and this was a heavy, cumbersome thing which probably would have stopped a charging rhino dead in its tracks. He didn't doubt that he could still muster up the stillness he'd once possessed, or the aim, but what he did wonder about was why it might become necessary.

And since he had it in the car, it might. Even his confused brain could work out that little one; their small band carried no dead weight, therefore if the rifle was there it was likely to be needed.

To shoot at what?

He would worry about it later because Dekker and the girl had arrived in Margherita de Savoia and the air pressure was changing, just as he'd expected it to, and soon it would all be over.

He wondered if he should go and watch and was on the point of draining his drink and going outside when he remembered Lot's wife. In the next half an hour or so there was going to be magic in the air and enough miracles performed to fill a whole book in what would one day become the new bible, but watching those things happen sometimes wasn't a good idea. Enrico didn't intend to be remembered as a pillar of salt. He knew where to stand when the time came and that was enough. He would keep his head down, do his job and reap the rewards.

Smiling to himself, Enrico Spagnol lifted his glass towards the heavens in salute, then drained his drink in one draught.

After he heard the first peal of thunder, he ordered another.

Chapter Twenty-Two
Margherita de Savoia

1

Thunder pealed and the first fat drops of rain began to fall as Paul lifted Katie out of the Jaguar. He knew what was going to happen here because he could remember it vividly from his first dream. He didn't know how or why it was going to happen and he hadn't dreamed the sequence of events, but he knew what it was.

Margherita was going to blow up.

'Hey!'

Paul turned. A grubby kid on a tatty bike was glaring at him from across the road. The boy's eyes were dark as if he knew what was going to happen too and hated Paul for it. Everyone he'd seen so far seemed to know and looked as if they wanted to kill him before he could bring devastation to their town.

'What?' Paul said, remembering that other kid – the one both he and Kate seemed to have run down and killed. Little Paulie Saunders.

'Away!' the boy shouted, cocking the bike's pedal and placing his right foot on it in case a speedy escape became necessary. 'You go! Away!'

'I wish I could,' Paul said, but he was talking to the boy's back. The kid was already speeding away in the direction of town.

Paul hefted Katie up into his aching arms as the rain increased. He thought of the alternatives. One of them – the one he'd dreamed – was to walk in the direction the boy had pedalled away in, towards the centre of the town, and the other was to turn away and head back for the open road. Paul badly wanted to do the second thing, but it was impossible. There were four people out there somewhere, following him. The two he'd seen speeding away from the fisherman's beach in Volos – the pair who had burned his apartment down and killed Sandra Rook – and the two he thought he had killed up on the plateau. He didn't know where they were, except that they were likely to be hot on his tail now that he'd been located, but he did know what they were capable of. All of them were likely to be armed and they wanted him dead pretty badly.

Which means, poke, that there's only one way you can go. If this godforsaken place blows up it isn't going to be your responsibility. Remember that.

Paul didn't want anything terrible to happen to the place whether it was his responsibility or not. Its inhabitants might not seem very welcoming, but they probably had good cause. In their collective unconscious the words: *Beware of the man who arrives in a Jaguar with a dead girl* seemed to be implanted and all they were doing was reacting to this message. He couldn't blame them for believing that he was the man responsible for what was going to happen: in a way, he *was* responsible.

But there was no good alternative.

Up ahead, in one of these streets, he knew, he was going to obtain an Alfa Romeo 164 – the car he had been sitting in, in his dream. He didn't know how he was going to get it – Alfas had good deadlocks and were impenetrable to the casual thief and difficult even when you had a full set of tools – but Paul was certain that he was going to find himself behind the wheel of one. Perhaps there was a chance of getting the car and averting the following disaster by coming back out of town as quickly as possible. In his dream it had only been a truck, but in his dream his mind had also told him that the town had blown up.

The dream was just a dream, poke! his goad told him. *Just a mish-mash of all sorts of things. Some of them were prophetic, some were allegory. In your dream, if you recall, the girl was alive and speaking and she died. Unless she comes back soon, you can call that part allegory.*

Maybe, Paul hoped, the dream was wrong and there were going to be no shadow-men. It was getting a bit late in the day for H to provide that demonstration of his power. Earlier it made sense; now, Paul already knew what H was capable of. Maybe none of it would happen.

He doubted it. The air pressure around him seemed to be increasing as he trudged down the wet street towards the town. Paul could smell rotten oranges and hot electrical wiring. The air was thick with the tang of positively charged ions; lightning was waiting to happen.

The sky flickered as Paul trudged past brick-built buildings which might have been warehouses or might have been flats – there were few windows and it was impossible to tell. The rain became heavier, soaking him instantly. Kate's hair swiftly became a tangled blonde rope and her white dress clung to her body, turning transparent. Her bare legs glistened golden-orange in the light from the street lamps. One of her red sandals had been dragged off her heel and was dangling from her toes, swinging with the motion as Paul walked. Moisture glistened on her face and parted lips. Paul ached for her. The words, *I love you!* leapt into his mind and he pushed them away savagely. It was too late for that. Soon it would be too late for anything.

Lightning flickered again, closer this time, and the thunderclap followed hot on its searing heels.

On the other side of the street someone shouted something in Italian at Paul. He glared in the direction of the voice. A middle-aged bald man in shirtsleeves was forking the sign of the evil eye at him, forefinger and pinky extended, middle and ring fingers folded into his palm. There was a heavy gold ring on his pinky. It was the first time Paul had ever seen anyone do this and the hatefulness of the gesture and the expression on the man's face chilled him. If there were many more like this in this town H wouldn't have to do anything at all except rescue Katie – the town's inhabitants would pull Paul apart and burn the pieces.

He looked away from the man and trudged on, ignoring the shouting that followed him. *How could they know?* he asked himself, but there was no good answer. They *did* know and that was enough.

The rain streamed from broken gutters and downpipes, steamed on the street's warm tarmac and formed rivers at either side of the road. Storm drains began to overflow. Paul's espadrilles were two heavy sodden masses on his feet. He paused and kicked them off. The pavement was still warm beneath the cold rainwater.

He passed a supermarket and its owner, an ancient man in a white apron, ran out and shouted a stream of abuse at him in Italian, following him down the road and yapping at his heels like a dog. Paul got the message, loud and clear.

A fat woman who smelled of fish blocked his path. Two tiny children hid behind her, peering at him around her bulk. She said something to him and Paul shook his head. He moved to the road to pass her and she side-stepped him and remained in his way. Car horns blared and somebody shouted at him from a Lancia.

Paul's blood pressure surged. 'Fuck off,' he said, smiling icily at her.

The woman might not have been able to speak English, but she understood the danger that glittered in Paul's eyes. Her expression rearranged itself from defiance to fear. She moved aside, reached behind her and pressed her children to her back, and let Paul pass.

Paul passed a side street and peered down it for the Alfa which didn't look as if it was going to appear after all. The pressure inside him increased and the pocket of high pressure air that seemed to surround him grew heavier.

You won't get her! Paul thought, in case H could hear him.

She's mine and I won't let you have her.

The rain seemed to have brought the Italians out in their cars. When Paul had arrived, the streets were almost deserted but now they were filling rapidly with cars. The increase in the amount of traffic wasn't just large, it was phenomenal. Paul knew that a jam would block the town soon and that he wasn't going to be able to drive away quickly as he had planned. This part of the dream was going to turn out to be prophecy too.

Paul's ears began to ring with the pressure. He wanted to *click out* and be able to forget the anguish but he was still a good few notches down the scale from that happening. His tolerance seemed to be growing. He paused, stood Katie on the ground, held her up with one arm while he groped in his pocket with his right hand. The ten pfennig piece he withdrew didn't feel like a magical talisman at all. It felt like an ordinary German coin of small denomination. Paul put it into his mouth, the way a Vietnamese soldier would insert his neck-chain Buddha before he went into battle. It had a brassy taste. It still didn't feel very lucky and Paul didn't know why he'd done it . . . until he realised that the ringing in his ears had stopped and his mind had cleared a little. The pocket of high pressure that surrounded him seemed to have faded slightly. The coin was somehow partially masking him from the activity going on around him. Paul didn't question this because two important things happened simultaneously.

One of them was that his Alfa 164 pulled up at the side of the road just ahead of him and a pretty Italian girl in a shiny metallic dress got out, and the other was that Paul was struck by lightning.

2

Except that it wasn't ordinary lightning. The flash was white but not blinding, there was no following thunder, and Paul had the sensation that it had happened internally rather than externally.

His muscles all spasmed and his feet might have momentarily left the ground. Paul felt a whack like a jolt of static electricity at the tips of the fingers of his left hand and then Katie was falling.

They got her! he thought.

'Where am I?' Katie wailed. 'What are you doing to me? Oh, Daddy, don't do it any more. It *hurts!*'

Paul realised it was not Katie's voice as he ran towards the girl in the metallic dress, his heart sinking, because now Katie was alive again, just as she had been in that first dream. Lulu Kaminsky had not returned to inhabit Katie's body, but someone had. Whoever it was had the voice of a terrified little girl.

The girl in the metallic dress had been standing beside the driver's door of her car, her mouth dangling open and her car keys and open clutch-bag dangling from her right hand as she watched Katie shudder-kick her way across the pavement like an epileptic in the throes of an extremely violent fit. Her left hand was hovering in the air just in front of her mouth, as though ready to clap down and stifle a scream, should one find its way out of her throat. She had long fingernails which were exactly the same shade of red as Katie's sandals had been before the water had soaked them, Paul realised as he ran at her.

The girl turned towards him as he closed in on her and began to shrink down, unconsciously making herself a smaller target. She couldn't have been any older than nineteen, she was very pretty, she didn't have the hateful expression with which the town's elder folks had regarded Paul, and he did not want to kill her, either now or later.

He skidded to a halt in front of her and snatched the keys from her hand. The girl squealed, crouching against the side of the Alfa. Paul dashed back to Katie, who was lying face down and writhing like an injured spider, got an arm around her waist and hauled her off the ground.

'Get out of the way!' he shouted at the girl in the metallic dress as he hurried back towards the car.

'DADDY, *DON'T*!' the thing in Katie's body squealed, struggling.

The girl in the metallic dress was too terrified to move. Paul reached down, grabbed her dress where it tented between her breasts and heaved her out of the way. The girl sprawled across the wet pavement and stayed there. Paul glanced up and down the street, saw people hurrying towards him and juggled the bunch of keys in his hand until he had the ignition and doorlock key between his fingers. For a few frantic seconds he stabbed the key at the lock and missed it. *Relax*! he screamed at himself, but his own tension was not the problem. Katie was kicking and wailing and whenever he got the key close to the lock, she would jolt against him and the transmitted motion would move it away.

'Hold still!' he yelled.

'Don't hurt me any more!' Katie screamed shrilly as Paul jabbed the key at the lock and missed again.

'Let her go, you bastard, you're hurting her!' the girl in the metallic dress called in English. Paul turned back towards her. She was wrong. They were all wrong. He was not the villain of this piece; what was going to happen was not his fault. Why didn't they know? He badly wanted to snap her neck now; to twist her head around until she stopped accusing him of things he wasn't doing. 'Shut up!' he shouted and the brassy ten pfennig rattled against his front teeth. 'Just shut the fuck up!' And the word *up* left his mouth and took the lucky coin with it. Paul's mind did a slow roll as he watched it hit the pavement and skid through the water all the way across to where the girl was now getting up. She snatched it from the ground and threw it at him. It hit the side of the car, fell into the gutter and was gone.

Feeling absurdly vulnerable now the coin was lost, Paul turned away from her and stabbed at the door with the key again. This time it found the slot and wiggled itself in. Paul yanked the door open, threw Katie in across the driver's seat, face down, put a hand on each of her buttocks as she clambered up on to her knees and tried to back out again and pushed as hard as he could. She shot across the car, hit her head on the passenger's door and collapsed, sobbing.

'You *bastard*!'

Something cold touched the back of Paul's neck and he ducked forward as it slipped across, jabbing an elbow out behind him, knowing already what had happened. The girl in the metallic dress had got up and attacked him with something. His elbow hit the girl in her midriff and the air shot from her lungs. 'Hoohh!' she shouted.

Paul backed out of the car, stood and turned. The girl had straightened much more quickly than he would have expected. Her left arm was clutched to her stomach but her right was slashing through the air towards him. Paul reached out and yanked the girl's arm out of the air while it was still a good two feet away from hitting him. The tiny shining thing he tore from her fingers was a minute Swiss army knife. In her rush of bravery and her haste to rescue the girl she thought Paul intended to hurt, she had opened the wrong blade of the knife. The thing she'd tried to sever the back of his neck with was the nail file. Paul could feel the stinging cut at the back of his neck but it was probably little more than a scratch.

The girl spat in his face.

Paul *clicked out*.

In less time than it took to blink, the girl's neck was clutched firmly in his right hand and his fingers were pressing into her windpipe. For one terrible moment Paul thought his hand was working independently from the rest of him. He watched the muscle swell between his thumb and forefinger, saw the veins and tendons pop up on the back of his hand as his fingers bit into her neck.

'I DON'T WANT THIS!' he screamed. 'GET AWAY!' His right hand shook the girl. Her eyes bulged and her limbs flapped as if they were boneless. Then he felt his fingers uncurling. He pushed the girl away, hard. She sat down on the pavement, clutching at her neck and coughing.

Paul turned away from her, shoved the sobbing Katie back into the car again, and got in beside her.

'Daddy, *please*!' Katie squealed.

'Shut up!' Paul shouted, shoving the keys into the ignition and twisting them. The Alfa started first time. The radio came on, loud. Paul turned it off because he knew that Valerie Masterton would begin to sing opera in a few seconds if he didn't, and it wasn't *Un bel di* at all, it was a godawful day. He turned on the wipers, hit the throttle, put the car in gear and pulled out into the traffic without looking behind him. People instantly found their horn buttons to provide him with a little Napoli night music – except this was the Margherita version of that well-known tune. It sounded the same.

'SHUT UP!' Paul shouted, and found second gear. The traffic was still moving. With a sinking feeling that felt like being on an elevator all the way down into Hell, Paul realised that the road they were on was one way, just like in the dream.

At least the traffic was moving. It wasn't fast enough for Paul's liking, but it was fast enough to keep any of those people who had been approaching him on foot from having good ideas about running after him and catching him up.

Lightning flashed and thunder roared. Rain hit the windscreen as if someone was out there throwing buckets of water at the car. Between each wipe of the blades, the road ahead turned into a distorted mirage.

'Where am I?' Katie asked tearfully.

Paul glanced over at her as the traffic came to a standstill. He pulled the handbrake up and was not terribly surprised to see an ancient coach jostling its way along the near-side of the Alfa. What was happening outside was all old news. What was happening *inside* was another matter entirely. None of this had featured in that first dream. In that, he had been frantically trying to bring Katie back to life. Now, he was sitting beside her body while someone else inhabited it. That someone else had brown eyes. Even the shape of Katie's face seemed to have altered to accommodate that person. That person looked – and more importantly *smelled* – very much to him like it was a little girl. It was a good smell, a smell that was at odds with all the bad odours surrounding him. Looking at the strange discrepancy that had appeared on Kate's face, hurt him. Her skin seemed to have another face superimposed upon it, but this new face was smaller and nothing seemed to fit except the eyes.

'You're in Italy,' Paul said. And thought, *And you're already dead and I'm going to have to kill you all over again to get rid of you*. He didn't know whether he could do it or not.

'You're not my daddy,' the girl said. She turned and looked at him and her face was shocked and pale. Tears ran from her brown eyes.

Paul shook his head. 'No, I'm not,' he said.

'My daddy hurt me,' Katie said.

Paul nodded. The traffic moved forwards and inched along with it. On the near-side of the Alfa the coach was pressing closer and its thick, stinking fumes were beginning to taint the air in here.

'I'm not dead, am I?' the girl asked as Paul stopped the car again. She wiped her nose on her arm. 'I thought my daddy killed me and it got dark and I got squished up and it hurt and I couldn't find my brother Nicky. I still don't know where he is, but I can sort of *feel* him. Am I big now?'

'Yes, darlin',' Paul replied. The best thing he could do was to reach over there and squeeze the life out of her right now because if she stayed for much longer he wasn't going to be able to do it. He knew that. He also knew that H knew it and that was why this child had been put here.

'Are you going to hurt me?' the girl asked, her brown eyes dark and fearful.

Paul didn't reply.

'Do you know what happened to make me come here and get big?' she asked, frowning. 'I feel a bit better now I'm alive again. I was squished up in a dark place and it hurt. I thought my daddy had me in his bag.'

The words *squished up* and *in his bag* rang a bell for Paul. He tried to put the thought out of his mind and couldn't. 'What's your name, sweetheart?' he asked. Beside him, the Fiat Strada drew up. Paul glanced out through the window at it. The woman driving it hadn't yet begun to shout and gesticulate at him, but she would, he was sure of that. There was no way out of the car now – he was blocked in on both sides.

The girl hitched in a shuddering breath. 'My name is Clara Defoe and I'm eight, and I live in Bude,' she said slowly. 'But something bad happened to me. Do you know what?'

Paul didn't know exactly what had happened to her, but he could take a good guess. Up on the top of the hill in Skiathos where he had rescued Katie, he had found passports in both the dead men's pockets. One of them had been called Peter Defoe. In Peter Defoe's wallet he had found a picture of a family mugging for the camera. On the back of the photo had been written: *Me, Denny, Nicky and Clara, EuroDisney, August 1992.* Also in his pocket had been a plastic bag which had contained the flattened face of the girl called Clara. Dear old Peter had slaughtered both his children – and probably his wife too – and had brought Clara's face and fingers with him to Greece. Paul wanted to scream. Instead he asked, 'How was EuroDisney?'

Katie looked at him, astonishment written across her face. 'How did you know I went?' she asked. Her innocent and surprised expression cut him deeply. How could anyone do something like that to an eight-year-old girl who had eaten candy-floss on a trip to EuroDisney?

And how are you going to kill her again? his goad asked.

Paul shrugged, and inched the car forward. 'Just a guess,' he said. Tears were beginning to sting his eyes. He hoped Katie and her friends were out there somewhere across the void ready to take this child when he sent her away again.

'I can't remember what happened,' the girl said. 'I remember before, and I remember my daddy hurting me terribly, but I can't remember afterwards. I thought I was dead. Have I been asleep a long time?'

When Paul turned to her again, her face had settled. It was

the face of the eight-year-old he'd seen in the photograph. She even had the birthmark over her left eyebrow he'd used to identify the face in the plastic bag. He looked away quickly.

'Yes,' Paul said, 'you slept for a while. And your daddy isn't going to hurt you any more. We won't let him.'

The traffic rolled forward a little further and stopped again.

Paul's heart began to race. The girl smelled clean and pure. He didn't want to do it. 'Come over here,' he said.

Suspicion lit in the girl's eyes and she pulled away from him. 'Why?' she asked.

'I want to give you a cuddle, that's all. Make you feel better.'

'You're going to hurt me!'

Paul shook his head. He could feel the eyes of the woman in the Strada burning into him. 'I don't want to hurt you,' he said thickly.

'You're crying,' the girl said, brushing the wet hair out of her face. She looked as if she'd never seen tears in a grownup's eyes before. Her fingers found her seatbelt and unclipped it. 'Don't be sad,' she said, moving towards him. 'I'm sorry.'

'I'm sorry too,' Paul said, and held her, rocking her back and forth, 'I'm so sorry.' He pulled away from her, cupped her face in his hands and kissed the tip of her nose.

Clara began to cry too. 'It isn't right, is it?' she said sadly.

Paul shook his head sighed. 'No, it isn't. It isn't right and it's not fair and I hate them for it.'

And his hands slipped down to the back of her neck and his thumbs found her throat and started work.

3

Afterwards, he knew what had upset the woman in the Strada in his dream. Clara had not died gracefully. She had bucked and kicked and fought to stay in the body that H and her father had forced her to occupy. It took a good two-and-a-half minutes before she stopped resisting and another minute or so before Paul allowed himself to let go of her.

He glanced at the woman in the Strada who had evidently watched him throttle the girl to death. When their eyes met, she began to shout and gesticulate while on the horn she beat out what might have been a morse code representation of the words she mouthed.

'No spikka da lingo,' Paul muttered sourly, remembering having said the very same words in his dream. A quick, hot anger drove a spike into him and he badly wanted to get out of the car, go over there, yank open the driver's door of the Strada and scare the shit out of the stupid woman. He would not have to speak. His physical presence would do the trick.

And, still conforming to the rules of the dream, Paul rolled down the electric window on his side of the car and glared at the woman through the driving rain.

The woman's quick mouth stopped working, hung open for a second and then snapped shut. The high-pitched blipping of the Strada's horn ceased and after a moment the woman looked away. When Paul glanced over at her again she was staring resolutely out of the windscreen, minding her own business.

'Good!' Paul spat venomously and wiped tears from his eyes. Scaring the woman hadn't made him feel much better, but it had relieved a little of the pressure he was under.

4

And now, at this moment of your dream, you got to work on Katie and tried to bring her back, old poke, his goad reminded him. *It might be an idea not to do that this time because you know what happened before. Perhaps you just ought to wait for her to come back of her own accord.*

Paul remembered very well what had happened during the dream and he didn't intend to work himself into a frenzy trying to bring Katie back because it hadn't worked properly then and it wasn't likely to now. If Katie was coming back, she would arrive when she was ready.

And that's a very big if, old poke, isn't it? his goad replied. *Do you think she's going to come back at all? Or do you think it's all over now? She's been gone for a long, long time.*

But Paul *did* think she would come back. He couldn't allow himself to think otherwise. He also thought that she wasn't coming back until after Margherita de Savoia had blown up. That was something he was going to have to deal with alone.

The traffic moved forward again and Paul moved the Alfa along with it, gulping in deep breaths and forcing himself not to think about what he had done to an eight-year-old girl called Clara because it made him feel dirty inside, and trying not to believe that the shadow-men would get him this time, even though they hadn't in his dream. It was all electrical somehow, and now that his only insulator – his lucky ten pfennig – had gone, he had no protection at all.

He willed his heartbeat to slow, peeled his hands away from the Alfa's wheel, and rolled on without steering, realising distantly that he'd been holding on to it so tightly that his knuckles had stiffened. Waiting, and knowing what was coming next, he massaged away the hot tingling in the palms of his hands which had probably been caused by his fingernails digging into them, then walked his index and middle finger down his back across his trapezius muscle – the one that always stiffened when he was behind the wheel of a stolen car.

And the traffic rolled on, a lane chock-full of it on either side of him and another before him.

What if . . . Paul started to think, and the words were knocked from his mind by a thunderclap. Lighting sizzled across a building just over the street and tiles flew from its roof. Behind Paul a cacophony of car horns began, as if the lightning had melted their wiring so they were permanently turned on.

They're trying to come, poke, his goad told him as the pocket of heavy air around him increased its pressure. *What if you have to bring her back now to stop all this?*

And Paul couldn't let the thought go. He was going to have to give her heart massage and mouth to mouth, just as he had in his dream, because if he didn't drag Katie back, H was going to send his shadow-men through her to . . . *to what? Blow up Margherita? To kill you would be a little more likely, don't you think?*

'He didn't kill me before,' Paul said to himself.

But he will now, so bring Katie back.

The urge to drag her to him, just as he had done in his dream, and to blow life into her and massage her heart (for what good that exercise would do) was almost irresistible. Katie was dead beside him, another life squeezed out of her – another life that H and his merry men had sent. The air pressure around Paul was popping his ears and making them sing like a diva and it was so heavy he could hardly draw it into his lungs which meant that he was still in H's range and that H was going to send something else through Katie soon. And the only way to prevent that happening was to get Katie herself back into her body.

Yet in spite of the evidence and the screaming urge he felt to do something, Paul resisted. Bringing her back before she was ready might be dangerous. He had to wait.

Rain sheeted the windscreen and bounced from the Alfa's bonnet in a million fractured droplets. The wiper flicked quickly from side to side, no longer managing to clear the screen.

'Come on, sweetheart, wake up!' Paul urged, smelling the bad smells, and fighting the feeling of claustrophobia that was building in him. His heart was beating so furiously and so fast that as he spoke, the sentence was broken up into its phonetic component parts. 'Come back to me, Katie!'

But Katie wasn't ready to return. Paul thought of the ten pfennig piece lying in the gutter under a stream of water and felt a terrible urge to go back and search for it. None of this should be happening. He should have been in Naples by now instead of being suckered into coming here. This was where H had wanted him to come – had arranged for him to come in some strange way. This was H's strongest point and his best chance. Katie was away and he was going to send something

581

through her which would kill Paul. He wasn't going to need the four who were following or the others who lay in wait to take back the girl. It was all going to finish right here. Enter one shadow-man, exit one Dekker.

Paul rolled the Alfa forward with the traffic and stopped again, still with the coach on one side of him and the woman in the Strada on the other. He peered out of his open window at the woman, who was staring resolutely forwards. She had seen one murder, and apparently didn't intend to attract his attention and become the next victim.

A sudden gust of wind drove rain into his eyes. The weather was spitting into his face in the same way as the Italian girl had. Paul turned away, wiped his eyes and reached out towards Katie. Her skin was soft and silky. He gently shook her slender arm, feeling the bone beneath the thin muscle. The arm was limp.

'Katie!' he urged. '*Wake up!*'

And Katie kicked. Both her legs jolted a single time. Paul waited, his hand still touching her arm. A tiny pinprick of hope began to shine. She was coming back! Her legs started to judder. Her hands trembled and spasmed and her neck muscles tightened, first raising her head and then tossing it back and forth.

'C'mon, sweetheart, you can do it!' Paul urged.

In front of the Alfa the traffic rolled forward twenty feet. The drivers of the cars directly behind let Paul know they weren't terribly happy at the delay by simultaneously hitting their horns.

Paul tore his eyes away from Katie and pulled forward. Another gust of wind threw water into his face as he pulled up and without thinking about it, Paul pressed the button to wind up the window. The pane got halfway up and inside the door – at the same moment that Katie went limp again – the motor began to labour. The glass slowed and Paul smelled the acrid odour of melting insulation.

This was another thing he had already lived through in his dream, another thing that was the same and yet slightly different. H, or whoever had broadcast that vision of the future to him, had corrupted it enough to be sure that when it finally happened, Paul wasn't going to be forewarned and forearmed. He didn't know whether he should keep his finger on the button and keep Katie immobile, or let it off and allow her to start moving again.

You can't make Katie short-out with a dodgy electric motor! Paul told himself, but he could and he was and he proved it to himself by taking his finger off the button, just as he had in his dream.

Katie spasmed as though she'd been hit in the stomach with a poker. Her feet began to hammer on the floor.

Paul hit the button again. The motor complained and got hot. A wisp of smoke puffed up through a tiny gap in the window's rubber seal.

Katie instantly went limp.

But who are you keeping out? H or Katie herself? What if she's trying to come back?

There was no way of telling. What had happened in his dream might have been what would happen now, or it might have been a bluff.

If you take your finger off the button, something will bump the car and then there will be another lightning strike and Katie will get out of the car and start coughing up sprites or shadow-men or whatever you want to call them.

But that might have been a lie. If he took his finger off the button, Katie might return. Bluff or double bluff?

Paul was as taut as a racquet string. All his muscles were locked up tight, his heartbeat was in the one fifties, his head was pounding and it was getting more and more difficult to suck in the thick air that surrounded him. His sense of smell had gone – the odour of the melting insulation in the window-winding mechanism had swamped every other smell in the car – and his ears were screaming. 'I don't fucking well *know*!' he shouted and drove his free fist into the Alfa's fascia. Plastic cracked and Paul groaned in despair as he realised he'd done this in his dream too.

The whole situation was paused. He was pausing reality by

keeping his finger pressed on the window button and nothing could happen until he released it. *How long?* he thought crazily. *How long can you sit here and hold this button in place?*

And then it didn't matter any more.

Because the Alfa suddenly wriggled on its suspension as if something had gently bumped it from behind and the suffocating pocket of high-pressure air that had been surrounding him, abruptly vanished. The pain in his ears was excruciating. Paul screamed and clapped his left hand to his ear as he doubled up, but he kept the window-winding button depressed.

Beside him, Katie started to jolt and shudder as if she was being whipped. Inside the driver's door, the window motor began to shriek. Blue smoke puffed out from the switch and it grew hot under Paul's finger.

Fuse will blow! he told himself. *Fuse fuse fuse!*

The switch began to melt under his finger and the heat grew tremendous. The car was swamped with the smell of rotten oranges. The hot spot under Paul's forefinger ate into his skin and he finally yanked his finger away from it, screaming.

The temperature inside the car plummeted from somewhere in the region of twenty-eight Celsius to what must have been a good ten below zero and lightning hit the car. The flash seared Paul's eyes – or rather his brain since there was no after image. It was worse than last time and much much worse than the dream. It wasn't Katie, it was H. Paul had lost control and now it was too late to do anything about it.

As the lightning struck, the Alfa's wipers juddered to a halt halfway across the screen, the electric window motors inside all the doors wound all the windows down half an inch, the lighting circuit fuse blew putting out the headlamps, and the air was instantaneously filled with the acrid smell of ozone. The doors unlocked themselves, the engine coughed and died and the radio suddenly began to play Puccini's *Un bel di* from *Madame Butterfly* at full volume.

Too late! Paul thought as the temperature inside the car plummeted another ten degrees. *Too late!*

And *clicked out*.

The pain ceased. Paul's mind cleared of all thought and his internal damage register lit up and reported no serious injuries. Paul gasped in a breath of icy air and expelled it in a white plume.

The car began to jolt as if something massive was dancing on top of it. The traffic ahead of the Alfa began to pull away and after a moment when the only sound Paul could hear was car horns, drivers started to squeeze by the offside of the car.

Katie's head was thrown back now and a terrible sound was coming from deep in her throat; a rising, urgent, animal noise that sounded a little like a small girl's impression of the sound a jet might make as it powered down the runway. Except that when she hit the top note, her voice kept on rising. She was grasping and kicking and writhing as if she was wrestling an invisible octopus to the death. One of her arms flew over towards Paul and struck him in the face before he could protect himself. There was no pain.

Rain was falling through the car now, as if the roof had been torn away. Paul looked up at the headlining which was still unmarked. Water was soaking into the fabric, pooling and falling, but the outside rain was coming straight through as if the roof didn't exist.

The deafening opera playing on the radio suddenly dissolved into a wave of static. Lightning flashed again and the distorted stereo sound quietened into the empty static hiss Paul knew so well: the Telecom void. Somewhere off in the distance he could hear a small, burbling crossed-line voice, the words of which were tortured beyond recognition. Echoing pops and hisses came and went.

'Katie?' Paul heard himself ask.

The distorted voice in the distance rose in pitch and then fell silent.

'*Katie!*' he said urgently.

A shower of small, white pebbles fell through the roof of the car. Paul leaned closer to the radio and his hand touched one of the stones. It felt as if it had been deep frozen throughout eternity.

A pair of scissors materialised beneath the car's headlining and fell into Katie's lap. The blades were crusted with frost. Paul snatched them away from her in case she picked them up and they froze to his hand. He blew on his fingers, peeled them away from the freezing steel and tossed the scissors into the back of the car.

I can't get back! Katie's tiny voice said through the radio. *They're blocking me and I can't come back!*

'Try!' Paul shouted. 'Just try!'

I don't know what to do!

'Neither do I!' Paul yelled. 'Just keep trying!'

Outside, the coach pulled away from Katie's side of the car. Paul hit the lock button because he already knew what would happen next: Katie would try to get out of the car. The Alfa's locking circuit was out of commission, which wasn't much of a surprise under the circumstances. It didn't fit the dream he'd had, but none of this did either. A steady stream of cars was passing the stalled Alfa on both sides. All of their drivers seemed to feel it was their duty to let Paul know how much trouble he was causing and what a dim view they took of it. This was the least of his worries. There was the knowledge in the back of his mind that those people who had seen him knock down the girl and steal her car had now had enough time to walk here, *en masse*. He had driven less than a mile since taking the car and they were still on the outskirts of Margherita.

He twisted the key in the ignition. The starter turned, but the engine did not catch. Several ball point pens and sheets of writing paper fell through the solid roof of the car.

Katie's body struggled with the invisible force.

Paul twisted the key again.

A large, live fish fell through the car between Paul and Katie and lay between the front seats, gills working and tail flapping as it lived out its last moments.

Lightning flickered again inside Paul's head.

He tried the ignition again. The Alfa's engine caught, coughed and died. 'Fuck you!' Paul shouted.

A single coin fell into his lap and forced a cold spike into him. Paul glanced down, intending to brush it away from him, then snatched it up. It was his not-so-lucky ten pfennig. He blew on the coin until the frost was gone and popped it into his mouth. It tasted of brass and rotten oranges.

Help me! Katie called through the stereo system, and then her voice was washed away as Puccini began to play again.

Paul turned the ignition key.

Bright blue light flashed to the right of the car. Once, twice, three times. Paul glanced through the frosty window to what he thought was its source and if, in his present state, his heart had been capable of sinking, it would have done so. Outside was the very thing no one driving a stolen car ever wanted to see. The car with the blue flashing beacon on top was a black and white police cruiser with the word *Carabinieri* written down the side.

5

Paul tried the ignition once more and a string of linked paperclips fell out of the car's roof.

'Oh!' Katie said, and stopped moving.

Paul looked at her, then glanced at the police car. Its occupants were getting out. In a moment or two they would also be getting their guns out of their holsters. Paul's hand went to the waistband of his jeans and withdrew his own gun – the one the immigration official had dropped into the car. He had shoved it down his waistband when the Jag broke down and promptly forgotten about it. He had never shot a man before but the part of him that now had control wouldn't hesitate if it became necessary.

Paul opened his door, and as though this simple action had caused it, Katie came to life and began to claw at the door handle on her side of the car.

Like fucking magic! Paul thought.

'Katie!' he shouted, but it wasn't Katie doing this: Katie was trapped somewhere in the void between two planes of existence. Something else was inside her body.

Paul leaned to her side, grasped for the back of Katie's grubby summer dress and yanked her away from the door. But Katie was suddenly alive and strong and intended to leave the car no matter what. She pulled hard against him and the back of her dress tore out of his hand, as its cheap material ripped. Her fingers finally got to the door handle and with the agility and grace of a young gazelle she leapt out of the car.

'Out!' someone shouted from behind Paul, and then he was being pulled backwards from the car.

Paul hit the tarmac face down and tried to scramble to his feet, but one of the cops kicked him good and hard in his ribs. He felt this pain. Bells rang on his damage register. Paul lashed out behind him with the gun and was lucky. Mr Kick's second blow was coming in and the barrel of the gun connected with his shin. The cop shouted. The other cop took hold of Paul's hair and yanked his head backwards. Paul struck out at him and his arm was caught in a firm grip. The cop pulled hard and Paul was tugged up to his knees and bent over backwards so far that he found himself gazing up at the second cop's face. That face was forty or fifty years old, olive-coloured and weather-beaten. It sported a walrus moustache on a lip which without it would have looked half an inch too long between nose and mouth. The guy's eyes were dark.

'Drop the gun!' he said in Italian, then in English: 'Drop the gun!'

'Get fucked!' Paul replied around the brassy coin. It rattled against his teeth. He struck out in an arc with his left elbow and got lucky again. It hit the cop's patella. The cop yelled and let go of Paul's gun arm, but not his hair. The other cop was up again now and squaring up for another kick – this time into Paul's unprotected stomach. Paul looked down his nose and saw the cop's leg go back for that touch of added force. A kick like this was going to rupture his stomach.

Paul flicked the gun into the air above his head, hoping to catch the first cop's wrist and make him release his grip. This time he missed. He was still kneeling and bent backwards and wasn't going to be able to get to his feet in time to avoid the incoming blow, so he simply pulled forward as hard as he could, yanking the cop behind him along by his hair. He lost some of it as he moved and his damage register noted that there were one or two points where his scalp might be pulling away from his skull, but there was no other way. He swept his gun hand around in front of him as the kick came in and let his right wrist absorb the impact. He jabbed his left elbow back again and caught the cop's groin. The cop yelled and let go.

Paul caught Mr Kick's next shot at him in both hands, then stood up, pushing the leg as far into the air as it would go, and then a little further. He felt the jolt as the man's hip dislocated, then let go. Mr Kick fell on to his back, screaming.

A gun fired and Paul's left hip lit up. He spun around, not yet feeling the pain from what was only going to turn out to be a graze if his damage register was correct in its estimation.

The cop who had been pulling his hair was sitting on the wet tarmac in a pained little ball. His left hand was pressed to his crotch and his right was holding out his gun towards Paul. A single wisp of smoke curled from the gun's barrel and vanished into the rain. The expression on the man's face suggested that he could not believe he'd shot a man from a distance of less than five feet without having killed him. It also suggested that inside the next second he was going to try to put that to rights.

'You shot me, you motherfucker!' Paul heard himself say in surprise, but he only heard it distantly. His right arm was already on its way down to the cop's gun. The barrel of Paul's gun hit the back of the hand with which the cop was holding his own piece. Paul struck hard enough and fast enough to break enough of the bones in that hand to stop it being able to *hold* a gun for the next month or two, let alone fire one.

The cop's gun fired as Paul hit it and the bullet took out the

Alfa Romeo's rear window. The cop shouted in pain. Paul stepped forward, tore the gun from the man's broken hand and threw it as far away as he could manage. He flipped his own gun around in his hand and coshed the policeman over the head with it, not using quite so much force this time. It was enough. The cop fell and was going to have quite a headache when he woke again.

Paul got back to Mr Kick before he'd got his own gun out of his holster. He leaned down as the man fumbled with it, put his gun into his left hand and swiped at the side of Mr Kick's jaw with his right. It was a haymaker punch and it was slow enough for any self-respecting fighter to avoid. Unfortunately for the policeman, he was currently looking out through what must have been a red haze of pain and didn't appear to be in a fit enough state to avoid an oncoming tortoise, let alone a punch which by street-fighting standards would have been classed as blindingly quick.

The sensation of jarring knuckles and tearing skin was quite satisfying, a distant part of Paul realised as he quickly surveyed his work. Mr Kick's jaw looked as if it had broken. Here was a man who, throughout the remainder of his life, was unlikely to be able to chew gum without a tiny click in his jaw reminding him of Paul Dekker.

He threw away the second cop's gun and began to trot down the wet street in the direction he knew Katie must have gone. Back towards town.

6

The traffic was heavier now and the rain harder. Throughout the fight he'd had with the cops, cars had passed, none of them stopping and some of them sounding their horns as if the spectacle of two policemen fighting with a criminal was a regular occurrence and only a minor inconvenience.

Paul touched his burning hip, found blood on his fingers, then craned his neck round to look as he ran. The bullet had torn his jeans across his left hip and cut flesh. It was little more than a scratch.

Paul clicked back in again and ran on, ignoring the teeming rain that sizzled on the tarmac and soaked him, and the blaring of horns that racketed and echoed around him and behind him where the cops and the stalled Alfa were. He could feel the full weight of his injuries now, but he would not stop running no matter how much it hurt. He could not see Katie, but he had no doubt at all that this would change very soon. What would happen after that was anyone's guess.

The buildings that rose on either side of the wide road were ancient and dirty and seemed to be empty. The street-lighting was minimal. There were pavements both sides of the road, but in both directions on both sides of the road they were chock-full of cars, some parked, some weaving their way past the parked ones as they tried to beat the jam.

'Katie!' Paul yelled, not knowing whether the real Katie could hear him across the void. 'Come back!'

Paul saw the truck before he saw Katie. It had stopped in the centre of the road and there were cars squeezing by on either side of it. Paul increased his pace. If he could get there before it started happening . . .

You could do what, exactly? Squeeze her throat until she dies again? She hasn't really come alive again this time, has she? They're using the split part of her as a gate for their sprites. Strangling her isn't going to do any good this time, poke, because there's no one home to send away.

. . . perhaps he could drag her away before it started.

Paul spotted Katie, silhouetted in the beams of the truck's four headlights. The words *natural disaster* occurred to him and he wasn't quite sure if he'd thought them or not. Katie could not easily communicate with him while she was away, but a mental picture of her had grown in his mind and it was this image of her that was mouthing these words. He did not understand them.

Paul closed in on her, not knowing what to do.

Rain was misting in halos around her as she stood tall, legs astride, hands on hips in front of the truck, but this time she was not facing it down, but standing with her back to it as though challenging something that stood on the wet tarmac in front of her.

Behind her the truck driver leaned on the air-horns and the loud low bellow sounded ominous. And just as he had in the dream, the driver switched the truck's lights on to main beam, and turned on the spot and fog lamps, creating a wall of light before Katie.

Her drenched blonde hair hung in a glistening tangle down her back, her thin summer dress clung to her body, transparent in the inverted vee her legs described. Her bare arms and legs shone golden in the headlights.

Katie was back. She was changed and she was back in her body. She might have been lovely before, but compared with the way she looked now, that earlier incarnation had been homely. In that moment she was the most gorgeous thing Paul had ever witnessed. There was a *perfection* about her which made him ache; which, he would not be willing, but *glad* to die for. In that moment of incredible beauty she looked as though she had been newly struck from one of God's own personal moulds and placed there by His hand.

Katie looked like an angel.

'Paul!' she gasped. 'Don't come any closer! Not yet! It's wrong! It isn't finished!'

Paul stopped about ten feet away from her, facing her in the centre of the empty stretch of tarmac. Cars passed on either side. He gulped in air, finally realising why she didn't want him any closer. She had fought her way back into her body despite the fact that H was trying to keep her out while he used it as a channel, and now she was having trouble hanging on. She was battling with something in a place which might have been inside her body or which might have been somewhere out in the void.

Paul went a little closer. Katie tilted her head back and

moaned. The sound was worse than the hollow lowing of the truck's air-horns. It sounded as if she was simultaneously suffering every torture man had ever devised.

When her head dropped again. Katie's green eyes were gone and the black orbs of H's angel glared from her face. 'You lost her, old poke!' Katie's mouth said.

And then Katie was back again. Paul started towards her. 'Don't!' she warned, and Paul stopped.

Katie's body began to shimmer. For a moment Paul could see through her to the truck's radiator grille, then it steadied. Katie screamed and doubled over. Behind her, the truck driver blasted the air-horns again.

Paul hesitated for a moment, then ran to her, pulled her upright. Her flesh was warm. 'Katie!' he said.

Katie turned her head towards him and looked at him with the raging eyes of H's angel. The powerful smell of burning wiring filled his nostrils. 'It's a no win situation for you, pipsqueak,' the male voice told him. 'The girl is mine. Give her to me now and you'll live. Refuse and you'll die now and suffer in hell.' One of Katie's hands took Paul's own right hand and she placed the other on the split in his jeans. Then she was sinking in her nails – where the bullet had ripped his skin and where the climber had tried to saw off his forefinger. It hurt. Both areas began to bleed and cold seemed to be pouring into him through his blood.

Paul ignored it. He pressed his nose against Katie's, looked deep into the Hell that raged behind the angel's black eyes and said, 'Take her away from me . . . if you think you can.' He knew what he had to do next. He reached up to Katie's mouth with his left hand and gently opened her jaw. Katie's mouth was now the blackened misshapen thing that belonged to Henry Tyler's angel. The lips were seared and the teeth were gone and the tongue was a melted grey blob. She reeked of charred flesh and over-stressed wiring.

'She's mine,' Paul said, and opened his own mouth and kissed Katie, deeply, pressing the lucky ten pfennig piece into her mouth. He felt a small shock as the coin touched her burned tongue like static snapping at him, then it was all over and H was gone.

Katie tasted warm and sweet.

She stopped scraping at his wounds and her hands found his head and pulled him to her as she kissed him back, pushing the coin back into his own mouth.

Then she pushed him away. 'Quick!' she said. 'Get away from me!'

Paul staggered away from her as she doubled over and coughed like an expert smoker, long and hard and loose. The coughing stopped abruptly and then Katie bent forward as if she'd been struck in the stomach. Then she stood up, an expression of surprise on her face.

'I think we did it,' she said. 'I think we stopped it happening. You drove H away and I think I stopped him bringing the sprites through. They were the reason I didn't want you near me. I didn't want one to get inside you. If it had, you'd be dead. I tried to tell you, but I couldn't get a fix on where you were. They can't hurt you directly unless they get inside you. They're natural disaster things.'

'The shadow-men?'

'The sprites. The things he was trying to birth. I think he was hoping that you would either swallow one, or be killed in the mayhem when he set them free. I don't think he'll try again now that I'm back, but if anything happens to me again . . . don't kiss me. I can't do it without you.'

The truck driver gunned the engine and sounded the horns.

'Are you okay now?' Paul asked. 'Can you stay in your body this time?'

'I think so,' Katie said, slowly. 'I don't know. I'm not quite straight yet.'

And then her face clouded. She stood up straight and closed her eyes. Air-horns blasted behind her. The truck driver had rolled down his window now. He leaned out and shouted at Paul, waving his arm to indicate that he should get his girl out of the road.

'Katie?' Paul asked.

Katie's chest hitched and her stomach spasmed as if she were going to throw up, but she made no sound. She opened her mouth and the black substance appeared at the back of her throat, rising slowly from her gullet like a viscous liquid.

She had been wrong about how firm a grip she'd had on herself. Paul moved away from her, his heart sinking. It was too late to do anything now except stay alive. A part of him whispered that this might have happened when he was kissing her. And then what would have happened to him? He would probably have ended up like the two he'd killed when he rescued Katie. He'd seen this same odourless black substance trickling from their mouths. Apparently H could slot them into dead bodies and call them his own.

Paul watched in awe as this part of his dream came true before his eyes. The stuff slid up Katie's tongue, blanking parts of her flesh from view as though they didn't exist. The substance reflected almost no light at all. It flattened and stretched over her teeth and quickly coated the contours of her mouth. When the inside of her mouth was filmed with the substance, it became thinner and faster and ran out over her bottom lip, sheeting her chin and neck like a smooth layer of soot.

Margherita's going to blow up, Paul's goad told him needlessly.

Like a living thing – which it was, Paul supposed – the substance sought its way beneath Kate's dress and spread rapidly out across her shoulders and down her chest between her breasts where it gathered at her heart in a distinct bulge.

Paul watched, powerless to do anything to prevent it, as the substance filled Katie's mouth completely and flowed out in a thick living cable which snaked down her body and pooled on the ground to her left.

The pool, only visible as a black hole in the wet tarmac, grew rapidly, forming an oval which stretched and elongated then began to pull itself in, drawing its edges closer together at certain points.

Cars were passing all around Paul; they mounted the

pavements to get by and weaved past, angrily sounding their horns at the obstruction, but no one seemed to notice what was going on.

Paul watched the black pool drawing itself into the man-shape, separating one lower pool into two pointed legs while the other end grew a round head, narrow shoulders and pointed arms.

In his dream only a single pool of this substance had been expelled from Katie's mouth, but now it was happening for real, H was going for broke. The first sprite was almost complete now and had sheared itself off from the thick black cable that was still coming from Katie and was only attached to her by the thin strand that ran to her heart. But the substance was still coming out of her mouth, more quickly now, and was reaching the tarmac, filling a space then breaking off again and doing another. It was like watching someone squeeze off big dollops of thick black icing from a huge cake decorating set.

There were five there now, and another forming.

The truck driver was climbing down from his cab, presumably to move Katie physically.

The first sprite was complete now. It was shadow-thin and shaped like a child's cut-out paper-chain man. Its slender limbs narrowed to points and it had no hands or feet. The second sprite was rapidly taking shape. This one grew a head and shoulders first, while its body shape narrowed and stretched. The rest were still crawling pools.

'Run away!' Paul shouted at the trucker.

The trucker was short and fat and pissed off. He replied in Italian and strode towards Paul as if he meant business. When his eyes lit on Katie he stopped dead in his tracks and stared at her. One of his hands found his head and he began to scratch it, in what looked to Paul like a cartoon representation of puzzlement.

'Get away!' Paul shouted, motioning at the man. '*Run!*'

The trucker turned to face Paul and began to talk in Italian. The words were not important – the tone they were spoken in conveyed the driver's emotion quite adequately. Fear.

'Run!' Paul shouted.

One of the strands of black substance that connected Katie's chest to the pools of darkness on the tarmac began to shimmer in rainbow colours. On the ground, the first sprite was enveloped in a wave of tiny golden lights, which twinkled briefly, like the lamps of a distant valley town glimpsed from a mountain top. The string which connected it to Katie dissolved into wisps of dark smoke which were driven away by the rain and the golden lights vanished. The sprite flexed its flat limbs and slid effortlessly away. For a moment Paul could see it, a darker patch on the dark tarmac, then it was gone.

The trucker had seen enough. When Paul looked up, intending to shout at him again to run away, he was sprinting through the traffic towards the far side of the street.

The second sprite was almost finished. It had shaped its round head into a profile with a sloping forehead, sharp hooked nose and a small twisted mouth, and as Paul watched it burst into the brief golden firework display.

Across the road, the trucker leapt on to the pavement – and fell into the dark hole that opened before him. The hole was waist deep. As the trucker pressed his palms into the wet pavement to push himself up again, the hole heaved itself shut like the jaws of a trap.

Paul looked away.

The second sprite slid away, then the third. The black substance had stopped pouring from Katie's mouth now, but there were still three sparkling strings connecting her to the remaining sprites.

Across the road where the severed torso of the trucker lay, the wall of the building fell, showering huge slabs of brickwork down on to the passing traffic. Within two seconds, the traffic on that side of the street had become a huge tangled mess of brickwork and twisted metal which grew rapidly as more cars ploughed into it.

One of the sprites slid up over the truck's front bumper and flattened itself across the radiator grille. All the truck's lights died.

Away in the next street there was a huge explosion. High above the roof tops Paul saw a gout of flame reach up into the night.

Across the road people were running back and forth, trying to avoid being killed by falling masonry and flying cars while they pulled people from the wreckage.

The truck's radiator fractured and clouds of steam billowed out, followed by jets of coolant. A second later, the truck's engine tore itself apart and its tyres began to burst, one by one in deafening explosions, each one lowering a different corner. The big wing mirrors twisted and exploded in clouds of glass.

A man hurrying past the truck fell to the ground screaming, his face in tatters.

Another sprite broke away from Katie.

The truck's windscreen exploded, showering Paul with glass.

From behind the truck there was the huge tortured sound of a building being subjected to forces it was unable to withstand.

A section of tarmac suddenly vanished and the truck bounced down into it, its suspension squealing horribly as the ground beneath it lowered and it sank.

Behind it, Paul caught sight of the screeching building. Its front wall bulged horribly outwards and was now interlaced with gaping cracks.

In the lane behind Paul, cars were still moving. A VW, moving impossibly fast as it wove its way through slower traffic, was heading towards where Paul and Katie were standing, no longer protected by the bulk of the truck.

Another sprite left Katie.

Paul watched the path of the VW – surely the same one through which the door of the cab had flown in his dream. That wasn't going to happen here because the truck was now flush with the street; its doors could not fly off. In that instant, Paul thought he knew what *was* going to happen. The car was going to run down him and Katie.

Way down towards the town centre, a building exploded.

More people were milling about in the street now, some

screaming, some staggering dazedly in no particular direction, some standing before the bulging building and staring up at it as though they couldn't believe that their senses were telling them.

The VW drew closer, knocking a running man aside like a skittle. Paul glanced at Katie. There was still one strand of that null substance attaching her sternum to the last sprite.

Across the street the building fell, spewing debris out across the street. A Ford swerved to avoid it and the VW hit it, bounced off, ran on to the kerb, hit another car, bounced back and was rammed by a Fiat which burst into flames.

The VW shot forwards, hit a slab of masonry and took off.

Paul watched it all as if it was happening in slow motion. The VW did a gentle curve through the air, the trajectory of which was going to bring it back down where Paul and Katie were standing.

Feeling as if he was running under water, Paul dashed forward to pull Katie out of the way, not knowing what would happen to the sprite that was still attached to her and not caring.

His arm hit the strand of black stuff as he grabbed her and yanked her out of the way. It burned like acid. Paul ran a few steps as the VW hit the spot where they had been standing and folded up.

The area surrounding the truck was filled with crashed and burning cars and injured people. Back down the road into town the collisions were continuing, interspersed with the dull *crump* sounds of buildings falling and the sharper sounds of explosions.

'Katie!' Paul shouted. The remaining sprite whipped and thrashed across the wet road at Paul's feet, like a pike with a hook buried in its maw. It passed over his bare feet, scalding them, and Paul leapt away, letting go of Katie who fell to the ground. As soon as Paul released Katie, the sprite twinkled with golden light and broke free.

A middle-aged man whose face was sheeted with blood ran

up to Paul, grabbed the front of his shirt and began to scream in his face. Paul pushed him away and he came back as though magnetically attracted. Paul hit him. The man fell.

Paul picked up Katie, distantly noticing that the sprite that had buried the truck had now back-filled over it and replaced the tarmac in big crazy-paving chunks. For a moment he gazed back down the road towards town. Before him lay what looked like Armageddon. The tangle of wrecked and burning cars went on for as far as he could see. People were running like headless chickens, some of the nearer ones falling into holes in the road which opened before them, swallowing them up. Every second building seemed to be falling and the ground beneath Paul's feet was moving uneasily as if some of the sprites were busy excavating under the road, perhaps preparing to sink the whole town.

In the distance, the low rain cloud was tinged a flickering orange with fires. The racket of explosions as the sprites ruptured and lit gas mains and brought down buildings made it sound as if Margherita was being subjected to the worst aerial bombardment since Dresden. Most of the street lights were out now and Paul thought that pretty soon they would all be gone. Pretty soon the population would all be gone too.

I didn't want this, he thought as he turned away from the mayhem. *I didn't want any of this to happen.*

But he had come here and it *had* happened.

How many more notches on the old six-gun will this make, pard? his goad asked him. *Ten thousand? Twenty?*

Ahead of him, away from the town, the road was clear and the buildings were undamaged. Paul adjusted his grip on Katie and began to trudge through the rain, back towards where the Alfa 164 would be standing, alone in the middle lane of a one-way street.

Chapter Twenty-Three
Sniper

1

Enrico Spagnol stood in the doorway of a deserted warehouse on the far side of town, sheltering from the rain while he waited. A bottle of Jack Daniels stood on the step beside him, its cap off, but he had vowed not to drink another drop of it until the danger had passed.

He had got the urge to drive out here about twenty minutes ago, and he was learning to trust the sudden hunches he kept getting just lately because they always turned out to be the right thing to do. He suspected that this was because those impulses were planted squarely in his brain by the subliminal thought network that he and his compatriots shared.

There had been a change of plan. Enrico had suddenly known this, as certainly as he'd known he'd only managed to force down a single triangle of the pizza *ai funghi* that had been cooling on the table before him in the bar. Somehow – and he didn't know what had happened to cause it – the situation had changed. Apart from an odd discomfort which was caused, not by the booze making his bowels ache, but by a logical deduction he could have done without, Enrico accepted this. What puzzled him about it – and caused the discomfort – was the obvious fact that something had gone wrong.

And that something must have gone quite badly wrong because instead of killing Dekker (if it became necessary) and delivering the girl to the border, he was to shoot both of them.

Which meant, by deduction, that the divine embodiment H Tyler was fallible. Fallible was not a word Enrico was comfortable with when you applied it to the coming master. Divine beings were not supposed to be fallible.

He had sat and thought about it for a while, drawing parallels between the struggle his band of disciples was going through and what had happened to the last divine embodiment and his disciples. Jesus had not been infallible. It was surely something to do with having to inhabit a human body. When you were incarnate and walking the earth, limitations must be placed upon you. Jesus had had human qualities and presumably H had them too. And although being incarnate seemed to be a necessity in order to intervene in – and shape – the affairs of human beings, there were distinct drawbacks to it. Like the inability to be infallible, for example.

Now that Enrico had cleared up this matter, another of his doubts was assuaged. The angel had taken a ruined body which had no sight, and although the deity inside what had once used to be Henry Tyler was able to perceive things on several different levels, Enrico had worried about the body's missing eyes. Surely it would have been better to have miraculously restored the body, facial damage and eyes? Now he understood that another of the angel's limitations was that it could not perform such actions until its adversaries had been vanquished. When Dekker and the girl were gone, all this would change.

And, looking forward to a world where there were no doubts and no sudden changes of plan, Enrico had paid his bill and walked through the rain back to where the Ford had been parked. Things weren't quite settled yet, but tonight they would be finished with.

2

In spite of the thunder and lightning and the strange smells in the air, Enrico hadn't quite realised how far things had advanced until he reached his car and turned out on to the main road.

The road was packed with traffic and it was raining so hard he could barely see out of the windscreen. A part of him noted that if it came to the point where shooting had to be done, visibility was going to cause him a few problems.

Enrico drove carefully, skirting several accidents that had happened – presumably due to the rain – and dodging the bedraggled swarm of pedestrians who were striding up the road amongst the traffic. There were men and women and children, none of them wearing wet weather clothing or using umbrellas. The procession seemed to be led by a small boy on a bicycle who rode on the pavement just ahead of a pretty girl in a short metallic dress that clung to her like a second skin.

The group seemed significant somehow, but Enrico wasn't equipped to work it out. The rifle was on the back seat of the car and the better part of his mind seemed to be carrying on a telepathic conversation with it, in the same way as he once used to do before a target competition. If you were going to shoot – either to kill or to hit a small and distant paper target dead centre – you not only had to possess a good eye and an ability to remain perfectly still, you also had to have the total agreement of your weapon. The weapon had to cease to be an encumbrance that weighed you down and distracted you and turn into a mere extension of your eye and fingers. If you were any more conscious of it than that, you were going to miss. This was the first time Enrico had been near a gun for years and although this rifle was a big clumsy thing, he was certain he had won its tacit agreement and was looking forward to putting it to his shoulder and eye and peering down its scope.

It wasn't until he was almost a mile outside the town centre that Enrico realised the gravity of the situation. Up ahead of him was mayhem. In the centre of the road, a truck was sinking into the ground as if it stood on a hydraulic platform that was being lowered. A building had fallen on the right-hand side of the road, crushing cars. More cars were piling into the wreckage as if their drivers could not see the obstruction ahead of them.

Frowning, Enrico barged his way into the left-hand lane, which was still moving past the point where the truck was sinking like a setting sun.

He had to mount the kerb in a couple of places when several minor accidents occurred in the centre lane as those cars stuck behind the truck tried to barge their way into his lane. On his right, as he pushed forward, a building began to bulge like an expanding balloon. Something way behind him exploded with a *crump*! and the air pressure in the car rose, making his ears pop.

And there, right before his very eyes, were Dekker and the girl. Enrico crawled past them, gazing out of the passenger window of his car as he passed. He recognised both of them straight away, even though he'd never laid eyes on them before. There was a strong surge inside his head which seemed to end with the kind of *blip* noise you heard in war films about submarines, but Enrico didn't need this to inform him who they were.

Dekker was standing about ten feet away from the girl looking as if he wanted to run to her, while she stretched and bowed in the headlights of the sinking truck. A black cable of something Enrico thought he ought to recognise was falling from her open mouth and pooling on the ground. Something at the girl's feet shimmered with tiny pinpricks of golden light.

And then Enrico was past them. Shaking with fear and excitement, he put his foot down and hurried up the road ahead.

A couple of hundred yards further up the road, he had to swerve to avoid a black and white Carabinieri cruiser which was backing down the road towards him, see-sawing wildly as though its driver didn't have proper control over it. Enrico wondered why it hadn't turned round. He passed the car, glanced at it in the rear-view mirror and watched as its driver lost control and the car smacked into a wall.

He looked back again just in time to see the Alfa 164 parked in the centre of the road ahead of him. Enrico hit the brakes, pulled hard on the wheel and missed the open driver's door of the car by a whisker. The Ford began to skid, but Enrico was ready for it and corrected it before it could get out of hand.

This was the car. He knew it in the same way as he'd recognised Dekker and the girl Katie. This was the one they would be coming in, if they made it.

And when he arrived at the right place, he pulled in to the side of the road, spun the top off the bottle of Jack Daniels and drank, long and deep.

3

And now he stood here in this doorway, waiting, sure that they *were* going to come after all. One of H's human failings was that he had underestimated the power of his adversaries. Enrico wasn't surprised. He wouldn't have thought it possible that two people could do so much.

Dekker and the girl were causing terrible devastation in the town. Over the past five minutes he had heard explosion after explosion echoing around the sky and mingling with the thunder. The breeze that blew from the town smelled of many fires and carried the sounds of sirens and distant screams and shouts.

Listening and waiting, Enrico had begun to understand the terrible truth about Dekker and the girl. He already knew they were dangerous, but the extent of their power was a revelation. A deep and all-encompassing anger grew within him at what they were doing to this pretty seaside town and its inhabitants.

He leaned out of the doorway and drew a bead down the road with the rifle. In his arms, the weapon did not feel quite as heavy as he had expected it to, or as ill balanced. But the doorway was not a good place to shoot from. He would be firing at an angle to the target and that wouldn't be any good at all. To score a kill – or two kills – he wanted to be square on to the target. When he heard the car's engine start, he would step out of the doorway, walk to the centre of the road, lie down on his stomach and elbows, in exactly the same way as he had always done when shooting, then he would compose himself. There would be ample time.

And he would not be in danger because he was wearing black. In this light and weather Dekker would not see him lying there at all.

Enrico didn't expect to be hit by the car after he'd killed Dekker because he was going to shoot while the car was still a hundred metres or so away and once its driver was dead, the car would veer off and crash long before it had covered the remaining distance.

And the beauty was, he wouldn't even have to see Dekker to kill him. All he would need to see was the car's windscreen. He intended to put the bullet through a spot in the screen which was eight inches lower than the roof and a foot to the right of the pillar. He had measured the windscreen of the Ford he had hired and that would have centred the bullet between the driver's eyes and the bottom of his nostrils. In an upright position the bullet would have entered his head through the bridge of his nose; if he had been slouched, it would have probably gone through his forehead. Enrico doubted that the seating arrangement in the Alfa he was going to shoot at would be very much different. A few inches either way, perhaps, but he had plenty of vertical leeway. Dekker wasn't going to be up to much, even if the shot went low enough to hit his mouth. The lateral allowance was tighter, but people driving cars tended to keep their heads upright and in one place – especially if they were driving in foul weather like this.

He wasn't going to miss.

And if there was time, he would squeeze off another shot at the corresponding position on the passenger's side of the car. It didn't really matter either way if he struck or missed the girl – or even if the crash that followed did not kill her. Enrico had visions of dragging her out of the car, putting the muzzle of the rifle against one of her eyes and watching as he blasted what was left of her brain away.

She and Dekker were a pestilence and when they turned up here, Enrico Spagnol was going to take a great delight in removing them both from the face of the planet.

He thought about it for a few seconds, then stooped and picked up his bottle of Jack.

The glass neck of the bottle was cool and good against his lips.

The burning liquid was even better.

Chapter Twenty-Four
Margherita In Decline

1

Paul hadn't gone more than ten paces before he realised that the sprite he'd caused to break off from Katie prematurely was following him.

It was hard to see in the flickering light – which was now being radiated by little more than the odd car headlight still shining and the flickering flames of burning buildings – but he spotted its misshapen form trail over a kerb and vanish along the side of a building. This sprite had a chunky unformed head which flowed into its shoulders and one of its arms was shorter than the other. Paul didn't know how much power it would possess in this state and he wasn't keen on finding out. It had blistered his foot by simply passing over it and he didn't care to visualise what it might do to him if it flickered its way beneath his clothing.

He adjusted his grip on Katie, who'd slipped off balance, and quickened his pace.

Over to his right a window exploded outwards and Paul ducked as hot glass fragments whickered through the air close to him.

He spotted the sprite again a few seconds later, ahead of him this time. The thing didn't seem keen on coming into contact with him again and it occurred to him that physical contact might hurt the thing as much or more than it hurt him.

Paul turned the ten pfennig over in his mouth and prayed to his patron saint that this was the case.

He wasn't surprised when the ground trembled and wrenched itself apart in front of him – he had fixed the spot where he'd last seen the sprite and had half expected it. With a noise like a thousand tons of granite tearing away from another thousand tons, the tarmac opened in front of him in a ragged split that ran from one side of the road to the other. The fissure was less than two feet wide. Paul looked down into it as he stepped across and his mind rolled. The crevice was very deep and the red stuff that seethed down there looked very much like volcanic lava. It also looked as if it was rising. A blast of hot, sulphurous air hit his nostrils.

And you wondered if it would be weak, he told himself.

Paul glanced about him, in case the shadow thing was nearby, didn't see it, and began to run. His progress wasn't very fast, but the car wasn't too far ahead. He glanced behind him and wasn't surprised to see steam pluming from the red gash in the road as rainwater fell into it.

You know what's going to happen next, don't you, poke?' his goad asked. Paul thought he did and increased his pace.

A building crashed into the road in front of him. Paul turned away from it while it fell, sheltering Katie from the airborne debris. The ground beneath his feet began to shudder, like a huge monster slowly waking. The air pressure increased as, away in the distance, a huge and ominous rumble began.

Paul turned back to the pile of rubble and began to climb over it, fighting to keep his feet as it shifted and rearranged itself. For a second his ankle became wedged between a large chunk of brickwork and a piece of concrete lintel. Somewhere beneath the pile, the sprite realised it had him trapped and made a move. The whole pile shifted in a rolling wave. The lintel moved away from the masonry and Paul yanked his foot out of the trap before it could close again and bite off his ankle. He half ran, half leapt across the moving debris, expecting to fall and be crushed at any moment and being constantly surprised to find himself not only still alive, but still on his sore and bleeding feet with Katie held firmly against him. If there was anyone alive in the world at this moment who needed a tetanus shot more than Paul Dekker, he would have been very surprised.

Behind him, the low rumble rose in volume until it was massive. He could hear it and he could feel it in his chest.

This is one of those places, Paul thought as he struggled to keep his feet. *One of those places like the ring of stones in Skiathos, but connected in another way, somehow. That's why he brought you here. It's a place where he's strong, where he has influence. A place where he thought he could kill you and get Katie back.*

And then his goad added, *Or kill you both if he* didn't *get her back.*

The rumbling noise reached a crescendo and stayed there. The rubble beneath Paul's feet was alive with vibration. He looked back. Over to his right on the far side of the town, the thing he had been expecting happened.

The earth erupted in a huge column of smoke and burning debris and molten orange rock. Where before there had been flat arable land, a fault in the earth's crust was making itself known. A volcano had formed.

Closer – too close, in fact – red hot lava was welling out of the crack he'd leapt across thirty seconds earlier.

Paul leapt down on to wet tarmac and ran.

He passed the police cruiser that had stopped beside him earlier. It was now embedded in the wall of someone's house, its back crushed and its bonnet hanging off. Both its front wheels were off the ground. Neither of the cops was in it – or nearby. Paul was thankful for that.

The sprite that had been trying to prevent him from reaching the Alfa seemed to have exhausted itself now. The car was in sight, about a hundred yards ahead, and since the thing had brought down the building, Paul hadn't seen it and nothing else had happened. He was thankful for this too.

Rubble and sparks showered down on him as he reached the Alfa. He yanked the passenger door open, suddenly realising that since the car hadn't wanted to start before there was no good reason why it should now. He put the thought from his mind and ran round to the driver's side of the car. The dull and rainy sky glowed orange with a thousand fires and on the other side of town, where liquid rock was being flung into the air, the clouds seemed to be boiling away.

As Paul got into the Alfa, the sky lit blindingly with a multiple strike of lightning and a cannonade of thunder pounded his ears.

Paul didn't know whether or not he had expected to find the Alfa's keys still in the lock, but there they were, as if they had been waiting for him.

Volcanic ash fell on to the car's bonnet like burning butterflies.

Paul offered a silent prayer to St Cunt, took a deep breath and twisted the ignition key.

Nothing happened.

C'mon, car! he thought, *Don't let me down now*!

The Alfa lurched as if something soft had hit it. Paul glanced in the rear view mirror and saw nothing but a geyser of hot lava shooting into the air from the crack in the road. He twisted the key again and the Alfa's engine turned, resisted, then gave in and started. Paul hit the throttle, selected first and dropped the clutch. The Alfa's wheels bounced and skittered across the wet tarmac, its tyres hissing, its engine screaming, then it dug in and shot forward. Paul corrected its course and breathed a sigh of relief.

2

Enrico Spagnol heard the car's engine roar and left the shelter of his doorway. There were things happening that were beyond his ability to comprehend. Although a major part of southern Italy suffered from earth tremors and a little volcanic activity, it was supposed to happen on the other coast. As far as he knew, Margherita wasn't situated directly on a fault in the earth's crust, and as far as he knew the nearest place where volcanos were likely to erupt was Sicily where Mount Etna dozed fitfully. Surely none of this was supposed to happen?

But it *was* happening, whether it was supposed to be or not. Way down on the other side of town the ground was puckering up as the earth reached to kiss the sky and expelled boiling subterranean juices. Closer, molten rock was spurting from the street in long hard pulses as if someone had severed one of the earth's arteries.

The whole town seemed to be on fire now. Things were exploding and falling back there amongst the glow of the blazes, the clouds of steam and smoke and the sheeting rain. All human noises were lost beneath the horrendous rumble of the volcano as it rose slowly from the earth, seemingly already fully formed and rising as though on a lift. Thunder rocked the skies and lightning burned a dozen snapshots of the orange-tinted roiling clouds on to Enrico's retinas. It was like Hell come to earth.

And Dekker and the girl had brought it here.

Clearing his mind of all thought – which wasn't difficult given the circumstances – Enrico walked to his chosen position in the middle of the road and lay down. The tarmac was alive beneath him, flexing and juddering with the transferred shock of what was happening further away. The surface was warm and the rain was steaming off it. It didn't matter. None of it mattered. Enrico spread his legs, made a steady brace with his elbows, put the rifle to his shoulder and his eye to the scope. The rifle felt firm and cool in his hands. Enrico began to converse with it in that magical two-way mode which suggested weapons had minds and voices of their own, and he began to feel very calm and very still. The aches and pains of his rusty joints faded, and effects of the alcohol in his bloodstream vanished and Enrico allowed himself to merge with the personality of the gun. They now had a single purpose – were a single item, in fact. And that single item existed only to kill.

3

Paul changed to second, let out the clutch and glanced in the mirror at the mayhem he'd brought to the quiet seaside town. He could not allow himself to be affected by it, could not allow himself the guilt he wanted to feel, because it would weaken him somehow. H knew his Achilles' heel and had gone for it relentlessly since that first nightmare. The voice of his goad – now smaller and less insistent – was trying to ask him, *How many more notches will this be on the old six-gun, pard?* and Paul knew it, but he didn't allow the words to form and he didn't think of their meaning. He was not culpable. This was H's crime.

He tore his eyes away from the tableau of Armageddon behind him and looked ahead, peering through the windscreen against the driving rain and the falling dust. Pieces of debris were raining down on the car and scattering up the windscreen. The road ahead could barely be seen.

Something black flitted sideways across the windscreen and for a moment Paul thought it was the tattered remains of a black plastic bag, borne by the wind. The thought died in his mind before he finished thinking it.

Because the passenger door of the Alfa was torn off.

You wondered what had happened to that last malformed shadow-man, a clinical part of his mind told him, *and now you know. It got in the car with you!*

The Alfa shot to the left as Paul compensated for the immense tug of the door being ripped away, and he corrected, his foot already on the brake. The car slid and he caught it, putting it back where it should have been.

Katie's dress was whipping in the wind and her hair was alive, writhing in Medusa-like snakes. She was leaning towards the open door and she wasn't belted in. Paul reached over for her, grabbed a handful of her dress and yanked her back into the car.

In front of the screen, the wipers curled away from the glass, quickly twisting themselves into corkscrews which wound and unwound with the movement of the wiper motor. The sprite slid up the windscreen and for a moment its malformed head was directly in Paul's line of sight. Its mouth snapped like an angry turtle and slivers of glass were scraped from the screen. Then it was gone.

Don't let it get in the engine! Paul prayed. *Just don't let it stop the car!*

Katie groaned. Her left arm spasmed, clawed at the air then fell on to Paul's arm. It stung as though he'd brushed against a jellyfish. Paul pushed her away.

The Alfa's remaining windows all rolled down. Their motors continued to screech after the glass was down as far as it would go and the smell of burning wiring hit Paul's nostrils. The Alfa's rear window cracked into frosted chips and fell into the back of the car.

Paul hit the throttle and took the car up to third gear.

The sprite flowed across the screen again and dipped down the Alfa's bonnet.

Katie gasped. A shower of tiny sea shells rained down on Paul from somewhere above his head.

'Katie?' he shouted.

The Alfa's engine began to labour.

It's under the bonnet! Paul's mind warned.

The car began to misfire, and Paul changed back down to second and hit the throttle hard. The Alfa picked up and rock-eted down the road, its headlights now flickering.

Something damp fell on to Paul's shoulder. He glanced down at it. It was a live crab. He flicked it away, his mind reeling. Surely none of this could be happening?

The car's headlights grew brilliant then flicked out.

Fuse gone, Paul thought crazily.

Lightning flickered and he saw something lying in the road a few hundred yards ahead of them: a dark shape which looked like a piece of tree trunk.

You ought to know what that is, Paul told himself, but it was gone now, and only remained in his eyes as an after-image. He was driving almost blind now. There was a flickering orange glow suffusing the rainy street but it was only dim and Paul's vision still had garish blue stripes across it from the lightning.

'Paul!' Katie said.

He turned to her as his hands and feet changed up a gear. The Alfa was picking up speed. A distant part of Paul hoped that the road ahead was as straight as it looked.

Katie's mouth was working and her arms and legs were jittering and clawing. A faint smell of vanilla was drifting from her. Paul didn't know what good she could do if she came back now. She might simply leap from the car to birth more sprites, for all he knew.

The Alfa's engine began to labour again and the car slowed rapidly.

It's got to run out of energy soon, Paul assured himself, but he doubted that there was any limit to the malformed sprite's power.

The sprite slipped out of the gap at the back of the bonnet and swept up the windscreen, blocking Paul's view with pitch darkness. The screen crazed. Paul hit the brakes.

'NUUUUHHH!' Katie screamed. And then her hand was reaching out for the windscreen where the sprite was plastered against it.

The glass fell away beneath her touch, showering down on Paul's legs in tiny burning scraps. When her fingers touched the sprite, it lit up in a rippling explosion of rainbow light and vanished. The Alfa's engine picked up.

Katie fell back against her seat, moaning.

'You okay?' Paul yelled. 'Sweetheart?'

'*Coming back*! *Hurts. Look out!*'

Paul heard a sound like material tearing, then distant lightning flickered and he saw the thing in the road again. This time he realised what it was. It was a burning man. A burning man who was pointing a rifle at him.

4

Pieces of Enrico Spagnol were alight. This fact did not interest him and he realised it only distantly. He didn't know how it had happened, only that it was to do with Dekker and the girl Kate. Hot things had fallen on him and in spite of the driving rain, those things had set fire to his clothing. But Enrico was a weapon now and could not feel the pain. He would hurt later, but later wasn't a word that currently held any meaning for him either. He was here and he was now. A machine with a single purpose. Stillness and aim.

The car had been in his sights for more than two hundred yards. The things that had happened to it while it came towards him were of no interest except in terms of how they affected his sighting. Once or twice Enrico had seen something dark pass over the car, as if pieces of it were simply vanishing and reappearing. The passenger door had left the car as if it had been blown off with explosives and the car had skidded across the road, but Enrico had swung with it, matching its movements.

Now, just as the car reached the point where he had intended to shoot, the dark shadow across the windscreen burst into a million points of shimmering light and vanished.

In the back of his mind, Enrico heard the girl scream and received a simple message across the disciples' mental network that informed him that H had taken a setback and lost control.

Enrico was on his own.

In the following two seconds, his telepathic connection with the other disciples was severed and his mind started to peel itself away from the rifle, allowing his body to report the pain it was experiencing. And the pain was horrendous. His hair was smouldering, his back and legs were burning and the right sleeve of his jacket was on fire.

With a supreme effort Enrico forced his mind back towards the cool steel of the gun, because those two people in the Alfa that was coming towards him were responsible for all this. And once they were gone there would be no pain. Once he put them out of the world's misery, a new age could begin.

Enrico found the optimum spot on the Alfa's windscreen, held the gun there and pulled the trigger. The rifle barked like a surprised dog and jerked back into his shoulder. The Alfa's screen shattered. Enrico's hands worked the bolt, expelling the cartridge and popping another into the chamber. The Alfa slewed off to one side, skidded off a wall and came down the street towards him. Enrico put the second slug in exactly the same place as the car steadied. If the first shot hadn't blown off Dekker's head, the second surely had. All he was going to have to do now was wait until the car turned over or stoved itself into the wall, then make sure the girl was finished too.

Watching the car heading towards him, and fully expecting it to stop long before it hit him, Enrico Spagnol rolled over, extinguishing the fires on his body, and got to his feet.

5

Kate came back at the exact moment that Paul realised the burning man lying in the street was aiming a gun at him.

She arrived back in her body in a flash of light that Paul saw inside his skull rather than with his eyes, a noise that threatened to shred the auditory part of his brain, and she was accompanied by a shower of freezing pebbles and a cold shockwave that hit Paul just to the left of his navel.

'Paul!' she shouted.

And Paul screamed. The flesh where the force hit him instantly became a mass of seething pain. His shirt had been ripped and an area to the left of his midriff had swollen to the size of an orange. It was bleeding horribly as it tore apart. Paul doubled over, clapping both his hands to the site. Pain lanced his fingers and he tore them away again, distantly aware that he was no longer driving the car and that it was surely headed towards a wall. This didn't matter. Nothing mattered except that swollen ball of seething flesh. Because he knew what the trouble was now. When Katie had come back, she had drawn more with her than a shower of pebbles. She had brought back all the pins and needles that had existed in Margherita de Savoia and they had materialised, not above his head, but in a ball beneath his flesh. And now those slender and pointed pieces of steel were bursting their way out of him again, tearing at his flesh like living things.

Above his head, the windscreen exploded and a bullet zinged through the car, hitting metal and whining as it exited through the gap where the Alfa's rear window had been. Paul barely noticed it.

Katie screamed again and both her hands closed around the ball of spikes in Paul's midriff. Paul's pain grew to a screaming brilliance as she touched him.

The Alfa jolted up a kerb, skated along a wall which tore into its metalwork, bounced off and jolted back down into the road. Another shot ricocheted through the car.

Katie's fingers sank into Paul's flesh. Paul's vision turned white.

And then the pain was gone.

He tried to sit up and couldn't. Above him, Katie had hold of the wheel. 'Hit the gas!' she shouted. 'Quick!'

Paul stuck out his right foot, jolted the brake pedal then found the accelerator. The car shot forward, hit something with the metallic *thock!* noise which Paul knew so well, then jolted twice as first the front wheels ran over it, then the back wheels followed.

'Brakes!' Katie said.

Paul hit the brake hard and kept it there until the Alfa came to a juddering halt and its engine stalled.

'I'm sorry!' Katie sobbed. 'I'm so sorry, Paul!'

Paul pulled himself up and looked at the site of the damage. His shirt was ripped to shreds and covered in blood around the area, but his flesh was smooth and unbroken. It felt a little sore when he touched it but seemed otherwise okay.

'I didn't mean to bring that stuff,' Katie said. 'I don't know how it happened. I sent it back where it came from.' She shook her head and shrugged then added, 'I think.'

Paul glanced at her. 'Welcome back,' he said, turning to look over his shoulder. His midriff ached when he moved. The bulge in the road about fifty feet behind him was one of H's guys. That much was certain. Another certain thing was that he wasn't yet dead. His arms and legs were moving as burning debris showered down on him.

Can you? Paul's goad asked him. Paul thought he could.

He took the car out of gear and turned the ignition key. The Alfa's engine started. Its idle was rough, but at least it was running.

'He's one of them, isn't he?' he asked.

Katie nodded. 'Four following still,' she said. 'Not far behind.'

Paul selected reverse, dropped the clutch, swung the wheel hard round and applied the clutch and handbrake. The Alfa skidded round through a hundred and eighty degrees. Hell was burning in Margherita.

'We haven't got much time,' Katie said.

'I know,' Paul replied, putting the Alfa into first and dropping the clutch.

The car rapidly closed on the damaged man and Paul braced himself for the impact.

6

Afterwards, Paul went back and looked. This was one man who wasn't going to bleed black stuff and come back to life. His head was crushed beyond restitution. He gazed at the elongated, squashed skull for a few seconds, brushing pieces of burning ash from his hair and shirt, then he turned and looked back at Margherita de Savoia. There was burning lava spurting from the volcano, there was thick ash falling like snow, there were clouds of smoke and steam and there was darkness.

Feeling cold, and very old and tired, Paul went back to the car, got in and began to drive.

Chapter Twenty-Five
Jake and Double A, Fighting Back

1

When Double A woke up it was daylight outside the speeding Pop. He didn't know if it was the same day as he and Jake had killed two people or another day entirely. That episode seemed distant, as if it were something he'd dreamed about a week earlier. In fact, when you stopped to think about it, the whole shooting match seemed like a bad dream. He felt as if he'd been travelling in this noisy car almost all of his life.

The inability to think straight upon waking was nothing new to Double A and there was a tried and tested method of curing this problem. One that he adhered to whenever possible. All you had to do was shove something white up your snout and your mind would become amazingly clear. He felt in his pocket for one of the bags of speed, then looked stupidly at his hand when it returned empty. *Mission unsuccessful!* his grubby fingers reported. This was impossible.

The window was open on his side of the car. The breeze coming in at him was hot, and Double A suddenly realised he was drenched in sweat. He peered out at the landscape. The last thing he remembered being outside the car was mountains and tunnels. This looked more like England. Hampshire, perhaps. Weild, where his grandparents had lived, looked rather like this. *Except that it didn't get quite this warm*, he told himself as he wormed his right hand beneath the waistband of his jeans. If the dope wasn't in his pocket, it must

620

be down his underpants keeping his balls company.

But neither of the bags was there either.

The Pop shot by a filling station which, according to the signs, sold a brand of petrol called Agip. This was a new one on Mrs Anthony's boy. A sign just after the service area claimed that Rimini was forty-five kilometres away. Huge stiff cogs inside Double A's brain started to turn. One of his girlfriends had gone to Rimini on holiday once. He was pretty certain that this particular part of Italy was called the Adriatic coast. And according to the map they'd bought, the Adriatic was the sea on the right-hand side of Italy whereas Naples was on the left.

Wondering about this, and beginning to panic about his speed, Double A searched all the other places he might have put the bags. Then he searched them all again. 'Jake,' he finally said, *where's my speed?*'

Jake glanced over at him. His face was pale and drawn. 'Bang, you're dead!' he said. 'Bang bang. You're dead. Don't talk. Dead men don't talk!'

'My *speed*,' Double A said, his mind whirling. Something was terribly wrong with Jake but he didn't think he could apply his mind to the problem without first kick-starting it with some of the white stuff.

'I'm fighting,' Jake said – apparently to himself. 'You caught me and now I've got a hold on you too. I won't let you go! *Christ*, it hurts, chicken. Don't talk to Anthony, Anthony's dead.'

'Speed!' Double A whined.

'Gone! All gone!' Jake half screamed. 'Like the guy in the Audi who was chasing us. I'm hanging on! I won't let the bastard stop me!'

Double A couldn't take any of this in. 'What's *wrong?*' he asked desperately.

Jake turned and grinned at him. His eyes were glassy and his face was so pale it was almost translucent. His nostrils were ringed with white powder. He screwed up his face in what would have been a comical parody of concentration under different circumstances – here it was chilling. 'I don't know what's real and what ain't any more. Sorry, chicken, he's got me. Can't think. You're supposed to be dead. I'm trying to fight him.'

'Who? What are you on about?' Double A screeched, almost beside himself. He thought he was beginning to understand and he badly wanted to be wrong. It wasn't merely the fact that Jake had been keeping himself awake with God knew how much speed and had come apart under the strain. It was worse. Much worse.

'The fucking radar man!' Jake said. 'He kept sweeping for us with this . . . it's like a radar beam that goes through you and when they touch you with it, you know that they know where you are. And he found me and put himself inside my head and – *oh, Christ, it hurts!* I gotta hang on. He wants to go, but I gotta keep him in my head.'

Jake drew a deep, shuddering gasp of air. 'I won't,' he breathed.

'Jake! What's happening?' Double A demanded.

'Catch twenty-three,' Jake groaned. 'You're dead and I've still got to kill you. I won't do it. I'm pressing down on him. I got him pinned.'

'Stop the car!' Double A shouted.

'I ain't gone mad, ducks,' Jake said. He took his foot from the accelerator and the car began to slow. 'I won't hurt you.'

'Okay,' Double A said, sounding a good deal more confident than he felt. He had experienced that strange sensation of being searched for himself, back in Switzerland, and had managed to draw himself away from the beam. Whoever was sending it – and that didn't take very much working out, even when your mind was as muddy as his currently was – had hooked Jake and now he was battling for control of his own mind. The good news was that this had been going on while Double A was asleep and Jake hadn't hurt him yet. The bad news was that he didn't expect this to continue for long. The guy trying

622

to do Jake's thinking for him had already told him that Double A was dead and Jake half believed it.

'It's all wrong,' Jake moaned. His voice sounded a little more like his own now. Double A tensed as his foot hit the accelerator again.

'I thought we were stopping, Jake,' he said.

Jake glanced over at him as though surprised to find him still in the car. 'I got him pinned,' he grunted. 'No time to stop. Late. Don't panic.'

'I want to get out of the car,' Double A said, hearing the fear in his voice. 'I've got to take a leak.'

'He says you're dead,' Jake said. The Pop was getting faster.

Double A's mind was spinning. 'I'm not dead,' he said, 'and I have to piss.'

'The radar man says you're dead,' Jake said. 'I got lost after we got through into Italy.' He sounded as if he were ashamed of it. 'We went to a place called Genova and it started to rain. Ain't never seen rain like it. Couldn't see out the window. Traffic on all sides going mad. I couldn't find my way out again. Not for a long time. I tried to wake you up and you wouldn't come awake. He said you were dead. Help me, chicken, I don't know what's what any more.'

'Stop the car and I'll help you,' Double A said. 'Please, Jake.'

'I don't wanna hurt you,' Jake said. His foot lifted off the accelerator and the car began to slow again.

'You promise you'll help me?' Jake asked.

'Yes,' Double A said, with as much certainty as he could muster. But he didn't think there was anything he could do and his paranoia was already presenting him with a plan which went along the lines of: *Find an excuse to get him out of the car, then drive away without him.*

Jake shook his head. 'No, it's too late. We ain't gonna do it. I can't grind the fucker down. I'm too tired and he's there all the time, yakking and jabbering. And you know what? *I think he's me.*'

'Could I have my coke, please?' Double A said. He couldn't

think straight and he was aching for a snort. One good blast would clear his sleep-befuddled mind and perhaps allow him to make sense of everything.

Jake shook his head. 'Gone,' he said, 'threw it out the car before the Italian border.'

For a moment Double A felt as though he had been slapped by a huge icy hand. He had often used the word 'mortified' and now he knew its true meaning. There had been enough speed in those bags to keep him high until Christmas and Jake had tossed it out of the car – presumably in case the customs people wanted to search them. He couldn't believe this had happened, not even in the crazy world he had been flung into. Then he remembered the rings of powder around Jake's nostrils and something twanged inside his head like a rubber band. In the following moment he could have shot Jake, and probably would have if there had been a gun in his hand. Jake still had the coke and he didn't intend to give it back. A white rage lit behind his eyes. 'No, you didn't, you lying bastard,' he shouted, *'you've been shoving it up your nose!'*

'Don't upset me, chicken,' Jake softly. This was the tone he used when he wanted to scare people. It seldom failed to get the desired result.

Double A's righteous rage left him in an instant, like a light bulb that has blown. Fear flooded in to fill the vacuum. Jake *had* gone crazy. The car was still moving at around thirty miles an hour, which wasn't quite the speed Double A would have preferred to make the jump out, but he would go for it anyway, if it became necessary. Double A got ready to jump. His right-hand fingers closed around the doorhandle.

'GET OUTTA MY FUCKING HEAD!' Jake shouted. 'MAKE HIM JUMP! MAKE HIM JUMP! NO, I WON'T MAKE HIM JUMP, YOU CUNT, HE'S MY FRIEND! DON'T!'

Double A drew away from him, pressing himself against the door. He was going to be injured if he got out, and he was going to roll down the carriageway, not the verge, because they were driving on the wrong side of the road and his door opened on to the fast lane.

'I ain't gone mad, chicken,' Jake hissed. 'He's getting me again. Help me!'

'What can I do?' Double A pleaded.

'DON'T!' Jake shouted. His left hand shot under the dash and came out clutching one of Double A's plastic bags of speed. There was cocaine in this one. Jake glanced over at Double A, his face blank, pulled the bag open, thrust it to his nose and snorted in a deep breath.

Then the bag was falling into his lap and his fist was clenching. Double A watched in horror as several hundred pounds' worth of cocaine spilled from the bag. An eye-blink later, Jake's left fist stove into his ribs. It felt as if a grenade had exploded there. It hurt like a bastard. Double A wanted to scream, but didn't have any breath; he wanted to dive out of the car, but his energy had all been sapped by the single snapping blow to his ribs.

'I WON'T!' Jake screamed, his voice breaking. His fist wavered in the air, as though he was trying to stop himself using it again.

Double A turned as the next blow came towards him and this one hit his shoulder. It hurt almost as much. *Just keep your face out of his way*, Double A's mind was screaming, *because he's killed two people just by punching them on the jaw.*

Double A caught the next punch Jake threw and held on to Jake's fist with both his hands while he tried to pull away. Jake was tremendously strong and Double A was yanked out of his seat and across towards Jake. He was distantly surprised to see that tears were streaming down the man's face.

'I can't stop,' Jake moaned.

And Double A surprised himself again. He let go of Jake's big fist and swiped out at his agonised face with the flat of his palm. The blow was clumsy. It hit Jake over the nose and open mouth and didn't so much make a sharp slapping noise as a gentle pop as it came away from his lips. Jake's nose began to bleed instantly and a bead of blood bloomed on his bottom lip.

His face rearranged itself into an expression of horrified surprise.

Double A slapped him again. 'Stop the car!' he shouted, pulling himself away.

And to his surprise, Jake pulled on to the hard shoulder and let the Pop roll to a halt.

Double A leapt from the car at the same instant that Jake threw himself out of the driver's door. He started into the road and a Fiat shot by, its horn giving a remarkable example of the Doppler effect at work as it sped by. Double A glanced down the long two-lane carriageway, saw that he wasn't going to get across in one piece for a good long while yet, and decided to leg it down the hard-shoulder. He glanced to where he thought Jake would be running round the car for him and was surprised to see Jake, not coming at him at all, but leaping over the fence at the side of the hard-shoulder and into a field.

Double A watched in stunned disbelief as Jake ran right into the middle of the huge field of ripening corn and threw himself to the ground. He was now hidden from view by the corn. Double A watched the spot where he'd fallen, because his paranoia was busy suggesting that Jake might be crawling back through the long crop on all fours, but there was no movement which suggested this was happening. After a few seconds Jake began to shout again, giving his position away.

Double A listened to him for a few seconds, then went back to the car.

2

Things didn't begin to fall into place for Double A until after he'd snorted a couple of hefty nostrils full of cocaine. He'd gone back to the car with the simple intention of whacking himself into the driver's seat, starting the engine and high-tailing it out of there before Jake had a chance to come back and kill him. And if it hadn't been for Double A's deeply ingrained thrifty nature, which was the result of having lived most of his life without having two coins to rub together, this was exactly what would have happened.

But the moment Double A yanked the door open and saw all that snort lying on the seat, the avaricious side of him kicked in and he knew he wouldn't be able to drive away until he'd scooped up what he could and put it back into the bag from which it was spilling. There was also the contributory factor to be considered that his mind and body were screaming out for a good hit.

Double A checked on Jake, who was still lying in the field shouting unintelligibly, gauged that he had a little time left to play with and set about scraping the powder back into the bag. When that was done, he put his nose to the fabric of the seat and snorted, like a dog who has detected a very interesting smell. While he was hoovering the remaining powder from the seat where Jake had spent the last twenty odd hours sitting and sweating, he *did* detect some odours – all noxious. Double A didn't think about them and when the scattered powder was almost all gone, he threw another couple of heaps up his nose from the bag to drive those bad smells away.

He sealed and folded the bag and put it back in his pocket, already feeling chipper and letting his mind rev itself up a few notches. Soon, its dumb tickover would become a smooth purr. While he was waiting for that to happen, he got the crowbar from the back seat in case Jake came thundering back.

And as the banks of ready lights in his brain finally began to flicker and light, Double A began to make things fit together. Jake had shouted that he wouldn't 'make him jump' because he was his friend. Which suddenly seemed to suggest that Jake wasn't just rambling after having blown his mind away with an excess of speed, but that he was answering a command someone had given him. Jake had also yelled that he 'couldn't get the fucker out', and that he was 'there all the time yakking and jabbering'.

And he was on about the radar sweeping round so they know where you are, Double A's mind told him. *Funny how you can't put two and two together unless you goose your nervous system with something chemical, isn't it? Soon, you won't be able to function without it.*

But Double A – who now knew that Jake had been mentally ensnared by the bad guys who had fastened on to him with that psychic radar beam – knew better than the voice of his conscience: he was *already* unable to function without being artificially perked up. A warm trickle of blood ran from his right nostril and Double A sniffed it back up. He didn't know how long he was going to be able to continue to live at this pace, but he would damn well make sure that it was until this little escapade was all over. Somewhere in this country Paul Dekker was fighting to keep a girl from the baddies. *The* girl. The one Double A had been offered in return for betraying Jake. The girl was special – he didn't know how or why – but that dream had been enough to convince him. If there was any way little Double A could prevent them from getting her, he would do it. Which left him with a brain-teaser to consider.

Out there in the middle of that field, Jake was lying on his back hollering at the thing inside his head. Double A could now drive away without him . . . which might be exactly what the baddies wanted him to do. On the other hand, he could think of no course of action he could take to help Jake shake the thing out of his head – and if he just hung around waiting for Jake to do it on his own, he might be endangering his own life, because Jake might attack and kill him. Or another of the bad guys might show up. Or nothing might happen at all, except that vital time was wasted, making him too late to meet Paul and the girl. They were already headed towards the wrong coast for Naples.

Double A got the map he'd bought in the service area in Switzerland and unfolded it with trembling hands, while he rolled the problem over in his head, searching for its weak point.

The problem was seamless. Any course of action might be damning, as damning as doing nothing was going to be. And according to the map, they were indeed on the wrong road for Naples. Jake had been heading in the right direction last night if what he'd said about being lost in a place called Genova was true. Since then they'd come all the way back across the top of Italy and were now approaching the Adriatic coast.

So what do I do? Double A asked himself, sniffing back another trickle of blood. He wished he had some gum. It wouldn't have helped him concentrate, but it might have given his suddenly lively jaws something else to chew upon other than the insides of his cheeks.

'GET OUT GET OUT GET OUT!' Jake screamed from across the field.

Double A folded the map – in all the wrong directions – threw it into the back seat of the car and got out, badly wanting to do something and not knowing what. There was a large scrape all down the driver's side of the Pop that he hadn't noticed until now. It looked as if Jake had shunted another car off the road last night just like he'd claimed.

Double A fingered the deep dents in the Pop's bodywork, half his mind calculating the repair procedures and costs while the rest of his mind wrestled with the problem of what to do next. If it were a movie, Double A would get the urge to run to Jake, tug him upright and shout into his face that he had to come back because Double A loved him. The bit about love would do the trick – it always worked in films. Double A imagined himself shouting, 'I love you, man!' into Jake's distant eyes. In a way it was true. The urge to put this into action was almost irresistible, but Double A fought it off. It was too sappy to work in real life. Real life was pretty good at fending off declarations of love and friendship. Jake would probably whack him in the jaw and kill him, without even realising he was doing it. Exit one speed freak.

The idea that rose afterwards was equally as appealing, but it presented difficulties of its own. Double A grinned grimly. This one fitted into the dog-eat-dog reality which precluded declarations of love. This one would work – if he could only get Jake to chase him.

Double A set the crowbar down on top of the Pop, leapt the low fence and strode out across the field.

Jake was on his arched back in the centre of a flattened patch of corn. Looking at him filled Double A with cold fear.

Jake's legs were under him, pushing his hips into the air as if he was fucking an invisible woman who stood astride him. His face was white and sheened with sweat. He was pulling a variety of expressions that wouldn't have looked out of place on a gargoyle. His lips writhed like two small injured snakes, trying to wriggle away to safety. His fingers were tearing at the corn. He looked like a man who had swallowed a good dose of strychnine.

Or snorted, Double A's paranoia chipped in. *Perhaps you were right about the hot shot old Reuben had arranged for you. What if they buried the bad stuff beneath the good in those plastic bags? What if Jake got down to the poison?*

Double A cut the thought off, because if Jake *had* got down to the poison, his little friend was shortly going to be lying beside him doing the same convulsive dance of death.

'Jake!' he shouted.

'Get off me!' Jake moaned.

Double A drew a deep breath. 'Get up, you motherfucker!' he shouted. 'Stand up! Stand up and hit me, you coward. Where's your killer instinct now? Come after me!'

'Hurts!' Jake moaned, twisting his hips and falling to the ground on his side. He began to bend backwards, arching his back further than Double A would have believed possible. He fully expected to hear Jake's spine snap at any moment. His little plan didn't look as if it was going to work after all. He was just going to stand here and yell at Jake while Jake died.

Double A danced from foot to foot with frustration. 'Jake!' he shouted in desperation. 'I love you, man!'

The big Hollywood scene did not follow. Jake merely bent backwards a little further while his face did a passable impression of Popeye.

Double A's whirring mind threw up another idea for him to

consider. That idea was that the thing you first thought of was usually the right thing and everything else was bullshit. Therefore, Jake was not dying of strychnine poisoning at all, but dying of fighting something that was inside his head, trying to vanquish his mind and take control of his body.

So what? Double A screamed at himself.

If Double A had a muse – and unless there was one of the hitherto unknown variety *car fixer* he seriously doubted it – it chose this moment to shit all over his head. Double A had been inspired before. Usually it was the type of inspiration that told him that three more rum and blacks poured down the throat of this girl would see him getting laid tonight, but this was different. It hit him like a hot shower and a part of him knew that this was not shit but gold.

So make Jake throw in the towel. Stop him resisting!

It was so simple a moron could have thought of it. The trouble with logic was that when you were coked to the max it went out of the window and left you groping for things that ought to have been obvious. Like what he ought to shout at the thing trying to take Jake over.

'I'm taking him back now,' Double A announced, uncertainly. 'You can just piss off, you second-rate shithouse,' he added, gaining confidence and ignoring the part of him that was insisting he was crazy for shouting at a dying man when he should have been helping him to stay alive. He *was* helping Jake stay alive. The first thing he'd thought of was the right one.

Jake writhed on the ground, groaning.

'You bastards can't win,' Double A said, suddenly finding his mouth full of words. He let them run. 'You don't know what you're up against here. We've already killed off three of your goons. Some of them two or three times. You keep sending 'em, we'll keep mowing 'em down. Send 'em dead or send 'em alive, it's all the same to us. You just keep sending 'em. Except you're running low now, aren't you? How many more do you have, big guy? Not as many as you need, do you? You're outnumbered now and me and Dekker and Jake are coming after you. I won't stop even if you get the others. I'll be out there and I'll be coming for you. And as you well know, little Double A is bad news.'

Double A listened to himself saying all this and realised it wouldn't fool a little old lady. The strange thing was the more words that tripped off his tongue, the greater his own belief in himself became. By the time he'd declared that he was *bad news*, he could see himself tracking down the baddies in the Pop and squashing them, one by one.

'And I'll tell you something else, shithouse, if you don't get out of Jake's head, I'm going to make you sorry, because I'm going to hurt Jake now and I think that you'll feel that hurt too!'

'Don't, chicken!' Jake said in a strangled sob. His eyes were rolled up so far Double A could only see the whites.

Double A walked around to the front of Jake and kicked him hard in his taut belly. Jake hissed in pain. 'I'm fighting!' he said. 'I'm fighting him!'

'Let him have you,' Double A said. 'Stop fighting him. Let him take you!' He kicked Jake again, in the balls this time. Jake squealed. 'Lose the battle and win the war, Jake. Understand?'

And as Double A aimed another kick at him, Jake went limp.

He's dead! Double A's paranoia informed him, but he knew this was not the case. He didn't know whether Jake had understood or not, but it didn't matter now – he had finally caved in under the onslaught. The thing inside him now had his mind. And just as he had anticipated that thing was angry.

Double A grinned as the lights came back on in Jake's eyes and he sat up, roaring.

Jake had been fighting to stop himself hurting his friend and he wouldn't have chased Double A back across the field to the car while there was still a breath left in him. But the thing driving him would.

Which was exactly what Double A wanted. He could have brought the crowbar and knocked Jake unconscious here, but he wouldn't have been able to drag him back to the car. This way, all he had to do was keep clear of Jake until he got back to the road . . . and then let him have it.

Worry about that when we get to it, he told himself as Jake lumbered to his feet. 'Come on then, sucker, let's see what you can do!' Double A shouted. Jake charged forward, but unlike Double A, he was not a man built for speed and grace. His clumsiness was legendary. Double A leapt aside and Jake fell headlong into the grass.

'Get up, fucker!' Double A shouted, and this time left it a little longer before he began to run. Jake was no match for him. By the time the big man fell again, they were fifty yards closer to the car.

Jake picked himself up again as Double A danced in the corn in front of him. He trotted slowly forwards, fists swinging, and Double A bobbed and weaved before him, dodging slow punches as he backed away, drawing Jake ever closer to the fence.

Jake began to find his stride while they were still fifty feet away from the car. His blows were getting sharper and his movements more fluid. Double A twice found himself a whisker away from stopping one of Jake's killer blows with his jaw.

Fucking thing wants to kill me so bad, it doesn't realise where I'm taking it! Double A thought. *That's because it knows it's gonna stop you before you get to where you wanna go*, his paranoia told him.

Overconfident, Double A told himself, ducking a haymaker right. Then he found out that Jake wasn't the only one whose confidence level was too high. He didn't see the left jab that followed the sweeping right at all. But he felt it as he fell to the ground. It felt as if someone had injected quick drying concrete into his stomach and lungs. His breath was gone, there was no way of drawing another and the concrete was crushing the rest of his internal organs as it set.

Jake bent over him, clearly intending to hit him while he was down. Double A rolled away. Jake stepped forward and one of his fists flashed down and hit Double A's bony right shoulder. The pain was tremendous. Double A found his breath, rolled away again twice, gasping as his shoulder hit the ground, then pushed himself up into a sprint-start position and ran. The punch that hit his pelvis as he rocketed forward didn't so much hurt as provide a little extra acceleration.

When he thought he was a safe distance away, Double A turned. Jake was still lumbering after him, moving like a machine.

'Come on, fucker, that didn't hurt!' Double A lied. The fence was behind him now. When Jake was close enough, Mrs Anthony's boy leapt over the fence and leaned against the door of the Pop, waiting for Jake.

'I'm going to kill you,' Jake said when he arrived at the fence. The voice was angry. It did not belong to Jake.

'You the guy with the fucking radar beam?' Double A asked, trying to appear nonchalant. It was difficult when all you wanted to do was scream in pain. He distantly congratulated himself on doing a passable job, if not a good one.

Jake paused at the fence. 'Dekker's dead,' he said.

Double A nodded sagely. 'And where's the girl?' he asked. 'You've got her too, I suppose?'

Jake didn't reply, merely started to climb the fence.

'Let me tell you this, sunshine,' Double A said, ignoring his mind which was screaming at him to get the crowbar and let Jake have it before he got over the fence, 'Dekker is not dead and you don't have the girl. If you did you wouldn't be bothering with me and Jake. If you'd won, you wouldn't be trying to stop us.'

'Dekker's dead,' Jake said, jumping down from the fence and landing heavily on his feet. He stumbled and caught himself. 'And so are you,' he added.

Double A waited for it, his heart hammering in his ears and his fingers twitching. He had used this modus operandi on Reuben and the guy who was driving Jake ought to know about it. Perhaps he did. Or perhaps he didn't. Double A had another idea. Today was his day for being inspired apparently.

'Who are you?' Double A asked.

'Jake,' Jake said.

'Really,' Double A said. 'Who are you *really*? Just tell me who you are before you kill me.'

Jake frowned. 'I'm Jake,' he said in the other guy's voice.

Double A nodded slowly. Jake had fought back and fought back well. The other guy – the mental domination specialist with the psychic radar – had taken some damage. He wasn't sure about his own personality.

'Who else?' Double A asked. 'You're someone else too, aren't you?'

Jake took a hesitant step towards him, his face clouding. 'Jake?' he said.

'I think you're fucked, sunshine. Old Jake's hurt you, hasn't he?'

Jake shook his head as though he'd just said the wrong thing and knew it. 'No,' he said, thoughtfully. Then his face cleared. 'I'm Gary. Gary Richman.'

At which point Double A snatched the crowbar from the roof of the car and hit Jake across the crown of his head. 'Go home, Gary!' he yelled as Jake collapsed.

4

For a few seconds Double A stared down at Jake thinking, *What have I done?* because Jake had fallen like a man with no bones and hadn't moved since. Then he heaved in a breath and Double A relaxed.

Getting him back into the car wasn't easy. Jake weighed upwards of fourteen stone and Double A around eight. To compound the problem, Double A was going to have to get him into the passenger's seat through the driver's side because carrying him round to the other side of the car was going to be impossible. He tried feeding Jake's legs into the car first, then lifting his body, and when he found he wasn't strong enough, sat Jake down with his back to the door, got in the car, took him under the armpits and heaved him in, bracing his legs against the door frame. It was slow and Double A's injuries stuck him like knives, but eventually Jake's arse made contact with the seat. Double A rested for a while, then heaved him across into the passenger's seat, wriggled out from beneath him, got out of the passenger's door, went round the car and pushed Jake's limp legs off the driver's seat and into the footwell on the other side, finally twisting him round into a sitting position. He put Jake's seatbelt around him, fastened it, then climbed wearily back into the driver's seat of the Pop and started it up.

He treated himself to some sulphate when he found it under the dash, then drove away.

5

'Where are we?'

Double A turned towards Jake. They had been driving for less than five minutes and he had expected Jake to remain unconscious for some time. 'What?' he said, surprised.

'Where are we now?' Jake asked, his voice urgent. 'Are we going the right way?'

Double A shook his head. 'No, we're going the wrong way. I'm looking for an exit off this motorway so we can turn round. This ain't the way to Naples.'

'We ain't going to Naples no more, chicken,' Jake said. 'This is right. If you haven't turned off, this is right.'

'This goes to Rimini!'

'That's where we're meeting Paul.'

'Naples, surely?' Double A complained.

Jake shook his head and winced. 'Not now. *Rimini*. Did you have to hit me so hard, chick?' he added, fingering his head.

Double A glanced across at him. He didn't look any the worse for his tap on the head with the crowbar or the kicks he'd collected in his stomach. There wasn't even any blood on him. 'What happened?' Double A asked. 'You didn't tell me.'

Jake sighed. 'That fucking radar beam thing found me last night,' he said. 'I'd got down to that Genova place and it started pouring with rain and there were cars every-fucking-where and it just hit me. I'd already felt it sweep past me a couple of times and I kinda ducked it somehow. It was like I knew it was looking for me and I pulled away from it. Get me?'

Double A did get him. He told Jake about his own experiences back in Switzerland.

Jake nodded. 'Same thing,' he said. 'Got any more of that supercharged snuff, chicken? I couldn't half do with a sniff.'

Double A handed him the bag of cocaine, told him not to overdo it and cursed himself for sounding like his own mother.

Jake snorted some of the coke, about as clumsily as he did everything else. Some went up his nose; most fell between his legs. He sneezed three times, wiped his nose and announced that he felt better. 'So there I am, in this place in the rain, and this guy latches on to my mind. I get this terrible scraping feeling inside my skull like someone's at it in there with a rasp, then I get a picture of him sitting in a country lane in a Bentley, his fingers pressed to his temples like he's got a headache. Then the next minute the bastard is inside my head, talking to me like he's on the phone. And everything he says sounds true. I won't tell you some of the things he said, but they were all scary. Then he tells me I'm going to lose my sense of direction and it's like I'm hypnotised or something. The moment he says it, that's what happens. Then he goes quiet, but I can feel him up there in my head, sniggering as he watches me go round and round in circles trying to get out of that fucking place. If I'd had that gun, I would have pulled up and blown out my fucking brain, just to get rid of him. It was horrible, chicken.'

'What happened after that?' Double A asked. Rimini was now only twenty-five kilometres away and getting closer every second. Double A had a bad feeling about it. He thought Gary Richman would be putting in another appearance when they arrived. Either that or they would meet Paul Dekker and the girl, and the moment they all came face to face there would be a big surge of electricity or something and they would all be zapped away, like bugs in an electric pest killer.

'Next thing I know it's dark and I'm on this winding little road with the sea on my right. I know I'm going in the right direction because that sea is where it's supposed to be. This little road went up through some high hills and there was this sheer drop down to the sea. A couple of hundred feet or so. And I thought, "Christ, Jake, you don't wanna get too close to the edge here or you'll go right over." And this fucker in my mind pipes up and says, "That's exactly what's going to happen to you, Jake."

'And then this car is coming up behind me. It's an Audi Quattro. I don't know how I knew; he might have told me or something. The guy that's driving it is one of *them* – he might have told me that too, but I know anyway. I even know the guy's name: Roger Graham. I know all about him. He's an intelligence officer in the forces and he's gone AWOL to fight a war he thinks is more important than any war that's ever been fought so far. He's left his wife. Her name is Derry. This guy has driven all the way down here to kill me and you and to take the car out. I know all this the moment I see his lights in the mirror, and then my guy starts telling me all the things I have to do to avoid being killed and I know all of them are wrong but I start doing them. Then I get it back for a second. I kinda started fighting, y'know, with my mind. I was fighting for my life. For our lives.

'And the Quattro comes alongside us on the wrong side of the road and I know it's gonna try and poke us off the edge so I hit the brakes, hard. They're some fucking anchors you put on this babe, chick. Nearly went over the fucking handlebars! And the Quattro pulls in in front and lays on his brakes, but he's slower to stop than us, and then I'm in the wrong lane with him on the outside, closest to the drop, and I keep him there. He brakes, I brake. He accelerates, I match him. Move for move. And the guy inside my skull is screaming and I'm starting to see things in the road ahead. Lights coming towards me. Big holes in the road. And although I can see 'em a part of me is going: "They ain't there, Jake!" So I keep driving and I'm hitting them and they aren't there and it's like my brain is being tore apart from the inside.

'Then we're on this hairpin bend and the guy in my head

tells me that if I try to put him over the edge here, then I'm going over with him, and a part of me knows it's the critical moment so I slam over into him and he goes. Just like that. Through the barrier and over the edge. Goodbye, Roger Graham. The guy in my head is insane with rage now and I send out a thought telling him that he's got one less goon to chase us with now and I know this one ain't coming back, 'cause he bites down on my mind like his teeth are inside my head. Fucking *hurt!*' Jake shook his head.

'Then what?' Double A thought he knew the rest. Jake had started to cram speed up his nose in an attempt to stop the pain and rid himself of his mental passenger.

'Then I suddenly realise we ain't gotta go to Naples any more. There's a change in their plans. I picked it up from matey-boy in my skull. They stopped Paul getting to Naples and took him somewhere on the east coast. It was one of their main places or something. They had a good chance if they took him there, but he came away from it. I knew that. I picked it up. And do you know what else?'

Double A shook his head.

'He took another one of 'em out down there. I felt the guy go. It was like a steel cable stretching inside of me and then snapping. I felt Paul kill one of 'em!' he said proudly. 'And then the guy in my head starts talking to me, softly, and he's telling me how good things could be if I was to do the dirty on you, chicken.'

'Kill me?' Double A said.

'I wouldn't do it. I get to this place called La Spezia and there's this road called the S63 which goes to a place called Reggio and I sent this guy a thought saying, I dunno if this road is the right one to where I wanna go, but I'm taking it and you can't stop me. Then I stop and pull your bags of dope out of your underwear and tamp two thumbs full up my nostrils, because I know it's going to be a long night and the guy is going, "Right you are, Jake, you take this road," and I know it's a double bluff – he's telling me to take it because he thinks if he says to, I won't. So I do. Get me?'

639

Double A nodded. A sign said that there were only twenty kilometres to Rimini. And then the fun was going to start in earnest. He was getting a distinct feeling that none of their little band was ever going to see England again, whether or not they outweighed the opposition. The bad guys were going to be saving their best until last. He was certain of that. He was also certain that if Gary Richman found his way into *his* skull he wouldn't be able to handle it like Jake had. 'Then what?' he asked.

'I can't tell you some of the things I saw and heard while I was driving along that winding mountain road. Visions, they were. Stuff that's gonna happen if they get that Katie back. Her name's Katie, the girl Paul's trying to get back to England. I'll tell you this though, chick, if we don't come out of this lot on top, we'll be better off out of it. And all the while this guy is trying to make me push you out of the car and I'm fighting it. After that it's hazy. I remember telling you I'd dumped the supercharged snuff because I wanted to keep it to myself and after that all I remember is pain and you shouting and telling me to let go. I wanted to kill you then. I know that. I really did want to tear you apart.' He shook his head.

'Don't worry about it,' Double A said.

'Thanks for what you did,' Jake said. 'You're a hero.'

'Tell me that again this time tomorrow,' Double A said. He took the bag of cocaine back and snorted more of it, then passed it back to Jake. Rimini was only fifteen kilometres away now and they were both going to need to be as hyped up as possible because of the information a tiny nagging part of Double A's mind was trying to impart. It might have been what Jake would have called a premolution, or it might simply have been his overwrought mind making things up, but either way Double A believed it.

Later on today in Rimini, one of them was going to be shot.

Chapter Twenty-Six
Rimini

1

The change in the light disturbed Paul and his eyes opened long before his mind began to wake. The question *How far behind are they now?* was wheeling around somewhere behind and above him, but Paul didn't ask it because he seemed to be still asleep and dreaming. He was in a room, lying on a bed which had soft pillows and crisp white sheets that smelled fresh.

The change in the light had been caused by Katie pushing back the drapes and opening the balcony doors. She stood between the open doors, silhouetted against the bright light, her back turned to Paul, and her arms holding back the diaphanous net curtains that hung between the drapes and the doors. She was naked and perfect. A gentle breeze swirled the net curtains around her body and toyed with her mane of blonde hair which hung between her shoulders, descending to the middle of her back in a tousled V. There were no marks on her now to mar her pale perfection. Katie had returned unblemished and pristine.

Paul watched her for a while, growing hard for her as the memories of what had happened last night came floating back to him as if all that had been a dream too. The blurred memories came in no particular order. They had driven the ailing Alfa out of Margherita, where as if by magic it had ceased to function – less than a hundred yards away from an XJS Jaguar coupé. Katie had opened the car and made it run – Paul couldn't quite recall how it had been accomplished – all he could remember was its leathery smell and the way the driver's seat had cradled him when he climbed in. The drive had been long and fast. He seemed to remember stopping several times at toll booths, but he didn't think he'd paid any tolls. Katie had somehow arranged this too.

Although it had to have happened less than four hours ago, the memory of arriving at this hotel was almost non-existent. He could recall climbing stairs and watching, exhausted, as Katie put the key in the door and opened it, and he could remember standing in a hot shower with her while she spoke gentle words to him and laid her soothing hands on his hurts, but after that there was nothing.

'How far behind are they now?' Paul asked. His voice grated like rusty machinery.

Katie turned. The light behind her made a halo around her hair. Paul couldn't see the expression on her face.

'They're close,' she said quietly. 'But there's still a little time.'

Four following, Paul thought.

'Jake and Double A will be here soon,' Katie said. 'An hour, perhaps.'

'Here?' Paul asked, realising with a start that he didn't know where *here* actually was. 'Are we in Naples?' he added.

'We're in Rimini,' Katie said.

'Where's that?' Paul heard himself ask.

'On the Adriatic coast. Your friends are coming here now. You told me about them on the way up here. Jake and Double A. They sensed you'd be here and not in Naples.'

Paul nodded. He did not recall telling Katie *anything* yesterday night after Margherita. Neither did he have the faintest idea why Jake and Double A had changed direction. Or why Double A was coming at all. As far as he was aware, Jake had been intending to travel alone to Naples. By air.

'And when they arrive?' he asked.

Katie shook her head. 'I don't know,' she said. 'We just have to do what we can.'

'Will it be enough?' Paul asked.

'Some of the others are gone,' Katie said. 'I don't remember much from when I was . . . away . . . but I do know that. We're not doing badly but they'll still be strong. I don't know if we'll be stronger. I don't know what I can do. Not yet.'

She came back across the room, as lithe as a panther, and sat down next to Paul on the bed.

'You got your legs back,' he said.

Katie smiled down at him. 'I'm back, full stop,' she said. She laid a hand on his chest. It was warm. She smelled faintly of vanilla. 'I don't know how much time I have,' she said.

'We'll fix it,' Paul said thickly. He was trembling. A part of him wanted to cry and he didn't know if it was shock caused by what they'd already been through, fear of what was to come, or because he was hopelessly in love and he knew that God wasn't going to answer the prayer he'd sent back in the hotel room in Igoumenitsa: *Please God, I want her back when you've finished with her*.

Katie nodded. 'We'll fix it,' she agreed.

Paul gazed up her suddenly feeling dizzy, as if he might fall into those green eyes and be swept away. *Don't do this*! his goad advised. *Don't let it go any further. It isn't right!*

And then Katie's warm, sweet mouth was against his and her hand was pushing the sheet off him and encircling his erection. Her touch was electric. She pulled away from his mouth and looked at him with an expression of love which tore at his insides. 'Don't let me go!' she urged. 'Stay with me forever!'

Paul's mind emptied itself as Katie's moist mouth found his neck and moved down to his chest. Her hair fanned out around her head and traced tingling lines down his stomach as she squeezed and pumped his cock and explored the contours of his belly with her tongue. He almost reached the point of orgasm when her lips closed around the head of his penis but Katie didn't let it happen. She kept him teetering on the edge for an age, working at him while he moaned and writhed, holding him tightly until he stopped dry-pumping and then starting again, expertly bringing back the fizzling feeling of impending orgasm with her soft lips and flicking tongue and grating teeth. When his mind was swamped and reeling with ecstasy, she drew him deep inside her mouth and pumped at his cock. Paul soared across the edge and came, long and hard, but Katie didn't release him, didn't let his erection subside. He gasped as the waves of pleasure turned to discomfort, and the discomfort changed to an exquisite agony.

And then Katie let him go, straddled him and guided his erection into her. She was slick and snug. Her hips thrust hard at him, taking him deep inside her, and she pressed her mouth against his, her tongue seeking his. Paul tasted his own semen, and then he was coming again and Katie was throwing her head back, squealing and bucking against him as she reached her own orgasm.

Paul felt his mind dissolving as his penis pumped hard and his flesh lit in tracers of tingling ecstasy. He thrust deep into her and she pushed back, forcing his hips down against the bed. Then she was winding her arms around him, finding his mouth with hers, pulling her to him. Paul's orgasm ceased and started again. He gasped air into Katie's lungs and sucked her own moans from her throat. There was an instant during which he felt as if he was plummeting towards the ground from a great height at incredible speed and then he wasn't only inside Katie's body, he was inside Katie herself. And she was inside him. He felt her orgasm as if it were his own. It was as if they had merged into a single entity, writhing in a fizzling sea of ecstasy. Katie was screaming inside Paul's head and her voice was *his* voice and his was hers.

It lasted for what seemed like an eternity.

2

'C'mon, get up!'

Paul opened his eyes. He was on the bed naked, and he was hard. Katie was dressed and prodding him in the chest. He felt as if he'd slept for a week.

'What happened?' he said, confused. He stretched and was surprised to find that he felt rested and well.

Katie smiled at him. 'Jake and Double A are here. I just saw the car go past the window. It's an old one that's been done up, isn't it? Purple. It's got a big scrape down the driver's side. Get up. If we're quick we'll get out of here before the others arrive. I can feel them. They're close but they aren't in town yet. Hurry up.'

You dreamed it, poke, his goad informed him. *It was all a dream and just as well.*

'Did anything else happen?' Paul asked, pulling himself up. He felt extremely stupid and embarrassed asking the question, but he had to know.

Katie dipped her face towards his and kissed him lightly on the lips. 'Yes, something else did happen,' she said, smiling. 'You gave yourself to me. All of you. You're mine now, for ever, amen. And I'm yours. You've been entrapped and there's no going back. I'd tell you I love you, but that would be old news now, wouldn't it?'

Paul shook his head, knowing what she meant and not knowing at the same time. He pulled on his underwear and jeans. The split was still in his jeans where the bullet had grazed him, but the broken skin on his hip had healed – as had his other hurts. Again he got the impression that he'd been asleep for a great deal longer than the four hours his watch told him he had. *Maybe you took time out in Heaven, poke!* his goad told him. Paul pulled on his tee shirt and shook his head, trying to clear it.

Katie looked at him with clear green eyes and he felt a surge of bitter-sweet love for her. It was going to work out all wrong. She was going to be taken from him. He didn't know what he would do afterwards.

Katie's face became serious. 'It's been going on a long time, Paul. Longer than either of us know,' she said. 'You can feel that, just as I can, can't you?'

Paul nodded dumbly.

'We'll be together again,' she said. 'I promise you that. No matter what happens. We'll be together again. Okay?'

'Okay,' Paul said, looking away from her eyes and trying not to break down in tears like a jilted fifteen-year-old. Katie had just said goodbye.

'I love you, Paul,' she said.

'Sure,' he said, looking down at his bare feet. There was a pair of white leather loafers on the floor beside the bed. They had straps across them and little gold buckles. They were the kind of shoes you only ever saw on the feet of people who owned yachts and very expensive cars. They were probably hand made somewhere in this country. He had no idea where they'd come from. He assumed they'd been in the last Jaguar he and Katie had taken. He slipped his feet into them and hooked them round his heels, thinking about how comfortable they were, to keep his mind from considering Katie's words. What was happening seemed a terribly high price to pay for knocking over one little kid on a bike when the accident had been the kid's own fault.

Except that you didn't just knock him over, did you, cowboy? Paul's mind said. *You killed him and drove away.*

3

They stood on the steps outside the hotel, watching as Double A cruised back down the street in the Ford Popular, its engine rumbling like an angry tiger. Paul was surprised to see that the sea was directly across the road from the hotel he had just left. The long sand beach was divided up into sections with fences and arches. Each section sported sun-shades of different colours. It looked as though you had to pay to go on any of the beaches. On the strip of sand nearest to him, there were a bunch of Italian teenagers playing volleyball.

Paul sniffed the air and smelled sea-salt and car exhaust and trouble. He glanced up and down the street and didn't see anything threatening.

Double A gunned the Pop's engine as he crossed the road into the oncoming traffic and drew into the kerb and the volley-ball players all stopped in their tracks as one man and gazed admiringly at the unfinished Pop.

The car's passenger door opened and Jake threw himself out, stumbled and fell on the pavement. 'Paul!' he shouted as he lumbered to his feet. 'Quick! In the car! *Watch out for the red Merc!*'

Paul grabbed Katie's arm and dragged her down the steps behind him. The red Mercedes Jake had been shouting about was a couple of hundred yards away still, but it was closing quickly. The distant car-thief part of Paul coolly noted that it was a 300E-24, 220 horse power 24-valve and that it was going to be difficult to shake off now that it was behind them, even in Double A's tweaked Pop. He hoped the car handled well, because it looked as if it was going to come down to out-manoeuvring the Mercedes.

Paul got to Jake before he'd picked himself up and yanked him from the ground. Behind the Pop, the red Mercedes slewed across the street into the oncoming traffic, which peeled away from it as it cruised slowly and irrevocably towards the back of the Pop.

As if in slow motion, Paul put his hand to the waistband of his jeans, intending to draw the gun and shoot at the car before it reached them. His hand touched his stomach and reported that the gun was absent.

Still in the hotel room, cowboy. You forgot to pick up your six-shooter! Paul's mind told him.

'MONSTER!' a voice screamed from Paul's right.

Jake yelled, 'LOOK OUT, THE BASTARD'S GOT A GUN!'

Double A was climbing out of the car now, screaming at Jake to get out of the way because he was going to get shot if he didn't. Katie was half turned away from Paul, gazing at the steps of the next hotel down the street in the other direction. Paul caught a glimpse of what she was looking at as he wheeled around to face the man who had shouted.

A guy was coming down the hotel steps, a blank expression on his face and a shiny silver revolver in his hand. Sunlight glinted off the gun's barrel as the man assumed a shooter's wide-legged, double-handed firing stance. Paul only saw him for a moment but it was long enough to recognise him as Peter Defoe, the man who carried his dead children's faces with him in a plastic bag; one of the two men Paul had killed when he rescued Katie in Skiathos. Paul already knew who had shouted 'Monster' without having to look. Dick Stevens, ex-mountain climber and full-time crazy who thought he was a monster spotter. The man who had tried to cut off Paul's fore-finger up on that hill.

Both of these men were supposed to be dead.

This is it then, old poke, Paul's goad told him as he gazed at the man coming down the street towards him. *Empty-handed and surrounded by dead people with guns. Butch and Sundance would have been proud of you!*

Jake was ahead of Paul now, lumbering towards Dick Stevens, while Double A screamed at him to hit the ground. Paul saw what Jake was trying to do and felt both absurdly grateful and terribly angry about it. Dick Stevens was trying to draw a bead on Katie and Jake was blocking him.

Now what? Paul asked himself. He heard the Mercedes pull up behind him and didn't know which way to turn. In front of him a man was shortly going to shoot Jake, behind him another was aiming at Katie, and the people in the Mercedes were about to get out and join in the fun and games. Paul took a pace back-wards, pressing himself against Katie's back to give her another shield. Any second, Jake was going to fall.

Paul's vision wavered. For a moment he thought he was going to faint, then his heart squeezed hard and he *clicked out.* Except that this time something else happened too. There was a warm uncomfortable feeling across the inside of his forehead, as if someone had inserted a finger into his brain and was gently pushing it through from one side of his head to the other. It was a strange and somehow *erotic* sensation.

Paul!

This time it wasn't his *farmer-oppozite* voice but Katie's. Paul had no time to think about the fact that she was inside his head talking to him as if she were a part of him because the moment he understood it was happening, his vision began to waver again. It broke up into a billion coloured speckles that flew away from one another with dizzying speed, like an expanding universe, then the universe abruptly collapsed and congealed and Paul's vision came back.

Except that now he was looking in two directions at once. He could see Jake striding purposely towards Dick Stevens and he could also see Peter Defoe on the hotel steps squeezing the trigger of his silver revolver. *He sent his daughter back and made me kill her*, Paul thought, and his anger reached the point of vaporisation.

And then it was gone, as though it had been torn from him by an immense field of gravity. Up on the steps where Defoe was in the process of squeezing off his first shot at Katie, a huge shower of pebbles appeared from nowhere and racketed down around him like hailstones.

The shot whistled over Katie's head.

Again! Paul thought.

I'm trying! Katie replied.

Double A darted through the gap between the back of the Pop and the front of the Mercedes as its driver's door flew open and a leg came out. He threw himself at the door and it swung back. From inside the car, someone screamed a curse in German.

Erich! Paul thought, and didn't know how he knew. The guy getting out of the passenger's side of the car was called Josef. Paul – or Katie, if he was getting his information from her – knew this too.

Double A yanked the Merc's door open again and slammed it back on Erich's leg.

Paul felt the odd sucking sensation again inside his head and up on the hotel steps Margherita de Savoia's collection of pins and needles materialised in Peter Defoe's hands. The man screamed and let loose two more shots. One of them ricocheted off the pavement in front of Katie and whined its way past Paul's left ear and the other lit sparks on the roof of the Pop.

The other one! Paul thought, but either Katie couldn't manage it, or there wasn't time. Dick Stevens fired and Jake spun round, already falling. Blood bloomed from his right shoulder.

'MONSTER!' Stevens roared.

Then Paul was running at him, running faster than he had ever run before. Through Katie's eyes he saw Double A fling himself across the roof of the Mercedes and into Josef who was out of the car and aiming his own gun. Double A caught Josef's arm and the gun fired into the air. As Paul leapt over Jake and Dick Stevens brought his own gun up again, he saw Josef club his weapon down on Double A's head and heard Double A scream.

The driver's door of the Mercedes flew open and Erich flung himself out, rolling across the ground, his hands together and his gun pointed towards Paul and Katie.

Katie sucked at Paul's mind again and two things happened simultaneously. Peter Defoe's silver revolver winked out of existence and the sleeves of Erich's jacket burst into flame.

Paul's mind slid sideways, rolled then steadied and settled . . . just in time to realise he was too late.

Dick Stevens had his aim, his hand was steady and the gun's trigger was moving backwards. Paul was going to run into him, but by the time that happened, Paul's brain would be minced meat.

Katie! he screamed.

Oh God, I can't do it again! Katie said inside his head.

Paul looked up into Dick's face as he took his last ever step. Time was almost standing still. Dick Stevens' face was drawn into a crazy expression of madness and concentration. There were furrows on his brow. One of his eyebrows was raised and the other was lowered as he squinted one eye almost closed. His open eye had no iris, just dark pupil, behind which Paul thought he could see tiny pricks of rainbow-coloured light shimmering. His mouth dangled open and there was a trace of the black, null substance stringing from his upper teeth to his lower ones like spittle. There was an incredibly sharp smell of rotten oranges. Dick's finger tightened on the trigger and a white, swirling scene lit up in Paul's mind: Dick Stevens trudging through deep snow in a blizzard, the barely breathable air around him freezing his nostrils and searing his lungs as he followed the footsteps of the last of his party – Jenny Richt – to the edge of the precipice over which she had walked. For a moment he felt – and understood – Dick's pain and grief. Then the scene faded and he heard Dick think, *Now I'll have my darling Jenny back!*

And the gun boomed, slowed in Paul's ears to the massive, rolling sound of a huge tidal wave hitting a seaside town. The gun's muzzle flashed like a lighthouse.

All over, Paul thought, *it's . . .*

4

Double A's vision returned in negative, fading in like a strip of monochrome film in developer. There was a big pounding pain at the crown of his head where the gun had smacked into him, and the warm feeling of freely flowing blood rushing down through his hair. The big German guy had hold of his throat with one hand and was punching the gun towards his face, barrel first, with the other. Double A knew what was going to happen when it hit him. Most of his front teeth were going to be smashed out and the force would probably take out all his rotten and filled molars too. The barrel would go so far down his throat that he would gag, and then the guy would fire the gun and put him out of his misery.

And everything would be lost.

Double A realised all this, just as he realised that his premonition about either he or Jake collecting a bullet had come true, and he reacted in less than half a second.

He saw the negative image of the gun coming towards him and smacked out his left arm, distantly surprised at how strong and determined you could get when you were an eye-blink away from becoming a dead person. His wrist bone hit a much stronger wrist bone coming in the other direction and the pain was sickening. The gun went off and the muzzle-flash singed his face and hair and the noise tore away the hearing in his left ear.

If his throat hadn't been choked off, he would have screamed. Instead, he kicked out hard with his right foot, then brought his bony knee up hard.

He heard someone shout through the ringing in his good ear, gauged that he'd had some measure of success and repeated the operation, twice.

It wasn't until the hand had been removed from his neck and Double A was on his way to the tarmac that he realised the German had lifted him clear of the ground by his throat. He gulped in air, simultaneously kicking and hitting out at the negative world that surrounded him while he tried to writhe away.

His vision began to clear after the second breath and Double A saw that the big German was bent double before him, his hands pressed to his crotch, his gun on the ground between his feet. Double A could barely believe that this was possible. He didn't think about it, just reached for the gun. The German kicked out at him and connected with his sore – and probably broken – left wrist again, just as his fingers touched the gun. The weapon skidded away and Double A pounced on it.

Then the German was down beside him, shouting angrily as he tried to get a grip on Double A's writhing body. Double A was not strong, but he was wiry and quick and packed full of speed and now he became as slippery as an eel. The German hit him a few times and each blow hurt horribly, but none of them slowed him. Double A felt the knees of his trousers tear against the road surface, felt the skin rubbing from his elbows as he wriggled away from the German and thought, *Isn't it about time someone came along and tried to stop this happening? Where are the fucking police when you want them?*

On the other side of the car, the German whose leg Double A sincerely hoped he'd broken, was babbling, half in English, half in German. The gist seemed to be that he was burnt and it hurt. *Good!* Double A thought.

The German grabbed hold of his right hand, yanked it back across his body and sank his teeth into Double A's wrist. Double A pulled against the pain, and the German's teeth simply dug in harder. Double A was now lying on his face with the German along the left side of his body, and his right arm pulled across the small of his back, pinning him down.

Ignoring the pain where he was being bitten, Double A wriggled and got his left shoulder under him. From there it was an easy move. He flipped himself over, threw out his left leg and found himself straddling the German. Somewhere during the movement, the man had released the grip he'd had on Double A's arm. His teeth were stained with blood.

Double A jammed the gun barrel against the man's cheekbone so hard that he felt bone crack, then he pulled the trigger.

And nothing happened.

Double A looked at the barrel of the gun against the German's cheek in a moment of disbelief during which his mind informed him that guns had things called safety catches and that the safety catch on this particular gun was on, then he pulled the weapon away from the man's face and brought its butt down on his forehead. The German stopped moving instantly.

Killed another one, Double A told himself, and considered blasting his brains out in order to prevent him from coming back to life again. He looked for something that might have obviously been a safety catch, didn't see one, and then he was up and running back towards the Pop, because he heard the girl's voice inside his head telling him to get back inside at once.

The man shot Paul Dekker just as Double A reached the door of the car.

5

. . . it's all over, Paul thought as Dick Stevens pulled the trigger and the gun's muzzle-flash seared his eyes. He thought the pain inside his head was the bullet passing through . . . until he finally realised that the flicker he'd seen following the shot being fired had not been a glimpse of the bullet at all but something else.

It had been two disturbances in the air: one as Dick Stevens' gun had vanished from his hand, and the other as the bullet was snatched out of reality and thrust into nowhere.

Paul was travelling too fast to stop. He ran into Stevens and both of them sprawled to the ground.

Paul! Come back to the car! Quick!

Paul scrambled to his feet, shaking the climber's clawing hands away from him. As he moved away, one of Stevens' hands caught the nape of Paul's neck and dug in, his fingernails piercing the skin. Paul elbowed the hand away and spun around, not just intending to hit the man, but intending to damage him so badly he wouldn't ever come back again. And in that moment he *could have* done it. An image of this leapt into his mind. In it he had already gouged out Stevens' eyes and was now forcing his fingers down through the sockets and into the man's brain. He could feel bone being crushed beneath his fingers, flesh and brain tearing away.

But Paul did not throw the punch for which his fist had so readily balled. When he saw Stevens, his fist unclenched and he took a pace back, unable to take his eyes away from the man.

The climber's left foot seemed to be stuck in the concrete paving slab – not stuck *to* it, but *in* it, as if the concrete had become liquid then solid again after the man's foot had sunk into it. On its own it would have been bad enough, but Stevens didn't seem to be aware of it and his right leg was pushing hard as he tried to run towards Paul.

And like Rumplestiltskin, after his name had been discovered, Stevens was tearing himself apart. His trousers and underwear had torn at the crotch and his cock and balls hung to the left of the split that had appeared just off the centre of his pubic bone.

'Monster!' he shouted, his bent right leg finding a grip on the pavement and straining against his trapped left.

Paul heard the awful splitting sound and hoped it was the material of the man's clothes he could hear and not the flesh being rent. The gaping slit in Stevens' crotch grew, unzipping his body like a rotten banana. Paul watched the wound travel up his abdomen like a live thing, was unable to tear his eyes away as Stevens' leg dug in and pushed – and his intestines tore and began to fall from his body, unravelling like streamers.

'Monster!' he roared. 'Jenny! Where's my Jenny?'

Paul turned away from him and ran back towards the car, vaguely aware that there were knots of people all around him, all frozen into a surreal tableau as they watched Stevens tear himself into what was soon going to become two halves. Double A was on the passenger's side of the car, his head streaming bright red blood as he helped Jake into the back seat. Katie was standing with her back to Paul, her head bowed and the index and middle fingers of her right hand pressed to her temple as though she was searching her mind for something she'd forgotten. There was a small throng of Italians grouped in a semi-circle before her, their eyes dreamy and beatific smiles on the lips. Behind those, the German called Erich Spiegel, his arms still smouldering and his hair now in singed and matted clumps, was clawing his way back to the Mercedes through a group of onlookers who parted to let him by like the Red Sea was supposed to have done for Moses.

Further back than that, two or three of the guys who had been playing volleyball on the beach stood in their trunks watching Peter Defoe undergo a similar fate to the one Dick Stevens was suffering. Peter Defoe was trying to free himself a little more energetically than the climber had and quite a bit more of him was spilling out on to the pavement. The volley-ballers seemed to have noted this and were standing back far enough not to get splashed by anything nasty.

Hurry, I can't hold it for much longer! Katie said inside his head.

Paul sprinted the last few yards and ran out into the road, knowing that he was going to be expected to drive.

He threw himself into the Pop, found the ignition and had the engine running by the time Katie got into the car. She had spots of high colour on her cheekbones and her face was sheened in sweat. Her eyes were glassy and distant.

Paul found first gear, looked at the stalled traffic all around and drove the car on to the pavement.

'Get them out of the way!' he said to Katie, and felt that tugging sensation inside his head as she siphoned off his energy to help her.

People began to scatter as the Pop lurched on to the pavement and gathered speed. Over the racket of the car's engine, Paul heard a single woman begin to scream and knew that Katie had released whatever hold she'd had on the bystanders. Suddenly the air was filled with shouting and wailing. Paul felt Katie slip away from his mind. A cold and empty vacuum seemed to have been left behind.

Dick Stevens lay on the pavement before the Pop in a tangle of intestines and organs. He was split in two right up to where his neck joined his skull and the halves of his body were at right angles to one another. The black substance was trickling from him in lifeless tendrils, blanking out sections of the pavement. But unlike Defoe who this time was gone for good, Stevens was still alive and still kicking.

Paul glanced in the mirror after the Pop had lurched over him and grunted when he saw that the climber had finally been made to lie down and die. There was no feeling of vengeance having been done and the tiny spark of satisfaction he felt was quickly extinguished when he realised the Mercedes was running and mounting the pavement, a hundred yards behind them.

Paul hit the throttle, let his mind go blank and turned into a driving machine.

Chapter Twenty-Seven
Robert Farmer Takes a Trip

1

For the next half an hour, Paul was unable to consider anything but the task of shaking off the Mercedes, which clung to the tail of Double A's Ford Popular like a limpet. He finally accomplished it by doing a wheel-shrieking hundred and eighty-degree power-on turn, dodging the Mercedes as its driver threw it head-on at the Pop and then hammering off down a side road, after which he took each turn in the opposite direction to the ones he estimated the Mercedes would be taking. It had worked before when he was being tailed, and it worked again now. When he was certain that the two Germans (who surely had to be two *dead* Germans by now) weren't going to come sailing round the corner towards him at any moment, he pulled the Pop over to the side of the road and stopped, took stock of the damage, leaving the engine running just in case.

Double A's face was a red mask, but the blood flow seemed to have stopped and the mask was deepening in colour. 'I'm fine,' he said, 'and just as soon as I can get my baggie out of my pocket and toot some supersnuff, I'll be even finer. But don't even bother asking me what happened, because I'm not sure. But I think we ought to get old Jakey baby here to a quack as soon as possible. He stopped a slug.' Double A shook his head. 'I knew one of us would, but I thought it would be me.' He glanced at Jake and then said, 'And I wish it *had* been.'

'Shaddup, chicken,' Jake said. His hand was pressed tightly

657

to his shoulder and there was blood between his fingers. 'I'll be all right, Paul,' he said. 'Just get us the fuck out of this country and into another one. I'm sick of being here. People have been trying to kill me ever since I arrived.'

'What about your arm?' Paul asked. He felt horribly guilty. The back of his neck had bled a great deal and the back of his tee shirt – and probably the car seat – was sticky with blood, but compared with what had happened to Jake and Double A, whose business this most certainly *wasn't*, it was hardly a scratch. If anyone should have been badly wounded, it was the person who was currently sitting in the driver's seat.

Jake moved his hand, slowly and carefully. Paul saw him fighting not to grimace. 'I was lucky,' Jake grated. 'It went straight through my shoulder muscle and out the other side. Didn't hit an artery, didn't break any bones. Hurts like a bastard, but it ain't life threatening. I'll be fine. Just let me keep the hole plugged up until it stops bleeding and I'll be just as good as new.'

Paul turned to Katie. 'You okay?' he asked.

She looked at him and nodded. Paul felt that warm, probing sensation inside his head again. He didn't realise how good it had felt that first time until now. *I'm fine*, Katie thought to him.

The words, *Don't leave me*, came into Paul's mind, except that this time they were his own. He kept them at the edge of his consciousness until they vanished. He didn't know whether Katie had intercepted them or not. He hoped not. He didn't want her to know exactly how smitten he'd allowed himself to become.

Too late to stop me knowing, Paul, she thought. *I've known for a long time.*

He looked into her clear green eyes. They were moist with what would have become two large tears if she hadn't blinked them away.

Paul's insides felt as if they were being crushed in a vice. A part of him hoped he would die when this was all over because in that moment he knew without a shadow of a doubt that Katie was going away: and living on a planet where there was no Katie was going to be a very cold and lonely existence indeed. Since they'd made love – and since he'd felt her presence inside his head – he'd felt as if they were bound together in a way that was deeper and more significant than the promise he may or may not have made to her.

Claptrap, he told himself and pushed the thought away. But the crushing sensation did not cease.

'Can you do anything for Jake?' Paul asked.

Katie shook her head. 'I've only got a limited amount of power and I think I've already used too much.' She turned to Jake. 'I'm sorry,' she said. 'If I thought I could, I would try anything for you.'

Jake did a one shoulder shrug. ''Sokay,' he said. 'I'll survive. There is something you can do for me, though. What me and old chicken back here would really like, is for you and Paul to tell us what the fuck is going on. We worked some of it out, but . . . y'know . . .' He grimaced.

And as Paul put the car in gear and drove away, Katie began to tell them.

2

Paul didn't begin to smell trouble again until just before the border crossing between Italy and Switzerland, and when he did, it wasn't the smell of the trouble he anticipated at the crossing and it wasn't an odour that suggested the Germans' red Mercedes was catching up with them.

It was the same strong smell of blood he'd had before discovering his mother's and the Cindy dog's mutilated corpses, and it was nothing to do with the smell of drying blood that was coming from two of his three passengers.

Paul was thankful there was no radio in this car because he didn't know if he could stand hearing voices calling to him again at the moment.

'Anything wrong?' Katie asked him. She had been silent for a long while, staring out at the lengthy stretches of straight road that were throwing themselves beneath the rocketing Popular. Paul thought that she had been considering what the future might hold for her.

Everything's wrong, Paul thought, but Katie did not enter his mind to receive this thought. She hadn't done that since they left Rimini. A part of Paul had solemnly told him that she would never do it again. It was one of the conditions of her returning. Katie had hinted at this herself, while she and Paul were explaining to Jake and Double A exactly what was happening. The two men had soaked it all up with hardly a comment. When the story had been told, they had asked no questions, just retreated into a kind of shell-shocked silence. Now, five hundred odd kilometres and three hours later, they were both sleeping, Double A with his blood-masked face on Jake's good shoulder, and Jake with his head lolling forward and his right hand clamped to his bullet wound. The pair of them looked messy, but Paul didn't expect either of them to die.

'Smell it?' Paul asked, raising his voice over the roar of the car's engine. *Of course she doesn't, poke, she's saving herself*, his goad put in bitterly. *And she won't take it from inside your head because it's against the rules*. Katie had broken the rules by making love to him. She'd told him after Jake and Double A had fallen asleep. She'd broken the rules by *falling* in love with him, too. It wasn't supposed to happen and she was frightened that it would make everything go wrong. She wasn't supposed to have used the force she had been imbued with to control the actions of humans – and she had done exactly this with the onlookers in Rimini, keeping them empty-minded until the danger had passed *and* she had caused Erich Spiegel to burn. None of these things was supposed to happen and Katie had done them all. And now she was worried that she had somehow corrupted herself and, as a consequence, she wasn't going to have enough power left to finish the job.

Katie shook her head. 'I don't smell anything different,' she said. She didn't look at him. She didn't have to, just like she didn't have to tell him it was over between them; a love affair that had stopped shortly after it had started. Sometime in the hours between Rimini and Milan, Katie had begun to have doubts and everything had changed.

'Don't worry about it, sweetheart,' Paul said, trying to put thoughts of her and the growing smell of blood out of his mind. He thought about their chances for a few seconds and then put this out of his mind too. It was wrong. It was all wrong.

Paul thought about the car instead of thinking how they were going to get across the border without any documentation. The '59 Ford Popular that had stood in the workshop of the Miles Carriage Co. for so long was a very special vehicle. Paul hadn't expected Jake and Double A to turn up in it, and under normal circumstances he wouldn't have been seen dead in it (if being seen dead was still a phrase that could be used – and Paul strongly doubted it in the light of the past few weeks). But being seen *at all* in the car was something that had been puzzling him. They had passed two Carabinieri cruisers and one belonging to the Polizia on the way between Rimini and here and each time Paul had expected trouble. Word must have gone out about what had happened in Rimini: the police would know about the Pop and would surely be looking for it. But it had sailed past the police cars without being noticed. Double A hadn't known what he was doing when he'd applied those three coats of purple paint to its body. That stuff was surely no ordinary two-pack purple paint; it had apparently rendered the car invisible to the boys in blue.

There were other things Double A and Jake had excelled themselves at while putting the Pop together and Paul began to notice them now he thought about it. There was the three and a half litre V8 Rover engine, for instance. These motors were usually okay in lightweight two-seater cars but when you shoe-horned them into something the size and aerodynamic shape of the Popular they tended to lose a little. But not this one. In his time, Paul had driven some very expensive cars that could sprint a bit, but this one could surely hold its own amongst any of them. The zero to sixty time had to be somewhere in the region of six seconds, and the engine didn't lose anything much on the way up to the ton and beyond. The tuning Jake and Double A had done had worked amazingly well; the gearbox and limited-slip differential matched the V8 perfectly, but there was more than this. Paul couldn't recall being in a car that had better roadholding than the Pop. It handled like it was running on rails. The car was a gem: its whole wasn't just greater than the sum of its parts but it had that little extra too. And that little extra was its feel and the way it seemed to fit Paul as well as his old leather driving gloves had done. The Pop might have been built for him and him alone. The car seemed to know him and welcome him into its driver's seat. It was a car that wanted to work for him without having to be coerced or persuaded, a car that had one boss and knew who that boss was. Whatever else happened, Paul didn't expect the Ford Popular to fail him.

On the side of the road a sign warned that they were approaching the frontier. Paul meant to crash through without stopping. He didn't know whether or not it would work, but they weren't going to talk their way through with two passports between four of them. There was every chance that the border police would be on the lookout for the Pop anyway, even if the Italian cops had missed it. Jake had related the tale of what had happened to him and Double A in the motorway service area in Switzerland. Word might not have got to the border quickly enough to stop Jake and Double A getting out of the country, but they would surely know all about the Pop and its murderous occupants by now.

'Paul?' Katie said softly.

Paul turned to face her. It was no good telling himself she wasn't the most beautiful woman he had ever laid eyes on, because she was and a blind man would have seen it. Framed by a rich tangle of blonde hair, Katie's sad face shone with an inner light. Her skin seemed to have a golden glow and her clear green eyes drew him, making him ache inside. It was like gazing into a crystal-clear body of endlessly deep water that you knew would be warm and welcoming when you slipped into it. You could fall into those eyes without causing the merest ripple . . . and vanish into a blissful eternity.

Katie really did look angelic.

Paul looked back at the road, feeling the vice tighten on his insides. *Sucker,* he told himself, because his goad, as Jake might have said, had shut up shop and shit in the shutters.

Paul felt the strange pressure in his head again; the sensation of another person easing their way into the very core of him. The feeling was both uncomfortable and unbelievably erotic. It was like having a missing part of you put back; a part that would not only make you whole again, but give you something extra. Paul gasped. He ached for Katie to be there, and his mind screamed for the completion of the act the way it had earlier when Katie had kept him teetering on the edge of orgasm.

Then he resisted.

Let me, Katie said inside his head.

Paul didn't reply.

I love you, Paul. Let me in!

The rules, Paul thought.

Katie surged inside his head, breaking into spray across his mind like a wave against a sea wall. She put her hand on his thigh, close to where his erect penis was aching for her touch. *Fuck the rules,* she said in his mind. *I want you. You're mine and I love you. Fuck the rules and fuck everything else. I can't do this without you and you can't do it without me. I want you, Paul. Let me in.*

Paul glanced at her. There were tears in her eyes and Paul suddenly knew that she must feel exactly the same way as he did. The whole situation was horrendously painful. It was a bad thing; a doomed relationship. It had been doomed from the moment he'd answered the phone. Perhaps even prior to that. Katie was dead. She wasn't really alive again, not even now that she'd come back complete with a heart that beat and blood that flowed through her veins and arteries. She had been given a little extra time to fix the mess she had made and then she would be dead again. It was a terrible price for her to pay and an extortionate one for him. He hadn't asked to fall in love with her, just as he hadn't asked for the kid on the bike to sail off the verge in front of a stolen car he was driving. The price for killing the kid was having to help Katie, and the price for helping Katie was going to be living the rest of his life in pain. Paul hated whoever was responsible for setting it.

He looked away from her and back at the line of cars up ahead at the border. *Ain't life a bitch?* he asked her.

And let her in.

It was ecstasy.

3

Live now, pay later, Paul thought bitterly as he stopped the car. There were four packed lanes going slowly through the frontier post and now he realised that his plan of crashing through had been impractical. He might have been able to stall the Swiss passport cop for a while until the road ahead of him was clear and then make a break for it, but the chances were that the guards – and there were many of them in evidence this evening – would start to shoot. And Paul didn't want that to happen.

Katie had a better idea, she told him. From now on she was going to throw away the rule book and simply do whatever was necessary. She said she didn't know what the consequences would be later and she didn't care. The worst thing that could happen to her, she said, was that she would be separated from Paul – and that was going to happen anyway.

Paul didn't mention the fact that he could think of worse things – like losing to the black angel that they were heading towards and then spending an eternity of agony in whatever part of Hell it was master of, because that could have been construed as negative thinking of the type with which H and the huge golden thing that was cramped inside his body would have been very pleased. There were three ahead and two behind now. Seven of H's disciples had gone. Seven had fallen to four and the others would follow. Whatever was going to happen afterwards couldn't be allowed to affect his thinking on the business in hand. What all this was about had nothing to do with his feelings for Katie or hers for him. What it was to do with was nailing the fuckers who had killed his mother, his ex-wife and almost all his friends: sending the bastards back to whatever hole they had crawled out of before any other towns ended up like Margherita de Savoia. If mayhem was what H and his parasitic angel wanted, it was what they were going to get.

Look how tough you're talking now you've got your girly back, he told himself, and grinned.

The car in front of the Popular edged forwards and Paul followed. They were two cars away from the crossing point now. So far no one had come screaming towards them waving a gun, but the border guards were being particularly vigilant today by the look of it.

'What do we do?' Paul asked, weighing up the pair of officials who were inspecting the German-registered BMW in front. One was inspecting the passports of its occupants and the other was leaning into the car's boot, up to his elbows in suitcases and camping gear. Both the men wore guns. They were both in their mid-thirties and didn't look particularly fit. If it came to a fight, Paul would be able to put hem both out for the count in less than ten seconds. For what good it would do. There was somewhere in the region of fifteen other guards going about their business nearby.

'Leave it to me,' Katie said, and flashed a sunny smile at him.

In front of them the border cop extricated his arms from deep beneath the baggage and slammed the boot lid shut. His partner handed back the passports and gave the driver a curt nod in the direction of Switzerland. This, apparently, meant that he was free to enter their country.

When the BMW had cleared the diagonal lane, the nodding cop repeated his economic head action to indicate that Paul should put his car in the space. Paul understood why they'd put these dog-leg lanes through the border shed – it was so you couldn't take a flying run through without stopping. If you decided to cross the border this way, you would have to slow right down to get through the tight diagonal lane then straighten your car again before accelerating away. This would give the police here ample time to draw their guns and shoot you.

Paul gunned the Pop's engine from a rough idle to a smooth (but still noisy) 2500 rpm and slipped the clutch, letting the car creep forward – a slower engine speed would have meant the Pop jerking forward and stalling. The Pop was not your average family saloon.

Both customs men, who apparently didn't know about the lumpy and gutless tickover you got from having a high-lift cam in your engine, interpreted the engine sound as meaning that this driver was going to be troublesome even if he didn't try to make a break for it, and unclipped their holster straps. Paul saw the nodding one thumb the safety on his weapon. A part of him wanted to break that thumb clean off the man's hand.

Leave it to me, Katie said inside his head and for a moment Paul thought she meant to do as he'd just thought. Then he grinned at himself again.

Mr Nod, who was accustomed to receiving the documentation he wanted from the left-hand side of the car and didn't intend to alter his routine for a foreigner, went to Katie's side of the car, 'Passports,' he said.

Katie reached up to the sun-visor where Jake and Double A's passports were lodged and handed them to the man, smiling.

His buddy, the boot-searcher, came up beside him scowling, saw Katie and smiled at her.

'There are only two,' Mr Nod complained.

'That's right,' Katie said. 'There are only two of us.'

'Quattro,' the boot-searcher said, shaking his head and pointing at Jake and Double A. The smile on his face didn't say that if two more passports weren't produced in very short order there would be big trouble, it said that surely the gorgeous lady had made some kind of mistake.

'Two,' Katie said. 'Duo.'

Mr Nod's hand hovered over his gun. 'Where are *your* passports?' he asked.

'Those *are* our passports,' Katie said sweetly. 'Look again. Mr and Mrs Stephen Miles. They are our pictures. We have no passengers.'

'But these are the passports of the men in the back,' the boot-searcher insisted, looking over his partner's shoulder at the documents. The smile had gone. Concern had taken its place. This was a man who didn't want to be nasty to such a pretty girl, but whose sense of duty was deeply ingrained.

Paul's feet twitched at the pedals. He had to fight not to deck the accelerator and make a run.

Mr Nod's hand closed around his gun and began to withdraw it.

It isn't working, Paul told himself. *She's run herself dry.*

'Get out of the car,' Mr Nod said.

Now where have I heard that before? Paul asked himself. And then Katie was drawing power from him. A sharp ice-cream pain lit behind his eyes and was gone. Paul felt as if he was being swept away by a river.

'Me and my husband,' Katie said. 'The Mileses. We have a passport each because we travel separately quite often. You can see it now, can't you?'

Mr Nod glanced at the passports one more time and his mouth fell open. The gun wavered in his hand and found its way back to his holster. He began to talk rapidly in Italian to his partner.

Paul's mind steadied and he breathed a sigh of relief. He glanced over at the men who seemed to be arguing with one another. The boot-searcher was pointing at Jake and Double A.

Mr Nod shrugged and turned back to Katie. 'Excuse me, but these are not good pictures of you,' he said apologetically, showing both open passports to Katie. Paul looked at them and was surprised to see the photographs were no longer of Jake and Double A but of Katie and himself. Both images were blurred, and had a kind of moving quality to them like a television picture about to perform a roll.

'But they are us,' Katie said.

Paul watched the photographs steady and sharpen.

'And the two men?' the other cop asked. His expression of concern now looked rather like an expression of deep discomfort. He was no longer a man dealing with a mistake a pretty girl had made, but someone who had been dragged to the edge of his sanity and who was currently teetering on the brink staring down at the abyss while a force he didn't understand nudged him in the small of his back.

'Two men?' Katie asked.

The boot-searcher pointed uncertainly into the back of the car. Katie looked over her shoulder, turned back to him and shrugged. 'I don't understand,' she said.

The guard put his right hand to his temple. 'There were two men,' he complained. 'I saw them and I saw their passports and now they are gone.'

'Did you see them?' Katie asked Mr Nod. Paul was impressed by the amount of astonishment and disdain she had managed to work into those four words.

Mr Nod knew when he was beaten. He *had* seen them. He might still be able to see them, as far as Paul knew. But even if there had been two live crocodiles in there eating babies, Mr Nod was way beyond the point of admitting it. His partner had seen people who were no longer there, the occupants of the car seemed astonished about it, and that was enough to prove to him that whatever he *thought* he'd seen a few seconds ago, wasn't what he actually *had* seen. If he argued the toss and his colleagues turned up and couldn't see the two men in the back of the car or their photos on the passports he was going to be facing a medical retirement, the details of which would trudge around behind him for the remainder of his life.

Mr Nod shook his head, handed Katie the passports, stepped back and gave a curt nod towards the country of his birth.

As Paul drove away, he noticed the man wiping his hand on his trousers, as if the passports he'd been holding had somehow left stains on him.

4

For a time, as Paul hammered up the fast lane of the N2 towards Luzern at slightly more than a hundred and thirty miles an hour, he believed that they were going to get a clear run home and that the increasing smell of blood was the odour of the final showdown approaching. Katie couldn't smell anything, not even when she pressed herself inside his head, and Jake and Double A who had both woken when Paul had stopped for petrol were unable to smell at all because both of them were using a great deal of amphetamine sulphate as a kind of analgesic.

Jake was silent while Double A prattled on about nothing in particular and Paul was worried about him. The wound in his right arm had stopped bleeding but Jake looked sick and worried.

'What's wrong?' Paul asked.

'They're at it with that fucking radar beam again,' Jake said. 'Don't you feel it? I been trying to duck it, but they're gonna catch me with it sooner or later and then they'll know where we are.'

Paul remembered his own mental battle with Gary Richman. A sensation of increased air pressure and a scraping ache inside his skull had been the precursor of that attack and he hadn't felt anything like that happening since. 'Katie?' he asked.

Katie shook her head. 'I can't feel it,' she said.

'I can,' Double A said. 'It's like they're sweeping through the wavebands looking for the one where your mind lives. I have to keep ducking it too, but I'm getting pretty good at doing it. All you have to do is kind of suck yourself down. Don't worry, Jake, they won't get you, and you ain't driving anyway, so it won't matter if they do.'

'It might,' Jake said.

And Paul thought he was right. Jake might be hurt and weak, but if Richman gained control of him he could still do a lot of damage. Like delivering a left-handed rabbit punch to the back of Paul's head, for example. Jake had never hit Paul, but Paul had seen him hit others. Jake hit very hard indeed and Paul didn't relish the thought of trying to keep the car on the road if Jake attacked him.

'Can't you do anything, sweetheart?' Paul asked Katie. 'Mask us or something. Put Richman off the track?'

Katie shrugged. 'I could try to find them,' she said. 'But I'm frightened to do it. He and H are too close. I don't know what would happen. I want to keep away from H until I'm ready.' She thought about it for a while. 'I'll try,' she said. 'Jake's important. I know that. We all have to get back in one piece to win, so I'll risk it.'

There was a meaty slapping sound from the back of the car. Paul glanced in the mirror as Katie spun around. Jake had clapped his left hand across his eyes. 'Too late,' he said. 'They found me.'

Paul slowed the car and put it in the slow lane between a camper and a truck. 'Should I stop?' he asked.

'The Germans are behind us,' Katie said. 'Twenty miles or so.'

'You didn't say,' Paul said.

'You knew they'd be coming,' she replied. 'They haven't gained on us in the past two hours so I didn't say anything.'

'You've been tracking them,' Paul said.

Katie shrugged. 'It isn't the same as taking on Gary Richman and H and the other one from here. If we stop the Germans will be on us in ten minutes.'

'Nothing's happening,' Jake said. 'Don't stop. They found me but they didn't do anything to me so keep going. I'll shout if anything happens. Then you can stop and drop me off and fuck off without me.'

'We won't have to do that, Jakey baby,' Double A said

quickly. 'We'll see you're all right. Here, shove some more of this up your great snout.'

Paul swung the car out into the fast lane again and put the accelerator to the floor. He glanced at Katie. 'Who is the other one?' he asked. 'You said, H and Gary Richman and the other one.' Suddenly it seemed very important to know. It was as if everything was going to hinge on this.

'I don't know his name, but he's the first and the strongest,' Katie said. 'H is helping them change. They're becoming like me. Neither of them are ordinary men any longer. They're something more . . .'

'They're metamorphosing,' Double A said from the back.

'Meta-what?' Jake asked.

'Changing into something else,' Double A said. 'Like what caterpillars do.'

'Christ,' Jake said.

'And him,' Double A replied. 'And . . .' he tailed off.

'Me,' Katie said. 'Except I'm done.'

'This guy . . .' Paul said.

'You know who he is, Paul?'

Paul thought he did. 'The guy who's been chasing round killing off everyone I know,' he said, thoughtfully. 'The guy who killed my mother and left his brown leather brogues behind him to incriminate me. What's his name?'

Katie shook her head. 'I don't know,' she said.

'I do,' Jake said distantly. He spoke in a series of small grunts as if he had to strain each word from his lips. 'His . . . name's . . . Robert Farmer . . . and he used . . . to . . . be a . . . bank manager.'

The smell of blood increased ten-fold. The man's name burned itself into Paul's mind like a red-hot branding iron and as it happened, Paul felt himself rearrange internally. It was as if until Jake had spoken those words, his mind had been full of cracks like an ancient piece of china that had suffered rough usage. And the pieces that the cracks ran through had been separated from one another, causing Paul to become a fractured personality; a man whose mind had many facets, all at war with one another. He had been denying this since the day he'd killed the kid on the bicycle – little Paulie Saunders. And now, as the words *Robert Farmer* impressed themselves upon him, those cracks disappeared and the pieces of his mind slid, lined up, steadied and knitted themselves together in a seamless whole. Paul was suddenly certain his mind was healed. He didn't know how those words had accomplished it, but he had his suspicions. Robert Farmer was his. His own target. His own chance to atone. This sensation was so strong that Paul hardly noticed the change of atmosphere that had taken place around him.

'How do you know?' Katie asked, her voice concerned.

'I . . . dreamed . . . it,' Jake grunted.

Paul! Katie called inside his head.

I dreamed it too, Paul thought back. *Must have done. Know the name.*

I can smell it, Paul. I can smell blood!

'And . . . do . . . you . . . know . . . what?' Jake grunted.

Double A said, 'What?'

Paul heard his voice as if from a thousand miles away. He already knew what the *what* was going to turn out to be and he didn't know if he was going to have time to stop the car before it happened.

Do something! he mentally screamed at Katie.

I don't know how to stop it! she screamed back at him.

'What?' Double A asked. 'Jake? You okay, man?'

Paul hit the brakes but there was a string of traffic to his right stopping him getting back into the slow lane. 'Get out of it, you bastards!' he shouted at the traffic. He twisted the button for the Pop's left-hand trafficator and hit the horn. The little orange swing-arm flipped up out of its socket and lit, but the traffic didn't break to let him through.

'I can see him coming and I can't stop him,' Jake moaned. 'I tried, Paul. I've been trying since they spotted me, but I couldn't stop it. I'm sorry!'

'What's going on?' Double A screamed. 'Jake! What the fuck's happening?'

Paul saw a space a hundred yards ahead of him a good five seconds before it had appeared. Cursing, he hit the throttle and the car rocketed forward. They weren't going to make it. He wasn't going to get off the road quickly enough to deal with what was going to happen.

The back of the car began to creak. Somewhere around the point where the headlining came down to meet the sides.

Can't happen here! Paul screamed. *There aren't three ninety-degree angles! There aren't!*

But somewhere in the car there were three ninety-degree angles and they were being used.

And right before Paul's eyes, his gap in the traffic opened up . . . and closed again as the driver of the car in front of the space heard the Pop's horn and slowed down.

5

'*Jake! What the fuck's happening?*' Double A screamed as the sound of bending metal came from the headlining above him. Beneath him the rear bench seat lurched. Paul threw the car to one side and hit the horn. Double A fell into Jake and pushed himself away. Jake's nose had started to bleed and Double A didn't know if the speed had done it or if it was something else. The atmosphere in the car seemed to have become heavy.

'Sorry, chick, I'm sorry!' Jake groaned and took one of Double A's hands and squeezed it. Jake's big strong hand was cool and moist.

The seat moved beneath Double A again and its springs twanged and rattled. '*Jake! For fuck's sake, man!*'

'Too late,' Jake said.

The car swung again, to the other side this time. Paul swore. Jake pushed himself away from Double A. 'Get away from me, boy!' he yelled.

And in the gap between them the back of the bench seat pulled down, peeling itself away from the seat back. There was something in the gap that looked like mist, except this wasn't swirling like smoke, it was crawling as if it was alive.

'What is it?' Double A shouted, wishing to God that someone was going to tell him he was having an hallucination. No one did.

In the front seat, Katie made a small sound that might have been a cry of grief or surprise or fear, then turned around and looked over her shoulder at the dip in the seat between Double A and Jake. The expression on her face was scary.

In the long second that followed, Double A's hyped-up mind had ample time to list several more things about Katie that frightened him terribly. The first was that she could no longer be construed as an ordinary girl. Double A had heard the whole story about what had happened to her, but until now his mind had classed her as a girl to whom things had happened. She might have had extra powers or whatever, but basically, when you got down to the nitty gritty, she was still only a girl, even if she had been brought back from the dead.

Now, Double A realised that his mind's attempt at understanding the situation had been hopelessly misplaced. For one thing, Katie was perfectly still. She was completely unaffected by the powerful forces as the car slewed from side to side, cannoning him and Jake towards, then away from the smoky gap in the seat. She wasn't resisting the movement with her muscles the same way as he and Jake were, she just stayed where she was as if those gees the car was pulling as Paul tried to get it into the slow lane didn't act upon her at all.

And in the space of that second, Double A also realised that Katie was lit wrongly. She seemed to be shining – or glowing at least – as if she were basking in the light of a bright follow-spot. *Or of another sun*, his mind jabbered. The effect made Katie look twice as real as everything else in the car. There was an area around her, close to her body and head, where this increased force of reality ceased and ordinary reality began and Double A tried very hard not to think about it because at certain points along that ragged edge which reminded him of torn paper, he could see beyond Katie and into what he thought might be another world.

Katie's eyes sparkled green as though they were alive and Double A felt as if he was being drawn towards them. *You could literally fall into them and vanish,* his crazily reeling mind told him.

She wasn't a woman at all, or even partially a woman. In that moment, Katie was an angel and nothing else.

Then the moment passed and Double A was shouting at Jake in terror as the girl in the front seat started to do something. She wasn't moving, but Double A could feel the force of what she was doing pushing him away from the gap in the centre of the bench seat. Double A was crushed against the side of the car. It felt as if a bulldozer in low gear was compressing him and Double A thought it might kill him. Katie was changing reality. Trying to prevent that living smoke from crawling out of the car seat.

Trying and losing, Double A realised as his last shout was squeezed out of his body.

The pressure on Double A ceased and was followed by a series of ear-popping changes in the air pressure and a series of bright shocks which lit his brain like a fusillade of flash-guns going off. Double A was blinded. Someone shouted that they didn't have enough power, and it might have been Paul or Katie or someone else. The voice was slowed down and indistinct and it grated against his eardrums like a rasp.

The car lurched again. From what seemed like miles away, he heard the sound of car horns . . . and seat springs protesting. The car lurched again, again throwing him towards Jake. He bounced back off something solid and his vision cleared.

Paul had got the Pop on to the hard shoulder at last and was braking hard but Double A didn't know what good it was going to do now because a huge bean-shaped bubble of what looked like glass had formed on the seat between him and Jake. Its surface was warm and flexible. Inside it, the smoky vapour he'd seen crawling up from the seat was thickening and swirling furiously, like a time-lapsed movie of an angry weather front.

'What *is it?*' Double A heard a terrified voice screech. A moment later he realised it was his voice.

'Sorry, chicken,' Jake yelled from the other side of the growing bubble. 'Can't stop it.'

The whole process, from the moment that Katie began to fight, to the point where the bean-shaped bubble stretched into something that suggested it was about to become man-shaped, had taken less than five seconds.

What happened next happened while the '59 Ford Popular was still five seconds away from rolling to a halt. For Double A, the process seemed to take about an hour. It was the worst period of his life because he saw it all unfolding before him, he knew what was going to happen and he was absolutely powerless to prevent it.

Double A smelled rotting fruit. He watched in horror as the cloudy substance inside the bubble thickened and curled back against itself several times. A pink tube formed at the edge of the bubble and was whisked away. The process repeated itself again and again, its pace increasing until the movement was impossible to follow. The stuff in the man-shaped bubble was now moving in a frenzied blur and a dark shape was beginning to grow. Inside two seconds the thing was whole and fully formed. It turned its head towards Double A, then towards Jake.

And the bubble vanished.

If Double A's body hadn't been full of speed, his heart jabbering like a machine gun and his blood pressure high enough to give a hill-climber a good challenge, he might have fainted at what happened. He had expected a drooling monster from Hell, teeth and claws poised ready to tear them all apart with a single sweeping slash. What he got was worse.

What he got was a smiling, even-featured man dressed in a sharp business suit and wearing brown leather brogues on his feet. His hair was neatly clipped and his hands were clasped in his lap.

Double A screamed at the insanity of it, distantly realising that the man who now occupied the seat between him and Jake was surely Robert Farmer who had once been a bank manager. He was a big, fit-looking man who obviously spent a great deal of his time working-out but Jake would surely kill him with a single punch.

'Hi, guys,' Robert Farmer said in a well-modulated, friendly voice. 'Now we're gonna have us some fun!'

GET BACK!

Double A heard Katie's voice inside his head and felt the edge of the jolt that followed it. He was glad the bolt of power – or whatever it was – hadn't been directed at him.

Robert Farmer tensed and winced. 'Dear, dear, you're not being very cooperative about this, are you, Katie?' he said. 'There's still a chance for you with us, you know. It doesn't have to be this way.'

The Pop jolted to a halt. 'He's come for me,' Paul said, turning around. Double A glanced at him and then looked away. The expression on Paul's face wasn't just white rage, it was a cold, still, murderous look which spiked ice into your eyes.

The thick atmosphere inside the car consisted of many layers of fear and hatred and hope and fury, and way beneath all of them, Double A could sense the massive struggle that was still taking place between Katie and Robert Farmer as she fought to expel him from this place and he fought to retain his grip. Double A thought Farmer had the edge. He certainly spoke as if he did.

'Actually I've come for all of you,' Farmer corrected. 'Nice as it is of you to volunteer to show the others the way. I'll take you first, if you wish.'

'Outside,' Paul said, throwing open his door.

Jake had told Double A a little of Paul's history during the long drive down here and he was able to imagine this particular scene being played out in pubs and clubs over the years. He doubted that many people who had accepted this challenge and followed Paul outside had been able to come back in again afterwards.

'As you wish,' Farmer said confidently. 'I'd like to be able to promise that I won't hurt you, but on this occasion I am unable to. It's going to be very painful for you, Paul, and it's going to do me a great deal of good. I've waited a long time to catch up with the man who stole my two XJS Jaguars. Yes, Paul, *old cowpoke*, it was you. I don't suppose you remember, do you? No, but I do. The first was three years ago and the second was, ahh, about a week and a half before I killed your mother and her little pet doggy. Crime really doesn't pay, does it, *old poke*?'

Paul didn't reply, just leapt nimbly from the car.

Throughout this short, one-sided conversation Double A had considered striking out at Farmer and had decided that it would not be of any use whatsoever. Their chances of staying alive depended solely on Paul. Double A glanced at Jake and realised that he had thought the same thing at the same time. But Jake had reached a different conclusion entirely. Double A saw Jake twist round and thought, *Kill him, Jake!*

And Jake's left fist flashed out of nowhere.

6

Paul got out of the car feeling very cold and very strong. His mind was clear and calm. Katie had stopped drawing power from him after she commanded that the man go back where he'd come from, and Paul knew why. Robert Farmer had not gone back and if Paul was going to have to fight him, he would need all the strength he could muster. And he had that strength. His body was thrumming with power. If Robert Farmer was going to try to kill him, he was going to have a very difficult job on his hands. And he might just get a nasty surprise.

Paul turned back just in time to see Jake throw a short, stabbing left hook at Farmer. The punch connected with the bank manager's jaw and made a meaty *thock!* noise. Farmer's head snapped back. A surprised expression crossed his face but he didn't lose consciousness as Paul hoped he would and he didn't vanish back to where he'd come from.

'*Fucker!*' Jake cried and hit him again, harder this time. The force of the punch threw Farmer into Double A who brought a fist crashing down into his crotch.

Paul could feel Katie pushing at Farmer with her mind, and knew that her grip on him was weakening. Farmer was very strong indeed.

Paul saw Jake's next left hook closing on Farmer's face as if it were happening in slow motion. This time Farmer reacted. His right hand came up out of his lap and Paul got a good long look at the weapon that had done so much damage to his mother and the Cindy dog. And also, he presumed, to Freddie and Amy. It was a matt black stiletto that was no more than four inches long. Its pin-prick point was so sharp it was hard to see and both its finely honed edges glinted dangerously. It wasn't the kind of knife Paul had imagined Farmer had used to make such a mess of his mother, but now he saw it, he understood. The knife wasn't large but it would surely slip through flesh and muscle just as easily as a scalpel. It was a precision cutting instrument.

To Paul, it looked as if it was happening in slow motion, but Jake didn't see the knife at all, not until it had sliced almost all the way up the inside of his arm, from wrist to elbow, peeling flesh and muscle away from bone in a single long slough. The blow hit Farmer, but by the time it arrived, it was little more than a weak, open-handed slap.

Jake took his arm back, looking at the skein of dangling bleeding flesh with an expression of total astonishment. The blood that had flicked on to Farmer's face and hands, broke up into oily globules that were absorbed into the man's flesh.

'*JAKE!*' Double A screamed.

'Run, chicken,' Jake said, looking away from his arm and back at Farmer. 'Better run now!'

And then Jake shouted and threw his mangled arm at Farmer once more. Flesh fell as Double A scrambled out of the back of the car, across the front seat and out on to the hard shoulder.

'Motherfucker!' Jake screamed. He twisted away from Farmer,

brought up his right arm and thrust out his elbow. Paul saw blood bloom in the bullet wound. This time Farmer's stiletto went wide. Jake's elbow hit him hard in the mouth and when it came down again, had one of Farmer's front teeth embedded into it.

Katie scrambled out of the car and ran towards Double A who was heaving and moaning on the bank beside the road.

Paul considered going back into the car and knew that it would be a terrible mistake. It was too late for Jake now. Much too late. Inside the car, Farmer's stiletto flashed and Jake's neck began to gout blood. Jake screamed.

Oh God, I'm sorry, Jake, Paul thought.

And Robert Farmer turned away from Jake and started to climb past the tilted driver's seat. Jake threw himself off the seat and grabbed him, clinging on to his waist with his good arm. Jake weighed a good fifteen stone, but Farmer dragged him out of the car behind him as though he weighed nothing at all. Blood was shooting out of Jake's severed carotid in quick, high-pressure squirts that spattered the car and the hard shoulder. It was soaking into Farmer's clothes and vanishing. A small trickle of blood ran from Farmer's own mouth and was being absorbed by his skin, disappearing as quickly as it arrived. The stiletto flicked down and scored a deep line across Jake's wrist, but he didn't let go. Amazingly, he was fighting to find his feet.

Paul stepped forward, snapped a blow into Farmer's face and got his fist out of the way as the stiletto flickered towards his wrist.

'We'll see, you fucker!' Paul shouted. 'We'll see who's better than who!'

Farmer's eyes cleared. Blood ran from his nose and vanished into his skin. 'You can't win!' he said. 'Can't!'

Behind Farmer, in his dying moments, Jake found ground under his feet, dug in and pushed hard. Farmer tottered three steps closer to Paul, both his arms flung wide as he tried to keep his balance.

Paul saw the opening and reacted to it, moving quicker than he'd ever done before. Feeling as if he was watching all this from a distance, he darted into the space and hit Farmer with his left hand. It was a clean blow and it landed right on the spot he'd chosen and travelled upwards slightly. Alone, it should have been enough. The blow caught Farmer beneath his nose and smashed the better part of the gristle it was composed of up and back, through his eye sockets and into his brain. Paul couldn't stop and didn't *want* to stop. His right fist followed, hooking into Farmer's jaw as the man tottered unsteadily, surely dying. Farmer's jaw was slack when the punch connected with it. Paul heard the crack it made as it broke. Farmer looked confused but he didn't go down. Blood poured from his shattered nose and mouth and disappeared into his skin.

Behind him, Jake slid to the ground, the pulses of blood at his neck growing weaker.

Paul snapped another right into Farmer's bottom jaw, pushing it further to the left than it had any right to be. Hit it again and heard the skull snap.

Farmer took two steps backwards, fell over Jake, hit the ground, rolled and lay still, face down, his hands twitching.

'Bastard!' Double A shouted, then retched.

And Robert Farmer began to push himself up off the ground.

Paul was on him in a second, his mind white with rage. He squatted on Farmer's back, caught hold of his hair and smacked the man's shattered face down into the tarmac, again and again.

7

'Stop it! Paul, stop it!' Katie shouted. Paul looked up at her and realised he had no idea how long he had been smashing Farmer's face into the ground. He was exhausted, he ached from head to foot and the tendrils of pain which were sneaking up into his arms from his hands suggested that at least one of the bones on each of his hands was cracked, if not broken.

He let go of Farmer and climbed off him. The man's head rolled around. There was a red pulp where his face had been.

'Get back in the car,' Katie said. 'I have to finish it.'

Paul didn't know what she meant. There was nothing to finish here. This episode was all over. 'Jake,' Paul croaked. The body of his best friend lay at his feet in a large pool of blood which was darkening quickly in the sunshine. To the left of him, cars and caravans and trucks were swishing by as though nothing worth mentioning was happening here.

'We can't take him,' Katie said. 'He's gone, Paul. He's gone and he won't be coming back. Please, get in the car and let me finish it.'

Paul looked at Jake and then at Farmer and purposefully emptied his mind. He walked back to the Pop on legs that felt as stiff as stilts and got into the driver's seat.

Double A was in the back of the car, sobbing.

Wearily, Paul turned to him. He took hold of one of Double A's skinny arms, dragged it away from his tear-stained face and looked him in the eyes. 'You did good,' he said. 'You and Jake both did good.' It wasn't enough, and he knew it, but Paul didn't have any more words. Jake might have been Paul's best friend, but his relationship with Double A was deeper. Much deeper. Jake had been a kind of surrogate father to the kid. What could you say to a guy who had just seen his father figure hacked to death; who was currently sitting in a pool of his father's blood? *Life goes on*, didn't quite fit the bill – especially when it could be either or both of them next.

'I didn't thu-think it wuh-would end like this,' Double A sobbed.

Paul squeezed his hand and blinked back tears of his own. 'None of us did,' he said. 'I'm sorry.'

'Duh-does she have tuh-to?' Double A moaned. 'Does she have to do that?'

Paul frowned. A second later he understood what Katie had meant about having to finish it; what Double A meant about not having thought it would end like this. He fought off the urge to look out of the window at her, even when he felt her begin to siphon off power from him.

Paul and Double A stared at one another. Paul trying not to cry and losing the battle and Double A looking at him with eyes that pleaded for it not to happen.

The noise, when it came, sounded like a car tyre exploding. Something soft splattered against the side of the Pop. Double A's grip tightened on Paul's hand. A second later there was another explosion.

'Goodbye, Juh-Jake,' Double A said.

And Paul began to cry.

Chapter Twenty-Eight
Bad News in Bad Pieterstal

1

On the one and only campsite the sleepy German spa town of Bad Pieterstal had to call its own, Derek Davis put down his Richard Bach book on the power of positive thinking and began to poke at the embers of the barbecue with an immersion heater thermostat, thinking positively about the amount of heat they were likely to produce.

If Hans or Ricky the Swede or Jacques had been here, they would have had a great deal to say about the barbie and none of it would have been positive. The chicken that was suspended over it, wrapped in foil, was still dripping red juice after two hours and showed no sign of browning whatsoever.

But Ricky the Swede had retired to his motorhome to smoke dope, Hans was pottering about in the ladies' shower room fixing a leak and Jacques was two miles away, up in the village of Bad Pieterstal where he had gone almost ninety minutes ago to extract as many cigarettes from the machine as he could for the minimum amount of money.

For a French chef, Jacques had a way with machinery. For one thing, he had kept his ancient (and souped up) Renault 12TL Gordini on the road way past the point at which its life would have been curtailed if Jacques had been a kind man, and for another, he regularly returned from the village with upwards of a hundred cigarettes which had cost him the price of a single pack. He had either been caught in the act, or the local police had pulled him in again. The German police hated the car, but since Jacques had it registered in France there was little they could do about it except complain.

Derek pushed some glowing charcoal into a heap beneath the chicken and rotated the dripping bird. It would be ready by ten if it didn't rain. Perhaps.

He glanced up at the tree-lined mountains that surrounded the valley and sniffed the air. It smelt like rain, but then it *always* smelt like rain in this little neck of the Black Forest. There were clouds in the sky, but they weren't joined up – or *holding hands* as Jacques would have had it – and Derek thought he was safe. From the weather, if not from the chicken which looked as if it was going to be served rare.

He stood up and went back into the rickety caravan he laughingly called home, in search of a beer.

There were several half-written letters laid out on the trestle which stood beneath the caravan's canvas extension and Derek glanced at them as he passed on his way to the bucket of cold water that served as a fridge. One was to his kids, who were in Staffordshire with his first wife, another was to his second ex-wife, and the third was to Sandra Rook with whom he'd had a three-week love affair on the Greek island of Skiathos back in May.

I'll finish them later, he thought guiltily. He cracked the tab from a can of beer and went back outside, trying to shake off the feeling of negativity that was trying to steal up on him. Things only went wrong if you allowed them to. Ask Richard Bach.

The British couple – Alice and Bob – wandered past and Derek greeted them.

'Could you tell Hans we'll be staying another three days?' Bob asked, pausing.

'Sure,' Derek said, smiling. Hans spoke no English at all and Derek acted as the campsite's unofficial translator. It made introducing yourself easy and often led to the making of friends. Derek viewed himself as a man whose sole purpose in life was to do good for people. And while being a centre lathe turner in a small village in southern Germany wasn't exactly conducive to spreading happiness on a large scale, it was better than a kick in the bollocks. And provided you didn't mind walking up very steep hills, the countryside was perfect. The topography of Heaven itself would have a job to beat some of the views you could see from the top of the mountains.

Derek watched Bob troll off towards the showers, then poked at the embers of the barbecue, fighting off the strange feeling of melancholy that was trying to steal over him. He didn't get depressed any more. His old problems could not find him here in this lovely spot.

Derek didn't realise his mind had flung itself back to the bad old days until he'd spent a good while remembering, and then, even though he cast the memories forcefully aside, it was too late to disremember again. Derek thought that the taint of those old days would stay with him until he had slept.

Things had stacked up on Derek while he was still married to his first wife. Events had seemingly conspired, placing layer after layer of weight upon him, and he hadn't been able to cope. He had been thinking negatively. And negativity was self-fulfilling. It sucked badness towards it like a black hole. Then, one summer's day in Bath, right before his very eyes, the world had folded itself up and vanished.

They had repaired him, of course, but the mending had been makeshift and temporary, like a rubber patch on a bicycle's rotted inner tube. The repair hadn't lasted. They repaired him three times in total; gave him three new personalities. The first had crumbled in the divorce courts when his wife got her decree nisi. Derek had vague memories of having been dragged out of the boot of a woman's car in which he had hidden afterwards, while the woman stood there and screamed. The second personality had folded under the weight of his relationship with his new wife and the third had vaporised while he was on a bus to Coventry. Derek had climbed off the bus with no memory whatsoever of who he was, where he was going or where he'd been.

After that, Derek had re-built his own personality. And when he was strong enough he had begun to run. It had been successful. Just as long as he kept thinking positively things would turn out okay.

Except that it was becoming increasingly difficult to think positively.

Derek forced thoughts of his troubles out of his mind and looked up at the cloudy sky, just in time for the first fat rain-drop to fall into his eye. A second later thunder racketed around the mountains.

Gonna be a storm, he thought. *It's closing in.*

And then he heard a different kind of thunder.

2

This one's for you! Derek thought, standing up. He distantly wondered why he hadn't thought, *Here come fresh customers for Hans*, or *Christ, listen to that!* and had no good answer.

On the other side of the hedge, the road ran alongside the triangular campsite for a distance of perhaps three hundred metres. It wasn't uncommon to hear maniac drivers roaring by at a speed which was much too fast for the narrow and winding road, but Derek had never been subjected to this level of noise before, or seen a pair of headlights moving so quickly on the other side of the hedge.

The car that those headlights belonged to was going to come into the campsite, Derek knew without a shadow of a doubt. It was coming for him – in what way, he wasn't sure. A part of him was suddenly as terrified as he had ever been, and another part, for some deep and unknown reason, rejoiced.

Bellowing like a wounded lion, the car shot along the side of the campsite. Derek followed the flicker of its headlights with his eyes, thinking, *It's going too fast to make the turn! It'll roll!*

And the car flashed past the turning, its roaring engine note rising to a scream as its driver selected a lower gear and hit the gas.

Derek watched its tail lights vanish around the bend in the road, then listened to it tearing up the air as it wound its way up towards Bad Pieterstal. The crushing disappointment he felt was tempered with something that might have been relief.

When the noise had faded to nothing, Derek sat down again, shaking his head and wondering what had gone wrong. A hundred feet away from where he was sitting, the curtains in the back of Ricky the Swede's camper parted and Ricky peered out, a huge seven-skin joint hanging from his mouth. Derek waved and watched the hot end of the joint wobble, then grow brighter as Ricky took another puff. Ricky flipped him the finger and the curtains closed again.

It'll come back, Derek assured himself, and wasn't sure he wanted it to.

3

Lightning flashed, way over the mountain, and the sound of thunder took a long time to get to where Derek was sitting. It seemed as if the storm was following the car. It would probably be going through Nordrach by now, Derek thought. He had expected it to get up into Bad Pieterstal, then turn around and come back, in the same fashion as everyone else arrived at the campsite. Almost no one came straight here unless they knew where it was.

Droplets of rain were raising ash in the barbecue and vaporising with tiny hisses when they touched the charcoal that was still glowing. Derek picked up the rod-thermostat and poked the embers viciously, as if doing this would remove the disconcerting *déjà vu* feeling which his mind seemed to be mirroring, so that it wasn't so much as if it had *happened before*, as feeling like it had *happened before it had happened before it had happened before*. A picture of a burning car kept trying to pop into his mind to accompany the sensation and he fought it off.

Think positively, he told himself and pictured Richard Bach, not at his desk writing *Jonathan Livingston Seagull* but at the seminar where Derek had first listened to him speak about the power of the mind. He used Bach's spotlit figure as a shield to keep negativity at bay while he thought about the girl who had written to Bach telling him how dearly she wanted to be an airline pilot and how Bach had encouraged her and sent her a little money to get her started. That girl was now the captain of a Jumbo jet which only went to show . . .

That she was lucky, a small voice said in Derek's mind.

. . . that if you could harness your imagination, anything was possible.

The image of the burning car swept the picture of Bach away in flames.

And Derek heard the distant roar of the car coming back down the mountain.

This time it slowed as it approached the turning, but it didn't slow quite enough. The car, which was purple and dented and covered in dust and looked as if it had once been a Ford of the fifties before someone had got to work on it with fat tyres and air-scoops and other 'refinements', slid sideways as its driver wrenched the wheel round. Gravel flew and the car's engine roared and its wheels spun, and for a moment Derek thought it was going to slide straight into the deserted house that stood on the corner and burst into flames. The feeling was so strong that it wasn't until the car skidded to a halt ten feet away from him that Derek could believe he hadn't actually seen that happen. He could still see the smashed wall of the house burning with the petrol that had sprayed up it after the collision.

The car's headlights blinded Derek as he stared into them. He stood up, wanting to run away and knowing that he could not. Someone in that car needed him. Of that he was certain.

The car's headlights went out and it stood there, its low engine sound now a sick, idling throb. It reminded Derek of a race horse he had once seen on the Kingsclere downs after its early-morning exercise. The horse had been lathered with sweat and steaming. But its muscles had been pumped up and it had looked as if it would have run forever if its jockey had asked it to. The car had the same look about it. Tendrils of steam wafted their way from the front grille and the exhaust was surely broken, but the car looked as if it could run another five hundred miles if it was necessary.

Except that this car was going to burn.

Derek shook his head and walked towards the car. Over in the camper, Ricky peered out again.

The Ford's engine stopped, leaving Derek's ears ringing with silence. Then the driver's door flew open and someone fell out on to the dusty track. That someone didn't look anything like Derek had expected. He wasn't quite sure *what* he'd been expecting, but it was something a lot more power-ful (*and troublesome*) than this. The guy picking himself up from the ground was around five foot eight tall and looked as though he'd been on the kind of low-cal diet that had been all the rage in prisoner of war camps during what his father had called The Big Bastard. He was an emaciated bag of bones to whom something terrible had happened. His face was sheeted with dried blood – and dust as well, now that he'd fallen – his hair was matted and there were drying stains all over his clothes.

Before the man had even spoken, Derek had mentally show-ered him, bound his wounds, fed him and dressed him in a set of his own clothes – which would hang on him like a big suit on a broomstick. During this second, Derek's mental reserva-tions – and all his doubts and negative thoughts – left him. Here was something he could (and would) do something about. Life had seen fit to deliver someone in need of help to him and he would help that person.

The guy got up, stumbled against the side of the car and held on. 'Quick!' he said.

And fainted.

The guy didn't so much fall as curve gently down to the ground. Derek sprinted the last few steps towards him and knelt beside him, checking the pulse in his throat. The guy was alive. His pulse was fast and weak but a cursory examination assured Derek that he wasn't too badly damaged. He was bruised almost everywhere Derek cared to look and there was quite a gash in his scalp, but he wasn't about to die.

'I don't fucking believe this, man!'

Derek looked up at Ricky the Swede whose long blond hair was still wet from the shower he'd taken an hour ago. Ricky's eyes were red-rimmed and he stank of cannabis. 'It's happening,' Derek said. 'Help me lift him.'

But he didn't need Ricky's help to pick the guy up – Derek's nine-year-old from his first marriage had weighed about as much as this the last time he'd swept her from the ground. Sandra Rook, his Greek goddess who weighed nine eleven, was a good stone heavier.

'Quick,' the guy moaned. His eyes fluttered.

'It's okay,' Derek told him. 'I've got you. You're gonna be fine.'

'After . . .' the thin guy moaned. 'Close.'

'What's he say?' Ricky asked distantly. He was peering inside the car from a safe distance as though he expected the open driver's door to snap at him like a crocodile if he went too close.

'Nothing much,' Derek said. 'Come on, let's get him inside my 'van.'

'Wait,' Ricky said.

Derek spun back towards him. In his arms the man moaned that something or other was 'catching up'.

Ricky looked worried. He held up his hands, palms outward, like someone miming a sheet of plate glass that stood in front of them. 'He didn't say anything?' Ricky asked.

'He's only half conscious, for Christ's sake,' Derek said. 'What did you want, a formal introduction?'

'I just wondered . . .'

'*What?*'

'. . . because of the blood on him . . .'

'Christ, man, hurry up!'

'. . . if he said anything about how these two people in the back of the car got dead.'

'*More* people?' Derek asked.

'Two . . . unless this hashish is a little stronger than I thought. Will you check?'

Ricky said this as calmly as he might have done at work when requesting that Derek give a second opinion on a perfectly machined spigot.

Derek checked, already knowing what he was going to find.

'What do we do?' Ricky asked.

Derek knew Ricky didn't want the police around because of the dope in his camper. There was a lot of it. The local police were keeping tabs on him – had been since he arrived.

'Take this one, put him in my caravan, I'll look at the others,' Derek said, and thrust the thin guy into Ricky's arms before he could protest.

Ricky's eyebrows did a comical dance of surprise when he felt the man's weight, then he bore him off towards Derek's caravan.

'Hide!' the guy whispered thickly. 'Coming!'

Derek tilted the front seat forward and climbed into the back of the car. There was a great deal of blood there on the bench seat with the two bodies. In the dim light provided by the site's one and only street lamp, Derek only saw it as dark patches, but he could smell it and it was sticky on his fingers.

This is all wrong, he told himself.

And it didn't start to make sense until he realised that neither the man nor the girl who were on the back seat, entwined like deceased lovers, was actually dead. Both of them had steady pulses.

Derek backed himself out of the car, tilted the front seat down and climbed into it. The guy had said three intelligible words, which were: *quick, coming and hide*. And the car had been going very fast.

As if, in fact, it was being pursued.

Wondering what he was getting himself into, and instantly deciding that whatever it was, it was the right thing, Derek found the ignition and turned the key. The car roared into life. He blipped the throttle, put his foot on the clutch and found what he hoped was first gear, then let the clutch out. The Pop jolted forward and stalled. Derek cursed and wished he'd taken the driving lessons Jacques had offered. He knew what you had to do, but he couldn't do it.

He tried again and this time the car shot four feet towards his caravan before stalling.

And as he turned the key to try again, a car turned off the main road and on to the gravel track. Its headlights swept through the interior of the Pop and Derek's heart sank. Whoever was chasing was here, and he wasn't going to be able to do a damn thing about it. He hoped it would be the police, and knew that it was a vain hope.

Derek wound the key in the ignition and stood on the Pop's throttle. The car roared indignantly. He floored the clutch, ground the gears as he looked for first and missed it.

Behind him, the oncoming car's headlights pinned the Pop like spotlights on a prisoner caught on a barbed wire fence. The car drew up directly behind and Derek glanced in the mirror and saw its door open at the edge of the bright headlight beams.

He gunned the Pop's engine, thrust the gearstick to where he had found first gear – to where first gear no longer seemed to be. The car made a horrible metallic screeching noise until he stopped forcing the stick.

Too late! he thought, because he'd seen the films and he knew what happened to those prisoners caught on the fence after they were lit in the glare of spotlights. Someone opened fire on them.

The door of the car was yanked open. Derek smelled Gauloise smoke.

'What are you trying to do?' an accented voice asked in English.

Derek looked up towards the source of that voice, not even allowing himself to think about its tone or about the cigarette smell or the person who had spoken the words.

He could have wept with relief when he saw that the swarthy

face belonged not to some murderer but to Jacques. Derek had never been so relieved and pleased to see anyone in his whole life.

Derek threw himself out of the car. 'Quick,' he said, 'help me get these people out of here, then get the car round behind the shower block. Someone's going to be here shortly, looking for it.'

4

The Mercedes didn't turn up for another fifty-five minutes and when it did there were four people sitting round a dying barbecue waiting for it: a German, an Englishman, a Swede and a Frenchman. Derek thought there ought to be a joke about that, but he couldn't bring one to mind. What he *could* bring to mind was the story that the thin guy – whose name was apparently Double A – had told him. And if any of that story was right (and Derek had started to believe it from the moment he'd picked up the girl called Katie and taken her into the shower block) someone here was likely to get hurt.

Derek and Jacques, who had spent the better part of forty minutes with Double A, first feeding him little sips of water, and then aiding him in the shower block while they tried to revive the comatose Katie and Paul Dekker, had not told the whole story to the others. Between them, they had concocted a thin tale of mistaken identity and gangland thugs and although it hadn't rung true in Derek's ears while he told this part of it, the others seemed satisfied. It went down, Derek estimated, better than the truth might have done, and although Hans and Ricky weren't enamoured of the idea of facing down the two thugs who were chasing the English people, he was sure they would like it a lot less if they thought those thugs were zombies.

While he and Jacques and Double A had showered Paul and Katie, dressed their wounds then dressed them in fresh clothes, Derek thought his senses might have deserted him again. But Jacques was there and Jacques had never had a doubt in his life and he believed it all.

Something had happened, Double A had said, after a man called Robert Farmer had killed his friend Jake. It was to do with a mental battle between Paul and Katie and someone called Gary Richman. Derek didn't quite understand the rules of this combat, but according to Double A's theory, the upshot of it was that both of them had lost consciousness and could not be woken until it was finished. Both the girl (who seemed to affect you in a strange way when you touched her, or even looked at her for too long) and the man had strong, steady pulses and were breathing evenly and regularly, but they remained unconscious, whatever you did to them. Double A said he thought the time was getting short and if he didn't get them back to England inside two days it would be too late.

It was all strangely confusing and it all had the clear ring of truth.

And the truth was, Derek knew, as he watched the Mercedes roll into the drive, that there was an angel and her two helpers in the shower block and all of them were wearing his clothes. There seemed to be a kind of finality in the act of washing and dressing two of those three people, as though Derek had lived his whole life simply to do this.

And he had been rewarded for his efforts. He didn't know whether it had also happened to Jacques or not, but when he had stared hard at Katie's naked and perfect body he had seen something around it that looked like a ragged tear. A rip in reality where it might have been opened to allow her access. And through that fault area, Derek had caught a glimpse of something special.

Something that might have been Heaven.

And if he died now, as he thought he would, he would die happy.

5

'Rain didn't come to anything, did it?' Derek said in German as the men approached. 'We had thunder and lightning and thought there would be a storm, but it passed. Sometimes they do.'

'This is them?' Ricky asked.

'Oui,' Jacques replied.

Hans simply nodded slowly.

'Where are they?' Erich Spiegel asked.

'What did you say?' Jacques asked politely in German.

'The English. Where are they?' Josef Spiegel demanded. 'We don't want any unpleasantness. We know they are here.'

Hans shook his head. 'Which English?' he asked in German. 'We have eight camping.'

'Dekker and the girl and the other one,' Josef said. 'You know which English.'

The four looked blankly at one another. Derek picked up his thermostat and poked at the barbecue embers. His heart was hammering in his ears. He shook his head. 'No one here called Dekker,' he said. When he looked up again, he was looking at two men holding guns.

'Why do you have black teeth?' Jacques suddenly asked.

Erich stepped forward and jabbed the gun towards him. 'Bis du ach gut im Kopf?' he asked. *Are you still right in the head?*

Derek assumed the unspoken part of the sentence was that he was unlikely to be after a bullet had passed through his brain. Jacques appeared to think about this. 'Oui,' he said, 'et vous?' A grin that was less than a thousandth of an inch away from being maniacal was fixed to his face.

Derek could suddenly feel a snap of energy in the air surrounding them. It was as though he'd become precognitive to the tune of about ten seconds so that he could sense movement which hadn't yet happened. The atmosphere was thick with the potential energy of six people about to try to kill one another.

Josef tilted his head to one side as if he was listening to a distant voice and frowned. He spoke in German. 'They're in the shower block,' he said. 'Richman has them pinned down. Easy targets but watch for the boy. He doesn't have the boy.'

Derek saw Erich's finger tighten on the trigger and knew that the two men intended to kill all four of them. His heart leapt into his throat and the words *What am I going to do?* skated across his mind, but it was too late for thought, because Jacques was already getting up and his chair was falling over behind him. Derek noted with distant surprise that he was following suit. Josef's gun swung to a spot that seemed to be roughly in the middle of Derek's forehead and steadied. Hans shouted at the top of his voice and beside Derek, Ricky was falling forwards towards the ground.

And behind the shower block, the engine of the Ford Popular roared into life.

Josef's gun swung away from Derek as the car slid sideways around the corner, its lights on high beam and its engine roaring.

Derek felt as though the movements he had sensed – the ones he and his little group were now making – had been planned to the last detail. He knew them all intimately as if he had rehearsed them time and time again and they seemed fixed, as though no other course of action was possible. The word *choreography* slid past his mind and the pictures of the burning car lit again inside his head. In the eye-blink of time it took for him to leap out of his seat and smash head-first into Josef's chest, Derek knew none of it was going to do any good. The car would burn. Whatever he and his friends did, the car would burn.

Derek stove into the German and as they went down realised what Ricky had been doing when he'd slid out of his seat. It was a schoolboy trick that Derek himself had participated in on more than one occasion. The Swede had snaked round behind Josef on all fours and stopped, giving Derek a human bridge to push the man over. The force of the fall smacked Derek's mouth against the German's chin. His teeth bit deep into his lips. It hurt very badly. Josef twisted himself to his right and his gun went off, close enough to Derek's ear to deafen him.

Another gun fired and Jacques screamed, 'MERDE!'

Derek pushed himself back from the German as Ricky scrambled over towards Jacques. Josef squeezed off another shot at the car and its engine died.

'DON'T!' Derek screamed. In his mind the car was alight. He was now crouched over Josef who – unbelievably – was ignoring him in favour of shooting at the stalled car. Derek punched the man's gun arm with his left fist as Josef fired his next shot. It was like hitting a piece of steel. The man's arm didn't even waver. The bullet lit sparks on the Pop's bonnet and its windscreen imploded.

As he had done at those key moments in his life when his personality was about to dissolve, Derek howled hopelessly and brought both clenched fists up to his face like a child throwing a tantrum. The battle was lost and he could feel himself fading.

Something cold touched his face. As the next shot fired, Derek opened his eyes and saw that the rod-thermostat was still clenched in his right hand. It was an eighteen-inch 'stat from a thirty-six inch immersion heater. Its diameter was a little larger than that of a pencil. As though he was moving in slow motion, Derek looked from the 'stat to the German and back again. The 'stat was blackened with ash from a hundred barbecues. The German's eyes were blackened with death.

The next time the gun roared, the sound seemed to go on forever. While the noise tore at his ears, Derek turned the 'stat up the other way in his fist with his left hand and looked back down at the German.

Derek felt very strong when he brought his hand down. He had the force of a tidal wave, the speed of a hummingbird.

The narrowed end of the thermostat pierced Josef's eye, instantly turning it into a black, oozing mass.

Josef turned his head back towards Derek, fixing him with his good eye. Something golden and horrible looked out of that eye at Derek. The gun came back towards him. He screamed and pushed at the 'stat.

There was a brief feeling of resistance as the thermostat met

698

bone, then an odd falling sensation as the bone gave way and the thermostat slid into Josef's brain.

Derek felt the thing inside Josef let go. The German's body twitched once and relaxed. A strong smell of rotting fruit wafted up from him.

Derek threw himself off the German and, feeling as though he was made of jelly, got to his feet.

Ten feet away from him, the other German was standing and pointing his gun at the Pop. Hans lay at his feet, curled into a ball. Ricky was sprawled across the steps of Derek's caravan, a fist-sized hole in his forehead, and Jacques was limping towards the man with an axe in one hand and his sheath knife in the other. Behind him, down the length of the campsite, people were flooding out of their tents and caravans, eager to see what was happening. Derek noted distantly that none of them seemed quite so eager to lend a hand. No one whatsoever was hurrying in this direction.

Jacques was covered in blood and looked hurt, but the German seemed to have taken the worst of the damage. There was no hand on his left wrist and the right side of his face hung in darkly glistening tatters.

Derek watched Jacques closing on the German, watched him sweep the axe around in a big, slow arc, knowing it was going to be too late.

The German fired his last shot a moment before Jacques beheaded him.

And behind Derek the Pop burst into flames.

6

Derek had never seen a car on fire and he was surprised that a motor vehicle contained enough combustible material to burn with such ferocity. He screamed at Jacques that they had to get the people out of the car, but he knew that no one inside could possibly be alive. The inside of the car looked like Hell itself. Nothing could be seen other than the bright orange flame which swirled and raged. It leapt out through the Pop's open windscreen in long tongues which seemed sentient and eager for more fuel.

Derek ran towards it and stopped, still fifteen feet or so away, his hair and eyebrows singeing with the intense heat.

'Get back!' Jacques yelled in German. 'The tank will blow!'

'*WE HAVE TO GET THEM OUT*!' Derek screamed and thrust both his fists against his teeth. *Wet blanket*! he thought. *Get a wet blanket and cover yourself so you can get them out. You can't let them die! Not now!*

Derek ran back towards his caravan, intending to drag the duvet off his bed, soak it at the tap on the side of the shower block and dive into the car to rescue its inhabitants, refusing to allow himself to believe two obvious truths – that it couldn't be done and that it was too late anyway.

The thing that saved his life happened as he reached the steps of his caravan and leapt over the body of Ricky the Swede who was never again going to ask to have his fine lathe work checked.

The '59 Ford Popular that Double A and Jake had spent so much time restoring and 'rodding, blew up with an explosion that would be heard as far away as Strasbourg.

The shockwave knocked Derek clean off his feet and whipped his head into the side of his caravan, denting the aluminium panelling and knocking him unconscious.

Way down the campsite, a single voice began to scream.

Derek dreamed of angry angels causing thunder and lightning and death.

Chapter Twenty-Nine
The Gift of Cynthia

1

In the space of one very short hour, Jacques Ellimot's day off work had changed from being just another mundane rest day in which he did all the usual boring things to one that he would remember for the rest of his life.

In those sixty minutes, Jacques, who described his religion as that of a born again atheist, and who broke a good eight of the ten commandments whenever possible, had heard an impossible story he believed to be true, he had gazed upon what he thought was the face of one of Heaven's angels, and had seen the glowing fires burning in the dead eyes of two of Hell's servants. And although he had not undergone a religious transformation, Jacques, who would swear to his dying day that he had always remained neutral in the battle between good and evil, had quickly discovered which side his inner self leaned towards.

Without having to think about it, he had accepted the story the Englishman called Double A had told him, knowing it was the truth. And he had fought for the side of good, telling himself it was simply because the girl was lovely and the Germans were ugly and that because it was the side his friend Derek had chosen to join. Derek was a good judge of character.

There was more to it than this, he knew, much more, but Jacques would have to think about it later, just as he would have to think about what he'd done to the German later – there was no time now.

Because his German had shot the car before the axe had taken off his head and the car was on fire and Derek was running towards it, apparently intending to rescue its occupants.

'Get back!' Jacques yelled. 'The tank will blow!'

'*WE HAVE TO GET THEM OUT*!' Derek screamed.

For the first time in his twenty-eight years, Jacques became telepathic. Later he would tell himself that it was through fear of what might happen to his friend, and later still he would tell himself that it had been the product of his imagination, but now, Jacques clearly heard what Derek thought next. *Wet blanket*! he screamed to himself. *Get a wet blanket and cover yourself so you can get them out. You can't let them die! Not now!*

Jacques dropped the axe and sprinted towards Derek's caravan, knowing he wasn't going to get there ahead of his friend, but intending to stop him carrying out his crazy and impossible plan. If there was one thing that was a dead certainty, it was that no one inside that blazing car was going to be alive to be rescued. When Derek came out again, carrying the blanket he was going to get, Jacques would restrain him. Forcibly if necessary.

It can't be done and it's too late! Jacques mentally shouted at his friend.

Derek reached the steps of his caravan, leapt over Ricky's body . . . and the car blew up.

Jacques dropped to the ground a moment ahead of the shock-wave. The world collapsed under a horrendous booming roar.

When he looked up again, it was raining. Not pieces of burning metal and fabric – and possibly pieces of body – but good honest clean cool rain. Thunder cracked and echoed around the mountains. Up ahead, the Ford Popular was a two foot high tangled piece of rent metal which smoked and steamed in the rain.

Derek was on the ground beside his caravan, lying close to Ricky who had been killed by the German's first shot. Jacques had suffered the dubious delight of having seen his brain flying away from his head in shreds and thought the image would stay with him forever. Ricky was dead and gone, but Jacques didn't know about Derek. What he did know was that he had to go and look in the trees on the far side of the tangle of steaming metal as quickly as possible because the impossible thought that *it isn't over yet* sounded in his head like a gong and something else had to be done.

2

On the far side of the drive upon which the Ford Popular had exploded was a strip of grass, behind which stood a line of trees about four deep. Behind these were bushes and then the bank of the river.

Jacques skirted the smouldering car and ran across the grass, leaping over pieces of twisted and steaming metal. 'Où êtes-vous?' he shouted as he ran into the stand of trees. He didn't know who he was calling for. If the girl was, by some miracle, in this little wood and still alive, he would take her all the way back to England himself. There would be no question. And it was going to have to be the girl, because if she was lost, the war was over.

'Katie?' he called, peering into the darkness.

Thunder rocked the sky as if in reply and the rain began to fall more heavily, sizzling through the leaves like a thousand pans of frying food.

'*Katie!*'

And then he saw legs on the ground before him, dressed in Derek's denim jeans rolled up at the ankles. For one terrible moment Jacques knew that the legs were all that he was going to find of the body, then he realised that the remainder of it was shielded by a low bush.

'Katie!' he shouted, bending over and taking the ankles and dragging the light body from beneath the dark bush.

Except that it wasn't Katie, it was Double A.

'Something went bang. Knocked me down,' he mumbled.

Jacques dropped to his knees. Double A didn't look hurt.

'You got out from the car?' Jacques jabbered, his grip on English slipping. 'You alive got out?'

'Yes,' Double A replied. 'The bastards blew it up, didn't they? Christ, man, my head hurts. I think I bashed it.'

'Vos amis? Your friends?' Jacques said. He groped for the words. 'They couldn't got out?'

'They weren't in,' Double A said thickly. 'Still in the showers. Drove the motor round to get the Germans. Was going to run 'em down. Didn't happen though. I got out the car after the first shot hit it. Knew it would blow. Don't ask me how.'

'We must get you away,' Jacques said and hauled Double A to his feet.

'The Germans?'

'Morts,' Jacques said. 'At last.'

'Thanks,' Double A said.

Jacques found both his hands and squeezed them. His hands were strong and warm and hard and so much like Jake's that Double A found himself wanting to cry.

'You must leave,' Jacques said carefully. 'Something will happen here if you don't get out. Something that will stop you until it is too late. This I feel strongly. You must quickly go!'

He turned away and dragged Double A along behind him by his hand.

'Can't go,' Double A complained as they reached the track. 'No car.'

'Voilà!' Jacques said and swept his free hand out in an arc towards his own car.

Double A stared at it in disbelief. It was a delapidated Renault 12TL Gordini which had surely finished its good years around 1975. It looked like something you'd hire for a tenner a day from Rent-A-Wreck in Peckham – except that those cars looked more roadworthy . . . and they weren't painted down both sides in psychedelic-coloured patterns.

'You take my car. The keys are in and the tank is up full. There are three thousand French francs in the lining of the head. She is fast and reliable. She will serve you, Anthony. Now quickly! Something will happen. I will to the shower block go. Bring her round.'

3

Double A glanced wistfully at what remained of his pride and joy. The loss of the car hurt, but what was worse was the loss of thousands of snorts of what Jake had called the old super-charged snuff. Double A's head ached, his body felt wrecked and the loss of Jake weighed on him like a thousand tons of concrete. Some of that coke or sulphate would have done him a power of good. He wished he'd had the presence of mind to stuff it into his trousers before he'd got out of the car. Then he put the thought out of his mind and turned back to the Renault.

The rain suddenly increased its force as though someone up there in the sky had opened the tap another turn. It came down hard and apparently in long streams. *Stair rods, Jake would have said*, Double A thought, and splashed across the wet grass to the car.

The Renault was shot. Double A realised this the moment he opened the driver's door. It sagged almost a quarter of an inch on its hinge. He climbed in. The seat might once have given some support, but those days had long since passed. Double A felt the hard floor of the car rise up to meet the bottom of whatever foam was left in the seat. The floor felt hard beneath his bony bottom. It was like sitting with your arse halfway down a toilet and Double A couldn't see over the steering wheel. He shunted the seat forward, which helped a little, adjusted the mirror, wriggled himself into a more comfort-able position, found the keys and twisted the ignition. One lonely wiper juddered its way across the screen and halted. *Shit!* Double A thought. He twisted the key a little further and the engine started. It sounded good. Its note was smooth and low and promised power. Double A brightened a little. When the wiper began to work again, he brightened a little more. For some obscure reason, Jacques had fitted a maple steering wheel to the car. The wood felt good under Double A's hands and the wheel had no play whatsoever, which meant the steering would be responsive. It was no '59 Pop, but it was beginning to look as if it might actually do the job.

Double A revved the engine, put his left hand out for the gearstick and smacked his knuckles into the door. The car's stick came out of the dash. Double A found it after a brief, frantic search and after another found reverse gear. He let the clutch out and the car moved backwards, turning more gracefully and smoothly than it had any right to.

Double A found first gear and rolled slowly past the dead Pop and round behind the shower block. It was raining so hard now that even with the one wiper on full speed the screen was not being cleared.

Jacques and Hans were waiting for him at the door to the men's shower room. Double A backed the car up to the door, pulled the handbrake on and got out, leaving the engine running.

'Okay?' Jacques said.

Double A nodded, realising that his headache was going away. 'Fine,' he replied.

'You are happy to take her?'

'If you're happy to let me,' Double A said.

'She is my gift to you,' Jacques said. 'Her name is Cynthia. If you treat her well, she will treat you well in return. Maybe you will bring her back to see me one day?'

'Sure,' Double A said, more confidently than he felt. 'You'll get her back when we're done.'

'You win,' Jacques said. 'You make sure you win. Now let's get your friends into the car.'

4

Katie and Paul both looked as if they were in a very deep sleep. Both their faces had slight frowns, which both deepened

706

into furrows when they were moved so they were no longer touching one another. Double A watched Hans and Jacques carry both of them to the car and made sure that their hands were clasped together when they were set down in the back seat. He wasn't quite sure what had happened to them, but since they'd been out of it, he hadn't sensed that mental radar beam of Gary Richman's searching him out, so he supposed the pair of them were engaging him in some kind of mental battle to keep him occupied until they were taken home. This was what he had told Jacques and Derek, who was still unconscious (but whom Hans said was going to be okay), and it was the best explanation he'd been able to come up with.

It could, of course, have been wrong. The Germans had found them here, hadn't they? And according to Jacques, something nasty would happen to prevent them leaving if they didn't go soon, which meant that H still knew their whereabouts.

'Okay,' Jacques said when Double A was back in the car. 'Now you go. Quickly and safely!' He bent down to the open window, took Double A's shoulders and kissed him on both cheeks. Then he handed Double A a gun. 'It belonged to the German,' he said as Double A looked at the weapon. 'Keep it. You might need it. Now get them home and win the war. For us. We will be thinking of you!' he said.

And with those words ringing in his ears, Double A put the gun down on the empty front seat and drove away.

5

Double A turned left on to the road and headed back down the mountain the way he had come, knowing now that he hadn't driven here to Bad Pieterstal because he was lost but because it was necessary. In some peculiar way, the place had called to him, dragging him there, as it had tried to on his way down.

Something else he understood, as he peered out of the windscreen at a road which was now more of a river, was what Jacques had been worried about. The rain, for which the adjective *torrential* seemed too feeble, was making any speed greater than twenty miles an hour impossible to achieve, and it was pouring down from the mountains and out on to the road which either meant that Double A was soon going to run up against a flood which he would not be able to pass, *or it might just be a . . .*

Double A rounded the bend and hit the brakes because the other thing, the thing he'd just been going to verbalise to himself, had happened.

. . . landslide, he finished as the Renault's waterlogged brake pads skidded across wet discs without gripping at all.

Double A pressed harder on the pedal and the brakes bit, juddered and smoothed. The Renault stopped six inches away from the fall of rock that had slid out of the side of the mountain and blocked the road.

So now what? Double A asked himself, but he already knew, was already opening the car door to go and look at the angles and gap at the bottom.

The big, almost flat, sheet of granite that lay against Double A's side of the rockfall looked very much like a ramp. It was inclined at an angle of thirty or forty degrees and it was perhaps ten feet from where it touched the road to where it ended at the top of the heap.

Double A walked up it, realising that it wasn't as smooth as it looked. The pile of rubble on the other side of the sheet spread about ten feet down into the road. There were two huge boulders on the tarmac down there where the rubble ended. They were about eight feet apart. If Double A was going to jump this obstruction with the Renault he would have to try to arrange things so the car came down between them and not on top of either of them or even *into* either of them. And then there was the four-inch face where the tilted end of the sheet met the tarmac on his side. It was a stunt that would have made Eviel Knievel cry if he'd been asked to perform it in dry and sunny conditions, let alone at night in this rain in a beaten up Renault

12TL, even if it did have the suffix Gordini.

Double A clambered back down the ramp knowing he couldn't do it, and knowing he was going to try anyway.

What the fuck, he told himself, *the car will fall apart long before you get to the top.*

He got back into the car, checked on Paul and Katie, who were still out of it, then strapped on his seat belt.

Okay, Cynthia, he thought to the car, *I'm gonna be asking you for a favour. We're gonna have to make a big jump here and I want you to see us all across it. With any luck, no one will ever have to ask you to do anything like this again. But we all need you to see us across this one and we need you to get us back to England afterwards. If I thought there was any other way we could get by, I'd do it, but I don't think there will be. I think if we were to turn round and try to find another route, that one would be blocked too. So please, Cynthia. Please, please and pretty please.*

He gunned the car's smooth engine and reversed up the road and back around the bend. It didn't matter that he wasn't going to be able to take aim up the granite ramp until he rounded the bend because in these conditions you wouldn't have been able to see what you were looking at even if the road had been straight.

Double A paused when he estimated he'd gone back far enough. *Okay, girl?* he asked and gunned the engine. The single wiper paused and started again and Mrs Anthony's boy took this as a sign of the car's assent. It was about as good as he was going to get, by the look of it.

Double A hit the throttle and plummeted down the hill into the dark night, bringing Cynthia quickly up through the gears. The car was moving at forty-five miles an hour as it reached the bend and all Double A's senses screamed at him that they couldn't possibly make the turn. The tyres were going to lose their grip and aquaplane Cynthia and all who sailed in her right off the road. Or she would roll. Or he would oversteer and crash into the rock face.

Cynthia dipped alarmingly but didn't lose her grip or her

position in the centre of the road. Double A could barely see anything at all now. The rain was coming at him horizontally and the shelf of granite was little more than a huge dark hulk looming in the car's headlights.

Go! Double A screamed to himself as Cynthia levelled, and thrust his foot down hard on the accelerator. The car speeded up, and in the moment directly before it hit the slab of rock Double A wondered if he ought to be praying and realised it was too late.

Cynthia's front wheels hit the edge of the rock with a horrendous crash that had surely burst both tyres, bent the wheels flat and driven the suspension out through her wings. The steering wheel tried to tear itself away from Double A's leech-like grip and failed. Double A was suddenly leaning backwards at an angle of forty degrees or so, staring up into blackness and rain, tinted gold by the car's headlights. Cynthia's rear wheels mounted the ramp and the car bucked, throwing its back end into the air. The rear wheels hit the rock face and then all Double A was conscious of was the tremendous tramping vibration as the car shot forward and its suspension tried to deal with the irregular surface.

Then they were flying.

The car was in the air for less than three seconds, but for Double A it seemed like a lifetime. Still under power, Cynthia's driving wheels spun beneath her, humming. The car's body complained as Cynthia reached the zenith of her trajectory and altered her attitude from going up to coming down. The single wiper flip-flapped against the screen and the car's smooth engine note decreased as Double A let the power off.

There was time enough, as the car came down, for Double A to realise they were no longer travelling level. The car was listing slightly to the right, which meant it was going to hit the ground on its offside front wheel. He had time to conclude that it might be a very good thing to turn the steering wheel slightly to the right, because when that single front wheel hit the force was going to thrust it to the left. In the moment before the car hit the ground, Double A made the adjustment and gritted his teeth.

Landing was worse than taking off had been. The front wheel Double A had made the adjustment for did hit first, but it came down in a pile of rubble and yanked the steering wheel in the opposite direction to the one which he was compensating for. It tore from his grasp and slid rapidly through his fingers.

Double A's side of the front of the car slammed down and the rear wheels followed. The steering wheel slid back the other way and Double A caught it and seeing one of those two large boulders looming up on his side, wrenched it to the right. Cynthia fishtailed and Double A put the gas on, screaming inwardly as the rear of the car slewed round towards the rock. The back of the Renault smacked into the boulder and bounced off. Double A corrected the skid, caught the oversteer and straightened. And the road grew smooth under the car's wheels.

'Did it I did it I did it!' Double A screamed, his foot automatically finding the brake pedal. He pulled the car up, and looked over his shoulder. Paul and Katie were still out cold. They lay in a tangle in the back. Paul had slid halfway down into the footwell and was pushing the front passenger seat forward. His head was in Katie's lap. There was a small cut on his cheek where he'd scraped it on something. It was bleeding, but not badly. Double A looked at him, offered a silent prayer of thanks to Cynthia and any gods who might be listening, thought about trying to straighten the two of them up, concluded that he wouldn't be strong enough to do it, then got out into the pouring rain to inspect the damage. Cynthia's rear wing was badly dented just behind the wheel and her boot lid was buckled and would probably never open again, but the wheel wasn't fouled and the tyre was whole and serviceable. The rest of the car seemed fine. Even the lights were all still working.

'Holy fucking *smoke*,' Double A muttered, glancing back at the impossible jump he'd made. He began to tremble. Then he began to shake. He held up his hands in front of him. They looked as if they ought to be attached to someone suffering from Parkinson's disease. They fluttered like two nervous birds. He knew that if he didn't soon get back in the car and start driving he would faint dead away with the shock and exhaustion so he hurried back to the driver's seat on legs that gave about as much support as two elastic bands and collapsed into it, pulling his legs inside the car with his hands.

For a few long seconds, Double A didn't think he was going to be able to work the pedals. His feet juddered and danced on his ankles of their own accord and when he got his left foot on the clutch pedal his leg would not provide the power to push down. He took two deep breaths, warned himself that if he didn't soon leave he was going to have another rock fall to contend with, and managed to calm his legs enough to get going.

6

Progress was slow. Cynthia didn't seem to have suffered too badly at all from her jump: there was a stiff spot in the steering but Double A counted himself lucky to have any steering at all at this point. Other than that, she seemed fine. The engine ran just as smoothly as before and the car's grip on the almost flooded roads was impeccable.

Poor visibility was one reason that Double A couldn't take the car above ten miles an hour, but the main problem was that the rock falls he'd predicted had already happened – and were still happening. None of them were of the extent of the one he'd had to leap over, and you could squeeze past, or carefully drive over them. Double A had to stop only once to roll a couple of large boulders out of his path.

Oppenau, where the low mountains flattened out into small-ish hills, was only a few kilometres away from Bad Pieterstal, but the journey took the better part of an hour. The main street through the village was now more like a river.

It got worse as Double A eased the car towards Oberkirch and at times the water level rose high enough for it to creep into the car through the bottoms of the doors. Double A drove very slowly and carefully. While boulders in the road could be skirted, water could not and if he went too fast he would make a bow-wave which would eventually swamp the engine. If the car's electrics got wet and water got into the carbs through the air filter, Cynthia would be going precisely nowhere for quite some time.

The rain didn't lessen until Double A saw the sign pointing towards Strasbourg and the A4-E25 motorway and then it abruptly changed to a light drizzle, as if someone somewhere had flipped a switch to turn it down.

Double A thought he knew who that person might be.

Tough one, H, he thought, on the off chance that the person responsible was listening. *You didn't stop us there and you won't stop us at all now. It's getting too late for you, old pal. Much too late.*

But in spite of this faked-up bravado, Double A wondered. He nursed Cynthia through the deserted border post into France and through the empty night-time streets of Strasbourg, his every sense concentrated on the sound and feel of the car.

It wasn't until he was on the motorway – or whatever the French called it – that he began to think that there was nothing much left in H's arsenal with which he could stop them. It looked as if there was going to be one final battle, and it also looked as if the black angel was saving himself for it. Double A didn't know what would happen when they got back to England and he didn't allow himself to think about it. His job was to drive.

He pulled up at the toll ticket machine, got out of the car and grabbed the ticket and got back in, realising that for the first time in living memory he felt hungry. He drove through the gate and put his foot down, adding more surprising infor-mation to that thought about his sudden and unusual desire for food. The first was that he was straight and had no come-down from the speed he'd snorted all the way from Switzerland to Bad Pieterstal. The second thing was that he could actually breathe through his nose without it hurting. This wasn't exactly true, he admitted to himself after testing it once or twice – it stung a bit and the back of his soft palate was sore. It was, however, a large improvement on feeling as if someone was slicing away at his olfactory nerves with a sharp knife, which was the usual way of things.

Another surprise was that he could smell. The sharp odours of sweat and old wet carpets mainly, but it was unusual enough to be faintly exciting.

But the thing that really knocked the head of Mrs Anthony's little boy for a sixer was that he felt no desire whatsoever to stuff chemicals up his snout because he was feeling very good without them, thank you very much. Tired, perhaps, and most of him ached dully, but his mind felt as if it had undergone a rigorous spring cleaning: fresh and sparkling.

Wondering what good this was going to be to him if he was going to die within the next twenty-four hours or so, and finding that he didn't particularly expect to die, he brought Cynthia up to a smooth seventy miles an hour. Then to a wind-whistling eighty and there was still more to go.

The car started to vibrate a little when he'd toted it up to the ton, so Double A dropped it back down to around ninety-five. Cynthia seemed happy to keep it there and Double A drove, watching the trees and bushes and barriers flicker past at the edges of his vision in a long, blurred procession.

It wasn't until after the first toll booth (where Double A paid the ticket with some of Jacques' francs that were crammed into the 'lining of the head' in stiff wads of hundreds) that he realised the main difference in him was that he was no longer paranoid and scared shitless. Or even faintly worried, come to that. Somewhere along the four thousand odd miles he'd travelled all that had been blasted out of him. Double A knew then that if it became necessary that he should die, he would accept it without question. Things would either work out for him or they wouldn't; worrying about the future wasn't going to help at all.

And now he'd realised this, he felt supremely confident . . . and ravenously hungry.

A couple of toll booths after passing through Reims, Double A pulled in to fill Cynthia with petrol and bought three ham salad rolls from the shop's chill cabinet. By the time he passed the turning off for Arras he was hungry again and fairly glowing with confidence. Nothing untoward had happened at all.

They were going to make it home.

7

Double A parked Cynthia in the crowded Sealink Ferries car park in Calais at a little after six-thirty in the morning. He thought it was Friday, but wasn't sure. What day it was didn't matter, even if it turned out to be the thirteenth.

'We're here,' he announced. The better part of him felt as if he was still hammering along the motorway. The whistle and hum of Cynthia eating tarmac still rang in his ears and his body buzzed with the vibration.

He turned to check on Paul and Katie, expecting them to wake now he'd got them here. 'Paul?' he said. 'Katie?'

There was no response. He prodded Paul in the ribs. The guy's body was nail-hard. It was like poking a tree trunk. Double A shook his shoulder, wondering if Paul would be able to move when he did finally wake. He'd spent the better part of six hours kneeling in the footwell, his body twisted to one side and his head in Katie's lap. Double A suddenly realised that the circulation in Paul's legs must have been cut off for all that time and a picture of the man's pale feet turning black lit in his mind.

Too late now, if it has happened, he told himself. He spent several seconds trying – and failing – to rouse Katie, then gave up. He pulled a couple of wads of francs from the rip in the headlining, took the car keys from the ignition, checked that the handbrake was on (and put the car in gear just in case the handbrake was faulty), got out and locked the doors.

At the reservations counter he discovered that there was a space for the Renault and three passengers on the Stenna

Fantasia which would be leaving in forty-five minutes. He paid for the tickets with Jacques' cash and was told to queue at gate two as boarding would be starting shortly. The girl behind the desk didn't ask to see any passports, but Double A imagined that someone would before they let him on the ferry. He didn't have a clue what he was going to do then. Carrying the tickets in a hand that had suddenly become very sweaty indeed, Double A hurried back to the car.

Paul and Katie were still unconscious, still in the position in which he had left them.

'Why don't you bastards wake up?' Double A asked as he started the car. Cynthia's engine purred and Double A drove slowly to join the queue of home-going holiday-makers at gate two.

Twenty-five minutes later, he drove the Renault on to the ferry, surprised at how easy it was. No one had mentioned passports at all. As long as you had the tickets, they would let you on.

What he was going to do now about Paul and Katie, he didn't know. One of the crew members waved him into a slot behind a red Sierra and Double A drew up close to it, wondering if there was a blanket in the car with which he could cover the others – they weren't going to be allowed to stay in the car during the crossing, he was certain of that, and if anyone spotted them in the condition they were currently in, there was going to be hell to pay.

And even if I can cover them up, how the fuck am I going to get them off at the other end? he asked himself. *These guys might not want to see passports, but the British people certainly will. No one gets into England without documentation.*

'Paul?' he said, shaking the man who until a few days ago he'd known as Stephen Miles of the Miles Carriage Co. 'For fuck's sake, I'm *stuck*! Wake up, will you!'

Chapter Thirty
Channel Crossing

Paul heard Double A shouting that he was stuck across what seemed like a great distance. The journey back to himself, however, seemed to be less than a millionth of an inch. He felt his mind snap back into position and his eyes opened. He thought, *It's okay, we're on water*, and had absolutely no idea what it meant. There was an odd sensation in the lower half of his body – or rather there was a disconcerting *lack* of sensation down there. It felt as if it didn't exist; as if he'd been amputated from the top of his hips downward.

'You awake?' Double A asked, then nodded to himself and added, 'thank fuck for that.'

'Where . . . *are we*?' Paul asked, his senses all screaming that the smells were wrong, the lighting was wrong, and that this wasn't even the right car. The last thing he remembered was driving away from the spot where Katie had put paid to Robert Farmer and Jake and feeling that awful scraping sensation start in his skull. Katie had begun to draw power from him again – so quickly and violently that this vision had broken up and faded to grey. He could remember pulling over to the hard shoulder, then, after that, nothing at all.

But it was all right now, apparently because they were *on water*.

'In the ferry!' Double A said. 'Katie, wake up!'

You're crippled, Paul's mind informed him. He pushed himself up from Katie and gazed down at his twisted hips and legs, frantically trying to recall how he had become so seriously damaged. 'What happened?' he gasped.

'No time!' Double A said. 'Tell you later. We have to get out of the car. C'mon, Katie, wake up!'

Katie moaned and complained thickly, like a woman being dragged back from the deepest part of her sleep cycle.

Paul tried to move his legs. Double A had said something about a ferry. They were on a ferry. 'Where to?' he asked, using his hands to lever himself into a sitting position.

'Where to, *what*?' Double A asked. 'The guy's waving at us! For Christ's sake, man, we have to get out.'

We're on water, Paul thought and suddenly recognised his surroundings. They were in a car – a strange car – on a boat deck, not unlike the one from which he'd stolen a Jaguar from a couple called Phil and Barbara.

'What water?' he asked. There was an unpleasant aching sensation of cold stealing into his thighs. He badly needed to urinate.

'What?' Double A asked.

'*What water*?' Paul demanded.

'The channel. We're in Calais and we're getting ready to sail home.'

Paul was stunned. He almost asked how he'd come to be here, but the answer was obvious: Double A had driven them here from Switzerland. Somewhere along the way, for some unknown reason, he'd dumped the Pop and picked up this left-hand drive Renault.

The feeling of cold had reached down to Paul's knees now and there was a hot tingling sensation sweeping down after it. Paul distantly understood that he hadn't become crippled at all – he was merely suffering from the worst case of pins and needles in the history of mankind. Then he remembered what Katie had mistakenly done to him in Margherita and made this the second worse case of pins and needles ever.

'Paul?' The voice was Katie's. He turned towards her, his buttocks and bladder screaming. His legs felt as if they were on fire.

'Are you okay?' she asked, tension giving her voice an edge. Her eyes were dark, her face concerned. She looked bowstring taut.

Paul nodded. 'Fine,' he said. It wasn't exactly the case, but it would do.

'Your head? It's okay?'

Paul shrugged. 'About as okay as it gets these days, yeah.'

'It doesn't ache?'

'Not at all,' he replied.

Katie relaxed, then threw her arms around him and pulled him to her. 'Oh, Paul,' she said into his shoulder. 'I thought I'd hurt you. I've been pulling and pulling at you and didn't think there was anything left. I thought I'd dragged you past the point where . . .' she sobbed.

'I'd die?' he said.

Katie drew back and looked at him, her eyes brimming. 'It doesn't matter,' she said.

'What's happened?' Double A asked.

Paul thought he knew. 'Richman. The radar guy,' he said. 'He's been trying to stop us. Katie's been fighting him back.'

'All this time?' Double A asked incredulously.

'H was feeding power to him,' Katie said. 'I had to draw from Paul to stop him. I thought I'd drawn too much.'

'You . . . uh . . . killed him?' Double A asked.

Paul shook his head. 'Water,' he said. 'For some unknown reason he can't get to us while we're on water.'

'Look, are you getting out of this car or *what*?' an angry voice wanted to know.

Paul looked up at the sailor who was glaring into the car. He was a big, red-faced, bearded guy dressed in jeans and a shirt.

'Only everyone else is in, the ramp's up and we'll be sailing in five minutes. You can't stay down here during the voyage.'

The sailor looked from one of them to the other, then peered down at the floor. 'A gun,' he said in a small, surprised voice. He began to back away. 'You've got a gun,' he repeated.

'Hold on,' Katie whispered to Paul. 'It's one of the kids' toys,' she called after the sailor. 'It's plastic.'

Paul felt the power being drawn from him and knew that Katie was using him to save herself. A vacuum seemed to form in his mind where the force had been drawn out. Katie only used a brief burst and the vacuum filled almost instantly. Paul wondered for how long this would be the case. There had to be an end to it somewhere.

The guy came back smiling.

'Hand him the gun,' Katie whispered to Double A.

Double A scooped the gun from the floor on the passenger's side of the car and held it out the window for the sailor. It was much too heavy to pass for a toy.

The guy took hold of it, nodding. 'Oh,' he said as though he suddenly realised the truth. 'If it was heavier and it wasn't made of plastic it'd look just like the real thing,' he said, hefting it round into his hand and pointing it at Double A. 'Good toy. Where'd you get it?' he said.

With a mounting horror, Paul watched the scene unfolding before him. At any second, the sailor was going to pull the trigger of what he thought was a toy gun and Double A's head was going to explode like an over-ripe tomato. He wanted to tell the man to give the gun back, he wanted to shout at Double A to duck, but his voice wouldn't work.

Is the safety on? he screamed mentally to Katie. *For Christ's sake, don't let him pull the trigger!* But either Katie didn't hear his thoughts or didn't have time to react.

'Pow!' the sailor said and fired.

The shot passed so close to Double A's head that Paul saw his hair ripple. It flung itself through the Renault's passenger door panel, ricocheted inside the door and presumably shot upwards into the ledge that supported the window glass, because that glass now fractured into a thousand pieces and fell into the car in a sparkling shower.

The sailor seemed conscious of none of this. He had apparently missed the gun's recoil, the noise, the muzzle smoke, the terrified squeak that the now ashen-faced Double A had let out, and the fact that the car's window had disintegrated.

'We got it in Germany,' Katie said calmly.

'*Good toy*!' the sailor enthused. ''S got caps in it 'n' everything! Know how to make things, those Germans,' he said admiringly. He handed the gun back to Double A who put out a hand that was visibly shaking to receive it.

'We'd better get out,' Katie said.

Paul's legs were like tree stumps, but he managed to follow Katie out of the car. Double A was holding on to the door, looking as if he expected to collapse the moment he let go of it.

'Okay?' Paul asked, stretching his legs and feeling the blood rush back into them.

Double A shook his head.

'Want me to hold you up?'

'It'll be all right,' Double A replied and slammed the car door.

As they walked towards the staircase to the passenger deck, the sailor called after them. 'If you want to get that bust window fixed, I can give you the name of a good garage in Dover!' he yelled. 'Cheap!'

'Later!' Paul called back. 'Where did the gun come from?' he asked Double A. 'And the car?'

It took most of the crossing for Mrs Anthony's boy to explain.

Chapter Thirty-One
Showdown Time

1

Gary Richman found Paul's mind the moment that Cynthia's wheels touched the quayside. Behind him in the rear seat, Double A gasped and Paul knew that he was sharing the awful scraping sensation which felt as if your brain was filing its way out of your skull with a rasp. It hurt like a bastard and Paul expected it to get worse. His eyes began to water.

Katie had told them to expect it to happen. She had also told them that he and Double A were going to have to deal with it themselves because she would be handling the immigration and customs officials.

Trying to ignore the pain, Paul put the battered Renault into one of the queues of cars that were heading towards the customs shed and crawled along after the car ahead of him.

'*Jesus*,' Double A hissed and Paul glanced at him in the rear-view mirror. He was pale and his face was sheened with sweat. He looked as if he was in agony.

Beside Paul, Katie's face was blank and her eyes distant as she stared ahead, already concentrating on the uniformed figures in the customs hall. Paul badly wanted to ask her if she could do anything for Double A, but didn't speak in case her concentration was broken. She'd told him not to try to link with her unless he felt her reaching for him and not to speak to her unless she spoke to him first.

Paul didn't know if she was feeling the scraping pain too,

but he did know that Double A had been passed the shitty end of the stick to hold during the journey. However much the pain hurt Paul, it was going to be hurting Double A that much again, because on the ferry Double A had pressed something into Paul's hand and said, 'I think this is yours. It fell out of your mouth when I put you in the back of the car in Switzerland.'

Which might have been a silly move for Double A to make, because the thing was Paul's lucky ten pfennig piece and it was currently clamped between two of his molars, lighting a tiny electrical charge between the fillings in his teeth, and somehow, he thought, affording him a measure of protection against Richman's mental onslaught.

'Seagulls,' Double A moaned as Paul shunted the car forward. 'The *seagulls*!'

'It's okay,' Paul told him, glancing in the mirror at his pained face. 'We're here. It's okay.'

Double A didn't seem to hear him. He ducked and waved his hand in front of his face, as though batting something away.

Paul wondered if he should take the coin from his mouth and put it into Double A's, then feeling like the world's most practised bastard, and hating himself for it, decided against it. His job was to drive the car and he didn't think he would be able to do it without the coin in his mouth.

Sorry, kid, he thought. *I'm truly sorry.*

'Get 'em away from me!' Double A moaned, cringing.

Ahead of Paul the queue moved forward and he rolled Cynthia along behind it.

Double A threw himself down on the seat, sobbing. 'I didn't!' he said vehemently. 'I *didn't* kill Jake! No! Take those gulls away!'

How the hell are we going to get past these immigration people with Double A in this state? he asked himself, and the rasping pain at the crown of his head increased.

'You *can't* send him back!' Double A moaned.

And Paul was being waved forward by one of the officials. His heart sinking, he drove into the shed and stopped, then wound down his window.

'Passports?' the guy said.

'Again?' Katie suddenly asked.

The guy slapped his forehead with the heel of his hand. 'Sorry,' he said, 'I already saw them, didn't I? Do you have anything to declare then?'

'*Jake*!' Double A moaned.

'No,' Paul said, and his lucky ten pfennig slid out of his mouth. In the fumbling second it took to catch the coin and put it back where it had to be, Paul saw the windscreen of the car vanish and a huge seagull with a dripping black beak dive-bombing him.

'What's a fake?' the customs guy asked, frowning. He peered into the back of the car and seemed not to see Double A at all.

Paul felt Katie suck power away from him. The monstrous seagull momentarily flickered into existence ahead of him. As the vacuum in his head filled, the gull vanished. Paul's mind spun.

'Looks like a real one to me,' the customs man said admiringly. 'I'd have sworn black was white that this was a genuine "E" type Jag. What is it, fibreglass?'

'GRP,' Paul heard himself say, suddenly understanding that the customs man hadn't been looking at Double A at all but had been studying the bodywork of what he thought was an 'E' type Jaguar. 'All the original running gear though,' he added.

'Nice car,' the guy said looking as though there was something he ought to be remembering but couldn't quite put his finger on.

'*Jake*!' Double A moaned.

'So you said,' the customs guy nodded. 'Okay, sorry to have held you up, but I just had to look at the car. Drive safely now.'

Paul gazed up at him, not quite believing what he'd heard.

Get out of here, I can't hold it much longer! Katie yelled inside Paul's head.

Paul hit the throttle and drove away, tyres squealing. When he glanced in the mirror the customs man was staring at the car, beaming and shaking his head.

'Did it,' he said drawing a deep breath and feeling his heart slow. 'Thanks, Katie.'

'It isn't over yet,' she replied in a small voice. 'Something's happening to me now and I don't know what it is.'

'H?' Paul asked through gritted teeth as he swung the car through the traffic. Up ahead on the other side of the road was Freddie Simmons' garage. Just after it, Paul knew he was going to drive by the little restaurant where he'd told Freddie he was retiring. It seemed like a hundred years ago now.

Katie shook her head. 'Not H, and not Richman. I think it was making that immigration man see a Jaguar with only two people in it. I used up too much and now my body is doing something strange. Something's happening inside me and I'm frightened. I'm changing, Paul. It feels like my insides are dissolving. I don't know what'll happen. Promise you won't leave me, Paul, whatever happens. Promise you'll protect me, always.'

'I promise,' Paul said.

Katie turned to him, her face gorgeous and tragic. Even now the terrible scraping inside his head had been joined by a series of short buzzing sounds that he thought might soon become words, Paul's mind was clear enough to read that aching expression. It meant that Katie expected to die. Paul's guts twisted and he knew that the exquisite and tortuous pain of loss he felt was worse than anything H could do to him. A cold black rage began to grow inside him. Not just for Gary Richman and H, but for whoever had sent all this to him.

When Katie spoke, she already sounded defeated. 'I know it's wrong and I know it's probably ruined everything, but I couldn't help myself. I love you, Paul. And I'll love you forever. They must have known. Surely they must have known. I'll come back to you, Paul, I promise I'll come back.'

'I love you too,' Paul said, but Katie's eyes were distant now and she did not seem to hear him.

'YOU BASTARDS!' Paul shouted, throwing the car out into the oncoming traffic to pass a slow Mini.

'Seagulls,' Double A moaned. 'Eating me.'

Paul serpentined the Renault through the busy traffic, heading for Folkestone and the M20. From there, if the M25 wasn't jammed, Cambridge was two, maybe two and a half hours away. If his present level of rage could be maintained over that period of time, Paul thought he would be able to knock down the door of the house in which H was holed up and tear his head right off his neck, using only his bare hands.

The short buzzing sounds inside his head began to clarify. Now Paul could identify them as being words, although they were indistinct and sounded like the Dalek voices you sometimes heard on a crossed telephone line. *Never happen*, were the only two he could pick out. They were being repeated in almost every short sentence.

'*Hurts!*' Double A moaned.

Paul glanced in the mirror and looked away quickly because the view out of the back of the car was no longer the busy A20 from Dover to Folkestone, but the oddly lit landscape of a town nestled in rolling hills that he'd last seen in Italy when Richman had latched on to him the first time. It was the place Paul had thought might just be Heaven.

It isn't Heaven, the sizzling crossed line words assured Paul. *That would never happen. Never happen never.* He glanced in the mirror again and the vision – or hallucination – was gone. The Telecom void voices abruptly vanished. Paul nodded and swung the Renault around a van, cutting in before it a little closer than he would have liked. The van's driver beat out an angry message on the horn and flashed the headlights.

You know she's just using you, poke, don't you? Paul thought as he pulled away from the van. *You know she doesn't care about you or what happens to you. What has she done, except cause you grief? She only needed you to get her home and now she's pulled away from you, hasn't she? Do you think she'll live up to all those promises she's made to you? Do you really think she will?*

Paul didn't.

He glanced in the mirror again and saw a huge seagull swoop down out of nowhere into Double A's face, beak first. He felt the movement of air caused by its beating wings on the back of his neck, felt Double A's blood spatter him as the bird's beak drove into flesh.

It doesn't have to be like this, he thought. *It really doesn't. All you have to do is put the girl out of the car and it'll all stop. She doesn't love you. She's dead, for God's sake! She's just been using you, old poke, and when she's finished with you, she'll cast you aside like a worn out piece of clothing.*

'Hurts!' Double A squealed. Behind Paul, bird wings fluttered and webbed feet scrabbled against upholstery.

It doesn't have to be like this, cowboy!

Paul saw a garage ahead of him. He would pull in there, heave Katie out of the car and drive away without her and it would be all over.

Nice idea, he told himself, and felt his left foot move from the accelerator to the brake pedal. A seagull swooped down from the sky, folded its wings, passed through Cynthia's windscreen as if it didn't exist, and plummeted between Paul and Katie into the back of the car. Paul heard the soft thud and squawk as it stove into Double A. Double A moaned like a child and an image lit in his head of little Paulie Saunders rolling up the bonnet of a stolen car, his hands going *thock thock thock*! on the paintwork and leaving bloody imprints after them, and Paul felt as if he had been slapped around the face with a wet towel. His mind cleared instantly, the smell of burnt electrical insulation filled his nose and he realised that Richman had been thinking those last thoughts on his behalf.

When Paul spoke, his voice sounded ancient and papery and very, very dangerous. 'Nice try, Gary,' he said. 'But I'm coming for you and you won't stop me now. You can't stop me, Gary, neither you nor your good friend H.'

Paul bit down hard on the ten pfennig; hard enough for one of his back teeth to groan as if it might split. The weak electrical tingle became a bright toothache shock and he felt Richman leave go of a part of his brain. 'Hope it hurt you, Gary,' Paul said through clenched teeth. 'It's gonna hurt you a lot more when I arrive.'

3

Five minutes later, when Paul hit the M20, Gary Richman left Paul and the searing pain in his skull subsided to a dull ache.

'Oh, Jesus, thank you,' Double A moaned from the back seat. 'It hurt. It really hurt. Is it over?'

Paul pressed hard on Cynthia's accelerator and the car moved smoothly up to eighty as he guided it into the fast lane. 'He'll be back,' he said, 'and I think it's gonna be worse next time.'

'Katie! What about Katie?' Double A asked.

Paul glanced at her. She was slumped back in the seat and although she still seemed to be breathing, her eyes were closed. He doubted that he would find a pulse if he were to search her wrist for one. The painful twisting sensation of loss found his guts again and Paul found he wanted to cry. He shook his head. 'I don't know,' he said. 'She said she was in trouble and then she glazed over.'

'Will she be okay?'

Paul shrugged. 'She's done it before and been okay, but this time . . . I don't know. All we can do is carry on and hope for the best. That's all anyone can do when it comes down to it,' he added bitterly. 'Ain't life sweet?'

'You like her a lot, don't you?' Double A said. It was a statement rather than a question. Paul nodded, not turning round and not looking in the rear-view. I'm sorry about Jake,' he said. 'I liked him a lot too. He cared about you, y'know.'

'Paul?'

'What?'

Double A took a deep shuddering breath. 'Are we going to . . . y'know . . .?'

'Win?' Paul asked. 'I dunno. We're gonna give it a fucking good shot though. Someone will remember it as the battle of a lifetime, but whether it'll be us or them, I really don't know. And whether we'll survive if we win . . . I don't know that either.'

Double A was quiet for a time and when he spoke again his voice was so heavy with sadness that the tears welling up in Paul's eyes overflowed and ran down his cheeks. 'We're going to lose Katie, aren't we?' he said.

Paul nodded, blinking his vision clear. 'I think we are,' he said. 'I think we are.'

For the next forty minutes Paul became a driving machine, devoid of all feeling and thinking of nothing except the car he was in, the road ahead and the positioning of the traffic around him. He drove fast and accurately, bringing the three of them another mile closer to the Black Angel every forty-five seconds.

4

Paul broke out of his semi-hypnotic driving trance between junction eight and nine on the M11 motorway between Bishop's Stortford and Saffron Walden, and thought, *Showdown time*. The final battle in the war wasn't going to begin and end at H's house in Cambridge after all.

It was going to start here.

He offered up a silent prayer to St Cunt of the Car Thieves and hoped he'd got out of bed on the right side this morning because he was going to be needed.

Katie was still unconscious (and if you cared to look at her carefully, which Paul most certainly did not, *sagging* as if her bones were dissolving) and Double A was sitting in the back of the Renault cradling the gun that had almost put an end to his life.

'Hang on!' Paul shouted.

And just as his ten-second precognitive driving talent had suggested it would, the big silver Ford Granada he was about to overtake suddenly slewed out into the fast lane, a whisker ahead of him. Paul hit Cynthia's brake pedal a fraction of a second before the Ford's driver hit his, and flung the Renault into the middle lane spot the Ford had just vacated. Double A rolled across the back of the car, hit the side and shouted.

'Put the safety on the gun!' Paul yelled as the Ford came back across towards the middle lane, matching the Renault's speed exactly. In his time, Paul had come up against lunatics who would try this kind of thing for fun, but he doubted that the grey-haired business type in the Granada Scorpio belonged to this breed. This particular lunatic probably didn't even realise what he was doing: someone else was in control of him and his car now.

Paul braked hard, saw a potential gap in the slow lane and went for it. The cars parted to accept him, and as he had done when the crazed cop was chasing him, Paul drove right over to the hard shoulder and throttled away, wishing the gap shut. Cynthia leapt forward. Paul glanced in his mirror, saw the gap closing and knew that the Granada driver was going to try to push through it anyway. The car at the back of the gap was an old blue Datsun and its driver braked hard as the Ford came at it. For half a second Paul believed that the Datsun had done enough, then both cars leapt into the air, the Granada spinning towards the bank and the Datsun out into the traffic.

Paul put Cynthia back into the slow lane, saw a space in the centre and went for it as the stop lights of the car directly in front of him lit for no reason at all. He hit the throttle hard and yanked the wheel to the right and felt the jolt as the Renault's damaged rear wing clipped the bumper of the braking car. Cynthia slewed away from the point of impact and Paul caught the skid and threw her into the fast lane to avoid another harshly braking car. There was fire in the distance behind them now, as cars piled first into the rolled Datsun, then into one another.

Cynthia flashed past a yellow Ford Fiesta, which joined the fast lane and gave chase.

'It's catching up!' Double A yelled and when Paul glanced

into the mirror, he yelled again: '*In front!*'

H and Richman had gone for broke now. The huge articulated truck that was a hundred yards ahead of them in the middle lane and moving at more than seventy, swung out into the fast lane cutting the road away from a group of three nose-to-tail Sierras, all in the same white colour. The only groups of cars Paul had seen that travelled in that fashion were unmarked police cars on driver training exercises.

In less than a second, two of the three white cars were crushed to half their width against the collapsing central barrier and the third was cartwheeling down into the oncoming traffic on the other side of the motorway. The truck jack-knifed and its trailer swept round across all three lanes ahead of Paul. Upwards of ten cars stove into it. Paul swerved into the centre lane, braking hard, dodged a car coming at him from the slow lane, and got over on to the hard shoulder where there was a way past the wreckage no more than six feet wide. Something hit the trailer and exploded and burning petrol rained down on the Renault.

Double A shouted as a car rolled towards them and Paul dodged it.

With Cynthia in flames, Paul wormed his way past a stray tangle of wreckage, heading towards the gap. A second later they were through and clear.

'We're on *fire!*' Double A shouted.

Paul ignored him and hit the throttle, peering through the flame and smoke on the bonnet as the Renault gained speed. *Don't fail me now, Cynthia*, he told the car. *Please don't let me down!*

Burning petrol oozed up the windscreen as the car got faster and the rubber seal began to melt. Paul took it up to sixty-five in third, changed up to fourth and hit seventy. Then eighty and the flames started to gutter and go out.

'It's gonna be okay!' Double A yelled, his disbelief apparent in his voice.

Thanks, Cynthia, Paul told the car. 'Don't speak too soon,' he told Double A, 'there's a few more miles to go yet and it'll probably start all over again when we catch up with the traffic.' He could already see cars in the distance ahead of him.

'So don't catch up with the traffic,' Double A suggested.

Paul thought about it and lifted his foot from the accelerator, letting the Renault's speed drift down to seventy, then sixty. It seemed horribly slow and a part of him ached to put his boot back down hard, but he resisted, wondering why the cars ahead weren't slowing as he did.

'I don't think they're going to try that particular trick again,' he said as the first fire engine dashed past on the down lane. He wondered how many lives had been lost in the past few minutes and expected his goading voice to wake up at any moment and tell him he was culpable. But the *farmer-oppozite* voice was gone and Paul didn't think it would be coming back again. At some point during this seemingly never ending shit-storm, the two halves of Dekker had somehow welded themselves back together.

For what good it's going to do, Paul thought, sniffing and smelling something he couldn't quite put a mental finger on. It reminded him of ant hills for some reason.

And suddenly the car was filled with flies.

They didn't fly in through the broken window on Katie's side of the car, or arrive by any normal means whatsoever. And there didn't seem to be any period of time as the transition was made. One moment Paul was wondering what good being sane again was, and the next – as if to prove that he was still crazy after all – he was waist deep in live, buzzing, crawling bluebottles.

Double A began to scream and thrash like a man who has just parted with sanity on a long-term basis.

Paul took his foot off the accelerator as the top fifty or a hundred layers of flies took to the air. His vision darkened with a thousand buzzing bodies. They were crawling in his nose, invading his ears. Insects crawled between his lips and crunched when he moved his jaws.

Paul held the steering wheel straight with one hand and let

the car slow while he plunged his other hand down into the seething mass and groped for the window winder. He sucked in a breath through his tightly clenched teeth and his air was choked off with fly bodies. His left hand found the winder and he quickly rolled the window down. Flies left the car in their thousands. Paul spat the bodies away from his teeth and took another breath, using a little of it to snort the insects out of his nostrils.

The car was down to about twenty miles an hour and still slowing. Paul found the door handle and yanked it, pushing the door open. The insects left the car in plumes, like thick black smoke.

'Get them *away*!' Double A screamed, his voice frantic.

'Don't fire the gun!' Paul warned, through clamped teeth as the car slowed down.

A second later, Double A did exactly that.

The first words that found their way into Paul's mind were, *He's shot Katie*! For a moment he was certain that in desperation Double A had fired blindly into the seething swamp of blue-black insects and hit her, and was certain that this was what Richman and H had intended. It wasn't until his mind finally registered that the faint crash of breaking glass that had occurred at the same instant the gun roared that he realised Double A had actually shot out the Renault's rear window. The breeze running through the car increased and the living swirling tendrils of flies abruptly changed direction, now sweeping over Paul's shoulder towards the back of the car.

'SPEED UP!' Double A shouted.

Paul let go of his door and put his foot down, hard. By the time Cynthia hit fifty, the majority of the flies had been blown out of the car.

Paul spat dead insects from his mouth and wiped away their remains from his face and eyes.

'Okay,' Double A said from the back seat. 'We're okay. We're gonna be all right now!'

But they weren't going to be all right now because almost as soon as Double A had spoken, Paul had begun to smell burning electrical insulation and rotting oranges again. This time it wasn't a faint taint to the air, but an all-encompassing, gut-wrenching stench that made you want to forget everything else, thrust your head out of the window and throw up until you lost consciousness.

There was a momentary sensation of downward pressure during which the Renault crouched as though a huge, unseen hand had pressed on it and Paul's ears popped and his sinuses crackled. Paul was distantly aware that he felt drunk and dizzy and that the awful rasping sensation inside his skull had begun again but in comparison to the smell these things were a minor hindrance.

'We're slowing down!' Double A yelled. 'Don't stop, Paul! Don't let the car stop!'

Paul drew what were left of his wits back to him and glanced at the speedometer. There were dead flies squashed all over it. He scraped them aside with his right hand index finger, noting, in a kind of dream-like stupor, that the cut in it where Peter Defoe had tried to saw it off up on the plateau was bleeding again. Even though the flesh was healed and unbroken, it was bleeding again.

Stigmata, a voice said in his mind and Paul wasn't sure if it was him, his goad, or someone else.

Out there in front of him, in a world that had become as soft as rubber and in which your thoughts flowed like treacle, the speedo read twenty miles an hour. This was not fast enough. Paul hit the throttle and watched the speedo indicate thirty, then forty, then fifty. He changed up to fourth. Sixty. Sixty-five. Seventy.

'Paul! We're running off the road!'

Double A's voice cut through him like a chainsaw. Paul looked up and was surprised to see the central reservation barrier quickly closing on him at an angle of thirty degrees or so. He felt as if he had just woken up. He opened his mouth to shout and his hands tightened on the wheel, but the subconscious part of him that dealt with the driving was ahead of him. He turned the wheel, catching the car as it shimmied and lifted its nearside rear wheel. The wheel thumped down and the car jolted hard to the side. Paul anticipated this and corrected again, nursing the Renault back to a smooth, straight course.

You'll have to try harder than that, he thought.

A half-formed image shimmered in his mind, in the same way as it had during his last battle with Gary Richman. When it cleared this time, it was not an image of Richman sitting in his Bentley Mulsanne Turbo, his fingertip placed lightly against his forehead, nor was it an image of the blackened shell of Henry Tyler, his eyes gone and his mouth melted to grey gristle. It was an image of the angel itself.

It was massive and golden and naked, alien but somehow man-shaped. Its body was taut and perfect, its face achingly beautiful.

And its eyes burned with the fires of Hell.

Paul could see Gary Richman's face in the shape of the angel's own face, could see H's tortured features there too as though the angel had somehow absorbed both of them. And worse, as the angel moved its head, Paul could see others he recognised: his mother; Freddie Simmons; Amy.

How do you like me now, old poke? the angel said, its voice no longer grating, but smooth and musical. *Do you still think you can face me? Still think you can fuck with me, cowboy?*

'I'm coming,' Paul said. 'You won't stop me.'

You won't even get here, small fishy. There are eight more miles between us and with each closing yard my influence increases and yours decreases. You won't win. Give it up, Paulie.

Paul's heart squeezed hard, once, twice, three times. He clicked out. His mind cleared and a cold rage swept through him. 'Don't you ever call me *Paulie!*' he hissed.

I'll take her from you. Bring her here and I'll take her, old poke. You won't prevent it. It'll be the ultimate agony for her, when I tear her from her living shell, you know that, don't you? It'll cause her pain beyond measure and you'll hear her tortured screams and be able to do nothing to help her. And then I'll take you, old poke. You don't know the meaning of the word suffering yet, but you will. You'll suffer throughout eternity, cowboy. You'll beg for my mercy.

'So why are you trying so hard to stop me from reaching you?' Paul asked coldly. 'Wouldn't be because you're not so sure of the outcome as you say, now would it? Wouldn't be a case of an empty vessel making a great deal of noise?'

Don't even imagine you have a chance, old poke, the angel roared.

And there was that tone again, the one Paul had recognised in his first dream. The desperate seething anger of someone who wanted to scare you away because he didn't want to take it all the way to a fight. The voice of bluster. The voice of someone who wanted you to believe he held all the trumps when he knew damn well he didn't.

'I don't have to imagine anything,' Paul said. 'I *know*. Like I told you before, I fuck with whoever I want to. And I'm coming to fuck with you now, empty vessel.'

Then come! the angel said angrily.

And left Paul.

'What the fuck was all that?' Double A said shakily. 'I could hear someone talking.'

'I think we just got ourselves an easy ride into Cambridge,' Paul replied.

'Was that . . . *him*?'

Paul nodded. 'That was him. You still want to come all the way?'

Double A thought about it. 'Yes,' he said. 'For Jake and for you but mainly for . . .'

'Katie?'

Double A sounded embarrassed. 'Yeah,' he agreed.

'It's okay,' Paul said. 'I know what you mean. And how you feel.'

736

'Do you think we'll die?' Double A asked.

But Paul didn't answer the question because the inside of the car was suddenly flooded with white light and intense heat. Katie had woken up.

6

The metamorphosis Katie had been undergoing during the journey up from Dover was complete. The flash of white light and heat died away just when Paul thought he wasn't going to be able to stand it any more. He was certain the hairs on his right arm had been singed away.

Paul glanced over at her and remembered the words she had said to him back on the ferry between Greece and Italy. *Angels are different. They're not human. I am human and I can never be an angel. They're going to give me the powers but I'll still be Kate Straker underneath* . . .

And Paul had thought she had received all those powers back in Margherita – and he had been wrong. And he was no longer certain that she *was* still Kate Straker underneath. Where before she had looked as if she'd been lit by a follow spot, she now seemed to be radiating a golden glow of her own. What before had looked like physical perfection now seemed coarse in comparison. Before, she had been achingly beautiful: now it tore your heart apart to look at her.

Katie sighed. 'Paul,' she breathed and he felt himself falling into the crystal clarity of her cool green eyes. He looked away quickly. She put her left hand on his right forearm and Paul felt the power she'd siphoned from him being returned. Her hand was cool but the energy pulsed into him in slow, warm waves that tingled through him with orgasmic intensity. For a few seconds Paul felt an ecstasy which wasn't dissimilar to the sensation he had when they'd made love.

And then it was over.

'You okay?' he asked, glancing at her. It was like glancing at the sun. After-images remained on his retinas when he looked away. He felt as if the changes that had taken place here ought to have distanced them, but the opposite seemed to be true. He felt a fierce love for her that seemed greater than any emotion he had previously experienced, and somehow, that love was being returned.

'I'm fine,' she said in a voice that was too small, too girlish and too frightened to be coming from that vision of an angel.

She ought to have wings, a tiny voice said in the back of Paul's mind. *They're all that's missing*.

When he looked at her again, she was smiling ruefully. 'I'm frightened,' she said, 'that's all. I feel . . . kind of . . . funny. Like I'm suddenly too big for my body. And there's all this . . . power. It's like I'm looking out through sheets of white lightning. I can see H as though I'm already there in his house.'

'We'll be there soon,' Paul said. 'Ten minutes or so. I don't know where to go when we turn off the motorway. Guide me.'

'Okay,' Katie said shakily. 'And whatever happens when we get there, remember, I love you. Remember you promised not to leave me. I'm still in here underneath all this. Little Katie Straker is still here and she still loves you.'

Paul didn't reply because he knew his voice would be choked if he did. Katie couldn't have made it much plainer that she was saying her last goodbye without actually saying it. He simply drove Cynthia the Renault, following the directions that Katie gave him while he tried not to think of failing.

And the closer they got, the more difficult this became.

7

The street on which H's house stood was deserted. Turning into it was like driving into a wall of syrup. There was a huge resistance as if the Renault and its occupants were a pole of a huge magnet and H's house and those inside it were like a pole which repelled them. Cynthia's engine began to labour immediately and Paul thought that if he took his foot from the accelerator the car would be pushed backwards right out of the street. The atmosphere pressed down like a ton weight and the acrid smell of burning electrical wiring filled the car.

'Almost there,' Double A said, and his voice was as child-like and frightened as Katie's had been.

Paul changed down to second, then to first as the Renault's engine protested. The car's single wiper burst into mad life, whacking back and forth across the screen at what must have been twice its fastest speed. The washers sprayed two hard jets at the screen and the pump began to scream as if it was being tortured to death. All the car's indicators came on at once, ticked on and off and went out. One by one the lights came on, glowed brightly for a moment and went out. The washer motor made a sick squeal and ground to a halt. The wiper motor seized in mid wipe and the blade snapped off and clattered away down the bonnet.

The radio turned itself on at maximum volume. The hissing static void filled itself with a thousand distant voices and then, just as Paul had known she would, Valerie Masterton began to sing Puccini's *Un bel di.*

Mayhem, poke! H's grating voice said across the opera music. *Welcome home!*

A moment later, as Paul twisted the radio's volume control so hard that it broke off in his hand – and left the music still playing – all four of the car's tyres burst.

'Up ahead!' Katie shouted over the noise and pointed at what Paul recognised as H's house.

Slowing, the Renault crawled towards it, now firing on only two of its cylinders and moving at less than ten miles an hour.

And although it was impossible, little Paulie Saunders was in front of the car on his bike, his feet off the pedals and his shock of blond hair dancing in the wind as his face lit with the terrible realisation that he was about to die.

'NO!' Paul shouted as the boy rolled up the car's bonnet, leaving bloody handprints. For a second the boy's face was against the screen and Paul was gazing into his dead eyes.

How do you like it, pipsqueak? H grated inside his head. *Do you like it just fine?*

Then the boy was gone.

'Mayhem!' the voice said from the radio.

'Stop the car!' Katie said, but the car was stopping of its own accord. The engine coughed a nasty rattling metallic hack, jolted twice and quit with a musical noise like glass shattering.

Katie leapt out of the car and stood on the pavement, looking at the hedge around H's front garden, fifty feet ahead of her.

Paul climbed out of the Renault as its suspension collapsed and Double A scrambled out after him, clutching the gun to his chest as if he expected someone to tear it away from him at any moment.

'Okay?' Paul asked him.

Double A shook his head. Paul knew exactly how he felt. He glanced over at Katie who should have been an ordinary pretty girl in her mid-twenties dressed in someone else's torn jeans and tee shirt, but who looked like a gorgeous being from another universe, and he tried not to see the ragged gap in reality that traced a line around her like a cut-out from a newspaper.

Katie began to walk up the pavement towards H's house and Paul and Double A hurried after her.

I don't want you to touch me, ever again! Amy's strident voice suddenly said inside Paul's head and then it was joined with the voice of Freddie Simmons saying, *What you* can't *do is retire!* Then the policeman Stephen Jones saying, *She told us you were unpredictable and that she was frightened of you!* And his mother saying, *Paul, you always were a sucker for a girl in distress!* Then his own voice rang in his ears: *I get mad and something clicks in my brain and it's like there's molten metal in front of my eyes. When it clears something bad has happened, usually to someone else. Don't make me show you.*

And Paul suddenly knew he could and *would* do whatever was necessary. As he followed Katie towards the house he became cold and still inside.

The Bentley Mulsanne Turbo in which Gary Richman had sat, while he searched them out and fought battles with their minds, was parked in the road a little way away from the house. Its tyres were all flat, the windows were cracked and opaque and the paintwork was crazed as if it had been subjected to a great heat. Paul could almost recall how this had happened. Almost but not quite. He thought he and Katie might have had something to do with it. It had probably happened while they were fighting Richman from a car that Double A was driving towards Germany.

Katie walked towards the drive, her tangle of golden hair alive in a wind that didn't exist. It was the only sign that the repellent force was at work on her. Paul and Double A followed her, bent forward against the force as if they were walking against a gale.

She paused at the gates and turned back, watching them with clear green eyes as they fought their way towards her. Her face was pale and frightened.

'Showdown time,' Paul said as they caught her up. There was a red Lotus Eclat in the drive. He remembered it from the ferry when he'd linked with Katie. It had belonged to her ex-boyfriend, Chris. The seemingly irrepressible car-thief part of Paul that would forever be searching out chances recalled that the keys were still in the car. Paul sent up a quick prayer to St Cunt who had seen him safely back from Greece but whom he doubted was going to have much influence here.

'What's going to happen?' Double A asked. 'What do we do?'

'No plan,' Paul said. 'We just go in and see what happens.'

'Is that a good idea?' Double A said.

Paul looked at him for a second, searching him out. Then he nodded. There were no chinks in Double A's armour; the kid was in for it and would go all the way – it was about the only thing Paul was certain of at the moment. 'Nope,' he said, 'it isn't a good idea. Have you got a better one?'

Double A shook his head.

'Come on,' Katie said softly and turned into the drive.

'Lambs to the slaughter,' Double A said.

Showdown time, old poke, Paul thought and followed Katie.

The repellent force vanished the moment they crossed the threshold of H's property. Paul fell to his hands and knees and fancied he could hear H laughing as he got up, his palms now cut and his knees undoubtedly scraped and bleeding inside the borrowed jeans he was wearing. Blood welled up out of the healed-over scar in his index finger. He wiped it on his shirt and looked at the house's overgrown front garden, searching the long grass for any sign of a nasty surprise and knowing there wasn't any need for one. The nasty surprise was waiting inside the building.

The bungalow nestled in the garden like a singed bug. The whitewashed window of the room on the left – in which H would be waiting – was smeared with soot from the fire which had happened when the computer equipment had melted down. In the garden there was a split tank and broken pipework which had once conveyed liquid nitrogen coolant to the machinery. Tiles were missing from the roof of the bungalow and here and there were thin black scorch marks, as if the fire had swept through the whole building, somehow without gutting it. The odour of fire was strong, but the electrical smell was stronger.

As they moved to the side of the drive to pass the Lotus, Paul caught sight of a figure squatting on the steps that led up to the recessed front door, and shouted a warning. Like a presidential bodyguard, Double A was in front of Katie with the gun pointed at the man in less than a second.

'It's okay,' Katie said softly, 'he isn't there any more.'

And as they drew closer Paul understood what she'd meant. The man was – or used to be – Gary Richman. Paul had been right when he'd thought that Richman had been absorbed by H's angel; what was left of Richman was a mummified husk. It sat on the steps in an expensive suit, its dried hands clasped around bony knees. It had only happened this morning but the body looked as if it had been there for a thousand years.

'Fuck a duck!' Double A whispered. 'If he's dead, there's only H left, isn't there?'

Paul shook his head. 'One more,' he heard himself say. 'One more to make a total of twelve. Eleven have gone, H is still here, so there's one more.'

'Charles Robinson,' Katie said. 'A doctor from the hospital. He was one of the first. He's been looking after H. They're waiting, and we don't have much time.' She went past Richman and up the steps to the front door, which hung ajar – presumably to allow them access. Paul followed her with Double A close behind him.

'How much time *do* we have?' Paul asked.

'Minutes,' Katie said, pushing the door open wide. The hall inside was blackened with soot and the reek made Paul's stomach close like a fist.

'What do you mean?' Double A whispered.

Paul knew exactly what she meant. Katie was only going to be able to carry the power that was coursing through her for a limited time. She was glowing like a six-volt torch bulb connected up to a twelve-volt battery. And everyone knew what happened to bulbs that burned that brightly. After a while the filament melted and they went out. Paul could smell the subtle scent of that irreversible process taking place, right now, even with all the other terrible odours in his nose.

'She means we have to be quick,' he said, trying not to think about her simply fading from existence. 'We're ready,' he told her and thought, *I love you!*

I'll come back to you, Paul! Afterwards I'll come back.

Paul wasn't certain whether he'd heard these words inside his head or if it was just wishful thinking. And there wasn't time to dwell on it because Katie strode down the hall and flung open the door of Henry Tyler's secret room.

9

Between the second that the three of them burst into the room and the time the gun went off, there was a moment of silence that seemed to last an eternity.

The room was exactly the same as it had been in Paul's vision of it. Along the far wall was the burned out hulk of the Cray computer. Two melted visual display units stood on a charred bench in front of it, along with what had once been a keyboard but which now looked as if it was fashioned from candle wax; it had melted, run and set. The ceiling was blackened with soot, the acrylic carpet was now something that looked like cracked toffee and over by the whitewashed window, in the top right-hand corner of the room, through which the angel had entered this universe, the geometrical impossibility still existed. The two walls and the ceiling curved back on themselves and opened into the room like a sooty three-petalled flower.

H sat on a tubular framed chair beneath the wrecked corner, the last of his disciples crouched on the floor beside him like a faithful dog. The small, fresh-faced man wore a white hospital lab-coat and Paul assumed he was here to cater for whatever bodily maintenance H needed. Paul gauged the man, estimated that he was in his late-twenties and that he would prove to be nothing more than a hindrance. Despite the crazed and hateful expression on the man's face, he was a doctor and not one of H's fighters. Paul knew the man would fall at the first blow.

H himself looked incapable of movement but Paul could feel the raw power coming off him in thrumming waves. He seemed to be generating a sound that was almost sub-sonic; you couldn't quite hear it, but you could feel it in the soles of your feet and the pit of your stomach.

Paul felt the hairs pricking up at the nape of his neck. It was impossible to believe that anyone so horrendously damaged could still function in any way. H was naked and horribly burnt. All the hair was gone from his charred body and head and what was left of his scalp looked like scraps of crisp cellophane. Beneath these trembling pieces of skin Paul could see the dark, damp bone of his skull. Singed flesh hung in his empty, blackened eye sockets and his mouth looked as if it had been modelled by a child with a bag of butcher's scraps. H's left arm

744

ended in a misshapen black blob of gristle, his penis was gone and his right ankle tapered down into a point. There was no sign that he'd ever possessed a foot on that leg.

But during that silent moment before the gun went off, and Paul was proven wrong about the doctor, he realised something that surprised and shocked him more than the devastation in front of him, or the power that emanated from H. There were two electrode pads taped to H's chest, one either side of his heart. At first sight, Paul had assumed that the two tiny wires that ran from the pads went to a cardiac monitor. Now, as he looked at the wires a second time, his mind was jarred into making a series of unbelievable connections.

The two thin wires, which Paul had at first thought were insulated with brown plastic, were actually shellacked, like the winding wires you would find in the armature of any electrical motor. And the wires were hot. They had burned two brown runnels into what was left of the flesh of H's chest. Paul could plainly smell the hot insulation. But it was where the wires went that made his mind reel. They crossed H's chest in a diagonal and ran down to where his upturned right hand lay on his thigh.

And clasped in H's loose fingers was the nine-volt Duracell battery to which the wires were attached.

Paul was looking at the Duracell in disbelief, half-formed ideas whirling through his head about how the angel was using the battery to alter H's body chemistry – or perhaps even to keep the body alive – when the moment of silence ended.

Double A screamed, '*He's got a gun!*'

Paul tore his gaze away from the little nine-volt radio battery just in time to see the blond-haired doctor's hand flash from his pocket and not soon enough to act.

Double A fired three times. Plaster flew from the wall behind the doctor's head in chunks. All three shots went wide.

Paul sensed movement beside him, realised Katie was going forward towards H and the doctor and threw out his right hand, intending to grab her arm and drag her out of the line of fire and knowing it was going to be too late. Paul was moving extremely quickly, but his arm seemed to take an age to reach her.

Crouched beside H, the doctor's hand wavered as he steadied the weight of the black revolver. While Paul reached for Katie he watched the doctor's face change from the epitome of concentration to a savage snarl, watched as his eyes changed to the raging one's of H's angel, watched as his finger tightened on the gun's trigger. Paul knew that this shot was not going to miss.

On the other side of him Double A fired again . . . and Paul heard the *clack!* of a hammer striking an empty chamber.

The doctor's gun boomed as Paul's hand found Katie's arm, clamped itself on and dragged her violently towards him.

Too late! H's voice crowed as the gun fired.

Katie's head snapped back and a section of her skull flew off, trailing a hank of yellow hair. Paul heaved and she slammed into him, spraying his face with warm blood. A section of her skull had gone from her hairline up towards the crown of her head. The hole it left was about an inch and a half in diameter and Paul could see the surface of her brain through it, bleeding and peppered with shards of bone.

Paul felt as if his heart was being torn apart inside his chest. 'KATIE!' he screamed.

I'm okay, her voice said inside his head. *I'm alive! Now let me go!*

'How do you like it now, pipsqueak?' H said as Katie tore herself away from Paul and tottered towards him.

The doctor's next shot hit Katie in the waist, just above her hip. The bullet passed through her, out of her back, and buried itself in the wall beside Paul. Katie staggered to the side but kept her feet.

A moment later Double A stove into the doctor and the two of them rolled across the floor hissing and spitting like a pair of tom cats.

Katie stopped in front of H, her legs wide and her arms held high.

'*Go now*!' Paul heard her say. Her voice seemed tiny and distant, as if she was saying it from another room.

H stood up. When he spoke it was with the voice of the angel. MORTAL! he said contemptuously. YOU ARE MINE NOW! His eyeless face turned towards Paul. CAN YOU FEEL HER FEAR AND HER PAIN? he asked.

And suddenly Paul could, as if he had *become* her. The pain in his waist was a terrible grating ache, the agony in his skull like a spike of ice, but the freezing, paralysing terror was worse.

AN ANGEL? COULD THIS BE AN ANGEL? DOES THIS HAVE ENOUGH POWER TO DEFEAT ME? I THINK NOT.

Static sounded in Paul's ears. *Help me, Paul*, Katie's frightened little girl voice pleaded, coming to him on rolling waves of white noise. *He's hurting me!*

Paul's rage finally overtook his fear. His rapid heart rate hammered up through the one fifties and sixties and into the one seventies. Then it paused, squeezed hard three times and Paul felt himself yanked viciously around inside his body as he clicked-out. His mind cleared.

TOUCH HER AND YOU'LL BE SENDING HER TO ME, the angel warned as Paul ran towards her.

But Paul didn't intend to touch her, he intended to touch H. With a great deal of force.

'Bastard!' he heard himself snarl.

Paul hit H hard, but the burned man didn't budge. It was like throwing yourself at a tree except that trees didn't burn like acid when you came into contact with them. Paul grabbed hold of H's good arm and his internal damage register reported that his clothes were close to the point of combustion and that his hands were getting singed, but there was no pain. There would be no pain until he clicked back in again. H brought his right arm up, lifting Paul from the ground as if he weighed nothing at all, but Paul held on. There was no chance of prising the battery from H's clenched fist, but he wasn't going to have to do that. All he had to do was tear the wires from H's chest.

'*Go back*!' Katie yelled, her voice pathetically small.

Paul shot out his right hand towards H's heart. H realised he was going for the wires and brought up his left hand to shield them, but Paul was faster. His fingers closed around the wires and yanked them away, while his damage register reported that they were burning deep into the palm of his hand.

At the moment when the electrodes tore away from H's body there was a blinding blue flash, a sharp acrid smell and a sound which may or may not have been a short, sharp yelp of pain. Something hit Paul hard in the chest and he felt himself falling backwards. A moment later he thudded to the floor, the breath knocked from his body.

And Paul clicked back in, thinking, *I did it!*

10

And Katie began to scream.

Paul pushed himself up to his elbows and as his vision cleared he realised he'd been wrong. He hadn't accomplished anything at all and now it was too late.

H was bent double, his ruined face pressed into Katie's midriff, his good hand biting into the bloody flesh at her waist. Paul could see her blood meeting the charred flesh of his fingers, sparkling in golden points of light which glittered all the way up to H's shoulder before they vanished. Katie's head was thrown back and her hands were clawing at the air. The left side of her face was sheeted with blood from her head wound. The area of cracked reality around her seemed to have extended but there was no golden light shining on her through it and nothing could be glimpsed beyond it except what looked like an angry purple sky.

'No!' she moaned piteously. 'No . . . *don't*!'

And the centre of H's back lit in points of golden light, which formed a chain and rose from his skin, pivoting as if joined to him at his pelvis. As they swung to the vertical, they melded into one another, stretching and shaping themselves until they became a long, flexing, articulated shaft which mimicked his spine.

Every cell in Paul's body screamed at him to help Katie and he tried to force himself from the ground. Gravity seemed to have increased tenfold in the room.

Behind him the gun fired again and Double A gave a brief curse.

Tendrils of light extended themselves from the golden spine, like growing nerve cells, and as Paul tried to force himself from the floor he watched the angel begin to take shape while the reality of his own universe altered. Behind H and Katie the walls faded like photographs undeveloping themselves and turning back to black paper. Except that it wasn't quite black. There were shapes and colours there; things that Paul didn't want to see. A bruised purple sky which was angry with clouds began to form around them as the angel grew out of H's pelvis. Rolling black hills spread out into the distance, lit with the half-light of approaching thunderstorms. H's secret room ended about three feet before Paul and became another world, or perhaps another universe. Looking into it made his mind reel. A stinking wind blew into the room from the other world, ripe with corruption.

Then the angel was whole from its head to its waist, where it tapered down into H's body. It slowly turned its great head towards Paul. Its eyes raged with fire. *How do you like me now, pipsqueak?* it asked. *Watch me take your angel from you! Watch me bring you mayhem and agony!*

Get up! Paul screamed at himself, but he couldn't move and didn't know what he could do even if he did get to his feet. Double A was close to him now, screaming something that Paul couldn't quite understand, forcing something cold into Paul's hand.

The angel placed both its hands on H's hips and pushed down. For a moment nothing happened and Paul realised the thing was still not able to break free of H's body. Then he heard H's bones crack. The angel roared in what Paul hoped was a great deal of pain.

'Shoot it! Shoot it!' Double A screamed in Paul's ear. '*Shoot the fucking thing!*'

Come to me! the angel said, and enclosed Katie's damaged head in its hands and bent her forward so that her face was against H's back. It placed its hands about nine inches apart above Katie's pelvis and drew them slowly into the air.

And Katie rose from her body, naked and perfect and glistening gold.

'NO!' Paul screamed.

'Shoot it, man!' Double A shouted. 'I can't, my wrist's broke!'

Paul brought the gun to where he could see it. It looked like a toy. In comparison to the terrible world that lay before him, everything on this side of the divide looked insubstantial, grey and unreal. He doubted that the gun would be of any use whatsoever.

And Katie linked to him.

The overwhelming cocktail of emotions and exquisite agonies he suddenly felt almost made him lose consciousness. It was like having a skyscraper suddenly thrust into his head. He suddenly understood that the battle between Katie and the black angel could only be perceived inwardly. That battle was an agonising fight for survival as the angel's life force tried to overwhelm Katie's.

Help me! she said.

And Paul looked out of her eyes into the raging hell of the angel's. And Paul began to fight in the only way he knew how. He found Katie's left fist and snapped it up into the jaw of the angel. The flash of the impact stung his eyes. The angel roared and the pain inside Katie increased. Paul jabbed Katie's left hand into the angel's solar plexus, followed blind with another right that found its mark and felt the angel leave Katie.

By the time it returned – with enough force to break the link between Katie and Paul and send him back to himself with a ferocity that stunned him – Paul had been linked with Katie for long enough to discover what he had to do. It was going to hurt him more than anything had ever hurt him before, but there was no alternative, of this he was certain.

The angel's delaying tactics had worked and they had arrived after its point of maximum power had been reached. Katie's power had always been limited and she'd used it too freely. It wasn't great enough to defeat the angel now. But it was enough to aid it. And in a few more seconds the angel would overcome Katie and absorb enough energy to allow it to walk in this world, free of the constraint of a human body.

There was no alternative.

'SHOOT IT, MAN!' Double A screamed.

His heart breaking, Paul slowly brought up the gun and aimed it across the border of two universes. Over there, purple clouds were roiling in the sky and a fetid wind was blowing.

I'm sorry, Katie, he thought, and feeling very cold and very old, pulled the trigger.

The shot was good.

Katie's head exploded like an egg hit with a hammer and her body flew off H's. Katie's golden astral form winked out of existence. It didn't shimmer, it didn't hang in the air long enough for her to turn to him and mouth the word 'goodbye', it simply vanished.

The angel roared and swung to face him in the moment before Paul fired his second shot.

'Suck on this,' Paul said, holding the gaze of the angel, and pulled the trigger again. Beside the angel H's head shattered.

The angel broke free of H's body, shot into Paul's universe in a roaring blaze of flame, hit the wall and shattered into flaring fragments.

In the other universe, purple clouds peeled away from one another to show a pale sky. A moment later a double bolt of lightning hit the ground off in the distance. The double strike travelled in perfectly straight lines, moving much faster than anything Paul had ever seen before. The sound that followed instantly shook the ground beneath him so hard he thought the house would collapse.

And while his eyes were still blinded by the searing power of the lightning, the opening to the other world vanished.

11

Some time later, still half blinded by the lightning and totally crushed under a billion tons of aching grief, the weight of which he knew would never be lifted from him, Paul sat amongst the small fires – which were gradually becoming larger – staring at the body of the girl he'd loved more than anything else in the world. His Katie. His angel.

It was all over and he'd won but the price for it had been much too high. He felt neither elated nor redeemed, but as if he was dead inside, like one of H's walking corpses. It was all too crazy and too unfair and he didn't think he could face carrying on in a world where there was no Katie.

Fuck it, he thought and lifted the barrel of the gun to his right temple. The muzzle was still warm from his earlier shots.

We'll be together again, Katie, he thought and tightened his finger on the trigger.

And a gentle hand moved the gun away from his head.

'Don't do that, man,' Double A said softly. 'I already lost everyone else I liked. I don't want to lose you too.'

Chapter Thirty-Two
Alonissos

1

'I got your batteries,' Double A announced, from somewhere inside the apartment.

Paul was sitting in the shade on the verandah reading a month-old newspaper for what must have been the hundredth time. Cambridge had been subjected to a bout of freak weather and seismological activity during which the town had suffered lightning strikes to several buildings and earth tremors that had reached a scary 4.1 on the Richter scale. There had been quite a lot of damage to property – including some of the older parts of the university – but only one death, as far as the paper knew. The death was that of a man identified as Henry Tyler, a noted computer scientist. He had been discovered in the front garden after his house had been struck by lightning and burned to the ground. According to the paper, Tyler had also been struck by lightning because when he was found, his body was 'shrivelled and apparently mummified'. A near neighbour, who had told the paper that 'some of Henry's friends had just left the house when the lightning struck' had identified the corpse.

Paul wondered just how well the neighbour had known H Tyler. Not well enough to know that the body belonged to Gary Richman apparently.

The newspaper, a quality, went on to relate instances of strange weather and seismic activity all across Europe within the previous fortnight, such as the tragedy in the small Italian seaside town of Margherita de Savoia where nine thousand people were killed, and the freak floods in the Black Forest, and went on to conclude that perhaps *Gaia* was no longer a terribly happy force.

Paul had read all the English language newspapers over the past month, then read them again in case he'd missed anything, then read them again after that. But the strange weather and unexpected movements of the earth's crust had ceased as abruptly as they had started and none of the papers carried reports of a girl who had turned up from nowhere minus her memory. He no longer expected this to happen, but he still searched the papers, just in case.

Paul folded the paper and put it down on the table.

Double A came through the big glass doors to where Paul was sitting, both his hands held out in front of him – he'd walked into the closed doors twice since they'd been here, bloodying his nose on both occasions. Paul looked up at him. Double A had gained a deep golden tan and about twenty-eight pounds since they'd arrived. He looked fit and healthy and handsome. There had to be scars hiding in him somewhere, Paul knew, but they didn't show. Double A had a girl now, too. She was Greek and her name was Helena. Paul hadn't met her yet, but he thought he would approve when he did.

'I left the batteries on the drainer in the kitchen,' Double A said. 'It's as hot as a bastard out today, ain't it? Think I'll mosey on down to the beach now.'

'Okay,' Paul said.

A flicker of concern passed across Double A's face. It was just a flicker, but Paul saw it and the fact that someone still cared for him almost made him cave in again. He owed a great deal to Double A. The kid had spent the first fortnight looking after him like a nurse. It had been Double A who had taken the gun away from him, led him out of H's house, sat him in the Lotus and driven him away; Double A who had run round getting forged passports and plane tickets; Double A who had re-established the identity of Mr Stephen Miles, sorted out the problems with the missing plastic and sat and talked to the property agencies about long-term leases and rentals in Greece. All Paul had done was sign his name on documents and cheques. It was all he was capable of at that time. He hadn't been able to begin to piece himself together again until they'd arrived here.

'You coming today?' Double A asked.

Paul shrugged. 'Maybe later,' he said thickly, looking away.

'I'll be there till three anyway,' Double A said. 'See you later, maybe.'

2

The apartment that Mr Stephen Miles and Mr Andrew Smith had rented for three months stood on a terrace high above the harbour and one-horse main town of Alonissos. They had come to this particular island because they couldn't go back to stay on Skiathos and this was as close as you could get. Paul looked down at the still blue water in the bay and thought he knew what he would do today. The same as he'd done yesterday and the day before that and the one before that.

There was a motorboat moored down there in the bay with a seventy-horse outboard attached to the back. It too was on a three-month hire to Mr Miles. Later, Paul knew, he would walk down there, get into the boat, start the motor and bounce across the waves to Skiathos, moor at Troulos and walk up through the pine trees to the blackened plateau where he'd first laid eyes on a girl called Katie Straker. The place where he had fallen in love.

And like before he would sit there in the ashes, staring at what remained of the blackened stones while he waited for the tube to descend from the sky so that Katie could keep her promise to him.

I'll come back to you, Paul! Afterwards I'll come back.

The words rang in his ears, just as they had done since the moment he'd shot away Katie's pretty head. Each time he slept he saw her, alive again and whole and smiling and walking towards him, her arms outstretched to receive him. And each time he woke, he woke with tears in his eyes.

Paul got up and went into the kitchen to look for the batteries Double A had bought him. Two blister packs of Vidor MN1500s lay on the drainer. Paul smiled. Double A had only brought back Duracells once. That was a brand that Paul didn't use any more. He broke open the pack, took two of the batteries out and went upstairs to his bedroom.

The nine-band short wave Saisho he'd bought in the airport on the way here stood on his bedside table along with the not-so-lucky ten pfennig piece he'd found in his trouser pocket when it was all over and a worn pair of Katie's red sandals. He'd found those shoes in the Lotus on the way back to London and kept them close to him ever since, just as he had kept the memory of what else had happened during that journey.

While they were hammering down the M11 towards London, Double A had turned on the car's radio to see if there was any news about the crashes. Paul remembered him saying he didn't think the road would be clear yet and that he intended to divert to the B roads because he didn't want to get stuck in a jam. Paul didn't remember whether or not they'd turned off the motorway and gone into London on the back roads but he did remember what had happened when Double A switched on the radio.

The car had been filled with the empty hiss of the Telecom void.

And in the moment before Double A had punched one of the pre-set buttons and found a radio station, Paul had heard Katie's faraway voice calling to him.

I'll come back to you, Paul.

He took the dead batteries from the Saisho, inserted the fresh ones, replaced the cover and tried the radio. None of the short-wave channels were any good, but if you tuned it high on the FM air-band – around a hundred and thirty-five megahertz and between the places where you would pick up aircraft transmissions – you sometimes heard things that sounded like distant voices. Sometimes, one of those voices sounded like Katie's.

Paul turned the radio off, picked up his backpack and put it inside. He took one of Katie's red sandals and put this in the pack too, then picked up the other and looked at it, his heart in a vice.

The darkened shape of Katie's foot was worn into the shoe. Five toes, the ball of her foot, the unmarked gap of her instep and the smudge of her heel. Paul knew he would be able to smell her if he put the shoe to his nose: a faint aroma that seemed to consist of honey and vanilla had permeated the leather.

I'll come back to you.

Paul put the other shoe into the backpack, went downstairs, added cans of Coke and an ice pack, slung the bag across his back and went out into the bright sunlight.

There was a girl down on the jetty staring out across the water towards his boat. She was wearing a white dress from which the sun reflected, searing Paul's retinas. Her back was turned to him. A mane of long, yellow hair tumbled down between her shoulders in a vee.

Paul felt his heartbeat begin to rise and checked it. This had happened before. He had imagined he'd seen her in Gatwick airport, in a shop in Skiathos, on the beach here in Alonissos. Each time he had been crushed.

Paul walked carefully down the steps, staring at the girl and not daring to believe; not allowing himself to imagine that she was staring at *his* boat out of all the boats that rested on the gentle water.

For a few moments, when the steps descended behind a lower terrace of buildings, he lost sight of her. He fought the urge to hurry, telling himself that when the harbour came back into view, she would be gone, telling himself that not even a good and just God would allow such a thing to happen.

But when he cleared the row of buildings, the girl was still there, still staring thoughtfully out towards his motorboat. Paul's heart started to hammer in his chest and this time he didn't check it. The pain was going to be exquisite afterwards, he knew that, but he let the glimmer of hope in his heart fan itself into a tiny flame.

I'll come back to you, Paul, Katie's voice repeated in his mind.

And, hoping for a miracle, Paul walked slowly towards the girl in the white dress.